THE BEAUTY OF DESTRUCTION

Cardiff Libraries
www.cardiff.gov.uk/libraries

Llyfrgelloedd Caerdyd
www.caerdydd.gov.uk/llyfrgelloed

THE BEAUTY OF DESTRUCTION

Gavin G. Smith

GOLLANCZ

LONDON

The right of Gavin G. Smith to be identified as the author
of this work has been asserted by him in accordance with
the Copyright, Designs and Patents Act 1988.

First published in Great Britain in 2016 by Gollancz
An imprint of the Orion Publishing Group
Carmelite House, 50 Victoria Embankment,
London EC4Y 0DZ
An Hachette UK Company

A CIP catalogue record for this book
is available from the British Library

ISBN 978 0 575 12721 0

1 3 5 7 9 10 8 6 4 2

Typeset by Deltatype Ltd, Birkenhead, Merseyside

Printed in Great Britain by Clays Ltd, St Ives plc

The Orion Publishing Group's policy is to use papers that
are natural, renewable and recyclable products and made
from wood grown in sustainable forests. The logging and
manufacturing processes are expected to conform to the
environmental regulations of the country of origin.

www.gavingsmith.com
www.orionbooks.co.uk
www.gollancz.co.uk

To Yvonne,
for her evil brand of patience.

Prologue
The Walker

The twisting, multi-storey bridge had uselessly violated the rock of the ridgeline. The Walker was almost used to the nonsensical angles, the shadowy corners that stretched away from the eye, the optical illusions that weren't actually illusionary. He clambered through an irregular arch, only banging his head twice, and made his way across the bridge, high over terraced spore fields that weren't what they had once been.

The city was the last bastion of life. The remnants of humanity had flocked here when there had been nothing else left, though they were little more than animals now. They had separated into subspecies – herd, predator, parasite humanity – but they remained in the city. Urban living, it seemed, was part of some shared race memory; the fleeting pretence of something approaching civilisation.

The Empty Bridge was still one of the main thoroughfares into the city, though it saw little use these days. The Immortal Mr Jenkins was still there, however. He was something between a rat and a monkey, with a narrow, buck-toothed, but undeniably human face. Sometimes he claimed to be a witch's familiar, or a particularly wilful homunculus, and at other times he claimed to be the King of the Rats. Mr Jenkins was standing on the bench that ran down the deceptively crooked bridge in one of the more low-ceilinged areas. He was absently turning the bodies of a number of spitted, blackened, rat-like bodies over a small rubbish burner while looking towards the living tombs at the centre of the city.

'Mr Jenkins?' the Walker said cautiously. Mr Jenkins turned and ran an appraising eye over him before a smile appeared on his face.

'I'm pleased to see you. Such a day for visitors. I don't think the stones themselves can remember the last time that happened.' He was eyeing the skull shells that the Walker was carrying. 'Now, what can I do for you on such an auspicious day?'

'Food and screaming demons,' the Walker said.

Mr Jenkins narrowed his eyes. 'I see. The skulls bonded?' the grotesque little creature asked.

The Walker nodded.

'One will get you something to eat and two more will get you the bound service of a demon.'

'I need more than one,' the Walker said irritably.

'I don't doubt it, I don't doubt it at all. Well yes, I 'spect we'd all like an army of screaming demons for a hardened skull-shell or two, but that's not the way economics works, is it? With the emphasis on economy, and don't you go thinking you can negotiate with a sword, you know there's more of me where I came from. Besides,' he waved at two of the cooking rat-like things, their faces deceptively human, 'these are fresh. Me wife, queen of my harem and my heart mind you, just popped them out last week.'

The Walker tried to remember a time when this would have disgusted him, but frankly he needed to eat.

The centre of the city was bathed in hard destructive light from the red heavens. Twisted spires, which had reached for the blood-coloured sky, started to fall. Mr Jenkins watched, appalled. The skull shells clattered onto the bench next to the creature.

'Now,' the Walker said.

'Right you are.' Mr Jenkins turned and ran into the inky blackness of one of the bridge's oddly angled corners. The Walker watched the spires fall as he chewed on one of the cooked creatures. Moments later Mr Jenkins reappeared from the darkness. The lines around his small grotesque eyes had deepened, there was more white in his fur.

'They don't like what's happening,' Mr Jenkins said, between grunts of exertion. He seemed to be tugging on the corner's inky darkness. 'They know the city's sleep has been disturbed.' Slowly the darkness started to coalesce into a form.

1
Ancient Britain

Tangwen stumbled through wasteland that had once been dense forest, before collapsing to her knees in a cloud of grey dust that defied the weather. Tears ran from her eyes as she vomited.

There was a dividing line. Just to the north of her the forest started. Everything south was a grey wasteland that the driving rain was turning to mud. All along the demarcation line were the crumbling remains of the creatures that Crom Dhubh, the Dark Man, had drawn from Andraste's poisoned womb. The warped forms created from the beasts, plants and even the rocks of Ynys Prydain, the Isle of the Mighty, were returning to their original state, robbed of the animated life the goddess's magics had provided.

She touched her neck. It itched painfully as the mouth that had grown there during the battle with Andraste's spawn started to heal over with new skin. When the goddess's magic, her seeds, had tried to transform Tangwen into one of her brood.

She drew a painful breath as sobs wracked her body. A shadow fell across her. She wiped the vomit from the corner of her mouth with the back of her hand and looked over her shoulder. Britha was standing there holding the little girl from her village. The one who had survived the wicker man, the march north, and Andraste's spawn. Neither the girl nor Britha looked like they were ever going to let go of each other. The girl was quiet. She had seen too much to cry. Britha grimaced in obvious pain; some of her flesh still had a life of its own.

'I remembered her name,' Britha said quietly. 'It's Caithna.'

Tangwen nodded. She tried to speak but could form no words.

'I've killed too much ...' Tangwen finally managed. Britha looked down at the younger woman and nodded. She gripped Tangwen's shoulder with her free hand. The skin looked pink and raw, new, almost as if it was still in flux. 'What now?'

'Now? Now we start to fight each other.'

Tangwen nodded again and looked down. A small flower had grown through the mud.

There was little of the *gwyll*'s fortress left. Whatever the Muileartach's spawn hadn't pulled down had collapsed into the crater created by the Red Chalice. All that was left was one of the watchtowers and part of the rear wall. Despite the rainwater trickling down the side of the crater the chalice was still where they had left it, in a growing pool at the bottom. Britha was sure she could make out the raindrops that hit the red metal turning to steam.

They had wasted no time. The warriors and the survivors were regrouping in the woods to the north of the ruined fortress. Those who wanted the chalice, who wanted the power it offered, were all here regardless of their fatigue.

Britha was disappointed to see that Ysgawyn, *rhi* of the Corpse People, was still alive. His warband had burned and murdered in Crom Dhubh's name, back when they had thought it meant power. They had changed sides when their master had abandoned them. Now that his retinue numbered only two warriors the *rhi* was looking for any opportunity to increase his fortunes. Of all of them Ysgawyn looked the least weary from his exertions in the recent battle.

Guidgen was the *dryw* and leader in all but name of the *gwyllion*, the forest tribe whose land they were on. He looked ready to collapse into the crater, despite being one of those who had drunk of Britha's blood to receive the gifts of the chalice's magic. The bearded, wizened old man may have been imbued with the powers of speed, strength, vitality and healing that the cup offered, but it was obvious the battle had taken its toll.

Germelqart, the short, once portly, Carthaginian trader was tugging at his beard, a worried expression on his face. He was looking anywhere but down into the crater at the chalice. It had been Germelqart and Britha who had spoken with Goibhniu, the god in the chalice who had claimed to be the servant of other greater gods long since gone.

Anharad, the highborn Trinovantes woman who was friend to Tangwen and had helped lead the survivors to eventual safety, was trying not to glare at Britha. The Pecht *dryw* knew that the older women hated her for siding with the Lochlannach, the Otherworldly raiders. They had slain Anharad's family and imprisoned her in the wicker man as part of the sacrifice to the Llwglyd Diddymder, the Hungry Nothingness, the dark god that Crom had tried to summon to eat the sky.

Mabon, Anharad's grandson, the only surviving member of her family, remained close to his grandmother. Britha saw that he had a shortsword now and had clothed himself in a patchwork of boiled leather armour. Despite the raggedness of his attire he held himself as a warrior, though Britha knew he had not said a word since his parents had been killed and he had been taken as prisoner from the boys' camp.

Britha noticed that Anharad was standing quite close to Bladud, known as the Witch King. The heavy-set, bearded bald man wore the black robes of a *dryw* once more, despite having been cast out. Britha knew that Bladud, *rhi* of the Brigante, had ambitions to be the *bannog rhi*, the high king of the Pretani. He wanted the chalice for himself.

Finally there was Tangwen. The younger woman, a small, wiry warrior and hunter with spiked hair from the Pobl Neidr, the People of the Snake, swayed on her feet as if she was about to pitch forwards into the crater. This was despite the fact that she had drunk of her blood as well. Britha could see the ravages of the magic on Tangwen's wiry form. It had fed on her flesh – she looked emaciated and would have to eat soon. Warriors and landsfolk alike had decreed Tangwen should be guardian of the chalice.

Along with Britha, still holding onto Caithna, they formed a rough circle standing around the edge of the crater. Britha had no illusions about why Caithna would not be parted from her. The girl had been frightened of her but terrified of the spawn of the Muileartach. In such times it made sense to seek the protection of someone as frightening as the Pecht *dryw*.

There were so many of them missing. Kush, the Numidian warrior, had been killed by Crom Dhubh in Oeth, the Place of Bones. Sadhbh, the Iceni scout, and Nerthach, Bladud's right hand, had fallen in the same place. Teardrop had been killed by the Ettin in the wicker man. She herself had helped Bress kill Fachtna, her lover and the father of her daughter – now taken from her by the *dryw* of the Ubh Blaosc. She touched her stomach as she thought of her stolen daughter. She knew that Bress, Crom Dhubh's champion and warleader, held the control rod that would allow her to open a trod back to the Otherworld where the *dryw* of the Fair Folk kept her unborn child. She would take the rod from Bress if she could. From his corpse if need be, as they had both done with Fachtna. Old lore and newer magic, however, told her that she was once again with child. The dread she felt at this was because the father was Bress.

Her people were gone. Cruibne, her *mormaer*, Feroth, the war leader and all but a father to her, Talorcan, the quiet tracker. And Cliodna. So many in such a short period of time.

'The blood of our fallen hasn't yet cooled. This is unseemly,' Guidgen started. The *dryw* was right but Britha had respect for his cunning. Guidgen knew he was fatigued. He would want more time to recover so he could bring all his wits to bear on the coming argument. Bladud, however, was as much warrior as he was *dryw*. He thought to strike while his enemy was weakened.

'And yet you are here,' Ysgawyn pointed out in a tone less courteous than one would expect when speaking to a *dryw*, even for a *rhi*.

'If this isn't resolved quickly then it will cause trouble among us, and we still have a greater threat,' Bladud said. Britha could hear the fatigue in his voice as well, but something told her that he had planned this before the battle.

'It has already been resolved,' Guidgen said. 'Tangwen has guardianship of the chalice until the threat has passed.'

'Tangwen did an admirable job in safeguarding the chalice and protecting Germelqart and Britha while they worked their magics; we owe them much, but the agreement held until we had dealt with Andraste's Brood. This we have done. We need to decide what happens with the Red Chalice now,' Bladud told them.

'You said it yourself,' Guidgen muttered. 'Tangwen was a worthy guardian, let's leave her as such.'

Britha glanced at Tangwen's face. She did not think the younger woman was listening to them. Britha had seen the same look on warriors before. She was locked in a prison of fatigue and the memory of her experiences. This would have been the first time she would have had the luxury to reflect on everything that she had seen, everything she had done, since the wicker man, if not before.

'I notice this time we are not having this discussion in front of everyone,' Britha said.

Bladud looked over the crater at the black-robed *ban draoi*, meeting her gaze easily. 'Nor do I have my warriors at my back,' he pointed out.

Britha noticed Anharad and Ysgawyn nodding. *No, but you brought allies*, she thought.

'There is still the matter of the Lochlannach and Crom Dhubh. Let us leave things as they are until we have dealt with them and then we can fall on each other.' Guidgen's tiredness was telling in his lack of subtlety. There was no trace of his normal wry smile.

'Some of us are strong enough to keep going even after the exertions of battle,' Ysgawyn said.

Bladud glanced over at the *rhi* of the Corpse People. He did not look pleased. Guidgen closed his eyes. For the first time since Britha had met him he looked his age, his normal vitality gone.

'I did not see you in the battle, *rhi* of two,' Guidgen said, then he opened his eyes, bloodshot. He stared at the bristling Ysgawyn.

'Enough of this,' Bladud growled, raising his voice enough to be heard across the crater, over the rain. 'I am well aware of the threat that Bress, the Lochlannach and this Crom Dhubh pose ...'

'Are you?' Britha asked. Normally she would not interrupt a *rhi* in such a way. It wasn't that she lacked the authority to do so. It was just that it showed a lack of respect to their station. 'You have not fought them. They raided little of your land, as far as I can tell. You were not at the wicker man. I think you know little but what you've been told.' Caithna was growing restless in her arms. Presumably cold and hungry, but the young girl showed no sign of wanting to be put down yet.

'If we are to fight them then more of us will have to drink from the chalice,' Ysgawyn said, almost managing to keep the eagerness from his voice. Britha glanced at Tangwen. Normally the young hunter would counter anything said by Ysgawyn; she had borne witness to the depredations of the Corpse People, she hated them and their *rhi*. Instead she just swayed on the edge of the crater, looking up into the sky, the rain falling on her face.

'We will certainly need the magic of the chalice to fight the Dark Man,' Bladud said, and then spat to avert evil. 'Magic that must be shared.'

'And controlled,' Guidgen said. He pointed at the chalice. From their position on the lip of the crater they could see its bubbling, liquid, red metal contents. 'We have the means of our own destruction here if we are not careful.'

'Control requires strength,' Bladud said. 'We have proven time and time again that we are the strongest.'

'Bladud has our support,' Ysgawyn said. Again it was a sign of Guidgen's tiredness that he laughed in the so-called *rhi*'s face.

'All three of you? That's an impressive warband.' Britha could not hide the contempt in her voice.

'And where are the people you swore to serve?' Ysgawyn asked. 'Is that the only survivor there in your arms?'

Britha opened her mouth to retort, but no angry words came. He was right, after all.

'The Iceni are with me,' Bladud told them. This was significant. After the Brigante, the Iceni were the largest tribe that had answered Bladud's summons to fight the monsters. They were powerful and warlike.

'And the Trinovantes,' Anharad said. Mabon nodded at his grandmother's words.

'And you can speak for them?' Guidgen said.

'I have some influence,' Anharad said.

'We are to be wed,' Bladud told them, and suddenly he had the attention of all but Tangwen. Britha guessed that Anharad had underplayed just how important she was to her tribe.

'Congratulations,' Britha said.

Guidgen laughed bitterly. The old *dryw* turned and looked to the south at the plain of mud that used to be his people's wooded land.

'After we have dealt with the Lochlannach you will need strong allies,' Bladud told the old man. 'All the southern tribes will.'

'Allies yes, rulers no, tyrants certainly not,' Guidgen said. 'And we have already had this discussion. The chalice was given to Tangwen to safeguard because we would have fallen on each other with sword and spear if we did not. Nothing has changed. We still have a threat that we need to deal with.'

'So you see war between us when we have dealt with the Lochlannach?' Bladud asked. Britha sensed a trap in his words.

'There will be war if you insist on ruling all,' Guidgen said angrily. 'There is always war when a *rhi* wants to own more than they can see from the highest point of their land. We should use the chalice and then throw it into the deepest part of the sea.'

'Things like the chalice have a way of finding their way back into the hands of mortals,' Germelqart said quietly.

'We need its power to defeat the Lochlannach,' Bladud told them.

Britha laughed bitterly. 'You are assuming that you can defeat the Lochlannach,' she said.

'Andraste's spawn and the Lochlannach have proven that we need to be united ...' Bladud said as if Britha hadn't spoken.

'But not ruled—' Guidgen started.

'I understand the danger of the chalice's power,' the Witch King continued. Ysgawyn turned to look at Bladud, distrust written all over his face. Bladud ignored him. 'Can we come to an accord?'

Guidgen peered through the rain at the Witch King. 'An accord that will benefit you, no doubt,' he said.

'Of course.'

'I don't mind an agreement that benefits you and yours; I object when it is to the detriment of all else.'

'Bladud may have forgotten that your people crept into our camp as we slept, slit throats and stole the blood of many, including children,' Anharad started. Bladud was making calming motions with his hand. 'I have not. You need to remember that he can take the chalice whenever he wants.'

Britha saw Germelqart sigh. She understood how he felt.

'We would murder him and flee with the chalice.' Britha was surprised at just how strong Tangwen's voice sounded. She was staring straight at the Witch King. She was more surprised when she looked up and saw Bladud smiling.

'At best it would bring dissension in your forces before you face the Lochlannach,' Britha added.

'Indeed,' Bladud said. 'Before the battle we sent messengers out to all the tribes asking them to meet us in the valley of the Mother Hill where the entrance to Annwn and the Place of Bones is. We could also send a message to Ynys Dywyll. I am assuming that you will abide by the judgement of the council of *dryw*?' Bladud asked. Britha knew Ynys Dywyll, or the Island of Shadows, was a place far to the west where the southern *dryw* were trained. It was also home to their council and arch *dryw*.

Guidgen did not answer. Britha could tell by the firm expression on his wizened face that the old *dryw* was less than pleased. Britha wasn't sure what Bladud hoped to gain from this. He had betrayed the *dryw* when he had pursued power as a warrior, leader, and ultimately *rhi*. She had heard that he had been satirised, censured and then cast out, though he still wore the robes and used the influence. She could not see the council on Ynys Dywyll ruling in his favour if they were anything like the *dryw* in her homeland to the north.

'And you will accept the council's judgement in this matter?' Guidgen asked.

'Of course,' Bladud said. Britha knew that if Guidgen refused then Bladud would have reason to turn on him and the *gwyllion* for rebelling against the council. The Red Chalice was a thing of power; magic and the Otherworld should be their responsibility anyway.

'I'm surprised you would seek their guidance,' Guidgen said suspiciously.

'I do not have to,' Bladud said.

'We all had a part in retrieving it,' Britha pointed out.

'Aye, while you tried to betray us,' Ysgawyn spat.

Britha looked down to hide the look of shame on her face. She had tried to bargain for the rod she needed to return to the Ubh Blaosc and her stolen, unborn daughter.

'And you weren't there,' Tangwen said, staring at the *rhi* of the Corpse People.

'We could claim it as a spoil of war from you,' Bladud said evenly. Suddenly everyone went very still. The only sound was the rain in the trees just to the north of the ruined fort and the constant drip of water as Bladud's threat settled in. Britha noticed Tangwen's hand go to the hatchet pushed through her belt. She felt Caithna grip her more tightly.

'Or?' Guidgen managed between gritted teeth.

'Or we seek the guidance of the *dryw* and we leave the chalice in the hands of Tangwen and Germelqart until they send someone to make judgement.'

'Britha as well,' Tangwen said, slurring the words slightly in her tiredness.

'She cannot be trusted,' Bladud said. He sounded almost sad. Tangwen opened her mouth to protest.

'He's right,' Britha said. *I would give the chalice back to Bress if I thought it would mean I could see my daughter.*

'The Red Chalice is the responsibility of the *dryw*,' Bladud said, glancing over at Britha as he did so.

'I grow tired of this; speak plainly,' Guidgen told Bladud. 'What do you want?'

'Your support,' Bladud said.

'Against the Lochlannach? Gladly.'

'I mean your oath of loyalty.'

Guidgen stared at Bladud. Britha had never seen the old *dryw* so angry before. She suspected that he would have struck the Witch King, had it not been for the muddy crater in the way.

'False tongue! Deceiver! Liar!' the old *dryw* spat. Bladud narrowed his eyes but controlled himself with great restraint. They weren't words you called a warrior lightly. 'You swore—'

'That we would not conquer you. We are negotiating over the Red Chalice. Have the events of the last moon taught you nothing? Show me a stronger leader and I will step aside. Or he may challenge me and kill me in single combat.'

'We will aid and follow your leadership for—'

'No!' Now Bladud became angry. 'This does not work! You know this does not work! If everyone wants one rule for themselves we are divided.' He pointed at Guidgen. 'That is just you putting your arrogance and the arrogance of your people before the good of all!'

Guidgen stared at Bladud. The old man was shaking with rage. Britha had to give Bladud his credit. Guidgen was wily but Bladud had completely outmanoeuvred him.

'I will take this to my people,' Guidgen muttered with little grace before turning and stalking out of the ruins.

Bladud watched the old *dryw* walk away before turning and nodding to Britha and then starting to walk back to camp himself. Britha wondered how much it cost him to leave the chalice at the bottom of the muddy crater. That said, it would not be seemly for him to scrabble around in the mud. Ysgawyn smiled and then followed the Witch King.

'The child,' Anharad said, nodding towards Caithna.

'I will look to her,' Britha told the other woman. Anharad looked less than sure but started back towards the temporary camp. Mabon followed. 'Her name is Caithna!' Britha called. Anharad stopped. Something in the set of her shoulders told Britha that the other woman was feeling her age. The highborn Trinovantes woman did not turn around, and after a moment or two she continued on her way.

Britha sagged, overcome by a sudden wave of fatigue, and she realised just how hungry she was. She looked to Caithna. The girl had fallen asleep.

'I do not mislike Bladud ...' Germelqart started.

'But you would not trust him with the chalice,' Britha supplied.

The Carthaginian navigator nodded. 'I do not think I would trust anyone with it.'

'Except yourself?'

Germelqart looked up at her. 'I would not trust myself with such a thing.'

Britha noticed that Tangwen was staring down into the crater at the chalice with a look of loathing on her face.

'I had better go and get it then,' she muttered quietly to herself. She started to climb down into the crater and almost immediately slipped. By the time she had made her way through the mud to the chalice she was covered in filth from head to foot. Her fingers curled around the red metal and she lifted it out of the mud.

He felt heavier with each step up the bone spiral staircase. It had been several days since the Dark Man's last summons had crawled into the back of his head like a sickness. Bress hoped each time that it was the last. That his master would finally let him go, but he knew that it would not be the case this time – if indeed it ever would be.

Crom Dhubh was standing on the top of the tower looking out over the boneless, drifting bodies in the huge subterranean lake. There were no carrion eaters here, and little current to carry them away from the isle of rock that the skeletal tower grew from, deep in the huge cavern.

'They did it, didn't they?' said the pale warrior with the long silver hair. He held his master's gaze when the Dark Man turned back to look at him. 'They defeated the Muileartach's Brood?'

'I was as much their father as that slug was their mother,' Crom Dhubh said, his voice a silk corruption. 'Does my children's destruction please you?'

'They will come for you,' Bress said.

'It does not matter, they can do nothing to me. Your Loch-lannach can distract them until I am ready. The war will not be fought here.'

'You will travel to the Ubh Blaosc?' Bress asked.

'Me? No, they could destroy me. You will travel there. You will

12

die there, but you will make the Ubh Blaosc's location known to the Naga.'

'How?' Bress asked, showing no reaction to the news of his imminent death. If anything, he found himself struggling not to show excitement at the prospect.

Crom's expression of consternation looked alien on his face. 'That is the question.'

'You called them before.'

'Relics from this world. The Ubh Blaosc is too far.'

'What of the one in the cave, to the south and east?'

'A frightened old creature, if it still exists, if my children did not consume or transform him. I have not heard his mindsong again. No. I think the answer lies in the body of the dragon.'

2
Now

Six Months Ago

The trees had been sucked towards the portal and some residual energy still played over the stones as lightning. They were standing there in what were thought to be period-appropriate clothes, all of which were armoured, though to Crabber they didn't feel right without an energy dissipation grid woven into their fabric. His neunonics reached out and found a painfully slow connection to a painfully primitive communications network. He started to assimilate information on this world. Search routines filtered through the masses of information. They knew what he liked.

'I think there's a habitation nearby,' his attractive, if dead-eyed 'partner' said.

Crabber just smiled, and let the hybrid assault weapon hang horizontally on its sling down his front.

'I guess we'll have to kill them, then,' Crabber said.

'It will be cleaner just to rewrite their memories.'

'You're being well behaved. That's not your reputation.'

His 'partner' turned to look at him. 'You know as well as I do, the job's all that matters.'

Crabber nodded. 'You ever think about what we could do here? Just with what we have in our heads, in our bodies? We could live like kings, like gods. After all, we've been sacrificed; we're just betas, clones – the real us are living large with the money they were paid for us doing this pre-programmed work. I say fuck 'em.' His 'partner' looked down at him. Programmed or not, Crabber could still detect the slightest trace of contempt for him. 'Couldn't break free, huh?' Crabber said quietly.

'What's that suppos—'

If anything his 'partner' was faster, but Crabber had the drop on him. The shorter, squat, unnaturally broad-shouldered bounty killer with the offset head had his sidearm out of its holster and fired first.

He'd changed the magazine in the pistol for the nano-tipped bullets he was supposed to use on the target. He put two in his 'partner's' head while the taller human was still stepping back and bringing his hybrid weapon to bear. The bullets beat hardening skin and armoured bone. Their nanite payload started eating grey matter. His 'partner' spasmed, staggered backwards a few more steps and then hit the ground, shaking. Crabber was standing over him and put another two rounds in his head. He reached down and took the taller human's magazine of nanite-tipped bullets and his grenade magazines – those would be hard to come by. Then he set the self-destruct code for the neunonics and liquid hardware, dropped an incendiary grenade on the corpse, and walked away.

Alpha Crabber and Patron had made one mistake. They had let him say goodbye. His reconstructed man-plus body had a second hard-tech neck on it. It contained some very illegal corpse-hacking hard- and nano-ware. If he severed someone's head and put it on the stump, the 'ware in his neck grew into their neunonics, hacked their liquid hardware and interrogated them. For a laugh, it also provided an artificial larynx and enough electrochemical stimuli to reanimate their head briefly. So they could see what he had done to them. Crabber was in a tough business. He needed a laugh every now and then.

Normally, however, Little Crabber lived on the secondary, hard-tech neck stump. An automaton, which was just a head designed with a complementary personality. The head was packed with electronic and immersive hard- and liquidware. Basically, Little Crabber handled the hacking for him.

Beta Crabber had been surprised when Alpha had agreed to let him say goodbye. He guessed the Alpha had assumed that Little Crabber was onboard with the plan to sacrifice the Beta. It seemed that the automaton's loyalty programming hadn't been as specific as it should have been. The programming had to allow for dealing with clones because their business was dangerous, but having two clones up and running was highly illegal. Patron didn't seem to care about that. Little Crabber was just as loyal to the Beta as he was to the Alpha, and he didn't like seeing him slaved. He had downloaded an attack program to go after the meat-hack.

Of course that hadn't helped his 'partner'. So he had to die.

As white phosphorus lit up the night behind him, illuminating a forest of broken trees, he drew his knife. He had heard panicked voices after the gunshots. Doubtless they were investigating the lights emanating from the ancient stones. He might not have much time but he was going to enjoy himself.

Beth felt like someone had beaten every inch of her body with hammers. Even as she struggled to deal with the pain it started to recede. The technology inside her flesh was healing her. Instinctively she was aware of just how damaged she was. She was starting to feel very hungry. Like a machine, she needed fuel.

Du Bois helped her get to her feet. For some reason his leather coat, shirt, and even his jeans did not look soaked through. His clothes seemed to have repaired themselves as well. The last time Beth had seen him he'd been lying on the roof of his Range Rover with a broken spine. Despite everything they had been through, even his shoulder length, sandy-blond hair didn't look all that out of place. He looked undernourished, though. His sharp cheekbones normally made his face look aristocratic; now they made it look angular and gaunt. Beth was up to her waist in water looking out at the choppy Solent. She was standing on the road that ran down the seafront in Southsea. The road had been completely swamped. She could barely make out the top of the remains of South Parade Pier, which du Bois and the strange bag lady – who had put the alien technology into Beth's body – had destroyed when they had fought. There was no trace of the huge and very alien creature that she knew lived under the water. The one she had been inside. She could make out smoking wreckage in the water to the west of them, a sinking warship.

Talia! Selfish bitch! But Beth knew her sister was gone. Talia was with the creature, or part of the creature. She wasn't sure which. Her sister had joined the cult that seemed content to live as some sort of parasite within the alien. She staggered a little, trying to assimilate it all. She had been caught up in events: car chases, gunfights, alien creatures. It was only now that she had a moment to try and think it through. She tried to sit down in the water, borrowed weaponry still hanging off her on slings. Du Bois helped her back up with one arm, the other holding his carbine at port.

'You want to go into shock,' du Bois said. 'That's not unreasonable. The nanites, however, are trying to counteract your body's biochemistry. You'll be fine.'

Nearby a woman's body floated on top of the water, and as Beth swayed she could see the gunshot wounds that had killed her. She also saw the thing that had tried to grow and pull itself out of her flesh. Beth was vaguely aware of many phones ringing in the distance.

'Did you ...?' Beth managed. Du Bois followed her eyes to the floating body.

'I killed her,' du Bois told her quietly. 'I did her a favour.'

For a moment Beth had a hysterical urge to attack du Bois. Punch him, kick him, claw at him. Just as soon as the feeling of hysteria came, it disappeared in a way that felt unnatural. She didn't think that was the way that emotions, feelings, were supposed to work. Blue eyes looked down at her, du Bois's expression grim.

Beth was suddenly aware of just how itchy her skin was. She scratched at it.

'What is that?' she asked, the unpleasant sensation distracting her for a moment from everything else that was happening.

'It's sporing,' du Bois told her. 'It's trying to make new life. The itching is your body's defences warring with it, protecting you.'

They heard raised voices, cries of terror and the sound of breaking glass, then an agonised scream followed by more of the same.

'What the fuck is going on?' Beth demanded. Despite all the strangeness she had seen, she was struggling to understand what was happening. She couldn't stop anger creeping into her voice.

'I don't know. All the phones started ringing at once. If I had to guess, it was some sort of attack on the communications infrastructure.'

'Portsmouth's?' Beth asked, almost hopefully.

'The world's,' du Bois told her. He was no longer holding her up. He was checking all around them, his carbine at the ready.

'I don't know what that means,' Beth said in a small voice. Du Bois saw some figures moving on the other side of the now-flooded boating pond. He sighted on them with the carbine and then lowered it. They were too far away to be any real threat. He glanced back to Beth.

'Yes you do. It means that anyone who answered their phone when it rang was subject to the attack. I think they were driven insane.'

'But that could be—' she started.

'We need to go,' he told her, and started wading back towards

Alhambra Road where the Range Rover had been parked. Beth didn't move.

'Go where?' she demanded. 'Everything's fucked, isn't it?' Du Bois turned back towards her, still looking around. 'I mean, you've just told me that the whole fucking world's been driven mad ... right?' She sat down in the water. It practically came up to her neck. 'And the only thing that's stopping whatever it is that's growing out of everyone else is the little machines inside us, right?'

'We don't have time—' du Bois started.

'Wrong! We've got all the fucking time! Because unless I've misunderstood, it's the end of the world, right? And the only people not going to be affected by these ... these spores are people like you! Well, I'm sorry, but that means a world entirely populated by either the mad or wankers!'

For a moment Beth thought she saw du Bois's resolve falter. Then his face hardened again.

'Your sister has gone, and that means the only hope humanity has at all is in the genetic sample I took from her. That sample is in the hands of the Do As You Please clan. They are a group of psychopathic children who use the same kind of technology that runs through your body to turn people into their fantasy playthings. They tried to take your sister, they tried to kill us, they turned all those people into their slaves and made us kill them. Even if we are all doomed I will not have them profit from our fall.' He all but spat the word 'fall'.

Beth opened her mouth to argue but as she did something occurred to her, and with it guilt.

'Maude and Uday!' she said, standing up.

They had seen the people warping and shifting as they made their way back to the Range Rover. Human bodies as cocoons consumed in the act of birthing. Flesh ran and flowed, distended mouths were frozen in silent screams.

'Will these work?' Beth had asked quietly, referring to the recently soaked guns du Bois had loaned her. She felt like her gorge should be rising, that panic should overwhelm her, but instead she felt strangely and artificially calm; sedated yet somehow still aware.

'Not reliably,' du Bois said, intent on checking the local areas, his SA58 FAL carbine at the ready. As they made their way down the flooded, narrow Alhambra Road, away from the now-submerged beach, they could see more of the locals staggering, sliding into the water as the new forms tried to pull themselves free of their host flesh.

'Is it an invasion?' Beth asked.

Du Bois considered this. 'More like an infection,' he said, sparing a look of contempt for the dead thief floating in the water close to where they'd left the Range Rover.

Beth climbed into the passenger seat. The door had been torn off by one of the creatures that had accompanied the cult when they had come for her sister on the motorway. Du Bois sighted his weapon on some of the transforming locals who were close to the vehicle. Beth could hear the sounds of violence in the distance. She felt numb. Du Bois handed her the carbine and climbed into the Range Rover, starting it up. With trained precision Beth checked and then readied the weapon. Du Bois put two magazines within easy reach. There was an explosion in the distance. Beth looked around, her eyes freshly wet.

The water had come as far north as Campbell Road. The Range Rover was creating a wake with its passage as they turned into the tree-lined street. One of the locals, a new face growing out of his own, staggered towards the open passenger side and Beth kicked him away with a look of distaste.

As they had passed through Clarendon Road, and then Albert Road, the two main shopping areas in Southsea, what they had seen looked halfway between a riot and the shell-shocked aftermath of a bombing. Parts of the city were already burning. Some people appeared to have been driven to violence, either against themselves or others. Many, however, just seemed to be wandering in a fugue state, waiting for the spores to infect them. Beth felt like her skin was on fire. She had noticed du Bois scratching his skin red-raw as he drove, though it healed moments later. He looked even gaunter now.

Beth clambered out of the four-wheel-drive, splashing into the water, carbine at the ready, swinging it round to cover the closest of the once-people. She'd put the two extra magazines into the pockets of her sodden combat trousers.

'They will be infected,' du Bois said quietly as he climbed out of the other side of the Range Rover.

'We don't know that,' Beth said through gritted teeth.

'Even if they haven't been so far, they have phones, don't they?'

Beth blinked back tears. She heard two suppressed shots. She glanced back at du Bois. Both the hopper-mounted, shrouded, snub-nosed .38s were in his hands. He had shot one of the creatures as it slithered too close to him. There was something serpentine about the new birth.

'You people have to kill everything, don't you?'

Blue eyes met her own. She couldn't read his expression but he followed as she went into the four-storey townhouse.

They had fused. Uday and Maude had become mother and father to one organism. Beth had turned away and fled the lounge. Even among the agonised, twisted flesh, even after the assault on their minds, somehow Beth was sure she had seen an accusatory look in Uday's remaining dark eye. Beth's family had been a curse to both of them and yet they had been kind, they had befriended her despite what her sister had done to Maude. They were just two students who hadn't seemed to ask much of the world.

She squeezed her eyes tightly closed. Information came unbidden to her, information she had effectively been programmed with. She opened her eyes. She could see du Bois through the doorway into the lounge, raising one of his arms. He was about to execute them. Put them out of their misery.

'Wait!' Beth cried. Du Bois didn't look at her but he didn't fire either. 'Your phone, you can record their consciousness.' It was information she had assimilated from the vast data packets du Bois had sent her when he had needed her help to fight the DAYP in Old Portsmouth. He hadn't had time to edit the information and had sent her pretty much everything. She knew that the phones du Bois and people like him carried were capable of whole brain emulation. They used a mixture of electromagnetic resonance scanning, infrared light pulses and infrasound to map and record a brain, effectively downloading a copy of the original human consciousness. 'You also have access to cloning facilities, don't you?'

Du Bois hesitated. Suddenly he looked tired.

'Even if there are any Circle facilities left, it's not that simple, and they certainly wouldn't allow them to be used for this.'

'Are they not valuable enough?' Beth demanded.

'No,' he said simply. Beth glared at him. 'Do you want me to lie to you?'

'Fine. We can still record them, right?'

This time du Bois sighed. 'It's not them any more. Even if they have minds left the spores will have corrupted them and the human consciousness is a complex thing, it takes petabytes of data, and that's assuming my phone hasn't been corrupted.'

'Please,' Beth said very quietly from the hall. She still could not bear to go back into the lounge. She watched as du Bois lowered his arm. She tried to ignore the wet ripping noises coming from the fused bodies. It looked like du Bois was studying the thing that Uday and Maude had become. Finally he nodded and took his phone out. Beth actually sagged from the relief. She pushed open the door to one of the bedrooms and went to sit on the bed.

'No,' du Bois said. 'The world has just become infinitely more violent and you have soaked all my weapons in the salt effluent of the Solent. They need to be stripped down and cleaned. Take the carbine with you and keep it near. This is going to take a while.'

Beth opened her mouth to argue and then closed it again. She walked out of the bedroom and left the flat.

It was busy work. Beth had known that. They would almost certainly need the weapons but she was sure that du Bois had asked her to do this to keep her mind off her friends. The problem was it didn't. She had stripped down the Accurised Colt .45 first. She had done it practically unconsciously. Her fingers seemed to move of their own accord, the practiced movements of a military veteran unlearned, a technological cheat. It was something else she found herself feeling absurdly guilty about. She had heard du Bois tell McGurk that the .45 had been a present from an officer in Delta Force, who she now knew were an American special forces unit.

As she stripped and cleaned the .45 calibre Heckler & Koch UMP sub-machine gun in the back seat of the Range Rover she felt like she was going through the motions. She knew that trying to record Maude and Uday's consciousness was clutching at straws. She had always wondered why people *bothered* in post-apocalyptic films. When everything and everyone was gone, when existence was beyond miserable, what exactly were you living for? Was the simple urge to exist that strong?

As she finished reassembling the UMP, she glanced across the street. There was a man in a raincoat watching her. He looked sad somehow. The side of his face was bubbling but he showed no sign of feeling the pain. She stopped and looked over at him. He was a little older than her. He had the kind of dishevelled attractiveness that she used to like, or at least he would have if his face stopped moving of its own accord. Their eyes met. His hand came up to the bubbling flesh on his face. Beth wondered who he had been before things so utterly beyond his control had fucked his life. She looked away first and pretended to busy herself with the Benelli M1014 semi-automatic shotgun. He had gone when she looked up again.

Beth felt something hit the Range Rover, rocking it. She climbed out, bringing the butt of the carbine to her shoulder as she did so. Something rolled in the muddy water, an indeterminate form in a caul-like membrane. She raised the carbine to her shoulder and sighted on the thing, but lowered the weapon again. The gunshot would bring du Bois running and she wanted him to concentrate on the job in hand. She knew there was a suppressor for the carbine and the UMP somewhere in the vehicle, but she also knew that even suppressed guns weren't as quiet as they were made out to be in films. She slung the carbine and drew her great-grandfather's bayonet. She stood on the thing, pushing it under the dirty water, then, bending down, she pushed the bayonet into its centre mass. It writhed but the only noise from it was a low squeal that sounded like air escaping from cooking meat. Some of the dark fluids that leaked out of it into the water looked a little like blood. She straightened up and looked in disgust at the ichor covering her bayonet. Then she looked around the road. She could see more of the horrific transformations going on in the street, and in the houses as she looked through the windows. It was only then that she wondered why she had killed the creature.

Du Bois was standing on the other side of the Range Rover looking at her. Again she could not make out his expression.

'Did you do it?' Beth asked. Du Bois nodded. 'I need pr—'

'I did it!' he snapped. 'For what it's worth.' Beth regarded him. It didn't seem like he was lying but she suspected that meant nothing. 'You can either trust me or not.' Something in his voice told Beth that he wanted her to believe him. She just nodded. Maude and Uday's continued existence was something she needed to cling to. 'Are you ready?'

There was no question of her not accompanying him. 'I need a few minutes to sort out the shotgun,' she told him.

Du Bois nodded. He picked up the UMP and went round to the open concealed weapon cabinet in the vehicle's boot. He changed the magazine. Beth knew he was loading it with sub-sonic rounds. He affixed a long tubular suppressor to the SMG. It made sense; less chance of drawing attention to them.

As Beth stripped down and cleaned the shotgun, she wondered if her dad was alive. He had been weak and ill. She hoped that he had answered the phone when it rang and the shock of whatever had screamed at him had killed him. It was probably the kindest fate that this brave new world had for her father.

Du Bois only had to kill one more of the things before they were ready to go.

She was belted into her seat, one foot on the Range Rover's running rail, weapon at the ready. It reminded her of footage she had seen of the wars in Iraq and Afghanistan, but this was Hampshire. She was still soaked to the skin but the cold and the wet didn't seem to bother her any more.

The roads were carnage, multiple pile-ups and crashes every-where. Physically and mentally damaged people wandering the tarmac. More than one of them had thrown themselves at the Range Rover. She guessed that many hadn't answered their phones while driving, but enough had to have caused chaos.

Du Bois used the Range Rover's off-road capability to avoid the worst of it where he could, and the vehicle's power and armoured weight to shunt cars out of the way when he couldn't. Beth tried not to think too much about the bleeding, staggering people wandering between mangled, often burning wreckage. It had all gone so quickly. She had lived in Bradford during more than one riot. Civilisation had seemed little more than a surface façade to her, and prison had confirmed this. Alien entities or not, somehow this devastation didn't seem to surprise her as much as it should. She still found herself blinking back tears. Trying not to think about the few genuine friends she had in Bradford. She felt du Bois look over at her but he didn't say anything. Instead he concentrated on driving the Range Rover up a grass verge on the side of the northbound A3 to avoid a tangled mess of cars and an articulated lorry.

A small convoy of military vehicles drove past them heading

south on the other side of the dual carriageway. She knew they would be of no use.

'Where are we going?'

There had been some military presence in the ugly red-brick town of Aldershot. People who hadn't been able to access phones for one reason or another, Beth guessed. They were very jumpy and had nearly fired on the Range Rover but there was almost a sense of order in the old military town. There were also bodies in the street. Du Bois had shown them the special forces warrant card he carried and they had been allowed through. He had to talk his way through several more checkpoints as nobody was risking using radio, or any other form of electronic communications. Each time Beth had found herself subconsciously ready to fire if it looked like the situation was about to turn nasty.

They were driving across the runway at Farnborough Airport. She could make out figures on the runway. They appeared to be wandering aimlessly across the concrete. In the distance they could make out the wreck of a civilian C-130 Hercules transport plane. Beth hadn't seen any more plane wreckage but she had to assume that if the entire communications structure of the planet had been compromised, then thousands upon thousands of planes all over the world must have crashed. The areas surrounding airports would look like battlefields. Even with all the technology expanding her mental capacities she was struggling to deal with the scale of what had happened.

'Don't think about it,' du Bois told her, reading her mind. 'Concentrate on the task at hand.'

'You used to be a soldier, didn't you?' Beth said.

'A very long time ago.' Beth had to strain to hear him.

Du Bois steered the Range Rover into one of the smaller hangars on the edge of the airfield. It was empty. She saw du Bois visibly sag in his seat.

'An aircraft?' she asked.

'A suborbital transport. We could have been in America before the DAYP.'

Absurdly the idea of travelling to America seemed even more extraordinary than what was happening all around her. 'Surely all this has messed them up as well.' Perhaps her sister's all-important genetic material was already at the bottom of the Atlantic.

'They have access to the same kind of protection we do. But until we know for sure we have to behave as if there is still hope.'

'The thing in the Solent, it did all this?' Beth asked. The question seemed to trouble du Bois. It seemed there were things that he didn't want to think about either. 'It didn't, I don't know, it didn't feel all that malevolent.'

'There are others. If they've ...'

Beth looked at him expectantly but he did not continue. 'Can you think of a good reason not to tell me everything?'

'Yes,' he said simply and then took his phone out of his pocket.

'Wait, what the fuck are you—' Beth protested, but du Bois switched it on. The hangar was filled with the sound of electronic screaming too loud to be coming out of a normal phone's speaker. Beth clamped her hands to her ears. There was a feminine quality to the sound. Du Bois, grimacing, switched the phone off.

'Are you trying to drive us both mad?' Beth shouted at him.

'Our communications are often carried by human mediums for convenience's sake but the Circle has its own satellite network and it's very secure.'

'But it's been compromised, right?'

Du Bois frowned. 'I don't think that's what everyone else heard when they answered their phones. That wasn't them.'

'What was it?'

'I think that was Control, one of the Circle's AIs, artificial intelligences, and I think it was in pain.'

'So they can't tell you what to do?' Beth asked. She had expected anger but instead she saw momentary confusion on du Bois's face. Then the ground shook. They stared at each other. For a moment Beth wondered if the thing in the Solent had burrowed through the earth and was coming for them. She followed du Bois out of the hangar and into bright light.

It looked like a white sun was rising in the south. Her vision darkened, polarising, and she swallowed hard.

'Is that a nuclear bomb?' she asked. Even to herself she sounded like a frightened little girl. Du Bois nodded. 'Portsmouth?' He nodded again.

'A tactical nuke, probably delivered by an artillery shell. All the missiles will be compromised. If I had to guess it was probably fired from Salisbury Plain. The British aren't supposed to have tac nukes.'

'Your Circle?' she asked as a warm wind blew across the

runway. She was aware of the radiation she was soaking up but she also knew that the technology inside her could easily handle it.

'They certainly have the resources for something like this.'

'Will it ... will it deal with the problem?'

'Possibly,' du Bois said. He didn't sound convinced. He turned and walked back towards the Range Rover.

'Where are we going?' Beth called, unable to turn away from the fading light in the south.

'London.'

3
A Long Time After the Loss

He may not have had the soft-tech augments or the combat neunonics gifted by the Dark Mother but he felt exhilaration, not fear. He may have been on the bottom rung of the hierarchy according to the Murder Darwinists, still unproven, but he wanted to kill. He wanted to find out if he could taste the tiny machines in the blood, the machines he had heard stories about but didn't quite believe in.

He was small, lean, and pale from his time in the dark. They'd been fed little and had to fight for that. He looked down at the chitinous, barbed, spear-like weapon grafts. He knew if he fought enough, killed enough, then one day he could have hands. Maybe even a name. He knew the name he wanted but he would have to live up to that one. As a neophyte he knew he was little more than a hunting animal.

The neophytes of the rival street tribe were loping towards them, some of them on two limbs, others on more. He was out ahead of the rest of the Darwinist neophytes; he leapt up onto the wide, low lip of the catwalk, the gas clouds far below him looking like they were trapped in glass. The first enemy neophyte swung a fused, club-like limb at him. He somersaulted sideways over his opponent. Landing behind him, he twisted and rammed the spear-graft into his enemy's back. His first kill happened so quickly, so instinctively, he barely registered what he had done, let alone had time to savour the warm splash of red.

Both of his graft arms were dripping, his pale naked body was spattered in blood. He could hear the older Darwinists coming up behind him, the rough bark of projectile weapons as they put injured neophytes out of their misery. He used his boot to push an enemy with mandibles off his spear-graft, the barbs tearing at the flesh as they were ripped free. He strode towards the ziggurat. The way the stepped building's smart matter opened for him reminded him of sex. He stopped for a moment. He knew he should not go any further, that was for the higher ranks, so they could receive their gifts. He was gripped by a compulsion, a wanting. He wanted to know what was in there. He speared the dead enemy neophyte again, an offering, and then dragged the body through the opening.

He didn't really understand the feeling of disappointment at the plain, empty chamber inside the ziggurat. He let the corpse of his victim drop to the floor. He heard a cracking noise. He looked down to see black tendrils growing from the floor into the enemy neophyte's head.

'Do you want hands?' He didn't understand the inflection in the words. He was always told what he had to do. It almost sounded like there was some kind of option here. Despite the clattering of the mandibles and his victim's apparent base-male gender, there was something feminine and seductive about the voice emanating from the corpse. He wasn't sure if his blood-stained erection was from the killing or the sound of the voice.

He ran through the options. He was supposed to earn his hands through acts of blood. He would be killed if someone or something outside of the Murder Darwinists provided them, therefore if he wanted hands he would have to prevent this from happening. It seemed simple once he had thought it through. Making a decision was still something of a new experience.

He almost cried out as the tendrils grew from the smart matter and pierced the pale flesh of his leg, but pain was a friend, a teacher; sweat still beaded his bloody skin. He felt movement in his body, then the pain in the barbed spear-grafts made him stagger and almost fall to his knees. He watched them change. He found himself looking at four fingers and a thumb on each hand as the last of the chitinous barbs sank into his flesh, the matter transformed and reused.

'I . . .' the neophyte started. 'I want more.'

The corpse started to buck on the floor, its chest caving in as its base matter was harvested to make an egg. One of the Dark Mother's 'gifts'. The neophyte plunged his hand into the chest cavity, fingers closed around the egg and he yanked it out, his fist still red but now dripping again. He held the egg in front of his eyes and watched it 'hatch', the harvested carbon changing at a molecular level, growing and transforming into his gift. A projectile weapon, a large frame, old-fashioned revolver, a tumbler pistol.

'That is mine.' Suddenly he was standing in the shadow of a bulky figure in the ziggurat's doorway.

'I don't think I'm a neophyte any more, Evisceral.'

'The first half of your statement is correct. Hand me the gun, neophyte.'

He continued to stare at the red dripping gun held in his fist. The tumbler pistol couldn't belong to Evisceral. It felt like it had always been his. It was an extension of his new-grown hand, little different from the weapon grafts.

'I want a name,' he said, still not looking at the Murder Darwinists' leader.

'You will get rendered down for this insolence,' Evisceral told him. There were other named members of the Darwinists crowding around behind him. Nobody ever did anything like this. Everyone knew their place.

'When I rest, behind my eyes, I see a tower of bone.' He turned to look at Evisceral. 'Do you see a tower of bone?'

For a moment the gang leader didn't seem to know how to respond, then his face hardened. 'Give me the gun, neophyte, now!'

'I have a name now.' Ever since he had slithered, wet and half grown, from the smart matter exo-womb in the walls, he'd heard whispers that his genetic code came from the Bad Seed line. 'My name is Scab.' He levelled the tumbler pistol at Evisceral's head and squeezed the trigger, nice and sweet.

Scab wasn't sure why the memory of his first kill had come to mind. He was not one for dwelling on the past and this ... glory that he was witness to, even holographically, despite having witnessed it in action himself, was still a thing to behold.

They were in a windowless, stone-walled, open plan room, part split-level lounge and part conference room, high up in the hundred-mile-long habitat that was the Cathedral, the Church's base of operations.

At first Scab had thought the ten-foot-tall golden armoured form of Churchman was an automaton. Perhaps it was the bulbous tinted visor between its shoulders that changed his mind but Scab was beginning to believe it was some sort of exoskeleton. He was sitting on a throne-like chair against the interior wall.

The Monk, whose name was apparently Beth, was Talia's sister. This meant that she had been alive before the Fall and the loss of Earth. Or at least her original body had – Scab had killed her at least twice himself. She was leaning against the wall to the left of Churchman. Tall, lean, athletic looking, her head completely shaved. She was dressed in a simple black *gi* and was watching the holographic display with a look of concentration.

Talia was sitting on a mouldable cushion affair, low to the floor, staring in horror at what the hologram was showing. She was wearing a leather corset with a lace dress underneath it. The dress had a flared skirt. Her clothes were all in black to go with her hair and her eye make-up.

Elodie, his sometime consort, a feline intrusion and kick-murder specialist, was reclined on a chaise longue the room had grown for her from the smart matter. She had been body sculpted to look almost human except for her feline eyes, ears and the dark downy fur that covered her body. In her chitin-style armoured bodice and thigh-length boots, she looked as elegant as she looked bored. The feline was inspecting her envenomed nails and ignoring the holographic display. Her long, animated hair braid, ending in a spike, was swishing from side to side impatiently, like a tail.

The chair that the room had grown for Vic, his seven-foot-tall, hard-tech augmented, insect partner, actually looked comfortable. Scab had tried to subtly hack the room's smart matter to make the seat less so but the Cathedral's security systems were more trouble than they were worth for something so petty. Vic was staring at the holographic display, mandibles agape in what Scab suspected the 'sect thought was a human expression of horror. Scab knew it for what it was, a humanophile's affectation. Vic was trying too hard. Again.

Scab's personal satellite, a small black sphere containing sensors, electronic warfare hard- and software, and a laser normally used for personal point defence, hovered on its anti-gravity motor just over his left shoulder. The P-sat provided information on his surroundings and the other people in the room via interface with Scab's neunonics, but it was the hologram that had most of his attention. He was watching a star being consumed by what looked like a swarm of squirming black bacteria or maggots. It was the thing he had seen in Red Space when they had found the Seeder ship Talia had been on. The thing he had summoned with the girl's blood and the blank Elodie had stolen from Mr Hat, the diminutive lizard bounty hunter with the god complex who was pursuing them. Watching the swarm consuming a ship, even a fleet of ships, was one thing. Seeing it eat a star was another. He watched the red sun grow dimmer and dimmer in the black sky. It was a level of destruction far in excess of even what he had wrought as an Elite. It took him a moment to realise that the feeling spreading through him was his under-utilised sense of wonder.

'Beautiful,' Scab found himself saying. Talia looked at him, horrified. Vic shook his head, another human affectation. The rest of them ignored him, though he couldn't shake the feeling that Churchman was staring at him through the tinted visor.

'That thing ...' Talia started. The fear in her voice was unmistakeable. Scab could smell it on her. He was sure that before the Fall she'd had some kind of experience with the thing. The image was becoming darker as the sun was consumed. Finally the room was almost dark. He suppressed his feelings of contempt when he heard Talia sob.

Suddenly they were bathed in the orange glow that illuminated all of the Cathedral, though Scab would have preferred the blood-coloured light of Red Space that lay outside the Church's hidden base. Two of the walls, apparently smart matter, became transparent. The interior facing wall looked down on the cloudy fifteen-mile drop to the dolphin pools far below, the main chamber of the Cathedral. The now-transparent smart matter wall on the other side of the room looked out on one of the gothic flying buttresses, its foundations far below in an asteroid. One of the three capital ships present at the Cathedral, each one the size of a small city in its own right, was passing outside – silent, ponderous and balletic. A heavy boarding/ground assault shuttle was setting down on the landing platform embedded into the massive flying buttress.

'What is it?' Vic asked.

'We don't know,' Churchman's deep, obviously modulated voice boomed. 'We know it consumes matter.'

Talia's face scrunched up in concentration as she wiped tears of eyeliner off her face.

'Conservation of energy ...' she managed. She seemed to be dredging through some long-distant memory. Scab turned to look at her. The Monk could not hide the expression of surprise on her face. 'What? I liked physics at school.'

'The teacher was attractive, wasn't he?' the Monk said, smiling.

'Fuck off,' Talia muttered.

'What does conservation of energy mean?' Vic asked.

It took Scab a moment to realise the odd noise emanating from Churchman's exoskeleton was a sigh. 'Is that information not in your neunonics, Mr Matto?' Churchman asked.

'Obviously not,' Vic said irritably. 'Or I wouldn't have asked.'

'No, it doesn't seem very important these days, but then the uplifted races are a parasitical species,' Churchman continued. The Monk rolled her eyes.

'What's that supposed to mean?' Vic demanded. The 'sect

31

seemed to have overcome his fear of being captured by the Church, judging by the way he was speaking to Churchman.

'That we have spent too long relying on the benefits of S- and L-tech ...' the head of the Church started.

'L-tech?' Vic asked.

'What you call S-tech is actually two kinds of technology. Seeder tech is the soft-tech, the biologically derived technology of the alien progenitors of the uplifted species. L-tech is the hard-tech, the material technology such as Mr Scab's energy javelin, and the technology from which the Cathedral itself is derived.'

'What does the L stand for?' Vic persisted.

'Lloigor,' the Churchman told the 'sect. Vic shook his head. Scab had never heard the name before. Talia looked mystified, but then she would, and Elodie was still examining her nails.

'All we know about them comes from examining their technological artefacts and talking to the frequently damaged or corrupted AIs within those artefacts, the Lloigor's machine servants. As far as we can tell they lived in a universe that predated ours. They ascended but did not survive the destruction of their universe.'

'Are you saying that Scab's energy javelin is older than the universe?' Vic asked.

'No. More likely, when the Lloigor's machines bridged into this universe they did so with some kind of assembler with a powerful AI driving it. One of the original AI's offspring or descendants would have created Mr Scab's weapon, which is among one of the least of their technologies.'

'We may look for these artefacts,' Vic said. 'They may be powerful enough for the corporations and the noble houses to fight over, but that doesn't make us parasites.'

Scab started to laugh as he realised what Churchman was telling them. 'Everything?'

'Everything of worth. Bridge technology, our information and communication infrastructure, nanotechnology, material science, augmentation of our bodies, all of it is derived in one way or another from L- or S-tech. With a little help from social conditioning we just stopped trying. We're too lazy, too self-absorbed, and too busy trying to crawl all over each other for a slightly bigger slice of shit that we can't be bothered to develop our own science and technology. And why should we, when we can just cannibalise the remnants of more advanced alien civilisations?'

'Well that's fucking depressing,' Talia muttered. 'Surely you're trying to improve on it.'

'Mostly we're trying to reverse engineer it. The Seeders and the Lloigor were so far in advance of us that any progress made outside of these walls tends to be for privatised profit rather than the betterment of all.'

Scab frowned. He didn't really understand what Churchman was talking about. People only ever did things for gain. There was no betterment of all because the person next to you was just competition for resources, unless they could be used in a way that meant they contributed more than they cost. That was just the way people were, regardless of their species or gender. It was the way things had always been.

'And this place, your secret base, it's L-tech?' Vic asked. Scab heard Elodie sigh.

'Yes, but this isn't just our base. This entire facility is basically one big telescope. We use bridge technology to study real space from here,' Churchman said. Suddenly Scab found himself paying more attention. He noticed Elodie look up from her nails as well. There was a slack-mandibled expression on Vic's face. It was clear that it was going above the 'sect's head.

'Why?' Vic asked.

'What do you mean "why"?' the Monk asked, exasperated. 'To find things out, expand our knowledge.' Scab knew enough about his 'partner' to know the 'sect was confused. Information was only useful when it could be used for gain. Knowledge for the sake of knowledge would make no sense to Vic. Like seemingly everyone else in Known Space, Vic had very little in the way of curiosity.

'Why a cathedral?' Talia asked. The golden armoured form shifted slightly on the throne to look at her.

'A crucible for the transformation of man,' Churchman said.

'But apparently not women,' the Monk muttered.

'Conservation of energy?' Scab asked. His head was starting to throb.

'Talia?' Churchman asked.

Talia's face screwed up in concentration. 'Energy can't be created, or destroyed, only transferred. Something like that.'

The Monk was smiling.

'Close enough,' Churchman said. Scab was pretty sure that if Churchman had a face he would have been smiling in a patronising manner.

33

'But you said it consumed matter?' Vic said. Scab assumed the 'sect was taking an interest because Talia was.

'Yes. Consuming matter and energy is the only time that it seems to interact with the visual spectrum, but we think that is merely a side effect of its true purpose,' the armoured form's booming voice explained.

'Get to the point,' the Monk told him. It took Scab a moment or two to realise the odd modulated noise was laughter.

'It is consuming dark energy,' Churchman said, then paused expectantly. Talia looked confused, as did Vic, though again Scab was sure he was just aping Talia. Elodie still looked bored.

'You know nobody knows what that means,' Scab growled.

A rasping sigh emanated from the armour. 'But they should.' Churchman sounded sad. 'In that it's relevant to this discussion. Dark energy is the force responsible for the expansion of the universe.'

'So if it's being consumed, it's slowing the expansion?' Talia asked.

'Yes,' Churchman said. Talia looked pleased with herself. 'If enough of it is consumed then it changes the critical density, which was already quite carefully balanced, and the universe starts to contract.'

'But this would be over a vast amount of time, right?' Talia asked.

'At the moment,' Churchman said. 'So far these attacks have appeared random, spasmodic, perhaps even reflexive. They can be stimulated, which we're sure is what happened to you in Portsmouth.' Talia brought her knees up to her chest and hugged them tightly. Scab noticed the Monk move as if to comfort her sister but then think the better of it. 'But these attacks are increasing in frequency. Entire star systems gone, and if what we believe is correct, that is just a by-product. If they continue to increase exponentially we could be looking at the Big Crunch in the very near future ...'

Scab started laughing. He couldn't help himself. He doubled over in his seat. Everyone was looking at him now. Acid tears fell from his eyes to sizzle on the carpet. Eventually he managed to control himself. He sat back, sniffing. Talia looked appalled, Vic was staring at him, the Monk looked angry.

'The sociopath act is getting boring,' she told him. Scab just smiled, saying nothing.

The Monk opened her mouth to continue her harangue but Churchman held up one massive armoured arm. 'Beth, please.'

'So it's breaking the law of energy conservation?' Talia asked. The armoured form inclined his upper body slightly in what Scab assumed was supposed to be a nod. 'How?'

'Some kind of naturally occurring bridge effect,' the Monk said, anger in her voice, still glaring at Scab. 'One theory is that it is some kind of sentient singularity.'

'We've seen it bridge,' Vic said. 'When we ...' He looked over at Talia. 'It bridged into Red Space.'

'It's taking the dark energy from Known Space and bridging it somewhere else,' Churchman told them.

'Where?' Talia asked.

'Maybe here,' Churchman said, pointing out through the transparent smart matter wall to the swirling crimson gases of Red Space. 'For all that we utilise Red Space for its coterminous short cuts, we understand little about it, and it defies analysis. It could be expanding. It could be utilising the dark energy in some other way. We do know that Red Space is a younger universe where different laws of physics apply, and that it was artificially created by picking a baby universe out of the quantum foam and inflating it.'

'How do you know that?' Scab asked.

'Discussions with ancient AIs in L-tech artefacts.'

'Created by whom?' Talia asked.

'The Seeders. It would have required an amount of energy beyond belief. Perhaps this thing that is consuming Real Space is the mechanism for such creation. Perhaps Red Space has always existed as a parasite on our universe. But we do know things are changing. Redshift has become blueshift in living memory.' Everyone was looking blankly at him now, with the exception of the Monk, who was staring at the ceiling in frustration, and Elodie, who was still studying her nails. Another sighing noise emanated from Churchman's exoskeleton. 'The universe, Real Space, humanity's home, is contracting, becoming smaller, starting to collapse in on itself.'

'And this thing, the squirming maggoty thing, that's what's causing it?' Vic asked. Churchman nodded. 'What is it?' Vic asked.

Neither Churchman nor the Monk answered for a moment.

'We don't know,' the Monk said.

'Is it intelligent?' Scab asked.

The Monk looked over at Churchman's armoured form. Scab had the feeling that the Church's leader was trying to decide whether or not to tell them something.

'Some of the AIs seem to think so,' Churchman said. Outside, the capital ship was almost past their position, its manoeuvring engines glowing brightly, subsidiary craft zipping about it as maintenance automatons crawled across its hull like insects.

A piercing cacophony suddenly filled the room. Scab grimaced slightly and he saw Vic jerk back. Elodie hissed and looked up. Talia grabbed her ears and curled into a ball. Only the Monk showed no reaction. Then the noise was gone.

'What! The fuck!' Talia shouted at Churchman. 'I'm not ... bionic like everyone else!'

'I am sorry, I wasn't thinking,' Churchman rumbled.

'What was that?' Vic asked. 'Was that it communicating?'

'It's a signal within the cosmic microwave background radiation of the universe. We shifted it up sixty or so octaves so humans could hear it.'

'Is that it talking?' Talia asked.

'Screaming,' the Monk said. There was silence. 'Its presence in the CMB means that it's existed since the birth of the universe.'

'You make it sound like it's God,' Talia said quietly.

'No,' Churchman said simply.

'Does the Consortium know? The Monarchist systems? What are people doing?' Vic asked, more than a hint of panic in his voice.

'Don't you get it?' the Monk asked sarcastically. 'Nobody cares now. It's not what you're bred for.'

Vic stared at her. 'What's that supposed to mean?'

'Besides,' said the Monk, glaring at Churchman. 'We've been covering it up.'

'What? Why?' Talia cried.

'Because people don't look for solutions any more,' Churchman said. 'They have been conditioned to look for someone to blame. It keeps them divided.'

'The Consortium care about conspicuous consumption, the Bluebloods about decadence, everyone else is somewhere on the survival-self gratification spectrum,' the Monk added.

'How did it get like this?' Talia asked.

'It was going this way before the Fall,' the Monk said quietly.

'And it has been given some guidance,' Churchman added.

'Who by?' Talia asked.

Scab was desperately trying to recall the name of the man they had met under the influence of Key. The tall man. The one who had hired him to steal Talia's cocoon in the first place. But neither meat nor neunonics could remember him, which shouldn't happen.

'The organisation that became the Consortium, and their leader. The man you know as Patron, though he has had many other names,' Churchman told them.

Talia was staring at him. 'That makes no sense. He's helping that thing?'

'As far as we can tell he serves it,' Churchman told her. 'All his actions seem to be about stopping any organised resistance against it.'

'Why?' Talia asked.

'He has some kind of connection to it. We suspect the connection causes a great deal of pain. Beyond that we don't know.'

'This all seems ... I don't know, so abstract. It's too big,' Talia said. Her voice sounded small.

'Patron said I owed him. What has this got to do with me?' Scab asked. Churchman started to answer but the killer held up his hand. 'I have a better question. So what?'

The Monk was glaring at him.

'Mr Scab, I'm sure that nihilism as a way of life is all very exciting as an adolescent but—' Churchman started.

'Think of what you've just described. What's worth saving? We were grown by the Seeders, these biotech gods. Why? Slaves? Pets?' Churchman didn't say anything. He didn't need to. 'And we've done nothing with our existence. You said it yourself. We're parasites.'

'There is a great deal more to this universe than the uplifted races.'

'Let them save it then,' Scab said as he got up and walked towards the door.

'Mr Scab, you're greatly mistaken. We're not asking you to do anything. You may stay here and live in comfort if you wish, or you may have the location of the Cathedral removed from your memory and your ship's, and you can take your chances back in Known Space. We'll make you as rich as Croesus if you wish. Of course, Miss Luckwicke will have to remain with us.' The massive armoured form shifted slightly to look down at Talia. Talia looked up at Churchman and then her sister. She smiled and then nodded. Churchman turned back to a seething Scab. 'I'm intrigued, were you honestly arrogant enough to think we would let scum like yourself anywhere near possible solutions for this? I am simply doing what I promised and providing you with answers to whatever you wish to know. I am sorry if they do not live up to your expectations ...'

'On the contrary,' said Scab. 'God is real and it's about to eat everything. Good news, we'll be leaving soon. Just a few more pieces of business. My ... Benedict?'

'As I'm sure you can imagine, our resources are stretched a little thin at the moment but we will help you track down and deal with the possessed Benedict on board the *Templar* ...'

'You have his backups here,' Scab said, cutting Churchman off. The massive armoured form shifted in his throne-like chair again. Scab was sure that he was being stared at, despite the tinted visor.

'You're worried about leaving some trace of yourself, aren't you?' the Monk said, unable to keep the disgust from her voice.

'I suspect that this will be difficult for you to understand, Mr Scab, but I'm not wiping Brother Benedict's backups. I'm not going to murder him out of some sense of genetic insecurity on the part of his psychopathic father.'

'Why not?' Scab demanded.

The Monk laughed humourlessly.

'Because it's not the decent thing to do,' Churchman told him.

Now Scab started to get genuinely angry. 'What the fuck are you talking about? It's going to happen. You decide how hard you're going to make it on yourselves,' he said, quietly.

'Do you honestly think we're frightened of you?' the Monk asked. Scab turned to look at her with his dead eyes. He felt calm and cold now, like he always did before a fight.

'The next time I kill you it might be in a way you can't walk away from,' he told her. She laughed.

'Don't threaten my sister,' Talia told him, though she was obviously frightened. The Monk couldn't keep the look of surprise from her face.

'No,' Vic said. Scab turned to stare at his 'sect 'partner'. 'You can go if you want. If they'll have me, I'm staying.'

'That's not how this wor—' Scab started.

'You are most welcome, Mr Matto,' Churchman said.

Scab smiled. 'She doesn't give a fuck about you. She was using you.'

Talia looked down at the floor. Out of the corner of his eye he could make out Elodie smirking. Scab's olfactory sensors picked up on Vic's pheromonic misery.

The 'sect nodded, another human affectation. 'I know.'

Scab walked out of the conference room.

'I'm bored,' Elodie said. 'I don't like being bored.'

4
Ancient Britain

You did not fight in winter. Britha was no warrior, but she did know this. In winter your greatest enemy was the cold. In autumn you returned from raiding to tend to the fields and harvest for the cold, dark months when the dead could be heard on the wind. Crom Dhubh and the Lochlannach had given them little choice, it seemed.

She was sat on an outcrop overlooking a flat plain in a valley between steep hills, many of which were edged with rock escarpments and cliffs. The chill she felt wasn't just from the cold air. The valley ran from east to west. She could make out the Mother Hill at the western end. She had since discovered that the hill had been sacred to the southron tribe's Mother goddess, Cuda. It had been a place for the dead and the ravens when she had been there last. Now the magics that ran throughout her flesh allowed her to see movement in the fort atop the hill. She knew they would be the Lochlannach. She could not, however, make out the cave that was the entrance to Annwn where lay Oeth, the Place of Bones where Crom Dhubh dwelled.

There were a number of small settlements, mostly clusters of roundhouses and granaries. Closer to the west end of the valley, in the shadow of the Mother Hill, she could see a small village with its own longhall but she knew it was deserted. Even from this far out she could make out that much of the farmland was overgrown. The crops had not been harvested and the frost was killing them.

She tried to suppress the irritation of seeing the field rot, sheep, aurochs and smaller cattle left to roam free. She suspected that there were so many of the beasts wandering the valley because the wolves, bears and lynx knew that the western end of the valley was inhabited by the corrupt and unnatural.

With one hand Britha pulled the furs she had bartered for

tighter around herself. The other grasped the longspear that she was leaning on. It was mostly a memory of cold. Even the shaved side of her head did not feel the cold as she once had. She had decided to keep her hair as it was. They did not trust her, so they may as well fear her. Her odd appearance went some way towards accomplishing this.

Below, the warband snaked into the valley. The scouts, mostly women of the Iceni with their lynx headdresses, and ash-painted members of *gwyllion*, had gone in first. Only a few of them had carried weapons blessed by the Red Chalice – though perhaps empowered was a better word. Or even cursed. The scouts certainly didn't lack for courage in Britha's eyes.

There were outriders spotted around the high ground watching over the warband as they entered the valley. After the final battle with the Muileartach's spawn they had continued marching north. Each night as they camped Bladud had called his advisors to him, which now included herself. They may not have trusted her but it seemed they had started to value her wisdom, her knowledge.

They had sent scouts into the wasteland in the south. Goibhniu had been true to his word. The land there was starting to recover. Natural plant life seemed to be returning, albeit unnaturally fast. Bladud was reluctant to send people back into the wasteland to live and Britha had agreed with this.

They had discussed what to do with the survivors who marched with them. Bladud had spoken to all the landsfolk. He had told them he would send them to their homes in groups if they lived north of what the southrons were calling Andraste's Wasteland. If they had lived south then they could go and seek new lives in the north, for the Lochlannach's raiding had left many lands short of people to work them. Bladud had said they were welcome in Brigante lands. He had, however, explained that if they stayed then they would become spear-carriers and would fight. He left the appeal of vengeance against the Lochlannach unsaid. Many had stayed, and now Bladud had an army, one that was very loyal to him. He had become the saviour of Ynys Prydain. Britha had wondered how generous he had been to the bards who sang of his victory across the land. More warriors from the different tribes had come to join the fight, following stories of glory, magics and power. They could scarcely credit the stories told by those who had lived through the wicker man and the children of the Muileartach's onslaught.

'Act like a *rhi* long enough and everyone starts to believe you,' Britha said quietly to herself, her lips curving up into something that came close to a smile. She had to admit to liking the Witch King, even having a degree of respect for him, but he was dangerous because he was greedy and too ambitious. However well intentioned he might be, he wanted to tell others how to live. That could only end in war.

She had been aware of Tangwen's approach for some time now. The small, wiry warrior scrambled onto the outcrop with her.

'Did you climb up here?' Tangwen asked. There was disapproval in her voice but the hunter also sounded and looked tired. She had gone into the valley ahead of Bladud's warband with the scouts. Britha knew that the younger woman was doing just about anything that didn't require her to take time to think, or sleep.

'I am pregnant, not crippled,' she told Tangwen. 'Where is the chalice?'

Tangwen managed a raised eyebrow at the change in the conversation. 'Germelqart has it.'

'And if some of the warriors decide that they want it?' Much of their conversation these days seemed to be about the chalice and its whereabouts.

'They will need to be stronger than me, faster than me, and more cunning than a snake to keep it, and if so then they deserve it. It would not be good for Bladud to hear you taking such an interest in the chalice,' Tangwen warned. Britha suspected that her constant enquiries were making the other woman nervous. Britha glanced at Tangwen. She smelled of leather, and sweat and the cold earth.

'I will be discreet with my enquiries and speak with only those who I trust.' *Even though they will not, can not, trust me,* she left unsaid.

'Look at these fools,' Tangwen spat. The warband was slowing. Starting to form into a rough circle as they prepared to camp for the night. The hunter and warrior were staring at a number of chariots struggling over rough ground; some of them had to be carried by the landsfolk. Britha laughed.

'Warriors have to have their trappings,' Britha said. She

42

understood the reason for it but often wished they could be more practical.

'This is no terrain for chariots,' Tangwen muttered. Britha had agreed with Feroth on the matter of chariots. The only good terrain for them was a really flat beach. Though even then the chariots hadn't done the Cirig much good. They could hear shouted commands and landsfolk being bullied in the frigid night air. The *ban draoi* glanced up the valley.

'There's flat ground further to the west,' Britha pointed out.

'Bress will not fight us in open battle. He is not like other warriors; he seems only to do that which will bring him victory, no matter if it's the right thing or not,' Tangwen said. She glanced over at Britha. 'But you would know that better than me.' Britha suppressed the urge to flinch, as if the younger woman had slapped her. 'He will fight from the fort on the Mother Hill, or in Annwn itself. There's not much reason for him to leave Oeth.'

The first snowflakes drifted down out of a darkening, pregnant sky. Tangwen looked up at the older woman.

'Are you still a *dryw*?' she asked, and then glanced down at Britha's stomach.

'As much as Bladud is a *rhi*,' Britha said, angry despite herself. Once she would have castigated Tangwen but she understood why the other woman had asked the question. *And still dryw enough to be asked to conduct a wedding ritual,* she thought. Though she had been the second that Bladud had asked. Guidgen had refused. There was only so much humiliation that he would put up with.

'I have not forgotten what I swore to you,' Tangwen said after a while. Her voice had softened. Her words reminded Britha of another moment of weakness, of Tangwen telling her that she would help Britha on her impossible task: to steal back her never-seen daughter from the Otherworld. Britha wanted to release the young warrior from her oath. She wanted to destroy the false hope of ever seeing her daughter again. Instead she said nothing.

'Let us go and find Anharad then,' Tangwen said. She started to climb down off the outcrop. The air was filled with falling snow now.

Tangwen felt the looks, and thanks to having drunk from the Red Chalice, could actually hear the mutters as they made their way through the camp. The warriors who had not fought with them against Andraste's spawn looked too clean and well fed to her jaded eyes. She heard the words they called Britha. She knew they thought Tangwen too young and weak to hold onto such power as the Red Chalice. She knew she would have to kill some soon. Or Britha would. The *ban draoi* was pretending that she couldn't hear them describe her as their enemy's whore, but as her pregnancy became more obvious Tangwen knew that one of them would be stupid enough to say something. She did not wish to kill any more of the people that stood with her. Britha had no such qualms. So far the newcomers had been kept in line by those who had fought with them against the spawn of Andraste, those who had seen Tangwen fight and had seen the magics of the chalice unlocked. She still didn't like the feeling of all those eyes on her as they made their way through the camp.

They found Anharad close to the centre of camp. Bladud and the rest of the Brigante were conspicuous by their absence. A number of the new warriors were of the Trinovantes tribe and Anharad was well known to them. She was deep in conversation with the warrior who commanded their contingent. He looked young for the responsibility but the network of scars down one side of his otherwise handsome face, and the claw-like ruin of his left hand, told her he had seen battle.

Mabon was nowhere to be seen but Caithna, the young girl from Britha's tribe, was sitting on a barrel just outside the skin-and-branch shelter Bladud had made for his wife-to-be. The snow was coming down steadily now and sticking to any surface that wasn't being churned up by heavy boots. Tangwen smiled at Caithna and the girl looked terrified. Even though Tangwen had cared for the little girl, Caithna had also seen her kill to maintain discipline, to keep more people alive, because she had to. The girl was considerably less afraid of Britha, despite her position as a *dryw*, her bizarre appearance, and her black robes. Caithna stood up and ran to Britha, peeking out at Tangwen from behind the *dryw*. Absently, Britha stroked the girl's hair. Tangwen caught the unhappy look on Anharad's face at Caithna's actions. It was quickly replaced with a look of distaste.

'I am no more pleased at this than you are,' Britha said.

'Then why did you agree?' Anharad snapped. The highborn Trinovantes woman had no love for Britha.

'It seemed churlish to refuse,' Britha said.

'That didn't stop Guidgen from doing so,' Anharad pointed

out. Tangwen could see by the set of Britha's mouth that the *dryw* was getting angry. 'There will be *dryw* with the rest of the Trinovantes ...'

'Well, perhaps if Bladud wasn't so quick to marry—' Britha started.

'Both of you be quiet!' Tangwen said. Britha turned on Tangwen, her face like thunder. 'I'm sorry, but if we are to spend the night together among the trees ...' Britha's expression softened a little. Tangwen could practically feel the discomfort coming off the Trinovantes warleader in waves. She turned on him. 'And why are you still here?' she demanded. 'Have you a cunt between your legs as well? Do you wish to walk among the trees and sacrifice to the gods for a virile young warrior to fill it?'

'What? No!' the man sputtered.

'Perhaps you would be wed to Bladud and see yourself ploughed on the morn?' Anharad demanded. The warrior went a red bright enough to make out in the fading light. She was surprised the snow in his moustache wasn't turning to steam.

Britha took a step towards him. 'Or perhaps you seek to learn the magics of women?' she asked in a low, dangerous voice. 'Would you know of the power of the moonblood? Do you wish me to fetch my sickle so I can harvest the fruits between your legs that you may learn?'

The warrior fled with as much dignity as he could manage. The three of them started laughing, and even Caithna managed a smile.

'And the funny thing is Clust would not think twice about facing a Lochlannach shield wall on his own,' Anharad said between gasps for breath. 'Utterly fearless in battle.'

'Unmanned by women's words. It's a wonder we ever get pregnant at all,' Tangwen said without thinking. Anharad stopped laughing and her eyes went wide. Britha turned to stare at Tangwen, but then the *ban draoi*'s face cracked and she started laughing again.

Relieved, Tangwen knew that the laughter could not heal the dislike the two women held for each other, but it might make the night that bit more tolerable.

'Call this heather ale?' Britha demanded, looking at one of the jugs they had taken with them into the woods. 'I've pissed better than this!'

'I'm not drinking that,' Anharad said. There was more laughter from the three of them. They were now drunk enough that almost everything seemed funny.

'My mouth hurts,' Tangwen complained.

'It's because you haven't laughed in so long,' Britha said sombrely and then the mood was broken. The silence stretched out, becoming uncomfortable. Caithna was wrapped in fur and asleep in a bough of the tree they were sat by. They had made a fire in a root-lined bowl at the base of the tree. It was bitterly cold but not even Anharad, who had not drunk from the Red Chalice, seemed to be feeling it, though she too was wrapped heavily in fur. Some of which was so fine that Tangwen assumed it was a gift from her husband-to-be. The Trinovantes woman was also wearing a heavy wool dress that was obviously new, and a new ring, torc and headband of interlaced spun gold. All this, better food, the chance to bathe and groom, and not being harried by monsters across the land had revealed Anharad's beauty despite her years.

'Give me that,' Anharad snatched the jug from Britha. For a moment Britha seemed confused as to where it had gone. 'After all, I'm the one that needs to be drunk enough to get married in the morning.'

'Aye, I just need to try and remember the ritual,' Britha said. 'I should do it in my own tongue. I mean, how would any of you know whether you were being wed or told how to make heather ale? I mean proper heather ale, not that shite.' She nodded at the jug Anharad was drinking from.

'Thought it was good,' Tangwen said and then frowned. She wasn't sure that the words she had used were what she had meant.

Anharad lowered the jug and wiped her mouth with the back of her hand. 'Aye,' she said, and looked down.

'Is this what you want?' Britha asked. Tangwen looked up. Suddenly everything was serious and Britha seemed oddly sober. 'I'm supposed to ... it's one of the things I have to ask this night.' Perhaps not that sober.

'I ...' Anharad started. Then she took another long swig from the jug.

'Can I get some of that?' Tangwen slurred.

'I had thought that my children, and my children's children, would have been enough ...'

Anharad handed Tangwen the jug. Tangwen took a long swig from it and immediately regretted it.

'Myself and Gwern believed we had made something. We had increased the fortunes of our tribe. Increased our village's and our own standing among the Trinovantes. We had become wealthy. Our people had plenty, yet we had not become fat and lazy. Our warriors trained hard, they raided and practiced warfare, yet we never warred needlessly. We had brought up our daughters and sons well and they would continue the work we had done once we had seen our last sunrise. Then it was all taken away.'

Anharad took the jug from Tangwen. The older woman's face was wet with tears now. 'And that's the thing that galls me the most. I could accept if another tribe had done this to us, if the Iceni had attacked from the north.'

Tangwen could hear the fervour in Anharad's voice as she leaned forwards, the flames in the fire reflecting in her eyes.

'We would have given them such a fight, but if they had won it would have been because they deserved it. There was no chance with the Lochlannach. They were good fighters but we could do nothing against their magic.' Anharad was glaring at Britha. Britha reached down and took the jug from the other woman and took a long swig of it. 'It's over a child, isn't it?' said Anharad. 'That's why you betrayed us?'

Britha turned to stare at Tangwen. Tangwen managed to feel absurdly guilty, despite not having said anything to Anharad.

The Trinovantes woman nodded. 'I would have betrayed all for my children, which is why you must know I'll see you dead if you do anything that will harm us.'

Britha stared at the other woman. 'I have never seen her,' she said quietly. 'They took her before I had a chance to.'

'Does anyone ever see the Horned God?' Tangwen asked. 'Let alone get ploughed by him on these nights?' Many newborns were supposed to be the children of the Horned God. It was why on the night before the wedding the betrothed was accompanied by two others, ideally one of them being the *dryw* that would perform the marriage ritual.

'I've seen some foolish lovers and husbands-to-be running around the woods naked with antlers strapped to their heads, but I've never seen the Horned God in all the years I have done this,' Britha said, 'Though my people try ... tried to avoid the gods.'

And with good reason. Other than her Father, all the gods Tangwen had encountered, in one way or another, had brought them nothing but ill.

'You didn't answer her question,' Tangwen said to Anharad. She did not want to talk of gods. It would have her thinking about her Father again.

Anharad wiped the tears from her cold skin and shivered under her furs.

'There's a reason weddings are for the summer,' Britha said, not unkindly.

'He has enough power and you hand him more,' Tangwen said, sounding serious despite herself.

'Has he not earned everything he has?' Anharad snapped back, but Tangwen could hear the defensiveness in the older woman's voice.

'Aye, he has,' Britha said. 'Including his satire and casting out. He has taken oaths in the past not to wed, and he has broken those oaths. Why would he not do the same to you? He cares about the words of an oath only, not its meaning. Look what he did to Guidgen and the *gwyllion*.'

'Have you never broken any oaths?' Anharad asked. Britha opened her mouth to answer angrily but then closed it again. 'Do you think he is an evil man? Or is it because he is not evil enough for you?'

Britha bristled.

'Enough, I beg you,' Tangwen complained. 'Anharad, Britha must ask you these questions.'

'And the more honest you are, the more likely you will get what you want from your marriage,' Britha said irritably. 'Despite what you may think, we are not here to judge you.'

'And yet you are no friends to Bladud,' Anharad pointed out.

'I like him well enough,' Britha admitted. 'But I would not be living under his boot. The same cannot be said for your tribe.'

'I like him less since he started to count Ysgawyn as an ally,' Tangwen muttered.

'He is no fool, he can see Ysgawyn for what he is,' Anharad said, but she did not look at either of the other women. 'Everything I ... we sought to build has been snatched away. I am not like either of you now. I am no longer beautiful ...'

'What matters that?' Britha asked. 'That is not what we are about.'

Tangwen barely realised that her hand had covered where the acid scar on her face had been before the drinking of Britha's blood had healed it.

Anharad fixed Britha with a long, hard look.

'Easy enough for you to say,' she told the *dryw*, who looked genuinely confused. 'By all accounts you can still catch the eye of a *rhi* yourself.' Britha opened her mouth to retort. 'Peace, please. I have been strong enough. I do not have that many winters left. I would live them out in as much comfort as possible and see Mabon well placed. I do not think Bladud will be a tyrant, I will add my word to his with the Trinovantes but in the end it will be their choice.'

'It is dangerous,' Britha started cautiously. 'For a woman of—'

'For a woman who has seen as many winters as I have to have children?' Anharad laughed. 'My days of giving birth have passed long since. He has another wife in the north who has provided him with children. He may have other wives if he wishes, lovers; it makes little difference to me as long as I have primacy.'

Something about this whole conversation bothered Tangwen. As a warrior among her people she counted as much as any other warrior. She did not like the way Bladud seemed to be the important one in the marriage. She could see that Britha looked uneasy as well.

'His first wife will not like this,' Britha said.

Anharad shrugged. 'By all accounts she is young, pretty and docile. Who knows? Maybe I will teach her to respect herself, but if she troubles me I know a number of recipes that are difficult to trace. I'm too old to call her out with sword and shield, I think.'

Tangwen was appalled but Britha just smiled and looked down.

'But I tell you this much.' Anharad turned to stare into the fire. 'I will see the Lochlannach, Bress and this Crom Dhubh dead first.' Her spit arced into the fire and sizzled.

Tangwen swallowed.

Britha nodded. 'I go to seek the Horned God,' the *dryw* said.

'Are you sure you can fit another child in your belly?' Tangwen asked and both she and Anharad laughed.

'You go too far, little snake!' Britha said, unable to keep the smile from her face as she left the fire and walked into the woods.

Britha lifted her robes and squatted. She did not feel the cold as she once had but the draft on her hindquarters was still an unpleasant experience. Steam rose from the snow that had settled as she made water.

'So your friend would see me dead?'

Britha actually cried out as she stood bolt upright, looking around frantically for her spear. She had left it leaning against a nearby tree. She found it and grabbed the weapon as Bress stepped into the faint moonlight that filtered through the branches.

'Britha?' Tangwen called from the fire.

The *dryw* could see the warm glow of the flames through the bare wood. They were supposed to have been left alone but since Anharad was with them Britha knew that the copse of woods where they performed their pre-wedding vigil was surrounded by Brigante and Trinovantes warriors. Of course they would not be difficult for Bress to slip past.

'I'm fine,' Britha called back to Tangwen. 'I slipped.' She wasn't sure why she lied. Her spear was levelled at Bress. The last time she had seen him she had run him through with the weapon. Even so, even though she had helped him kill Fachtna, even though he had denied her the rod that she needed to get back to the Ubh Blaosc, she could not deny how he made her feel.

'It is not right—' Britha began.

'Really? Another lecture on how I should behave? Are you sure you are in a position to sit in judgement?'

'Not on all, but even a slave is in a position to sit in judgement of you!' Britha snapped, trying to ignore how much she wanted to lie with him. 'For you are the lowest of all the slaves.' Bress was circling, making her turn to keep the tip of the spear between them both. She tried to remind herself of all that he had done. How he had all but wiped out her tribe, but she wanted to grab him by his hair, ram him against the closest tree, and take him.

Bress nodded towards the spear. 'I can take that from you any time I wish.'

'Draw your sword, let's end this now,' Britha spat, but it was bravado. Even with her own skill, even with the magics of the chalice inside her and the demon imprisoned in the spear whispering to her, hungry for gore, she knew she was no match for Bress. 'You lied to me. You said that you would take me back to the Ubh Blaosc!'

Bress made a claw with his hand and nodded towards her belly. 'I could tear it out of you now, like I tore out your friend's heart.'

Britha tried to blink away her tears. It was the cruellest thing he had ever said to her.

'Kill it with tansy. It will only live to do Crom Dhubh's bidding.'

Britha heard someone running through the forest towards her. Her attention was diverted for a moment and Bress was gone.

Tangwen almost slipped over in the snow as she came to a halt next to the *dryw*, a hatchet in one hand, her dagger in the other, looking around frantically. 'He was here, wasn't he?' she demanded.

Britha did not answer. Instead she looked through the trees towards where she knew the cave entrance to Oeth lay.

Bress staggered against the wall of the cave and sank into a crouch, hugging his knees, his tall, thin frame wracked by sobs. The Lochlannach stood sentry at the mouth of the cave paying not the slightest bit of notice to their master.

Eventually he straightened up and walked over to the mouth of the cave. From there he could see much of the valley. It was dusted in white and seemed to glow in the moonlight. It was still snowing, though the cloud cover had disappeared, making it bitterly cold. To the east, far in the distance, he could make out the fires of Bladud's warband.

Staring at the camp, Bress drew his dagger and ran it across the palm of his left hand. He went to first one and then the other Lochlannach guard. They were unmoving as he smeared his blood on their faces. She was right, he was a slave and his master wanted him to travel south, to return to where they had grown the wicker man from the very roots of the earth, to search the corpse of a dragon for a way to summon others. She was right that he did not have the courage to disobey the Dark Man, and now he lacked the courage to do the deed himself.

He had given the two Lochlannach one simple order: kill her.

You leave soon. It was not a question. The guilt that the words crawling into his skull made him feel was absurd. If Crom Dhubh wished to know what Bress had just done there was nothing Bress could do to prevent it.

'Yes,' Bress said out loud.

Summon the remainder of your forces before you leave. The presence was gone. Bress had stopped feeling the residual nausea a long time ago. He closed his eyes and reached out to the south and the east.

In a copse of woods on the banks of the Tros Hynt rows of Lochlannach turned and faced the west and started to march. Giants rose out of the water and stepped onto land, pushing trees aside as they went.

A freezing mist had formed in the lower ground and in bowls on the surrounding hills in the morning. Britha recognised that she and Tangwen should have felt much worse than they both did, though she observed that once again the young hunter had avoided sleep.

As she wrapped the holly around Bladud and Anharad's arms, both of them wearing crowns of mistletoe, Britha noted that the Trinovantes noblewoman, with her bloodshot eyes, looked as tired and hung-over as befitted a bride on her wedding morn.

5
Now

Du Bois knew it was ridiculous to get attached to objects, particularly for someone as long-lived as he was, but he was going to miss the Range Rover. Absurdly he found himself worrying if Alexia had damaged his Vincent Black Shadow. He was worried about his brother ... his sister. Despite her augmentations she was not ready for a situation like this. Nobody really was.

The roads into London, however, were just too jammed with wreckage. Much of the Heathrow area, and indeed the westernmost parts of London, was on fire from what must have been a rain of falling planes.

From raised ground they had caught sight of the M25. It had become one big bumper-to-bumper traffic jam interspersed with huge piles of wreckage. Some of the road was burning and the drivers seemed to have formed tribes and were battling each other across the roofs and bonnets of their now-abandoned cars.

Du Bois had parked the Range Rover in a back street just off the A30 by a Kawasaki dealership. He had taught Beth how to smear her blood onto her clothes. The nanites in her blood used the matter in her clothes to replicate themselves. Her clothes looked the same but, like his, would harden when they were hit and distribute the kinetic energy of blows and bullets. He provided her with some simple webbing that could carry ammunition for the Heckler & Koch USP and the Benelli M1014. Then he shut and locked the concealed weapons locker and ordered it to destroy the remaining ammunition they couldn't conveniently carry. Du Bois tossed an incendiary grenade into the Range Rover and walked away knowing that he had just started yet another fire.

They walked in through the glassless windows of the bike dealer – it seemed people had got there before them. Du Bois smeared blood onto two of his keys and passed one to Beth.

'I'd say I can't ride a bike, but that's not true any more, is it?'

Beth said, her boots crunching on broken glass. Du Bois glanced over at her. Beth was solidly built, quite heavily muscled. Her face was plain but not as unattractive as she seemed to think it was. He didn't really approve of the Celtic-style tattoo creeping up her neck, though it matched the interlocking knotwork design painted on the back of her leather jacket. Her dirty, dark blonde hair was tied back in a ponytail. 'Where are we going?'

Du Bois reached one of the remaining bikes and straddled it. 'We're going to see the King of London,' he muttered, unable to keep the distaste from his mouth. 'We need transport.' Beth just frowned. Blood changed the shape of the key as he slid it into the Enduro's starter. The bike fired first time and he gunned the throttle.

'You want to go to London? After what we just saw?' she demanded.

Du Bois said nothing.

'Look, my father ...' she tried.

He could see the guilt all over her face. There was no need to mask his own as the only bit of guilt he felt at having killed her father was the pain that it would inevitably cause her.

'I think you should stick with me for the time being,' he said. 'But it's up to you.'

When he roared out of the showroom Beth was following.

At one point on the ride into London they had found themselves on a deserted, sunken, dual carriageway. At the top of the grass banks on either side of the road a firestorm had raged. Ash rained down on them like snow and only their augmented bodies had enabled them to breathe. It was strangely beautiful. Du Bois had glanced behind him to see a look of wonder on Beth's face.

They had made their way through the city towards Kensington. They had seen a few people in the streets. Many of them had seemed lost and had little idea what to do. There was some sort of migration towards the centre, however, and every Tube station they had passed had been crammed with people. He had seen double decker buses lying on their sides but some of the underground trains still seemed to be moving and full. The streets were jammed with abandoned cars. Only a few of them had been wrecked, or burned, though the sky was full of smoke. They'd only had to avoid a few attacks. Still, du Bois found himself using all his concentration to navigate the streets. This at least stopped him from becoming angry thinking about whom he was going to see.

They'd had to dump the bikes when the press of people became too much. A military convoy was making its way down Kensington High Street between the designer shops and pricey cafés. Challenger tanks and Warrior armoured personnel carriers with eight-pointed stars painted on them crushed expensive German saloons and Italian sports cars as their tracks rolled over them. The armoured vehicles had loudspeakers bolted to them, playing something that du Bois's internal systems assured him was a form of music called UK Grime. The soldiers were handing out SA80 assault rifles, ammunition, and other weapons to young men and women wearing shell suits. As one of them ran by, du Bois could see that he had shaved off an eyebrow and crudely tattooed a postcode just over his eye.

There were bodies hanging from lampposts, street names carved into their flesh. Directly across the road he saw a table of young men outside a café. They had salon-groomed beards and hair. They were wearing tweed and very tight trousers. They were studiously ignoring each other as they frantically tapped at their phones. Du Bois wondered for a moment if they were communicating with each other via text instead of talking, or just describing the firefight on whatever passed for social media on the corrupted internet. A stray, or perhaps not-so-stray, bullet caught one of them in the head and he fell sideways off his chair, spilling his latte.

Du Bois and Beth backed further into the doorway of a designer make-up boutique. Du Bois glanced behind him to see naked men and women painting make-up on their bodies in a way that reminded him of tribal war paint. There was a severed head on the floor of the shop.

Beth's eyes were wide. Again it looked like her body wanted to panic but the technology in her system was fighting it. It had been so long since he had first been in a battle that what was going on in Kensington High Street barely registered with him. Though the battle's location did feel a little incongruous.

'Beth?' du Bois asked. She ignored him. He was pretty sure she would be shaking if the nanites in her body hadn't been controlling her biochemistry. He wasn't surprised that she wanted to shut down. The fight with the Do As You Please clan in Portsmouth had been one thing. They had obviously been evil and they'd taken her sister. What was happening here was on such a massive scale as to be abstract. Du Bois had no doubt that Beth was tough. He had seen that first-hand, but there was only so much a mind could take in one go and this whole situation had been engineered to drive humanity insane.

'Beth!' du Bois hissed louder.

Beth jerked round to look at him. 'What's the fucking point?' she demanded. There was the snap of bullets passing close to them. A nearby car bounced on its suspension as holes appeared in its bodywork and the remaining glass in its windscreen shattered.

'I'm sorry to break this to you, but people lived like this all over the world before today. Just because it hasn't happened in your country for a while doesn't mean you can just give up!' He knew it was harsh but he suspected it was what she needed at this moment.

'What's your fucking postcode?' an almost guttural, south London accented voice demanded.

Du Bois glanced over at the young man with the tattooed postcode above his eye. His hair was shaved into a pattern that du Bois suspected was supposed to be a Tube map. He looked very young. Du Bois found himself reminded of the root of the word infantry. London was at war, it just didn't seem to know who with. It was a horrible inverse parody of the blitz spirit.

'Do you think there's any way I can convince you of the imbecility of fighting over an address?' du Bois enquired.

'Yeah? Well there's no oil in Lambeth, is there?' the postcode soldier told him. Du Bois just stared at the youth as he raised the SA80 to his shoulder. Du Bois didn't like that the boy seemed to know how to use the weapon, that it was trained at his head rather than where he was wearing more armour, and that the boy knew enough to keep out of reach. 'Now, what's your fucking postcode?'

'I'm a tourist,' du Bois suggested.

He practically felt Beth wince behind him. The boy started to squeeze the trigger. Du Bois started to move. Three red holes appeared in the boy's chest and du Bois was aware of the sound of suppressed gunfire. Hot metal shell casings bounced off his face. The boy staggered back and fell to the floor. Beth was staring down at him, looking stricken as she lowered the suppressed UMP. Du Bois saw her swallow hard.

'I—' she started.

'He was going to shoot me,' du Bois told her.

'It was barely me doing it … it was like I was on automatic …' She flinched and jerked the UMP up to cover a sprinting girl who reached down to grab the fallen SA80 as she ran by.

Du Bois brought his weapon up and moved off. Beth followed only a moment later. They were making their way past the front of an art deco building containing a number of high street clothes shops. It looked like the roots of trees had pierced the ceiling of the building and grown down through the floors of the shop. It didn't seem to be deterring the smartly dressed, middle-aged female looters.

They turned right off Kensington High Street and onto Derry Street. The street battle seemed to be heading east towards Kensington Gardens.

Du Bois led Beth to a door in the side of the art deco building and looked into an empty reception area.

'It's their worst nightmare, isn't it?' Beth said, nodding back towards Kensington High Street. She still looked like she was struggling to hold it together.

'What is?' Du Bois asked, distracted. He had his carbine at the ready.

'All those south London scrotes rampaging through the nice parts of the city.'

'Yes, this apocalypse seems full of irony. I don't think there's a "they" any more. Beth, are you with me?' du Bois asked.

'I don't know what we … what I'm doing.'

'Surviving.' Du Bois stepped into the reception area, scanning all around. Beth followed, the UMP at the ready, the shotgun slung down her back. Du Bois accessed old plans of the building. It had been a while since he'd had to come here and he had never used the stairs before.

'I think I've seen some of these people on the telly,' Beth said. The room was full of beautiful people, all of whom had the look of someone faintly famous. Du Bois's internal systems were identifying most of the partygoers as micro-celebrities from reality or talent shows. 'Now I want to start shooting,' she added. All of them seemed to be trying too hard to have a good time. They were coated in sheens of sweat and desperation.

'Fucking arsehole,' du Bois muttered. They were standing in

a glass-fronted restaurant looking down on a roof garden with a stream running through it. Beth gawped at a pelican wading through the water. There were more micro-celebrities sat in deck chairs on the level below.

The restaurant provided a great view of London's rooftops. Smoke was rising from many places in the city. There were holes in the dome of the Royal Albert Hall, and the big wheel that was the London Eye burned.

'He'll be in the Spanish Garden,' du Bois said, and went down the stairs.

Beth followed, looking around, seemingly confused by what she was seeing. 'Don't they know there's—' She only just managed to stop herself.

Du Bois led her through an open area where a DJ was playing insipid music and more of the partygoers were dancing.

They came out into a garden with fountains. Vines climbed the Moorish inspired architecture that surrounded the landscaped area. It was quiet here. Decorative stone and ornamental flora deadened the sound of the disco. There were small grottos with comfortable sofas all around the garden. A number of the party-goers were engaged in various intimate acts in the grottos while paparazzi photographed them.

Du Bois pushed his way along the raised path at the edge of the courtyard to one of the nooks. He could hear The Doors playing 'Five to One'.

The music was coming from a modified walking cane. He was lying on one of the sofas, naked, but little of his nudity was on show due to the masses of hair and beard. He wore coloured sunglasses and was surrounded by a detritus of drug paraphernalia and empty bottles. There was a *Buckaroo Banzai* comic lying, open, across his expansive, beard-obscured gut.

'He looks like a fat John Lennon,' Beth muttered, clearly unimpressed. The figure opened his eyes with a start.

'Is John here?' he asked.

'He's dead,' du Bois said viciously. 'Hello, Gideon.'

Gideon looked around the Spanish Gardens.

'Who are all these people? I don't think this is what I meant.' He sounded a little frightened, though he had always seemed somewhat disoriented.

'How is this old hippy going to help us?' Beth asked.

'I'm not a ...' Gideon started. 'This has been done to me.' He glared at du Bois. He was starting to sound like he was more with it. 'Can I offer you some drugs?'

'I'm fine,' Beth assured him.

Du Bois raised his carbine to port and lit a cigarette with the lighter in his free hand.

'What do you mean "this has been done to you"?' she asked. 'Someone forced you to be a hippy?'

'I'm not a ... well, yes. It's a thematic prison.' Again he glared at du Bois.

'This guy's not a friend of yours, is he?' Beth asked. Du Bois and Gideon continued to glare at each other.

'Gideon here is a fantasist, a less malevolent version of the Do As You Please clan—' du Bois started.

'I'm nothing like those—'

'His father was an actual scientist. He was with the allies when they liberated Europe and came across the Nazis' cache of S-tech. Gideon inherited the cache.'

'Tell me, Malcolm, do you really believe that, or do I just need an origin story? I'm curious, did my brother work for you in the end? He thought that technology had the potential to free us from brutality as well.'

Du Bois noticed Beth looking at the wall that separated them from the rest of London. The surrounding foliage was doing a good job of deadening the sound of the city's death. When she turned back Gideon was staring intently at her. Du Bois could see her discomfort growing.

'Didn't work out so well for him, though,' said Gideon.

'Let me guess, all things aspire to chaos? That's all you had to offer,' du Bois snapped, angry with himself for getting enmeshed in this old argument.

'Entropy,' Gideon said quietly, still staring at Beth.

'Your brother thought what you wanted him to think. At least until you killed him,' du Bois spat.

'You killed your own brother?' Beth asked, though there was little in the way of recrimination in her voice.

'A number of times. It was complicated.'

'It was the wish fulfilment of an insecure child given to day-dreaming. The problem was his access to the tech meant that he could effectively live out his fantasies,' du Bois explained to Beth.

'That's not quite—'

'He engaged in some rather unpleasant psychodramas with

friends, acquaintances, people he saw as enemies, and most distastefully, his own family. If I'm being charitable, he got carried away.'

'Except none of that is true,' Gideon said, turning away from Beth to look at du Bois. 'Is it?'

Du Bois had forgotten the unease he felt around this man. He couldn't believe that with everything going on right now Gideon could still unnerve him.

Gideon turned back to Beth. 'They have no idea what I am so they invented stories, added me to their personal mythology and imprisoned me with stolen technology.' He raised his hands, gesturing around him.

'There are worse places,' Beth said quietly.

'They might not fear change, but they wish to control it.' Gideon faced du Bois again. 'How's that going?'

Beth was looking between the two of them. 'So what happened?' she finally asked.

'They made me a cliché. I was an agent for change, and they turned me into a sixties throwback. I can't conceptualise anything beyond this.'

Du Bois was laughing but there was little humour in it. 'Oh yes, he wanted to be a physicist, a science hero, and a rock star. He wanted to have adventures but adventures have victims. He wanted to be an assassin, because assassins are cool, but that meant people had to die ...' He could feel Beth looking at him. He knew there was something in his voice, as if he wasn't so sure now.

'Bad people,' Gideon said quietly.

'In your opinion.' Du Bois took a drag on his cigarette angrily.

'You see, Beth—' Gideon started.

Du Bois saw Beth narrow her eyes. Du Bois couldn't explain how he knew her name either.

'—Some of the people I killed weren't very nice. They were just the sort of venal, corrupt, greedy arseholes that the Circle liked to recruit and I killed them properly. With a little needle.' He turned back to du Bois. 'They weren't coming back from that, were they?'

'Tell me, do you still believe all that bullshit you used to spout?' du Bois demanded.

'Well, everything since 1969 does seem to have been something of an anti-climax.'

Du Bois felt his patience slip away. 'Here we go! Whining about your failed revolution! All the proponents of which either sold out, or died of what amounted to self indulgence!' He nodded towards the sonic cane, which was now playing 'Celebration of the Lizard'.

'Are you missing feudalism?' Gideon asked, smiling under the beard.

Beth couldn't help but laugh.

Du Bois glanced at her irritably.'At least we got things done,' he said weakly.

'Trapped in the same mindset for a thousand years? I'm not sure that good organisational skills are justification for tyranny.'

'What you and your ilk fail to understand is that someone has to be in charge, or what happened with your revolution is the end result ...' He knew Beth was looking at him, eyebrows raised.

'It wasn't my—'

'... nothing!' du Bois snapped.

'It's a trap, isn't it?' Beth said quietly. Both men turned to look at her. 'There's a point in time, I don't know, like when you become aware, or excited by the larger world, and then we go on to compare everything to that moment in history and never quite realise that nothing can live up to when we were all young and beautiful.'

Du Bois and Gideon were both staring at her. She was turning red with the attention. Du Bois wondered if she had ever truly believed that she was beautiful.

Gideon slumped back on his soiled sofa. 'Why are you here? There's an apocalypse going on, don't you know?'

'I need to get home, and then to America.'

'So? Aren't you the ultimate henchman of the ultimate conspiracy? You have more resources than I do. Besides, I only deal in retrotech, which I thought you would have known.'

'We have to go to Bradford as well,' Beth told him.

Du Bois wanted to object, but instead he looked down and said nothing. When he looked up Gideon was leaning forwards, staring at him.

'Is this your new Grace?' he asked, pointing at Beth.

Du Bois frowned. He felt Beth looking at him.'I don't know what you're talking about.'

Now Gideon frowned. 'Are you out of favour, du Bois?'

'Just out of contact,' du Bois said evenly.

Gideon studied him. Then he leaned back in the chair. 'You turned me into a seedy little dealer for S- and L-tech ...' he said.

'We tolerated you, nothing more.'

'Nevertheless, dealers get paid.'

Du Bois smiled. 'I can give you what you want. It's the apocalypse; aren't you supposed to be the messiah? Perhaps this time they'll actually nail you to a cross.'

Gideon started laughing. 'Do you think I'm stupid? I've been trying to slip my thematic bonds since '77. I was free two hours ago. I know that the Circle have more important things to do than check up on me right now.'

Du Bois's face fell.

'Please,' Beth said quietly.

Gideon pointed at her. 'You ... you remind me of someone. I just wish I could remember who.' He looked around at the guests at his party. 'This wasn't what it used to be like. I don't think I like these people.'

'They're still people,' Beth told him.

This seemed to make up Gideon's mind. He stood up and started pulling on clothes that looked a little too small for him but would have been stylish more than forty years ago. Though even forty years ago there would have still been too many ruffles, flares and high heels in the other man's outfit for du Bois's taste. Gideon slid an odd-looking pistol into a shoulder holster and then threw on a black velvet car coat.

Beth looked at du Bois and shrugged. Du Bois just shook his head.

Du Bois and Beth watched as Gideon strolled down Kensington High Street past urban phages with broken teeth. Outside an architect's office a group of lost and broken well-dressed men with tears in their eyes attempted to trace the cracks in the pavement.

Gideon led them into Kensington Gardens. Du Bois was aware of children in romper suits, feather headdresses and war paint, carrying bows in the undergrowth. He was hoping he wouldn't have to shoot any of them.

As Gideon headed towards a small copse of trees to the cacophonous sound of the park's parakeets, du Bois noticed a trail of ash-like carbon coming from the other man. His beard and much of his hair were falling off, his fat was deflating. His clothes were changing, his car coat becoming a hip-length jacket from Lee Roach, shirt and trousers by Gieves & Hawkes of Savile Row. A pair of Rochester 'Albion' Chelsea boots, by Jeffery West, completed the ensemble.

Du Bois was keeping an eye on the young children stalking them in the undergrowth as Beth and Gideon pulled scrim netting off a Westland Scout light helicopter. Gideon climbed in first and started the pre-flight checks.

The helicopter took them up over the park. The sun was just beginning to go down behind them. Only as they flew over the rooftops could they start to understand the full extent of the damage. The city was spotted with the burning craters of plane crashes on the Heathrow approach corridor. Entire streets had been demolished. Gideon had to fight to control the helicopter as banking Tornado jets flew over the city at near rooftop level. The roundels on the tails of the aircraft had been painted over with black flags. Something dropped from the planes and suddenly St Paul's roof was silhouetted against a horizon of flame.

Du Bois was leaning out of the helicopter, one foot on the skid. This reminded him of Vietnam, Iraq, countless other unhappy places around the world. He remembered when Gideon had come close to engineering a US invasion of Britain as a protest against the Vietnam War. The airframe of the Westland Scout was shaking violently. Du Bois had been in enough helicopter crashes in war zones to start to worry. The matter of the helicopter was transforming, turning itself into a more modern aircraft, an MH-6J Little Bird.

Then they were coming down in the grounds of a nineteenth century brick-building complex. It looked like a large private house attached to a chapel, or a small church. High walls topped with electrified razor wire and heavy, metal gates protected the complex.

Next to where the Little Bird had landed was a Hawker Siddeley T4A. A two-seat trainer version of the Harrier Jump Jet V/STOL aircraft. It had been given a bright, psychedelic paint job and was fully armed.

Gideon turned to look at du Bois and grinned.

'Why would you do that to an aircraft?' du Bois demanded.

'I know, it seems so retro now, doesn't it?'

'It doesn't have the range—' du Bois started.

'It isn't what it seems. That's basically a shell for an L-tech aircraft. It has enough stealth capabilities to avoid casual detection, though it may struggle to hide from the capabilities of the Circle. But that's okay, because you're just out of touch at the moment, right?'

Something about the way that Gideon said it made the skin on the back of du Bois's neck prickle. Beth had climbed out of the helicopter and was standing by the Harrier, looking at it with a mixture of awe and worry.

'Have you seen Alexia?' du Bois asked.

'Now there's a girl who knows how to change with the times.' Gideon leaned in close to du Bois. 'I like your sister, I mean *really* like her.' Du Bois gritted his teeth but managed to control his temper. 'I haven't seen her,' Gideon finally said.

'Do you have a way to find her?'

'Looking? But you know, the indolence.'

Du Bois just glared at him.

Gideon felt the downdraught ruffle his hair as the Harrier rose above the trees. He could hear the war beyond the walls. He was just about ready for the modern world. He wondered if he should get a new guitar.

6
A Long Time After the Loss

They watched Scab walk out of the conference room. The Monk had to admit there was a certain amount of defiance in his exit, however much she wished to put it down to sheer petulance. She glanced at Churchman. Despite the golden armour she knew him well enough to know he was disappointed. However ruthless he had to be, she knew the years had softened him, while the rest of Known Space had just got harder.

'He's insane,' Talia said quietly.

'So you slept with him, then?' It was out of her mouth before she realised she'd said it. It was an ancient reflex. It was the repressed anger over the words they had exchanged the last time they'd met. Talia looked like she'd been slapped.

'You haven't changed!' Then Talia was storming out of the room.

The Monk banged the back of her head against the transparent smart matter of the internal wall. Everyone was looking at her now. Even Churchman had turned in his chair. Elodie had stopped examining her nails and was grinning at her.

The Monk pushed herself off the wall and followed Talia. She felt someone grab her arm. She broke the grip and moved away, turning, instinctively ready to fight. Vic, the big insect, was standing over her.

'Maybe I should go and speak to her?' he suggested.

'Really?' the Monk blurted, more out of surprise than anything else. She shook her head. 'Okay, fine.' She turned and left the room anyway and 'faced the Cathedral for Scab's whereabouts.

It took a moment for the Monk to realise that the horrible rasping noise was Scab singing. She was just about able to make out the words.

'Every time I plant a seed, He said kill it before it grow, He said kill them before they grow.'

He was walking around the upper corridors in the Cathedral's roof. Where he walked the floor was turning transparent so he could look down at the clouds in the massive habitat. It had started to rain below. A light cruiser was rising up through the dark clouds. The Monk recognised the cruiser as the *St Andrew*. She didn't like the ship's AI.

'Oi, wanker!' the Monk shouted.

Scab ignored her. He was wearing an ancient pair of audio crystals in his ears that would impair his hearing but there was no way he couldn't be aware of her, particularly with the black sphere of his P-sat bobbing along on its AG motor after him.

She increased her pace and reached for his shoulder, grabbing him and yanking him around. It was, of course, what he had been waiting for. A rapid flurry of strike, counter strike and attempted locks. She thought she had the upper hand for a moment as her strong fingers closed around his neck and she lifted him off his feet and slammed him into the wall. Then she felt his fingernail push through her hardening, armoured skin. Her eyes met his: cold, dead.

'What's wrong with you?' she demanded. But she knew the answer. He was just perfectly adapted to live in this age. He probably didn't even understand the question.

'You think you can kill with impunity and still be a good person?' he asked. The Monk was asking herself why she had gone after Scab. From interrogating Benedict/Scab she knew there was no reasoning with him. He wasn't going to listen to a lecture and resolve to be a better person. There was barely a person there. He was little more than a malignant psychopathology as platform for weapons. She would hate him if there were anything there to hate.

Is this foreplay? She had no idea who had initiated it. They were kissing. She felt her *gi* tugged open as she fumbled with his flies with too much eagerness. She 'faced the Cathedral asking it to divert people from the corridor, not that Scab would have cared.

'It's like fucking a corpse I made,' he whispered romantically. Teeth bared, she hit him, hard. He swayed and almost fell over the vertiginous drop; she felt him enter her.

*

The Monk was leaning against the wall holding her head as Scab pulled his trousers up. She was remembering threatening Benedict/Scab.

Why do I have some sick attraction to this psycho? She was disgusted with herself. Scab stood for pretty much everything she hated about this age. *It must be some residual holdover from Game*, she told herself. They had lived on Game as lovers, albeit with different personalities.

She looked up to find Scab watching her. She couldn't read his expression. He nodded once and started walking back the way they had both come. Below them the *St Andrew* was still hovering. She could make out the statuary, the blister-like weapon batteries and the lines of its energy dissipation matrix on its thickly armoured hull. Scab reached the end of the corridor and nodded to someone just out of sight before turning the corner and disappearing from sight.

The Monk was trying to clean herself up, her *gi* in disarray, when Elodie stepped around the corner. The feline glared at the human. The Monk closed her eyes and let out a groan. Her day wasn't going well at all. When she opened her eyes Elodie was much closer to her.

'Seduction by being his murder victim? Think if you let him kill you often enough he'll start to like you?' Elodie enquired. 'Pretty sick, not to mention servile and pathetic.'

'Okay look ...' the Monk started. 'I unreservedly apologise for fucking your boyfriend—'

'He's not my boyfriend!' Elodie spat.

'Fine, whatever,' the Monk said. 'Let's assume it was a momentary lapse in judgement – to the point of insanity – on my part. I'll apologise again and then we can all forget about it. Perhaps to the point of editing our memories after I've bleached myself down.'

'He's in love with her,' Elodie muttered. She did not sound entirely rational. It was at odds with the calculating professional that the Monk had come to expect. 'He thinks I don't know.' She didn't even seem to be talking to the Monk now.

'What are you talk—' the Monk started. Elodie's padded hands were on either side of her face now. The feline's mouth pressed against hers. The Monk's lips parted before she had a chance to think. Elodie's tongue probed her mouth for a deeper kiss. The Monk pushed the feline away so hard that soft-machine augmented muscles threw Elodie across the corridor and into the other wall. The feline bounced and landed crouched on all fours, hissing. The Monk's hands dropped to her knives, though she intended just to switch on her coherent energy field if Elodie attacked her.

'What the fuck?' the Monk demanded when she managed to become verbal again.

Elodie straightened up. The Monk was astonished when she saw tears in the feline's eyes as Elodie moved towards her.

'Please don't make me hurt you,' the Monk said.

'You've hurt me enough!' Elodie yowled. It was practically a caterwaul. Then the feline spat at the Monk. The Monk tried to shift out of the way but Elodie was too close. Then she ran away.

The Monk watched her go as she wiped spit off her face. She had her neunonics run an internal diagnostic to make sure there was nothing unusual in the saliva.

'Are you okay?' Churchman asked over a 'face link. The Monk groaned internally.

'Does everyone know?' the Monk snapped over the 'face link. She almost asked him if he had enjoyed the show but she knew who she was really angry with. She was trying to think of a quicker, more destructive way she could have complicated her life. She was struggling to come up with anything.

'Well, the Cathedral, myself and Miss Negrinotti.'

'Ideally I'd like to keep it that way.'

'Mr Scab is leaving,' Churchman told her. *Good*, she thought. 'I have agreed to provide him with upgrades for his ship and a lot of black credit.'

'I hope he's taking that fucking cat with him!'

'Beth, we've discussed speciesism before. You know the guidelines,' Churchman gently scolded. 'Are you going to speak to Talia?' Churchman 'faced.

You mean apologise? 'Unless you need me I'm going to go and visit with friends,' she 'faced back. *Bravely.*

'I understand that we are often attracted to people who aren't good for us,' Churchman started. 'But ...'

The Monk pushed herself off the wall, waving her arms about over her head as she started to make her way towards her rooms. 'I'm really not in the mood for a paternal discussion right now!' she shouted out loud, 'facing it at the same time.

*

Elodie was waiting outside Talia's room as Talia and Vic approached.

Talia looked up at Elodie suspiciously. Vic was all but hovering over the human protectively.

'Girl time,' Elodie told the 'sect. His puppy-like adoration for the human girl was contemptible but she was impressed he had stood up to Scab, even if it was with the de facto backing of the Church. He wasn't nearly as frightened of her as he was of his partner/captor.

'I've got nothing to say to you,' Talia said. Elodie knew the jealous girlfriend act wouldn't work with the younger sister. Talia had a better idea of what Elodie was like.

'Look, I'm not going to pretend that I like you. In fact, if I was more aware of your existence I'd probably spend a moment or two feeling disgust for the way you explore the most extraordinary levels of weakness and victimhood, but who has the time?'

'As always, lovely speaking to you,' Talia said, and started to move past the feline.

Elodie took hold of her arm.

'Get your fucking hands off me!' Talia snapped, and tried to shake Elodie's hand off. Vic moved to intervene.

'I don't like you but there are some things … Look, I have siblings as well, and what your sister has done ain't right.' Elodie didn't like the way that Vic was looking at her.

'What do you mean?' Talia asked.

'I'm home!' Beth called as she entered the flat. The same peeling wallpaper, the same posters, worn furniture, empty wine and cider bottles and the smell of the last meal greeted her. She knew she had effectively trapped herself in the past. She always felt faintly ridiculous at the way she looked in the immersion. The way she used to look. The boots, combat trousers, band T-shirt and the painted leather jacket that she wore like armour. Beth had never realised what a pain having hair was until she'd shaved it all off.

She walked into the lounge. Maude looked up at her, smiling. She was sitting on the floor surrounded by books, though the television was on and her laptop was open on a social media site.

Uday was sitting on the sofa with a mug of tea, watching the television. He looked up at her, eyebrow raised.

'Rough day at the funfair?' he asked.

'You've no idea,' Beth said. 'You look hard at work.' He stuck his tongue out at her.

'Chavs still giving you trouble?' Maude asked. Beth couldn't help but laugh. 'I'll make you a cup of tea.'

'Oh, don't fuss, Maude, she's a big girl. She can look after herself.'

Maude pulled a face at Uday and then got up to make Beth a cup of tea anyway. Beth plumped down into one of the two sofas in the flat and just let banter and gossip wash over her.

They weren't Maude and Uday. They were simpler in so many different ways. Of course they had been corrupted. The Seeders had driven them insane and then the spores from the thing in the Solent had infected their flesh. When she had come to the Cathedral they had done their best to reassemble their personalities and then create an immersion environment for them to grow and live their lives in. Good lives, pleasant lives, lives she felt they had deserved, doubtless like billions of others had. At least, she told herself that was what she had done. Sometimes she wondered. She hoped and prayed this wasn't for her benefit, her entertainment, a place of refuge for days like this.

She had expanded the time parameters of the environment. Thousands of years had been mere months in the immersion. It contracted and expanded when she was going to visit so it complemented their narrative. The AI ran a parallel story for Beth and seamlessly integrated it with her neunonics when she put herself into the immersion but that was it, the rest she left to them and the AI.

Maude handed her a tea. The immersion never got the taste right. At least she didn't think it did, she was several clones and many soft-machine augments away from her original self. God knows what she had for taste buds now. Still, sometimes it felt like millennia since she'd last had a good cup of tea.

The pocket of her leather jacket started to vibrate. Beth frowned.

'It still gives me a warm fuzzy feeling that you decided to join us in the twenty-first century and buy a phone. I know it must have frightened you and all, what with all the demons in the tiny box,' Uday said.

Beth gave him the finger and answered the phone.

'I think we probably need you down here,' Churchman said,

although he sounded like Ted, who had run the Clarence Pier amusements in Southsea. He had been a large, fat, cheerful man and he had stood up for her when she had needed him to.

'Bollocks!' Beth said and hung up.

'Some big dipper-related emergency?' Uday enquired.

'I thought we were going to watch *Strictly*!' Maude said, pouting.

'I'm going to tell all the other emo kids you watch *Strictly*,' Uday threatened.

'I told you, I'm a goth!'

'I'm going to tell all the other retro-emo kids that you watch *Strictly*.'

'Sorry, kids, I've got to go,' Beth said, getting up and leaving the lounge to the sounds of protests and bickering. She closed the door of the flat behind her and dropped out of the immersion.

The Monk's place was at the apex of the roof. She had the smart matter make it look like it had a low-beamed wooden ceiling, stone walls and a polished, bare-boards floor; a kind of open plan, rustic attic. She was lying on her very large and comfortable bed.

'What?' she 'faced Churchman, but she already knew. The Cathedral had sent images from outside her attic to her neunonics. Talia was hammering on the door and shouting. The Monk closed her eyes and made a moaning noise. 'How did she know where I was?' But she knew that answer too..

'Did you want me to lie?' Churchman 'faced back.

'Obviously,' the Monk muttered, but she didn't 'face it. With a thought she had the smart matter start to extrude a comfortable Chesterfield from the floor. She sighed again and opened the door with another thought. Talia stormed in.

'You fucked Scab!' she shouted at her sister. Her face was red with the kind of fury that only family can really cause. It was just like being back at home.

'That fucking pussycat ...' the Monk muttered. 'I hadn't realised that you and he were an item, I thought that, y'know, it was casual ...'

'That I'm a slut?' Talia was still shouting.

Porn actress and occasional whore, actually, the Monk thought but decided to keep it to herself.

'I thought you and Vic ...' she said instead.

'He's a friend.' Talia thought for a minute. 'And an insect!'

71

Beth had seen it before, the 'friends' trailing her around, manipulated into doing what she wanted. Beth knew that she had been in the wrong, that fucking Scab was a bad idea for so many reasons. Even so, she found herself getting angry. She almost administered herself a slight sedative. Almost.

'Oh, so Scab's yours as well, is he? Someone else who's off limits because you say so? Perhaps you should take to spaying them like your insane fucking cat friend!'

'Elodie doesn't ... What do you mean someone else? We were never competing, anyone I had was always out of your league!'

Beth actually rocked back on her heels. 'You haven't fucking changed, have you? Are you angry because I fucked the biggest arsehole in Known Space before you got to him? Why am I not fucking surprised? I'm astonished you didn't offer to give Patron a blow job the moment you saw him!'

Talia had her hand on her hip now. Her mask of fury had grown cold. 'Well, at least I don't have to have surgery to make myself pretty enough to steal men.'

'I've been cloned ... it's optimised for the things I do.'

'The violence, you mean? Really?' Talia asked mock-innocently. Then she leaned in closer to her sister. 'Then tell me. Why did you have yourself cut to look like me?'

It felt like a slap, no, like a bucket of ice water thrown over her. She had to make a conscious effort not to look round for a mirror, though she would have had to create one from the smart matter.

'What are you talking about?' Beth finally managed.

'Did you think I wouldn't notice? Scab obviously did.' The Monk could see the vicious look of victory on her sister's face. 'And we were never actually related. You decided to look like me.'

'I don't ...'

'How long have you had to convince yourself of that?'

Beth had forgotten just how much better at this Talia was. Even before she could control her temper, she had never hit her sister. Talia's words were always too hurtful.

'You want to know why I like Scab?' Talia asked, her voice like brittle ice. 'Maybe I'm just trying to find a boyfriend you can't kill!'

Beth went cold. She could not believe what she had just heard, even coming from her sister.

'That's what you do now, isn't it? Kill. So nice you chose to experiment on my boyfriend!'

'He was going to kill you,' the Monk said quietly.

'Maybe. You certainly got a taste for it, though, didn't you?'

So it was just going to be about inflicting pain now. 'Why don't you ask yourself how many died because of you?'

'I didn't ask—'

'For any of this? To be born? I mean the people who died because of selfish decisions you took. You know I spoke to Maude and Uday about you.' It was with some satisfaction that Beth noticed her sister at least had the decency to look guilty at the sound of Maude's name. 'Whore.' Beth just breathed the word. She knew there was no coming back from this. She was too angry to care. *Why? Did you have yourself sculpted to look like her? Even a little bit?*

Talia's expression had grown cold again. 'I'd rather be a whore than a mass murderer. You and Scab are made for each other,' Talia said evenly. 'How the hell can you judge me?'

Talia turned and walked towards the door. Beth wanted to tell her to stop. To keep the door closed. To try and speak to her.

The door opened and Talia walked out. The door closed. Beth stared at it.

Talia managed to make it some of the way down the corridor before she stumbled and had to lean against the wall. Then the tears came. It felt like she would never be able to stop them.

The terrifying multi-directional elevator/transit monorail journey to her room had been almost enough to shake Talia out of her misery and anger. Almost.

The Cathedral's unobtrusive AI had let her know that she could configure the room however she wanted. For now it was enough that she had a bed and an assembler with a half-decent recipe for vodka and marijuana.

'Ms Negrinotti is here to see you,' the polite AI announced over Joy Division. Part of the wall became a screen. The feline was standing by the door.

'Brilliant,' Talia muttered, sniffing and trying to wipe tears and snot off her face with the back of her hand. 'Can you tell her to go and fuck herself please?'

'I shall certainly convey that you do not wish to receive visitors at the moment,' the AI said. The screen disappeared. 'I do apologise. The security to your door is being overridden, would you like me to alert the militia?'

The door to her room slid open and Talia sighed. Elodie strode in. Talia considered lobbing the half-drunk bottle of vodka at the feline but decided it would be a waste of good vodka.

'Fuck off,' Talia told her. She couldn't even muster much in the way of venom.

Elodie held her hands up. 'Look, I know we got off on the wrong foot—'

'Wrong foot? Wrong foot!' The feline had to duck as Talia flung the vodka bottle at her. It bounced off the wall and fell to the thick carpet, only to be absorbed nearly immediately. 'You have been a total ... cunt to me since the moment we met!'

'Yeah, okay. Look, I'm sorry. Scab and I go way back. It wasn't easy. I mean you're really pretty, I mean not now ...'

'Piss off.'

'But normally; I have to stake my claim. And it's not just me – none of us are nice when we do that, humans, lizards, 'sect queen, but felines are the best at it.'

Talia could see this. It wasn't the first time that someone had tried to make her life difficult because they were jealous of her.

'Okay. So?'

'So we're territorial, but you're crew. We fight but I'll protect you against outsiders.'

'Who? Beth?' Talia sighed. 'She's not an outsider, she's my sister,' she said miserably. 'And possibly an alien.'

'He doesn't love her, you know.'

Talia was surprised that Elodie would even suggest such a thing. 'Well no, obviously, he's incapable. It was just a sleazy f—'

Elodie sat on the edge of the bed.

'He's in love with the ghost of the ship.'

Talia frowned. 'What are you—'

'I had a brother who did something similar to me,' Elodie said. 'It really hurts, doesn't it?'

Talia nodded.

7
Ancient Britain

The valley in the shadow of the Mother Hill was white with snow now. They had seen little of the Lochlannach. They either stayed in the fort, or were occasionally seen scuttling around the mouth of the cave that led to Annwn and subsequently to Oeth on the island in the cavern lake.

Tangwen was bored. She did not think that she liked going to war. Among her people warfare was raiding, and then, when they were tracked back into the marshes, ambushes. Since she had agreed to help Britha, Teardrop and Fachtna, they had seemed to do little but run and fight. Although there had been a lot of talking and arguing as well. All this waiting, however, made her want to leave and do something else. It gave her too much time to think about the things she had done. Sleep came easily but it was not restful. She saw the faces of those she had killed. Not in battle, but to prove points, to enforce discipline. The killings had saved lives in the long run, so she told herself, but she wondered if it had just been easier to kill those who got in her way. Even if she had left she knew her dreams would have gone with her. Besides, she had responsibilities again. Though nothing as well defined as seeing the survivors of the wicker man to safety.

As soon as they had arrived in the valley, Bladud had sent well-protected foraging parties ranging far and wide across the surrounding countryside. It seemed that the Lochlannach had been content to leave alone the food supplies of the villages they had attacked. Bladud's foraging parties had harvested what they could, though much of it had already spoiled on the stalk. They took what stores they could find, though much of that had been allowed to run down before the impending harvest. Where they had done well was with livestock. There had been a goodly amount of cows, some pigs and aurochs, and many, many sheep. Rarely had a warband had so much mutton to eat.

She was sitting on a fallen tree next to a trail of churned up, now frozen, mud and animal shit that led east from the camp, out of the valley, when the newcomers arrived. The snow was coming down heavily again. It was already halfway up her calves. There was little visibility and their emergence from the flurries might have surprised someone who had not drunk of Britha's blood, but Tangwen had heard the sound of creaking wood and iron-shod horses on the frozen earth, and smelled leather, frozen sweat and beasts long before she saw them.

The warriors rode small but sturdy looking ponies, and had either small round shields or large oblong ones hanging from their horses. They all had longswords at their sides and casting spears in leather sheaths hanging from their saddles. They carried their longspears – which meant they were ready to fight – but the tips of the spears were pointing down, which meant they were prepared to talk first.

They were small, dark-haired men and women wrapped in cloaks and furs. They wore plaid trews and the men had neatly trimmed beards and moustaches. Few of them wore armour of leather or metal. She wondered if the blue woad tattoos she saw creeping above necklines and onto faces would keep them safe. Many tribes painted themselves for war, ritual, and to hide themselves, but to permanently mark the skin in this way meant one thing: the warriors from the far north had travelled to join them.

Behind the horses came the chariots for the warriors of higher rank. Tangwen remained unconvinced of the practicality of chariot warfare. She knew they were useful in the right circumstances but you had to be very lucky, or going up against a particularly stupid opponent, to get those circumstances. And they were of no use in the marshes she had grown up in.

The first chariot was reined to a halt in front of her. The charioteer was at odds with the rest of the northerners. She was tall, blonde, blue-eyed. Tangwen thought her face would have once been attractive were it not for the puckered scar tissue and the angry expression.

Standing on the back of the chariot was a small man, only a little taller than Tangwen, with a surprisingly slight build. He wore a fine cloak and had a thick gold torc around his neck, which must have been cold against his skin in this weather. She wondered if they had changed just up the track to make an impression, though they were mud-spattered and frost-covered, which told of a long journey this day. His shield was well-made but showed signs of extensive use. Chunks were missing from his scalp and his face; his mouth had been cloven at some point in the past and left a mess of broken teeth, but his beard was neatly trimmed and oiled. He had clearly taken a lot of time with the beard. Tangwen recognised a *rhi* when she saw one.

The *rhi* spoke but it came out as a mush of words. Despite the gifts given to her by the chalice, she could not understand what he was saying. She sensed rather than saw movement to her right. She glanced over to see a stooped figure in a brown robe with a tasselled hood covering their features walk out of the flurries, leaning heavily on a staff as gnarled as their form looked. The bent figure was clearly a *dryw*.

The *rhi* was speaking again, slower but still in the language of the Pecht. 'Little girl, do you know Britha, *ban draoi* of the weakling Cirig people?' was what Tangwen was pretty sure the man said. His look spoke of his utter contempt for her. Tangwen raised an eyebrow at being called 'little girl' and looked down to check she was still carrying weapons, wearing armour, and generally comporting herself as a warrior. She was.

I guess my fame as a mighty warrior has not spread as far north as I had hoped, she thought, a small smile curling her lips. She knew she should take offence, challenge the *rhi*, fight his champion, but she was trying to avoid killing members of her own warband as much as possible.

'Something funny, girl?' a rasping voice demanded from underneath the *dryw*'s hood.

'Yes,' Tangwen said simply, though with less respect than one should perhaps use when addressing a *dryw*. She wondered if the *dryw* had somehow heard her smile, as the tasselled hood covered her eyes. Behind the bent figure she could see the northerners' spearmen and women. Unlike the warriors, they wore armour of leather and a few had metal armour, though it looked ill-fitting and much repaired, so she assumed it had been the spoils of war. Tangwen waited for the *rhi* to introduce himself. He did not. Instead he turned and looked through the snow towards the camp. Tangwen smiled again. In many ways it was lucky that they had met her first. Almost anybody else would have challenged the *rhi*. She had assumed that was the point. Make an entrance. Display strength. Gauge the strength of your opposition. 'Well, I'll just go and fetch the weakling for you.'

Tangwen pushed herself off the tree trunk and walked towards the camp. She heard a comment about the southron tribes arming their girl-children and heard answering laughter from the mounted warriors.

Tangwen sighed when she heard the raised voices. She recognised Clust, the Trinovantes warleader, arguing with Garim, Bladud's husky, thickly bearded new second. The Brigante lieutenant looked like a younger, less scarred Nerthach, but he was no replacement for the big grizzled warrior who had been the Witch King's strong right arm. The similarities between Garim and Nerthach just made Tangwen miss Nerthach all the more. She had liked the big man, though she had only known him a brief time before a touch of Crom Dhubh's strange sword had utterly destroyed him. She hoped his soul had made it to Annwn, but somehow she doubted it.

Clust and Garim were arguing about the precedence of their tribes in the initial attack. They were standing under an open skin shelter that had been erected for councils. A crude model of the area had been made from snow on a hastily assembled, rough-hewn table. Bladud looked resigned, and Britha looked like she was ready to kill one, or both, of the warriors.

'There's an idiot here to see you,' Tangwen said, cutting across Clust and Garim's angry exchange. Both the warriors looked up, furious at the interruption, but they kept their peace when they saw who had spoken.

'I have sufficient here, thank you,' Britha spat. Bladud laughed as Garim and Clust coloured.

'This one asked for you by name.' Tangwen saw the frown on Britha's face deepen. It would not be the first group to join their camp who had heard of her infamy. 'He's from the far north, one of your people. A *rhi*, I think.'

'One of the Pecht?' Britha asked.

Bladud was watching the exchange.

'Yes, very rude.'

'A small man, badly scarred but a perfect beard?'

'Aye, that sounds like him. You know the fool?' Tangwen asked. She saw a smile spread across Britha's face.

'Aye, aye I do and he fights all his challenges himself, so don't call him fool to his face unless you want to kill him in an unfair fight.'

'There's a *dryw* with him. An old, bent woman, keeps her features covered,' Tangwen told the other woman and saw Britha's face fall. She heard her mutter something that sounded like: 'Will nothing kill her?' in her own language.

'Let us go and meet these guests who do not introduce themselves,' Bladud said, amused.

'Your manners are not improving!' Britha shouted through the snow, her breath misting. She stopped by one of the horses pulling the Pecht leader's chariot and whispered to it, patting it, much to the charioteer's visible displeasure. The short *rhi* climbed down out of the chariot and walked towards Britha, his scars forcing his mouth into a grimace. 'I think I have told you about this before.'

'What could a poor excuse for a *ban draoi*, from a tribe I would have taken as slaves if they had the courage to live further north, tell the likes of me?' the *rhi* demanded. Bladud's eyes widened and Tangwen gasped, her hand falling to her hatchet and knife, but Britha was smiling and the small man's face seemed to split open. It took Tangwen a moment to realise he was grinning. Britha embraced the smaller man.

'It's good to see you,' Britha told him. She tried to blink away the tears in her eyes.

'We need to talk. I've come seeking my people,' he told her.

Britha nodded but the small man seemed to read the answer in her expression. He clenched his fists, squeezing his eyes tight shut, remaining teeth grinding.

'All of them?' he managed.

'We'll talk later,' Britha managed.

He opened his eyes. 'You've been down here too long, you've got soft,' the Pecht *rhi* told her.

Bladud opened his mouth to say something. Tangwen was pretty sure that he wasn't used to being ignored like this.

'She has not grown soft.' The horrid rasping voice came from under the bent *dryw's* hood. 'She is with child.'

Britha wiped the tears away with the back of her hand as her face hardened.'Eurneid,' Britha said coldly.

'Is that all you have to say to me, child?' the bent *dryw* demanded. 'No explanation of what you have done to yourself?

Perhaps you have been hanging around with the likes of *him* too long?' Eurneid nodded towards Bladud. Tangwen felt the Witch King bristle at her side.

'You know who I am then?' Bladud asked.

'I know what you are, false *dryw*!' Eurneid spat and then pulled her hood down.

Tangwen managed to resist the urge to spit and make the sign against evil. The woman was the oldest person that Tangwen had ever seen. She looked like she should have died many summers past. Her skin was so thin Tangwen could see the network of veins underneath. Her eyes were grey, staring orbs, utterly devoid of life, and obviously sightless. Tangwen knew this was one of the hags that she had been told of, one of those who flew with the spirits of the unquiet dead on Samhain-night.

'Even an old blind woman can tell that.' She turned back towards Britha. 'We will hear explanations for your state later. You will be coming back north with me for judgement among the oaks. In the meantime that ... thing ... that darkness in your belly needs tearing out of you.'

Britha touched her stomach. Tangwen had her hatchet in her hand suddenly; she was barely aware of having drawn it.

'I'll saw your face off and wear it to frighten the children before you touch me,' Britha said, but her voice trembled slightly. Tangwen was surprised to hear fear in the older woman's voice.

The *rhi* had his hand on the hilt of his sheathed sword, as did a number of his warriors.

Eurneid turned to face Tangwen. 'You would draw a weapon on a *ban draoi*?' she demanded.

Tangwen tried hard not to think too much about those she had killed at the holy place on the Isle of Madness. 'I'll kill any who would threaten harm to a *dryw* in my presence,' she answered, nodding towards Britha.

'This one isn't a *dryw*, never was,' Eurneid spat.

'Who's this idiot?' the northern *rhi* asked, looking at Bladud.

Tangwen saw Eurneid glance at the short Pecht irritably. She was pretty sure he had asked the question to interrupt the old woman.

'This idiot can speak your language,' Bladud said dryly. If he was irritated by the insults then he was masking it well.

'Good, it'll save me having to sully my tongue with yours.'

'Presumably this is someone who thinks it's interesting to be obnoxious?' Bladud asked Britha. Britha smiled again, though Tangwen could tell she was still troubled.

'No, this is someone who has earned the right to say whatever he pleases atop a pile of corpses,' the Pecht *rhi* explained.

'I like him, he can stay,' Bladud told Britha. Tangwen had to suppress a smile at Bladud's cleverness, once again.

'Bladud, called Witch King—' Britha began. Eurneid gave a snort of contempt. '*Rhi* of the Brigante.' Bladud cast a sideways glance at her – presumably he had expected to be introduced as *Brenin Uchel*, high king. 'May I present Calgacus of the Bitter Tongue, *mormaer* of the Cait, a tribe from further north than my own.'

'I have told you before, I mislike that name,' Calgacus said. 'I am Calgacus of the Perfect Beard!' he announced. Britha laughed, as did Tangwen. Even Bladud had to smile.

'You have had truck with the gods.' Eurneid's accusation was like a pall over any humour. 'You know that is against our ways.'

'We weak southrons do not fear our gods so,' Bladud replied waspishly.

'Because you did not fight them as our ancestors did, because you bare your arses to them, because you are servile, and because you are not very bright.'

'I tire of this lack of courtesy. What do you want?' Bladud snapped. 'If you are just here to cause discord then be on your way, or we will use you as practice before we fight the Loch-lannach.'

'Is this one like Cruibne? Wishes to be high king? Ideas above his station?' Calgacus asked Britha.

'That is not what Cruibne wanted, as you well know,' Britha said.

'And my deeds speak for themselves,' Bladud said evenly.

Tangwen was struggling to read the canny Witch King. He was rising only to things he could not ignore.

'I have come for my people,' Calgacus said.

Bladud looked to Britha.

'I only know of one that yet lives,' Britha said quietly. 'And he is in the service of Crom Dhubh.' She nodded up the valley.

Tangwen saw the pain etched across Calgacus's ruined face at Britha's words.

'As you have been,' Eurneid spat.

Tangwen found herself wondering how the hag knew that. Calgacus studied Britha but said nothing.

'I will vouch—' Bladud started.

'Your words mean nothing, oathbreaker!' Eurneid snapped.

Now Tangwen could see Bladud's simmering anger. She knew this game. The *dryw* would use the freedom her position provided to say things to the *rhi* others could not to put him off-balance. She had rarely seen it played so blatantly and with such venom.

'I would have vengeance, then, and this traitor must be dealt with!' Calgacus announced.

'They are enslaved by the Dark Man's magics,' Bladud explained.

'This one was freed but chose to become a slave again,' Britha said.

'Like you?' Eurneid asked slyly.

'I have never been a slave,' Britha said irritably.

'Except to your cunt!'

'Which one of you has the bitter tongue?' Tangwen asked as she dropped her hatchet back into the loop on her belt. She still felt a thrill of fear at talking to a *dryw* so. The hag turned her head to look at Tangwen with blind eyes. Tangwen found herself involuntarily holding her furs tighter around herself despite not really feeling the cold.

'That is the second time, serpent child. One more and I'll snatch your tongue from your pretty head.'

'This serves us nought,' Bladud said. 'If you can fight with more than words then you may join my warband.' He emphasised the word 'my'. 'If not then prepare to fight or be on your way, as you like. It makes no difference to me.'

Calgacus regarded the Witch King carefully, then he smiled his awful smile.

'So you have a spine, then?' the Pecht *rhi* asked. Bladud smiled as much through exasperation as amusement. 'You should consider yourself lucky I have no use for a Southron warband, though I do need more slaves.'

'For someone with a reputation for straight talking you certainly take a long time to say anything.'

The smile disappeared from Calgacus's face. Tangwen was aware of the Cait warriors shifting all around them.

'If, and I mean if, you prove strong enough to lead this warband then we will fight alongside you.'

Bladud nodded and then looked to Britha. 'Deal with this,' he said, before turning and walking back towards the camp.

Tangwen felt Britha bristle but the other woman said nothing.

It just seemed to appear out of the flurries of snow. A shaggy, white-furred creature with the face of a man's corpse. Her hatchet was back in her hand, her dagger in the other.

'Hold!' Calgacus snapped in a voice used to being obeyed. Tangwen felt Britha grab her arm.

'Look again,' the older woman said. The man had limed his face. He wore thick woollen trews and a thick woollen *blaidth*. He had tied a bearskin to himself and that too had been limed to blend with the snow.

'One of my scouts,' Calgacus told her. Tangwen felt a moment's embarrassment. He was doing the same thing she had done herself many times. 'Selbath?' Calgacus addressed the scout. The man pointed north into the flurries of snow.

'The fair folk,' the scout, apparently called Selbath, started breathlessly. Calgacus looked sceptical at mention of the fair folk. Tangwen assumed he meant the Lochlannach. 'Coming across the ridge. Saw them with my own eyes. They make for the fort.'

Now she looked at him, Tangwen could see he was covered in sweat and panting for breath.

'How many?' Calgacus demanded.

'More than fifty. I didn't stay to count. They knew I was there.'

Calgacus looked surprised, as did his tall, blonde charioteer. There was muttering from the mounted Cait warriors.

'And you ran?' Calgacus asked. The man nodded, still trying to catch his breath. 'Aye, well can't say as I blame you. They don't call you the Timid for no—'

'There's more!' Selbath cried.

Calgacus looked like he had been slapped, so surprised was he at the scout's interruption. Tangwen was aware of something but she wasn't quite sure what it was. She looked around. Some snow fell off a tree. The naked branch was shaking.

'I'm sorry,' Selbath pointed to the east, the way the Cait had come. There was a tremor in his arm. 'Giants,' he said.

Now through the lime and the exhaustion Tangwen could see the man's terror. Tangwen felt her own bowels turn to ice as she remembered the battle on the beach in the shadow of the wicker man.

'Calm yourself,' Calgacus snapped. Tangwen's eyes narrowed as she peered into flurries of snow. Some of the horses whickered nervously. 'These southrons aren't that much taller than us.'

Tangwen thought she saw something through the snow, a huge shadow, though she wondered if her mind was playing tricks on her. Then the first horse reared. A Cait warrior was deposited into the snow on his arse, hard.

'He means giants,' Britha said. Tangwen could hear the tension in the other woman's voice. The ground shook from an impact, and then another. Snow fell from naked trees, winter birds took to the wing despite the weather. Selbath, called the Timid, ran.

They loomed out of the flurries, towering over people and panicking beasts, warped and gnarled, faintly human in shape, each footstep creating an explosion in the snow. A number of the Cait's ponies bolted. The spearmen and women backed away from the huge figures but to their credit did not break. Those with control of their mounts reached for casting spears, arrows began to stud the giants' flesh, but the huge creatures paid no attention.

Tangwen was crouched, feeling useless. She didn't even have her bow. Britha was looking up at them, one hand across her belly, a knife in her other hand. Calgacus dared the shifting chariot to grab his spear and shield even as his charioteer sought to control her team. Only Eurneid moved towards them.

'Eurneid!' Calgacus cried, stopping just short of giving a *dryw* an order.

'Even the Otherworld know not to harm a *dryw*!' the old woman called.

'They are no respecters of—' Britha started, just as one of the giants stood squarely on Eurneid.

The giants, however, did not attack. They just walked by and continued past the camps where there were more cries of warning and fear. They paid no attention to more arrows and casting spears studding their deformed skin. Then they were swallowed by the flurries of snow again. Though the ground still shook.

Tangwen swallowed hard. She could hear the frightened muttering from among the Cait warriors.

'Master yourselves!' Calgacus shouted, though Tangwen was pretty sure that the Pecht *rhi* was more than a little disturbed by the show of force he had just seen. 'Remember where you are!'

Tangwen fell in beside Britha as the black-robed *dryw* moved forwards carefully. Calgacus joined them moments later, two of his warriors with him. There was barely anything left of Eurneid. She was a mangled red mess in a very deep footprint, barely recognisable as having been human.

'There's a lesson in this somewhere,' Calgacus mused. Tangwen couldn't shake the feeling that the Pecht *rhi* was more than a little relieved.

She was aware of movement on either side of her. Warm red liquid spattered her cold skin. One of the Cait warrior's faces had been cut off. The body staggered backwards a few steps and then stumbled to the ground. There was a figure moving quickly towards her. He was a solid, well-built man, wearing no armour and little protection from the cold, a longsword in one hand, a dagger in the other. Tangwen was aware of movement on the other side of her as well. Calgacus was between her and the swordsman. He was moving forwards, punching his small round shield into the swordsman's face.

Tangwen turned. The other Cait warrior was already reddening the snow. A second swordsman was stabbing his longsword at Britha's belly as she threw herself backwards. Tangwen heard the sound of wood hitting flesh behind her. The hunter threw herself forwards, swinging out with her hatchet at the second swordsman's blade. The axe head caught the blade and yanked it away from Britha but the man just turned, the dagger in his other hand snaking out towards Britha's belly. Tangwen was aware of the sound of metal splintering wood behind her as she collided with the second swordsman. They hit the ground together, sliding through the snow. Tangwen howled and spat as she fought frantically. Her skin and the flesh beneath it smoked as his blade cut into her, and she felt the agony of its venom in her blood. Her dagger found his throat before he could do more harm, then her hatchet found the top of his head as he shook beneath her.

Tangwen stood up, spinning round. Calgacus had split the first attacker from hip to shoulder with his unpolished, blued iron blade, and had turned from him because none could survive such a blow.

'No!' Britha cried, running towards the first attacker, dagger in her hand. Tangwen was running as well but she knew she would not be there in time. More of the Cait warriors were sprinting towards the fight. Calgacus started to turn but he was just a man, and they were fighting those who had the blood of gods coursing through their veins. The first swordsman's wound was closing. Tendrils of red metal were knitting the bloodless wound together again. Tangwen felt her body flush with fever as the magics of the chalice fought with the magics of the venom on the blade that had just slashed her.

The first swordsman swung for Calgacus but as Britha reached the Cait *rhi*, the attacker changed the angle of his blow, aiming for her. Tangwen had already thrown her hatchet. The spinning axe flew between Calgacus and Britha, narrowly missing them both, and hit the swordsman just under his right shoulder. It was enough. A screaming Britha parried the longsword on her way in, then rammed her dagger into his chest before the force of her charge sent them both sprawling into the snow.

Britha was sitting atop her attacker now, holding her dagger in both hands as she stabbed down again and again with all her strength, turning his chest cavity into a red ruin. She screamed, tears rolling down her face. Tangwen had seen this before. She knew that sometimes pregnant women had problems controlling themselves. It was one of a number of reasons that she had always preferred the tansy cake.

She glanced back at Calgacus. He looked badly shaken. The Pecht *rhi* looked between the dead Cait warriors.

'Those were two of my best men,' he muttered in his own language. Then he looked at the two dead swordsmen. 'I didn't kill him.' He sounded appalled. 'That blow would have felled a boar.'

'And I'm just a southron girl-child,' Tangwen said, smiling. 'Guess you're not quite as tough up north as you like to boast,' she couldn't resist adding. Calgacus just stared at her.

Britha stood up, using the sleeves of her robe to wipe the tears off her face, smearing her skin with blood as she did so.

'He sent them to kill the baby,' she said. Her voice was cold and hard once more.

8

Now

The retrofitted Harrier Jump Jet was easier to fly than some console games were to play. They could have downloaded and assimilated instructions straight into their neuralware from the plane itself had they wanted to. Though cramped, the cockpit had been made more comfortable and behind their seats there was a secure, armoured storage compartment that could be ejected. The plane's engine looked like something out of a 1960's spy film. Du Bois had told her that this was probably because Gideon had grown it from some kind of L-tech nano-factory that just needed to be given design specs and fed matter. When du Bois had transferred knowledge straight into her neuralware he had provided her with a great deal of conventional knowledge, but he had kept much of his hidden world of secret organisations and alien technology to himself. She understood why. He had wanted a weapon to help him out of a fix. She had been that weapon. He hadn't, however, wanted to betray his employers.

They had kept low. Hugging the contours of the landscape, nap-of-the-Earth flying, she now knew this was called. The Harrier's stealth systems were engaged. Du Bois hadn't wanted to draw attention to them, though he had tried to re-establish contact with his employers several times, to no avail.

Nap-of-the-Earth meant they got to see more of the country close-up as they headed north. They spent a lot of time flying through smoke. They saw mobs in the streets of suburbia, towns and villages; geometric arrangements of bodies in fields; and lots of wreckage. Sometimes the places they flew over looked deserted. There were quiet places, particularly in parts of the countryside, where she could imagine there was nothing wrong at all, then she would see piles of decapitated bodies or some other atrocity.

Beth wanted to cry, but her body was now too efficient to

waste liquid like that. She was pretty sure that she didn't want to, couldn't, live in this world. Du Bois had tried to talk her out of going to see her father, though he hadn't tried very hard. She knew he was probably right. This wasn't going to have a happy ending. The flight north had been very quiet. All of Beth's friends had phones and access to the internet. If anything she had been the most Luddite of all of them. She tried not to think of what they would have become now. It was little consolation that they were too far from Portsmouth to be hosts for the spores of the monstrosity under the waters of the Solent.

Beth wasn't surprised that Bradford was burning. Racial tensions had spilled over into violence more than once in the city's past. Removed of inhibitions, racially motivated violence was revealed for what it really was: a convenient excuse for base, primal behaviour. Culture and skin colour had nothing to do with the open street warfare they saw beneath them as du Bois banked over the town centre. In some ways it was nothing new for Beth.

Du Bois brought the Harrier down smoothly in Peel Park. The park was in a basin on the hills just north of the city centre. There were a few lost souls wandering the area in various states of dress. A number of them looked like they had been attacked but they kept their distance.

They secured the plane and headed up Harrogate Road. It was lined with sooty, grey stone Victorian terraces. Nobody bothered them, possibly because the weapons they were openly carrying put them off. Even the insane instinctively understood a zero sum game when they saw one.

Her key still worked. Beth opened the door a crack and then leant against the doorframe, her eyes squeezed shut. Du Bois had his back to her, looking up and down the steep road. A badly beaten, naked man staggered past, leaving a trail of blood behind him.

'You don't have to go in,' du Bois said quietly. Beth steeled herself and pushed her way into the house. It still smelled of stale cigarette smoke and the cold damp but there was something else there as well. That was when she knew.

It could have been worse, she thought. It hadn't been peaceful. Even through the cloud of flies Beth could see that he had been frightened when he had died. She wasn't sure what she had expected but she was surprised he'd had the strength to cut his own wrists.

Her neuralware was providing her with all sorts of information. Her father's dead body reduced to data. She tried to shut down the process but it was like trying not to think. The lack of rigor mortis and other factors were suggesting a rough time of death. This had happened before the world had been driven mad. Her father had killed himself after her last visit. After she had taken the hope of seeing Talia from him.

'I did this,' she said, mostly to herself.

'No,' du Bois said quietly from the doorway. Beth glanced back at him. He looked troubled. 'There's nothing you can do here now. We need to go.'

Beth turned back to look at her father. 'Why?' she asked quietly. She was trying to remember his smile. Trying to remember hearing laughter in this house. Even when her mother had been alive, even before they had known she was ill, she couldn't remember laughter or smiles. Beth wondered how much of that had been fear of discovery at having effectively stolen Talia. She knew the sudden surge of anger she felt towards her 'sister' wasn't fair but she didn't try to suppress it.

She turned to face du Bois; there was something in his expression that she couldn't quite read. Her face hardened.

'Let's go. I'm done here,' she told him. Du Bois nodded. Then the phone in the hallway started to ring.

The orbital habitat looked like a cross between a modern office building and a petrified biomechanical egg. The material of the habitat looked like contoured black marble. Mr Brown was looking down through a clear, coherent energy field at the burning Earth. He smiled at his own hyperbole. He knew it for what it was: the reflexive, spasmodic, instinctive lashing out of idiot gods.

As far as they could tell the diseased Seeder minds had accessed all the information on the internet. They had used data held by internet providers, social media, commercial data providers, marketing companies, blogs and used it to create information simulacra of people. Then the Seeders had created intuitive information entities to plot the simulacra's worst fears and driven them mad. Finally they had played humanity's dark electronic soul back to itself. That and vast, insane, alien intelligences trying to communicate had done the damage.

The developing countries and poorer parts of the world, places with less sophisticated communications infrastructure, had weathered this storm the best, but the insane part of humanity was reacting to years of blame and fear politics. The military-industrial complex had just had its inhibitions removed.

Mr Brown found himself unmoved. He was leaning on his opiate staff. The bags were depleting faster every day. He would never run out of the synthetic morphine while he had access to matter but even the vast amounts he was now consuming barely took the edge off his agony.

'Have we established contact? With anyone at all?' Mr Brown said out loud. They were keeping electronic contact to a minimum now. They had isolated and then purged their systems. The Control AI, corrupted, had been taken off-line and erased. Now they had to do the work the hard way. Augmented immortals plugged into ancient machinery.

'We have established communication with several of our operatives via tight-beam communication when we have been able to find them,' one of the immortals said from his contoured, organic-looking couch. The man had been a genius once. He had worked with electrical currents, magnetism and radio. Now his pale, hairless body was little more than the human drone component of a greater biomechanical machine.

'Du Bois?' Mr Brown's question was practically a sigh. Du Bois was a very capable agent but he was also a lot more trouble than he was worth. Du Bois was more than eight hundred years old. Mr Brown couldn't understand why the man hadn't outgrown rank sentimentality.

'There is an eighty-seven-point-three recurring per cent chance that du Bois was destroyed in Portsmouth. We have modelled a few predictions of his possible whereabouts, if he yet exists, and we are trying to sneak carrier signals through to the most likely locations,' the drone told him.

The Seeders had gone after the Circle's communications network first, presumably due to proximity and access. Kanamwayso had proven their weak point. They had lost the race against time. It was just a case of whether or not they could salvage anything at all, because this wasn't enough, not nearly enough.

'Attempting to establish contact now,' the drone told him. Mr Brown heard the sound of a phone ringing. He mused for a moment on how the machinations of the godlike could be turned on their head by the actions of a few spoilt brats and a young woman from the anus of Britain.

Du Bois and Beth stared at the old-fashioned, rotary dial phone as it rang. Beth walked out into the street and listened. She couldn't hear any other phones ringing with her augmented senses. She walked back into the house.

'It's for you,' she said grimly. Du Bois just stared at the phone. 'Can you ... we survive what happened to the others who answered their phones?'

'I don't know ...' du Bois said slowly. Beth was pretty sure it was the first time he had seemed unsure of himself, possibly even frightened. Then the frequency of the ringing changed. Beth's neuralware recognised it as Morse code. Slowly the rings spelled out the word Control. Du Bois picked up the phone and immediately both of them winced as something howled at them from the receiver. It sounded like millions of souls in agony, undercut with horrific, unknowable noises in the infra- and ultrasound frequencies normally unheard by humans.

'Hang up!' Beth shouted.

'Malcolm, can you hear me?' a voice asked.

Even over the screaming Beth could tell the voice was deep, resonant, cultured. She could see from du Bois's expression that he recognised the speaker.

'I can hear you,' du Bois said.

'Where is Natalie?' The voice on the other end of the phone had to shout.

'She has gone. The cult took her. Retrieval is not an option.'

The voice didn't answer. Beth didn't think she could take the screaming for much longer, and then: 'So it is over?'

Du Bois said nothing. Beth could see him struggling with something.

'Tell him about the clan!' she shouted at him. She wasn't sure why. Perhaps it was the closest thing they had to hope.

'Is that Elizabeth Luckwicke?' the voice asked.

'Yes,' du Bois answered. Beth could tell he was less than happy about admitting this.

'The clan?'

'We managed to take some genetic material from Tal ... Natalie but the DAYP have control of it.'

'I see. And in the unlikely event that they survived the awak-ening, do you have any idea where they would be?'

'I would imagine somewhere over the Atlantic making for their base in America. Can you provide us with transport?'

Beth frowned. They had transport. She opened her mouth to say something but du Bois motioned her to be quiet.

'We are struggling with resources at the moment,' the voice answered. 'I think you've done all you can from there. You should stand down, or whatever it is you military types do.'

Beth could see du Bois wrestling with something else. 'Alexia?' he finally asked.

'We do not know where she is. I am afraid she cannot be a priority. In other circumstances she would have been more than welcome. I am sorry,' the voice said. Du Bois sagged. 'You have been a good soldier, Malcolm. We, humanity, thank you for all of your service. There is just one more service we would ask of you, one more loose end. Do you understand?'

Beth frowned. She understood when du Bois looked at her.

'Yes,' he finally said and hung up. The screaming stopped. Slowly, du Bois raised his hands. Beth had stepped out of reach and had the suppressed barrel of the UMP levelled at his head.

'I'm not going to kill you,' du Bois said. Beth knew that she would be shaking if the tech inside her body hadn't been so ef-ficient.

'He said it,' Beth growled. 'You're a good soldier.'

'We're in no different a position to when I upgraded your neu-ralware in Old Portsmouth. There are standing instructions to execute anyone we had to use in that way as a possible security breach,' he explained.

'So why didn't you?' she demanded. The SMG hadn't wavered even slightly, her finger curled around a partially depressed trigger.

'You didn't deserve it. If everything hadn't gone to shit I would have purged you of tech, modified your memory and then made the argument to Control.'

'But you've been given a direct order now, haven't you, soldier?'

'You're no threat, the war's effectively over. You don't deserve this. It's nice to see you want to live, though.'

As Beth looked into his very blue eyes, she knew that he had to be a very accomplished liar. As far as she could tell he was some kind of immortal super spy. Spies had to lie. They lived in deception, but everything told her to believe him. Perhaps that was just a result of du Bois's tradecraft.

'If you want to walk, just walk, take the weapons. The tech will give you a considerable edge, the skills you need. Go up onto the moors, there will be other survivors.'

'Why didn't you tell him about the plane?' Beth asked, lowering the weapon. She knew he would have taken considerable killing anyway.

'I don't know,' he admitted. 'Things ... perhaps things haven't been right for a while.'

'Is there any hope?' she asked, looking down.

'Not much,' du Bois admitted. Beth looked back up at him.

'I've got nothing better to do right now.'

Du Bois started to laugh.

Mr Brown rubbed the bridge of his nose with thumb and forefinger.

'He's going to disobey me again,' he muttered to himself. 'That man! I really don't have time for this.' Mr Brown sounded genuinely aggrieved. He was cursing himself inwardly for not having more fully reprogrammed du Bois, but he had known it would have made him a less effective operative. His ability to improvise, his free thinking, had been his most valuable asset, but also his most troublesome.

'Find me someone on the British mainland and assets on the eastern seaboard of the US. I want to know what, if anything, is still up in the air over the Atlantic. If it's still up, I want a way to contact it. If not, I want an excellent prediction of where it went down.'

He hated that he still felt hope. The possibility of release.

It hadn't been as bad in Scotland, purely because it was less populated, and du Bois had taken the Harrier out low over the Irish Sea as he headed up the west coast between the islands. The glow in the east had been Glasgow. The entire city must have been burning.

They had caught a glimpse of a destroyer among the islands. It was enough for Beth to see the hull was blood-stained, festooned with bodies, and the ship had been flying a black flag with an hourglass on it. The destroyer had launched a missile at them but the Harrier's systems and du Bois's piloting had meant they had avoided it easily.

The weather had turned as it had grown dark. Beth was only just starting to realise how tired she was, fatigued and hungry. Despite the tech, physiology had its limits.

Beth felt the aircraft slowing. Her eyes cut through the darkness and she could see cliffs just ahead of them, white-topped waves breaking against the rocks. She arched her neck, looking up through the cockpit at the castle perched on the edge of it. She felt the armoured airframe flex as the Harrier ceased forwards momentum and started to rise through the spray.

'Where are we?' Beth asked.

'Home,' du Bois grunted. Despite the L-tech retrofitting, the wind was still buffeting the aircraft and du Bois had to wrestle with it. As they rose past the walls, Beth could see that the small castle required some work but for the most part had been well maintained. 'Given to the family by Robert the Bruce for some ... considerations.'

They were up over the castle, and Beth could see there was a keep built against the sea wall and then a small courtyard. Du Bois kept the plane hovering over the courtyard, though the wind was knocking it around. He seemed to be concentrating intently.

'Aren't we landing?' Beth asked.

'I'm just checking the castle's security systems.'

'Oh, isn't that dangerous?'

'It's an isolated system and I'm using a direct link, a tight-beam transmission from the plane.' The plane dipped forwards and then started to sink towards the courtyard. 'It's safe.' He sounded somehow disappointed as the Harrier's wheeled undercarriage touched down on the courtyard's cobbles.

'Everything okay?' Beth asked. If anything, du Bois had seemed more preoccupied than she had been during the trip.

'My Black Shadow is gone,' du Bois said. Beth assumed he was talking about a vintage motorcycle. The cockpit opened and both of them climbed out of the aircraft.

'Alexia!' du Bois shouted as he pushed the sturdy, metal-studded door to the main keep open. They were in a stone-floored hallway decorated with armour, weapons and large oil paintings of landscapes. Beth had half been expecting to see stuffed animals and family portraits. A grand staircase with dark, hardwood banisters led to the first floor and rain battered against the window over the landing. The weather notwithstanding, Beth was pretty sure this building was dark at the best of times.

'Must have been as cheery as my place to grow up in,' Beth muttered.

'I didn't grow up here. The only people who grew up here were servants' children and they weren't allowed in this part of the house,' du Bois said, sounding distracted. He'd slung the carbine across his back.

'Servants? Really?' Beth muttered but du Bois was ignoring her.

'Alexia!' du Bois shouted again.

'I thought you'd checked the security. Wouldn't you know if there was someone else in here?'

Du Bois had mounted the stairs and was running up them two at a time.

'There's a chance that she could have circumvented the security,' he answered distractedly. 'Make yourself at home.'

Beth had found the kitchen. It was already quite warm, presumably because of the Aga, and she'd managed to get a fire going in the large hearth. She had also decided it was the homeliest room in the house, the most lived in, probably because of the servants. The fridge and the pantry had been well stocked and with a lot of fresh food, so it must have been done recently. She wondered where the servants were now, as the castle would have been a good place for them to hide if they were still sane.

She had intended on having a snack. It had turned into a feast of bread, cheese, pickles, cold meats and a cold roast chicken. She felt like a pig but her body had apparently needed the energy and was going about efficiently converting it. She had also found an excellent bottle of Scotch. Now all she had to do was not think about her dad. She hadn't seemed to be able to program her neuralware not to do that.

'She not here, then?' Beth asked through a mouthful of bread and cheese as du Bois walked into the kitchen and put the carbine on the long oak table she was sitting at. He shook his head.

'Girlfriend? Wife?' It suddenly occurred to her that she didn't know anything normal about du Bois.

'Br ... sister,' du Bois said. Beth decided not to push further.

Du Bois sat down and started helping himself to food. She'd all but emptied the huge fridge.

'They're a pain in the arse, aren't they?'

Du Bois smiled. 'You've no idea.'

'We could look for her,' Beth suggested. 'I may not have had much luck ...'

'I wouldn't even know where to start. She was in Brighton some days ago ... Now? I just don't know. Besides, it won't make any difference unless we have an out.'

'What is that out? There are other things happening, aren't there? You said this wasn't all done by that thing in the Solent.'

'No, there are more of those things on the other side of the world, in the Pacific, and they are considerably less benevolent.'

Beth tried to think about this for a moment. She decided to take it at face value. It was just too far removed from being a con, or working the doors in Bradford, the things she was used to.

'Why does everyone want Talia?' Beth asked.

'She was the descendant of a bloodline infused with living S-tech. She is connected to the thing you saw in the Solent. It was a Seeder, though I suspect you were in the seedpod rather than the actual Seeder itself. To cut a long story short, the Seeders were corrupted but they hid some of their genetic secrets in a human bloodline thousands of years ago.' Du Bois took a mouthful of whisky. Beth was staring at him. 'I'm no scientist but it seems that the information required to utilise Seeder technology to escape our current situation is encoded in Natalie's DNA.'

'Why the fuck did you put all your eggs in one irrational, goth basket?' Beth finally asked.

Du Bois sighed, leant back in the chair, and spent some time chewing and swallowing a large piece of gammon.

'We didn't. She was one of a great number of children grown from the genetic information we had. We tried very hard to find her but it was difficult because your parents kept their heads down and maintained a low-tech lifestyle.'

'The other children?'

'Well, this generation would have all been young adults now, same age as Talia, though another generation was about to be born ...'

'Something bad happened, didn't it?' Beth asked.

'A terrorist organisation called the Brass City attacked all of our facilities. They're masters of electronic warfare, they were able to wipe out all the related information on the bloodline.'

'The children?'

'A tailored virus specifically designed to kill the bloodline and junk their DNA. The attack was so total, so successful, they must have thoroughly infiltrated the Circle.'

'That's you lot, right? The guy who ordered my death?'

'Yes. That was Mr Brown, he runs operations for the Circle.' Du Bois wouldn't look at her. Instead he poured himself a generous measure of whisky and drank a large mouthful.

'And finding my sister suddenly became a priority again?' Beth said.

'Indeed.' Du Bois raised his glass to her and then took another drink.

'So with my sister gone ...'

'Our greatest hope for survival lies with the samples I took from Natalie when we found her in the lockup, which is in the hands of a group of entitled, psychopathic nerds. Assuming, that is, they haven't ditched in the Atlantic. Which I suspect is the most likely result.'

'But you're going to look anyway?'

Du Bois stared at the dark, peaty whisky in his tumbler, giving the question some thought.

'I want to live. I want my sister to live,' he said at last.

'Will the Circle let you in on their evacuation plan?' Beth asked.

Du Bois shrugged. 'Probably not.'

'So we're just going through the motions?' Beth asked. The whole thing still seemed too ridiculous, despite her recent experiences.

'Pretty much.' Du Bois sagged in his chair. 'Look, you don't have to do this. You're welcome to stay here. Wait for Alexia, if she's in the UK she'll be making her way here. If I can find an out I'll come back.'

'The planet's fucked, isn't it?' Beth said.

'It's not ours any more and it's going to become exponentially more hazardous to human life.'

'You're going after those Do As You Please bastards?' Beth asked. She remembered tourist after tourist that she had been forced to kill on the streets of Old Portsmouth after the DAYP clan had enslaved them, turned them into zombies. She remembered the gunfight. They had acted like it was a computer game.

Like they hadn't been shooting at real people. She remembered them taking her sister. She was just a 'thing' to them, though perhaps they were no different to the Circle in that. And she remembered what it felt like to get shot, to die.

'I still don't have anything better to do,' she said. She thought of her dad. Blinked back non-existent tears and tried to smile before taking a mouthful of the whisky.

It had just been pure chance that none of them had been using the satellite phone at the time. There had been screaming from the cockpit and then the executive jet had nosedived towards the Atlantic. King Jeremy and the demon-headed Inflictor Doorstep had climbed out of their seats and dropped down the centre aisle towards the cockpit. Dracimus had curled up in a ball and screamed. The door to the cockpit was open. The pilot had blood pouring from his ears and blind red eyes. The co-pilot looked like he was trying to chew through his own cheek.

Technology had overridden panicked responses. The Atlantic was a flat grey plain interspersed with flecks of white rushing up to greet them. King Jeremy lowered himself down to stand on the plane's windscreen. It held. He'd never even seen this in an action film. It would be cool if they weren't about to die. Inflictor reached down and dug his fingers into the flesh of the pilot's arm. King Jeremy reached up and unbuckled the pilot's seatbelt. Inflictor dragged the pilot out of his seat and up into the passenger compartment one-handed.

With difficulty King Jeremy wedged himself between the seat and the instrument panel, grabbed the stick and began pulling it back. The strength of his sculpted body, designed after the muscle-bound characters he saw in his computer games, meant he was slowly able to level out the aircraft and he sat down in the pilot's seat.

Some hours later King Jeremy had put the autopilot on and bullied Dracimus into sitting in the pilot's seat to keep an eye on it. Jeremy had heard the wet tearing and snapping sounds but even so he was still impressed with the mess that Inflictor had made in the forward part of the passenger compartment, with the bodies of the pilot and the co-pilot. Somehow it hadn't sounded like they minded.

He had unplugged the pilot's and co-pilot's headsets when he heard the screaming coming from the earpieces. Dracimus had whined to know what was happening but Jeremy had no idea. As far as he could tell they had been subject to some kind of weird sonic-based electronic attack.

There were a number of satellite phone handsets in sockets built into the passenger compartment's furnishings. One of them started to ring, then it stopped as King Jeremy passed it, then another started to ring as he came level with that one, then as he moved on that one stopped and the next one rang. Inflictor snapped a bone and looked up at Jeremy.

'Don't answer it!' Dracimus squealed from the cockpit. It was this more than anything else that made King Jeremy pick up the phone. He heard the screaming. It would have been cool, like a horror film, if it hadn't grated so much. He moved to hang up when he heard the voice.

'Mr Rush?' a deep, resonant voice asked over the screaming.

'Don't call me that!' Jeremy snapped. He didn't want to be reminded of that boy. That loser.

'My apologies. Should I call you King Jeremy?'

'What do you want?'

'To discuss a deal, but first I think you need to understand the gravity of the situation.'

'KJ!' Dracimus's panicked voice was like nails on a chalkboard.

'Busy,' King Jeremy spat.

'You need to see this!'

Jeremy fantasised about ways to hurt Dracimus as he dropped the phone and stalked through the gore back to the cockpit. Inflictor stood up to join him.

Jeremy found himself looking down at the broken fingers of the ruined, smoking Boston skyline.

'It's like the introductory film in *Demon Seed*!' Dracimus couldn't keep the excitement out of his voice. Jeremy turned back to look at the phone he'd left lying on the floor. Another one closer to him started to ring.

9

A Long Time After the Loss

Privacy. There were many benefits to being a member of the Church but the Monk had often reflected that privacy, physical and mental, so unusual in the Consortium and Monarchist systems, was chief among them. The Cathedral was high security. It was protected by secrecy, and then a lot of firepower. All public areas, particularly work areas, were subject to surveillance. Domiciles were only put under surveillance if it was requested by their inhabitants, or the militia made a convincing argument to the legal aspect of the Cathedral's supposedly objective governing AI.

To the Monk's mind, Church conditioning wasn't a breach of privacy. Yes, you had to agree to the conditioning if you wished to remain in the Church when you came to your majority, and most did, but it didn't allow Church AIs, Churchman, or the militia to spy on your mind or your biology. Instead it wiped any sensitive information from your mind if you left, or were taken from, the Church. More seriously, it could damage and ultimately kill anyone who either tried to reverse engineer the information out of themselves, or were subject to such reverse engineering. Again, this was due to security rather than thought policing. Everyone was free to think and say what they wanted and once the door to your domicile was closed you were on your own and unmonitored physically and mentally. It was bliss. Even so, many thousands of years later she still appreciated it. More so after she had been away from the Cathedral for any length of time.

The information from the surveillance sensors in the public areas, however, was constantly analysed by some very powerful AIs. This was why, as the Monk made her way towards a bridge-capable telescope array on one of the flying buttresses, the Cathedral's AI was politely requesting access to the medical diagnostic systems in her neunonics. It seemed that the visual and heat sensors had detected signs that she was running a fever. She looked flushed, sweat beaded her skin in a way that it really wasn't supposed to for someone as heavily augmented as she was. This was almost certainly the sign of some kind of nanite infection and a tricky and subtle one to have avoided detection so far.

Churchman appeared in the corridor next to the Monk as she stepped out of the express traveltube. He was a hologram emitted from a projector the smart matter wall had just grown. She wasn't receiving direct neunonic 'faces right now.

'Beth, are you okay?' Churchman asked. There was no panel or control centre for the array. It was run by the Cathedral's distributed systems, which ran throughout the smart matter of the entire habitat. Everything could be neunonically accessed with the correct clearance, which the Monk had. It really made no sense for her to be walking towards what was effectively a wall. It seemed to take real effort for the Monk to turn and look at Churchman's hologram. Her face was beetroot red, her mouth a rictus grin as she tried to speak. Churchman triggered the alarm with a thought.

Limbs extruded from the floor, walls and ceiling and reached for her. Seconds later powerful, non-lethal weapon barrels were grown from the corridor wall and fed power and/or ammunition, nano-swarms spored from the wall, security satellites and militia personnel were scrambled.

Churchman's armoured form was running. He was just over forty-two miles away from the Monk. It could have been worse. The direct sensor 'face from the corridor next to the buttress showed him everything, audio, visual, heat, electrochemical, nanoscopic. It seemed to be happening in slow motion. She was in the air, extruded limbs reaching for her, taking hits from the weapons.

With a thought, Churchman opened the wall in front of him and leapt through it. He was seven miles above the ground level of the Cathedral. He triggered his AG drive.

Through his 'face sensor feed Churchman saw the Monk curled up into a somersault. A smart matter tentacle reached from the wall, snagging her leg. A thermal blade lashed out and the limb was severed. Beth hit the ground as stunners and EM-projected baton rounds hit her, barely staggering her.

'Where the fuck is Woodbine Scab?' Churchman snapped out

loud. It had been a while since he had been this angry, or, if he was honest, this frightened. He had his answer before he had finished asking it. Scab was overseeing the upgrades to the *Basilisk II*. With a thought Scab was wrapped in extruded smart matter limbs. The bounty hunter immediately started to fight: bleeding acid, using his nano-screen, and spitting liquid hardware to try to matter-hack the material holding him. Pythian attack programs and viruses were attacking the Cathedral's local systems. Militia and S-sats were speeding towards him.

In his 'face sensor feed the Monk bounced off one wall, the floor, then another wall. Churchman would have admired the balletic grace of her movements if the situation hadn't been so serious. She'd had millennia to hone her skills.

Churchman landed on the hull of a banking fast-attack frigate. Tiny molecular hooks on his exoskeleton's feet adhered to the craft's hull as its engines burned hard, scorching a mile of the Cathedral's internal smart matter wall. The craft shot forwards.

'Locate and secure all of Scab's crew,' Churchman 'faced.

The frigate was fast but not fast enough. Subconsciously he analysed the flight paths and capabilities of all the craft speeding to help him. The local area was illuminated with the harsh burn of engines all making for him or the Monk. He leapt. The Cathedral's AI requested permission to take lethal measures against the Monk. Even though she would be cloned, again, he hesitated. *But it's Beth*, some impractical, sentimental part of him thought. It was just a moment's hesitation.

On the 'face sensor feed Churchman saw an extruded smart matter tentacle grab her arm and slam her to the ground. Her right arm reached for the wall. A red flash. Red steam. The limb fell to the ground. The Monk didn't even scream. Restraints grew from the floor, encircling her body. Her bloody left palm shot forwards and she smeared blood against the wall. An EM-driven cannon round blew the limb off.

'No!' Churchman screamed and leapt again. He landed on a fighter that had just passed under the frigate. His boots adhered to the craft but its speed meant he had to grip a handle that had just extruded from the craft's hull.

Beth's blood carried an ugly matter-hack. Ridiculously expensive tech designed specifically to beat Church defences with one order. *Transmit*. The telescopic array opened a bridge and did just that.

The fighter's forward-manoeuvring engines burned, braking the craft to stop it crashing into the wall that even now was opening for Churchman. Churchman leapt from the fighter, the twin AG motors attached to his exoskeleton carrying him through the hole in the smart matter wall. As he landed in the corridor he could already hear the screaming.

'Let me go! I'm going to fucking kill him! You hear me, Scab! You're fucking dead!' The Monk was writhing against her restraints. Both her arms ended in bloody stumps. All the extruded weapons, several S-sats and a squad of nervous militia were covering her. She had already opened her neunonics to the Cathedral's AI. Her internal systems had been fighting the sophisticated meat-hack the entire time. It had worked because it had sequestered her, controlled her, rather than attempting to root out the Church's secrets, which would have triggered the conditioning. Her clearance and reputation had done the rest, allowed her to get as far as she had.

'I'm calm,' Beth said. Churchman was receiving her medical telemetry, she was anything but, though he couldn't see any remaining trace of the meat-hack. Her own, not inconsiderable, internal systems had tracked it down and destroyed it.

'Let her up,' Churchman ordered, 'facing instructions to the Cathedral to do the same. The AI, which irritatingly had facets of his own personality, protested, as did the militia squad leader. 'Now! And get medical assemblers on her arms.'

The smart matter released her as two of the militia affixed assemblers with graft attachments to the Monk's severed limbs. As soon as they had done that, Churchman picked up the protesting Beth and tucked her under his arm. Another AG-motor-assisted leap carried him out of the corridor and back onto the fighter, which was turning even as they landed on it. They would have to go slower this time. Beth had less protection than he did.

'I'm going to kill him this time,' the Monk 'faced him.

If he was being honest he had been more than a little disappointed in Beth for her liaison with Scab. It had seemed like the sort of self-destructive thing her sister would do. If, however, sex had been the vector for the meat-hack then he could understand the violation. Even if he had wanted to stop Beth from killing him, he wasn't sure he could. Except that it wasn't Scab who was missing.

The Previous Night

She could understand how it had happened. She knew when it had happened. It had been while Scab, Vic and that insipid human bitch had been on their Key trip. The Elite had come through the wall of the Monastery. A moment later special forces contractors were levelling weapons at them, and the tall, thin man with the deep voice and skin so pitch black it seemed to absorb light, was standing over her. He had touched her. Just laid a hand on her head. It had been creepy. It had also been a contact transfer for what she had assumed was liquidware with a nanite carrier.

She didn't want to think about how easily it had bypassed her internal security. The liquidware had assembled itself and integrated with her own. Basically it was information and a small, limited capability AI. The AI projected an image straight into her neunonics, overlaying what she could see in the real world. It was how she could still remember what Patron looked like because, subjectively, in her darkened room, he was standing at the bottom of the bed looking at her.

It didn't matter who she was, her capabilities, what she'd done; she still found herself clutching her legs to her chest against the wall as far away from where she perceived the AI projection of Patron to be. Despite the fear, her neunonics were running through the data on the rest of the liquidware that had invaded her system. It was information gathered by Consortium intelligence contractors, everything they knew about Church systems.

'I have a proposition for you,' Patron said, his deep, resonant voice making her feel part aroused, part nauseous. 'Would you like to be richer than Croesus?'

'Who's Croesus?' she asked. The AI projection of Patron sighed.

Her flesh itched like crazy but the assemblers had not fully regrown the missing parts of her limbs. As Churchman leapt from the fighter to the landing pad, where the sleek *Basilisk II* was berthed, the Monk made the considered and mature decision that she was going to kick Woodbine Scab to death.

Churchman put her down and both of them strode towards where Scab was struggling with his smart matter restraints. Security satellites, the heavily armed version of P-sats controlled by the Cathedral's AI, were so thick in the air above him it looked like the microcosm of a planetary blockade.

'Move!' Churchman snapped at the militia surrounding Scab.

Beth assumed that the tiny bits of smoking wreckage were all that remained of Scab's P-sat. The militia cleared the way. Scab was frothing at the mouth, toxic saliva making his make-up smoke. He looked like a rabid animal. There was nothing in his eyes that Beth recognised as human, let alone sane. He was surrounded by inert, in some cases warped, smart matter. His left arm was free. As they approached there was a glow from the tentacle holding his right arm. It was cut apart as the energy javelin cut through the smart matter as though it wasn't there.

Churchman moved first, with surprising speed for his metal bulk. A golden foot stamped down on Scab's right arm. The Monk heard the bone snap. Churchman was in the way, she couldn't get close enough to Scab. She suspected this was what he had intended. Churchman reached down and plucked the E-javelin from Scab's hand as the smart matter restraints released him. Scab started to move. Beth triggered her coherent energy field as spit gun needles and monomolecular discs ricocheted off Churchman's armour. Some of the militia backed away, taking hits on their armour. Churchman reached down for a struggling Scab and picked him up by his skull.

'This is what it feels like to be helpless!' Churchman's amplified voice shouted. He slammed Scab back into the ground, then picked him up again. The Monk heard Scab's armoured skull start to crack as Churchman squeezed. She was worried that Churchman was going to kill him before she could. 'Where is Negrinotti?' Churchman demanded. It was written all over Scab's face. He didn't have the slightest idea what Churchman was talking about. She accessed the Cathedral's systems. Negrinotti was nowhere to be found. She wasn't the only one.

Some Minutes Ago

It was almost a physical difference. Vic was still cautious but he could see an end in sight. Freedom from Scab, though he would need to survive the inevitable assassination attempt that would come from the severing of their partnership, as well as the booby traps that Scab had installed in his personal systems over the years.

Living in the Church wouldn't be so bad, perhaps even working for them eventually, though he intended to spend a great deal of time just relaxing initially. He would become a burden on their resources, a parasite. He was quite looking forward to it.

He was also pleased that Talia would be staying in the Cathedral, almost as pleased as he was about Scab leaving. He wondered if he'd taken the human-aping psychosurgery too far. Was he actually in love? He wasn't sure he was entirely enjoying the sensation. It did go some way towards explaining why he was walking down an arched walk towards Talia's room, once more carrying a surgical steel rose, a bottle of red wine, and a be-wildering array of narcotics. For some reason he felt this was his time. Perhaps they could consummate what so far they had only done in immersions. The wine had even been grown in hydro-ponic vineyards in the Cathedral! It wasn't from an assembler.

Vic let off a little spurt of pheromonic irritation as he saw Talia and Elodie emerge from the human girl's room. Elodie's P-sat was bobbing up and down on its AG motor at her shoulder. Vic tried to purse his mandibles – it didn't work – as Talia failed to notice him. Elodie, however, glanced his way and turned to lead the girl in the other direction.

'Talia! Elodie!' Vic called. It was a little odd, he had been cer-tain that the two females hadn't just disliked each other, but had in fact utterly despised each other. Vic couldn't be sure but vari-ous senses and neunonic analysis routines were telling him that there was something slightly off about Elodie's body language. Whatever it was, it was gone when Elodie turned to face him, smiling. Vic momentarily forgot about it when he noticed that Talia had been crying, yet again.

'What's wrong?' he asked. It had become a common greeting with them.

'Beth fucked Scab,' Talia said. She sniffed, and wiped some of her running eye make-up on her sleeve.

Yes! Vic couldn't help himself. He was still a little confused as to Elodie's presence.

'And you're ...?' he said, turning to look at the feline.

'She's been a real friend,' Talia said, turning to look gratefully at Elodie, who was smiling sympathetically. 'She knows what it's like to be fucked over by a sibling.'

'I mean, yes, I've been hateful to her, but she's still crew. I mean, I've practically sprayed all of you. You know how terri-torial we are, but it's compartmentalised, you know?'

His nano-screen and antennae were picking up something in the air, some ever-so-subtle nanites. He guessed it was some kind of nano-screen, perhaps a privacy or stealth screen.

Vic nodded understandingly. The tray and its contents crashed to the floor as he reached for his laser pistols and 'faced targeting information to his power disc, grabbing it from his back with his lower left arm. His P-sat fired once, the energy dissipation grid on Elodie's chitinous armoured bodice flared, and then it dropped to the ground. He flung the power disc and that also dropped to the ground. Elodie was moving, drawing her own weapons. It had all happened too fast for Talia to react. The targeting graphics overlaying Vic's vision were almost exactly in the correct place as he brought the twin double-barrelled laser pistols to bear; he was about to 'face the command to fire when the wall reached out, grabbed him, and partially enveloped him.

Talia started to run. Elodie swung her leg around and the sole of her high-heeled boot slammed the girl into the wall, holding her there. The position looked as graceful as it looked uncomfortable. It would have been impossible to hold any augmented person against the wall like that, but Talia wasn't augmented.

Elodie was still looking at Vic, partially encased in the wall's smart matter and unable to move. She burst out laughing. 'I put a back door into as much of your gear as I could on board the *Basilisk*. Nothing personal, I just like a bit of insurance when I'm working with other people. If your own defences hadn't been quite so good I would have meat-hacked you, but I guess you'll have to remain Scab's bitch,' she told him.

'You hacked the Cathedral's systems?' Vic asked, appalled, thinking of the smart matter that imprisoned him.

'No. The Church must have ordered us locked down. I'm running a stealth screen, which is spoofing their sensors, screens and security swarms,' Elodie explained. It was obvious to Vic that she was impressed with her own cleverness. Talia was whimpering, trying to get free. 'Shut up!' Elodie snapped, all trace of humour gone from her expression. 'I do not like you. The hours I have just spent listening to you whine have, if anything, just increased my disgust at your simpering existence. Normally I'd just meat-hack you but apparently you have to remain pure. So you do as I say or I'll hurt you in ways that will make your previous embrace of victimhood pale into insignificance. Do you understand me?'

Talia made more whimpering noises in answer.

'For fuck's sake.' Elodie removed her boot and Talia slid to the ground. The angry feline yanked the human to her feet and started dragging her down the corridor. Vic noticed that the feline had two black orbs, with visors adhered to them, attached to her belt.

'Why are you doing this?' Vic demanded.

'Greed, fear, being pissed off at Scab for dragging me into his shit, getting to see this whiny bitch vivisected ... Shut up! Plus wanting to be on the winning side, but mostly greed.'

Vic had to concede that they were some good reasons, though the vivisection seemed a little harsh. 'Elodie, don't do this,' he pleaded. He was seeing his opportunity to be the hero in Talia's eyes slipping, well walking, well being dragged away from him.

'Perhaps try and negotiate first, then shoot me?' Elodie shouted over her shoulder.

'Would it have made any difference?' Vic called after her.

'No!' Elodie grabbed Talia, who flinched at her touch, and then reached for the extruded handle of her P-sat, the AG motor pulling them both into the air.

The Monk had dropped the coherent energy field and re-opened herself almost entirely to the Cathedral's systems as she removed the assemblers and inspected new pink flesh. The AI was running extensive diagnostics, as were her own systems, repeatedly checking that she was not still compromised. Erring on the side of caution. The meat-hack had been delivered in saliva. It had happened when Negrinotti had kissed her. She knew the possible consequences of her slaved actions but she didn't want to face up to them right now.

'You're gonna fucking die,' Scab spat at Churchman. Churchman contemptuously turned his back on the bounty hunter.

'Talia's gone,' the Monk told him. Scab stood up. She could hear his bones resetting.

'That girl,' the deep amplified voice from the armoured exoskeleton muttered.

'The sensors can't find them,' the sergeant in charge of the militia squad told Churchman.

'Yes, we might actually have to fucking look for them!' Churchman shouted. Then he sent out an open 'face to everyone in the Cathedral. It contained images of Elodie and Talia.

The Monk could see Scab picking up the glowing E-javelin, looking at Churchman's back.

'Listen, wank stain,' she told the human killer. 'Negrinotti fucked you over just as much as she did us, maybe more so.

She took a half-assed stab at framing you. So you tell me what's important here?' Scab glared at her. 'Yes, nothing resolves a situation like a good glare! Priorities?'

Scab shared a 'face from Vic with Churchman and the Monk. The three of them started to move.

Vic was 'facing a situation report to Scab, Churchman and the Monk as the smart matter released him. He leant low, grabbing the power disc and the P-sat on the run. He clipped both pieces of equipment to his armoured frame and made sure they were completely powered down. He could reboot and run diagnostics later but he couldn't risk having them active again if he caught up with Elodie.

He was sprinting as fast as his power-assisted frame would allow. He drew his triple-barrelled shotgun pistol and broke it open, replacing the current load with saboted seeker micromissiles, and loaded EM, heat and visual pattern recognition targeting information into the missiles' limited AIs. They weren't AG-driven smart munitions but they'd do in a pinch.

'She's heading for the closest airlock,' Vic 'faced to the others.

'She's too smart for that,' Scab 'faced back.

'She had two suits clipped to her belt,' Vic replied. That didn't make any sense to him. Even if Elodie managed to get out then the Church would just pick her up in Red Space.

'She'll double back, head for somewhere less obvious,' Scab told him. Vic heard a distant bang. The sound of superheated air exploding. The laser Elodie's P-sat was armed with. He changed direction and wished he could trust his P-sat enough to use it.

Elodie practically had to jam one of her suppressed autopistols into the militia woman's visor and empty the entire clip. The visor cracked and a human head became a red cavity. Elodie returned the autopistol to its holster-clip and grabbed the advanced combat rifle from the militia woman as she fell to the ground. Two S-sats lay inert on the ground nearby, momentarily overwhelmed by her 'faced hack. She kicked out at the other militiaman trying to bring his weapon to bear, knocking him off-balance. Her P-sat fired at his animatic visor again and again, giving her enough time to empty the four grenades in the ACR's grenade launcher at the squad of militia that had appeared at the end of one of the corridors leading to the airlock. Talia was running again as the space suit struggled to grow around her. It was probably the bravest thing the girl had ever done. Elodie threw the ACR. It spun through the air and hit the human in the back, knocking her to the ground.

Proximity fuses triggered the grenades and they exploded in staggered airbursts. The force of the blasts sent armoured militia tumbling back down the corridor, bouncing off the wall. The other militiaman was still trying to bring his ACR to bear, the energy dissipation grid still glowing from her P-sat's laser. Elodie drove her claws into the visor, the heat having weakened it. Envenomed nails found flesh. He staggered away from her, screaming, dropping his weapon.

Above her, the smart matter floors and ceilings were peeling back, presumably to allow access to something she didn't want to have access. Angrily she stormed over to Talia and placed the visor in front of the girl's face. The suit grew round to meet it and hold it in place. She stood on Talia's back and forced her face-down onto the floor, then pushed the clawed fingers of her left hand into the viscous globe on her belt. The space suit started to grow up her arm. She had to get outside the Cathedral, transmit, and hope that Patron lived up to his promises. If not, she had been assured that she would be less well rewarded when she was cloned, though if Scab survived she knew he would come after her.

She heard the chemical propellant motors on the micro-missiles first. She looked up, drawing her still-loaded autopistol as she transmitted one of her utility hacks. Two of the missiles veered off, exploding in the ceiling and wall. The third hit her in the side. The force of the explosion spun her round, taking her off her feet. Her armour was cracked, her skin had hardened beneath it but shrapnel and the force of the blast had taken its toll. Her internal medical systems rushed regenerative nanites to the internal and external wounds. Incoming beams dressed pher in neon as the energy dissipation grid on her armour struggled to cope with multiple hits from Vic's laser pistols. He had them in his lower limbs as he sprinted towards her, his upper limbs reaching for her. He looked like he wanted to pull her head off with his power-assisted claws. She didn't bother firing back. Instead she grabbed Talia and pulled the girl in front of her – the spacesuit had hardened enough to protect Talia from the micromissile blast – and put the autopistol to her head.

'Dead woman's trigger, Vic,' Elodie told the 'sect as the space-suit continued to grow over her. Vic skidded to a halt.

With her free hand she attached the visor to the suit over her face. She reached into a pouch that had grown out of the suit and removed a handful of thermal seeds. She was aware of the smart matter ceiling still peeling open far above her.

'Do you think that Scab gives a fuck about your dead woman's trigger?' Vic asked her. There was movement above her. Elodie glanced up.

Vic watched as Churchman fell from the *Basilisk II* through the vast hole the Cathedral's AI had peeled open in the smart matter of the levels above them. His AG motors carried the exoskeleton down. Neither Scab nor the Monk were bothering with their P-sats, they were just plummeting.

Elodie made a decision. Vic started to move. The feline had made the wrong decision on so many different levels. Elodie raised her autopistol and fired a long burst into Scab's groin area. Vic had no idea if the bullets penetrated Scab's armoured clothing and then made it past the hardening skin armour, but when Scab landed he seemed angry.

Scab tore Elodie away from Talia and threw her against the wall next to the airlock. Vic grabbed Talia. The Monk triggered the coherent energy field generator and was enveloped in yellow light. Whether through spite or as a result of the dead woman's trigger, Elodie fired another long burst from the auto-pistol, this time at Talia. Vic started to turn. The Monk landed between Elodie, Vic and Talia. Bullets were halted by the energy surrounding the Monk, like insects in amber. Scab, screaming, rammed his spawn blade into Elodie's chest, and emptied all six rounds from his tumbler pistol into her face. She slumped to the floor, leaving a red mess on the stone-like wall. In a fury, Scab rammed one of his filed nails into the ruin of Elodie's eye socket. Vic knew he was releasing a virus into the feline that would torturously destroy her neunonics and liquid software, scramble any attempts at uploads, and hopefully junk any backups so she couldn't be cloned, depending on which system she was linked to in the attempt.

'I saved you!' Vic told Talia quickly.

'No!' Churchman cried as he landed next to Scab and then kicked him so hard that it sent Scab bouncing down the corridor.

The Monk switched off the coherent energy field and bullets dropped to the ground. She hugged Talia and the pair of them collapsed to the ground. The Monk kept her sister's head turned away from Elodie's body.

'You simple-minded fool!' Churchman continued berating Scab as the bounty killer tried to climb to his feet on broken limbs. 'We could have learned something!'

'No, really it was me,' Vic insisted.

The Monk took off Talia's visor. Vic wasn't terribly surprised to see that the girl was sobbing again.

'I'm so sorry,' the Monk told her sister.

Scab had somehow managed to stand. His leg didn't look right and there was a red stain across the front of his trousers. The E-javelin extended from his left hand.

'You keep playing with that and I am going to take it away from you,' Churchman boomed, and then he pointed at Scab's groin. 'And I think you may want to have someone look at that.'

Vic was trying to make up his mind whose side he was going to join in on when this kicked off.

'I had you shat out of a giant alien!' Talia suddenly howled at her sister and then sobbed into her shoulder. Everyone turned to stare at Talia and Beth, even Scab and Churchman.

'Yes, yes you did,' Beth said, hugging her sister, a smile spreading across her face.

Amplified laughter boomed from Churchman's exoskeleton. Vic's mandibles clattered together in mirth, though he suspected that all the insanity had finally broken Talia. Scab seemed wrong-footed by the levity.

'I think we've got other things to worry about,' Vic told his partner, and then to Churchman: 'What was she trying to do? You would have just picked her up outside.'

'She matter-hacked me, got me to use the telescopic array to transmit something.'

'What?' Scab growled.

'I don't think it matters,' Churchman said. 'Just that she transmitted. The only time Elodie paid attention to anything I said in the briefing was when I mentioned that the telescopic arrays have to be bridge-capable to observe Real Space from Red Space.'

It took a moment for the ramifications of this to hit home. Elodie had been taking Talia outside because she was expecting to be met there, because the transmission had given the position of the Cathedral away. Vic looked over at Scab and then screamed: 'Noooooo!'

They heard a sound not unlike a horn or a trumpet being blown, only deeper, warped, a million times louder, and undercut with screaming, though that may have been his imagination. Vic effectively went deaf as his damaged audio filters tried to shut down and protect what was left of his hearing. It sounded like the end of the universe, even if the universe in question was comparatively small and red.

Vic at least understood the glow from above before his multi-faceted eyes went black to protect them from the glare. It was the firing of an impossible amount of energy weapons.

'What ...?' he managed over the 'face link.

'That's the first of the Elite,' Churchman answered.

'The first?' Vic asked, too shocked to be terrified yet. He wasn't sure he wanted his sight to return.

'Transmit the location of the Cathedral to the Monarchist systems,' Churchman ordered on an open 'face.

'What?' the Monk demanded.

'It's over, Beth. The Consortium knows where we live. All that's left is mutually assured destruction.'

10
Ancient Britain

Britha was irritated. The irritation was getting close to anger. She understood why warriors behaved as they did. She understood the need for establishing leadership and position. She even understood that it could be wasteful. She had lost people she had liked, if not friends, to challenges resulting from drunken exchanges of words. She knew, but did not approve of, some warriors who encouraged such challenges, made it difficult for their victims to refuse, but only picked people they knew they could beat. It added to their reputation. Where possible she had engineered their downfall. She understood that, in theory, it made for stronger warriors as the weak were killed. She just wished that warriors had some common sense. Did they have to do this sort of thing when the warband was facing a dangerous enemy from the Underworld, aided by giants? For the most part Britha was happy to leave warriors to their own idiocy, except when it interfered with her world.

There was a stark beauty to the white, hilly landscape. Fortunately the landscape didn't look similar enough to her home to make her sick for it. The camp was a large village of skin shelters and churned up mud. A wall of frozen earth, wooden spikes, and a hastily dug trench that kept filling with snow, surrounded the camp. She stamped out of the camp past the rough-hewn log gate and onto a plain of snow, her black robes a contrast against all the white. She could just about make out the circle of people through the freezing mist. Every warrior and spear-carrier who was not currently guarding the camp, scouting, or foraging, was standing in a large circle in the field of snow.

'Move!' Britha snapped. There were some mutterings but people got out of her way. Once they would have leapt to obey her.

'This girl! This serpent child of a weak people! This back-stabber who stood back from the fight when the spawn of Andraste attacked!' There was more muttering from those gathered.

All of those who had stood with them at the *gwyllion*'s fort in the woods knew the truth of the matter, but the newcomers, who now outnumbered the veterans, did not. Bladud's paid bards had been hard at work. They were telling the Witch King's version of events.

'A known coward, who has only ever killed by deceit! She is a murderer, no warrior, and she has no right to hold the Red Chalice to be used for her gain, and the gain of her allies!'

Of course the chalice wasn't the reason given for the challenge. That had been some invented slight. Tangwen had done all that she could to avoid challenges but she had been backed into a corner by Madawg. She'd had to respond to maintain her position in the eyes of the other warriors. A position she needed to maintain guardianship of the Red Chalice.

'For shame!' someone shouted from the crowd.

'Who challenges me?' Madawg demanded. The cadaverous, pockmarked member of the now mostly dead Corpse People tribe was engaging in the ritual insult, the first part of the challenge. He had limed his face and armour, he had spiked his receding hair, and he had black dye around his eyes to make him look more like one of the dead. On the one hand Britha felt he was trying too hard, on the other she couldn't deny the impact of his appearance. She wasn't surprised when the owner of the voice from the crowd didn't step forwards, though she suspected it was more because they knew he had drunk of her blood. He was now one of the Isle of the Mighty's invincible heroes. Invincible until they met the Lochlannach, the giants, Bress, or Crom Dhubh himself.

Britha came to stand by Calgacus. She didn't think the northern *mormaer* was enjoying his time in the south but she felt comfortable among the Pecht. They were her people. The leader of the Cait seemed to have weathered the death of his *dryw* quite well. Britha didn't think that he missed her. Few, if any, had liked Eurneid. Britha herself had suffered at the crone's hands when she had been trained in the groves. She wouldn't miss the old woman either and suspected it was one less source of trouble to add to this particular situation.

She could see Anharad standing next to Bladud. The Witch King wore no armour, no sword, and the hood of his robe was up. He had clearly chosen to look more *dryw* than warrior or *rhi* for this occasion. Guidgen was standing among the *gwyllion*, looking furious. Germelqart was trying to make his way through the Cait *cateran*, Calgacus's warband, but was getting pushed around. Britha turned to look at Calgacus.

'Cease that and let the foreigner through!' Calgacus snapped. Grudgingly they let Germelqart pass.

'Do people become more unpleasant the further north you go?' the navigator muttered in Carthaginian.

'Is he casting magics?' Calgacus asked, more interested than afraid.

'No, he's just speaking another language,' Britha explained.

The crowd were waiting for Tangwen's response but she was saying nothing. She was wearing heavier armour than she would normally. She had a longspear and casting spears driven into the ground around her, and a shield that looked to be the same size as her was leaning against the longspear. Madawg wasn't a large man compared to many warriors, but he seemed to tower over Tangwen. Size wouldn't be the problem, however; he was sneaky, devious, and treacherous. Because of the ritualistic nature of the challenge she was being forced to fight with weapons she did not favour, though she had still eschewed a sword for the hatchet and dirk.

'And what of you, low man?' Guidgen demanded. Britha sighed. Guidgen had been canny, but it seemed that his responsibilities and trying to combat Bladud's machinations had worn him down. He was playing into the hands of Bladud and his allies. 'You who thrust your kinsman into harm's way in Oeth to save yourself?'

'Forgive me, aren't the *dryw* supposed to serve the people of Ynys Prydain and not their own petty ambitions?' demanded Ysgawyn, the *rhi* of the Corpse People. There were muttered agreements from the Brigante and some of the newcomers.

'I have been told what happened in Oeth.' Ysgawyn stabbed a finger at Guidgen. 'This one only cared about getting the chalice.' He stabbed a finger towards Britha. '*This* one betrayed us to the Dark Man.'

Calgacus reached for his sword and started to step forwards.

'He speaks the truth,' Britha said quietly in the language of the Pecht. Calgacus stopped, frowning. 'In that only.'

'And the *foreigner*,' Ysgawyn took some time to emphasise the word, pointing at Germelqart, 'was already known to the Dark Man and probably in league with him all along!'

Germelqart frowned but said nothing. Britha was less than pleased when she noticed that the Carthaginian had a leather bag over his shoulder.

'Is the chalice in that?' she demanded.

'Yes,' Germelqart said.

Britha lapsed into silence. She supposed it was safer than leaving it somewhere, or even hiding it. She glanced up at the fort on the Mother Hill and then towards where she knew the gateway to Annwn was, but all she saw was mist. They did not have time for this. They needed to be working together to come up with a plan to deal with their enemies, not engaging in this nonsense.

'You fight well with your tongue,' Tangwen said. Her voice carried and silence fell across the audience. 'But you insult all when you assume stupidity on their part. None here have forgotten you killing your brother to live. None here have forgotten the Dark Man's cock in Ysgawyn's mouth. I will not call him *rhi* because a *rhi* does not betray his people by making himself subject to another. I grow bored. Start fighting, or all will know you as a coward.'

Ysgawyn looked furious. Even Madawg, who often taunted to his advantage, looked angry. He turned and took a drink from a leather skin offered by Brys, the other surviving Corpse People warrior.

It was nice to see a smile on Guidgen's face again. There were more than a few cheers from the circle as well.

'I like the little girl,' Calgacus said. 'In fact I think I like the southron woman. I have seen her fight, she will kill this man.'

'Madawg is cunning and has drunk of the magic of the chalice from my blood as well,' Britha said.

'You have learned some strange ways down here. Putting foreign magics in your body.' Calgacus tutted. 'I'd rather be sodomised by a boar.'

'Aye, I've heard that said of the Cait,' Britha said, smiling. A number of the Cait *cateran* were glaring at her. Calgacus turned to glare also but she ignored them all and watched the fight.

Madawg had pulled a casting spear from the earth and spun to give his throw more force. Tangwen had grabbed her longspear and shield and started running the moment his back was to her. Madawg released the spear. Tangwen's huge shield looked

117

ludicrous being carried by the small warrior but it covered most of her body. The casting spear hit high on the leather-covered oak, forcing her to duck behind it. For a moment she was blind. Madawg had his slender-bladed sword in his right hand, his small round shield strapped to his left arm, his left fist clenched.

'Is she wed?' Calgacus asked.

'She's too much woman for you,' Britha said.

Calgacus considered this. 'Aye, you're probably right.'

Straight away Tangwen was in trouble. In truth it had gone wrong for her before the fight had started. Madawg had offered skilled and constant insult until she had been forced to challenge. That had meant he had been able to choose the manner of the challenge. Spear and shield initially, though his longspear lay embedded in the snow still, and his choice of shield had been misleading. Had Tangwen gone straight to her hatchet and dirk then presumably he would have used the longspear for its reach.

Madawg darted past the head of the longspear and swung out with his left arm, the small shield battering into the edge of Tangwen's own, staggering her. His sword reached behind the shield and cut across the back of her leg. Britha grimaced as she heard Tangwen cry out. Tangwen dropped the spear and threw her shield blindly at Madawg. Madawg battered through the shield. Britha reckoned that the slight man was relishing not being the smallest, lightest fighter in a challenge for once. He slashed out at Tangwen as she flung herself back, grabbing at her hatchet and dirk now.

She was not sure what they had been thinking when they had allowed Madawg to drink of her blood. She was sure she had seen better warriors but few who mixed skill and sneakiness as effectively as Madawg did. At least Tangwen was armed with weapons she was more comfortable with now, and had closed with Madawg. She was, however, favouring her uninjured leg. Madawg went for the weak spot. Tangwen swept her injured leg back, steel scraped against steel as she used her dirk to guide Madawg's sword away from her. Madawg changed the direction of thrust and his blade went through armour and opened a gash on her arm. There was another cry of pain from the serpent child. That was when Britha realised that he was playing with her. Tangwen was a hunter. Her people used guile and stealth when they conducted raids, or defended themselves. She was a capable warrior, of that Britha had no doubt, but in the challenges she had fought previously it had been the magics in her blood that had given her the advantage. Madawg had the same magics in his blood. It was clear that he was by far the better warrior.

Tangwen's head snapped to one side as Madawg's small shield hit her in the face. Blood flew from her mouth and splattered the white snow. Then Britha saw it. It had been well done, subtle. She was not sure that she would have caught it before she had drunk from the chalice. As Madawg's hand had passed her face he had opened his fingers. A fine yellow powder, doubtless a creation of Bladud's, had hit her in the face. Tangwen screamed, staggering back. Madawg kicked her in her wounded leg. Now he was just enjoying himself. Tangwen collapsed to the ground, obviously struggling to see, despite the healing nature of the magics that infused her body. Madawg thrust down at her. She crossed dirk and hatchet, desperately parrying the slender sword blade. Madawg stamped on her wounded leg. Tangwen howled in pain, sitting upright. The rim of the Corpse People warrior's small shield hit her in the face, breaking her nose, and opening a gash in her head. Britha glanced over at Bladud. He was motionless, his features mostly hidden by the hood. Madawg brought the sword back, readying the killing blow. Britha closed her eyes, fingers tightening around the haft of the spear. More than anything she wanted to intervene and rush to her friend's aid, but she knew she couldn't. That would play into Bladud's hands.

'I yield!' Tangwen screamed. Britha opened her eyes. Madawg was standing over Tangwen. He looked angry.

'Try and die with some dignity,' he spat.

'She fought well enough,' Britha said. She was addressing Bladud, not Madawg. There were muttered agreements from the assembled crowd.

'She didn't fight at all!' Madawg snapped.

'It's clear that she is no warrior,' Ysgawyn announced loudly. 'Clearly what skill she has is derived from stolen magics, and she should not be considered a warrior, nor treated as one and granted their privileges.'

Now there were more than a few angry cries from the crowd, particularly from those she had helped lead to safety, or who had fought beside her.

'She fought a challenge. She has yielded. How is that different from any other warrior?' Guidgen demanded angrily.

119

'She made the challenge after Madawg caught her masquerading above her station,' Ysgawyn retorted.

'That was not the reason given!' Guidgen cried. Ysgawyn looked confused, though it was clearly an act.

'Clearly it was a simple ruse, any real *dryw* would have the intelligence to see that.'

'Watch your mouth, boy ...' Guidgen spat, pointing at the so-called *rhi* of the Corpse People. Many of the *gwyllion* had their hands on their weapons now.

'Enough!' Bladud called. He pulled his hood down. 'Tangwen did all that was required of her. The matter is settled.'

'My insults stand,' Madawg cried, playing to the audience now. 'She has been judged by Arawn and her own weakling serpent god!' Then he turned to Bladud. 'I will rape her. She needs to know her place.' There were howls of fury from the audience now. Britha could see from the set of Bladud's body he was furious.

'That's not going to happen,' Britha said. She couldn't look at Tangwen, couldn't take the look of defeat and fear on the younger woman's face.

'It is my right!' Madawg all but screamed.

'This matter is over,' Bladud snapped. 'Your insults stand, nothing more.' If he had planned this then it had gone wrong. He may have weakened Tangwen's guardianship of the chalice, and by association Germelqart's, Guidgen's, and his own, but he had revealed himself to be in alliance with monsters.

'She should be made an example of so that others know not to pretend to be warriors with unearned power!' Madawg continued to harangue the Witch King. The Brigante present were grim-faced and angry. A significant number of the women in the crowd looked ready to attack, as did many of the men.

'Madawg,' Ysgawyn said quietly.

The furious warrior snapped round to look at his king. The anger drained from the champion's face. 'My apologies,' he said to Bladud, and bowed. 'My blood was up from the fight and the extent of her insult to those who risk all to protect the people.' He turned and stalked from the circle, leaving Tangwen still lying in the bloody snow.

Britha moved towards her. The hunter's wounds were like mouths, opening and closing as harming magic fought with healing magic.

Calgacus was shaking his head as he joined her. 'This I do not like; we are brought too close to the gods.' There were many others in the circle who had not witnessed Otherworldly magic first-hand before. They were spitting and making the sign against evil.

'We fight the gods,' Britha said quietly. She felt the Cait *mormaer*'s eyes on her.

'Well, they're going to write songs about us,' Calgacus finally said, looking away. 'You do not like these Corpse People, I think?' he asked. Though he had no idea what had been said in the exchange after Tangwen had yielded.

'No, I do not,' Britha admitted, though Brys, the greybeard among the Corpse People who had died at Oeth, had grown on her when she had travelled with them.

'I do not think I like them either,' Calgacus said brightly. Britha sighed as they reached Tangwen and helped her to her feet. The younger woman said nothing. Britha couldn't quite make out her expression as they started back towards where the Cait stood.

'That one has not finished with her,' Calgacus said. Britha looked around. Madawg stood with his *rhi* staring at Tangwen's back. 'Maybe I should kill him.'

'You can't beat him, he has drunk of my blood,' Britha said, then she glanced at Calgacus. She could see the look of distaste on his face.

'Girl,' Calgacus said to Tangwen, but she didn't answer. 'You didn't lose because he was a better fighter, nor even because he fights dirty, though that's part of it. You lost because he will do what you will not.'

Tangwen didn't even acknowledge the *mormaer*. Germelqart met them as they reached the rest of the Cait and took Tangwen from Calgacus.

'See them back to camp,' the *mormaer* told two of his warriors. Then he turned to Britha. 'Translate for me.'

She was paying no attention. The serpent child's lack of reaction was starting to worry Britha. The *ban draoi* noticed that there was no trace of the effects of the yellow powder around Tangwen's eyes. That had been the beauty of the ploy. The healing magics infused in Tangwen's own flesh would cover up Madawg's trick.

'Britha?' She looked down at Calgacus, and reluctantly nodded. The *mormaer* turned to face Ysgawyn just as the crowd was

121

starting to drift back to camp. 'Given their serpent tongue and their inability to fight, can I assume that we can ignore these weaklings, so frightened of life that they pretend to be dead? I am guessing this is so they can be overlooked among the fallen on a battlefield.' Calgacus shouted. Calgacus looked up at Britha and grinned.

Britha sighed and translated.

'Could you point out to our flea-bitten northern friend that we ignore those who talk in the tongue of animals, rather than the tongue of civilised folks?' Ysgawyn asked, smiling.

Britha raised an eyebrow. 'Are you sure?' she asked. Ysgawyn glanced at Bladud, who remained silent, and then nodded. Britha translated.

The Cait *cateran*, as one, charged Ysgawyn, Madawg and Gwynn, the other surviving Corpse People warrior. The only one who did not was Calgacus's tall, blonde charioteer. Britha had a moment to see the look of terror on Ysgawyn's face and then her view was obscured. Some warriors grabbed for weapons, others sought to get out of the way, not through fear so much as it being none of their business.

'Stop! Stop!' Calgacus cried. He looked furious. The *cateran* skidded to a halt. 'Did I say kill all?' Calgacus screamed. Britha glanced at the blonde charioteer. She was just shaking her head. 'We're not in the north! These are civilised lands. You can't do things like that, you'll scare them to death!'

The *cateran* walked back towards their *mormaer* apparently sheepishly. Then Britha saw Ysgawyn. Madawg had brought his sword up ready to receive the charge. Gwynn had grabbed a shield and drawn his sword. Ysgawyn was shaking and had wet himself. Britha knew that the *rhi* of the Corpse People, while cautious and calculating, was no coward. She wondered if his experiences with the spawn of the Muileartach and the Lochlannach had broken his nerve.

Calgacus turned to Bladud. 'I apologise. I will discipline my people.' Bladud's face looked like stone. Calgacus turned back to Ysgawyn. 'You'll catch your death if you don't get out of those wet breeks.'

Of course the *rhi* of the Corpse People couldn't understand what Calgacus had said. Britha translated for him.

'Back to camp, all of you!' he shouted at his men, and they turned to leave.

Calgacus had made his point but he had also taught Bladud a great deal about the Cait and their leader. It had been funny, effective, but obviously done as show of strength, and probably discussed amongst themselves before the challenge had taken place.

Britha frowned and looked into the mist. She was not sure whether she'd seen movement or heard it. She was about to shout a warning when three pyres burst into flames. They were set out in a triangle and had gone up so quickly that they must have been doused in oil, which meant it was an expensive display. The flames illuminated the mist. Those who had been making their way to the camp stopped and turned back to look. Standing between all three pyres was a figure, a man, in the brown robe of a *dryw*, hood pulled up enough so that the top part of his face was in shadow. His beard was short, well-trimmed. *Just enough of a beard that warriors will listen to him*, Britha thought. He carried no staff but a sickle hung from his belt. He stood confidently between the fires, his arms crossed. His sudden appearance, and that of the fires, made the warriors nervous but Britha knew that the *dryw* could not have done it all on his own. She glanced over at the stony faced Bladud again.

'I am Moren of Ynys Dywyll,' the figure called. His voice silenced those present. He sounded young but confident. 'I bring a message from Nils, arch *dryw* of Ynys Prydain.'

'What message do you have for us?' Bladud asked. It was a farce. She'd seen bards less well rehearsed. Moren pointed at the Witch King.

'You have been summoned for judgement over your past acts,' he said.

'I am here waging a war against a foe that is a threat to all,' Bladud explained.

'Are they not besieged?' Moren demanded.

'Not really,' Britha muttered to herself.

'They are,' Bladud said.

'Are you so important that you can deny the arch *dryw*? Are all else here incompetent and disloyal?' Moren raised his voice just a little. There was an angry murmur from the assembled warriors.

Calgacus was at her side. 'What is this?' he asked.

'Another ploy, it would seem,' Britha said.

'They are not,' Bladud said, letting a little anger creep into his voice. 'And I would not deny Nils, or the gods!' Bladud emphasised 'the gods'.

Britha could feel the trap tightening around her.

'I will leave the warband in the capable hands of my wife Anharad, and Clust of the Trinovantes,' the Witch King announced.

Britha explained to Calgacus what was happening.

'It's a sore thing to do, to leave your warband during a siege, but winter has set in early. I doubt we'll fight until spring,' Calgacus said. Britha knew that Calgacus was effectively trapped in the south until the spring came.

'Did you not see the giants? How their wounds close? The Lochlannach don't care about the snow, they don't feel the cold. The only mystery is why they have not attacked us already,' Britha told the *mormaer*.

'Britha!'

The *ban draoi* looked up at her name. It was Bladud who had called. 'It is rude to talk in another tongue when a messenger from Ynys Dywyll is present.'

'I was just explaining to Calgacus what is happening. He does not speak any of the southron languages.'

Calgacus beamed at the sound of his name.

'You have also been summoned,' Moren informed her.

'I'm sure you mean invited. Your arch *dryw* has no authority over me.'

There was an angry buzzing from the crowd. She noticed that Guidgen was smiling, however.

'As have all *dryw*!' Moren shouted. The smile fell from Guidgen's face. 'You will bring this Red Chalice with you.'

Britha turned to glare at Bladud. 'No,' she said simply.

'The agreement was—' Bladud started.

'The agreement was to leave the chalice in the hands of Tangwen and Germelqart until the *dryw* send someone to make judgement. Your words, Witch King, not mine. They have not. They have sent a messenger.' She pointed at Moren. She raised her voice. 'But if you wish to explain to your army why you would deny them their greatest weapon before a battle, then by all means do so.'

'You would mince words—' Bladud began.

'Like you? Yes, when there is the need.'

'You would deny—' Moren tried.

'Oh shut up,' Guidgen snapped, as he made his way towards Britha. 'The *gwyllion* stand with Britha on this.'

'But she has put herself beyond—' Moren tried again.

'Look, just because you can find some wood and oil doesn't mean we have to go along with your plan to kill everyone here,' Guidgen said. Britha thought he might have been laying it on a bit thick but she could see a number of the gathered warriors nodding in agreement.

'I do not understand this,' Guidgen said quickly to Britha. 'Nils is no fool and I can't see him ruling in favour of an oath-breaker like Bladud. He certainly won't hand over the Red Chalice to him.'

'Should we go?' Britha asked.

'I have no choice, but neither does Bladud, that's why I don't understand the play.'

'If the *dryw* have demanded the chalice then we should take it from those who would deny them,' Anharad shouted.

'Do you challenge?' Britha asked. Then in Pecht to Calgacus: 'I may need you to posture.'

'I thought so, I'm good at that,' Calgacus said.

The Cirig and the Cait had fought more than once, and come close to war on many more occasions. She was gratified that Calgacus was offering her unconditional support. It was probably because they knew her, and she was from the North, and even during the warfare and the raiding they had dealt fairly with each other. She was still quite pleased that Eurneid had been stepped on, however. She suspected support would not have been so forthcoming if the old woman was still alive.

'Will there be an actual fight?'

'Possibly,' Britha told him.

'How many on their side have drunk the power from your blood?' he enquired.

'Less than on ours.'

'In which case, still yes.'

Britha laughed. Guidgen was following the exchange. She would need to introduce them later.

'It is rude to speak in whispers,' Bladud said, and Britha felt a moment of guilt at this but Guidgen turned on Bladud.

'Your wife threatens war on those who would fight the Lochlannach—' Guidgen started.

'I did not—' Anharad cried.

Guidgen pointed at Moren. 'And this one claims that the arch *dryw* himself is in league with Crom Dhubh and would see us disarmed.'

'I said no such—'

'So we were briefly discussing strategy. My apologies. We are ready for your attack.' He looked at Britha who nodded to Calgacus.

'Form a shield wall now!' Calgacus snapped. The Cait *cateran* did just that. Guidgen nodded and the *gwyllion* readied their weapons. Guidgen walked into the circle. None of the warriors from the other tribes seemed to know what was going on.

'Those who fight with Crom Dhubh form up!' Guidgen shouted. Not even the Brigante seemed to know what to do. Britha was pleased to see the old Guidgen back. Bladud started clapping. Guidgen pointed at him. 'You wish to lead, Witch King, then lead. This is just divisive.'

Bladud stopped clapping. 'Whatever Britha may think, we are still subject to the gods. Tomorrow we travel to Ynys Dywyll,' he said, and turned to walk back to the camp.

Britha saw Guidgen sag for a moment. 'And if they attack while you are gone?' Britha asked Bladud's back.

'They are under siege,' Bladud called over his shoulder. 'I do not think you understand the ways of war.'

After all they have seen they still do not seem to understand the nature of their enemy, she thought. Still, she was sure the Lochlannach would only attack if it would be of advantage to Crom Dhubh, yet he had seemed interested in the Ubh Blaosc. For all she knew he had already attacked the inside-out world, though she could not imagine how even the Dark Man could fight all the magics of the Otherworld. Britha was half ready to leave them to their folly except that she did not have the strength to wrest the rod from Bress and Crom Dhubh herself. She would need the power of the Red Chalice and the help of Bladud's warband. She thought on the quickest way to get what she needed.

'I will come with you,' she told Guidgen, who nodded.

'Calgacus, will you look to Tangwen, help her keep the Red Chalice?' Britha asked.

'Aye, though I want no part of that thing. It seems to be driving all mad. This is no way to fight a war.'

Guidgen nodded in agreement.

'I will have my people do the same,' Guidgen said. 'We can

have Germelqart act as translator between my people and the northerners.'

Britha was once again looking in the direction of the cave mouth that led to Annwn. She could still only see mist.

11
Now

'Are you a really insecure person?' Beth asked as she walked into the secure gunroom in the castle's cellars. 'Could you not have collected wine or something?' There were weapons in racks, boxes of ammunition, bullet presses, workbenches, tools and an extensive ventilation system.

'It's a mixture of multiple redundancy, me never throwing anything away, and different weapons having different purposes,' du Bois told her, sounding more defensive than he had intended. She was looking at his old Nock flintlock pistols, his cavalry sabre hung underneath them, the broadsword he had carried to the Holy Land above those.

'I thought they only had the one purpose,' Beth said quietly, then she turned to him. 'Are you sure it's not a fetish thing?'

Du Bois ignored her and opened a polished wood case to remove his Purdey bolt-action rifle. Based on the Mauser, the walnut stock, engraved custom rifle was chambered for 7.62mm NATO, the same as his carbine. He'd had the end of the barrel threaded to accept a suppressor, and he'd mounted a Leupold scope on it. It may have been a hunting rifle designed for the rich, but it was so accurate that most snipers would have killed for it. He laid the moulded armoured back sheath on the work-bench next to it. He would secure that to his pack.

'You need to lose the submachine gun and pick something that complements—' he started.

'My eyes?' Beth asked. Du Bois had to suppress irritation but there was no humour in her words, she just looked sad.

'You've seen the world,' he said softly.

'I know. Look, I don't have your experience but I have the knowledge you downloaded into me. I know what I'm doing. Or something in my head does, anyway.'

He nodded. 'I'll be back in a little while,' he told her and made for the armoured door. Du Bois felt her eyes on his back as he left the gunroom.

It had been a dungeon once, even deeper than his converted cellar. It was a partially excavated cavern. The bars had been removed long ago. Crystal growths covered the wall, there were bookshelves everywhere, a large TV and several other monitors, a top-of-the-line stereo with a collection of CDs and vinyl, comfortable chairs and sofas. It was half nest and half recreation room. He could smell the familiar musky scent of animal in the air. One of the stripped-out adjoining cells was set up as a gym and training area, but it had been a long time since du Bois had learned any new fighting skills in there.

He shuffled out of the kitchen area. Du Bois was thankful he wasn't holding anything to eat. He looked stooped and old but du Bois was half convinced that was because he had decided to age.

'I thought you might be asleep,' du Bois said. The hissing noise was laughter.

'Who could sleep?' The humanoid creature had an arrow-shaped, ophidian head, reptilian eyes and fading, peeling scales. He was wearing a heavy coat and layers of jumpers, a hood was pulled up over his head, he wore a tightly wrapped scarf and even his serpentine tail was covered by a knitted tail warmer. All this despite how high the heating was cranked up.

'This is it, isn't it?' du Bois said. The serpent just peered at him, his tongue flicking out. One of his eyes looked a little milky. The creature lay down on one of the sofas and scrabbled around on a cluttered side table until he found a pair of thickly lensed pince-nez. Du Bois sat down in one of the armchairs opposite the serpent creature.

'A shame they attacked the internet, I thought. I had just found a number of rather engaging online games.'

'How many thousands of years have you been bored?' du Bois asked, laughing.

'I enjoy knowledge. I genuinely wonder which was the greatest invention, the printing press or the internet. I suppose it could be argued one was the progression of the other. I do like the smell of an old book, though, that said: funny cat pictures. Still, it would have been nice to have walked under the sun again. The real sun, not the pale distant thing that very occasionally visits these shores.'

'I think you could walk out there now. I don't think it matters.'

The serpent looked down and slowly shook his pointed head, his tongue flicking out again.

'I don't think I could. I think I have become ... institutionalised.' He looked up again. 'I'm too afraid of the madness. I am too afraid to die. Fear was ever my real prison.'

'Justified fear,' du Bois said.

The serpent looked away again. 'Perhaps, but it is no way to live,' he said quietly. The silence stretched out. Du Bois began to feel uncomfortable. 'You're not coming back, are you?' the serpent finally said.

'It seems unlikely,' du Bois admitted. It was strange how much he was going to miss this inhuman creature, so much a part of his life for so long. In some ways a better father to him and Alexia than his real father had been. 'There's enough food and fuel—' he started but the serpent held up a scaled claw.

'Alexia?'

'I don't know.' Du Bois knew the creature well enough to recognise the body language. The serpent was dealing with a deep sadness. Du Bois wondered how someone who had lost so much did not become inured to loss.

'There's someone else in the house,' the serpent said. 'It's not Grace, is it?'

Du Bois frowned. 'You are the second person to mention that name to me.'

The serpent stared at him. This time du Bois saw the anger.

'That bastard!' the serpent spat.

'He's removed someone from my memory, hasn't he?' du Bois said, and sagged. It was hard to miss someone you couldn't even remember.

'You worked with her for over a hundred years. I think, in many ways, you were like a father to her. He is a cruel man. I ... think I once knew more. Perhaps you should have left when my daughter did. Your vicious little cult used her as a brood mare, you know?'

Du Bois tried not to show any reaction but he could feel the serpent's eyes boring into him.

'She's dead, isn't she?' Du Bois looked up but didn't say anything. He knew it was written all over his face. 'Would you leave me?' It was all but a hiss, the equivalent of a human voice filled

130

with emotion, an old man asking for mercy in the absence of his daughter's killer.

Du Bois was surprised to feel the sensation of his eyes watering, though his augmented physiology would not quite let it happen. He stood up and made for the staircase.

'You could have treated me differently. I think he wanted you to.'

Du Bois stopped his foot on the bottom stair. 'You weren't a prisoner as far as I was concerned. We were protecting you.' He started up the stairs and then stopped. 'Is there hope?'

'Yes, ' the serpent replied. Du Bois turned to look at the reclining creature. 'Find the Ubh Blaosc,' the serpent said simply. Du Bois frowned and then continued up the stairs.

'Are you okay?' Beth asked when he walked into the gunroom. Du Bois nodded brusquely and then looked at her choices. She had picked a Mark 48 Mod 0 light machine gun. Chambered for the same 7.62mm round as his carbine and the Purdey. She had replaced the solid stock with a collapsible one and added a foregrip to the picatinny rail, and a holographic sight. She had also filled a number of the clip-on ammunition pouches with hundred round belts for the weapon.

Next to the Mark 48 was a Benelli M4 NFA with a collapsible stock. The shotgun was a shorter barrelled version of the M1014 shotgun she had already been using but with a five round tubular magazine instead of seven. She'd put the weapon onto a nylon back sheath that she could attach to a pack or webbing.

For a sidearm she had picked a Colt OHWS. The .45 calibre pistol was a failed competitor to become the handgun of choice for the US special forces. Its nylon holster held a suppressor. The rail under the barrel had a laser aiming module attached to it that she probably wouldn't need. All in all she had chosen well. Between them they had a good mix of ranged, support and close-in weapons, most of which used interchangeable ammunition. Du Bois took down two hardened plastic boxes of ammunition. One was 7.62mm, the other .45 calibre. He took one of the magazines for her .45, emptied it, and went to start loading it with rounds from the box. Beth stopped him.

'I'll load my own,' she said. Again du Bois was impressed.

'These are hollow points. Their tips have been filled—'

'With nanites,' Beth said. 'They're for killing people like us?'

131

'Don't load them in your weapon unless you know it's someone you can't kill with normal ordnance. Even then, we tend to put them down with a lot of normal rounds, close, and deliver a *coup de grace* with the sidearm. The nanite bullets kill but they are slow, and you want your target's ability to heal overcome by conventional means. Also, we don't have a lot of these. We can sort of make our own but they will not be as effective. You need to use them as sparingly as possible.'

Beth put the magazine down and backed away from the workbench, shaking her head and laughing.

'What?' du Bois demanded.

'This is ridiculous,' she said. Du Bois felt something snap inside him. Suddenly he was around the workbench and had grabbed Beth by the arms.

'Nobody cares you don't like guns, nobody cares that you don't want to kill despite the knives you carry, nobody cares that your father's dead, your sister's gone, nobody even cares that the whole world's fucked! They don't care because everybody is mad and wants to kill you! You'll be doing them a favour when you pull the trigger. But if you're coming with me then you need to do the same as the rest of us – wish you still got the shakes after the fact, and down a bottle of whisky when thinking about it gets too much!'

'Get your fucking hands off me!' Beth shouted and pushed him away, hard, surprising him. He banged into the workbench. He tried to master his temper. Control the instinct to counter attack.

'Get your head in this, because this is going to be like Wonderland to the DAYP,' du Bois said, calming down. He could see the anger in her eyes, one hand in her leather jacket, he assumed on the hilt of her bayonet. She was ready to go for him with a blade.

'That's all that's keeping you going, isn't it?'

'It's enough for now,' he said, more quietly now. The Ubh Blaosc seemed nothing but a distant myth. He shouldn't have asked the question. He didn't want to let hope in. 'You could have gone to the moors, or you can still stay here.' *He'd probably like that*, du Bois thought, glancing down. 'But I can't have you with me if there's doubt, or hesitation.' He looked up at her. Finally she nodded.

*

They had put together their kit. As much ammunition as they could realistically carry. It was all secured in webbing worn over their jackets. They had bled on their clothes, even on their underwear, not just to provide the material with armoured properties but to make it self-cleaning so they wouldn't have to carry extra clothes. Their packs mostly contained food in the form of concentrated calorific energy bars developed by the Circle, medical equipment in the form of matter-replacing drips, and more ammunition. On their backs, under their packs, they both wore military hydration bladders that contained a calorific energy-replacing liquid. They had also taken a mixture of grenades, which again were held in pouches on their webbing. Everything was secured, or taped in place to make as little noise as possible. Beth had also found a woolly watch hat to wear.

Then it had gone wrong the moment they had taken off.

As they rose out of the courtyard in the pouring rain, du Bois fighting the cross wind as soon as they cleared the walls and narrowly missing the east tower of the keep, all the locks engaged on the cockpit. The stick stopped responding and the autopilot took over. They rose quickly, getting buffeted through the storm. Realising something was wrong, Beth drew her .45.

'That'll just have a bullet bouncing around in here,' du Bois told her. The autopilot took them into the lightning-illuminated clouds. It showed them the inside of the storm.

'One of the nano-tipped rounds could eat their way out,' Beth suggested.

'I've a better idea.' Du Bois reached for the punch blade he wore disguised as a belt buckle. He had replaced the one he had used in Portsmouth at the castle. The blade could disintegrate into nanites designed to attack – effectively eat – their target. If he used it now it was unlikely he would get a replacement. As he prepared to punch it into the modified Perspex, the plane cleared the cloud cover. Above them the stars still seemed peaceful. Du Bois checked the altimeter.

'We would never survive a fall from here,' he told Beth. He heard her slump against her seat.

'Can we eject?' The tone of her voice suggested that she already knew the answer to this, and so did he. He tried anyway but his neuralware was completely locked out of the system.

'Your people?' she asked.

'I don't know,' he told her. Somehow it seemed a little too

sophisticated for the Circle. He wondered if Gideon had sold them out. He was worried about their altitude. If the Circle did decide they weren't happy with his disobedience, all they'd have to do was look out the window of one of the orbitals and they would practically see them. There would be few other aircraft at this altitude in the air now.

Cloud cover had been a blessing. It had prevented them from seeing what looked like entire countries on fire. Breaks in the cover had shown them smoking craters of glass where cities should have been. When they reached the Mediterranean they could see where it had overflowed, filling some of the craters. All the while du Bois felt the moments ticking away. He was struggling to come to terms with the scale of the destruction below. There had been a number of moments in his past when it had felt like the entire world was burning, but it had always been the changes in society, morals, which seemed to happen so quickly, that had bothered him the most.

In the seat behind him he heard Beth trying to stifle a sob. Her world had ceased to exist.

Du Bois wondered how much of what seemed to be cloud was actually ash.

'Northern Iran?' Beth asked. The modified Harrier had been losing altitude for some time now. 'I guess it's no more dangerous for us now than anywhere else.'

'Less of a communications infrastructure, arguably safer,' du Bois said.

'Do you know who's done this?' Beth asked.

'I think so.' Du Bois was pretty sure it was over for him. Though he questioned their priorities at times like this. 'I think you'll be okay.' The Harrier alerted them to the missile lock from a surface-to-air missile system. There was nothing they could do about it.

'Mr du Bois, or do you prefer Sir Malcolm?' the voice emanating from a speaker in the cockpit asked. It was deep, with an African accent, but even with the help of his neuralware he couldn't pinpoint a region. He suspected that meant the speaker's people no longer existed.

'Mr du Bois is fine,' du Bois said through gritted teeth.

'Do we fight?' Beth asked. He could hear the uncertainty in her voice.

'I rather hope you won't, Miss Luckwicke,' the voice said. 'We mean you no harm.'

'And nothing says that like a missile lock,' Beth pointed out.

'You could probably still egress the vehicle if you so wished, we are hoping to discourage that. All we wish to do is talk.'

'Then switch off the lock,' du Bois suggested. The lock disappeared. It didn't really matter. The point had been made. They were coming down in a dry, dusty, mountainous region. There seemed to be little sign of habitation in the area, although further away they could make out a few towns, smoke rising above them, the omnipresent pall of this new age.

The Harrier was dropping vertically now, turning on a horizontal axis as it did, giving them a full view of the surrounding snow-capped mountains. Beneath them they could see the ruins of an old castle, scaffolding covering a number of its walls. On the narrow ridgeline that led to the castle they saw the SAM emplacement that had been tracking them. Among the ruins a number of people carrying next generation assault weapons waited.

'I think I preferred your castle,' Beth muttered.

'The weather's nicer here,' du Bois pointed out. The sun was shining through a break in the clouds.

'I hope you understand that any resistance at the moment just amounts to wasting resources and ultimately ends in the conversation we had hoped for anyway,' the voice said as the Harrier's wheels touched down.

A gunman was waiting to help them out. His swarthy complexion suggested a Mediterranean or Middle Eastern origin. He had an old but serviceable looking tulwar strapped to his back.

'Miss Luckwicke, Mr du Bois, if you would come with me, please.' His English was accented but perfect. Other gunmen on the walls were either watching them or checking the surrounding area.

They weren't ordered to relinquish their weapons, and didn't offer.

The gunman led them into one of the partially destroyed buildings within the castle. It did not have a roof but offered a degree of privacy. Sitting on some exposed stone foundations were a pair of brass bottles with melted lead stoppers.

'You must be joking,' du Bois said. 'I'm not opening my systems to you people.'

He had been hunting them, and had in turn been hunted by

them, for more than eight hundred years. The Circle had been fighting them for over two thousand years.

'This is much more of a security threat for us than it is for you,' the gunman told du Bois.

'What's going on?' Beth asked. 'Who are these people? Terrorists?'

The gunman turned to look at her, irritation flickering across his face.

'Yes,' du Bois said unequivocally.

'Should we fight?' Beth asked. 'What will get us out of this the quickest?'

He could see no other way out. The gunmen were probably as augmented as Beth and himself were, with the tech they needed to take them both down. It was an odd play, though. If they wanted him dead then there were easier ways to go about it. He knew they didn't need him to betray the Circle, they had already done all the damage they needed to his possibly erstwhile employers. Part of it was resignation. It was only his need to destroy the DAYP that was keeping him going, really, and perhaps the faintest sense of hope. But there was curiosity as well. These people had been enemies of his since he had been mortal. He was intrigued to see how this played out. The gunman with the tulwar was watching him as he considered this, as was Beth.

'Open the bottle,' du Bois told the gunman finally.

The man let his assault rifle drop on its sling and slid the tulwar from the scabbard on his back. The curved sword's blade cut through the neck of the bottle. Du Bois heard screaming, his own, then he started to shake as if he was having a fit standing up. Then he collapsed as his neuralware was overwhelmed.

It was easy to become jaded about the world when you had seen the technological wonders and terrors that he had seen. Du Bois was almost relieved that his sense of wonder could still be engaged. It was overwhelming. He had never thought it would seem so real. He could taste the breeze sweeping down from the mountains that surrounded the city; smell the flowers from the many gardens and orchards within, and the spices from the bazaars. Hear music on the air, which sounded like a fusion of traditional Arabic and African music mixed with the beat of modern electronic music. Despite his prejudices he had to admit that it sounded sublime.

In front of him was one of the city's vast gates. It lay open. He found himself looking at the statue of a huge brass horseman. Du Bois assumed it was one of the city's guardians. Beyond that he could see the rows of tombs. If the Circle's intelligence had been correct then there were four hundred of them, all of them different, and all of them massive. They dwarfed the tombs of the pharaohs, each an external reflection of the mind resting – or imprisoned – inside. Some were grandiose and beautiful, some warped and hideous, others alien and difficult to look at. Du Bois knew that inside each of the tombs was an AI. Either one of those created by the alien Lloigor, their machines, or one created by human reverse engineering of L-tech.

Beyond the tombs were the spires, domes, and minarets of the city. Plants and trees grew on everything, water cascaded between the levels and everywhere he looked was life. It was more alive in many ways than the real world.

The walls stretched out on either side of them. Tall and metallic, a straight high wall above what looked like a curved buttress that ran the length of it. Interspersed along the wall were numerous huge gates, each the size of the one that du Bois was standing before now. Above each gate, in ancient Greek, were engraved the words:

Here was a people who, after their works, thou shalt see
    wept over for their lost dominion;
And in this palace is the last information respecting lords
    collected in the dust.
Death hath destroyed them and disunited them, and in the
    dust they have lost what they amassed.

Du Bois assumed the inscription was here for his benefit. He heard stumbling steps behind him and someone sat down hard. He turned round to see Beth on the ground just behind him, staring at the city. It looked like she was trying to speak. Both of them had appeared unarmed, dressed in what they had been wearing.

'I know what you said,' she finally managed, wonder and panic warring in her voice. 'But give me a minute here. A few weeks ago I was in a prison in the normal world, okay?'

Du Bois reached down to help her up. She was still staring at the city.

'What is this place?' she asked. Du Bois glanced behind him. There was a figure, minuscule against the huge gate, walking towards them.

'This is a simulation,' du Bois told her. 'It's not real.'

'Like virtual reality?' Beth asked. Du Bois nodded. 'It seems so real; fantastical, but real.'

'You experience the real world through your mind interpreting the information from your senses. All we have done is remove the requirement for senses. Experientially there is no difference,' the figure said as he approached them. It was the same voice they had heard in the Harrier. The man was about six and a half feet tall, dark brown skin, obviously of African descent. The loose robe he wore covered the smooth dome of his belly. By his frame, he looked as though he had once been powerful but was now going to seed. His head was shorn of hair and he had strips of what looked like polished copper embedded in the skin. His eyes were the colour of mercury.

'The mind knows the difference,' du Bois said.

'Have people become less deluded? Less prepared to believe what they are told just because it suits their worldview, regardless of the evidence?' the man asked.

'Kind of irrelevant now,' Beth said.

There was a fleeting look of sadness on the man's face but something about it seemed artificial.

'The mind knows the lie,' du Bois repeated stubbornly.

'Which lie?' the man asked. 'I think you should taste my cooking before you rush to judgement on such a thing. But I am remiss. I am Azmodeus, a bound servant of Solomon, peace be upon him. Welcome to the City of Brass.'

Du Bois felt Beth looking at him. 'These are your enemies?' she asked.

'Yes,' du Bois told her.

'No,' Azmodeus said. 'Your enemy and ours are the same. You call him Mr Brown.'

'He is a facilitator, nothing more. He handles operations.'

'There is no Circle, he is the Circle, and I think you know that. The old woman knew, even though he had rewritten her mind, as he does to all his slaves. That was why she left.'

'She did not join you, though, did she? A gilded cage is still a cage.'

Azmodeus smiled expansively and raised his arms, quicksilver eyes sparkling in the reflected sunlight. 'How can you call this a prison?' he cried. 'Treat me as your enemy if you wish. Hamad always liked you, and I called him a friend. Come, let us walk on the walls.' Azmodeus turned and led them to a platform in the shadow of the huge gate's mighty mechanism. They stepped onto the reddish metal and the platform started to rise. Beth was staring at the city. The complex interplay of buildings, canals, gardens, entire urban fields and orchards played out in front of them. Flat, with no horizon, it looked like a continent-sized city.

'I—' du Bois started. 'I respected Hamad. Under different circumstances . . .'

'He helped you, you know? Helped you track down Silas Scab.'

Du Bois frowned. That was an old name he had not thought of in a while. 'That was more than two hundred and fifty years ago.' He remembered the chalet he had taken the torch to in the Swiss Alps.

'Not the father, the son,' Azmodeus said, but again there was something artificial about the sadness in his voice. 'This was just over two weeks ago. It was another bloodline infused with the tech. A bad one.'

The missing time! He had come to in a car park in Birmingham. He had lost six weeks.

The platform reached the top of the wall and they walked out onto battlements the width of a motorway that went on and on towards the distant mountains.

'There's no ugliness here,' Beth said, looking at the city. Du Bois could make out birds and other larger winged creatures in the air over the city's majestic spires. There were huge ornate pleasure barges on the canal.

'Should there be?' Azmodeus asked.

Beth turned to look up at him. 'Yes, I think there has to be, sometimes. This is your way of surviving?'

Azmodeus just nodded.

'Hiding,' du Bois said.

'If it was as simple as one of you looking for an answer in the real world, and the other in here, why did you have to fight?' Beth asked.

'What an excellent question,' du Bois muttered. Again there was sadness on Azmodeus's face as he turned and looked out over the city.

'We have tried to save as much of it as we can. The knowledge

139

of humanity. Your knowledge,' he pointed out. 'Before they were destroyed we recorded the library at Alexandria, at Alamut as well, and many others ...'

'We took two different approaches. We could have co-operated,' du Bois said. 'These are the people that poisoned the crèches, burned the information we needed for the evacuation,' he told Beth.

'Religion, philosophy, capitalism, all of them, at some level, start as systems designed to help their adherents, tools for you to use. How quickly they become divisive, turn against you, or rather you turn them against yourselves.'

'I'm not in the mood for a philosophical discussion,' du Bois spat.

'Is he telling the truth? You've doomed us?' Beth asked. 'Why?'

'This is humanity's ark,' Azmodeus told them.

'This is a recording,' Beth said.

'What is more important? What is human? The animal or the emergent consciousness?'

'Both,' Beth and du Bois said.

'Obviously we disagree,' Azmodeus said.

'But then why not just disagree, why fuck up this evacuation?' Beth demanded. 'This is just the powerful making decisions for the rest of us based on their own messed up ... fucking ideas!'

'It was not an evacuation, it was the spreading of a disease.' Again there was sadness in his voice.

'In your opinion!' Beth snapped, but Azmodeus shook his head ponderously.

'You've known there was something wrong for some time haven't you?' he asked du Bois and yes, he had felt it, a kind of ache, a sickening realisation. So many signs that he had tried to ignore for so long, even before Hawksmoor's experiments. He saw the serpent's face, Hamad, the old woman. All of them had tried to tell him. Mr Brown's features swam in his memory, always indistinct, hard to remember, a shade. 'Loyalty is a virtue but it is not required when all of you have been betrayed.' Azmodeus was reaching for him.

Beth moved, she reached for weapons she did not have in here, and then delivered a roundhouse kick to Azmodeus that looked like it could have felled a tree. She might as well have been kicking the wall. She bounced off him.

Du Bois staggered as copper lightning played across his features. He sat down hard. He visualised new software architecture growing within his neuralware. It looked like it was made of brass.

'We can reveal what was hidden, we cannot return what has been taken,' Azmodeus told him. The memory edit he had done himself in a street in Bloomsbury was undone. Yottabytes of information cascaded through his mind. Souls. Scientists, scholars, engineers, architects, philosophers, doctors, artists, poets, recorded by technology masquerading as magic over more than a thousand years. His face was wet. He could cry here.

Azmodeus turned from him and looked out over the city, folding his arms behind his back.

Beth knelt by him. 'Du Bois?' she asked softly.

'I don't understand—' he started.

'Yes you do,' Azmodeus said quietly. 'There is no room for the likes of these in Mr Brown's world. He will continue his work, redesigning humanity and anyone else he encounters. Make them slaves to their own indolence, their own ignorance. Make it so they will not co-operate with each other, so they will turn against themselves rather than act in their own collective best interest. So he can manipulate them. So there will be no resistance to his will.'

'Was Mr Brown the one you were talking to at my house?' Beth asked. Du Bois could only nod numbly. 'What does he want?'

'We do not know. He may just be insane. The eldest among us, older even than Solomon – peace be upon him – believe he once touched something even more ancient than the Seeders, though younger than the Lloigor, and that shattered his mind. We believe that he is in a great deal of pain, but for all we know his thought patterns are now too different to our own for there to be understanding.'

'Is this the same thing that drove the Seeders mad?' du Bois asked. He was not sure he wished to hear the answer.

'He was the conduit for that. It is destruction, utter destruction in denial of the laws of physics. It is the thing that your sister called with her blood, Miss Luckwicke.'

'She always was a handful,' Beth said weakly. 'Can he be stopped?'

Azmodeus laughed. 'Would you save the world? I have always enjoyed hubris,' he said.

141

Du Bois could tell that Beth felt she was being mocked and wasn't enjoying the experience.

'We thought we had. We thought we had trapped him here on Earth, a danger in itself. This is why we murdered babies and our *Ifreet* burned the future. We attacked the Circle. We tried to cut the bloodline. We killed knowledge. It is considered a great crime here.' Again it looked like Azmodeus was wrestling with a great sadness at the destruction wrought during their attack on the Circle.

'But you could fight him?' Beth said, desperation in her voice.

'You are the last contact we will have with the outside world. We did what we could, now—'

'You hide!' Beth spat.

Azmodeus turned to look at her, the flash of anger somehow more genuine than the sadness had been. It was only there for a moment. 'Perhaps. We must do what we can to assure our survival.'

'Where is this place?' Beth asked. 'I mean you've got to have ... I don't know, servers or something.' The words sounded unfamiliar coming from Beth.

'We are diffuse. We exist deep beneath the Earth, in Atlantic trenches, a circle of stones in Iceland, an abandoned city in Jordan, the ruins of the snake kingdom in Cambodia ...'

'The diffuse part I believe,' du Bois muttered, wiping the tears from his face as he ran diagnostics on the foreign software that had been uploaded into him. Now he knew how Beth had felt in Old Portsmouth. He climbed unsteadily to his feet. 'He would never answer that truthfully.'

Azmodeus smiled indulgently.

'This might sound like a stupid question, but are you connected to the internet?' Beth asked.

'They were the internet a long time before there was one,' du Bois said.

'When these Seeders attacked it, could you have stopped it?' she asked.

Azmodeus's face was very serious now. 'Not and have been assured of success. Not without risk to this.' His hand swept out over the city.

'Cowards,' Beth spat. She turned to du Bois. 'I want to leave.'

'As I said, this is your ark. You can stay here if you wish,' Azmodeus told them.

Du Bois laughed. 'I have been a puppet for so long, but I can see the strings now. You want to make sure we go after the DAYP. Get Natalie's genetic data from them.'

'And destroy it,' Azmodeus said.

'But that can be used—' Beth started.

'What did the Circle order you to do with the souls in your head?' Azmodeus demanded.

'Destroy them,' du Bois said.

'And you didn't, because you know we are right.'

'No, I didn't because it was the wrong thing to do. There's a difference.'

'Give us the souls. We will keep them safe,' Azmodeus said.

Du Bois wasn't sure why, but he turned to look at Beth. She looked deep in thought.

'You can take a copy, can't you?' she finally asked. Azmodeus looked less than pleased. 'What fucking difference does it make if you're just going to lock yourselves in here?' she demanded.

'Yes,' he finally admitted.

Beth looked over at du Bois.

'I'm not sure I trust my own judgement any more.'

She looked less than pleased at this response. 'You take a copy. You also take a copy of two other souls inside his phone, but just a copy. They are fractured, they might have been damaged ...'

'By the Seeder attack?' Azmodeus asked. Beth nodded. 'We cannot risk contamination ...'

'Listen, arsehole, you just said you might have won going toe-to-toe with those things. I'm sure you can manage the dodgy souls of two fucking students, okay? You heal them. Then you give them the best lives your little computer game can manage. Do you understand me?'

'Do not speak to me—' Azmodeus started.

'Do you want the souls or not?' du Bois snapped.

'We're not going to risk—'

'Can you even remember what it's like to be human?' Beth demanded. 'There's fucking risk involved.'

'It's not human,' du Bois said. Beth frowned and concentrated for a moment.

'Azmodeus, the demon that Solomon controlled with his magic ring,' Beth said. 'Isn't that a myth, though?'

'He's either a Lloigor AI, or more likely a reverse-engineered human creation using the L-tech. Aren't you?' du Bois said. He glanced at the tombs.

'Oh no, Mr du Bois, I am one of the Lloigor AIs. Though I am a child of another mind and born after the birth of your universe.'

'If he ever inhabited a human body,' du Bois nodded towards the AI, 'then he possessed it through the tech.' Azmodeus grinned. 'But there are rules. So we will have your agreement and we will have your oath.' The grin went away.

Beth was staring at it. 'It's an alien computer?' she asked.

'Dataform, but yes.' And then to Azmodeus: 'What did you do to my head?'

'We were always more masters of the L-tech than the S. We have upgraded your neuralware. It should protect you from direct control by your erstwhile employers, and help against any attacks. We also upgraded the systems in your aircraft. It should help hide you. Your best defence, however, remains that they have other things to worry about, but I still think you should stay with us.'

Both Beth and du Bois shook their heads.

'Where can I find the Do As You Please clan?' du Bois said tightly.

Azmodeus concentrated for a moment. 'Right now, we do not know.' Du Bois was aware of receiving information direct to his neuralware. He was less than pleased about this. 'They were based in Boston.' Du Bois checked the information. It looked like it contained a lot of information on the DAYP, including an address. 'I think you should know that Hamad believed that it was Nethercott, the one who calls himself Inflictor Doorstep for reasons we cannot fathom, who released Silas Scab from his oubliette.'

Du Bois frowned. Azmodeus was referring to things he could not remember but had apparently been involved in. The picture of an insecure little boy, who had used the tech to burn out his humanity and dress himself as a demon, appeared in his mind's eye. Du Bois couldn't help but think that the DAYP were perfectly suited for this age.

'What are you going to do?' Azmodeus asked.

'Fight,' Beth told him.

He knew it was a woman despite the apparent heaviness of the boots falling on the stone stairs. He knew she could have been quiet if she had wanted to, just as he could have fought if he had wanted to, but he was old and he didn't want to live in this world any longer. This was better than any of the alternatives he could think of. He couldn't quite bring himself to regret his life of fear and hiding. He brought to mind all the humans he had known. In many ways the humans were the Seeders' most flawed creation, and most interesting.

He raised his serpent head to look at her. 'You don't know how sad it is that he sent you,' he said.

'Where is he?' He could hear the hate in her voice.

'You know we were friends once? We could talk. I could make us tea.'

She raised the suppressed Beretta. 'Where is he?' she demanded again.

'You know he would never tell me.'

The first bullet caught him in the chest. The world seemed to tip sideways and he collapsed against the couch. He could see her soaked, leather clad legs walking towards him. He could feel the bullet eating him from inside. She was standing over him now, the pistol pointed at his head. He wished he could close his eyes but nictitating membranes didn't work that way. He remembered the city. Fire filled his vision.

12

A Long Time After the Loss

The Monk's senses desperately tried to compensate for the light and noise above. There were so many different spectrums of destructive energy on display. Successive concussive waves trying to batter them to the ground. She unclipped the coherent field generator from her belt and attached it to Talia's, set a timer on the mechanism, and triggered it with a 'faced instruction. Her younger sister was still mostly blind and working by touch. A protective amber light surrounded Talia.

'The ship.' The 'face had come from Churchman. It took a moment for her to understand what he was trying to say. Something hit her, driving her to the ground. Bones in her shoulder broke and almost immediately started to heal. She'd been hit by a piece of the Cathedral, she realised as her sight returned, a piece of ornate masonry melting into the floor, being reabsorbed. She was appalled to feel the Cathedral shake around her.

'No P-sat!' Vic's 'face was practically a shout. Churchman picked up Talia. She was difficult to hold in the force field but Churchman's arms were big enough to cradle her. The Monk had her P-sat clip itself to Vic's shoulder and she grabbed hold of him. Scab was holding onto Churchman, heading towards the *Basilisk II* overhead. It looked like they were rising into pure light and noise. She was receiving no tactical data from the Cathedral, she assumed her clearances had been pulled after Elodie had meat-hacked her.

The yacht's forward ramp was open like a mouth as Vic landed on it. She hadn't dared to look into the light but she was aware of a focus for the Cathedral and the Church ships' weapons, something that was acting like a prism for all that destructive energy, something shaped like a person. It made her nauseous that the Elite couldn't be destroyed by all this fury.

Her sight started to return. She could see her sister was

lying down in the cargo bay, still encased in the amber light. Churchman was holding a struggling Scab against his neck.

'Don't kill the AI! Do you fucking understand me!' Churchman's amplified voice boomed. The thunder outside was dampened in part by the *Basilisk II*'s hull. Churchman let Scab go. The bounty killer scuttled away from him like an injured animal, his face painted in hatred.

She couldn't understand what was happening. The large, golden exoskeleton stood up and turned to look at her. 'Find the Ubh Blaosc,' he 'faced her. She felt her eyes start to hurt.

'Come with us!' Her voice was lost in the noise from outside the ship but she had 'faced him as well.

'You know I can't,' he told her as he walked past. He went down the ramp and stepped off it, his AG motors slowing his fall. The ramp closed and it went quiet.

The timer on the coherent energy field ran down and the amber light seeped away. Talia was trying to crawl, making a horrible moaning noise as she did. Blood was pouring from blind eyes and deaf ears. Nothing looked life threatening but her sister needed medical attention.

'We need to get out of here,' she snapped as she moved towards Talia. The tumbler round caught her in the shoulder. Her *gi* hardened, her skin hardened, but she felt the bullet drilling, chewing up flesh and technology, the explosion nearly tearing off her arm. She heard more reports from the tumbler pistol as she stumbled back and hit the floor. Suddenly there was a big, solid shape over her. Vic was staggering as round after round impacted into him.

'Scab!' Vic shouted.

'I'm going to fucking kill her! Kill them all!' Scab roared. Beth grabbed at the hilt of one of her bayonet-shaped thermal blades with her remaining working hand. Her medical systems were trying to repair the internal damage but she didn't have enough spare matter for the external damage.

Scab had the large, empty, smoking revolver in one hand and a straight-edge razor in the other, tears of rage in his eyes. He was moving towards Talia. The Monk was aware of waves of force battering the *Basilisk II* around but its internal gravity was keeping them steady.

Vic stepped over Talia, all four arms held up in as unthreatening a posture as possible.

'Please, Scab,' Vic said quietly. 'Is this the way you want to die?'

Scab stopped. He stared at Vic. The rage had transformed him. He didn't look human. It had been a long time since Beth had felt afraid like this. Scab was shaking. He screamed. It sounded like an animal in pain. Then he grinned at Vic and lifted the razor to his face. He made his smile wider and redder. Then he stormed out of the cargo area.

The dolphin sea boiled. Some of them had made it to their cryo-genic escape pods, bridge projectors opening the way for them out of the Red and into the Real. Many more were cooked.

They had sent the Elite first. Churchman had only seen the one. He was sure it was the sleeping clone of Scab, the one that Patron had called the Innocent. The Elite had almost made it to the Cathedral undetected, moving in an exotic physical state, but there was enough L-tech in the Cathedral's systems that they had found him. Shifting physical state again, the Innocent had tried to move through the Cathedral's walls. The semiconductor quantum dots – effectively programmable atoms – that the smart matter was constructed of made the walls seethe. They acted like piranha on an atomic level. Impregnated coherent energy fields had torn at flesh and matter, regardless of how exotic, as the Innocent tried to push through. Ancient alien signals tried to introduce viruses to technology derived from the same ancient sources, while similarly ancient and similarly alien diseases at-tempted to infect modified biology. The Innocent, caught in the grips of a tailored, violence-inducing nightmare, had pulled itself free of the Cathedral's walls and into a storm of light and force. Churchman knew that coming through the walls would have cost it. The Cathedral's internal weapons searched for a spectrum of energy, a physical state for the bullets to sneak their ordnance through. This was not a Monarchist habitat. The Church's access to S- and L-tech made them far from helpless.

Then the Consortium fleets started to arrive. Patron must have had some idea of the Cathedral's position after searching for it for all those millennia, for the naval contractor's ships to have got there so soon after Beth had broadcast the signal.

The Church's fleet had already been moving into position, though many of the smaller craft were inside the Cathedral, concentrating their fire on the Innocent. Their ships were vastly superior to the Consortium's. The Cathedral's external weapons were brought to bear as well. It seemed like every inch of Red Space around the Cathedral was filled with beams, EM-driven projectiles, or AG-powered smart munitions.

So much firepower had been unleashed that the first Consortium capital ship to reach the Cathedral had been destroyed in moments, its ponderous bulk silently coming apart.

Mass drivers fired meteorites full of servitors at the Consortium vessels. Each servitor was an armoured, wedge-headed, six-limbed predator that the Seeders had created for their own defence. Their crucified image appeared on Church ships, and in Church facilities all across Known Space. Lasers and particle beam weapons cleared a path for the meteorites, and the rain of kinetic harpoons and AG-driven smart munitions that preceded them. The harpoons and fusion warheads penetrated armoured hulls. The meteorites followed and the servitors were unleashed on Consortium military contractor crews.

It didn't matter. The Cathedral's vast energy dissipation grid was already close to being overwhelmed. The massive habitat glowed like a neon sign, smart matter bubbling in the heat, rupturing when fusion-headed AG smart munitions made it through the defensive laser batteries. Churchman knew the Cathedral's fall, the Church's fall, was only a matter of time.

He hid. He found somewhere unobtrusive to do the things he had to. Ordering the evacuation, wiping all knowledge of bridge technology from systems and minds, triggering self-destruct sequences on artefacts that just could not be allowed to fall into Consortium hands, destroying those AIs that could not escape, and murdering key personnel who knew too much – all done with a thought.

He was wondering why the *Basilisk II* had still not left. Then the prism of light that was the Innocent moved. Black energy lashed out from inside the light surrounding the Elite. Where it touched the wall of the Cathedral it fed on the smart matter to create a reaction. The front wall of the Cathedral, fifteen miles high, twenty miles wide, blew out. The force of the explosion destroyed Consortium and Church ships alike. The atmosphere remaining in the Cathedral became a superstorm rushing to get out. The dolphin seas stopped bubbling, immediately froze and became icebergs hurling themselves towards the cold red light outside. Manoeuvring engines burned brightly as the ships in the

Cathedral were thrown around by the storm. Some were bounced off the walls, some collided with each other and a number of the smaller craft were destroyed by the flying icebergs.

Molecular hooks anchored Churchman to the floor. Among the chaos of information he was receiving he had lost visual contact with the *Basilisk II* and the Innocent. There was a moment of panic but just a moment, then he found them. The *Basilisk II* was on heavy burn, flying against the storm, weaving in and out of huge chunks of ice and other ships, staying close to the floor of the Cathedral where most of the ice was concentrated. The Innocent was chasing them.

'All ships fire on the Innocent!' Churchman 'faced, dooming himself.

The Monk carried Talia into the lounge/command and control of the *Basilisk II*. The pool was still there but the dead dolphin had been removed. Her internal systems clamped down on a surge of vertiginous nausea. Every surface of the room was either transparent or showing visual feed from the heavily modified yacht's sensors. The fall of the Cathedral was playing out all around them. Scab stood in the centre of the room, a fixed, red, maniacal grin on his bloodied face. He still held the straight-edge razor, but the tumbler pistol had been put away, and there was a smouldering cigarette in his other hand now. He was listening to reggae, loudly. The Monk's neunonics identified it as 'Steppin' Razor' by Peter Tosh.

The *Basilisk II* dropped under a newly formed ice asteroid big enough to have destroyed the ship. The storm of escaping atmosphere buffeted the *Basilisk II* but the AG field kept them in place as if they were standing on level ground.

The Monk put her sister down on one of the poolside loungers. Talia was panicking, trying to flail around. She tried to calm her younger sister with touch but it was having no effect, not surprisingly. She tried 'facing a command to the ship for a sedative but found herself locked out of the systems.

Scab brought them out of, and above, the flying ice field, sending the ship back into a dive underneath a light cruiser that was firing all its weapons at something behind them. They made it past the cruiser and then it split apart as their pursuer flew through it. Something made of light, something that all the Cathedral's internal weapons seemed to be targeting.

'There's a fucking Elite chasing us!' Vic screamed, the air filling with the pheromonic equivalent of the insect shitting himself.

No, the Monk thought, *it's not chasing us. It's playing with us. It could finish us any time it wants.*

Then the *Basilisk II* banked hard towards one of the enormous stained-glass windows. The Elite chasing them drew a line of destruction with its weapon, never quite touching the yacht. More of the Church ships died. They seemed intent on getting between the Elite and the *Basilisk II*. The Elite burst through a frigate just as the stained-glass window opened for the yacht. They shot out into Red Space, light and destruction.

'He's trying to destroy me.' The Monk actually jumped as Churchman appeared in the lounge/C&C. He looked as he had when she had first met him. Perhaps his hair was a little longer, but he was dressed as a Catholic priest. Vic let out a little squeal and drew his shotgun pistol and shot the holographic representation of the *Basilisk II*'s new AI. The shotgun loads impacted the wall, but the smart matter quickly repaired the cosmetic damage. The hologram glanced irritably at the on-edge insect. 'I have information you need. Scab is trying to wipe me and the construct containing Maude and Uday. I uploaded it into the *Basilisk II*'s systems.' Then the hologram started screaming. Scab was staring at the Elite chasing them. It looked like a ghost drawn in violent energy.

The Monk was moving. She 'faced the hack to one of Vic's double-barrelled laser pistols, there was resistance but her hack had won out by the time she'd reached the 'sect.

'Hey!' Vic started but she'd unlocked the laser's clip and gained neunonic access to the weapon. 'He's the p—' The Monk got Scab's attention by repeatedly firing the pistol at his right shoulder. His suit jacket's energy dissipation grid lit up but was quickly overwhelmed and she blew a lump of steaming flesh out of his upper torso, staggering him.

'There are consequences!' Scab screamed at her as he raised his good arm. She shot him in the head, once. His trilby glowed, skin bubbled, but it wasn't enough to overwhelm his hat's energy dissipation grid. The screaming hologram disappeared.

'I will kill you,' she told him. Her P-sat was covering Scab as well. Talia threw herself out of the lounger, still panicking. Vic had his shotgun pistol in one hand, the other laser in another, a third was reaching for his lizard-made power disc. 'Don't—' but Vic levelled the pistols at Scab.

Ahead of them the manoeuvring engines of the *Lazerene*, one of the Church's capital ships, were burning brightly as it hove into view in front of them, glowing, its hull bubbling as carbon reservoirs tried to regrow the damage from the constant and total bombardment it was receiving at the hands of the Consortium fleet. Suddenly the *Basilisk II* was surrounded by light as what looked like all the Church capital ship's weapons fired on the Elite behind them. The Elite slowed, and pulsed. The Monk guessed it was cycling through physical states. Its weapons lashed out, flickering between different types of attack. Amber light appeared over different parts of the Capital ship's hull long enough to block or lessen the Elite's attacks. In other places rents appeared in the massive vessel's glowing, bubbling hull.

'Stop your attack on the AI and give me total access to the ship. Vic as well,' Beth told Scab.

'This is pretty good, Scab. You might not get better, but is this a good enough way to die?' Vic asked his erstwhile partner.

Churchman was getting information from all over the Cathedral. He was aware that the Consortium ships were inside the habitat now, though still taking heavy fire from the Cathedral's defences. The Consortium vessels were providing covering fire for troop landings. The Cathedral's smart matter was giving birth to more of the servitors and the gargoyle statuary, which were part of the smart matter masonry, were coming to life and dropping onto ships and soldiers alike. The servitors, gargoyles, and the remaining militia fought heavy combat automatons and Consortium contractor Thunder Squads, backed by the expendable penal legions.

The electronic realm was a storm of data raids, attack software and virulent viruses as AIs and electronic warfare specialists attempted to steal the Church's rapidly diminishing store of secrets. They would be too late, which gave Churchman some solace.

Part of his fragmented but attentive intellect was aware of the battle between the Innocent and the still wounded *Lazerene*. The capital ship had not fully recovered from Benedict/Scab's extensive electronic attack on its systems, though much of it had been refitted.

Churchman saw the Innocent attack the city-sized ship. The

Lazerene countered with coherent energy fields where it could. The energy demand was too high for a coherent energy field to cover an entire ship; even doing it piecemeal as it was now required it to draw on entangled energy fed to it by ancient alien crucibles orbiting in the corona of distant suns, drinking from them like vampiric scavengers. Only having a partial screen up, however, meant that the *Lazerene*'s own considerable firepower could be brought to bear on the Innocent, though the capital ship was taking a lot of fire from the rest of the Consortium fleet.

Somehow the parry and riposte of the coherent energy fields and beam weapons reminded him of jousting. He thought of St George and the dragon. He found himself cheering on the doomed dragon.

The Innocent dived into the *Lazerene*.

'My master has a question for you.'

The sensors in the golden exoskeleton that housed his corrupted body were extensive. He was barely aware of the figure standing behind him.

'Let him come here and ask it then,' Churchman said, and turned around. He had been standing in a corner deep within the maintenance tunnels that ran through the rock the Cathedral had been carved out of or, more accurately, grown from.

The figure was an eight foot tall 'sect with six arms and a scorpion-like tail. It was leaning on a spear that looked similar to the type favoured by tribal lizard warriors. The figure's voice had been female. Somehow the Consortium must have recruited a hive queen, though she had to have been extensively redesigned physiologically, as she was much, much smaller than most hive queens. She was, of course, clothed in liquid glass. Churchman loaded all his most virulent S-tech viruses into his matter, and what was left of his flesh, and all his most virulent L-tech viruses into his software and neunonics.

'I don't like talking to proxies, and I suspect your ratings would plummet if your own kind knew you were an arachnid.'

Churchman tried to 'face broadcast the 'sect Elite's arachnid augment to the evacuating ships, a tiny act of spite. He was not surprised to find the 'face transmission jammed.

'You toppled the god you believed in and replaced him with science. If your god had been real, how do you think he would have felt?'

'These are not your words, puppet. My god is real enough to

me, that is all I need. He would not judge me for idols. He would judge me for the killing and all the suffering I have caused.'

The black liquid glass on the Elite's face transformed itself to take on Patron's features. Churchman took a step back. It meant his ancient enemy was much more closely tied to the technology of the Consortium Elite than should be possible.

'You know this will be the last generation of bridge-capable ships ...' Churchman told Patron's visage.

'It does not matter, not now.' It was his voice. 'You actually sent for the Monarchists. You know what they are? Who he was?'

'You have to be stopped.' Churchman's modulated voice was quiet.

'I don't think you understand how many times I have done this. I cannot be stopped.'

Churchman wasn't sure what Patron meant by 'how many times' he had done this. The visage in the black, liquid glass of the Elite's armour actually looked sad for a moment. Churchman could not help himself, despite everything he had suffered at the hands of Patron, despite the suffering Patron had wrought on countless others. He still couldn't help but feel sorry for him.

'I wish things had been better for you,' Churchman told Patron's visage. The 'sect Elite nodded under her master's control. The large golden exoskeleton started to fall. Churchman had killed himself and wiped his mind and systems of all information that wasn't viral before the Elite even reached him. The clawed limbs penetrated the exoskeleton's heavy armour as if it didn't exist. The 'sect Elite lifted Churchman's shell off the ground and held the limp exoskeleton there for a moment. Then she started to peel him, looking for secrets. The viruses gave her a few moments pause.

'You abuse me, wound me, disobey me, and ask me to save you?' Scab demanded.

'Save yourself,' the Monk said. She didn't like the way Talia was rolling around on the floor close to the pool. Unaugmented, and if the ship's systems wouldn't help, there was a real danger of her drowning in the pool.

Behind the speeding *Basilisk II*, the *Lazerene* looked sick, its very matter warping to make it look like its leprous namesake. All of its weapons had stopped firing, though the capital ship was still taking a lot of incoming fire. Clothed in light, another one of the Church's three capital ships was trying to get into position to help the *Lazerene*, trading fire with the Consortium fleet and aided by the Cathedral's remaining local weapon systems. The *Lazerene*'s engines burned brightly. All of them, bar Talia, were aware of the 'face broadcast of the *Lazerene*'s ten-thousand-strong crew, screaming. They presumed it came from the Elite.

The Monk was trying every electronic warfare trick she knew to gain access to the *Basilisk II*'s systems, but nothing was working. Scab was too good at this kind of thing. She thought about trying to reason with him.

'The AI can lead us to answers. He knows things.' The Monk hated the pleading tone in her voice.

'If this is enough then let's end it here,' Vic told his partner. The Monk was pretty sure it wasn't a bluff.

'Not by you,' Scab said. 'I won't be killed by you.'

The *Lazerene* collided with the other capital ship, crushing some of the smaller screening ships between the two behemoths. Whether from the diseased matter that the Elite had infected it with, or from taking so many hits from the Consortium fleet, the *Lazerene*'s structural integrity finally failed. The capital ship's back broke. Huge lumps of debris spun from it as it split, the two parts of the craft scissoring down on the other capital ship, still trying to rise through the wreckage of its sister craft.

A section of the *Basilisk II*'s transparent smart matter hull magnified part of the wreckage. The Innocent burst from it like a parasitic birth. The Elite was making straight for them.

Scab gave them access to the ship. The Monk split her intellect again. Scab's viral attack on the AI and the construct that contained Maude and Uday's psyches was represented as a hydra. She clothed herself in armour like she'd seen an actress wearing in a film about Joan of Arc, and laid into the virus with her own attack programs, symbolised by her sword. Vic appeared looking like a character played by his immersion star namesake in one of the colonial immersions Matto had been famed for. Though the real Matto had only two arms. Vic's attack programs looked like a colonial era disc gun and twin tumbler pistols.

The Monk wondered if Vic found shooting at the Scab-faced hydra therapeutic. The beleaguered AI, badly bleeding, was attacking the hydra as well.

In the real world the Monk and Vic remained covering Scab

as he flew the *Basilisk II* with his mind. The Innocent had gone. Then the *Basilisk II* 'faced her all the warnings. The Elite was standing on the other side of the pool, black, liquid glass peeling from him and sinking into his flesh, revealing a beautiful Scab as a beatific young man. His transforming weapon was an oversized sword burning with black fire. The Innocent was very much awake. He reached for his uglier clone twin and started to walk across the pool's water towards him.

The Monk 'faced another timed command to her coherent energy field generator. Talia was surrounded with amber light again. She would live, at least until the timer ran down. Then the Monk tried hard not to soil herself. The air felt electric. She dumped drugs from her internal supplies into her system, all but tranquilising herself as she attempted to cope with fear and awe enough to function. Vic was backing away from the Innocent, the air thick with his pheromone musk. With a snarl, Scab extended the energy javelin from its housing in his right arm and moved towards the Innocent like a stalking animal. The Monk suddenly found herself in control of the *Basilisk II*.

The hydra was dead. All its heads cut off. The now pharmaceutically-calm Monk checked the AI to see how much damage had been done, how much memory had been lost. The other half of her mind accelerated the *Basilisk II*, seeking the path of least resistance towards the closest beacon corridor. She manoeuvred away from the larger ships, only picking fights with the smaller, faster craft that could keep up with the modified yacht. A frigate came apart in a hail of transferred kinetic energy, exploding fusion and hard light. All the while she was staring, transfixed, at the Innocent walking across the surface of the pool.

A howl of anguish and pain. An open 'face broadcast as a carrier wave for a sonic attack and electronic warfare. Ships with damaged systems suddenly found themselves dead in space. The *Basilisk II* was thrown into shade by huge projected black wings.

Fallen Angel had come to avenge the death of Horrible Angel, his lover, and/or possibly sister. The Monarchist Elite had died at the hands of another Consortium Elite Scab clone when the planet Game had been destroyed. Behind the Fallen Angel, the Monarchist fleet was emerging from the red clouds, engaging the Consortium fleet. The Innocent paused and then continued. Scab crouched, ready to pounce. The Monk saw something moving under the carpet, like a burrowing animal. The brass scorpion burst from the smart matter floor, its stinger curving over its body. The Monk didn't even see the sword move and bits of the scorpion were dropping into the pool.

'I'm frightened,' the Innocent said, as if confiding in them. There were more warning messages from the *Basilisk II*, strange information about the yacht's structural integrity.

'No, no, no, no, no ...' Vic said, backing away from something. The Monk knew he should have been able to control his terror with his internal drug supply. Then the Monk was aware of something else in the ship with them.

It floated in the air, a squat, roughly cylindrical automaton with various strange technological components protruding from it that the Monk knew to be L-tech. It too was clothed in black liquid glass. Ludwig, the Monarchist's machine Elite.

The Innocent stared at the other Elite, his face twitching as if in the grips of some horrible waking nightmare. Then black liquid glass seeped from his pores, clothing him again.

Sensor information from the ship told the Monk that there was some kind of transmitted exchange going on between the two Elite. The air shimmered with ghost ordnance. Both Elite seemed to be taking care not to harm the other occupants of the ship.

Scab was crouched like an animal, staring at the Innocent, looking for a weakness and opportunity. Then the Innocent was gone through the pool room's ceiling. Ludwig sank through the floor. Out in Red Space the two Elite cut loose at each other. Red clouds enveloped the *Basilisk II*. The last glimpse the Monk caught of the Cathedral was of it collapsing in on itself.

It gave Patron no pleasure to look down on Churchman's inert exoskeleton, but then nothing could give him pleasure.

Churchman's exoskeleton had been found by one of the Thunder Squads. Hedetet, the arachnid Elite, had been too busy fighting Fallen Angel during their retreat. The Monarchist Elite had fought like a fury, still seemingly inconsolable at the death of his sister and/or lover.

Parker was standing to his right on the bridge of *Semektet*, Patron's pleasure yacht. The fighting fish moved through the liquid software of the sculpted, transparent smart matter head that Parker had replaced his real head with. Patron had decided a long time ago that he would never understand fashion. On his left stood the most covert of the three Elite at his command. The serpent-headed woman clothed in black liquid glass was one of his oldest and most faithful servants.

'I would be interested to know why Ludwig helped them,' he said. Her serpent head nodded once and she sank through the deck of the yacht.

Patron turned to Parker, his personal secretary. 'It seems we may still have a use for Mr Hat after all.' He could not understand pleasure but he still felt these small disappointments.

13
Ancient Britain

They had been travelling for the better part of a week. They had crossed over into a mountainous country, the landscape completely white from heavy snowfall. Britha had seen hill forts, and fortified villages, but other than exchanging a few words in Pretani with the odd wool- and fur-clad shepherd they had pretty much been left unmolested.

When they could they had sought hospitality among common folk and the warrior classes. It was always given, though often begrudgingly. People were nervous. They had heard stories of the fair folk raiding and a warband of monsters from the sea. Britha's appearance, her red metallic tattoos, did little to ease their minds. Bladud, to his credit, tried to leave any landsfolk they stayed with richer than when they had arrived.

In the roundhouses and longhalls of the wealthier warriors the Witch King proved to be a fair storyteller. He was known to many of them and had travelled this way before. He was often greeted warily, though more often than not as a friend. He regaled them with the stories of the Muileartach's Brood, who he called the spawn of Andraste, and their current fight with the Lochlannach. He spun stories of mortal heroes facing the gods themselves. Stories that Britha knew could kill the young and the foolish.

They were in the territory of a people called the Deceangli. To Britha they seemed a timid people. She suspected that the majesty of their mountains, the starkness of their land offered so little worth the taking for other tribes that they were rarely raided.

Some nights they had hospitality, and others, like this one, they had found no hall. Instead they had found a shepherd's *bwthyn* in the high country of one of the snow-filled narrow mountain passes they were trying to negotiate. The *bwthyn* was little more than a wood-framed hut with a thatch roof, the walls reinforced with mud and dung, but it kept the wind off and there was a small pit for a fire. Even so it was a tight squeeze for Bladud, two of his bear-skinned Brigante warriors, Guidgen and two of the *gwyllion*, Moren, herself and Madawg. She had been somewhat surprised to see Madawg accompanying them. She had assumed that he would be left behind to try and steal the Red Chalice. The narrow-faced Corpse People warrior spent most of the time riding at the front of their little column in the company of Bladud and Moren, who were trailed by the two Brigante warriors.

Britha had come to the conclusion that she didn't like Moren very much. A *dryw* had to be knowledgeable, and at their best, wise. Often they had to be cunning and ruthless as well, but all of that was in the service of the people. She had met *dryw* like Moren before. He cared more for his own ambition than he did the people he served. What was more, he seemed to be firmly in Bladud's counsel.

She had spent most of her time on the trip so far in the company of Guidgen. She had drunk from the chalice, and he of her blood, so both of them were capable of dealing with the discomforts and the cold, as was Madawg. Certainly more so than Bladud. Britha could see the Witch King getting more fatigued with every day. Yet he had pushed for this journey.

It was a different fatigue telling on Guidgen, however. Britha wasn't sure when it had happened. Perhaps it was the confrontation with forces that previously he had only known abstractly through signs and omens. Perhaps it was the strain of constantly trying to counter Bladud's machinations, but despite the 'gifts' of her blood flowing through him, he seemed tired as well. He had taken to grumbling, and his exchanges with Bladud were starting to take the form of two bickering, crotchety old men. Most nights Britha felt like banging their heads together. She could see Guidgen's point, however.

Britha had also struggled to rest each night. She was filled with thoughts of the Lochlannach attacking the warband; fears that any chance of getting her unseen daughter back was slipping further and further away.

'I wonder if they are all dead yet?' Guidgen mused. It was a question he had asked most nights. Britha may have agreed with the sentiment but she was tiring of the divisiveness of his words.

They were, after all, huddled round the same fire, they all had the same frozen earth under their bony arses. Instead of rising to the gibe Bladud muttered something about going to make water.

'More like making yellow icicles,' one of his warriors muttered.

Bladud's departure from the cramped hut brought a blast of icy air with it. A moment later Britha made her own excuse and got up to follow. The Brigante who had spoken nudged his friend and, grinning, gave him a knowing look. The grin disappeared from the warrior's face when he saw Britha glaring at him. He looked back down into the fire and she left the hut.

It was snowing hard outside. Bladud was little more than a black smudge through the flurries. The wind carried distant howls. She was surprised there were wolves out in this, let alone hunting, but the winter had come early and all were hungry. Steam rose as urine hit the snow and Britha came to stand next to the Witch King.

'How is the child?' Bladud asked, his tone neutral.

She had to think about the question. She was aware that she was pregnant, she was being careful with her activities, though she would not have recommended this trip to anyone else in her state, even this early on. She had wondered briefly if she was trying to rid herself of the child, but when the Lochlannach killers had come for it she had known the answer to that question. She knew the magics imbued in her by the Red Chalice would safeguard the child. There was little difference now to how she had been before. She was not even sick in the morning. She did not wish to risk fighting, however.

'Fine,' she told the Witch King. He nodded, put himself away and turned back to the *bwthyn*.

'Who are you now?' Britha asked.

Bladud stopped and visibly sagged. 'I tire of these constant gibes. You tear at me like rats gnawing on the near-dead. All of this will be decided at Ynys Dywyll. This is no way to behave. Is it too much to ask to be left in peace during this journey?'

By the hut the horses whinnied nervously, their ears pricked back. Britha glanced at them for a moment. Perhaps they should post someone out here with a brand to watch the horses, though tightly packed together as they were they would be difficult for wolves to break, and their hooves would see off a pack until their riders could come to their aid.

'I'm not biting at you,' Britha tried to assure him. 'I understand that you are ambitious, though I see little point in trying to rule anywhere you cannot travel across in more than a day or two. But against the Muileartach's Brood you led, now you scheme, and this, this journey is a foolish risk. I may not like the way he is reminding you, but Guidgen is right. So I ask again, who are you?'

'We left capable warriors behind us—' Bladud started.

Britha touched his chest. 'But we took their leader away, and we left them divided, and we did not utilise the magics we have, and all this for the ambition of one man, it would seem. All would follow you in this, but few would wish to live in tyranny for their efforts afterwards.'

'So I am a tyrant now, am I? I have travelled over the seas. You would not call me such if you had seen true tyranny. Ask your Carthaginian friend.'

'Perhaps, but that is no reason to take the first steps down this path. To ally with low men like the Corpse People.'

'They are tools to be used, as they were for you, as by all accounts were the Lochlannach,' and he glanced down at her belly. Britha suppressed her anger. He was, after all, not wrong. This time he touched her chest. 'Both of us have served our own ends in this. Both of us have risked ruin. You for your child ...' He turned away from her and looked out into the flurry. There was more distant howling. He wrapped his furs tighter around himself.

'And you?'

'It's the training in the groves. We need to be so sure of ourselves because others need to listen.'

'But we spend twenty long winters and short summers learning the knowledge and wisdom we need for such surety.'

Bladud turned to look at her. 'And you are so sure that I am wrong?' Britha opened her mouth to answer and then closed it again. 'Why? Because of what we have always been told? All that means is that the knowledge is old.'

'There is a *Brenin Uchel* in a time of threat,' she said. 'All would follow you in this, even Guidgen—'

'Who is *rhi* of his people in all but name. He is little different to me in this.'

'He acknowledges that you are the best person to deal with the current threat, but he does not wish for his people to live under the heel of another tribe, and what is the point when you rule from so far away anyway? You would not know what he does.'

'And if the threat never leaves?' Bladud asked quietly. The wind tried to take his words and she had to strain to hear them. 'Far to the south and the east there are kingdoms many times the size of the entire land of Ynys Prydain. They became this size because demon kings conquered the lands of other tribes.'

'And you would become such a man?' she asked.

'How are we to fight them if ... when they come here?' He turned to look at her. Britha couldn't be sure but she thought she saw tears in his eyes. 'The spawn of Andraste, did you see what they did to my beautiful island? The desolation they left behind them?' Britha could only nod. 'We must be united. Find some-one better and I will step aside.' He leant in close to her, his face hardening. Britha had to resist the urge to step back. 'So don't pick at me, breed division among my warband, and pretend I am the enemy of the people of this land when you can just as easily work with us.' His voice was like cold forged iron. He turned and stalked away from her back towards the hut. Suddenly she was less sure of her opposition to him. One thing she did know. There had been no falseness in what he had said to her.

Bress followed the trail of blood through the cave system. He was travelling south away from the so-called Witch King's war-band. Crom Dhubh did not fear the Pretani, but in this case he had decided his slave should take the path of least resistance. Bress, however, was starting to wonder if his master had under-estimated the local tribes. They had proved resourceful, hardy, and had mastered what 'magic' they could find and used it well. They had done so at great loss to themselves. They had not quite frustrated Crom Dhubh's plans but they had caused his master to adapt them more than once now. That said, Bress was confused as to what the Dark Man's plans now actually were.

The cavern system was a ghost world he saw only in muted greens, whites and greys. There was little life down here. Nothing to distract him. He was left only with his thoughts as he climbed a rock face and pulled himself into an almost cylindrical pas-sage lined with stalactites and stalagmites. The passage sloped upwards, and a stream ran through it. He reached down for a handful of the crystal clear liquid. Drinking it he could taste the minerals in the water.

The trickle of water had been the only thing he could hear

down here. He had been moving as quietly as he could. Any sound he made had seemed invasive somehow. As a result he was very aware of a sudden skittering noise. It echoed down the passage and out over the larger cavern he had just climbed out of. It was unmistakably the sound of metal on stone.

Quickly Bress drew the dagger from the sheath at his hip and used it to make a nick in his skin. The cut didn't bleed. Instead it released the tiny 'demons' from his blood into the cave. He quickly sheathed the dagger and drew the hand-and-a-half sword slung across his back.

The wards that the blood demons drew in the air caught something. Other wards, not unlike themselves. Bress moved silently behind a cluster of stalagmites and watched. Whatever it was, it sounded small. His blood wards sought answers, but the other 'magics' in the air resisted. Some of his wards were consumed.

He frowned as he heard a crunching noise like stone being eaten. If it was feeding then it would be growing. Bress glanced behind him at the cavern. This might just be something old and forgotten, wandering through the bowels of the earth, or it might be something specifically looking for him, Crom Dhubh, or 'people' like them. If that was the case then confrontation would be inevitable, and he certainly wouldn't discover anything by avoiding it.

He stalked forwards quietly, but the wards of the stone-eating thing snagged him. It was like walking into a cobweb. He could see it now. A metallic parasite melded with the stone. It was sinking into it as it consumed more. It had sounded small the first time he had heard it, now it was the size of a cow. At his approach it pushed itself out of the stone and scuttled around to face him. Two metallic pincers snapped open and closed, and a dripping sting arched over the thing's back. Bress found himself facing a massive brass scorpion.

They had come down out of the high mountain passes, though they'd had to pay more than one toll to the Deceangli warriors who guarded them. They had descended onto a flatter coastal area that supported a number of farms.

The journey had proved to be hard on those who had not drunk from the chalice, or of Britha's blood. One of the *gwyllion* had lost two toes, and both the Brigante showed the black-skinned signs of the frost kiss. Bladud and Moren, both badly fatigued, had enough winter sense to keep themselves warm. This was no time of year to be travelling.

Britha had heard Bladud and Moren talking. Ynys Dywyll was off the coast. The western sea and the isle of the Goidels lay beyond it, but all she could see was thick, frozen mist. She had almost ridden into the water.

Moren had produced a horn from inside the thick layers of fur and skin he wore over his robes, and blew it. It seemed like the freezing mist swallowed the horn's sonorous note. He waited several moments and then blew the horn again. Eventually they saw a long dugout log boat appear out of the mist. The boat was being paddled across the glass-like surface of the water by a fur- and hide-clad figure.

'You will stay here,' Moren told the Brigante and *gwyll* guards that had accompanied Bladud and Guidgen. The Brigante started to protest. The two *gwyllion* looked to Guidgen, who nodded. Moren gave them directions to a local longhall where they would receive hospitality.

'Why does Madawg go with us?' Guidgen asked.

'He has seen Crom Dhubh,' Bladud told them. Britha heard something in the Witch King's voice. *Is he nervous?* she wondered.

'As did we,' Guidgen started.

'But he did not attempt to deny the Red Chalice to the people,' Moren pointed out. Guidgen was glaring at him. Britha wanted to wipe the smug expression off Madawg's face. Guidgen opened his mouth to retort but Britha put her hand on his shoulder.

'Come, all will be settled,' Britha told him and they climbed into the boat. Moren blew a different note on the horn and another horn answered them. The boatman – or woman, it was difficult to tell under the hood – paddled back into the mist.

Bress backed away from the brass scorpion quickly. He could not parry the snapping pincers; at best they would trap his sword, at worst snap it, so all he could do was avoid them. While he was concentrating on the pincers, the sting was swaying backwards and forwards as the scorpion tried to find an opening. He stepped backwards, and pincers snapped shut where his leg had been a moment before. The sting darted forwards. He ducked out of the way, batted at it with his sword, but it was fast. He had to throw himself to one side. He had run out of room. The scorpion scuttled around to face him. He backed up, though he instinctively knew he was running out of passage. Behind him was the thirty-foot drop into the previous cavern. It was ridiculous. This thing, this construct, was probably the most dangerous thing he had faced since arriving in this realm, with the exception of Fachtna during his *riasterthae* frenzy.

Bress was tottering on the edge of the drop. The brass scorpion continued forwards. Bress bent his knees and somersaulted backwards off the ledge and into the darkness. He was quite surprised when the scorpion pounced after him. The sting was powering towards his face. Bress risked a swipe at it mid-air, severing the tail just behind the sting. There was an odd metallic cry.

They landed. Bress tried to scramble backwards. One of the pincers closed around his leg. Armour hardened, skin and flesh hardened. The powerful mechanism sheared through them, stopping only at immortal bone. Bress fell back, bringing the sword down with a clumsy blow, the impossibly sharp blade biting into the creature's armoured carapace. He cried out, and shuddered, almost dropping his sword, as the smaller, sharper part of the scorpion's other pincer speared him in the side, and then the pincer closed, tearing a chunk out of his flesh. The scorpion darted forwards, pincer closing around his head.

This would be a poor way to die, he thought. He smeared his hand into the wound in his side and wiped it into the crack in the creature's carapace, willing his blood to do his bidding. He felt the pincer close around his face.

Deep in the mist, the water was still. They may as well have been nowhere. This felt more how Britha had imagined the crossing between worlds to be, before she had actually done it. The boatman, or woman, followed the sound of the horn. Fire flared, a faint glow in the mist and the boat changed direction slightly. Britha glanced at Moren. She wasn't sure if it was a signal fire or just an attempt to instil awe in their guests.

Britha could make out a beach. There were figures on it. Behind those she could make out what looked to be a very broad, black wall. As they got closer to the beach she could see that the wall was in fact a dense tangle of trees made naked by the winter. Standing in front of the woods were a number of women in dark furs, bearing burning brands, their faces painted with dyes of black and red. More fires burned deeper in the forest. She could hear the rhythmic thud of the *bhodran*. She glanced over at

Guidgen. He smiled and shrugged. Bladud, however, was starting to look very worried, his brow covered in sweat.

'Are you all right?' Britha asked. Bladud looked around at her.

'I ... this place is difficult for me,' he told her.

'Old age has not mellowed Nils' temperament then?' Guidgen asked, but not unkindly.

Moren glanced around at the sound of the arch *dryw*'s name. Bladud just shook his head.

Once they had landed, Moren led them through the thick tangle of wood. Many of the trees were oaks, though smaller than those on the mainland. Britha suspected that they had been shaped by the harsh winds blowing off the western sea. Egg-shaped menhirs were spotted throughout the forest. All of them had patches that were stained brown. There were people moving among the trees, most of them brown-robed, though there were a number of initiates in their white robes, and she had seen one other black-robed *dryw*. One brave woman had been tending to the carcass of a black pig on a cromlech, naked. Her hands pulling its entrails out, running them between her bloodied fingers.

'I hope they will cook that later,' Britha said. She had never agreed with sacrifice for the sake of it. It should serve some other purpose as well as that of trying to tell the future. Of course she'd had piss-all luck trying to tell the future anyway, other than guessing based on her knowledge of the circumstances at hand.

Coins, pieces of metal, broken weapons, jewellery, polished copper mirrors, and many other items adorned the trees, obvious offerings to the southern gods.

Another fire was lit in what looked like a large, roughly circular clearing. Moren led them towards it and brought them to a halt in front of the fire. On the other side of the flames Britha could see an old, frail man sitting on a litter made of wood and furs. He looked ill, and she suspected his legs were useless. His skin was covered with the spots that came with age and it was pale enough to display his veins. He had a long, wispy, tapering beard running down over an expansive gut. He was attended by three of the painted women, and two brown-robed *dryw* who looked as though they had been chosen because they had the strength to carry his litter.

Moren walked around the fire to stand on the old man's left side. Britha noticed the look of irritation the old man gave the ambitious young *dryw*.

Britha had seen the trick with the fire before. By having them look through the flames it forged a connection between those they viewed and the power of fire. The shimmer in the air from the heat made people think there was something out of the ordinary happening. She had used this tactic herself in the past.

'Again, Bladud? Do you never grow tired of punishment and hearing the word no? No, we will not put aside ancient laws that have stood us in good stead all this time just for you. No, we cannot make things as you would have them. No, we cannot remake Ynys Prydain in your image. No, you are not yet a god.' The old man's body might have been frail and crippled but his voice still sounded full of life. He was craning his neck, looking from side to side, trying to get a good view of the man he was castigating. The Witch King had his hood up, his head down. He looked like a scolded initiate. Britha assumed the old man was Nils, the arch *dryw*.

'This is about the chalice,' Moren said quietly.

The old man glared at him. 'That nonsense? Well, is it here?'

'Has my old friend grown so close to death that he does not have the time to introduce himself?' Guidgen asked. Britha was pleased to see him smiling again. The elderly *dryw* looked through the flames.

'Show some respect!' Moren snapped. Guidgen flashed the younger *dryw* another look of contempt.

'He is!' the old *dryw* snapped. 'He is the first in many months to not have spoken to me as if I was a twig who would snap at the sound of a harsh word.'

'Oh, this is foolish!' Guidgen snapped and walked around the fire. Britha could see the old arch *dryw*'s face light up when he saw Guidgen. Moren didn't look so pleased, however.

'I never thought to see you again. I thought you were too old to make the journey in this weather! What were you thinking?' Nils said. Britha moved round the fire to join them as well.

'It's good to see you again,' Guidgen said. They shook each other's arms and then Guidgen knelt to hug the older man. Britha saw him glance down at the old *dryw*'s legs as they broke the embrace. She suspected Guidgen was hiding his shock at the arch *dryw*'s frail appearance.

'Nils, this is Britha. She is *ban draoi* to her people, the Cirig. Who are ...' Guidgen trailed off.

'No more,' Britha said and nodded.

'Taken by the black *curraghs*, were they?' Nils asked. She nodded. 'I hear stories that you are a betrayer, that you have lain with our enemies from the Otherworld.'

'There is truth to them,' Britha admitted.

'But more truth yet?' the arch *dryw* asked, looking her up and down, a shamelessly calculating expression on his face.

She said nothing.

'I mislike how you look. It is strange, and I have never known anything dressed in black that came from the north to mean anything other than ill.'

Britha nodded, considering his words, then she leaned in closer to him. 'Do you think you'll snap like a twig if I break your back for discourtesy?' she asked quietly. He stared back at her.

'You dare—' Moren started.

'Obviously she does,' Nils said, meeting Britha's eyes, holding her look. 'And shut up, Moren.' Then he started laughing. 'I wonder if I can still sport an erection!'

'Well, I'll never know,' Britha said, straightening up.

'She carries the child of a demon inside her,' Moren told the arch *dryw*. 'You will have to sit in judgement as to whether or not it should be cut out and given to Nodens.'

'Oh, will I?' Nils asked, craning his neck up at Moren. 'I think you sometimes forget who the arch *dryw* is, but we make that clear now. I'm going to say no. I think the two-faced god has seen enough blood for the time being.'

'And yet look what has befallen—'

'Moren?' Britha said. The young *dryw* turned to look at her. Britha felt the satisfying crunch of his nose breaking as her knuckles made contact. Moren landed hard on his arse in the snow.

The other *dryw* from the island looked appalled. Nils clapped his hands together. 'Splendid!' he cried. Moren was rolling in the snow, trying to focus, speak, and use his limbs with little success. 'Now perhaps we've suitably awed our guests, so we can get out of the cold, see if we can find something soft enough for me to eat, and offer our guests some proper hospitality.'

Throughout it all Bladud remained on the other side of the fire, his hood up, and his head down. Madawg was standing close to the treeline, his hand on the hilt of his sword.

*

Bress sucked on the teat that the scorpion had grown. It fed him a disgusting grey gruel that was helping him heal and regrow his damaged and missing flesh. His casting had worked. The demons in his blood had sought out the construct's dumb animal mind and possessed it. Just before the possession had succeeded, a fire had burned through the brass scorpion's mind, destroying any thoughts, memories, and instructions it had known. He still did not know where it came from, whom it had served, and whether or not it had been looking for him.

He took his mouth away from the teat in disgust and moved around to sit against the wall, taking some of the food he had brought with him from his bag. His flesh had healed enough to function. His armour had mended itself as well, but was not quite as strong as it had been. The brass scorpion was smaller now. It had clearly used some of its form to repair itself and feed him. The teat was sinking back into the machine and its sting had regrown.

Bress came to a decision. With a thought he ordered the construct to bleed off much of its form. It shrank. Soon it was the size of a cat. It climbed up Bress and secured itself to his armour at his shoulder.

14
Now

Beth killed the first one with her great-grandfather's bayonet. She had instinctively partitioned her mind. One part of her was calm, able to assimilate her newly uploaded skills, use them with her technologically transformed body. She was the good soldier, the calm, detached killer. The other part of her was screaming inside, panicking as she jammed the World War One weapon into a living man's throat and felt hot, salty, red life course over her hand in time with the fading drumbeat of the man's heart. Regardless of the partitioning she knew that this was her doing. All the uploaded skills and tech did was provide her with the ability. She was giving the orders. She was the killer.

At the other end of the gateway to the long, thin yard that led to the DAYP's warehouse, the other guard was turning to face her when the top of his head came off, and he left a red smear on the wall behind him as he fell over. She carefully lowered the guard she'd killed to the ground. The other guard had been shot from a nearby rooftop that overlooked the warehouse just off Massachusetts Avenue. Du Bois's suppressed, bolt-action Purdey had sounded deafening to her augmented hearing on the quiet street.

Her first trip to America and she had come to a broken and burning Boston, dotted with plane crashes. As they had flown in she had seen a coastguard cutter sailing out of the mouth of the burning Boston River. A US Navy battleship, flying a black flag, had fired on them before continuing to shell the city, apparently at random. Du Bois had taken the Harrier down among the broken towers of the city to evade the anti-aircraft fire. Flying just over deserted ruined streets, through the smoke in Northend, she saw the golden dome of the State House, her neuralware providing the tourist information. Someone had written the word *Patriotism* in red across the building. Someone else had crossed out the second I and the M, and written the word *Redsox* underneath it.

They had taken small arms fire over Boston Common, where people dressed as Washington's blue-coated Continental Army, carrying modern military weapons, were lynching others in business suits. Du Bois gained altitude over the Back Bay area. The Central Artery Tunnels running under Boston had been blockaded with piles of stacked cars. Beth had caught a glimpse of movement in the tunnels. It looked like people were living down there. Du Bois banked right, heading north over Fenway Park. The huge baseball stadium looked packed for some sort of gladiatorial combat. Beth had felt as though she wanted to be sick but her modified body wouldn't let her. She knew this had been done *to* humanity but she couldn't help but wonder how much humanity had wanted it, whether this had always been lying beneath the surface, waiting for an excuse. She wondered about those who hadn't been on the internet, watching TV, or hadn't answered their phones. What chance did they have?

The DAYP's base of operations was an old book warehouse in an otherwise residential part of Cambridge in Boston's greater metropolitan area. It was only a few blocks from the strangely intact-looking MIT campus. Du Bois had landed the Harrier in Pacific Street Park, hopefully far enough away from the warehouse so the DAYP wouldn't immediately connect the Vertical Take Off and Landing aircraft to them, but close enough to make a quick getaway if need be.

Du Bois had wanted to go in but Beth had pointed out that as the most experienced shooter he would be better off providing overwatch. Du Bois had been unconvinced but had finally agreed. Beth wondered if she was trying to prove something to the centuries-old soldier.

Du Bois had taken the Model 0 light machine gun, and she had taken the SA58 FAL carbine with the underslung M320 grenade launcher. They had swapped over the modular ammo pouches on their webbing for the weapons as well.

Beth had tried to ignore the dead people with dogs gnawing at their carcasses as they moved through the streets towards the warehouse.

Now she moved to the other side of the gate, glancing up at the CCTV camera. She could see clearly in the darkness now, so she magnified her sight and saw where the lenses of the cameras had been spray painted over. The sophisticated card and keypad lock on the razor-wire-topped gate had been blown by what looked like an entry charge, according to her newfound knowledge.

Like du Bois and herself, the gunmen guarding the warehouse couldn't risk comms infected by the alien madness. They still might not know they were being attacked.

She had no idea what she was doing. Why she was helping du Bois. Why she was killing people in the streets of America. She should have stayed in the castle. There was no need to do this. Besides, if what Azmodeus had said was true, and du Bois seemed to agree, it was pointless anyway. Like pissing into a burning building. As she adjusted her grip on the SA58, at once familiar and completely alien, she wondered how much of this stemmed from the feeling of power her newfound abilities and all the weapons provided.

She had to find calm. Blank her mind, concentrate on the task at hand, no matter how insane.

She could hear movement inside the yard. It sounded furtive. She didn't think the alarm had been sounded yet. She heard another subsonic round in the air. Someone hit the ground on the other side of the gate. Beth wrenched the sliding gate open enough to allow her entry.

Beth stepped through the gate, the SA58 carbine snug against her shoulder, eyes piercing the dark, looking for more guards. She saw a pair of boots lying between two of the four black SUVs parked against the wall on the left-hand side of the yard.

She found herself looking down the barrel of a carbine. The gunman's goateed face seemed to cave in on itself and turn red as he collapsed to the ground when du Bois shot him.

There were two more guards further down the yard, backing away from the gate, presumably to warn more gunmen inside. They wore civilian clothes under body armour and military webbing. She fired three subsonic rounds and the first gunman went down. She knew the other was going to have time to fire but the top of his head came off as du Bois shot him from above and behind her.

Beth moved quickly down the yard, checking above, between the SUVs, glancing at the bodies, making sure they were dead. As she got closer to the safety door she could see a hole in it from another breaching charge, like the gate. The gunmen did not work for the DAYP. She wished she had radio contact with du Bois.

The sky lit up behind her. The report from the massive .50 calibre rifle would have startled her once. She heard masonry explode as the huge bullet turned it to powder with its passage. Her augmented hearing had worked out a rough area for the source of the noise. Another sniper had overwatch on the warehouse and was firing, presumably at du Bois. Her best analysis suggested he didn't have the angle to hit her. They knew she was here, though.

Flickering muzzle flashes from the rooftop behind her backlit her final approach to the warehouse's door. She heard the flat staccato crack of du Bois firing the LMG, presumably in a bid to suppress the sniper. The returning fire from the .50 calibre sounded like thunder as it rolled across the Cambridge rooftops.

Beth reached the door and pulled it open as she stepped to one side. Nothing. She risked glancing in. To her left she could see a collection of expensive looking customised cars, trucks and vans. She checked to the right but saw only the wall of a short corridor that branched out into a wider area. Nobody fired. Carbine up, she moved in. She immediately began taking fire from the far corner of the garage. She couldn't be sure but she thought that one of the shooters had his penis out.

Is he wanking over a car? A bullet hit her in the chest. Her clothing hardened. She couldn't breathe but she was still moving. She went down on one knee and fired the carbine's grenade launcher. The 40mm high-explosive, armour-piercing grenade punched through the side and rear of a van and exploded inside the pickup truck the two shooters were crouched behind. The force of the explosion sent the pickup truck tumbling back into the corner of the warehouse. She didn't know if the shooters were dead but they had stopped firing. Her diaphragm allowed her lungs to inflate again. She was up and moving along the short wall, rapidly ejecting the spent grenade casing in the launcher and replacing it with a flechette grenade.

She came wide around the corner into the open space, the central part of the warehouse. The corner was suddenly chewed up by gunfire. She had a moment to take in the situation. The open space was cluttered with various toys, from gym equipment to sex swings. There was a mezzanine floor with lots of monitors and computer equipment. On the ground underneath the raised platform were a number of servers that she guessed were full of alien madness now. Oddest of all, between where she stood and the mezzanine floor was a cage which looked like it had a big dead cat in it, though the shape of the animal was all wrong.

There were two shooters, one with a squad automatic weapon, the other with a carbine, firing at her from the mezzanine floor. They had fired on the corner as soon as they had seen movement, which was why she had gone wide. There were another two gunmen running for a heavy sliding door just past the platform. The sliding door was open a crack and she could see moving images on the wall in the next room.

She fired at the gunmen on the mezzanine, the carbine twitching between them. A three-round burst for each. But they had ducked down and the bullets just sparked off the metal framework. She risked a burst at the two fleeing gunmen, targeting graphics overlaid in her vision to show her where to aim. A round caught one of them in the body armour on his back; he stumbled and fell face-first through the doorway. Then her carbine jammed. It was a common problem with cold loads. Because of the cartridge's reduced powder charge the gun didn't cycle properly. Beth was using her left hand to sweep the carbine out of the way as she drew the Colt OHWS pistol from the holster at her hip, firing one-handed as she moved for cover. Both gunmen on the mezzanine were back up now. A third was firing through the crack in the sliding door.

It felt like she was being beaten in the chest with hammers. Something hot tried to tear the side of her face off. Her watch hat was torn from her head as she hit the ground behind a sturdy looking weight machine. The Colt was empty. She reloaded it quickly and hunkered down, part of her mind panicking, the other part assessing the shitty situation. *Christ, there are a lot of them.* She had been hit in the head but her hardened skull had deflected the 5.56mm round. Her body was utilising her fat reserves to create new matter to help with the wound.

Beth holstered the .45 and rolled out from behind the weight machine. Almost immediately she was hit again. She fired the flechette grenade from the carbine's grenade launcher. Effectively she had turned the weapon into a massive needle-firing shotgun. The SAW gunner disappeared from view. She swept the carbine to one side again as she re-drew her pistol. The other gunner on the mezzanine floor was staggering back. She knew she hadn't hit him. It looked like he had some sort of spike sticking out of his face but she only caught a glimpse as she fired at the gunner through the sliding door. The gunman ducked back out of sight. The slide locked back on the Colt, the weapon was empty again. She jammed it awkwardly back into its holster and grabbed for a stun grenade from one of the pouches on the front of her webbing. Pin pulled, the spoon flipped out, everything seemed to be happening slowly, the gunman reappeared, she threw the grenade, he disappeared from sight again, shouting a warning. Beth drew the Benelli M4 NFA from its back sheath, extending the stock with her left hand as she brought it over her shoulder. She turned her head and closed her eyes. Her audio filters made her deaf for a while to protect her from the explosion. The flash leaked through her eyelids, but again the tech dealt with it. She could still see fine when she opened her eyes again. She was up on her feet and moving forwards now. Beth glanced up at the mezzanine floor. Blood was dripping down onto the servers but there was no movement. She knew she wasn't doing this properly. She should have confirmed her kills, but then one person wasn't supposed to clear a building this size with so many bad guys in it.

She was through the crack in the sliding door. It looked like a man cave. Sofas everywhere, junk food, empty bottles, and it was snowing cocaine. The projector was hanging off its bracket but still projecting images.

The first gunman had blood coming from his ears. He was still blinking as he tried to bring his weapon to bear. The shotgun pellets removed his face as Beth shot him at near point-blank range. The other gunman, the one she had shot, was clawing at the holster for his sidearm with his left arm. Beth had thought she had hit his body armour, but it looked like the bullet had hit him in the upper right arm.

'Don't do it!' she shouted at him, overriding her instinct to fire. She knew he wouldn't be able to hear her, he would just see her mouth move, but he had to realise that she would kill him if he drew his sidearm. Beth wanted to know who they were, what they were doing here.

'Fucking bitch!' he screamed. His voice had the warped quality of someone who couldn't hear what they were saying. His face was red with hate. He wrenched his sidearm awkwardly out of its holster. Beth shot him in the face, moving forwards, and firing again before his body had hit the ground.

'Wanker!' She wasn't sure if she was angry at him, or herself for the things she'd done. She turned around and shot the other gunman a second time in the face. Working quickly, she collapsed the shotgun's stock and slid it into the back sheath. She reloaded and re-holstered the Colt, all the while keeping an eye on the sliding door, though she couldn't hear anything outside.

She removed the suppressor from the SA58 carbine, cleared the jam, checked the weapon, and then reloaded it with a clip of armour-piercing rounds. The images from the projector appeared to be the graphics of some military simulation first-person shooter game. It was like a horrible mirror. *That* thought had come from the borderline-hysterical part of her partitioned mind. The DAYP clearly had all the toys.

As she checked her weapons she tried to work through a few things that hadn't quite made sense. Her internal systems had identified a couple of the gunners. One was an ex-Ranger, the other an ex-Marine, both of whom had worked as civilian military contractors. They had still seemed able to work coherently as a team, yet one of them had possibly been masturbating over a car and she suspected that the two in here had been doing coke and playing computer games, which didn't seem normal. The one she had tried to get to surrender had obviously been overwhelmed with hate, enough so that any sense of self-preservation had abandoned him. All of which could be explained by a significant lapse in military discipline in the civilian world, compounded with drug use, but it still seemed a little odd to her.

She heard a noise outside. It sounded like a whimpering moan. She glanced out through the partially open sliding door. She couldn't see anyone moving out there. Carbine at the ready, she moved swiftly out, heading up the stairs to the mezzanine floor. She went to the SAW gunner first. His face reminded her, queasily, of raw hamburger. She stood over him and put two in his head to be sure.

The other gunman, the one with the carbine, the one she hadn't hit with the flechette grenade, also looked dead. The spike had hit him in the jaw, gone through his head, and the point had burst out of the top of his skull. It looked like a huge insect sting. She looked down over the open area. She saw the big cat again. She realised why it looked strange. Big cats didn't have bat-like wings. There was blood dripping from the cage. There were shell casings and what looked like bloody pitchforks scattered around it. Judging by its wounds the creature had been extensively tortured. It had a segmented, chitinous looking tail that ended in multiple stings like the one embedded in the gunman's skull. The creature had a human face. The face of an attractive woman. Its chest moved.

She double-checked and then double-tapped the contractors' bodies in the garage. One of them had indeed had his cock out. On a whim she had flipped open her Balisong knife and cut him, making sure there was some of his blood on the blade before folding it away again.

Now she was standing in front of the manticore's cage, because it was a manticore, a creature from Persian myth. Except this didn't look something from a medieval bestiary – few of those had bat wings. This looked like something from a role-playing game. Someone had done this with human and animal flesh to mimic a fucking computer game. Then the soldiers had come here and tortured the thing near to death. She still staggered back and nearly killed the thing when it spoke.

'Kill me ...' it managed weakly. The pained woman's face had rows of shark-like teeth.

'Shit,' Beth hissed. She couldn't believe they had left it sentient, still able to talk.

'Please ...' the creature begged.

Beth raised the carbine. The DAYP weren't here. This had all been for nothing.

'Who were ... are you?' she asked.

'My name was Elizabeth,' the manticore said. Despite the pain etched on her face, despite the abomination that was her body, Beth could see that she had once been beautiful. This had been an act of spite.

'My name's Elizabeth as well,' Beth said quietly. Beth was somehow appalled when she saw the other woman smile.

'What are the chances ...' According to her neuralware the accent was from New York.

'What happened?' Beth asked.

'Will you kill me?' Elizabeth asked. Beth nodded and the manticore continued. 'Oh, y'know, it's the usual story: girl meets alpha male wannabe, girl rejects said man-child, girl gets turned into a monster.'

'This was because you said no to him?' Beth asked incredulously. Elizabeth's answering laughter was bitter. 'Who?'

'He calls himself King Jeremy. There's four of them. Jeremy, Dracimus and Inflictor Doorstep.'

Beth raised an eyebrow at the name. 'You said four.'

'I think one of them got killed in England.'

'That was us.'

'Good.' The manticore was already in a great deal of pain. Beth didn't wish to draw it out but there were things she had to know. She glanced about, checking her surroundings. There was no gunfire coming from outside. Given du Bois's capabilities she assumed it was because he had killed the other sniper.

'Elizabeth, do you know where they've gone?'

The manticore's eyes closed as she took several ragged breaths. Beth was sure she was going to die right there.

'I think they've gone to LA,' Elizabeth told her. 'Something's happened, hasn't it? Outside. My family ...'

'I've got nothing good to tell you,' Beth said. She wanted to cry. 'Where in LA?'

Sadness warred with pain on the manticore's face. 'I don't know. King Jeremy's made a deal with someone but he doesn't trust them. He was talking about all sorts of crazy things, like submarines, nonsense, but he has some contact in LA.'

'Do you know who?'

'I'm sorry ...' Hearing Elizabeth apologise was heartbreaking. 'I think they were looking for an aircraft. They mentioned Boston Logan and some air force base.'

It wasn't much but maybe du Bois knew more.

'The soldiers, why ...' Beth asked, and then realised she didn't have a way to ask the question. They had tortured her.

'I dated a soldier once. He was troubled ... but he was sweet. These weren't soldiers. They were junior league sadists.'

'Why didn't you ...' she started. 'Your tail?' she finished weakly.

Elizabeth swallowed. 'I ... I wasn't supposed to ... not in here ... I got punished ...' There were tears on her still-beautiful face. 'Please ... I've had enough.'

Two more shots rang out. As she felt the carbine kick back into her shoulder the urge to sob was gone. A much colder feeling replaced it. She knew why she was in this now. What she had to do.

The ceiling of the warehouse was ripped open, concrete and expensive toys torn apart as they were thrown into the air. Beth dived out of the line of fire. Her neuralware analysed the sound as that of twin 25mm ADEN cannons firing. Like those mounted on the Harrier.

The air was filled with powdered concrete. There was more firing, but none aimed at the warehouse, fortunately. Beth ran to the door.

Outside in the warehouse's yard she looked up. She could hear the Harrier nearby. It sounded like it was hovering. There was more cannon fire. Beth moved quickly out onto the street, weapon at the ready.

She could see the Harrier now. Muzzle flashes were coming from the twin cannon pods mounted underneath the fuselage. She couldn't make out what it was firing at. She hoped it was du Bois flying it, though that certainly hadn't been the plan. There was movement at the Massachusetts Avenue end of the street. There was a crowd of people, most of them carrying improvised weapons, some of them with burning brands, sprinting down the street towards her. Presumably they'd been attracted by the sounds of violence. They were probably screaming and shouting but she couldn't hear them over the cannon fire.

Beth darted across the road and into the alley that ran down the side of the building that du Bois had fired from. She reached the external fire escape she had seen earlier, jumped for the raised ladder and pulled herself up. The cannon fire had stopped. Now she could hear the mob. She clambered up the fire escape as quickly as she could. The first of the mob rounded the corner of the alley. She didn't want to kill them unless she had to.

Beth reached the top of the building. The psychedelically-painted Harrier was hovering over a building across the street. As she watched, fires ignited under the aircraft's wings in the crayon-shaped rocket pods, and 68mm SNEB air-to-ground rockets shot into the top of an apartment building. A cascade of explosions lit up the roofline. Beth wasn't sure, but she thought she might have seen a figure leap from the apartment building, just a shadow backlit against the explosions.

Wishing she had a flare, Beth fired a long burst into the air, moving forwards as she did so, trying to get du Bois's attention. At least she hoped it was du Bois. She could hear people climbing the fire escape now. She let the carbine drop on its sling and pulled out the other stun grenade she had been carrying. She pulled the pin, let the spoon flip off, and held it. She cooked the grenade and then threw it at the Harrier and turned her head away. The grenade exploded in mid-air. The Harrier veered slightly and then turned towards her. Beth fired another long burst in the air and then quickly reloaded the carbine and turned to face the fire escape.

The first of the mob appeared. Reluctantly Beth raised the carbine to her shoulder, still backing away. The edge of the building disappeared, phosphorus drew laser-like lights in the night as tracer-tipped cannon rounds disintegrated concrete, brick and fragile human flesh. Beth sagged.

She felt the downdraught from the L-tech modified aircraft as du Bois brought it down to hover close to the roof. The cockpit hatch was open. Beth slung the carbine and leapt onto the wing, making the aircraft veer slightly towards the building. She crawled across the wing. She was pretty sure that she couldn't have done this with an unmodified version of the aircraft. In the street below, the people in the mob were throwing things at the Harrier. Beth climbed into her seat, the cockpit sealing after her, and the Harrier started to climb.

'What happened?' Beth asked. Du Bois had looked thin and haggard in the momentary glimpse she had caught of him. He had been injured and had healed himself.

'The sniper,' du Bois said.

'Cannon fire, rockets, you don't think that was overkill, do you?'

'Perhaps you can judge after you've taken a hit from a fifty calibre sniper rifle,' du Bois said a little testily. 'He's one of us, like me.'

'He works for your old boss?' Beth asked. She knew it would make him difficult to kill.

'Yes, his name is Josh Ezard. The older of us used to call him the American. He served with Rogers' Rangers during the Seven Years War, and then formed a particularly effective colonial militia to fight against the British during the War of Independence. He is an extremely good shot.' Du Bois sounded angry. The Harrier dipped forwards and then G-force pushed her back as the aircraft accelerated.

'So your old employer sent the contractors?' Beth asked. Du Bois didn't immediately answer.

'Contractors? Were they insane?'

'Maybe, but they were able to function if they were. I got some of their blood.'

Du Bois passed his phone back to her. It was not worth risking in terms of communication, but isolated it was still a useful tool.

'Just wipe the blood across the bottom of it,' he told her. Beth reached for her Balisong knife. When the base of the phone touched the blade it absorbed some of the blood and the display lit up.

'S-tech, some kind of puppeteer nanites,' Beth said. 'They were arseholes, though, nasty, cruel.'

'Just controlled enough to harness their insanity. Are you okay?'

Beth didn't answer his question. Instead she told him about the deal King Jeremy had made and where the DAYP clan were going.

'It sounds like they've made a deal with Mr Brown, but he'll double cross them. They're amateurs in this.'

'Do you know who their contact in LA could be?' Beth asked. There was another pause.

'I can't think of anyone, I didn't operate there much. I always hated the place. I might know somebody who can help, however, if he's still alive.' The Harrier was already heading west. 'If King Jeremy, I mean young Mr Rush,' du Bois corrected himself, she knew he disliked using the DAYP's assumed names, 'is after a submarine,' du Bois mused, 'he must think he wants to go to Kanamwayso.'

'Kanamwayso?'

'Where I think all this madness came from.'

15
A Long Time After the Loss

It had got very quiet in the *Basilisk II*'s lounge/C&C, in part because Scab was nowhere to be seen. This would normally have made Vic very nervous but he was beyond that now. The Cathedral was gone. His chance at peace was gone. He looked over at Talia. The Monk had fabricated electrodes and managed to get signals to the cortical language areas of her sister's brain. Of course it had terrified the girl, but the Monk had managed to soothe her and run medical extensions from the ship's assembler to Talia's eyes and ears. She had also administered a gentle sedative. Talia was still conscious but she was calmer now.

There was a moment when Vic looked at her, the girl from before the Loss who said and did such strange things, and he resented how she had complicated things. Or he tried to. Sure, Scab had always been a psycho, but they'd been doing all right before they'd got embroiled in this nonsense. They'd been rich, well, less in debt; successful, in terms of killing people with money on their heads; and respected, well, feared, though that had mostly been Scab. *No, he decided, things hadn't been good, just slightly less shit. Well, perhaps significantly less shit.*

She looked so fragile.

Bitch! he tried to convince himself.

'Beth?' Talia asked weakly.

She can hear! 'I helped save you!' Vic blurted out. The Monk and Talia turned to look at him and then turned back to each other.

'It's gone, isn't it?' There were tears in Talia's eyes. The Monk nodded. 'It was your home?'

'Yes, it was,' the Monk said quietly, taking her sister's hand.

'I'm sorry.' Vic wasn't surprised to see Talia's face dissolve into tears. He looked at the Monk. She leant down and stroked her sister's face, tucking some of her long hair away.

Vic didn't understand. It was the Monk who had lost her home of so many thousands of years, her friends, Churchman, and yet she was comforting Talia. Humans made no sense to Vic.

'Where's Scab?' Talia asked some time later. Both her eyes and ears were fully healed now. 'Now there's a question I'd never thought I'd ask.'

Vic had been draining the pool, converting the water into carbon for the ship's reservoir, making the lounge more lounge-like and once again trying, unsuccessfully, to program the smart furniture to be comfortable for 'sects.

'Did he die?'

Vic looked over at the girl. He was pretty sure she had been trying to keep her voice neutral. He wasn't sure if she wanted Scab to be dead or not.

'He's merged with the ship's smart matter,' Vic said. 'Probably. He might just be in his room.'

'Can we assume he can hear us?' the Monk asked. Vic nodded. Talia looked like she was concentrating.

'Elodie said something,' Talia said. 'About Scab.'

Vic saw the Monk tense at the mention of the feline's name. For all that she had done, Vic was pretty sure that the feline would be cloned on Ubaste, sans memory, and get on with her life. Nobody here had the time or the resources to go after her. He found he couldn't even get angry about it. They hadn't been neurally audited, or denuded of dangerous nanites, virals, software etc when they had arrived at the Cathedral. Apparently this was because of one of those strange social mores called courtesy. As far as Vic was concerned, and despite the Cathedral's otherwise excellent security, the Church had destroyed itself. What had they thought was going to happen, inviting them on board?

'Anything Elodie said would have been part of her plan to manipulate us,' Vic told her.

'That's the thing, it didn't really make any sense. She said that Scab was in love with the ghost of the ship.'

Vic's mandibles clattered together and he emitted a sound that he thought approximated a human giggle. He didn't think he'd got it right because both the women were giving him odd looks.

'This ship?' Vic asked. Talia shrugged.

'I don't know, maybe she liked him more than she was willing to admit,' the Monk said dismissively. Talia frowned at her sister. 'I think we've got more important things to talk about than Scab's love life.' Talia opened her mouth to say something but then seemed to think the better of it.

'Do you want to go and have sex in an immersion? I can make myself look more human.' He had just blurted it out. Vic cringed internally and wondered if there was some routine he could add to his neunonics that would stop him from saying things like this when he was tense. He wanted to meat puppet himself.

Talia's hand shot to her mouth as she tried to suppress laughter. The Monk was staring at him.

'Vic! She's my sister,' the Monk pointed out.

'That's terribly sweet but not right now,' Talia said. The Monk turned to look at her. 'What?'

'The Elite!' Vic cried, desperate to change the subject. Though he didn't really want to think about it. Ludwig, the Monarchist's automaton Elite, had killed him before. 'Was it trying to protect us from the Innocent?'

'It looked that way, didn't it?' the Monk said, somewhat grimly.

'Because the Monarchists still want Talia?'

Talia was looking between the two of them as they talked but otherwise remained quiet.

The Monk shrugged. 'That would make sense, I guess.'

'But?'

'Even fighting the Innocent, Ludwig could have taken her. I mean, either of them would have walked through us. The Innocent would have killed us all if he wasn't as fucked in the head as Scab.'

'The Innocent is asleep and living through a tailored nightmare,' Vic pointed out.

'Which makes him slow for a death god, largely due to a penchant for the dramatic.'

'Penchant?' Talia asked.

'I've had millennia to develop a vocabulary.'

'Okay, try and remember you're from Yorkshire though, and not the Harrogate part of it.'

Vic had no idea what they were talking about. The Monk smiled but it was obvious to Vic's facial recognition routines the woman was still in an awful lot of pain.

'Ludwig was supposed to be a found weapon, right?' the Monk said to Vic, all business now.

'I believe so,' Vic said.

'It's an L-tech automaton,' the Monk said. Vic nodded as if he knew what she was talking about. 'Augmented by Elite-tech, which is itself mostly reverse engineered S- and L-tech.' Vic nodded thoughtfully. 'You've no idea what I'm talking about, do you?'

'Well, I know what Churchman told us,' Vic said. There was a momentary change in the Monk's face at the sound of her friend's name. 'These Lloigor. I don't really get why you called it all S-tech.'

'Because they were trying to create a religion,' Talia said. The Monk looked at her younger sister, clearly surprised.

'She's quite intelligent, you know?' Vic said, trying to curry favour and somehow irritating both of them instead.

'A true religion,' the Monk told them. 'One based on science.' Even she didn't sound convinced.

'Not so true that you didn't want your origin myth to get all confused with those tricksy Lloigor,' Talia pointed out.

'Ludwig?' Vic asked. He was developing a sense of when the sisters were going to start arguing.

'We've found things like it before, but inert,' the Monk told him.

'What are they?' Talia asked.

'As far as we can tell they were part of an autonomous defence network that protected Lloigor facilities.'

Vic gave this some thought. Then he decided that he still didn't understand anything. He pointed at Talia. 'She's S-tech, right?'

'No,' the Monk said tightly. 'She's my sister. She is from a biological line that had S-tech spliced into it.'

'When?' Talia asked.

'The Iron Age,' the Monk told her.

'Oh.'

'So what did the Seeders have to do with the Lloigor?' Vic asked.

'Well, nothing as far as we know,' said the Monk, 'but like I said, Ludwig might not have come for Talia.'

'I have a question,' her sister said. 'If the Church controlled the secret of bridge travel, which was connected to me somehow, why did you sell it to the Consortium?'

Vic had to concede it was a very good point. He turned to look at the Monk.

'Originally the Monarchist systems and the Consortium had it as well. We managed to get organised first, however, after the Loss. Removing their bridge production capabilities was our first Crusade.' She said this with more than a little distaste. 'Very exciting. The thing is, by that point the Consortium had enough bridge-capable craft to be a threat to us, as well as the fledgling Elite, and we also needed to operate within the Consortium-held systems for access to S- and L-tech, and for social engineering and intelligence gathering purposes. We also needed the resources that the Consortium paid us to continue with our research and our operations. So we came to an uneasy agreement. We sold to the Monarchist systems to act as a counterbalance against the Consortium, and believe me they are not pleasant people either.'

'Looks like it came back to bite you,' Vic said. The Monk looked away and Talia glared at him.

'Churchm—' the Monk started. 'Do I really have to call you the *Basilisk*?' She seemed to be talking to the air. The *Basilisk II*'s newly uploaded AI, the one that Scab had tried to kill, appeared. His holographic presence was for Talia's benefit.

'Psychologically I think it would be better for you,' the AI told her sympathetically, and then with a pained expression on his face said: 'And strictly speaking, I am the second of that name.'

'I'm not calling you *Basilisk II*. You ... Churchman told me to find the Ubh Blaosc? I've heard the name before. I think that they were another faction with access to the tech before the Fall. What have you got on them?'

'Beyond it being the Irish word for egg shell, nothing, I'm afraid,' the AI said apologetically.

'Fuck's sake! Did that wanker erase it when he attacked?' the Monk demanded.

'It is possible, but I do not know.' The AI's hologram seemed to be looking past the Monk and Talia.

Vic followed his eyes and then jumped and almost reached for his pistols. Scab was standing close to the wall. The Monk and Talia turned and looked as well. The Monk tensed. Vic couldn't read Talia's response.

'If there's going to be more petty tantrums, let's just get it over and done with now,' the Monk said.

Scab walked over to the well-upholstered chair close to the sofa that Talia was lying on and the Monk was sitting on. Everyone's eyes followed him. He sat down, took out his cigarette case, put one of the pointless drug sticks between his lips, lit it and then exhaled. He regarded the Monk carefully and then leant forwards. 'So what do you want to do next?' he asked.

The Monk's eyes narrowed but it was obvious that she had no answers. They were still hunted, there was still money on their heads, they appeared to have once again garnered the attention of the Elite, and any allies had either betrayed them, or been destroyed.

'If I may make a suggestion,' the *Basilisk II*'s newly integrated AI said. Scab's face twitched. 'I think Mr Scab should visit his mother.'

Vic couldn't have been more surprised if Steven the Dolphin had spontaneously reincarnated in the lounge/C&C and started fellating Scab, not least because he knew Scab had been gestated in a Cyst exo-womb.

'I don't have a mother,' Scab said quietly. Vic could hear the tension in the human killer's voice.

Cyst was on the cusp of extinction in celestial terms, and it had been for a very long time. The cold gas giant's magnetosphere, which should have been stripped away millions of years ago, had been kept in place artificially. Most of its volatiles had been vampirically consumed by the megastructure that caged it. The planet was a huge sphere of sparse clouds of hydrogen and helium, with mega weather systems creeping slowly across it. The reflected light of its fading star made the gas clouds look white against a pale blue. It was a husk, a corpse world, it looked like the ghost of a gas giant and it should have been torn apart by gravitic forces a long time ago.

Initially thought to have been the site of the single greatest find of S-tech during the colonial era, Vic now knew that the hard-tech of Cyst's Cage meant that it was actually an L-tech structure. He was still getting his head round it not having been created by the Seeders.

The Cage was basically a massive network of broad walkways and ziggurat-style buildings at evenly spaced junctions, all of which were made of some kind of smart matter. The Cage moved counter to the spin of the planet in a way that seemed to contradict physics and meant that it should have been torn apart by centrifugal forces. Somehow this allowed the walkways to generate a gravity field of roughly 1 G.

The Cage harvested energy from Cyst's volatiles like a leech, and presumably had once done the same from the cooling of the planet causing compression, which in turn heated it up, allowing it to radiate more heat than it received from its star. It was theorised that Cyst had been some kind of fuelling station. Now there was just enough fuel left, apparently, for the Cage to continue functioning. Sooner or later that fuel would run out.

Such a feat of engineering had, of course, required a great deal of matter. The initial xeno-archaeologist expedition had theorised that rings and a number of moons, mostly system-invading planetoids trapped by the gas giant's gravity, had once surrounded Cyst, and that their matter had been used in the construction of the Cage.

None of which meant very much to Vic. What he did know was that the existence of the mega engineering artefact had naturally led to war between the fledgling Monarchist systems, the fledgling Consortium, and of course the Church, all of whom wanted it. This was despite the Cage pretty much defying all attempts at scientific analysis.

During the height of the hostilities, roughly a quarter of the planet's volatiles had suddenly disappeared, and more than three quarters of the crossroad ziggurats had suddenly emitted beams of superheated plasma powerful enough to cut through star ships and make their hulls burn in space. Suddenly Cyst's orbit had been full of wreckage.

The hostilities ceased. The belligerents were less worried about the destruction of property and personnel, and more worried that the utilisation of the planet's resources in such a way would significantly hasten its destruction. Without a way to use the tech for their own gain, the Consortium, the Monarchist systems, and (in theory) the Church, lost interest.

It had proved cheaper to leave many of the combatants and other support personnel behind on the Cage after the conflict. It was assumed that they would die out when their supplies ran out, or that whatever had attacked the ships would deal with them. Instead the ziggurats started to assemble food and other supplies, though the Cage itself had seemed to be implicitly encouraging competition for the resources through scarcity.

Things went feral quickly. Roaming gangs were formed. They fought for territory and resources high above the depleted gas clouds. Heretical cults sprang up. Many of them talked about the

Dark Mother. Those that died were harvested for DNA, and new inhabitant/combatants were born from exo-wombs in the smart matter of the ziggurats.

The population had remained reasonably stable, in part because of the constant warring. Newborns very quickly gained physical maturity and were often 'rewarded' with grafted weapons and used as hunting/fighting animals until they had proven themselves enough to become something that looked more like an uplift.

Scab had been born into this. Apparently he had been part of an already-existing bloodline. He had started his own street sect, dedicated to himself. His mixture of cunning, psychosis, grasp of strategy, and his fervent followers who offered a choice of convert or be tortured to death in a society that had been conditioned to respect strength, soon had him close to dominating the world. A situation that the Consortium, backed by the Church, could not allow.

The war was fought on the walkways, in the ziggurats, and among the still-dripping structures of fused and hardened bone and skin Scab had made from his victims. Church militia and Consortium military contractors had fought side by side, but it had been the Legions, the Consortium's penal forces, who had borne the brunt of the fighting. Poorly armed and equipped, they had been thrown at the hordes of cultists.

Eventually a Legion special ops team, aided by one of the Church's monks, had captured Scab. Vic was pretty sure it hadn't been Talia's older sister. What he didn't understand was why the Consortium didn't have one of the Elite deal with Scab, and why capture him? After his capture he'd had brain surgery, apparently to curb his excesses, and had been placed into one of the Legions. There he had worked his way up until he had been offered Elitehood.

Both the Consortium and the Church had maintained a presence above Cyst. A number of the Legions' special operations units were made up entirely of recruits from Cyst. The Church's presence was to monitor the L-tech artefact, in theory.

But this was where it all started, Vic had thought as he looked at the planet through the *Basilisk II*'s sensor feed, which was 'face linked direct to his neunonics. From this distance it looked like wisps of gas encased in a glass sphere, which was in turn in bondage. They were relying on the Church-upgraded stealth systems to keep them hidden from the Consortium military contractor fleets now stationed above the planet.

Part of the lounge's wall became transparent and the Monk got up from the sofa she'd been sitting on, concentrating, since they'd emerged from Red Space. Talia had been pacing and fidgeting. It seemed obvious to Vic, since he had cross-referenced her behaviour with the information he had on human psychology, that the pre-Loss girl was struggling to deal with what had happened at the Cathedral, and the amount of violence she had to face in general. Currently she was trying to cope by self-medicating with vodka and THC. Vic had already sent a request to the *Basilisk II*'s AI for virtual counselling for the girl, as she couldn't control her psyche in a healthy way with drugs and machinery like the rest of them could.

Part of the *Basilisk II*'s hull also became transparent and magnified the view of distant Cyst. The Monk, hands clasped behind her back, stood just in front of the image. Scab extruded himself through the ceiling, making Talia squeal with fright, and dropped into the lounge in a way that reminded Vic of the humans' simian ancestry.

'I've sent a heavily occulted tight-beam signal to Church assets in the system,' the Monk said. 'Nothing.'

'They're dead,' Scab said. They had picked up the information from news transmitted between the beacons in Red Space. The Consortium had moved unilaterally on the Church, a board-level decree, no exceptions. Military contractors, company security forces, and the Legions had attacked every ship, Church and facility they could find. Any Church members who resisted were killed outright, many others had killed themselves for one reason or another, those that could had run, the rest were being held in the ship or facility they had been captured in.

The Monarchists had, of course, offered sanctuary to all Church personnel, and were on the cusp of war with the Consortium for the first time in centuries, and were one Elite down.

'She spoke to me once,' Scab said. Everyone turned to look at him.

'Who?' the Monk asked.

Vic found that he had no patience for Scab's strange little utterings, regardless of how calm his erstwhile partner seemed.

'The Dark Mother.'

The Monk started laughing. 'Bullshit,' she told him.

Vic sighed and slumped as Scab's face tightened and he turned to stare at her. 'Leave him with something,' Vic 'faced privately to the Monk. 'Or all we'll end up doing is fighting until he kills us, or we kill him.'

Scab clearly saw something in the Monk's face, however, and he turned to look at Vic.

'What are you going to do when we get down there?' Vic asked.

'If we get down there,' the Monk mused.

'I don't know,' Scab said. He seemed strangely thoughtful. He turned to look at the magnified image of the hell he had grown up on.

'We can bridge into planetary space,' Vic said.

'The contractors will be scanning the planet, they'll target us from orbit,' the Monk pointed out.

'You think they'll risk it?' Vic asked.

'Kind of solipsistic to assume that the only other time that Cyst comes to life is for us,' the Monk said.

'Okay, "solipsistic"?' a more than a little drunk Talia said from the sofa. The Monk ignored her.

'What are we going to do when we get down there?' Vic asked. He was aware there was a whiny tone in his voice. 'Go sightseeing?'

The Monk concentrated, frowned and then turned on Scab. 'What did you just do?'

'Sent a transmission,' Scab told her.

'It's his ship,' Talia pointed out, earning herself a glare from her big sister. 'Oops.'

'For Christ's sake, we're trying to hide!' the Monk shouted at him. He turned to look at her.

'I know what I'm doing,' he said quietly.

'But we—'

'Please, send a tight-beam signal to these coordinates,' the *Basilisk II*'s AI said as his hologram sprang into life.

'What do you want the message to say?' the Monk asked.

'So it's alright for us to send a transmission?' Talia asked.

'Maybe you should stop drinking,' the Monk suggested.

'Not a chance!'

'A simple hail, but use a Church encryption,' the AI said.

Scab was suddenly more interested in the hologram.

'Which one?' the Monk asked, anger creeping into her tone.

'Any,' the AI said.

'Any!' the Monk snapped. Vic wasn't sure why but suddenly the Monk seemed very angry. The 'sect knew that she had worked black ops for the Church. It was starting to sound like she hadn't been let in on all of Churchman's secrets.

'If being angry with me helps then by all means please go ahead but I am not him,' the AI told her. 'I just look like him.'

'In which case I am going to call you Basil,' Talia said. Even Vic thought she was being a little insensitive.

In Red Space the most real thing about Cyst was the Cage, though the network of walkways and ziggurats looked, well, spikier, Vic thought. Against the red, gaseous background they looked like something from one of the highly stylised, more artistic immersions that he hated. Talia had described it as looking like a dark fairy tale. He'd heard the Monk use the word expressionist. He'd had to search his neunonics for the definition.

Beneath them the gas clouds were black, serpentine forms roiling around each other.

'I'm sure there's something down there,' Talia said again. The Monk just glanced at her irritably.

The return transmission had the same encryption as the initial hail and had simply contained a set of coordinates in Cyst's planetary space. It was obvious that the Monk was not overjoyed by any of this. Vic wasn't entirely pleased himself.

'I believe this is what Churchman wished us to do,' the 'sect had told the sceptical Monk.

The Monk was flying the *Basilisk II* at the moment. For some reason Scab had become passive and less of a control freak than normal. This was making Vic very suspicious. Very slowly the ship sank past the walkways and moved under one of the 'expressionist' ziggurats. The Monk was making more and more of the hull transparent at the same time. Red light, the colour of blood, flooded the large, open space lounge/C&C.

'Well, this could be over quickly,' the Monk muttered. Blue light cut a jagged gash in Red Space, and the *Basilisk* juddered as red vacuum and a weak helium/hydrogen atmosphere briefly interacted. With a thought, the Monk brought the extensively modified yacht up through the bridge and into Cyst's atmosphere just underneath one of the ziggurats. Vic was pleasantly surprised that the blockading military contractors didn't immediately destroy them with an orbital bombardment.

'I was born here,' Scab said quietly.

'They're all identical,' the Monk said scornfully. 'At an atomic level.'

Scab just shook his head.

'Is that supposed to be happening?' Talia asked. They looked up. A covered stairwell was growing out of the bottom of the ziggurat towards the top of their ship. The Monk was staring at it, eyes wide. Vic was aware of Scab moving the top airlock through the smart matter to meet the stairwell. Vic had to step to one side as an extruded stairwell grew out of the carpet to reach the airlock that the ceiling was peeling back to reveal.

He gestured for Talia and the Monk to go ahead of him.

'Maybe Talia—' Vic started, but shut up when she turned and glared at him. He followed Scab and the others up the stairs. He was surprised and a little uncomfortable that they weren't taking heavier armour and weapons.

The stairs led them into a large, sealed, black, inverted-step chamber, illuminated by subdued lighting emanating from parts of the ancient smart matter itself. Vic, still more than a little nervous, half expected the chamber of the stairwell to close behind them.

His nano-screen made him aware of it first, the sensitive sensors on his antennae a moment later. He turned as Scab and the Monk did. Talia was the slowest to react. Her hand came up to her mouth and she took several steps back.

The figure was formed of the same material as the smart matter itself, black, like oil. She looked like a tall, statuesque human woman: long hair, angular features, wearing a black leather corset, an ankle-length skirt, slashed at both sides for her long legs, which were clad in thigh-high, spike-heeled boots. Even made from the black, oil-like material, the woman's beauty was apparent. Her arms were held out towards them, a slight smile on her features.

'She looks like Kali,' Talia said in a voice full of awe.

'Mother,' Scab said.

'Alexia?' the Monk asked.

16
Ancient Britain

Of course nobody wished to leave the camp. They might have had ample food, ample firewood, but it was difficult to get past how cold it was, and they were living in shelters of branch and hide that the wisest among them had added mud to, to keep in the warmth. They daren't use the village because it was too close to the entrance to Annwn and the fort on the Mother Hill.

With Bladud gone the divisions between the tribes, and even within some of the tribes, was becoming more apparent. Anharad was capable, and doing the best she could, aided by the warriors of the Trinovantes and some of the less truculent Brigante, but the other warriors, the newcomers, had not heard stories of her in the way they had Bladud. In part this was because she had not been as generous to wandering bards as her husband had.

Challenges were a daily occurrence now. A number of them had resulted in either crippling or death. Members of the Cait *teulu* had fought more than their fair share of the challenges. Partly due to their belligerence and partly due to them being the most prominent outsiders.

It seemed moon-touched to Tangwen. Too long had warrior society clung to the idea that the challenges weeded out the weak and made the tribe stronger. All she saw were dead and crippled warriors that they would sorely need when they attacked the Lochlannach. She could have enforced discipline herself, she supposed, but she had no stomach for it, particularly after her humiliation at the hands of Madawg, which of course meant she was respected less among the other warriors. Instead she tried to avoid arguments, particularly discussions about the Red Chalice, and in general avoid Anharad and others of rank who might try and get her involved in these things.

Part of the problem was that the newcomers had no real idea what they were facing. Too many of them were here for glory rather than revenge. All they had were stories from those who had fought the Lochlannach or, more accurately, had been raided by them. Proud warriors scoffed at the stories, assuming they were exaggerations to justify defeat. Then a challenge was made, and ever on. She had considered the idea of taking some of the newcomers out to look for Lochlannach, but they didn't even have weapons that could harm them at the moment, and she was loath to start using the Red Chalice unless she had to. She might have been its guardian but Germelqart carried it most of the time. The chalice had saved them but it also caused a lot of trouble.

Among the warband there were still those who carried the cursed weapons they had used to fight Andraste's Brood. The smartest of them wrapped the weapons up and put them away until they were needed. Others carried them. They looked half moonstruck, and were quick to feed their weapons blood and bone. So more challenges were fought, and occasionally the sword or spear had a new owner that it whispered to.

Even if she could put together a group of newcomers with the right weapons, and Anharad allowed them to hunt the Lochlannach, and she could get warriors of various tribes to co-operate long enough, the Lochlannach were staying close to the fort and the cave. She did wonder where their food was coming from. Anharad and a number of the ranking warriors thought they were waiting for something. Tangwen was of the opinion that Crom Dhubh just didn't care about the warband camped outside his lair, and why should he when his sword destroyed utterly with a touch?

The Dark Man's sword was just one of the problems facing them. Assuming the warband didn't destroy itself, and some were already leaving, then they had a number of things to contend with, apart from the magic of the Lochlannach and Crom Dhubh. Where did they attack? The Dark Man had to be their target and this ended when Crom Dhubh and Bress died, however Britha might feel about the Lochlannach's second-in-command. If they attacked the cave mouth, then the Lochlannach from the fort would charge down and hit them in the back. The fort was a nightmare to attack, cliffs on two sides, steep approaches on the other two and very heavily fortified. Their best bet was to besiege the fort, try and tempt the Lochlannach out and take a second force against the cave mouth. Which of course meant splitting the warband, and inside the caverns, inside Annwn, the Lochlannach had all the advantages.

The giants. Fachtna had slain one in the grips of the most powerful *riasterthae* frenzy she had ever seen. Though admittedly all the other frenzies she had seen had just looked like warriors who were either really angry, really drunk, or had eaten a lot of the mushrooms that grew on cow dung. She did not think that any among them had the power that Fachtna had, as his magics had come from the Otherworld. She smiled at the memory of them lying together. She had lain with a prince of the fair folk. Admittedly it had been in a muddy ditch.

Then she remembered that he was dead. Twice killed by Bress, the second time with the help of Britha. None of which helped her come up with a way to deal with the giants.

This was one of the reasons she was sitting up on the south ridge, close to a wide ravine, thinking of the idiocy of abandoning your warband to travel to the far west at a time such as this. The other reason was the 'humiliation' of her defeat. She didn't want to be in the camp because it meant putting up with further insults or fighting.

It had stopped snowing. The whiteness of the landscape made it look stark and empty, but still beautiful. Although the presence of Oeth in the Underworld, beneath the earth, made her feel like the land was sick.

She watched a miserable Germelqart struggle through the deep snow towards her. She was also aware of Selbach the Timid trying to sneak through the snow towards her on her right.

Germelqart was spending most of his time in the shelter they had made. He was well treated by those who had fought against Andraste's Brood, but for many of the others he was too much the foreign magician, and Father had taught her that people feared what they didn't understand. She had been forced to intervene on more than one occasion, and his biting skull club had torn the face off a spear-carrier who had tried to steal the chalice. Tangwen couldn't prove it but she was pretty sure that Ysgawyn had something to do with the attempted theft.

Once she had come back early to the shelter they shared, to ask him if the chalice could help them deal with their enemies, perhaps using the same magics that had destroyed Andraste's Brood. She had found the Carthaginian on his knees holding up a brass bottle stoppered with melted lead. He had been talking to it. Germelqart had explained that he was praying to Dagon, the navigator's odd fish god. Tangwen had told him that he was very far from the sea. She never liked seeing anyone kneel before anything.

When she had asked about the magics of the chalice, Germelqart had warned her against asking too much of it. The god inside it had been prepared to undo the excesses of another god, Andraste, but too much would attract the powers of others like it, and make more problems. She had half believed him but had thought there was more to it than he was saying. He definitely seemed frightened of something. She did not wish to push the matter, however. Other than Father, her tribe's own, small god, she was of the opinion that the gods whose work she had witnessed were nothing more than a curse on this island. She would be satisfied if this Ninegal, whom Germelqart said lived in the chalice – though Britha had given him another name – a god of the forge by all accounts, could provide them with weapons that weren't too ruinous when the time came. They had enough problems with Bladud and Ysgawyn's visions of all-powerful warriors ruling Ynys Prydain for all time through the gifts the chalice gave.

She thought casually about putting an arrow close to where Selbach was trying to creep up on her but she couldn't be sure if she would have noticed him before she had drunk of Britha's blood. Besides, it struck her as the sort of thing the more obnoxious of the warriors down in camp would do. The ones who wished to capitalise on Madawg's triumph over her. Instead she waited until he revealed himself and showed little surprise, though she had to admit he was good. She suspected his skill in hiding came from the terror of getting caught. She noticed he carried no weapons. Though he had limed himself the colour of the snow and was wearing the similarly limed bearskin again.

He opened his mouth to ask her why she had summoned him. She held up her hand for quiet. She only wanted to have to explain this once. Germelqart had nearly reached them. She saw he had the bag with the chalice in it as she had asked.

'I mislike this,' the Carthaginian told her in his own language. Selbach was looking between them. Tangwen didn't like how she suddenly knew all these tongues; she'd had to work hard for all her other skills, and felt that people should have to work hard for what they had, otherwise they didn't value it. 'What if we are killed and the Lochlannach capture it?'

'Speak in the language of the Pecht,' Tangwen said in Pecht herself. Germelqart glanced at the Cait scout, who smiled at him uneasily.

'How do we know we can trust him?' Germelqart continued in the language of Carthage.

'We don't know if we can trust him,' Tangwen answered in Selbach's language. 'But I am going to behave as though I can because I'm tiring of all the mistrust among our own people in the face of *that*.' She pointed towards where she knew the cave mouth was.

Germelqart looked towards it uneasily. After the last time they had travelled to Oeth Tangwen and the others had questioned him on what he had known about Crom Dhubh, asked why the Carthaginian had called the Dark Man Sotik? Whatever Crom Dhubh had done when he stuck the tendrils from the stump of his finger into the navigator's head had removed all knowledge of the Dark Man. As much as she liked the navigator, she could not claim to know him well. He had seemed changed since then, however. Always one to keep his own counsel, he was now nearly silent, as though he had turned away from people for the company of his god in the brass bottle.

'I cannot be trusted,' Selbach said. 'I am a coward.' He seemed ashamed of himself.

'I need a coward today,' Tangwen said. Germelqart laughed. She didn't think he'd seen him do so since Kush had died.

'Then you are twice blessed,' Germelqart said in the language of the Pecht. 'What would you have of us?'

'Where did the giants go?' Tangwen asked. 'Selbach, you have hidden close to the fort. Even lying down you would have seen them?' Selbach nodded. She turned to Germelqart. 'And we have seen the path to Oeth through the Underworld. If the giants crawled they might get into the first cave, but they could not have got all the way through.'

'Are they not things of the earth, though?' Selbach asked. 'Could they not sink into it, travel through it?' He may have been cowardly but Tangwen was starting to think that he wasn't stupid.

Germelqart looked thoughtful. 'I do not think so. But they may just have gone elsewhere, bigger caves, woods, a body of water we have not found.'

'Or there could be another way into Oeth?' Tangwen said. 'We went the way we went the last time because Britha knew it. This whole land is riddled with caves. It would be strange if there wasn't another way to get there.'

'I'm not going to the Underworld!' Selbach cried.

'Keep your voice down,' Tangwen snapped.

'You wish to go searching caves?' Germelqart asked sceptically.

'I wish to track the giants,' Tangwen said.

'I know little about tracking, but they passed many days ago and there has been much snow since,' Germelqart said.

'But they were heavy, heavier than two aurochs,' Selbach said. Tangwen nodded. 'And when they killed Eurneid ...' He was trying to suppress a smile. Tangwen wondered if the horrible old *dryw* had made everyone miserable.

'They made a deep hole,' Tangwen supplied. She pointed down into the ravine.

'You found tracks?' Germelqart asked. Tangwen nodded. 'But why am I here? I'm no scout.'

'It doesn't matter how quiet and well-hidden Selbach and I are because of Crom's wards,' Tangwen told them. Selbach spat and made the sign against evil. She remembered the feel of walking through spider webs when they had first gone to Oeth. From that moment on Crom had known of their presence. 'I understand that the gods will not fight our wars for us, that we need to prove our strength to them for their aid, but we face gods and their magics.' Tangwen pointed at the leather bag with the chalice in it. 'Can this Ninegal help us hide from Crom's wards?'

Germelqart looked less than happy.

He ran. Bress had finally climbed out of the caverns and into wooded foothills. He ran through the snow-covered woods. It hadn't taken long to find the wasteland that the spawn of Andraste had left behind them. The snow hadn't reached that far south yet. The cold and the damp had packed down a lot of the grey dust. It was like running across wet silt, though his footfalls still sent up little clouds. He had seen no one, no animals either.

Poking through the unnatural grey mud were the first signs of regrowth. He knew that the Red Chalice had left the land fecund with life beneath the dust. The winds would blow it away eventually and come spring, when the sun shone and the rains fell, plants would grow again, the animals would start to return, and then, finally, so would the people. Until then it was a near featureless wasteland broken only by grey hills and occasional standing stones. The stones had been left untouched. They were waymarkers of ancient tech buried far beneath the earth.

He ran for days, taking only the occasional break to sleep and eat. He didn't like to think about where the food came from. It was as tasteless as the land was featureless. It just provided the sustenance he needed to keep going. He tried not to think too much about the boned corpses lying in the water around Oeth.

He came down to the summit of the hill and looked down at the coast. The three islands. Two of them separated from the coast by only thin strips of water, the other one by a much larger channel. Now all three of them were barren, windblown wastelands of grey mulch, though here and there some of the hardier plants were trying to grow through.

Without any remaining point of reference it might have been difficult to work out where the wicker man had stood in the water before it had fallen apart, except there was a ship close to, or over, the spot. It looked like a galley from the Sea of the Greeks far to the south. Except this one was made of brass. He glanced at the brass scorpion clinging to his metal-clad shoulder. Then he started running again.

Bress had slithered into the water among the dust-covered marshes between the two islands closest to shore. He had waited until the tide was going out and let it sweep him towards the ship. Much closer he could see the living metalwork of the vessel was very similar to that of the scorpion, still with him on his shoulder.

The ship's crew were all bundled up against the cold, but what little skin was on display was either swarthy, or various shades of brown, suggesting that they all came from the lands far to the south across the sea. They were a small crew for a vessel that size. Standing towards the rear of the galley, and not wearing furs like the rest of the crew, was a large, powerful looking, brown-skinned man. He wore a light-coloured robe split open at the front revealing a sizeable gut. Instead of hair he had bands of polished copper embedded into the skin on his head. From where Bress floated in the water, the man's eyes didn't look right either.

The water was much clearer than he remembered. He assumed that the seed of the Muileartach must have consumed,

201

or transformed, any life that had been in the water as well. This made his job more difficult. After all, this ship must have been there for a reason.

As the man slowly turned around, surveying his surroundings, Bress let the water slip over his head as he sank down. He could not breathe the water like some of the children of the Muileartach, but he was confident that he could hold his breath long enough, though it could take several trips to locate what he sought.

Finding his master's prize was easier than he had expected, but not for a good reason. The spear that Fachtna had used to slay the Naga dragon was ancient and powerful. It had killed the dragon, and the serpents melded with it in a rage. Crom had sent Bress to see if he could salvage something. The sailors in the brass ship seemed to want to finish Fachtna's job.

The dragon lay in the silt on the seabed, scaled, sleek, reptilian, obviously dead, and half buried. On its back, legs and pincers digging into the dragon's body, was another of the scorpions. Except this one was even larger than the one now clutched to his shoulder had ever been, even after it had consumed the rock. The arachnid's mouth consumed the Naga dragon's flesh. The sting and half of its tail was embedded deep into the dragon, and pulsed as if it was feeding something into the corpse. As Bress watched, the scorpion grew. The hindquarters of the dragon were rotting away in front of his eyes. Bress guessed that the scorpion was using the carrion it ate to create the poison it was feeding the dragon's body through its sting, as well as increasing its own bulk. It was a monstrous but efficient parasite destroying its host.

Bress checked all around him in the clear water but he couldn't see anything else. There was no way to approach the dragon without the scorpion parasite seeing. If it was a servant of those on the ship, as seemed likely, then it had just been told to do the one thing and didn't care about anything else. If it did react to him then he wasn't sure what he would do.

He looked up as he dived deeper and saw the bottom of the brass galley distorted by the water, but again there was no sign of him having been seen, or even of them looking out for anyone else. He felt his own much smaller scorpion crawling around his armour, seeking to be out of sight of the monstrous scorpion and the galley.

With a little difficulty he drew his sword, and with a thought the weapon started to change shape. The hilt extended, covering half of the blade, then thinned as it turned into the shaft of a spear, a much more practical weapon in the water. With another thought a barb grew from the shaft and pierced his skin, sucking in a little of his blood. If he was forced to fight the thing then he would try the same blood magic he had used on the smaller one.

Bress swam past multifaceted eyes of black glass as he made towards the head of the dragon. The scorpion gave no indication of having noticed him, as its mandibles tore away and fed the reptilian meat into its maw. Bress reached the head and used the spearhead to open the skin of his palm but it did not bleed. He put his palm against the dragon's head, felt the smooth, hard, cold feel of the scales against his skin. Then, with a thought, he used the blood magic that Crom Dhubh had taught him. Naga blood magic. There was very little fear in Bress, yet as the dead flesh of the dragon opened against his skin, pulling his hand into the corpse, there was a moment when he tried to pull away – but it had him, and the moment of fear stretched out into the closest he had been to panic in a long time ...

The flesh parted like a corpse giving birth. Bress fell through dead flesh and bone and into the dragon's skull. He was surrounded by rotting meat, felt it pushing against him, like he had been swallowed. He flailed, his hand touching one of the dead serpents still attached to the throne of bone it had grown into to meld with the dragon.

He could hear the gobbling, tearing noise of the scorpion. He looked down the dragon's gullet. Scythe-like brass blades tore through flesh, letting surprisingly little seawater in. He saw diseased flesh spreading through the corpse towards him. He was sure he couldn't have it come into contact with him. He felt around, trying to find the sac that held the dragon's brain, cursing Crom Dhubh in his mind and hoping the Dark Man could hear it. He touched what he thought was what he was looking for. More of the blood magic that he had been taught. He felt the sac rip and his long fingers wrapped around something that felt partly like shaped stone, as if it had been worked, and partly like flesh. Bress tore the stone/flesh thing out of the momentarily revived pulsing organ. The cavity he was in was starting to fill with seawater and other fluids. He jerked his hand away from where the rotting corruption had grown close to him. He tried to wriggle around, trying to concentrate, to suppress the fear, but this was too close to being swallowed, or unborn. He smeared his bloody palm on un-diseased dead flesh again and the contraction yanked him into the flesh.

Snow had covered the tracks but after they had found the first few and then worked out the enormous length of the giants' strides, tracking them became easier, though their efforts would be difficult to hide from any who chose to look themselves.

They had climbed down and followed the ravine. Then they climbed over the hills of the southern ridge, and curved round west, running parallel with the valley, always climbing.

The cave was in a narrow gulley, the entrance obscured by trees, though a few of those had been pushed aside and then put back in their normal position recently. The giants would have had to crawl to get into this cave, but not far into it there was a large crevice in the rock.

Germelqart had prayed to the chalice and then pricked his finger and dropped a little of his blood into the red molten contents before they went into the cave. Tangwen hadn't felt like she had walked through cobwebs as she entered, though her skin was itching, Selbach's too judging by the scratching. The Pecht scout had to be coaxed, quietly, into the cave. He was standing looking down into the hole.

'Even if I wanted to, I could not see down there to climb,' he said, crossing his arms.

'We could make it so you could see in the dark,' Germelqart said, quietly. Tangwen stared at the Carthaginian. 'Just so he can see in the dark.'

'Drink from that which makes slaves? I think not.'

Germelqart looked down into the hole. 'I could perhaps make the climb but I do not have your skills. I would risk discovery.'

'I'll go alone,' Tangwen said. She didn't relish the idea. Partly because two of them doubled the chance of any information getting back to the warband if something went wrong, and partly because she just didn't want to go alone.

'We will not offer this chance to warriors unless we are forced to,' Germelqart told Selbach.

'I have not drunk from the chalice,' Tangwen said. 'It is a great honour.' Selbach turned to look at her sceptically. 'Sorry.'

'We seek to avoid the attention of the gods lest we have to fight them again,' Selbach said.

'We are fighting them,' Germelqart pointed out. Selbach still looked unsure.

'Will it make me braver?' he asked.

'You're brave enough,' Tangwen told him.

She was more than a little surprised when Germelqart grabbed Selbach by his limed hair and cut a chunk out of it with his bronze dagger. She almost intervened. Selbach broke free and backed quickly against the rock wall. He looked angry, hurt and frightened. Germelqart held up the lime-stiff piece of hair.

'You understand what I am, a *magus* ... a man of power and knowledge, yes?' he demanded. Selbach nodded. 'Boast that you have drunk from the cup and the warriors will steal your eyes, but I will do something much, much worse. Do you understand?'

Tangwen wasn't sure if Germelqart was trying to trick the man into believing him or not, but she could see that Selbach seemed convinced. The Carthaginian reached into his bag and produced the Red Chalice. He held it out to the Pecht scout. Selbach stared at it, obviously frightened, but he reached out for the cup.

It was a long, hard climb in the white and green ghost light, though she was relieved that Selbach was a good climber. The Pecht scout still looked terrified as they descended into the Annwn, the Underworld.

He had, of course, panicked when the hot metal contents of the chalice had forced itself into his mouth and down his bulging throat, glowing under his skin. He had curled into a ball and refused to look at them. They had coaxed him up and he had a moment of wonder when he realised he could see in the dark.

They had left Germelqart in the cave above. The Carthaginian had prayed to the god in the Red Chalice to work his magics to hide Tangwen and Selbach from the Crom Dhubh's wards.

Tangwen wasn't sure how long they had been climbing for. All she knew was that her muscles ached. Below her she could make out a faint white glow. What she couldn't hear was the sound of water.

The bottom of the hole was another cave. It was set back from the edge of a lake. She couldn't see where the glow was coming from yet. She put her foot down onto stone. To her right the cave went further back into the rock, opening up into a much larger area. On her left was the lake. The white glow was light reflecting on thick, white ice where the lake had frozen.

Tangwen put one foot on the ice; it didn't flex, or crack, and felt solid under her foot, but ice had fooled her before. She stepped out onto the frozen surface of the lake, all her weight on it. Selbach was already crouched down on the ice. He said nothing but motioned towards the island in the middle of the lake.

The light itself was coming from Oeth. The isle looked stark black against the white of the ice, its tower of bone reaching up towards the jagged rock teeth of the huge cavern's ceiling, a tribute to the gods of atrocity. There was movement off to her left. One of the giants was walking across the ice. Two more of the creatures were standing on it as well. At first she thought that one of the stationary giants had suffered some horrible wound, its chest and torso sundered, its ribs split and peeled back, the open flesh and bone like thick bark. If she had not drunk of Britha's blood she would have believed this to be the case. She heard Selbach spit to protect himself against evil. Britha's blood allowed her to see further and better in the darkness of the Underworld. On the ice in front of the giant was a man. He was slumped as though dead, or asleep, though something that looked like roots, or the thin branches of a tree, or the veins that ran through skin, propped him up on his knees. They had grown from the giant and into the flesh of the motionless man.

Tangwen was appalled but the beginning of a plan was starting to form, a plan that threw up more problems than it solved at the moment, but a plan nonetheless. The ice could take the weight of the giants.

'We need to find an easier way to get down here,' Tangwen whispered to Selbach.

Fighting against the current, Bress had made it to the eastern island, the one the mad had inhabited. He had started running down the isle's west coast, trying to stay out of sight of the brass galley. This was made more difficult by the isle now being a grey wasteland.

Eventually he had to lie down and hide when the brass galley's invisible oarsmen started to row the strange metal craft between the two islands towards the coast.

From his position Bress watched as four horses stood up on the deck of the ship. They had torn themselves out of some kind of caul. They seemed completely docile despite being on the deck of a moving ship, and even from where Bress was lying he could see that they were magnificent creatures, completely unlike the native horses.

The brass ship closed with the coast as the horses were saddled. A ramp was lowered into the marshy shallows and riders, including the man with metal strips running through the skin on his head, led the horses through the shallows before mounting them. The riders headed north, leaving a cloud of grey dust in their wake.

17
Now

'If Rush is just going to meet your Mr Brown, is there even anything you can do?' Beth asked. Du Bois wasn't sure how to answer. He had been making this up as he went along. He was half convinced he was just going through the motions because he didn't know what else to do in the circumstances. He despised the DAYP but it was starting to look like it was the Circle that had caused the most damage.

Flying over the eastern seaboard had been depressing. Broken city after broken city, often with open fighting in the streets. Skyscrapers burning like candles.

The mid-west had been better. Entire swathes of it had looked untouched, though they had stayed away from built up areas and military bases. There were always reminders, however. A number of the farms they saw looked like they had been fortified. Du Bois guessed they were less likely to have been near phones or the internet when it had happened, though many farms used radio. He had seen a number of fields with disconcerting patterns drawn in them by combine harvesters.

The mountains had been best. Among the Rockies, the sky bright blue and almost cloudless above them, it had almost been possible to forget about what was happening, if you ignored the smudge, little more than a discolouration, in the north: Denver burning.

'We're heading south but LA's west, so where are we going?' Beth had asked.

What are you doing? he'd asked himself. *It's unlikely he's alive, if he is there are no guarantees he'll help you, and even if he does there's no guarantee he'll know what you need to know.*

'I know someone,' du Bois told her. 'He'll know people in LA.'

*

'Is this all coming from us?' Beth asked a while later. They were over desert now. They had overflown what du Bois had assumed was a Native American reservation. Their flight had sent a committee of vultures flapping into the air. The human carrion they had been feeding on were laid out in rows. Du Bois was pretty sure he'd seen a few muzzle flashes as they'd flown past as well. 'Is this just inside all of us?'

'Perhaps,' du Bois said. 'But we have, *had*, an emergent psychology that prevented us from behaving like this. Even if it was just a veneer of civilisation, we accomplished so much. That's what matters.'

'Seems kind of redundant in the face of the tech.'

Du Bois was starting to worry about Beth. It had been a long journey, and she'd had a lot of time to think.

'Technology is just one part of humanity's accomplishments, and the tech notwithstanding, what we have done from a standing start is astonishing. Then there's literature, art, symphonies ...'

He would work it out afterwards. A flash in the extreme ultraviolet part of the spectrum, invisible to unaugmented humans. The Harrier no longer had a wing. It seemed to be happening in slow motion. The aircraft was tipping towards the desert floor. With a thought, transmitted by touch to the aircraft's systems through the stick, du Bois ejected Beth, himself, and the storage compartment. Explosive bolts blew and they were rocketed out of the aircraft at an angle a little too horizontal for du Bois's taste. The desert floor shot by beneath him. Dirt and wreckage flew into the air as the Harrier bounced, spinning, off the ground. The seat fell away from him. He started to fall, he had a moment to try and right himself and then the parachute deployed. The earth came up to meet him way too quickly. He cried out as impact with the ground tried to push his femur into his chest cavity.

Beth was standing over him, Model 0 in hand, looking all around. He glanced to one side and saw an IV tube full of regenerative matter hanging off a piece of aircraft wreckage that had been embedded in the ground. His neuralware told him that he was pretty much healed now. Only a little time had elapsed. With a thought he cut off the IV's flow. It was arguably overkill to use one of the IVs for this. They were last ditch. He hadn't been that badly hurt, but he didn't say anything.

He sat up, brushing himself down. Beth had dragged the

armoured storage compartment closer to him. The Harrier was in a trench some distance away.

'Thanks for ejecting me first,' Beth said. 'I got off lightly.' He just nodded and stood up, making for the storage compartment. 'What happened? I saw that weird flash.'

'X-ray laser,' du Bois told her. He touched the storage compartment and unlocked it with a thought. 'Fired from an orbital platform.' He laughed humourlessly as she looked up.

'So we were lucky, then?' she said.

'No, they were slowing us down. If they had wanted to kill us they could have.' Du Bois was quickly and efficiently pulling his gear out of the storage unit and putting it on.

Beth glanced up into the clear blue sky again. The sun was beating down on them but all it was doing was providing energy. They regulated their own bodies' temperatures and the UV rays wouldn't damage their skin now.

'So they can kill us any time?' Beth said.

Du Bois shrugged. 'Easier in the air. They'll still be having comms problems but they can certainly fire on us. On foot it's a hammer to kill an ant.'

'And this is your Control?' she asked. He nodded. 'Could they know where we are going?'

'Possibly,' he admitted.

'Why didn't they just kill us?'

Length of service? he wondered, but he knew the Circle wasn't sentimental. 'I don't know.'

Finally he picked up the SA58 carbine and turned, heading south.

'So we're going to walk into this trap then?'

'Let's go and see if we can find someone to donate us a vehicle,' du Bois suggested.

'This would be much easier for you if you would let us know where you are,' the voice on the end of the tight-beam radio uplink said. King Jeremy had to admit that he was right.

The LAV III armoured vehicle had given them the edge in getting out of Boston, at least until they had come across other military vehicles. It had been cool to see what the 25mm chaingun could do to mobs of people, though. Stealing the F-22 Raptors had been exhilarating but it had meant leaving most of their gear, and their slaves, behind. The dogfight over Nevada had been less fun, despite their uploaded skills.

They had only been able to take the most valuable of the Lost Tech with them. That had, however, included the cornucopia, which meant that they could fabricate almost anything on a small scale, just by plugging it into whatever matter they wanted to break down. That had given them their not-so-small arms and the portable tight-beam uplink. It had also fabricated their clothes and armour so they could look more post-apocalyptic. Given the time, they could have modified the 6×6 Cougar armoured truck they had taken from a military unit turned brigand to fit the aesthetic, but they were moving too quickly.

They were somewhere in the Sierras now, looking down on California. In many ways King Jeremy loved this new world. They could be more overt but commuting was a bitch.

'My problem remains the same, Mr Brown,' Jeremy said. 'I don't know you, I don't trust anybody, and your story sounds like bullshit.'

Mr Brown had told them that the world was over. What had happened was effectively an alien attack. The same aliens the biotech was derived from, and it would get worse before it got better. All King Jeremy knew was that something bad had happened, and he knew alien technology existed. The rest wasn't that much of a stretch. This Mr Brown clearly knew about, and had access to the Lost Tech, and was offering them a way out. The problem was that King Jeremy was now having to deal with someone with at least comparable – and probably greater – resources than he had, but he seemed to be the only game in town. King Jeremy hated playing games he didn't know he was going to win. He was going to LA looking for an edge.

'Very well, Mr R ... King Jeremy, but we could have been on our way now if you trusted me.'

Or dead, King Jeremy thought. 'We'll see you at the rendezvous.' He handed the headset back to Dracimus.

'So they've got their own satellite network up and running?' the other human-looking member of the DAYP asked. He might have turned out to be a whiny bitch but he had been proving more useful than the normally reliable Inflictor recently. His demon-headed henchman was spending a lot of time looking to the west. King Jeremy had managed to get little out of him lately except the word 'ocean'. According to Dracimus, Inflictor had been spending most of his time watching the same surf film over and over again, or playing 'Shadows over Oceania'.

'Yeah, they've got all the toys,' King Jeremy muttered. He put the range-finding binoculars up to his eyes and looked down. On the road ahead he could see a small convoy of various off-road vehicles. They were driven by what looked like a collection of well-armed, overweight, middle-aged men who'd seen one too many road warrior movies.

'And no reason to share,' Dracimus whined.

'Have you got any better ideas?' King Jeremy asked, wishing he had designed the psychometric games he'd used to recruit members of the DAYP a little better.

'Yeah, we find a compound and set ourselves up as fucking kings, man! An army, a harem, we could rule America if we wanted, maybe even Canada as well.'

The bikes, pickups and buggies were getting closer. It was going to be impossible to avoid them. He had to admit the naked bodies strapped to the front of some of the vehicles were a nice touch. If he had time he would do something similar.

'Just get in the fucking truck,' King Jeremy snapped.

Tucson looked like London after the blitz. If London had been neatly set out in a grid, and surrounded by picturesque mountains.

'Well?' Beth asked from the bed of the pickup truck they'd stolen. They had stopped on a mountain road just inside the boundaries of the Catalina State Park.

'Too far to tell,' du Bois said. What he didn't like was that it was obvious that Tucson had been extensively bombed from the air. Entire neighbourhoods had been turned into a series of craters. Much of it was still burning, including parts of the state park. He could make out people and vehicles moving here and there, but no large mob movements that he could see. There was nothing moving in the air at the moment but they were trying to get to Davis-Mothan Air Force Base in southern Tucson, which seemed the most likely place for the planes to have originated from. It looked like it had been a military-assisted urban suicide.

'If we had the time I'd say leave the truck and conduct a reconnaissance on foot but ...'

Beth put the Model 0 LMG down and climbed out of the truck bed, into the truck's cab.

'What are you doing?' du Bois asked.

'Driving,' Beth told him.

'I thought we agreed I'm the most experienced driver.' He knew that until she'd uploaded the skill Beth hadn't ever driven.

'You're also the most experienced shooter,' Beth said, starting the engine.

'Beth ...'

'I'm tired of killing people!' she shouted at him.

They had tried to take the back roads to get to Tucson but it hadn't always been possible. They had been chased twice. Where possible, Beth had tried to disable the vehicles, but they had also been attacked, and they had killed the people the truck had belonged to. They had been infected by the alien insanity. There were still bloodstains on the vehicle.

Du Bois slung the carbine and climbed into the truck bed, going down on one knee and picking up the LMG. Beth pulled away and started heading down the winding canyon road towards the city. The air was full of burning embers from one of the nearer forest fires.

Du Bois had started to put it together as they got closer to the air force base. He had seen the wreckage of A-10 Thunderbolt IIs, close air support aircraft. Ugly bombers nicknamed 'Warthogs'. He had also seen the wreckage of MQ-9 Reapers – Remotely Piloted Aircraft. It looked like the drones had been mounted with air-to-air missiles. The Warthogs had bombed Tucson and then been engaged by the Reapers. It looked like it had been a hell of an aerial battle.

The base itself looked like it had been attacked from the air as well, but it was difficult to make out the extent of the damage as they weren't going to the base proper but rather to the Boneyard. This was a vast graveyard of decommissioned, mainly military aircraft parked in neat rows out in the desert.

The Boneyard was on their left as they made their way down the road that ran along the perimeter fence. It had been breached in a number of places. On the right were tracts of low rent housing. There was no movement on either side of the road other than the occasional vulture taking to the air. They had seen bodies along the perimeter fence, some of them in air force uniform; it looked as though most of them had been carrying weapons. There were also a number of military vehicles either riddled with bullets, or hit with heavier ordnance. On the inside of the perimeter fence du Bois could make out the wreckage of a number of unmanned ground vehicles, armed, mainly caterpillar-tracked drones.

'So the machines went mad? Because they were connected to the net?' Beth shouted from the cab.

'Stop the truck,' du Bois said. Beth pulled the pickup over. Both of them climbed out and du Bois handed off the LMG. Beth immediately started checking all around them.

'It looks like the air force personnel attacked the perimeter,' du Bois said and then shook his head. 'But they didn't do it well. Looks like they just sort of charged it.'

'There,' Beth said, pointing. A quadrocopter, a four-rotor drone, was hovering high above the centre of the Boneyard. It looked to have a number of camera lenses on it, multiple antennae, small parabolic dishes and it was armoured. 'Can you hear music?'

Their weapons were up and both of them were moving towards the closest cover, a bullet-riddled SUV, as a small, low, angular tank moved out between two extensively cannibalised B-52s and then turned rapidly in a cloud of dirt. It had loudspeakers mounted on it. They were playing music that du Bois's internal systems identified as 'Halls of Karma' by a band called Black Oak Arkansas. He didn't like how heavily armoured the drone tank looked, or how little cover they had against the M2 .50-calibre machine gun that swivelled to point at them.

'Du Bois?' Beth asked.

'I'm not sure we have the tools for the job,' du Bois muttered. The music cut out, much to his relief.

'So are you guys loonies as well?' the voice from the tank's loudspeaker asked in a broad Essex accent.

'You have to be kidding,' Beth muttered. Du Bois couldn't help but smile at the figure trundling towards them on a motorised off-road skateboard. His skin was tanned from time out in the desert sun. He was easily over six feet tall. He had a thick, black, slightly unkempt beard that made it difficult to gauge his age. He looked to be somewhere between his mid-30s and mid-50s, though du Bois knew him to be a lot older. He wore a white cassock with body armour over the top. The body armour carried ammo for the Mossberg 590 tactical shotgun that was hung horizontally across his chest, as well as for the nasty little FN57 he held, a pistol that fired a round that had more in common with rifle ammunition than handgun ammunition. He was also sporting an eighteen-inch-tall pink mohican.

'According to my files you come from a similar sub-culture,' du Bois said to Beth as the skateboard came to a halt in front of them and the mohicaned figure spilled off it.

'Big Malky!' the man cried.

'Please, don't ever call me that.'

He came to give du Bois a hug but the amount of ordnance hanging off them both got in the way. He settled for a hearty handshake.

'Do you know anyone who isn't a London arms dealer?' Beth asked.

The figure with the mohican looked mock offended. '*Moi*? From London?'

'He's from Essex,' du Bois told her.

'Oh, that's much better,' Beth muttered. Du Bois assumed there was some sort of north/south divide thing going on.

'Canvey, darlin',' he told her. 'And I'm a consultant *otaku* for the good old USAF, not an arms dealer.'

'But you still like your toys, right?' du Bois asked. He was aware of a number of tracked and armed drones in the vicinity. They weren't exactly covering Beth and himself.

'Always have, always will,' the odd-looking figure said. He turned to Beth. 'The first time a bit of the tech washed up on shore it was like ...' He made an exploding gesture with both his hands by his head and an accompanying sound effect. He looked somewhat manic. 'Like electric ...' He tapped his head. 'Y'know?' Beth was looking at him as if she had found a new, exotic, and not entirely safe animal.

'Beth, may I introduce you to Karma,' du Bois said. Beth somewhat reluctantly shook his hand.

'Is he one of yours?' she asked.

'Independent, darlin',' Karma said. 'Always have been, always will be. Hasn't stopped this bad boy from trying to recruit me more than once.'

Beth looked over at Malcolm.

'Karma was a wrecker. Born in the sixteenth century?' du Bois asked. Karma nodded. 'He found his first piece of L-tech after he and his friends lured a ship carrying it onto the rocks.'

Beth frowned. 'Nice.'

'I'm a changed man now. Let's get out of the sun, shall we?'

Karma climbed back up onto his skateboard and started trundling deeper into the Boneyard between rows of stripped down helicopters covered in a white vinyl/plastic compound. A number of the tracked drones fell in with him, all of them kicking up clouds of red dust. Some of the other drones accompanied Beth and du Bois. Du Bois tried not to think of them as armed guards.

'Out of the sun' was sitting on garden furniture under a parasol on the wing of an old B-1 bomber. Karma had put on sunglasses and was lounging in one of the chairs, smoking a hand-rolled cigarette, having poured them both a glass of homemade lemonade from a frosty jug.

Beth and du Bois had divested themselves of enough of their gear to be comfortable but both of them still had their sidearms. They had tried to position themselves so that between them they had three-hundred-and-sixty degree coverage. For Karma's part a number of the tracked SWORD drones nearby had line-of-sight to Beth and du Bois, and there were a few more rotor drones in the air. They looked like they were homemade but they had personnel defence weapons mounted underneath them.

'So what happened?' du Bois asked. 'The people went mad, started bombing the city? Then you sent the Reapers up after them?'

'Oh no, that would have been too easy,' Karma said. 'First all the active drones went mental, turned on everyone. Meanwhile I'm lying on the floor because whatever's hit the internet has caused me to have a fucking fit. So things get tense for a while. I manage to hit the backdoor kill switches I've installed on everything I've made. I junk some really nice computer tech. Isolate the systems on the second team and fire them up, by which point all the Warthogs are up in the air ...' Something passed over Karma's face. 'Full on military suicide, man. Shock and awe.' He swallowed hard. 'So me and the girls,' he nodded towards the closest drone, 'engage in a bit of a Charge of the Light Brigade. Fucking nightmare. Over and across the runway. I got fucking shot, man! I do a bit of work on the Reapers and then they're up in the air ...' He looked down. 'Some of those guys, the A-10 jockeys, they were friends of mine.'

'At the point they were dropping bombs on the city, there was nothing left of your friends,' du Bois told him gently.

'Yeah, but it didn't do them much good did it?' Karma asked

quietly. 'I mean, I don't know; I should go into the city, start looking for survivors or something ... Bring them back here, a little community in the planes or something.' It was obvious to du Bois that Karma hadn't got much further than that with his plan, but on the other hand it sounded like he'd had a busy few days.

'How'd you control them all if those things fucked the comms?' Beth asked suspiciously.

Karma nodded to the rotor drone hovering over the centre of the Boneyard with all the cameras, antennae and small parabolas.

'Tight-beam microwave transmission,' Karma told them. 'It goes up pretty high but it's still line-of-sight. Plus I upgraded their autonomous functions. Little something I wasn't going to share with US of AF. This shit was not going to the military-industrial complex. All the drones are basically dumb AIs.'

Du Bois was impressed despite himself. Single-handed, Karma had tried to stop the A-10s from bombing the city.

'Then the soldiers attacked you?' Beth asked.

Karma shrugged. 'The drones did most of the damage to them.' Du Bois could see that he was wrestling with something.

'That's got to require a lot of power,' du Bois said, pointing at the rotor drone acting as a communications conduit.

'It gets tired I send up another one, so they overlap, drop it down, recharge, repeat and rinse,' Karma told him, but du Bois could tell he didn't want to explain further. Du Bois assumed that Karma had a command post around here, he suspected it would be mobile, probably something the size of a lorry.

'What happened?' Karma asked after a few moments.

'The Seeders woke up,' du Bois told him. Karma nodded, a grim expression on his face.

'So just like that, then?' Karma snapped his fingers. 'We're gone.'

'What are you going to do?' Beth asked quietly.

'Well, it's all gone a bit *Mad Max*, hasn't it?' Karma said. Du Bois was now sure the mohicaned tech was trying to suppress strong emotion.

'We could use your help,' du Bois said. 'We might even have an out.'

Karma looked at him. 'They took my internet away. I really liked the internet. Besides, and no offence, I don't want to have anything to do with the Circle and that arsehole, Mr Brown. You

and ... you were just about the most tolerable of the whole lot.'
Du Bois frowned. He was sure Karma had been about to mention
this Grace person, the partner he couldn't remember. 'I'm going
to try and contact the Brass City. It's a virtual life for me. You can
try and assassinate me if you want.' Karma was looking straight
at him. The smile gone. There was just a moment of tension.
Du Bois was suddenly aware of the drones around him and the
weight of the .45 on his hip.

'We're out of favour,' du Bois said.

'That's putting it mildly,' Beth muttered. 'I was never a member; they want me dead, and they shot us down.'

Karma frowned. 'Then why aren't you dead?'

Du Bois had to admit that it was a good question. He didn't
have a good answer.

Karma looked between the pair of them and laughed. 'Want
an easier question? Given that resources are at an all-time
premium, what do you need from me, brother?'

'Do you know who the Do As You Please Clan are?' du Bois
asked.

'Yeah, a bunch of arseholes. They're a so-called uberguild
bunch of crooked, bullying pricks. Rumour has it that they're
heavily involved in online money laundering, supposed to be
responsible for a couple of real life player kills. I spent a lot of
time making their griefing lives miserable on a couple of the
multi-players we have ... had in common. So? You going to tell
me they're in the know?' Du Bois nodded. 'Makes sense.'

'It's not just online,' Beth said quietly. 'Kidnap, murder,
slavery and probably lots of other stuff I don't really want to
think about.'

Karma looked north towards central Tucson. Vast clouds of
smoke were still rising into the sky.

'Well, like I said they're arseholes, but in the big scheme of
things ...'

'They've taken something, something very important ...' du
Bois started.

'And you're not going to tell me what that is?'

Du Bois sat back in his chair and looked at Karma. 'Do you
want to know?'

Karma gave this some thought. 'Probably not,' he decided.

'If it's any consolation, this will probably piss off Mr Brown as
well,' Beth told him.

'So they're making for LA,' du Bois told him.

'Big city,' Karma said.

'I need to know who they might know,' du Bois said.

'It's a hollow place, man, there's not much there and I thought your people had the Pacific Rim sewn up,' Karma said.

Straight away du Bois knew it was a test. The *otaku* was suggesting that he knew about Kanamwayso, the Seeder city deep beneath the Pacific Ocean. If du Bois was still part of the Circle, he could expect a reaction. It wasn't much of a play. Had du Bois still been working for them he would have got what he needed from Karma and then come back, killed him and wiped any information he might have.

'Not really my sphere of operations,' du Bois said.

'Kept you all pretty compartmentalised, did they?' Karma asked. Du Bois was growing more uncomfortable with how Karma was behaving.

'Can you help us?' Beth asked.

'There's a guy, came out of nowhere about six months ago, and he cuts a swathe across East LA. Unites the Hispanic gangs but all of a sudden I'm seeing his footprint in odd places. The feds are looking at him for serious stuff that should be way out of the reach for a bush league gangbanger. He's got juice from one of the big Mexi cartels, in bed with the Russians, all sorts, and he's doing things he shouldn't be able to do ... I mean there are things in the jungles and mountains down south, man, you know that?'

'What's his name?' Beth asked.

'La Calavera,' Karma told her.

'Original,' Beth muttered. It meant skull in Spanish, but could also refer to the sugar skulls made for the *Día de Muertos*, the Day of the Dead, or a death's head moth, or even a rake. As in an immoral male hedonist, not a gardening implement.

'And you think he has access to the tech?' du Bois said.

'He was in all the wrong places, making all the wrong noises with a ridiculous amount of technical know-how,' Karma told them. Beth looked less than pleased, and to be fair du Bois had been hoping for a bit more himself. 'He's supposed to be a hunchback as well. That's all I've got. The West Coast has been quiet for years.'

'Know where we can find him?' Beth asked.

'Well, assuming he's not smearing his own shit in his hair like the rest of humanity, the last I heard he was setting up his own fiefdom in East LA. I don't know the city that well.'

'He sounds exactly like the sort of wanker that the DAYP would make friends with,' Beth muttered. Du Bois wasn't quite so sure. The DAYP struck him as wannabes who had got lucky. Karma knew his tech, if he was impressed then this La Calavera was probably the real deal. He wouldn't have just come out of nowhere. He must have been biding his time. Planning. Even the name wasn't as ridiculous as it sounded, he had tapped into the folk beliefs of what was presumably his community, and if he did have access to the tech then he could potentially have made their nightmares come true. Fear was the key to control.

'Sorry I can't help more,' Karma said.

'Well, that's not entirely true,' du Bois said. Karma sighed. 'We're going to need a ground vehicle. We can't risk an aircraft but people are still using the roads. We need to lose ourselves. Something with a bit of speed but armoured, armed as well, supplies, ammunition.'

Karma slammed his hands down on the arms of his garden chair. 'I fucking knew it! You're after my toys.'

'Do you have any nano-tipped bullets?'

'Only homemade and I draw the line at donating my own blood.'

Du Bois smiled and nodded. 'Have you heard anything about Alexia?' he asked.

Karma's face dropped. 'Her new band, Light, I don't like them, too heavy. I much preferred her seventies ...'

'Karma ...'

'I'm sorry, man.'

'What?' du Bois asked, pretty sure he didn't want to hear the rest of it.

'Last minute gig in New York, another band pulled out, it was all over their website.'

'So?' Beth asked. 'New York can't be any worse than anywhere else.'

'It's not there any more. It's just a smoking crater of glass filled with radioactive water. The firestorm set off forest fires all the way up the Hudson basin. I'm sorry, man, I liked her.'

Du Bois could feel both of them looking at him. He stood up. 'Excuse me, I need a moment.'

18
A Long Time After the Loss

Mr Hat was frightened. It was not an emotional state he was used to, nor one he enjoyed. He neunonically manoeuvred the *Amuser* around the strange interconnected rings of rock hanging in Red Space. Among the rings he could make out a large flat area with a circle of standing stones in the middle of it. There were figures moving around the circle, bizarrely, what looked to be four enormous exoskeletons, their bodies moulded to make them look organic somehow. They were of a type that hadn't been seen in Known Space since the colonial era thousands of years ago. Their skin looked a little like the bark of the decorative trees he had seen on some of the more upmarket Core worlds.

A ship was hovering in place next to the flat area on the interconnected rings of rock. It was extensively decorated in some pre-Loss, presumably mythological, style. Its cargo ramps were down and the large exoskeletons were pulling things from the cargo bay. According to the *Amuser*, the ship was a pleasure barge called the *Semektet*.

Patron had provided him with the coordinates. It had meant going off the beacon paths, something that hadn't filled him with joy. This was worse, this looked heretical, but then it seemed the Church had fallen. He'd seen propaganda all across the Consortium on every media-form. The Church had tried to leverage its competitive advantage. Monopolies were a sin against capitalism. There had been widespread uprisings by the faithful, but not as widespread as Mr Hat would have thought. The Monarchists and the Consortium were now on the edge of war.

None of which explained why he was here. He had managed to trace the *Basilisk II* to a sensor ghost found by a very old defence platform orbiting New Coventry. He had made Patron aware of this and Patron had told him that he would handle it. Now, as far as he could tell, New Coventry no longer existed. It had been removed from the navigation systems connected to his bridge drive. Not that anyone ever went there anyway, though he had done some freelance work for one of the planet's larger vigilante societies a little over seventy years ago. It was how he had first met Vic and Scab. He had heard rumours of system disappearances before but it was difficult to care if it didn't directly affect you.

Without any 'faced instructions Mr Hat brought the *Amuser* in closer to the flat area, taking the upright squashed spider shape of his ship between the rings of rock. The *Amuser* made him aware that he had broken some sort of artificial magnetosphere, and that he was in a breathable atmosphere now.

Mr Hat had two of his automatons with him, one male and one female. The male was pushing the bath chair. Mr Hat was tucked in snugly under the travel blanket. It didn't stop the feeling of disquiet as he was pushed down the ramp and onto the smooth but porous-looking dark rock.

The stones in the circle were illuminated from within, as if something bright enough to shine through rock had slid up into them. The light shone through disturbing abstract patterns carved into the stones. He saw a bright, glowing blue light, and expected the sensors on his skin and tongue to warn him of radiation but they didn't. A display of energy flickered between the stones. For a moment there was a sphere which looked so black it was as though there was less than nothing there. The sphere did odd things to light. Then there was a circle of water, illuminated by the lights of the ship and the stones. The water was so clear that Mr Hat could see the stone bed of the body of liquid as he approached the rings.

'Hurry now,' the figure with the crystal head filled with liquid software and exotic fighting fish shouted, or rather emitted. The fashion victim, as Mr Hat found himself thinking of the presumably human man with the crystal head, was standing next to the tall, dark, slender form of Patron. As Mr Hat watched, one of the four huge exoskeletons pushed what looked to be an industrial assembler into the water with a splash. It sank to the rock floor, anchored itself and started to push out material. One by one the exoskeletons climbed into the water. Finally two figures appeared from behind one of the rib-like rock rings, one tall and slender carrying some kind of cup – it was difficult to tell through the blue light – the other shorter and more deformed looking. They both leapt into the water. The light went out and Mr Hat was looking at rock again. The stones were no longer glowing internally either. Mr Hat did not want to think about the amount of energy he had just seen being juggled around by what he assumed was ancient S-tech. He did not like that he had been asked here to bear witness to this.

Patron turned to look at him as his automatons wheeled him over.

'Ah, Mr Hat,' Patron said. There were another two figures standing further around the circle from them. They looked similarly proportioned, but were dressed very differently to the two human-sized figures he had watched step into the water previously. His eyes and sensors would have magnified and analysed them but he stopped the processes with a thought. He decided the less he knew, the better.

'Patron,' Mr Hat said, bowing slightly, his huge stovepipe hat bobbing downwards as he did so.

Patron nodded towards the two figures standing by the edge of the stone circle. 'Your compatriots.'

Mr Hat sighed internally. He had already worked out that the deformed-looking one was a bounty killer called Crabber. He ran the less-than-subtle heavy take-down crew that had recently captured General Nix and his arachnid, princess-sect second-in-command, the Widow.

'If you're looking for me to go through that,' Mr Hat gestured towards the stone circle, 'then I am afraid I will have to politely refuse.' The fashion victim's carved crystal head turned to look over at Mr Hat. Patron studied him for a moment longer and then turned back to the circle.

'They are clones, as I'm sure you've worked out, and where they are going you would not fit in. Would you like to know what I'm doing?' he asked.

'Attempting to awe me into co-operation,' Mr Hat said. By awe he meant terrify. 'Co-operation you most assuredly already have as a result of paying me so well.'

'There are no ideals any more, are there?' Patron mused.

Mr Hat was slightly affronted. He had ideals. Admittedly he had chosen them to make himself more interesting, a gimmick for his bounty killing, but then why else would you have them?

'I was hoping to impress upon you the importance of what we are doing. There is a reason for everything.'

Mr Hat was starting to feel very uncomfortable about this. His neunonics were struggling to analyse Patron's voice, as they struggled to analyse everything else about the Consortium board member, but Mr Hat was sure there was some fervour in the voice, just a hint of the irrational. Then Mr Hat worked out who the tall figure was standing next to the clone of Crabber was. He had been extensively sculpted but there was no doubt it was him. It was like a cold hand squeezing his heart. His systems automatically administered an internal sedative to deal with the tiniest moment of panic. Mr Hat hoped he hadn't given himself away but this didn't make sense.

'The problem is perspective. I have done this so many times and each time I have made things that little bit worse.'

Mr Hat frowned, he wasn't sure he was following. 'Why?'

'An end to pain,' Patron said. Mr Hat could have sworn he heard just a moment of suppressed desperation in Patron's voice.

The stones were starting to glow from within again.

Mr Hat was trying not to think about what Patron had said. He wanted to leave, complete his job, and hopefully never see Patron ever again, but something had occurred to him, something on the edge of his understanding.

The ring of blue light, then the sphere again. This close he felt like it was trying to pull him in. The absence of light was so total that he had to neunonically shut down the perceptive part of his real meat brain to stop it from filling in the blanks with disquieting images. It was clear that the ionisation in the air, the lightning display between the stones, was in part the result of a monstrously powerful invisible coherent energy field that was keeping them safe from forces capable of tearing open reality. Mr Hat was of the opinion that soiling himself would have been something of a comfort. Then the sphere was gone. In the stone circle it was night, somewhere. He could see some flat, overgrown stones, arranged roughly in a circle amid woodland that must have cost a fortune in debt relief. Only the truly rich had so much money that they could waste it on something as frivolous as trees.

'If everything gets that little bit worse each time,' Mr Hat asked, 'then doesn't that mean each time, he's a little bit worse?'

The two clones stepped through the stones and down into the wooded area.

The tall, black-skinned man gave Mr Hat's question some thought. The blue glow faded out, and the wooded area was replaced with the dark stone again. 'Yes,' Patron finally said. Mr Hat couldn't shake the feeling that he looked troubled. 'Parker has some information for you.'

The Monk moved forwards and hugged the Dark Mother. Scab knew that she'd had a name, another name, once; the name he had used before they had taken him from this place and cut into his head because they were frightened. He couldn't remember that name now. That made him sad. He was disappointed that somehow the Monk knew her.

'Churchman ...' the Monk started.

'My brother was always ashamed of me,' the Dark Mother said. 'He needed to hide me. We found a way during the war and snuck me in here.'

'I think I worshipped you,' Scab said, still not entirely sure how he felt about this.

'I'm eminently worshipable,' the Mother told him. When she talked it looked like her mouth was full of oil. She turned to Talia. 'And this must be the young lady that all the excitement is about. Kali?'

'Sorry, I panicked,' Talia said. She seemed to be blushing furiously. Scab had no idea why. 'I have a near-overwhelming urge to curtsey.'

'Please try and resist it,' the Mother suggested. She made what Scab felt was an overly dramatic gesture and chairs started to rise from the floor. Describing them as organic would have done them a disservice. Biomechanical was more accurate; they had ribs. She gestured for them to sit down. Scab was faintly disappointed that Vic looked comfortable. 'I saw the Consortium ships attack the Church.'

'The Cathedral has fallen,' the Monk said. She was controlling her emotions but Scab knew how to look for pain.

'Churchman?' the Mother asked.

The Monk couldn't look at her. 'I'm sorry.'

'I see.'

Scab couldn't get any reading on the Dark Mother, however. His worship of her had been a moment of weakness. He didn't like Churchman's connection to her. Churchman had needed to suffer and die. He was trying to decide if he should transfer this to his apparent sister. In fact he wasn't sure what to do all round. What Churchman had told him hadn't satisfied him. The Monk should be dead. Vic should be locked inside a torture immersion on maximum time expansion, and he should have been looking for a way to capitalise on Talia. Despite his poor treatment at their hands he was still finding that there was something compelling about all this. There was something making him stay his hand despite how it lessened him in their eyes. Though that only mattered in as much as they did what he told them to. In short, he was curious.

Scab was aware of the Monk's surprise at the Mother's apparent lack of emotion at the news. She seemed to disapprove. Scab couldn't prevent the slight smile on his face.

'He sent you here?' the Mother asked.

'The AI. He uploaded information but ...' The Monk turned to look at him. Scab didn't want to think about the existence of the AI on his ship. He flooded his system with calming drugs so he didn't kill anyone.

'Churchman knew that to keep a secret you didn't tell anyone. Even the most secure system can be hacked.'

'Minds can be hacked,' Scab said.

She turned to look at him. 'I remember you when you were a baby,' she said, smiling.

It was strange, her words should have made him angry. They didn't. He couldn't really identify how he felt. Like when he saw the ghost, but different. He glanced over at Talia, and the smirk on her face did make him want to hurt something. 'So the fewer people you tell, the fewer minds to hack.'

'But he told you?' the Monk asked. Scab was sure he could hear hurt in her voice.

'Yes.'

'I'm sorry to interrupt,' Vic said. 'And these seats are lovely, could you download the specs to the *Basilisk*?' He was rubbing the multiple armrests.

'Of course, Mr Matto,' the Mother said.

'But is the *Basilisk* safe?' Vic undistracted himself. 'There are lot of Consortium ships in orbit here.'

'A very faint coherent energy field, Mr Matto. Nothing in, nothing out. They may detect the anomaly but somehow I doubt they'll try and investigate, or even connect it to you.'

Scab knew his partner well enough to know that the

explanation had disturbed the 'sect as much as it had comforted him.

'Tell me, did you like the things I made for you?' Scab asked. He thought he saw a change in her expression, just a moment of disgust, gone as quickly as it had come.

'Such devotion. It is as awkward as it is flattering.'

'Did he do something horrible?' Talia asked.

'He made structures out of skin and bone,' Vic told her.

Talia nodded as if it didn't surprise her. Scab envisaged her being peeled.

'You seem ... nice,' Vic went on.

'Well thank you, Mr Matto,' the Mother said.

'Now don't get me wrong, myself and Scab have tracked down some very polite and socially pleasant recreational killers who were capable of the most horrible acts, but I don't get that vibe from you.'

'Believe me, Mr Matto, I am capable of atrocity on a scale I think you would struggle to quantify,' she said. It was stated in a matter-of-fact manner, neither a boast nor a threat, but again there had been something there when she had said it. Some emotional response so slight that Scab couldn't quite decipher it.

'Well, that's sort of my point,' Vic said.

'You weren't a bad person, assuming it's you,' the Monk said.

'The Alexia you knew was uploaded into the ancient alien petrol station, if that's what you mean,' the Mother said. 'Time has passed. I shouldn't take anything for granted.'

'But this place is a place of atrocity and you were ...' The Monk trailed away.

'Shallow, a hedonist?'

'I was going to say a musician,' the Monk said.

'Oh, I hear music, even here there is beauty,' she said. Scab had to smile. They never understood that. 'But I think you mean why is Cyst like it is?'

The Monk nodded. Scab frowned. He had always assumed that his home just *was*.

'Cyst is a social experiment and a breeding programme.'

Vic, Talia and the Monk stared at the Dark Mother. Scab felt a prickling sensation at the back of his neck. He wasn't sure he liked where this was going. He lit a cigarette.

'One of ours?' the Monk asked. She didn't look like she really wanted to hear the answer.

'Not exactly,' the Mother told them. 'It's social modelling for the end of civilisation.'

'We've seen this before,' the Monk said sceptically.

'I can open this chamber up and you can try and survive twenty-six hours out there,' the Mother suggested. 'It's not the same.'

'What were you trying to breed?' Talia asked. Scab could smell her fear. The girl was looking at the walls like a trapped animal.

'Not what, whom. Someone perfectly adapted for such times ...'

'Me,' Scab found himself saying. Surprise was unusual. He tried not to have a facial expression. He mostly succeeded. It went very quiet in the ziggurat chamber.

It was Talia who broke the silence. 'At least that goes some way towards explaining why he's such an enormous bell-end.'

'Talia,' the Monk said. Warning in her voice. Her sister went quiet.

'Not you specifically, Mr Scab, well perhaps not you, who can be sure, but your bloodline, certainly. You are a bad seed, from a long line of bad seeds. Others may condemn you killing your own offspring. I do not. I see that as an act of social responsibility.'

'Then why make him?' the Monk demanded. 'Whose breeding programme is it?'

Scab could feel his heart speeding, starting to pound. He made physiological changes to slow it, to control his breathing. He wanted to hear this but he wanted to lash out as well. It was sounding too much like he had been manipulated, controlled, from birth.

'Do you know who Patron is?' the Mother asked.

'We've met him,' Vic said.

'That surprises me.'

'Why did he do this?' the Monk asked.

Scab wasn't sure how much more he could bear. He was gripping the chair's armrests tightly, trying to dig his fingers into the smart matter, the tip of his cigarette glowing brightly as he inhaled hard. It seemed strange that nobody else could hear the screaming, flailing chaos inside him. And it kept on happening. And it kept on getting worse.

'The Destruction?' the Mother asked, turning to the Monk. 'I know you know—'

'We've seen it,' Scab managed through gritted teeth. Now they were looking at him. He could feel veins bulging out of his forehead. He could smell Vic's pheromonic concern, his fear. Talia shifted in the confines of her chair, trying to move away from him. The Monk tensed.

'Scab ...?' Vic said.

'Control yourself,' the Mother said quietly. He wanted to but it was a struggle. 'It is something to do with Patron's connection to the thing that is trying to consume everything. My ... Churchman thought he was breeding a herald for it.'

'What?' Talia said, confused. 'Why?'

'Because things need heralds, apparently.' Scab heard irritation in the Mother's voice.

'That's why I was made Elite, after I had proved what I was capable of,' Scab said. The Mother nodded. 'But then why did they take that away?' He could remember so little, but he'd seen a habitat burn, its matter infected as it fell towards the planet, the coldness of vacuum all around him. It had been the closest he had come to peace.

'Because they found a flaw, and I think they have been trying to breed that out of you with each successive generation of clone.'

'What flaw?' Scab asked.

'You know what you are,' the Monk said.

'That's why you want to die,' Vic added quietly.

'You added this,' Scab hissed at the Mother. He didn't think he had felt this betrayed when Vic had turned on him.

The Mother looked down. *Was it shame?* Scab wondered.

'Not exactly, Woodbine. I did something worse.' She looked up at her son. 'I gave you a choice. I made you self-aware.' A black tear leaked out of the corner of one eye and made it halfway down her cheek before it was reabsorbed into the oil-like surface. 'The rest you worked out yourself.' Nobody seemed to know where to look. 'I'm so sorry.'

Scab's skin burned as tears ran through his make-up.

'On the eve of the war we had managed to work out enough about this place. It was simply a fuelling station, we suspect for a mega engineering project that never happened. Any Lloigor AI had long since departed. Patron knew that the abundance of energy and the smart matter could support a population, of a certain type, up to a point. What he didn't know was the

Church had worked out how to upload human consciousness into L-tech.'

'It was you who weaponised this place?' Vic said. 'Destroyed the fleets?' She nodded.

'But to reign over this atrocity ...' the Monk started. Scab couldn't understand what difference it made.

'Oh, there was a cost. I spent more than one millennium beyond insane.'

'Then why?' Talia asked; there were tears in her eye.

The Mother looked up at her. 'I always wanted to be a mother.'

Talia turned to him. 'Look, Scab, please don't freak out and kill me.' He was aware of the Monk shifting slightly. She looked as though she was about to tell her younger sister to be quiet. Talia turned back to the Dark Mother. 'I get that he's a hard case and unpleasant, but he's not that hard. Churchman beat him up and he's as nothing compared to the Elite, those guys are like gods.'

It took everything he had to not kill her right there and then. Break her down to red, wet constituent parts with his bare hands. The Mother turned to look at him, concern on her face. It was if she could hear the black screaming thing in his head.

'That's not the point,' the Monk said quietly. 'He's poisonous, corrupting.'

'He destroys everything he touches,' Vic said. 'Because he can't destroy himself on his own terms.'

'Patron wanted him to destroy,' the Mother said.

Would that have been enough?

'We wanted him to think. That was the conclusion he came to. He is a suicidal thought.'

'You want to upload my consciousness into that thing, don't you?' he asked quietly. *Would that be enough?*

'That's sick,' Talia said through the tears. It was the look of pity she gave him that broke him. He started to move. He found he was adhered to the seat.

'Please don't,' the Mother 'faced him.

Vic and the Monk were both looking at him. He tried to relax his muscles. He couldn't relax his screaming mind.

'It is your choice,' she told him out loud. 'To be honest, I wouldn't know how to do it anyway. The Destruction exists in a different physical state. I think uploading you into it was Churchman's idea.'

'Can't this place ...?' the Monk asked.

'Petrol station,' the Mother said peevishly. Scab had no idea what petrol was. 'There was a place on Earth that perhaps had the tech but it's long gone.'

'We can't just—' Talia started to object but he could see that the Monk was more than capable of doing just that if she had the resources. He glanced at Vic. The 'sect smelled of guilt, he was thinking the same thing.

'The Ubh Blaosc?' the Monk asked. Scab looked back at her, frowning. He searched the data in his neunonics. Nothing. 'Churchman had mentioned it in the past. He told me to find it. Do you know where it is?'

The Mother concentrated for a moment. 'No. I have only heard it spoken of once or twice before. It was supposed to have been a third faction who knew of the tech. They were said to understand how the stones worked.'

'The stones?' Talia asked.

'An ancient network of bridge portals,' the Mother explained. 'But I have never met anyone who has claimed to have met anyone from the Ubh Blaosc, although in all honesty I haven't been getting out much.'

'This doesn't make sense to me,' Talia said. 'And again I mean no offence to Scab, largely because I'm frightened he'll hurt me, but who hinges a plan like this on somebody like him?'

'Things have gone about as badly wrong as they could have,' the Mother said. 'The Church was set up to oppose Patron and to try and limit the Monarchists and the Consortium from abusing S- and L-tech. As soon as we became aware of the level of threat posed by the Destruction, the focus shifted to finding a solution to that. Woodbine was a contingency plan.'

'This is pretty much as fucking contingency as it gets,' Vic muttered. 'No offence,' he told his partner. Scab wondered if they thought that was a magical phrase of some kind that would protect them. 'It's too big, it's too much. It's just us now. The forces arrayed against us ...'

'That is a trick, and it has been played on humans at least since way before the Loss,' the Mother said. Even on his insectile face Vic looked mystified. 'I understand things were probably different in the hives, but then humanity dominated Known Space. Unless they are board members, or the top of the food chain in the Monarchist systems, all the humans you have ever met are the result of genetically engineered embryos taken from Earth.

231

They were bred to be easy to control, either through apathy, or greed in the pseudo-capitalism of the Consortium systems, or just programmed to serve the aristos as slaves, serfs, courtiers and playthings in the Monarchist systems.

'Some people can be hacked free of this conditioning, sometimes psychosis can free you of it,' she glanced at Scab, 'and I guess religion can help distract you from it in as much as it distracts you from being pissed on and told it's raining. Or at least that it's a different flavour of piss.'

The Monk looked like she was about to object but thought the better of it.

'This is just a slightly more sophisticated version of *my idea is better than yours*, isn't it?' Scab said, sounding calmer than he felt.

'I wondered if, when we started downloading and storing consciousness, when we became electronic, we left something behind. Maybe not a soul but some vital, ephemeral part of us, a connection of some kind.'

'The trick played on us?' Talia asked, mystified.

'That it's too big, that there is nothing we can do,' the Mother told her.

'Not all of us are massive, fleet-killing fuel stations with an army of killer children,' Vic said. 'You go face-to-face with something like Ludwig, or the Innocent, and tell me you're not helpless!' Vic was getting angry now. Scab knew it was because he was frightened.

'And yet you're still here, Mr Matto, and yet you're still here.' Her oil-like features frowned and she turned to look at Scab. 'A bridge has just opened in-system,' the Mother said. 'What did you do?'

'The transmission you sent,' the Monk said.

'I exercised my free will,' Scab explained. 'I told the *Templar* where I was.'

Benedict/Scab was on his way here.

232

19
Ancient Britain

The second day of their stay a low winter sun had chased the freezing mist away and revealed a landscape of white contrasted with the black of gnarled, leafless trees. Among the groves were various cromlechs, dolmens and several barrows that Britha assumed were for previous high-ranking *dryw*. Across the narrow strait were stark, snow-covered hills running up into mountains that reminded her of the more northerly parts of her homeland. In places the snow was stained red and the cut-open corpses of birds and other small animals could be seen.

Morning brought the normal bustle of any settlement. Animals had to be seen to, food had to be prepared, and because they were in the south, the gods had to be appeased. They had been well-treated, given food and drink. They had slept in the smoke-filled longhouse with everyone else, the smell of people mingling with last night's meal and the odour of the animals brought in to protect them from the cold.

Long after the rest of them had turned in, Britha had seen Guidgen and Nils, the arch *dryw*, talking late into the night. At first she had heard much laughter, and she had assumed they were reminiscing. Later their conversation turned low and serious. She could have listened to them but she chose not to. Just before she went to sleep she noticed that Moren was awake and watching Guidgen and the old arch *dryw*.

They were waiting for the arch *dryw* to summon them. One of the silent black-clad women had been assigned as their escort as they had looked around the groves. It was rude to discuss things in private. If you had something to say to one person then you shouldn't fear it being said to all. On the other hand, all knew that the *dryw* had to have their secrets. Eventually Britha tired of the black-clad woman being closer than her shadow and demanded to know if they were prisoners or guests. The woman looked less than pleased but she bowed and backed away from the *ban draoi*.

'So?' Britha asked when she felt they had a little privacy. Guidgen had looked troubled since he had awoken.

'Nils has seen his own death. He will not see another summer. He has the support of the majority of the council at the moment, but only just,' Guidgen said grimly.

'And Moren is manoeuvring himself to be Nils' successor?' Britha asked. 'He seems very young.'

'He is. Part of the problem is that Nils has the support of the older members of the Circle, but many of them are standing at the gates of Annwn as well, as I should be were it not for your blood coursing through my body. Nils says that the younger *dryw* support Moren because he ... I don't know, offers them things.'

Britha frowned. 'That is not right.'

'Nils wonders if they even believe in our ways at all, or just wish to honour themselves. He still thinks he can sway the council while he yet lives, but once Arawn has taken him ...'

Britha could see where this was going.

'He needs to appoint a successor while he is still alive?' Britha said.

'Yes, but all he would suggest are almost as near death as he is.'

'Except you,' she finished.

They stopped walking. On a nearby tree stump a raven pecked at the cut-open and peeled-back gizzard of a rabbit. The waste disgusted Britha. Guidgen followed her gaze.

'Moren seems to have little time for the people, the land, and the gods, except when it comes to killing beasts ...'

'And people?' Britha asked. Guidgen nodded.

'Nils hadn't heard from me in years. He thought I was dead. He was so happy to see me.' Guidgen had gone from sounding troubled to sounding miserable.

'Do you wish my counsel?' Britha asked. He nodded. 'You already know the right thing to do. If you do not accept then Nils will lead until he dies. Then Moren will demand the Red Chalice for himself. We have all seen what happens when *dryw* rot from the inside, when they abuse their power. Does Nils have enough to cast Moren out?'

Guidgen shook his head. 'No, he is sly, clever. Nils says that

234

Moren understands people's weaknesses and uses it to manipulate them.' He shook his head. 'I wish I had never heard of this chalice!'

'Things would be worse if you hadn't. The sad thing is I do not think that Bladud is an evil man. I think he is doing what he thinks is right. Unfortunately, that is at odds with what we think is right.'

'Think? What we were *taught* was right, what we *know* is right,' Guidgen said, as though he was trying to convince himself.

Britha was suddenly reminded of Bladud's words outside the *bwthyn*: *And you are so sure that I am wrong? Why, because of what we have always been told? All that means is that the knowledge is old.* 'We need to be sure.' She saw him shake his head.

'Gods, Crom,' he said, spat and made the sign against evil.

'We can fight him without you,' Britha assured him. He would be missed but Britha was convinced that he would do them more good here than in the shadow of the Mother Hill. 'There are others who can stand up to Bladud.'

'My people,' he said, and sat down hard on a flat stone sticking out of the snow.

'They are not children,' Britha said gently. He looked up at her with tears in his eyes.

'I have no family. They are children to me.'

'There was nobody else to lead the Brigante!' Bladud shouted at Nils, sitting on his litter. They were back in the clearing. Logs crackled in the fire but the cold air seemed to suck the warmth from the flames. All were wrapped up warm but had clearly been out in the cold for too long.

Moren stood on Nils' right. There were a number of *dryw*, most in brown robes, standing around the circle, or sitting on fallen tree trunks that looked to have been dragged to the clearing for that purpose. Those sitting on Nils' left all looked to be quite old, many of them leaning heavily on their staffs. Those standing on his right looked younger. All the black-robed *dryw* were sitting on the right. There looked to be many more black robes than a grove of this size would require. Madawg was standing a little distance behind Bladud in the tree line. The Corpse People champion had his hood up and a hand on the hilt of his sword.

'Nobody?' Nils asked. 'So you are *rhi* of a tribe of only one, are you? Well, that I can perhaps accept.'

'We were being pressed by the Corieltavi from the south, and the Parisi from the east.'

'You could have advised them.'

'They needed a leader!' Bladud had the look of a man desperately trying to explain something that seemed obvious to him.

'Which should not have been you because of the oaths you swore,' Nils said more quietly. 'And we have had this discussion too many times. If the Parisi or the Corieltavi had conquered parts of your territory it would have been because they were the stronger. It would have been their right. The same justification you have for bullying the other tribes into serving you. But we can never know if they were the stronger ...'

'Of course they weren't, we defeated them!' Bladud cried.

Britha raised an eyebrow. You didn't speak to a *dryw* like that, let alone an arch *dryw*. She didn't think she had ever seen Bladud so exasperated, not even with Guidgen, whom he had once punched.

Nils sat back in his litter. 'But they were subject to their oaths, they adhered to our laws, you did not. For all we know your leadership could have weakened us all.'

Britha understood the arch *dryw's* point, but she did not think it was so in this case.

'Sometimes I think you like to see us fight each other to stop any one tribe becoming too strong!' Bladud spat. Nils stared at the Witch King, a dangerous expression on his aged features.

'Bladud!' Moren snapped. Bladud struggled to control himself but finally he lowered his eyes in contrition.

'I apologise. I should not have spoken so,' Bladud said.

'Arch *dryw*, we have outsiders here. I know you wish to speak to them next, but perhaps they should leave until we have resolved this matter,' Moren said.

Nicely distracted, Britha thought.

'Be quiet, Moren,' Nils said, the contempt in his voice obvious.

Nicely handled, Britha thought, *if not very subtle.*

'You would have me weaken my tribe?' Bladud asked, calmer now.

'I would have you hold true to our oaths. I would have you do the right thing, the just thing. You were trained here. You, more than any warrior, any landsfolk, understand the reason for our laws, for the oaths. Strength is in oaths, not in feats of arms, not in military strategy. Without oaths, and the behaviour that such ties in the eyes of the gods engender, there is only tyranny and chaos.'

'Where were your oaths when the spawn of Andraste laid waste to the land, when the Lochlannach raided?' Bladud demanded.

'And what of after you have defeated them? When you try to rule more than you can see from the highest point in your land? When all the tribes fall to fighting among themselves, fighting you?'

'And when the next invaders come?' Bladud asked bitterly.

'Then a *brenin uchel* will be elected, and hopefully you will be able to advise him.'

'It is not enough. You are here. You have not seen what we face.'

'Enough. This is my judgement and we will not be having this discussion ever again. Do you intend to stay in southern Pretani?'

Britha was surprised to find that Nils was speaking to her. 'I do not know, it seems unlikely,' Britha said. She had not thought much beyond the battle with Crom, the rod, and the daughter the *dryw* from the Ubh Blaosc had taken from her.

'If you stay beyond the battle with this Crom Dhubh, then you will either join our Circle, which means honouring the gods, or you will remove your robe and claim that you are a *dryw* no more. You will not be entitled to the benefits and protections that such a station holds, nor may you offer judgements or advice in such a capacity,' Nils told her. Britha saw Moren smile but she had to admit it was a fair judgement. She nodded. 'If, however, you stay and join us then you may stay as one of the guardians of this Red Chalice.'

'Arch *dryw*,' Moren started, 'we discussed this ...'

'Furthermore, the warrior called Tangwen of the Pobl Neidr, and the foreigner known as Germelqart the Carthaginian, will also remain in guardianship of this Red Chalice, on the provision that they bring it here after battle is done with Crom Dhubh. Along with Britha, the Pecht, they, and only they, may decide how and when it is to be used until such a time as this Circle has had a chance to examine the accursed thing.'

'No!' Bladud shouted. Nils silenced him with a furious look.

'Bladud, once of Ynys Dywyll, who styles himself Witch King, we understand that your leadership of the army in the valley of Cuda is such that it would be difficult to remove you without working in favour of this Crom Dhubh. Bladud, you are to lead this battle and either die during it, or afterward renounce your position as both *brenin uchel* and *rhi* of the Brigante and return to Ynys Dywyll. I do not think you should have ever been a *dryw*, but it must be seen that there are serious consequences for oath-breaking. Better you are subject to them in this world than the next. Cythrawl is not so merciful as we are. Fail to either die in battle or return here, and all men, women and beasts will turn from you, and you will be hunted like a moonstruck wolf and your body burned. You will not be given to the land, instead you will wander it, blown by the winter winds, never to know your place in the Annwn.'

Britha could see Bladud struggling to control himself. The veins on his bald forehead stood out against his furious red skin. It was no thanks for all that Bladud had done for the people of Ynys Prydain, regardless of his motivations, but it could have been a lot harsher. She wasn't really sure what more Bladud could have expected.

'I will die in battle, and look for wisdom in the next world,' he spat.

'So be it,' Nils said.

'Arch *dryw*, this is not what we discussed,' Moren said, urgency in his voice. Bladud was staring at the younger *dryw* furiously.

'It is not what you discussed, that I was forced to listen to,' Nils said.

'The Circle should vote.' Moren sounded frantic now.

'Oh yes, I forgot that we have to do this every time you don't get your way, how tiresome. It's a wonder the Greeks ever get anything done. I mean, surely the point of having an arch *dryw* is because you trust them to make judgements? Would you see the position done away with? Perhaps I should be the last one?' There was uncomfortable shifting around the circle. Britha found herself smiling despite herself. Moren didn't seem quite sure what to say. 'No?' Moren didn't answer. 'Tell me, Moren, how are you going to win this vote if you can't insinuate that you are going to have old Gowin's niece sacrificed?' Nils nodded towards an elderly *ban draoi* sat to his left. The *dryw* was plump and looked as though she was normally quite a gentle and motherly woman, but she had a face like thunder now, and was staring at Moren with undisguised disgust.

'The child was strong and would have made a worthy sacrifice,'

Moren said. 'Perhaps if you had listened to me, and we had honoured the gods, the land would not have suffered so much.'

Britha could hide her contempt no more. 'You know what would make a strong sacrifice?' she asked. 'A *dryw* at the height of his power. I mean, if that's what you believe.'

'How dare you speak so in this sacred place ... !' Moren began angrily.

'We do not fear words here, Moren. Though perhaps you can explain to me why the gods of war would want an un-blooded child as a sacrifice?'

'I ... ah ...' Moren stammered.

'Or we could get on with the vote once you've finished trying to humiliate us in front of our guests. All those who would see my judgement as arch *dryw* ratified?'

Britha considered saying aye but she could not be bothered with the inevitable argument. Those to the left of Nils all said aye, as did Guidgen.

'He may not speak!' Moren all but screamed.

'Enough!' Nils shouted back. 'I sicken of your venom! It burns the ears of all who hear it! Guidgen was a member of this Circle long before you were shat out of whichever poor daughter of Cuda had the misfortune to bear you! He is a senior *dryw*! He has served the people under his responsibility and the land well! And you will apologise!'

Now Moren looked furious. It was the anger of humiliation. It was clear that Nils was at the end of his patience with Moren.

'I think not,' Moren snapped.

'He does not know me. It is fine,' Guidgen said. Nils flashed his old friend an angry look. The *gwyll dryw* looked worried. Britha could see his point. Whatever had happened before, Nils was now humiliating the ambitious *dryw*.

'You will apologise or you will be cast out,' Nils said quietly. There were a number of sharp intakes of breath. One of the younger *dryw* on the right made to protest, and two of the black-robed *dryw* stepped forwards. Moren held a hand up to stop them. He turned to Guidgen.

'I apologise.' It was barely a whisper. Then he turned and stalked into the bare trees. Most of the *dryw* to the right of Nils followed. Suddenly the arch *dryw* looked very, very tired indeed.

*

They intended to leave first thing in the morning. Word had been sent to the Brigante and *gwyllion* warriors who had accompanied them. They were to meet them on the other side of the strait with the horses. Britha couldn't make up her mind if this time had been wasted or not. Now, hopefully, there would be less arguing and they could get on with dealing with Crom Dhubh, and she could concentrate on finding the rod. This was assuming that the battle hadn't already happened and they were all dead. She had smiled and then admonished herself for her arrogance. *There's nothing to say they will not have succeeded without your presence*, she thought. The smile left her face. Arguably that could be worse. What then for the control rod and her way back to the Ubh Blaosc?

Once having so much to think on would have kept her awake, but her body seemed to know when it needed sleep these days. She wanted rest before the long trip home. Guidgen had decided to stay. She would miss him.

It was a noise that disturbed her sleep and suddenly she was very much awake. She felt the *dryw* asleep next to her grunt, fart, and elbow her as she moved. She looked around the room, the glowing embers of the dying hearth fire providing more than enough illumination for her eyes to see clearly in the ghost light.

And again. A scrabbling noise, but not like the inevitable rats. The arch *dryw*'s sleeping stall. She could see the bottom of a pair of fur-wrapped boots sticking out under the wool hanging across the stall's entrance. Britha heard another noise. She was up on her feet and moving towards the stall, quickly drawing her dirk.

'You!' Britha snapped, loud enough to wake all but the deepest sleeper in the longhall. Suddenly a figure burst from the stall. Slender, dressed in dark clothing, hood covering his head, rags covering most of his face. Britha moved towards him, but he ran out of the rear door of the longhall. Britha threw herself down next to the arch *dryw*'s sleeping stall. She put her hand over Nils' mouth, feeling for breath, but it was obvious that he was dead. There were fading marks around his mouth and nose from where he had been held. Britha stood up, looking around.

'What have you done?' Moren cried. He was standing on the planks that ran down the middle of the longhall, pointing at her.

'I woke everyone, obviously I—' she started. Others were sitting up, looking at her standing over Nils with a drawn dagger in her hand. Moren stamped forwards and looked into the stall. He looked down at the body.

'Frightened to death!' the *dryw* announced. 'She must have seen that he was old and weak and not fully in his own mind, shouted at him to wake him. Nils awoke to find her standing over him with a blade in her hand. It would have been enough.'

All around the longhall people were nodding at what Moren was saying. Britha resisted the urge to plunge her dirk into Moren, repeatedly.

'What would I have to gain from that?' Britha demanded. 'He ruled in our favour.'

'You are Bress's lover, are you not?' Moren asked. More people were nodding.

'What happened?' Guidgen asked, stepping forwards, his sickle in hand. The grief for his dead friend was already etched on his features.

'I awoke to see a figure in the stall. I shouted and drew my knife. The figure bolted. I went to see if Nils was well.'

'Let us check the rear door for tracks,' Guidgen said.

'And I'm sure we will find them,' Moren said. 'After all, people were using the door all night. That is not the question. The question is why would you speak up for this woman when she has been caught murdering a *dryw*?' There was muttering and nodding from the assembled *dryw* in the longhall.

'I have not been caught—' Britha started.

'We all saw him last night, trying to pour honey into the ears of an obviously infirm old man. Trying to steal the position of arch *dryw* from those who have served this Circle! And he brings one of Crom's killers with him, here! On this sacred ground! Before our gods!'

There were cries of agreement, as well as suggestions of what should be done with her. She was accused of the most heinous of crimes, the one she had tried to kill Fachtna for, killing a *dryw* and not just any but the arch *dryw*.

'All of you saw the dissent they have wrought, confusing an old man who has served the land, the people, and the gods well! Striking a *dryw* in defiance of our laws!' It seemed that she was to be tried by oratory alone. She didn't fancy her chances. She could see Guidgen tightening his grip on the sickle. She felt sure that *dryw* or no *dryw* he was about to swing it into Moren's belly. She caught his eyes and shook her head. She looked around the longhall and saw Bladud. He looked troubled but he was thinking; he had not condemned her yet but he held his peace.

241

She felt the draught as the front door was opened. Everything fell into place as Madawg entered the longhall. He looked around as though surprised to see everyone was up.

'Where have you been?' Britha demanded.

'Pissing.' He looked taken aback. 'Is that the business of foreign *dryw* as well?'

'Nils has been killed,' Bladud said.

Madawg's eyes went wide. 'Somebody killed a *dryw*?' He spat and made the sign against evil. 'Among our people that is a great crime.' He kept on looking at her as if he was frightened. Britha had to give him credit: it was a fine performance.

'You killed him, didn't you?' Britha asked him.

'No!' he shouted. 'I would never ...' He turned to Moren. 'She betrayed us when we went to take the chalice from Crom Dhubh. I was just out making water!' He sounded desperate, panicked, in a way that Madawg never sounded.

'This is a low man. We have seen his acts. He caused his *teulu* brother to—' Guidgen started.

'I think you have been consorting with serpents too long,' Moren said. *A sideways swipe at Tangwen*, Britha thought, *clever*. 'And you have not yet explained why you are defending someone who murdered our arch *dryw*.'

'Because she didn't—' Guidgen started.

'All saw her!' Moren shouted. 'I should warn you against weaving magics into your words. We are skilled in such things as well.'

Britha turned to Bladud. 'We have had our disagreements, but you know I did not do this,' she said. She was still angry more than anything else at the moment. She wanted to believe that Bladud would not have been involved. He looked at her. She could see the indecision warring on his face.

'There is too much, Britha,' he said, shaking his head. 'You were deep in the enemy's counsel.'

Britha pointed at Madawg. 'He rode for Crom Dhubh. His tribe worshipped his sickness as a god!'

'Why don't you hand over the dagger?' Bladud said. 'That would be a sign that you could be trusted.' Britha had almost forgotten it was there. What must she have looked like, the half shaved head, the metallic tattoos, the black robes, shouting with a knife in her hand. At least she knew Moren was no coward, standing this close to her while she was so armed.

'Of course,' she said, and punched Moren in the face as hard as she possibly could. By the time he hit the floor she was out of the back door and running through the snow.

She ran at an angle away from the longhouse but still heading east towards the strait between the island and the mainland. Barefoot, she barely sank into the snow.

They spilled out of the longhall's front entrance. Running, but often stumbling in the snow. Madawg, sword in hand, soon outpaced them, powering through the snow towards her. He would kill her so she could not gainsay his story. Her dirk against his fast slender blade, one that had been imbued with the power of her own blood. She would not stand a chance.

In the early hours of the morning, the freezing mist was back, hanging around the denuded trees and over the water. She could hear Madawg behind her. The others were much further back. She did not even look behind. She just kept running for the water. She had the longest legs, and in only her robe, with no boots, she was the fastest.

She could see the snow-shrouded beach ahead of her. She thought about the child she carried inside her. She hoped that the child would be protected as a result of drinking from the chalice. She hated to do this but she knew the child had no chance if Madawg killed her, or if she was sacrificed.

She took a deep breath and dived into the water. She knew it was noise that would give her away so she swam as deep as she could. She heard the sounds of other people jumping into the water behind her. She stayed under, swimming the way her senses told her was east, towards the mainland.

20
Now

The ECV – enhanced capacity vehicle – that Karma had provided for them was basically an up-armoured Humvee, the four-wheel-drive patrol vehicle ubiquitous to the American military. This particular one had belonged to Special Tactics, the USAF's special operations unit. They had asked Karma to work on it as a favour.

Karma had provided them with as much ammunition as they could scavenge from the base. He had given them jerricans of fuel and water. They had also managed to scavenge a lot of MREs, the nearly inedible but high calorie ready-to-eat ration packs used by US forces.

The ECV's front passenger door had been removed and an M240B general-purpose machine gun had been mounted on a swing arm. The vehicle had an armoured turret mounted on the roof. The turret housed an M134 six-barrelled minigun. Du Bois had taken one look at it and told Karma that it was not a practical weapon.

'Establish firepower superiority, brother,' the consultant *otaku* had told him.

'For a second or two,' du Bois said disapprovingly.

'It was used as the lead vehicle in Iraq. The minigun's for breaking ambushes,' Karma explained. 'More to the point, it's all I've got.'

What had happened next was a little odd, Beth thought. She sort of understood that Karma, and possibly males in general, were excited by hardware, but it had seemed to come out of nowhere. Karma had handed du Bois another assault rifle, a pistol, and ammunition for them. Weapons they didn't need.

'What are these for?' du Bois had asked.

'Backups, same calibre,' Karma told him. Even du Bois had seemed a little surprised.

They had worked into the night, deciding that they could take turns sleeping on the road. Her body required a lot less sleep now, it seemed. Karma had periodically disappeared to check on his drones. It was apparent that he had a command post somewhere, probably mobile, among the bones of the decommissioned planes, which he did not wish to reveal to du Bois and herself. She could understand that.

With new-found skills she had helped with the prep of the vehicle but as it neared readiness there was only so much they could do. After discussing it with du Bois she decided to check out the air force base next door for more supplies.

Carefully, the Model 0 LMG at the ready, Beth made her way onto the air force base. Bodies spotted the cratered runway. She tried to ignore the birds, rats, dogs and humans eating the carrion. None of them seemed interested in bothering her. The city to the north glowed from the multiple fires. Beth had been keeping busy. It had been easy to forget what had happened. How much they had lost. In the distance she heard a howl that her neuralware identified as a coyote. The howl was answered by dog packs and humans. She also heard the noise of distant gunfire more than once.

She was looking around the hangar area. Her eyes saw straight through the darkness. She moved towards the hangars quickly and quietly. The weight of the LMG was a comfort, its stock snug against her shoulder, the barrel moving wherever she looked. She passed a CV-22B Osprey tilt rotor transport aircraft. Presumably it had been of limited use for the bombing, and so had been left behind.

The first hangar she entered was huge and mostly empty, other than two of the A-10s. Her neuralware had provided her with the information on the aircraft as soon as she had seen them. Five days ago she wouldn't have had a clue as to what they were. It looked like they had been being worked on when the Seeders had attacked. They probably weren't capable of joining in the bombing of Tucson.

There was one other aircraft in the hangar. It did not look military. She approached it carefully. It looked like a civilian executive jet but her neuralware identified it as an EADS Astrium TBN. A rocket-propelled spaceplane that was supposed to still be in development. She frowned, moving closer. She couldn't quite work out why it was here. If the USAF was testing the aircraft it would most likely be stationed at Groom Lake in Nevada.

Then she walked through the cobwebs. For a moment it made no sense. She was out in the middle of a large wide-open area, nowhere for a spider to live. Then she realised that the sensation of walking through cobwebs was her reconfigured physiology's translation of walking through a blood-screen: a networked cloud of nanites floating in the air.

She moved quickly to the plane. It was locked up tight. She climbed onto the wing but she couldn't see anyone. She clambered onto the roof of the plane. It wasn't very subtle but she had to know if there was anyone still inside the air/spacecraft. She slung the LMG as she moved quickly along the roof of the spaceplane. She drew the Colt OHWS and replaced the conventional magazine with the one containing nano-tipped bullets. She checked in the cockpit but saw no one.

She cursed their inability to use comms. There was someone else here, and they had landed before du Bois and herself had arrived. She supposed that if the spaceplane's stealth systems were sophisticated enough and the Astrium was capable of gliding they might have landed unnoticed after they had reached the Boneyard, but she doubted it. Du Bois had said that he thought the Harrier getting shot down had been a delaying tactic.

She slid off the spaceplane and started running. She had walked straight into the blood-screen. They must know she had found the aircraft. She had to get back and warn du Bois.

Karma's command post and living quarters had the look of a technological nest to Mr Brown. The CP was on the back of a heavy expanded mobility tactical truck, an 8×8 military cargo vehicle with excellent off-road capabilities. Inside were the computers and communications equipment used to help control Karma's drone army. There was also a rack for the constantly cycling quadrocopters used as aerial transceivers for the tight-beam communications between the drones and the CP.

Much of the comms and computer equipment's electronic guts were spread across the cluttered floor of the HEMTT, presumably yanked out when the Seeders had awoken. Many of the individual electronic components would contain the ancient alien insanity.

Mr Brown was sitting in the padded leather chair in front of the panels of equipment. The chair had been modified with a joystick, cup holders and the like.

'And we are discovered,' Mr Brown mused. He was watching

a jumpy screen being constantly updated with images from one of the two Ripsaw drone tanks, as Elizabeth Luckwicke sprinted back towards the Boneyard. He glanced at another screen. A similarly updating image, shot by one of the MAARS drones and then transmitted by microwave, showed du Bois finishing work on the ECV.

'Just another victim,' said Grace, watching Luckwicke running back. 'Why don't we take both of them down? Mueller is almost in place, and Ezard's ready. We can neurally audit du Bois.' It was not the first time she had made the suggestion. Grace had become sloppier since he had split up her partnership with du Bois and made her hate him, but she had certainly become more fervent. She had a point, however. Having Mueller and Ezard take du Bois down and kill Luckwicke would be easier. Du Bois was the most difficult of his pawns, but after the Pennangalan and her sister, he was by far the oldest and most competent. He wondered if he was becoming subject to the same sentimentality that had cursed du Bois's life.

'For all we know he is still about our business, despite being told to stand down. Given the lengths he has gone to, it could be argued that he is showing real loyalty.'

The Pennangalan came off the workbench she had been leaning against. The light from the screens and the other electronic instruments in the cramped CP reflected off the beaten silver mask that covered her face. His oldest servant, augmented with Naga-tech, one of the twin serpent pirate queens of the Khmer Empire, now little more than a slave. He sensed her impatience. This elaborate charade was a luxury they didn't have the time for.

'Didn't you order her dead?' Grace asked, pointing the barrel of her Noveske Rifleworks N6 CQB carbine at the image of Luckwicke. 'Is that loyalty?' the punk girl demanded. The side door to the truck-mounted CP opened and Karma found himself looking down the barrel of two carbines. He sighed and climbed in, closing the door behind him.

'How much longer—' he started, and then saw the images of Beth sprinting back from the air force base. 'Well, at least the charade's over,' Karma spat. It was clear the bearded tech did not like him. Mr Brown was sure he had known why once, and could probably remember if he concentrated, but it wasn't important. He glanced at the bed Alexia du Bois was lying on. She had been put to sleep by an S-tech derived nanotech sedative

247

that had bypassed the protection of her internal systems. Alexia's immortality, and her being kept out of their business, had been one of du Bois's tedious conditions of service. Finally she was proving useful. 'Lying to him about her was cruel,' Karma said.

Patron's laugh was devoid of humour. 'Now he will be pathetically grateful to see her. Remember, we are just here to talk. Ideally he re-joins the fold, the price of which is Luckwicke's death, but to all intents and purposes we are the good guys.' Patron reached over and placed a finger on Alexia's forehead, delivering the signal to wake her by touch.

'Yeah, right,' Grace snapped, and then opened the door, jumping out into the sunlight.

'Du Bois!' Beth shouted.

He was standing just a little way beyond the ECV looking up a corridor of dirt between two rows of decommissioned B-52 bombers. He glanced behind him at the sound of her voice but then turned back to face something else.

She reached his side. Further up the corridor of red dirt she could make out five figures standing in front of one of the old B-52s. Karma was on the right. Next to the *otaku* was a leather-clad punk girl with multiple piercings, her mohican flat on her head and tied back. She was carrying a carbine with an under-slung grenade launcher.

Next to the punk was a tall, slender, but somehow still power-ful looking man. His skin was so black he was almost a void, though his features were not African, in fact they didn't seem to fit any ethnicity she had ever seen before.

Next to the black-skinned man was another woman. Tall, statuesque, strikingly beautiful, though there was something about her that made Beth think of the transvestites she had known working the doors in Bradford and Leeds. She wore black jeans and a fitted T-shirt with the name of a band on it that Beth had never heard of. She was smiling, beaming at du Bois. Beth was sure she could see a family resemblance.

The woman on the far left was the strangest of them. She was shorter than the other three women, wiry. She had long black hair tied back in what looked like a braided hangman's noose. She wore very practical outdoor clothes in subdued desert colours, and carried a Sig Sauer 716 Patrol Rifle also with an underslung grenade launcher. Her face was covered by a smooth silver mask with contours in the shape of facial features but no slits for eyes, nose or mouth. It looked perfectly form-fitting.

'Okay ...' Beth said. 'What do you want to do?'

'Hello, Malcolm!' the black-skinned man shouted. His voice was so deep it made her feel funny. The air seemed to shimmer slightly when he spoke.

'We could run,' Beth suggested, glancing back at the ECV.

'I like westerns,' du Bois said. It wasn't quite what she wanted to hear. He started walking forwards.

'Are you still sane?' the black-skinned man asked. Beth fell in beside du Bois.

'Do you like westerns?' du Bois asked.

'My dad did, so I didn't,' Beth said.

'Malcolm! Thank god!' the tall, beautiful woman shouted, and started to move forwards. The black-skinned man stopped her by placing one of his huge hands on her shoulder.

'Please let us speak with him first. If anything's happened to him we can still help him,' Beth overheard the black-skinned man say. She could listen to his voice all day, she thought.

'Mr Brown, let my sister go,' du Bois shouted at the tall figure. 'But you've seen westerns, right?' Beth had heard this last in her head. She had that feeling of walking in cobwebs again, her skin itched. She knew that communication via a blood-screen would only last so long before desert breezes carried the nanites away.

'Yes, I've seen westerns,' she answered with a thought.

'You put them down with conventional weapons, overkill, then you finish them off with the nano-tipped bullets. They will have at least one, but more likely two, snipers in place. One will be close in. He won't miss, you're going to get shot. Our only chance is that they want us alive. If he hits us with nanite-tipped bullets we've had it.'

'The one further away?' she asked.

'He will have a bigger gun but the bullets will have to travel longer distances. We need to keep moving because he will be able to deliver that overkill I mentioned.'

Beth was aware of the Ripsaw unmanned light tanks behind them. They were being flanked by two of the machine-gun-mounted MAARS tracked drones as well.

'This isn't good, is it?' They were still closing with the five figures who had started moving towards them.

'Tactically?' du Bois asked. 'No.'

249

Beth noticed he kept on glancing at the punk girl. Beth wondered if this was the Grace that Gideon and Azmodeus had asked about. She looked young, early twenties at the oldest, and was staring at du Bois with undisguised hatred.

'Objective?' she asked.

'Get Alexia to the ECV and run away,' du Bois thought back.

'Chance?'

'Effectively nil.'

'Sorry to go all Lando on you, buddy,' Karma said. Du Bois glanced at him but said nothing.

'I am not sure what is going on here, Malcolm,' the one that du Bois had called Mr Brown said. 'Suddenly there is distrust?'

'Well, strictly speaking I am in breach of orders,' du Bois answered.

'Yeah, didn't you ask him to kill me?' Beth said, suddenly angry. It had been such a casual thing, it seemed. He didn't know her. She didn't wish him harm, and yet he was prepared to snuff her out on a whim.

'My apologies, Miss Luckwicke, the exigencies of our work are difficult to justify face-to-face. You are carrying a lot of dangerous technology inside you. If, on the other hand, you are prepared to join us?'

The punk girl sneered. Punks had always given her trouble in the clubs. They were supposed to behave as if they didn't give a shit. Alexia looked worried. She was glancing between Mr Brown and du Bois. Occasionally she would look at Grace. It was clear that du Bois's sister didn't like what she saw on the punk's face.

'So?' du Bois asked. 'Everything is forgiven? I'm back in the fold? I have a seat on the life raft?'

Mr Brown frowned. 'Assuming we can get Miss Luckwicke's sister's genetic material back, then of course. I'm not sure where you would get the idea otherwise. Malcolm, is there something you want to tell me?'

'Alexia, walk towards me,' du Bois said.

'She looks pretty angry,' Beth said and nodded at Grace. She had the look of someone who was about to start a fight in a nightclub. She could hear the sound of the servos on the drones as they shifted their weapons slightly.

Alexia stepped forwards. Mr Brown put his hand out to stop her.

'Get your hands off me!' she snapped, pushed his arm away and went to move forwards. The woman with the silver mask had a Sig P220 at Alexia's head. Beth had barely caught the movement of the semi-automatic pistol being drawn.

Beth had the LMG against her shoulder pointing straight at the silver mask. Du Bois had taken his right hand off the SA-58 carbine's grip and was holding his hand up.

'Woah!' du Bois shouted.

'What the fuck are you doing?' Alexia demanded.

'Nanite-tipped bullets, as I'm sure you can imagine,' Mr Brown explained. He sounded sad.

'Okay, there's no need for this. We just take Alexia and go,' du Bois said.

Beth could hear the desperation in his voice. She was feeling quite desperate herself. Too many guns. She smiled. It was like one of the films her dad liked. A strange way for her to go out, cut down in a hail of gunfire. She decided she was definitely going to shoot Karma. She was pretty pissed off with him right now.

'And my question is, what's changed?' Mr Brown said, his eyes narrowing. 'Whom have you been talking to?'

'Look, everything's over, what possible difference could any of this make?' du Bois asked.

'Well, we appear to be in competition, Malcolm. You are on your way to Los Angeles, aren't you?'

'You let Alexia and Beth drive away, and I'll tell you what you want to know,' du Bois said.

'Tell?' Mr Brown looked confused. 'That's not really how we do things. The question is do you get shot a lot before I tear your mind open, or do you spare yourself and your compatriots a lot of pain? Put the guns down and submit to neural auditing.'

'I'm not doing that,' Beth said. She wasn't sure if it was the tech or not but her mind didn't feel so partitioned now. The knowledge of her death was liberating. She was grinning.

'Wow, this is really tense,' Karma said helpfully.

'So you're the new sidekick now?' the punk girl asked.

'Grace?' Mr Brown said.

Beth was pretty sure that this wasn't part of his plan. She didn't answer the punk. She certainly didn't like to think of herself as a sidekick, though she had to admit that du Bois called most of the shots.

'Is he your mentor? Father figure?' the punk continued. 'Has he tried to rape you yet?'

Beth actually stepped away from du Bois, though she kept the

Model 0 aimed at the woman with the silver mask.

'What?' Du Bois sounded appalled.

Mr Brown looked down, a pained expression on his face. He reached up to pinch the bridge of his nose between thumb and forefinger.

'Are you out of your mind?' Alexia demanded.

'Grace, we discussed this. I removed the memory of what he did so he could still function as an operative.'

'I didn't—' du Bois started.

'How would you know?' Mr Brown asked.

One thing that Beth was sure about was that Grace was absolutely convinced. She was aware of the look of concern on Karma's face as he looked between du Bois and Grace. It was also clear that the accusation had completely rocked du Bois.

'That the kind of person you want to die for?' Grace asked her. Just for a moment Beth glanced at du Bois next to her. He looked stricken. That didn't mean he hadn't done it.

'My brother is no more capable of raping someone than he is of unaided flight,' Alexia snapped. 'You, on the other hand, you piece of shit,' she said to Mr Brown, 'are completely capable of putting a memory like that in someone's head.' Beth saw just a moment of doubt on Grace's face but then it was gone. The memories would be too real, too raw.

'Oh yes, rape is a stretch for a mass murderer,' Mr Brown said.

'All of you are mass murderers,' Alexia spat. 'He still believes in chivalry, for fuck's sake! It's probably the reason his new chippy's still alive.'

'Hey!' Beth cried. 'I am trying to help you.'

'Sorry, I'm a little tense because I've got a gun to my head,' Alexia muttered.

Beth could hear one of the drones trundle to a halt somewhere behind her.

'Did he tell you that he killed your father, I wonder?' Mr Brown asked her. Something cold seeped through her. 'On my orders, of course, but nonetheless.'

Beth took another dangerous glance away from the reticle on the LMG's holographic sight. The guilt was written all over his face. There was not a trace of doubt in Beth's mind. This he had most certainly done.

'I ... I'm sorry,' was all he could manage. His outstretched hand dropped down.

Alexia was looking at them both, stricken.

'You've no idea what kind of man you're dealing with,' Grace told Beth. 'You need to put the gun down and walk away ...' She stopped and thought for a moment and then turned to look at Karma. 'Wait a minute, in the end Lando ...' The shotgun blast caught the punk girl in the side, spinning her round. Karma worked the action on the Mossberg M590 tactical shotgun, firing rapidly again and again into Grace.

Beth wasn't aware of making a decision. She was operating on unearned, pre-programmed muscle memory. Necessity meant better the devil you know. Du Bois would have to wait. She was moving forwards firing.

'Alexia!' du Bois screamed. He used his left hand to move his carbine aside. Alexia was ducking down low. The woman with the silver mask lowered the Sig P220, trying to shoot Alexia in the head as she drew a twin Sig with her right hand. Beth's three-round burst caught the silver-masked figure in the chest, staggering her. Her own augmented hearing picked out a gun shot from behind her. Karma was hit, he staggered back and was hit again. Something larger fired from further way, a hole appeared in the fuselage of the B-52 on her left, and there was an explosion of sand. Du Bois fast-drew his Accursed .45 from the holster on his hip and fired once. The bullet hit the masked women in her left wrist, knocking it back. The P220 fired, missing Alexia. Du Bois was re-holstering the .45. The nanite-tipped bullet was eating away at the masked woman's wrist. Suddenly Alexia had a long knife that looked like a small katana. The blade flashed up and the masked woman's left hand hit the desert sand still holding the P220.

'Run!' du Bois shouted at his sister as he brought his carbine up to his shoulder.

Of course the reason that western style gunfights probably only ever happened in the movies was that modern weapons, in the hands of people who knew what they were doing, made such activity a zero sum game.

Grace spun with the momentum of the shotgun blasts. Bringing the N6 up she fired a three-round burst at Karma, hitting him centre mass, his body armour, clothes and skin hardening as armour. Then one of the sniper's rounds tore part of his face off.

Alexia was sprinting towards du Bois and Beth. The silver-masked lady was rapidly firing her right hand Sig, round after

253

round hitting Beth. They didn't penetrate her hardening armour but each one still felt like getting hit by a hammer. Beth got shot twice in the back, rifle rounds, armour-piercing, it beat her armoured clothes and lodged in her hardening skin, too close to her spine for comfort.

She spun around to find the sniper. It looked like part of the desert had stood up. The ghillie suit he was wearing had camouflaged him. His face was painted in reds like the desert earth. He was firing his M14 rapidly at one of the tracked MAARS drones trundling towards him firing its own machine gun. Beth triggered a short burst at the figure. He staggered, then turned and ran from the drone, diving into the open door of one of the B-52 skeletons. The drone fired its four grenade launchers in quick succession. Air-bursting high explosive grenades followed the sniper through the old bomber's fuselage.

A round burst through the B-52 nearest to her and passed so close it would have opened her skin had she not been augmented. She was getting shot a lot in the back again, the force of the impacts driving her down on one knee. She managed to turn back, bringing the LMG up. The crazy silver-faced woman, her left arm still being eaten by the nanites in the bullet du Bois had shot her with, was firing her Patrol Rifle one-handed. Alexia cried out and went sprawling face-first in the red dirt as a round caught her in the back. Du Bois was firing three-round burst after three-round burst between the masked lady and Grace.

Grace was rocking with every impact but she emptied the rest of her magazine into and around Karma. Karma sat down, hard, covered in his own blood. Beth desperately wanted the masked lady to go away. In the distance she could hear more machine gun fire and the sound of the larger weapon. It seemed the drones were taking on the second sniper. Beth fired a long burst at the masked lady, the barrel of the LMG climbing with the recoil. She stopped firing, adjusted her aim, and repeated. The masked woman staggered back, but Beth kept on firing until she fell over. Throughout it all Mr Brown stood stock-still in the chaos.

Alexia sprinted past them as Grace turned away from Karma and fired the underslung grenade launcher, dropping the 40mm fragmentation grenade between Beth and du Bois. Beth and du Bois were both turning away from the grenade as it detonated. Beth was aware of tumbling through the air. The fuselage of one of the B-52s suddenly filled her vision and then everything went black.

Anything resembling sentience was still moments away for the suffering piece of meat. Pain first. Then identity. She was Beth. Her systems flooded with enough endorphins to cope. Then information. Her back was on fire, her insides were full of broken glass. A lot of the precious red liquid she usually kept on the inside was staining the already red sand. Dying hadn't felt this bad. The nanotech was trying to fix the broken machine. Her neuralware was letting her know how well that was going. She needed the answer to two questions. Could she move? And was her weapon functioning? She had been turning. The blast had caught her on the right-hand side and on her back. Her body had shielded the LMG. She pushed herself up and looked around. Du Bois was a moaning, blackened and bloody mess on the other side of the red corridor. Grace was walking towards him, changing the magazine in her N6. Du Bois's moans turned to howls of pain again as Grace lifted the carbine to her shoulder and fired a three-round burst into du Bois's groin.

'Die, motherfucker!' Karma screamed. He was sitting up, firing his FN57 pistol at Mr Brown, his bearded face a mask of hatred. He emptied the pistol's entire magazine into the obsidian-skinned figure. It looked like he was shooting into burned paper. Mr Brown turned around to look at Karma.

A section of the fuselage of the B-52 behind Mr Brown ceased to exist.

The Metal Storm gun, mounted on the SWORD drone in the old B-52 behind Mr Brown, had four barrels. Each barrel was loaded with superposed rounds. The projectiles were packed nose-to-tail, the electronically triggered propellant between each round. It meant a firing rate far in excess of anything even a minigun could muster. Karma had fired them all with a thought. The Metal Storm gun had made a fast moving wall of bullets. Most of which hit Mr Brown.

Mr Brown was looking at a flurry of black snow in front of him. He realised this was what passed for the human element of his body these days. It was extraordinary. He had felt the crude nano-tipped bullets that Karma had made with his own blood, and he had felt whatever had just happened. After all these years, after all this pain, it was extraordinary that he was still capable of sensation. Karma had succeeded in getting his attention. He really must try and remember what he had done to the man to get him this upset. He turned to look at Karma and unfolded.

A wet, tearing, cracking noise echoed between the B-52s. Karma looked like he had been reconfigured, in a red way. Pain lanced through Beth's head as she looked at Mr Brown. He no longer made sense. She tore her eyes away from him as nausea threatened to overwhelm her. She felt a tugging sensation on her back as Alexia landed behind her, grabbed the Benelli M4 NFA from the sheath on her back. Beth was bringing the LMG up but Grace had noticed the movement and was turning, bringing her N6 to bear. Alexia fired the shotgun. The cloud of shotgun pellets caught the punk girl in the upper torso and face, staggering her. Something exploded against the side of the B-52. The pressure wave of the explosion battered Beth and Alexia to the ground, robbing them of their breath. Grace was flung like a rag doll across the corridor of red earth between the planes. Du Bois lowered the carbine and slumped to the ground.

'Get to the Humvee,' Alexia managed between gasps, meaning the ECV. Beth nodded and managed to stand up. She started staggering towards the vehicle. Behind her, Alexia was trying to get her brother to his feet. The two Ripsaw drone tanks powered past them. She guessed they were using their upgraded, limited AI minds to act autonomously now. She glanced behind her. Du Bois was half staggering, half being dragged by his sister towards the ECV. Then, behind them, walking out of the clouds of red dirt, was Mr Brown. It looked like he was reassembling his form, folding back together, collecting himself from impossible places at impossible angles.

The Ripsaws started firing. One was armed with a .50 calibre heavy machine gun, the other a Mark 19 fully automatic grenade launcher. Mr Brown was engulfed in explosions. It was like the end of the world at the other end of the dust corridor. Then she remembered it was. She stumbled against the ECV, and used the armoured patrol vehicle to hold herself up for a moment before climbing into the driver's seat and starting the vehicle up.

As she watched Alexia drag her brother towards the ECV some thought was trying to push its way through the pain translation organ that used to be her brain. Alexia dumped her brother into the passenger seat. He was just about conscious. The ECV was in gear and accelerating the moment Alexia was in.

Beth saw movement in her side mirrors. The mangled remains of the two Ripsaw drone tanks tumbled by behind them. Then Beth remembered the outstanding business she had with du Bois. Her sidearm was still loaded with nano-tipped rounds. She drew it and put it to du Bois's head, still steering with her other hand, the cold fury overwhelming her. He had stood there with her over her father's corpse and said nothing. He had made it look like a suicide to cover his tracks. She felt the cold, folded steel of the long knife against the skin of her throat.

'That's my brother,' Alexia hissed from the back seat.

'He killed my father.'

It wasn't much of a world to live in anyway. Beth started to squeeze the trigger.

Hans-Jorge Mueller had learned his skills hunting in the Teutoburg Forest, honed them in the streets of Stalingrad, and perfected them with an infusion of alien technology and his work for the Circle. Even so he had been little use. He had either been firing blind into the artificial canyons of aircraft, or been pinned down by armed quadrocopters, or prevented from getting close enough to the edge of the control tower to shoot by indirect ground fire from the MAARS drones. The airburst HE grenades had played merry hell with him. As soon as he had killed one drone another had replaced it to make his life difficult.

The ECV was over a mile away and moving away from him. It would have to turn soon, which would provide it with cover from the rows of aircraft, and from there it could break through the perimeter and lose itself among the tract housing. There was another armed quadrocopter on its way towards him. This would be his best chance, though it was still effectively a blind shot. He had never liked du Bois anyway.

He squeezed the trigger of the Steyr IWS anti-materiel rifle. The barrel flew back in its shock-absorbing hydro-pneumatic sleeve, not unlike those used for towed artillery pieces. The 15.2mm fin-stabilising, discarded sabot projectile left the smooth-bore barrel at four thousand, seven hundred and fifty seven feet per second. It would take the round just over a second to travel the distance to the ECV. He let the weapon settle, exhaled and squeezed the trigger again.

The first dart-shaped, tungsten carbide penetrator flew through the back of the ECV. It made a tunnel through their supplies, hit the rear of du Bois's chair and blew much of his chest all over the windscreen. Only the reinforced nature of his augmented physiology stopped the hydrostatic shock of the impact from blowing all of his limbs and his head off his body.

Alexia had slid under the ECV's turret to get behind Beth to put one of her knives to the woman's throat. Her left arm was stretched out over the back of the passenger seat to steady herself in the moving vehicle. The second round caught her in the shoulder, tore through the corner of the driver's seat, and narrowly missed Beth's leg. Alexia's arm was spinning around the cab.

The Pennangalan was up and walking. Her own systems had stopped the nanites from du Bois's bullets from consuming her just below the elbow. She was hooked up to a matter IV but her arm would need to be regrown.

Ezard, still in his ghillie suit, was carrying Grace. She would live but was badly wounded and also hooked up to a matter IV.

Mueller was jogging across the runway towards them, also still wearing his ghillie suit. The enormous anti-materiel rifle had been broken down and was in a case on his back; he had a customised Heckler & Koch G3 rifle in his hands.

Mr Brown was watching a Reaper drone taking off from the cratered runway. In the darkness it was a silhouette against the backdrop of burning Tucson.

'So does anyone have anything that could shoot that down?' Mr Brown asked.

'I could waste bullets shooting at it if you like,' Ezard suggested. Mr Brown wasn't sure he was in the mood for the American's humour tonight.

They watched as the Reaper circled back towards the hangars and fired four Hellfire missiles. Even from as far away as they were, the multiple explosions rocked them back. They could feel the heat as bits of debris rolled past them.

'One last fuck you from Karma, I guess,' Ezard mused. The missiles had destroyed the spaceplane.

I really must try and think what I did to him, Mr Brown mused and then out loud. 'Yes, we really could have handled that better.'

21
A Long Time After the Loss

The fashion victim with a fishbowl for a head had 'faced Mr Hat the information before he had left the strange stone construction in Red Space. The personalities in the Psycho Banks that the Church had bought to help them profile Scab had been sourced from the Monarchist systems. They had, however, been hacked by intelligence contractors working for the Consortium. Nothing too overt. The hacks were designed to subtly influence the possessing psychos to behave in a way that would provoke Scab, and to be just predictable enough that if you knew what you were looking for …

Tracking the *Templar* in Red Space wasn't too difficult. Patron had paid to have the *Amuser*'s stealth and sensor systems upgraded. The *Templar*'s sensors were good, it was a Church ship, but the *Amuser*'s were now Consortium next generation. It didn't hurt that the *Templar* was a larger ship. Even so there were a few tense moments, when the light cruiser doubled back on itself. The *Amuser* was no match for the Church-built ship, and for a light cruiser the *Templar* was fast, which was one of the reasons it made such a good raider. If the pirate ship did discover the *Amuser* he wouldn't stand much of a chance and in Red Space all bets were off. Sensors didn't work right, and Mr Hat had no idea how well his stealth systems were functioning. He imagined their effectiveness would become apparent if his ship started to de-cohere all around him.

'So then all I have to do is steal a psychopath, one of the most revered bounty killers in Known Space, out from underneath a crew of recreational killer pirates in a state of the art Church warship,' the diminutive lizard muttered to himself atop his throne-like control column. The faceless automatons below him looked up to check if he was uttering some divine decree. 'Nothing,' he told them. It didn't happen often but sometimes he wished for someone real to talk to.

The bridge into Real Space was impossible to disguise. Anyone looking would know that a ship had just entered the Cyst system, and there were few reasons for visiting the Cyst system unless you were a combat-trained, adrenaline-seeking anthropologist. Still, the cool black of Known Space looked inviting through the blue-light-lined rip in the red gas.

As the *Amuser* emerged from the oddly cramped confines of Red Space, Mr Hat was half expecting to be destroyed by the waiting *Templar*. Nothing happened.

Manoeuvring engines took him away from the bridge point, trying to leave the residual sensor interference behind. Mr Hat knew he was exposed. He could make out the strangely small-looking gas giant with its striated bands of cloud and weather, the Cage wrapped around the planet, and beyond that the faint light of a dying star.

He drifted for a while, intelligent systems analysing passive sensor data. Two minutes in he received the incoming challenges from the blockading Consortium fleet around Cyst and got caught in their active scans, which made a mess of his own sensors for a while. He replied using a Consortium naval encryption. He did not tip them as to his knowledge of the *Templar*. Reading between the lines they were jumpy, which meant the *Templar* had entered the system and then disappeared. His passive scans made him aware that a number of the ships from the Consortium fleet had left the blockade and were saturating sectors of space with active scans. The searching ships were working in squadrons with more than enough ships to deal with a solitary light cruiser.

Mr Hat didn't understand the play here. The bridge point was presumably unguarded to try and entice original Scab in, but then the blockade would frighten them off, and why was Benedict/Scab even coming to Cyst? It might have been where Woodbine Scab had been brought up. It might even have been where Benedict was conceived after Scab's sect had learned how to meat-hack the biological restrictions on the inhabitants of Cyst's gender and ability to breed. But nostalgia?

'You are a fucking child!' the Monk shouted at him in the smooth, black, inverse-stepped chamber inside the smart matter ziggurat.

'I mean, do you just not understand what's at stake?'

'He just doesn't care,' Vic said sadly. The 'sect could see his point. It was too abstract for Scab. Whatever the Dark Mother had said it was all too big and was not really any of his business except for the bits where they were trying to kill him.

'You're a selfish little prick!' the Monk snapped and stalked towards Scab. Vic was pretty sure she was about to attack him.

'Beth!' Talia said, scared for her sister. The Monk stopped.

'How much further do you want to push this?' Scab asked the Monk evenly.

It was clear that the Monk sorely wanted to beat the shit out of Scab. She pointed at him. 'You're a sociopath with reasoning power a three-year-old would be ashamed of.'

'Don't you want to catch him? See him destroyed?' Scab asked.

The Monk stopped. It was written all over her face. She badly wanted Benedict/Scab dead, not least for having killed her. There was something else there as well. Once again Vic decided that humans were complicated. He glanced at Talia. She was looking nervously between Scab and her sister. The Mother was standing perfectly still.

'Maybe it's not as dumb as it sounds,' Vic suggested. 'The blockade fleets could take care of the problem for us.' Scab was already shaking his head.

'No, he's not that dumb. He won't come any closer with the ships in orbit.'

'So then what?' the Monk demanded. 'We're stuck here until the *Templar* leaves the system, or we get discovered, or we try and draw him out by making a run for the bridge point, or we sneak away in Red Space.'

'Can't you get closer to him in Red Space, and then, I don't know, jump out and surprise him?' Talia asked. Everyone turned to look at her in surprise. 'What? I've been paying attention. I practically used to be a ship, you know?'

'That only works up to a point,' the Monk told her younger sister. 'We can't see the *Templar* from Red Space, so we would have to know roughly where they would be. Even then, navigating to a point in Real Space from a point in Red Space, and vice versa, isn't an exact science without the fixed bridge points. We come back into Real Space too far away and the *Templar* gets the jump on us.' She turned back to Scab. 'And even with the *Basilisk*'s upgraded weapons, and even if we manage to get the

261

jump on them, the *Templar* is a Church warship. Besides, the *Templar* has the same bridge capability, and Benedict is aware of his dad's tactics.'

Scab practically flinched at the sound of the word 'dad'.

'We force a boarding action,' Scab told them.

The Monk looked at him, appalled. 'They have a crew of recreational killers!' the Monk shouted.

Scab just cocked his head as if he was trying to understand her. 'Vic and I have a way of getting on board,' Scab told her.

Vic sagged in his seat. He knew what Scab had in mind.

'And if they've analysed how we did it last time, and come up with a counter measure?' Vic asked desperately.

'No,' the Monk said, intrigued despite herself. 'The *St Brendan's Fire* was destroyed before we could work out how you boarded her.'

'It's not for the faint-hearted,' Vic muttered. 'And what if I don't want to do this?' Scab just ignored him.

'How do we get close enough to board?' the Monk asked.

'Talia's plan,' Scab told them. 'Except not in space.'

'In the atmosphere?' the Monk asked.

'We get the *Templar* running a search pattern, one that we can predict, then we bridge out and appear next to it.'

'How do we get it running a search pattern?' the Monk asked. 'You'd have to hide in the clouds, which would mean going deeper than the *Templar*, which you can't because it's a fucking warship, and we have a yacht, however high spec it might be. The pressure would crush us.'

'We exceed the smart matter's suggested tolerances,' Scab said calmly. The Monk looked at him like he was an idiot.

'Then we get crushed,' she said, as though she was explaining it to a child.

'And none of us will ever have to worry about anything ever again,' Scab said.

'Besides, they can just bridge into Red Space as well,' the Monk pointed out.

'Same problem. Without knowing where we are, we're just playing a pointless game of hide-and-seek. We have to convince them we're still there,' Scab explained.

Vic didn't like how this was going. The plan was starting to sound possible if you squinted at it just right.

'How?' the Monk asked.

'We lay autonomous AG smart munitions behind us,' Scab said.

'We have a limited amount of them,' the Monk pointed out. They could manufacture new kinetic harpoons, given access to raw material – they were pretty much just very dense aerodynamic lumps of solid matter – and they could replenish the energy for the beam weapons from a number of different sources, but the AG smart munitions were too complex to duplicate. The Church had provided them with a full complement, but they had used a few escaping the Cathedral. The assembler on the *Basilisk II* was good but it just didn't have the military specifications required. 'And even if you and Vic did get on board ...'

'I don't want to do this,' Vic said again.

'You'd just get swarmed by the psychos on board. Half of whom you took down in the first place. They'll have grudges.'

'We don't have to take them all out, we just have to hack the *Templar* sufficiently to allow the *Basilisk* to dock.'

'And then I come on board and smack them all up, yeah?' Talia asked.

'No,' the Mother said quietly, her voice cold and angry.

'Your people?' Vic asked Scab sceptically.

'We're not people,' Scab told the 'sect. Vic noticed the Mother looking at Scab. He couldn't make out the expression on her oil-like features.

'With my skills and your knowledge of Church security protocols we'll be able to stay alive long enough to hack the *Templar*.'

The Monk thought about this for a moment. 'That only works if I'm on the *Templar* with you and Vic. Who's flying the *Basilisk*, the nut jobs that live here?' She turned to the Mother. 'No offence.' The Mother didn't respond.

'Talia,' Scab said. Vic turned to stare at his partner. The Monk looked furious.

'Hell yeah!' Talia said. 'Oh wait, I can't fly a ship.'

'You just said you used to be one,' Scab pointed out.

Vic stood up, towering over the still-seated Scab.

'No,' the 'sect said. He could see where this was going. It had something to do with why Scab had been spending so much time merged with the ship's smart matter.

'Not this kind of ship,' Talia said, 'And I can't remember any of it anyway.'

'Trust me, you can do this. I will show you,' Scab told her.

'I said no,' Vic repeated. Nobody listened. His feeling of resignation, the constant, hard-learned pessimism, was being replaced
by something else: a feeling that he would normally control with
drugs and tailored biochemistry for his own safety, but not this
time.

'You don't engender trust,' Talia said. 'So, what? I get all the
computer stuff in my head?'

'No!' the Monk shouted.

Talia turned on her. 'I'm not a pet, you know? I'm not the
ship's fucking cat!'

'I'll take you into the ship and then you'll understand,' Scab
told the girl.

'I said no!' Vic screamed and yanked Scab out of his seat, lifting him off the floor. Scab had his tumbler pistol in hand, the
hammer pulled back, the hair trigger partially depressed. It was
aimed at Talia. The Monk started to move to interpose herself
between the gun and her sister, but clearly she knew she'd be
too slow and froze. Vic was shaking with anger.

'Why?' the 'sect asked quietly to his erstwhile partner/captor.
'Why?' the 'sect screamed.

'Who's faster?' Scab asked quietly. 'You want to end this?
We'll end it now.'

'Put him down,' the Mother said, steel in her voice. 'Now.'

Vic knew this was his time. He was so far beyond being frightened of Scab. He wanted to see what the stump of the human's
neck looked like.

'Vic?' Talia's voice sounded small and frightened. He slowly
lowered Scab to the floor.

'I don't care any more,' Vic told his partner, flooding his system
with calming narcotics. 'Do you understand me? I don't care.'

Scab looked over at Talia. 'Of course you do.' Vic followed his
partner's look. 'When you really don't, you'll be free.'

'You leave her alone, you understand me?'

'You've nothing to threaten me with,' Scab said. He glanced
over at the Mother. 'It's all been done.' The planetary avatar
looked down. He lowered the gun. The Monk moved herself
between Scab and her sister. Talia was crying and shaking.

'I don't think I can do this for much longer,' the human girl
managed between the sobs. The Monk was just staring at Scab
with pure venom as she held her sister.

'None of this matters,' Vic said. Scab laughed as he re-holstered his tumbler pistol. 'The *Templar* can't get past the blockade,' Vic insisted.

Scab took out his cigarette case, removed a cigarette, and lit it. Then he looked at the Dark Mother.

'No,' the Mother said simply. Only then did Vic realise that she had been quiet for the whole conversation because she had seen what was coming. Even Vic was horrified. 'You don't know what you're asking. You're talking about sacrificing a significant amount of the life of this planet.' Scab took another drag of his cigarette. The tip glowed.

'It's my price,' he told her.

'Have you planned any further along than this?' the Monk asked. 'I'm intrigued.' Scab ignored her. He just kept staring at the Mother, his mother, and smoking.

'I don't owe you anything,' the Mother told him.

Vic saw realisation dawning on Talia. 'How many people are on those ships?' she asked, appalled.

'Tens, maybe hundreds of thousands,' the Monk said quietly.

'Your need for revenge is not important,' the Mother said.

'You mean it's not important to you,' Scab said, and took another drag of his cigarette. Then he looked down, and tapped some of the ash off. 'You need to decide what is important to you. If you want me to take part in this idiocy you've concocted then this is my price.'

Something occurred to Vic. 'The *Templar* wouldn't come anywhere near us after something like that.'

'Things have changed since the war,' the Mother admitted. 'Their sensors will tell them that I won't be able to do it again immediately.'

'We can't kill that many people ...' Talia started.

'How many can we kill?' Scab snapped, making her jump.

'He doesn't care,' the Monk told her sister.

'How many people have you killed?' Scab asked the Monk. 'But that's okay because you had a cause?'

'It's not a justification, but it's certainly better than doing it because you're a selfish prick with less empathy than a stone!'

'And that's why you fucking lost. That's why everything you care about burned. Because you tell yourself lies, you set yourself limits, so you can see your reflection and not hate it,' Scab told her.

Vic took a step back. The last few weeks had been hard on

Scab. People had done things he hadn't wanted them to do. He was angry now. Genuinely angry. He seemed open, unguarded. It made him look raw somehow.

'Well, learn to hate your reflection.' Scab pointed up. 'Those are your enemies up there. They destroyed your ships, your habitats, your precious fucking Cathedral, and killed your friends. And you don't want to commit this crime because of some arbitrary limit on murder? Grow the fuck up.' He turned to the Mother and pointed at the seething Monk. 'How do you expect us to succeed at anything?'

The Mother stared at him. She too looked angry, like a god. 'Do they know?' Scab asked. The Mother just stared at him. 'Do they know I'm back?'

'Yes,' the Mother said, with apparent difficulty. 'They know and I don't know how they know.'

'Because you know. They can smell it. They're hunting animals. That's what you bred us for, right? You didn't want to be a mother, you wanted to be a goddess.' Scab spread his arms out wide. 'Was I everything you hoped for, *mother*?' He all but spat the final word.

'For Christ's sake,' the Monk muttered in disgust.

The Mother started sinking into the floor of the ziggurat. Part of the wall split open to become a doorway. Scab stalked out of it. Vic could see the Monk staring out through the doorway, the fear on Talia's face. Vic could feel their presence outside the ziggurat on his skin sensors, his antennae could hear them all breathing, but otherwise silent. Vic turned around. Scab was climbing up the ziggurat past the doorway. The 'sect could see them all pressed together. Human flesh turned to crude weaponry. Vic wasn't sure why but he followed Scab out and climbed onto the steps of the ziggurat. Four of the walkways intersected at the stepped structure. There were thousands of them. All eyes were on Scab as he climbed to the top of the ziggurat.

Vic had calmed down now. It was strange. Moments ago he had no longer been frightened of Scab. Being here, Scab's treatment at the hands of the Monk, had revealed Scab for what he seemed to be: a frightened little boy lashing out when he didn't get his way. Scab had found a new level to climb to. Vic was frightened again. And this had only been Scab's hobby as a teenager.

'I have come back!' Scab shouted. Cheering thousands answered him.

Mr Hat still couldn't quite believe what he had just seen. Thick lances of plasma had stabbed out from the Cage that surrounded Cyst like searchlights sweeping the night sky for the orbital blockade. Ships, big ships, heavily armoured battleships, bubbled, glowed and burst. For a moment Cyst burned like a sun, so much brighter than the dying star that hung in the distance. Then all that was left was the afterglow and the wreckage circling the gas giant as it was slowly pulled into the planet's gravity well.

Mr Hat was hissing, his maw wide open in surprise as his eyes compensated for the glare. This had all happened just over a minute or so ago. He became aware of Cyst being actively scanned on many different spectrums but he had the *Amuser* hold its silence. The scans had come from the detached search squadrons sent to look for Benedict/Scab's rogue ship and one other source. The *Templar*. As the glow subsided to reveal the gas giant surrounded by debris, the *Amuser* was picking up comms traffic but it was encrypted. Mr Hat thought they were Church codes but he wasn't sure.

It was the single most destructive act he had ever personally witnessed. He was appalled but he had an erection as well. With a thought the *Amuser* started moving towards the gas giant. Though he would hold off getting too close.

Benedict/Scab was looking at Cyst as the glow diminished, laughing.

'It's a trap,' Harold hissed. He looked rather natty in the three-piece, double-breasted suit. Benedict/Scab had always appreciated a good double-breasted suit, though he never wore clothing made of human skin himself. In his opinion, wearing skin that belonged to members of your own species was trying too hard. It looked good on Harold though, and after all, to the *Templar*'s lizard first mate a flayed human was just another dead mammal. 'As soon as we get close they hit us with the same thing.'

'Which wouldn't be much of a trap,' Benedict/Scab mused.

'Cyst has lost about a third of its mass,' the sensor operator, one of the few 'sects on board, told him.

Benedict/Scab thought it unlikely that the possessing Psycho Bank personality was a 'sect but he seemed quite content in the body, and all he asked for was kittens to play with when they captured feline children. He wasn't popular among the crew but he was a capable sensor operator. An image of the heat flow through the S-tech Cage surrounding Cyst was 'faced directly into his neunonics. He was aware of receiving comms but studied the animated telemetry first.

'It can't do that again,' the 'sect told him. 'Even S-tech material couldn't take it.'

'It deals with centrifugal forces that should tear it apart. The whole thing defies physics,' Benedict/Scab said. Unlike most people Benedict had actually studied physics. There was enough of him remaining for Benedict/Scab to understand the principles.

'I think you underestimate the amount of energy that just ran through the Cage,' the 'sect told him. Benedict/Scab was pretty sure the 'sect didn't have a name. 'For a moment it gave off more energy than some stars. That and the stress it's under,' the 'sect shook his head. 'It will need to cool down. Also whatever it did used about a third of the gas giant's mass.'

Benedict/Scab brought up an image of the planet. Telemetry was fed directly to his neunonics. It even looked smaller, though the Cage remained the same size. 'If it did it again I think it would collapse.'

It was clear the days of Cyst being left in peace were over.

Various scenarios were unfolding in Benedict/Scab's head from his 'face link to the *Templar*'s strategic and tactical simulation routines. Unless they were hiding a Church fleet in there, and if they were then they were very well hidden, he couldn't see what Scab was planning. Besides, the Church had other things to worry about at the moment, like being hunted by the Consortium.

'We have nothing to gain here,' Harold said.

Benedict/Scab sighed. Sure, being a pirate sounded like fun but the reality was that you had to walk a fine line balancing the wants, needs, and often-difficult personalities of his psychologically-compromised crew. You also had to kill them to make a point sometimes. Harold was useful and bloodthirsty, but he was wondering if a new pair of boots wouldn't rather elegantly make his point. *Too speciesist?* he wondered.

'Yes,' he said. 'Remind me, Harold, you were captured by Mr Hat, weren't you?' His lizard first mate didn't answer. 'We're going to move in closer. Keep as much of the planet as you can between us and those contractor squadrons and run as silent as you can.'

He opened the comms and saw his father/older self's features. Even he was surprised by the feelings of hate they engendered. The image had clearly been shot by a P-sat. It was on top of one of the ziggurats. Benedict/Scab could see the denizens of Cyst crowding round his father.

They should be mine. The thought had come unbidden.

'Let's end this,' his father/older self said, and that was it.

'He can't think I mean to face him one on one,' Benedict/Scab mused. Though he had to admit he wanted his father/older self to meet him, to be in the presence of something purer. He wanted to slay a king in front of his court. It would impress the denizens of Cyst, but he knew neither of them could be trusted enough for that to be anything even remotely approaching a fair fight.

He 'faced a copy of the comms message to all the crew, along with a referendum asking them if they were prepared to go after Scab. Scab and Vic had taken down a significant number of the possessing personalities, and those tended to be the really dangerous members of his crew. He knew, however, that the referendum would be seen as a sign of weakness, and he would probably have to kill some of them. He sighed. Enlightened self-interest just wasn't their thing.

22
Ancient Britain

Tangwen had spent most of her time in the Underworld. She was starting to get used to it, which didn't feel right. People should fear the Underworld, even if warriors had to learn to embrace that fear to a degree. Still, it was better than having to deal with the other warriors back at camp.

Whenever she went into the caves with Selbach, Germelqart had to wait for them above with the Red Chalice. The magics of the chalice, wielded by the Carthaginian, hid them from Crom Dhubh's wards. Germelqart had also found a way to use their own blood magic to lead them back to the surface, so they never got lost in the labyrinthine caves beneath the hills surrounding the valley. It was only in those moments, following the tiny lights through the caves, that she truly felt at peace with herself and the magics that had suddenly infused her life. However, both she and Selbach were sure that there was something else down here with them, something other than Crom Dhubh's forces. They had both heard and seen movement. Something small and fast, that didn't move like a rat, in a place where they had found almost no other life. Though they had managed to disturb a bear and a wolf pack on two separate occasions closer to the surface. It had been a shame to kill the bear, though the meat had been welcome, and the friendlier Brigante warriors had joked that she could become one of them. The carcass, even skinned and butchered, had been difficult to move. Unfortunately for the bear they had needed the cave.

Tangwen heaved herself out of the hole into the cave. Selbach was just behind her. She had dyed her clothes grey, as had Selbach, and both of them had painted their faces grey and streaked them with black. They looked like creatures of the earth, barely human. Tangwen was smiling, despite her aching limbs and shoulders. The smile faltered somewhat when she realised that Germelqart wasn't waiting for them. She closed her eyes and concentrated for a moment, the way that Germelqart had taught her. She could feel the web of magical wards, subtler than those of Crom's, stretching through the caverns below. There was nothing to suggest that the Dark Man had discovered their work.

Selbach was frowning, looking down at the rock floor. The snow encroached a little way into the cave. Tangwen could see Germelqart's tracks leading out into the ravine that cut its way through the southern hills bordering the valley. There were no other tracks, which was a relief at least. It looked like he had just wandered off, which angered Tangwen. He was supposed to be keeping a look out for them, and not just with the chalice's magics.

They had been working on the plan. Calgacus had been sceptical but had agreed to help. Guided by the *gwyllion*, the Cait warriors had left the warband, taking their chariots with them. The chariots had caused a great deal of difficulty for the Cait, much to the amusement of some of the southern warriors. They had also taken Twrch with them. The Parisi tribesman had been one of the survivors of the wicker man. He had been learning to work metal when the Lochlannach had taken him.

Anharad and some of the other warriors of position knew they were up to something, but Anharad trusted her and was content to leave Tangwen to it as long as she knew what was happening before Bladud returned. The sticking point, of course, was the Red Chalice. Nobody liked that it was out of the camp so much. Tangwen could understand their concerns. If the Lochlannach found them then there was a good chance that they would lose their greatest weapon. The Dark Man, however, seemed content to let them freeze and bicker among themselves.

Tangwen was starting to worry about Germelqart and the Red Chalice, though. He was inseparable from the chalice now. Even when not in the cave watching them through the vessel he would sit in his tent, blank-eyed, staring into its molten contents. Always quiet, the Carthaginian had become practically silent. She had wondered how much of it was being so far from his home, all his friends dead. For a moment she felt an ache as she remembered Kush.

Tangwen left the cave. She wasn't sure why she strung her bow and notched an arrow. Her grey form stood out against the white snow as she moved through the naked trees. Selbach followed a little way behind. He looked ready to bolt at any moment.

Germelqart was talking to a horseman. The horseman was wrapped up so tightly in thick furs that it looked like he feared the cold. Despite the layers of clothes Tangwen could see that his skin was a much darker brown than Germelqart's, though not as dark as Kush's had been. He had an unstrung bow, and arrows in an inscribed wooden case hanging from the saddle of his horse. A strangely curved sword hung from his hip in a scabbard, and he had a small round shield that looked to have been made of brass, an impractical metal for a shield, also hanging from his saddle. In fact the shield reminded her of the blades of Kush's axe. All of it looked too ornate and delicate to be of any practical use.

The horseman reached down towards Germelqart, but the Carthaginian shook his head and stepped back.

'So be it,' the horseman said, and kicked his heels into the horse's flanks. The horse took off at a gallop despite the deep snow. Tangwen hadn't recognised the horseman's accent and although she had understood the language, and knew it as an old one, she did not know to which people it belonged.

The horse looked slender and sleek, but not made for the harshness of Ynys Prydain during winter, though it had no problems making its way through the snow. Something about it reminded her of the red-eyed steeds from the Otherworld that Crom Dhubh had gifted to the Corpse People.

Germelqart did not turn around as she approached, though he must have known she was there. Selbach held back. He had been afraid of the foreign sorcerer since the Carthaginian had taken a lock of his hair.

'I am discovered,' the Carthaginian said as she came to stand by him.

'Who was he?' Tangwen asked. Trying not to make it sound accusatory.

'He was the servant of a demon and he wanted the chalice,' Germelqart told her, his voice flat. Tangwen's eyes widened and she spat and made the sign against evil.

'Do the gods not think that we have enough to cope with?' she asked. The last thing they needed was more trouble from the Otherworld. Germelqart just looked at her.

'Will this demon try and take it?' she demanded.

Germelqart turned to face her. 'He would have us give it to

272

him, but I think he will talk first. I think he may be right.' He touched the bag. 'Its power notwithstanding, I think there is only the madness here and the division it brings.'

She knew he was right. Suddenly she felt tired. Germelqart was right. Bladud was right. The warband needed and deserved the chalice. Guidgen was right. The chalice would lead to tyranny, however well intentioned its use. They were all right.

'It has to stay,' she told him, trying to keep the desperation out of her voice. Germelqart pursed his lips. He looked uncon-vinced. Tangwen narrowed her eyes. At first she had thought that Germelqart's eyes were bloodshot, but now she looked, she wondered if there weren't tendrils of red metal trying to creep into them.

'Look!' Selbach said. The three of them were making their way back down the southern ridgeline towards the camp. The Pecht scout was pointing at a figure on a horse making its way across the snow-covered fields to the north of them, towards the camp. The horse was clearly staggering, and then the beast toppled into the snow.

'Is that Britha?' Tangwen asked. There were people coming out from the camp towards the rider, who was trying to climb out from under the obviously distressed horse. Tangwen picked up the pace, kicking her way through the snow.

'Where are my husband and the others?' Anharad demanded. Mabon was standing next to his grandmother. He looked every inch the young warrior now, as Anharad looked the queen in her understated and still practical finery. Before he had left Bladud had given Mabon armour. A sword hung from the boy's hip as well. His arms were crossed, brows furrowed in distaste.

'Behind me. I rode ahead,' Britha told them. She looked thin and haggard, Tangwen thought as she entered the skin shelter. It was Britha's hag aspect. Tangwen was immediately worried for the child that Britha carried. A brazier and the press of people were keeping the shelter warm. 'Why are you surprised to see me back?' Britha all but demanded.

'I am surprised when someone who has been in the counsel of our enemy, someone who has drunk of the chalice, and been blessed by its magics, comes back without the people she trav-elled with.'

'Not just in their counsel,' one of the Trinovantes warriors said suggestively. There was answering laughter. Britha turned to give him a look that would have withered crops on the stalk. He stared back at her insolently. It was clear that she had lost the respect due her position, at least among some of the warriors.

'If you have an accusation to make, then make it. Then you can fail to prove it and owe me compensation,' Britha snapped. 'Don't pour poison into the ears of those here with insinuations. You insult all and disgrace yourself when you do.' To Tangwen's ears it was overly harsh but it was obvious that Britha was exhausted, despite her gifts.

'You killed a horse getting here,' Garim, the big warrior now in charge of the Brigante *teulu*, said.

'More than one,' Britha told him in exasperation but making her honesty look instinctual, as it should be.

'A Brigante horse which we will need to be compensated for,' Garim continued. Britha nodded impatiently. 'But it makes you look like you were running from something.'

'I was just hoping that you hadn't all been killed while we wasted our time,' Britha said.

'You need to look to that child in your belly,' Anharad said, nodding towards where the lump was more prominent on Britha's emaciated frame. Tangwen caught the flicker of guilt, but only because she knew the *ban draoi*, then Britha's face hardened.

'Or to dig it out,' someone muttered. Britha's head snapped round.

'Who said that?' she demanded, but all that met her were stony faces. 'Which coward said that and now hides?'

'Britha,' Tangwen said. Germelqart had only just caught up with her and was trying to push his way into the tent. Selbach was presumably outside avoiding all the people of rank.

'If you'll excuse me,' Britha said. 'I need to speak with Tangwen.'

'You have not told us the news of Ynys Dywyll,' Anharad said. There were nods from many of the assembled warriors.

Calgacus pushed his way into the tent. The small Pecht *rhi* made warriors much bigger than him step aside. His scarred, seemingly humourless, blonde charioteer was with him.

'Can you tell them what I say?' Calgacus asked Tangwen. She was pleased he had stopped demanding she translate. 'Poor hospitality this, that all of rank are called except myself.' He made a point of looking around. 'And the *gwyllion*, I see. Particularly,' he nodded at Britha, 'when it is my kinswoman returned from a fool's journey.'

Anharad at least had the manners to look embarrassed.

'I am about the business of Ynys Dywyll,' Britha said, 'and I need to speak with Tangwen, and Germelqart. Will you excuse me?' The Pecht *dryw* didn't wait. Instead she turned and pushed her way through the warriors who would not make way for her. One or two were shoved aside by Calgacus.

'Tangwen, we need to hear your plan,' Anharad said. 'Before Bladud returns.'

'Anharad, I ... you will, but peace, let me speak with Britha.' She turned and followed Britha out of the skin tent before Anharad could insist.

'What is it?' Tangwen asked as they fell in with the Pecht *dryw*. She noticed that Britha did not have her spear.

'I need to gorge myself, and quickly,' the *dryw* snapped in the language of the Pecht.

'My camp?' Calgacus asked.

'My presence may bring trouble your way,' Britha told him.

'Excellent!' Calgacus said.

'They will say I killed the arch *dryw*,' Britha told them. Calgacus and Tangwen stopped dead in the snow. Britha kept on trudging towards the Cait *teulu*'s campfire.

Britha told them her version of events on Ynys Dywyll as she gorged herself on the Cait's food. The warriors had looked on, appalled by her story, and the *dryw*'s gluttony. They spat and made the sign against evil as her form filled out again in front of their eyes.

They talked openly in front of the *teulu* because it was rude to talk in private and because among the southrons only Bladud, and those infused with the magics of the chalice, could speak the language of the Pecht.

Tangwen couldn't help it. There was some part of her that wondered if Britha had actually killed the arch *dryw*, or if perhaps this was a story. The *ban draoi* was certainly capable of killing Bladud, but everything she had told them, her actions, and the way she was behaving, suggested that she was being pursued.

'It's a sore thing to kill a *dryw*,' Calgacus said, and not for the first time. 'A sore thing indeed.'

Tangwen could believe almost anything of Madawg and the

Corpse People, but they had grown up in the same land that she had. You did not harm a *dryw*. It was the worst crime imaginable and only foreigners ever tried. When she had mentioned this Britha had pointed out that they had attacked her during the siege on the Crown of Andraste. Though, thinking back, Tangwen was more of the opinion that she had attacked them. 'So Bladud will come back here and ...'

'Probably burn me,' Britha said. 'Any trial will have happened on the isle. I'm assuming that Moren is arch *dryw*, now.' Britha all but spat the name of the young ambitious *dryw*.

'So why come back?' Calgacus asked.

Britha closed her eyes. 'The Lochla ... Bress has something I need. I had ... have another child, taken from me by the fair folk. Bress has the key to help me get her back.'

Calgacus raised his eyebrows. 'Eurneid used to scare the children, me included when I was younger, with stories of all the terrifying things that ride the night winds. It seems I had to travel south to find them all.'

'Bladud will demand the chalice,' Tangwen said.

Germelqart, who had been listening, no expression on his features, his eyes catching the reflection of the flames, stood up. 'It is time,' he said to Tangwen.

'Time for what?' Britha asked.

'To speak with a demon,' Tangwen said.

Calgacus's eyes went wide. 'Now this I have to see.' He stood up and reached for his sword.

'Surely this demon will just pull all our heads off and take the chalice?' Calgacus asked. He sounded quite cheerful for someone climbing a steep hill in pitch darkness. Tangwen, Germelqart, Britha, and Selbach – who was following them a way back – might all be able to see clearly in the night, but Calgacus had no such gift. Tangwen was thankful for the clear night and the three-quarters moon.

'For someone called Bitter Tongue you seem in love with the wonders of this world and the next,' Tangwen said, smiling at the short, northern *rhi*'s enthusiasm.

'These southern lands are exciting!' Calgacus said. 'And full of weaklings.'

Tangwen heard the sound of an owl on the wing. She turned back to look at Selbach. The scout was pointing up at an

escarpment that overlooked the valley. At first the figure standing on it reminded her of Kush. A tall, powerful man, with very
dark skin, and the features of those from far to the south, but
where Kush had been wiry, and slender, this man was heavy
set, fleshy and running to fat. Nor had Kush had bands of brass
embedded in the skin of his head. Most disturbing, however, was
the smooth, thick metal that curved round where one of his eyes
should be. The metal around his eye also seemed embedded in
his flesh. As they approached the man turned to look at them,
smiling. There was something in the brass around his eyes. The
material was like crystal but clearer, like looking through clear,
solid water without the obscuration of ice.

Just back from the top of the hill were three riders and four
horses. The magnificent horses seemed eerily still and silent. The
riders were clearly watching Tangwen and the others, but they
had no weapons in their hands. Calgacus waved at them. They
ignored him.

'This is no demon but surely a man who does not know when
to stop with adornment,' Calgacus opined loudly. Tangwen saw
Britha grimace. Germelqart looked less than pleased.

'I am a demon wearing the flesh of a man, bound into service
by my lord Solomon,' the man said. He spoke the Pecht tongue
perfectly. His voice was deep and rich, his accent strange, and
disappointingly not that similar to Kush's.

'Never heard of him,' Calgacus said, making it clear in his tone
that his lack of knowledge of the demon's lord was a personal
weakness on the part of this Solomon.

'Indeed,' the demon said. 'He is well known enough in his
land, and those surrounding them, but that is far from here. How
many demons do you have bound to you, great king?'

Calgacus narrowed his eyes. 'Do you make sport with me,
demon?'

'A little.' The demon's smile made it clear all was a jest, but the
smile did not quite make it to the one remaining good eye.

'Where I come from we do not consort with the gods. Demons
are lesser things, evil creatures from Cythrawl. Why would I bind
them to me?'

'Power,' the demon said.

Tangwen liked the raw honesty of the answer.

'I am sure that this Solomon is a mighty lord,' Britha started.
'But we are being rude.' She introduced Calgacus, Tangwen,

herself and finally Germelqart in order of their stations. She sounded as if the formality and politeness were proving a strain.

'And the other one?' the demon asked, looking down into the darkness.

'His name is Selbach the Timid. He is one of my scouts,' Calgacus told him. 'And we have still not heard your name.' Tangwen heard Germelqart's sharp intake of breath, answered by the demon's low rumbling laugh.

'Germelqart is known to me, though I have never met him,' the demon started. The others turned to look at the Carthaginian but he stared straight ahead. 'I am called Azmodeus, though my name is my own.'

'A poor frightened thing who will not say his name,' Calgacus muttered.

'It is kept for me by my lord and master.'

Calgacus turned to Britha. 'Why am I, as a *mormaer*, conversing with a slave?' he demanded. Tangwen was pretty sure it was for show. Trying to establish dominance. She saw Britha sigh. The smile had gone from Azmodeus's face.

'He is an honoured servant,' Germelqart snapped. It was unusual to hear the Carthaginian angry.

'Sounds like a sl—' Calgacus started.

'Enough!' Britha snapped. Calgacus turned to look at her, one eyebrow raised. 'I'm sorry, but we don't have time for this.' Then to Azmodeus: 'Please tell us why you have come.'

'May I examine it?' Azmodeus asked.

Germelqart took the chalice out of his bag and handed it to the demon. Tangwen's hand was on her hatchet and dagger. Britha was moving towards the demon, and Calgacus had his hand on the hilt of his sword.

'Peace, please,' Azmodeus said. Tangwen glanced over at the riders; they hadn't moved, hadn't drawn weapons. She was wondering why she had agreed to the meeting. Though she wasn't sure she had exactly. Germelqart just seemed dead set on this course of action.

With the chalice in one hand, the demon closed his eye and took a deep breath. There was a silver glow from his brass-encased eye.

'The small god in here is almost unbroken and whole of mind,' he finally said, exhaling. He held the Red Chalice up. 'So much power in here. It will drive all who know of it to madness.'

'And you would spare us this?' Tangwen asked. The demon turned to look at her.

'That's good of you,' Calgacus said.

'Tell me that you would not see yourself relieved of this burden and we will speak no more.'

Tangwen slumped slightly. She did not like Azmodeus holding the chalice because she knew she might have to fight to get it back, because they needed it, but even the vessel being in someone else's hands, however fleetingly, seemed like a weight lifted from their shoulders.

'We have seen this before. My master is a mighty sorcerer; we understand and know how to treat with the small gods.'

'There is a great evil here,' Britha said.

'I know,' Azmodeus said.

'We need the chalice, but we need allies as well.'

'We are not warriors, we are scholars,' Azmodeus said. Calgacus opened his mouth to say something but Britha motioned him to be quiet. 'However, if you would be prepared to give us this Red Chalice once you have finished your war, then we could perhaps come to an agreement as regards our aid.'

'How can scholars aid us?' Calgacus asked. The demon turned to look at him.

'The magics they have at their command,' Germelqart told the Cait *mormaer*.

Calgacus looked unconvinced, though Tangwen was thankful for him keeping his peace. Tangwen had to admit it was an attractive offer. Effectively it would become someone else's problem. She could see Britha considering the demon's words. Britha turned to look at her, the question in her eyes.

'And what of those already blessed by the chalice? And the weapons it makes?' Tangwen said.

'What is given can be taken away. Weapons rust away to nothing. Heroes blaze like fire, until the oil is burned away,' Azmodeus told them. 'The little god will give you much, you just need to be careful how you ask for it. They are very literal. It is like bargaining with the *djinn*.'

Tangwen had no idea what a *djinn* was, but his words were making sense to her. She was beginning to think she saw a solution to some of their problems at least.

'No,' Tangwen said. 'I thank you for your offer, and demon or not, I think it was honestly meant, but we cannot.'

'You would have this power for yourself?' Azmodeus asked. He sounded disappointed.

'I would give anything to never have laid eyes on the accursed thing,' she said.

'Then we have a solution,' Germelqart said.

She could hear the irritation in his voice, and something else. *Is it desperation?* she wondered. She turned to look at the Carthaginian. 'If we let them take the chalice, would you be going with them?'

The answer was written all over his face. Tangwen was starting to think that Germelqart needed some time away from the chalice. She turned back to Azmodeus. 'When we defeat Crom Dhubh, what then? Because there is more power like this out there, isn't there? The power to enslave, to make stronger, create demons, and foul weapons.' Azmodeus nodded. 'So what happens the next time? And there's your—'

'We mean you no harm,' Azmodeus said.

'Now.'

The demon held the chalice up again. 'A nation of undefeatable immortals? It will lead to madness and tyranny, however well intentioned its beginnings, and that madness and tyranny will spread.' As he said this Tangwen could not help but glance down towards the warband's camp. 'And then my lord and master will send me, and more like me, and we will become enemies. I would not see this.'

'Then it must be controlled,' Britha said. 'And they must be made to fear it.'

'And then it must be hidden,' Tangwen added.

'And only used when needed?' Azmodeus asked. 'I have heard this before.'

'We are as subject to weakness as anyone else, but we can try,' Tangwen said.

'I counsel against this,' Germelqart said. He looked at Calgacus for support.

'I mislike the thing. Our own strength and skill should be enough ...' The Pecht *mormaer's* voice trailed off. 'But I saw the giants.' Then he looked up at Azmodeus. 'And now I think you should give that back.'

Azmodeus looked down at the Red Chalice as though he was surprised to find it still in his hand. He studied it as though he was coming to a decision. Finally he held it out to Tangwen. She reached up to take it from him but he did not let go of it immediately. His skin was warm despite the coldness of the night. Now it was her he studied.

'Power burns,' he told her. 'Some who drink from the chalice may not be strong enough to contain the fire.' He relinquished the chalice.

It took her a moment but she understood. She glanced over at Britha, to see that the *dryw* had understood as well. She did not look happy. It was not a thing that either of them could do. She turned to look at Germelqart. He looked less than pleased but it was clear he also understood. Calgacus thankfully remained oblivious.

Tangwen looked over at the horses.

'They're very well behaved,' she said.

Azmodeus smiled. 'Alchemy.'

Tangwen nodded to the demon and turned to head back down the hill but she stopped.

'You know what we face is evil,' she said, looking over her shoulder.

Azmodeus did not immediately answer. 'I think it is more complicated than that. I understand it is a blight on all, but you refused our bargain.'

Tangwen nodded and continued on her way.

23
Now

Du Bois knew he was in trouble the moment he came to. The pain in his wrists and ankles told him that. On the other hand he was quite surprised that he was still alive. The last thing he remembered was Beth with a gun held to his head.

He was lying on the dusty ground. Looking around he could see he was on a dirt road surrounded by scrub undergrowth, interspersed with cacti. He could see mountains in the distance. He guessed they were somewhere in the southern Sonora Desert. It looked so peaceful. They were on high ground and he could see for miles. He approved. Beth would be able to see anyone coming. The only problem was it left them vulnerable to the Circle's air and space assets.

He felt weak but his neuralware told him that he was mostly healed. He had been out for the better part of eight hours. Beth had used up at least three of the IV bags feeding him replacement matter to allow his body to rebuild itself and heal. Du Bois thought this was a bit wasteful, bearing in mind he was now cable-tied at the wrist and ankles and had chains around his legs attached to the back of the ECV. It looked like she intended to drag him. It would never kill him. He couldn't say he was looking forward to it, however.

Alexia was lying face-down nearby. She too was cable-tied but then Beth had further cable-tied her wrists and ankles together, leaving his sister lying with her spine arched back in a stress position.

Beth herself was leaning against the back of the ECV, drinking from her canteen.

'I know you're both awake,' the ex-convict from Bradford said. 'I heard your breathing change.'

'Thank you for reattaching my arm,' Alexia said. Du Bois wondered how she had lost the arm. He wasn't even all that sure what had happened to him. According to his neuralware it was massive kinetic trauma to the chest. Mueller, he guessed, probably with one of the big anti-materiel rifles. Beth would have had to hold the arm to Alexia's stump and then use the IVs to help rebuild the matter. He wondered how many more of the IVs they had left. Though he suspected it might be a moot point for him now.

'Let Alexia go,' du Bois said. 'She's got nothing to do with this.'

'I don't want to hurt her,' Beth started. 'But—'

'Hurt my brother and I'll kill you,' Alexia said evenly. She really meant it. He could hear it in her voice. Du Bois felt a surge of affection for Alexia.

'So that's a problem,' Beth said. 'I'll leave her in the desert with some supplies.' Du Bois supposed it was the best he could ask for, given the situation.

'Bitch!' Alexia spat.

'You, on the other hand,' she told du Bois. 'You're coming with me. I'm not sure where I'm going—'

'The DAYP—' du Bois started.

'Shut up, shut up, shut up!' she screamed, and stormed over to him and started kicking him with her steel-toecapped para boots. She put the boot in like she knew what she was doing. A backstreet Bradford kicking from a bouncer in the middle of the Arizona desert. He felt a number of his ribs go, reinforced bone broken by augmented musculature. She stopped kicking him and staggered away from him, sobs wracking her body but of course no tears. 'Why don't any of you understand that what you do has consequences?' she screamed. 'Mothers, fathers, brothers, sisters, lovers, children, even just friends! Every single fucking person you kill! And now I'm just like you! There's no fucking good fight! Just people hurting other people!'

She might be right, du Bois thought. It had been such a long time since he had thought about it. He wondered when he had become a psychopath, or perhaps he was just numb now. He certainly wasn't a human any more, he realised.

'Beth—' Alexia started.

'He killed my father! And raped that girl!'

Du Bois knew he had killed her father. That had been his job, but the rape? Mr Brown would have had to have extensively re-written his personality and edited his memories for him to have been capable of that. Azmodeus had said he had removed the editing but could not replace what was missing. If this was still him, if neither Azmodeus nor Mr Brown had done something that fundamentally changed him, if they hadn't manipulated him further, then he just wasn't capable of it. He had taken his oaths seriously – to an extent he still did, some of them anyway. He remembered lying battered and bleeding in the streets of Acre because he had tried to stop members of his order from raping when they had taken the city. He remembered the censure he had received for his interference. He remembered his disgust. That was when he had decided to walk out into the desert. To go looking for an answer to his then-brother's plight. Had all that been a lie? Had Azmodeus left a rewritten personality intact because he was a better person now? Had he been even more monstrous?

'Did you kill her father?' Alexia asked.

'Yes,' du Bois said.

'Did it even bother you?' Beth asked. She sounded calmer but he could hear the emotion just under the surface.

'I felt no compunction about killing him,' du Bois told her. 'He was a child thief.'

'He thought you were breeding them for sacrifice! You were breeding them to harvest their genetic material!'

'What's she talking about?' Alexia asked.

'I heard what he said to you, the last time,' du Bois said quietly. Beth screamed. She stormed over to him again. Du Bois was expecting another kicking. *Do I want her to punish me?* he wondered. This time she drew the Colt. He found himself looking down the pistol's barrel wondering if it was loaded with the nano-tipped bullets. He could see her finger squeezing the trigger. Then she screamed again, lowered the pistol and fired once, kneecapping him. He screamed. The pain was appalling. Then augmented biochemistry stamped down on it. Only his armoured skin and reinforced bone structure had stopped the hydrostatic shock from the injury blowing off his leg. It wasn't a nano-tipped bullet, however.

Alexia was screaming at Beth, threats, insults, pleading. Beth was holding the gun against her own face, trying to calm herself enough to function. Beth pointed the Colt at him again, her face a red mask of rage. She stalked back over and stamped on his injured knee. He howled as the pain overwhelmed his augmented nervous system.

'I'm sorry I hurt you,' du Bois said, when he had recovered enough to use speech. 'And I have no excuse. I killed him because I was told to, because it was my job ...'

'He was on oxygen, you bastard! He couldn't even fucking defend himself!'

Alexia was staring at him, appalled. 'You killed a differently abled person?'

Now he was angry.

'What do you think paid for your lifestyle all these centuries?' he demanded. Alexia looked like she had been slapped. He looked back at Beth. 'I didn't like him, so I felt no guilt when I killed him. I barely thought about it.'

'Shut up!' Alexia shouted at him.

Beth threw herself down onto her knees next to him. She jammed the barrel of the gun against his face. He suspected she had thought this would play out differently. She would be calm, her anger a cold fury, and she would deliver justice.

'He was my dad! He might not have been much, but he was my dad! He wasn't even Talia's real dad and ...' Her voice tailed off. Her face seemed to crumple as it was wracked by a dry sob. 'You're trying to make me kill you, aren't you?'

'I'm sorry,' he told her. 'For you, but only for you, for my part in all of this. Do what you have to.'

Beth stood up and started walking back to the ECV. She opened the boot and dumped out du Bois's pack, as well as the rifle and the pistol that Karma had given them. He now suspected that Karma had given them the weapons because he had known that Alexia was still alive. Beth put them down on the ground.

'No, wait!' Alexia shouted. 'Don't listen to him! Don't do what you have to! You know that this is what that evil bastard wants! Right?'

Beth hesitated.

'Mr Brown was trying to drive a wedge between you both. Don't play into his hands, please. I mean, where are you going to go from here?'

Du Bois could see enough of Beth's face from where he was lying to know that she didn't have an answer.

'Maybe I'll just live in the desert,' Beth said quietly, looking around.

'He made a mistake, he killed the wrong person ...' Alexia started.

Du Bois cringed internally. Beth rounded on his sister.

'You know the first person I killed? He was my sister's boy-friend. He'd hurt her before, badly, and this time I was sure he was going to kill her. So I beat him to death, with my bare hands. I went too far, it was a mistake. They called that mistake man-slaughter and I went to prison. It wasn't premeditated, like your brother's *mistake*. See, where I come from what he did to my dad would be called murder, but there's no accountability for people like you, is there?'

'She's right,' du Bois said.

'Shut up, Malcolm, just shut up!' Alexia snapped. 'What about accountability for Mr Brown? Malcolm was just a tool.'

There was just a moment of indecision. Then Beth dropped the pack on the desert floor and laid the rifle and the pistol on top.

'What about Grace?' she asked coldly, and started walking towards the cab of the ECV.

'My brother did not rape that girl,' Alexia said. Du Bois was pathetically grateful to hear the total conviction in her voice. Beth stopped and turned around.

'Do you not think I've seen this before, the loved ones remain-ing loyal to the accused? Mr Brown was right. You kill in cold blood. You've probably killed thousands. What the hell differ-ence would one rape mean to you?'

'It's different—' du Bois managed.

'He may be a monster, but not that kind of monster,' Alexia said, cutting him off. 'I can tell you all the things that he's done that could prove this. He has no place in this century. His mind-set is medieval, he can rationalise killing all the people, and still think himself a protector of women. I'm telling you he didn't do it. This is one of Mr Brown's tricks, and you're giving him exactly what he wants. And then what? Are you going to go after the guy who actually ordered your father's death?'

Beth looked stricken. He could understand why. Mr Brown was too big, too alien. After what they had seen in the Boneyard, Karma's pretty extensive assassination attempt, he didn't even know what his erstwhile boss was. Let alone how to kill him.

'You were just going to take it out on my brother, weren't you?' Alexia said from her uncomfortable position on the ground.

'Were?' Beth asked. 'First I'm going to drag him.'

'Beth,' du Bois said, 'you know I can get out of this, if I want?' He held up his cable-tied wrists. She had taken the belt buckle knife but all he would have to do was chew open his skin and let the nanites in his blood-screen eat away at the cable ties.

'We might not know how to kill Mr Brown,' Alexia said, 'but let's at least fuck his life up.'

'If you want to kill me after, I'll let you,' du Bois told her, and right then, right there, he meant it. He could feel Alexia staring at him.

'Will you just stop helping?' Alexia snapped.

Du Bois watched as Beth unsheathed the bayonet. Part of him was hoping that she was going to stab him with it. It was the least he deserved. She didn't. Instead she cut him free. Then she held the blade in front of his face.

'You need to know I will never forgive you,' Beth told him. He nodded. She stood up. 'So did your groin grow back okay?' she asked. He didn't really want to think too much about Grace shooting him in his nether regions. The thought still made him flinch and the new flesh was still tender. He just nodded. His howls echoed over the desert as steel toecaps connected with new testicles three times in quick succession.

They had tried to avoid the main routes into Los Angeles as much as possible. The highways had looked as bad as the M25 around London had. Except some of the vehicles were moving and there were a lot more guns. Despite eschewing the main routes there had still been trouble on the road and they had left behind bullet-ridden vehicles with corpses inside.

They had travelled in an uncomfortable silence. Du Bois had sat in the passenger seat manning the M240B general-purpose machine gun. Beth had spent most of the time standing up in the ECV's minigun turret, ignoring the du Bois siblings. Ignoring her father's murderer. Alexia had done the driving. Du Bois had done a contact upload of his skills to his sister, much as he had with Beth in Portsmouth. Alexia had some skills of her own, but she hadn't been one of the Circle's operatives like he had. Physically she wouldn't be quite as capable or fast as he was, or as Beth seemed to be, and although she'd been in fights in the past she didn't have his experience. She would, however, be able to handle herself better than before.

Karma had given them a prototype Beretta ARX-170 assault rifle, again chambered for the 7.62mm that he and Beth were using in their principal weapons, and a Beretta 8045 Cougar semi-automatic pistol. The Cougar was chambered for .45 calibre rounds like du Bois and Beth's sidearms.

'Both Italian,' Alexia had said, unimpressed. 'They'll go with my shoes.'

They had raided an outdoor suppliers for practical clothes and footwear for Alexia, and then du Bois had shown her how to use the nanites in her blood to armour her clothes and make them self-cleaning.

Alexia had told him that after the surprise gig, she and the band had gone up to Ithaca, in the Finger Lakes region of upstate New York, to use a friend's recording studio. They'd had a limited window of opportunity, and had driven out of New York straight after the gig. If not she would have been caught when the nuke had gone off.

She had to wipe a tear off her cheek when she told him about the phones starting to ring. She had known there was something wrong but the rest of the band had answered their phones, or had been on their laptops, or tablets. She had been forced to kill two of them herself with her knives.

'I don't think we feel like real people any more,' she had told her brother. 'How can I have done that and still function? We're too old, too dislocated.' He thought she was right. He had been thinking a lot about all the people he had killed. It was a problem with perfect recall.

They had skirted the saline lake that was the Salton Sea. They had caught sight of Los Angeles as they had come over the San Jacinto Mountains. It looked a little darker than du Bois remembered it being. He could see the faint glow of distant flames in some areas, but the streetlights were still on, spreading out before them like a strangely regular constellation of stars. Some of the smaller sources of light seemed to be flickering on and off. Du Bois knew that was the muzzle flashes from gunfire, but from where they stood the city looked to have weathered the storm pretty well.

It was a different story when they finally made it into the city proper. In the daylight they saw broad avenues lined with palm trees and crucifixions. They saw pimps with prostitutes on leads with stigmata, piles of naked corpses at intersections, oily black smoke curling into the air accompanied by the smell of burning fat.

Behind the walls of gated communities with armed guards, micro-societies based on atrocity were being born. The highways seemed like a separate city, fighting its own war with itself, either at speed or in gridlock. In the poorer areas apartment blocks, streets, and neighbourhoods were all fortified. The American Civil War had broken out again.

The brutality had come out of the alleys and spilled onto the streets. It was in the open now. LA was revelling in its past misdeeds, putting them on display where once it had kept them coyly hidden. It wasn't titillation any more, it was self indulgence. Screaming was the city's ambient soundtrack.

The Los Angeles Police Department was mobilised and militarised, though it was difficult to imagine what laws they were enforcing. Du Bois had seen an LAPD armoured car pulling a line of chained-up prisoners. He couldn't shake the feeling they were slaves for auction. The ECV was reflected in the blank mirror-shade eyes of the police as they passed but it seemed they respected a well-armed, armoured vehicle enough to leave it alone.

Bloody street religions were breaking out on the corners vacated by the drugs trade. The dealers had moved into more respectable premises now: shops, bars, markets, warehouses and churches.

Du Bois watched as a bloody, naked man was chased down in the street, past the oblivious and uncaring. He all but knocked over a man dressed as Jesus carrying a cross. The naked man's pursuers knocked him over and started to carve his flesh. Jesus shuffled past. There was something faintly amphibious about the penitent.

'I always wondered what this place really looked like,' Alexia had muttered quietly from behind the steering wheel. Du Bois knew she'd seen some bad times in the city during the late forties, early fifties, and then again in the eighties.

Du Bois, Alexia and Beth were all running blood-screens, replacing the lost matter with sips from the high-energy drinks they carried with them. They had time to release the nanites slowly, through their pores. It was more than just the attack on the communications network that was affecting the city. They had detected the Seeder spores in the air. Du Bois knew they must have come from Kanamwayso. The nanites were sweeping in across the Pacific Rim, penetrating further and further into the

Americas, Asia, and Oceania. Eventually they would be carried across the world.

Du Bois's blood-screen had analysed the Seeder spores. Each of them was a tiny biological nanomachine. They were smarter, and more sophisticated than the spores from the Seeder in the Solent. They weren't simply about consumption and creation. The Seeders were reshaping the city, and eventually the world, in the form of humanity's own twisted reflection seen through the filter of vast, unknowable, alien minds long since driven irrevocably insane.

There had been killing. No matter how hard they tried to avoid it. How often they had tried to speed away. Bodies came apart when hit by the kinds of weapons the ECV was carrying. Their constituent parts splattered to the pavement as bullets tore through cheap tract housing. Du Bois was more than sick of it now. Though if anything there had been a lot less of it than he had expected. It seemed that the extreme social Darwinism of the city was respecting their show of strength. For a moment du Bois had wondered if the city somehow knew they were apex predators. Then he suppressed the thought as disgusting.

They had decided before entering the city that it was going to be unlikely that they would be able to reason with anyone who might know where La Calavera was. Du Bois had concentrated, programmed some of his blood, and then dripped it into a syringe before eating one of the high-energy bars. They could use the nanites in the syringe to try and compel one of the insane to talk, if they could find someone who had the information they needed.

They had found themselves in a tangled warren of hilly streets and narrow canyons. Many of the rundown houses had small cliffs in the garden, or were supported by stilts. Naked children ate road kill in the streets, while armed men and women in gang colours kept watch from the rooftops of apartment buildings. They had found someone wearing gang colours on their own. After a chase, du Bois had thrown himself out of the moving ECV and taken the gang member down. Alexia had parked up, bullets from the rooftops bouncing off their vehicle's armour. Tracers had drawn lines of light from the barrel of Beth's minigun to the rooftops. Devastatingly accurate suppressing fire ate through lowest-bidder building material and spread gunmen across the rooftops.

LAPD did not respond.

They'd only had to do it three more times before they found someone who knew where to find La Calavera. He might have been king of the city but he had moved out of the barrio.

The studios were still running. Du Bois didn't want to think about what kind of films they were making. They headed up Mulholland Drive. There seemed to be a party, bacchanal, or orgy going on in each of the huge houses set back from the road. The Hollywood sign was still intact as they made their way through the Hollywood Hills, skirting the Los Angeles basin, and once again looking down on the lights of the city. The road was very dark. Occasionally they saw terrified people in the head-lights as they darted across the road in front of them, trying to escape the parties in the big houses. They had seen well-armed private security personnel patrolling the area. One of the security operator's four-wheel drive vehicles had a badly bleeding young man tied to the bonnet. Du Bois suspected it was one of the escapees.

They were still travelling in silence. Beth had said very little since she'd repeatedly kicked him in the balls. The silence had become more and more tense as the road wound down into Laurel Canyon. Du Bois kept on glancing over at his sister. He wanted to ask her about her time in LA but he didn't.

Compared to the rest of the city, Laurel Canyon was very quiet. Du Bois wondered if that was because everyone was dead. Side roads ran up between quirky homes built into one side of the canyon, and they could see very little movement or light. That changed when they found the castle.

The whole place was lit up, an aggressive hybrid of Latino rap and extremely heavy metal booming from a PA somewhere. Bodies hung from the windows and faux battlements. Heavily tattooed, armed guards sporting gang colours patrolled the bat-tlements and the area in front of the 'castle'. The building even had its own drawbridge, which was currently down. Du Bois guessed it was supposed to be a Norman castle. It had a courtyard filled with muscle cars, pickup trucks and SUVs, many of which were currently having crude armour plate welded to them. Du Bois even caught a glimpse of a 6×6 military transport vehicle in the courtyard, but the whole thing, to his eyes, as a Norman, looked a lot more American than any European castle. Still, its defensive qualities were slightly better than the average house, and it provided a commanding view down the canyon.

'What do you want to do now?' Alexia asked.

'Are you okay?' du Bois asked, hearing the tension in his sister's voice. He got the feeling that she didn't want to look around at her surroundings. They were parked a little way from the castle.

'I don't like being here,' she said. 'What do you want to do now?'

'Drive up slowly, they start firing, back away. If they don't open up on us then turn the ECV around so we can get away quickly. Beth, I'll need you to cover me.' He took the absence of a reply as an affirmative.

The guards seemed confident despite an armoured and armed military vehicle creeping up the hill towards the castle. The guards by the drawbridge turned to watch them as they approached but they didn't level their weapons. One of them did run into the courtyard, however. Du Bois climbed out of the patrol vehicle. He had his carbine slung across his chest but no weapons in his hands. He walked carefully towards the closest guard. The guard laughed at his approach. Du Bois could see it in his eyes, in the piercings that pinched the flesh running up his bare, tattooed arms, arms that looked like the product of prison yard weights and steroids. The guard had answered his phone. This wasn't a person standing in front of him. This was the madness given human form, a platform for atrocity.

'You're brave,' the guard said in Spanish.

'I want to speak to La Calavera,' du Bois replied in the same language. The guard's laughter was little more than a humourless bark.

'See, people say things like that, friend, then they get to speak to him.' He shrugged over-developed shoulders. 'He's talkative. Then they realise they've made a mistake.'

'Please, help me?' It was a female voice. She sounded broken. The guard backed away, keeping his eye on the ECV. Du Bois turned to the figure walking across the drawbridge towards him with what he initially thought were two large dogs on leads. Du Bois's experience with the tech notwithstanding, it was one of the strangest figures he had ever seen, and he had a talking serpent living in the cellar of his home.

The figure was short, squat, hugely muscled, almost unnaturally so. It had very broad shoulders for its two heads. One of the heads was male, shorn of hair, the skin covered by a full-sized skull tattoo. The other head was female, a dishevelled, attractive brunette with tears running down her cheeks. She looked as though she could barely understand what was going on. Du Bois's eyes widened. It wasn't making much sense to him either.

'Help me.' Her eyes were pleading with him. The creatures on leads weren't dogs. They were people, in ragged, torn business suits, their physiology changed to enable them to move on all fours better. Their teeth and jaws had been surgically altered. They had tattoos of red open mouths on their faces, running down onto their necks to make them look more predatory. The two-headed figure held the chains of his mutated human pets in one hand, in the other, a ball gag.

'You remember her from TV?' the skull-faced head asked. Du Bois just shook his head, though his neuralware was telling him who she was. He assumed the male head was La Calavera. The woman was somehow this monster's victim.

'Please ...' she started, and then the ball gag was placed in her mouth, her eyes still begging for release. Du Bois found he couldn't speak. La Calavera yanked on the chains of the two surgically altered humans, bringing them to heel.

'You grow attached to dogs, even the cocks, but studio execs? I wanted some properly vicious animals. And they like it, *esé*, I mean they really like it. These are some hungry motherfuckers.' The skull wasn't grinning at him. Du Bois was calculating how to kill everyone here. In some ways he was impressed that even now he could still be appalled. La Calavera leaned towards du Bois, who had to resist the urge to step back. 'Nothing's changed, people have just lost some inhibitions.' There was nothing alien about the madness in the strange two-headed man's eyes. Du Bois did not know where La Calavera came from, how he'd got hold of the tech he had – the neck thing was something that du Bois had never even heard of – but his viciousness, his cruelty, was human-born. And he had his own blood-screen. It was more sophisticated than du Bois's own.

'The Do As You Please Clan,' du Bois managed.

La Calavera leaned back and pointed at du Bois.

'I know who you are. You famous, *mano*.' He seemed to be waiting for a reply. Du Bois didn't trust himself to do so. The woman's eyes. 'You know I was hired to kill you.' Now the skull-tattooed head had his full attention. 'Oh yeah, you listening now.'

'Who?' du Bois snarled.

'Relax, I don't need your kind of trouble and I have everything I want.' Du Bois opened his mouth. 'Now, don't spoil it all by being disrespectful up in my crib.'

'What do you want?' du Bois asked, barely controlling himself.

'Left alone, like I said. I don't need your kind of trouble.'

'Who hired you to kill me?' du Bois demanded.

La Calavera smiled. 'Tezcatlipoca,' he said. The Smoking Mirror, the obsidian god in Aztec mythology.

'Mr Brown?' du Bois asked.

'I told you what I know.'

'The DAYP?' du Bois all but demanded. La Calavera was shaking his head. 'Don't ...' he started angrily, but La Calavera stepped towards him.

'Don't bark at me,' his voice low and dangerous. 'You don't want me wearing your head.' Du Bois swallowed hard. He wanted to break this creature with his bare hands, but La Calavera's body looked so hard he wasn't sure he could. He didn't like being this close to him. 'We had dealings. I was a middle man, nothing else.'

'Who for?'

'Russians, down in Long Beach.' He reached into the pocket of the chinos he was wearing and pulled out a matchbook. He smiled as though it was a personal joke. Du Bois's skin crawled as they almost touched when he took the matchbook, checking it. There was an address scrawled on the inside. He turned and walked away. 'Hey, want to hang out some time?' La Calavera called as he walked away. 'You're welcome to the dogfight any time you want! It's a thing to behold.'

He could see Beth in the ECV's turret. She was shaking with rage. He looked at her and shook his head. He climbed into the ECV, half expecting Beth to open up with the minigun at any moment. Somehow she didn't.

'Turn around and drive slowly down the hill, stop when I tell you,' he told Alexia. With difficulty in the vehicle's relatively cramped exterior he pulled the bolt-action Purdey out of its sheath. He estimated the range and dialled it into the scope. It would be a quick shot, a hurried shot, uphill at an awkward angle. He worked the bolt and chambered a round. 'Stop.'

He stepped out of the ECV and brought the Purdey smoothly to his shoulder. Targeting graphics appeared in his vision. La Calavera was walking over the drawbridge back into the courtyard. The two-headed figure was almost obscured by the curvature of the road. Du Bois inhaled. The targeting graphics were showing a spot just above the head. Du Bois squeezed. The rifle jerked back against his shoulder. The gunshot echoed up and down the canyon. Matter flew from the second head, the woman's head, and she slumped forwards. La Calavera ducked out of sight. Du Bois climbed back into the ECV. They sped down the canyon, small calibre bullets bouncing off the patrol vehicle's armour.

24
A Long Time After the Loss

It was fucking nonsense. The Monk had no idea why she had gone along with it. In fact she pretty much *hadn't* gone along with the plan. It had been Talia's decision to pilot the ship. Scab had taken her into the smart matter. Apparently the *Basilisk II*'s smart matter had extruded non-invasive, or at least less invasive, superconducting tendrils that had grown in through Talia's ears. The tendrils were many times more effective than the electrodes she had used previously to interface with the ship and other technology.

Standing in the cargo area, wearing her light combat armour, shoulder to shoulder with the oddly still and quiet primitive human weapons who were the inhabitants of Cyst, she had to admit her sister had some skills. The *Basilisk II*'s gravity field was such that they barely felt the manoeuvres, but the Monk had been receiving a feed from the ship's sensors as Talia had put it through its paces. After her sister had got used to the ship she had weaved in and out of the Cage's walkways, soaring high up towards the edge of the gas giant's atmosphere and then diving into the gas clouds. She took the craft low enough to make it shake. She had bounced the heavily modified yacht off the continent-sized heavy weather. She had taken the *Basilisk II* low enough to make the smart matter flex, and to cause warning signs for structural integrity to appear in their neunonics, but still not as low as they would have to go.

'Does Mr Scab think the structural tolerance specifications are a joke?' the AI asked, appearing in her vision superimposed over the form of one of the Cystians with reversed knee joints, bone plates and barbed spears for hands. They were in the cargo bay; the lounge/C&C and all their belongings had been subsumed into the smart matter, their private rooms were gone. Instead they had made more space for the feral living weapons. The Monk looked over at Scab on the other side of Vic. The psychopath was wearing light combat armour as well. Vic had heavier armour that he had clipped to his already reinforced hard-tech frame.

'I can't believe that Benedict bought it,' Beth 'faced the ship's AI, or Basil as Talia had taken to calling him. 'He must realise it's a trap.'

'It's not much of one,' the AI replied. She agreed. Benedict/ Scab outnumbered them, outgunned them, knew all their best tricks and was capable of them himself.

Then why did I let this go ahead? she wondered.

'Are you sure you are not motivated by revenge in this?' the AI asked.

Am I? She glanced over at Scab again. *Is that it?*

'Is this conversation going to help me do the dumb thing I'm already committed to doing?' she asked. The feed showed them rising vertically above the gaseous bands of colour, towards the edge of the atmosphere again. The *Templar* was close enough that they had visual contact. Neither of them had started firing yet, it would be just a waste.

'I just wanted you to know that she is fine and will be safe as long as the ship is,' the AI told her. 'And she has priority in the case of ejection.' The Monk just nodded and then it started.

Mr Hat reckoned the *Templar* was about half a light second out when it fired on the *Basilisk II*. The light cruiser no longer looked like a Church vessel. There were still statues and reliefs on the smart matter hull of the ship, but now they were the things of nightmare. They had made the exterior of the ship resemble the interior of the disturbed minds that had possessed the crew. Presumably they had toned it down a little to make the ship more aerodynamic for atmospheric actions.

The *Templar* fired its long weapons, the particle beam projector and the fusion lance, but the *Basilisk II* was already rolling and heading down towards the Cage, and the gas clouds. The light cruiser maintained its speed through the debris field that had been the blockading Consortium fleet. The ship's laser batteries destroyed any wreckage that got too close. Sub-atomic particles hitting the magnetosphere created a coronal display that the *Templar* then burst through as it powered its way into the atmosphere.

The *Amuser* sank through the weak magnetosphere, all stealth systems active, trying to draw as little attention to itself as possible, using the debris field as cover. There was something wrong with the *Basilisk II*'s configuration. It should have been folded down tight, spare and aerodynamic. Instead it had been made larger. He wondered what they could be carrying that they felt was that important.

He watched as the *Templar* fired multiple laser batteries downwards, trying to create a grid of destructive energy to ensnare the fast, elegant yacht. It fired AG smart munitions and emptied racks of kinetic harpoons. Mr Hat certainly wasn't going to struggle to track the light cruiser.

The *Basilisk II*'s energy dissipation grid flared briefly as it flew through the lasers. Its own laser batteries, blister-like bumps in its smart matter hull, fired defensively, aiming at the friction-heated kinetic harpoons that were too close for comfort and the AG smart munitions, though the latter had initiated random chaos-fact-driven evasive manoeuvres. The yacht launched its own AG smart munitions but not as many as the reptilian bounty hunter had expected.

The *Templar* was heading straight down, hard burn. It looked like an arrow pointed at the planet's core as it tried to bring its big guns to bear on the smaller ship. It was lost against the massive bulk of the gas giant, little more than a pinprick of light. The *Basilisk II*, however, was using the Cage as cover. Even the fusion lance didn't touch the S-tech material that the Cage had been constructed from. As the two sets of AG smart munitions closed, they detonated into multiple submunitions, destroying each other in a spectacular, expensive, but largely pointless, display of light and force.

Benedict/Scab knew that the *Basilisk II* could outfly the *Templar* but only for so long. The ex-Church light cruiser could follow the *Basilisk II* in and out of Red Space, and if they tried to run then that left them vulnerable to the big guns. Still, he had to admit that whoever was piloting the *Basilisk II* was good. He assumed it was his father/older self.

The *Templar* dived between the walkways of the Cage, and then levelled out, picking up some ionisation from a megastorm weather front in the clouds below them. Lightning wreathed the ship and the energy dissipation grid glowed slightly. The *Templar*'s weapon operators were trying to bring the particle beam cannon to bear, using the lasers and the fusion lance to shepherd the smaller craft into firing zones, but to little avail. The *Templar* launched another hail of kinetic harpoons, a number of them hitting the Cage and disintegrating. Several of the harpoons hit the *Basilisk II*, however, and the visual feed showed the yacht's hull flowing as the carbon reservoirs replaced damaged armour. The forward lasers were lighting up the *Basilisk II*'s energy dissipation grid. They themselves were taking laser and harpoon hits but the bigger craft was just shrugging them off, powering through.

The *Basilisk II* rolled over one of the ziggurats and dived. Its engines glowed brightly, hard burn. Benedict/Scab smiled. They had them. He just wished there could have been an opportunity to board.

AG field or not, they were getting kicked around. The dive had made the Monk's stomach lurch until altered biochemistry had controlled the sensation.

The feed from the *Basilisk II*'s sensors showed the massive bands of colour below them. They looked solid from her current perspective. It felt as if the yacht was getting beaten with giant hammers as kinetic harpoons impacted into the rear of the ship. The external feed showed the rear of the *Basilisk II* glowing neon, venting light and heat as lasers played across its hull. The thick white light of the fusion lance shot past them and into the cloud. It had probably missed by some distance but it had felt close.

With every impact the growling intensified. The Cystians were becoming more restless. The Monk tried not to look around, tried not to show any weakness. The last thing they needed was a fight on the *Basilisk II*. She felt as if she was standing in the middle of a herd waiting for a stampede, except the herd were all predators.

Talia was jinking the craft around a bit, trying to not be where the *Templar* was sending ordnance, but it was mostly a straight dive now. They were rapidly outpacing the light cruiser. The *Templar*, in comparison, looked as if it was slowly falling towards the gas cloud.

And then they were in among the clouds of hydrogen, helium and methane. The clouds made little difference to the *Templar* – the feed from the ship told her the light cruiser was bathing the yacht with active scans.

A laser hit a pocket of methane the size of a capital ship, and just for moment the inside of the clouds was illuminated by flame and then snuffed out.

'It's beautiful,' Scab 'faced. The yacht was being buffeted. The Cystians were making more noise. Little of it sounded like language to her ears, but it did sound like fear.

'Want to speak to your troops?' the Monk 'faced to Scab. He ignored her. Her vision was filling with warnings from the ship but so far they were warnings about exceeding the hull's stress tolerances rather than actual hull integrity warnings. That changed when she saw the smart metal hull flex inwards. Suddenly she wished that they hadn't made the *Basilisk II* bigger, that they weren't carrying all that extra, feral, biomass. The feral biomass who were becoming more and more frightened, and trying to back away from the hull despite being packed in tight.

'Well, this will be a shitty way to die,' Vic said. He sounded more resigned than frightened. The Monk suspected that he had run out of fear after the fall of the Cathedral and his close encounter with the two Elite. He had seemed particularly terrified of the Monarchist's L-tech machine Elite, Ludwig.

'The *Templar*'s levelling off,' the AI said. She checked the feed. The *Templar* was two miles above them. Talia took the yacht deeper. The smart matter was definitely bulging inwards, reaching the limits of its elasticity. The automated warning messages were becoming positively alarming. The *Basilisk II* levelled off. The Monk felt the ship slow significantly as Talia attempted to bleed off heat and lower the ship's EM signature as she engaged the stealth systems. Her sister dropped AG smart munitions behind the yacht, leaving them hovering in the gas clouds.

The yacht was now relying on passive sensors; fortunately the *Templar* was giving them a lot to go on as it rained harpoons and lasers down into the clouds, and saturated the area with active scans. The Monk still didn't like the way the hull was bending in. From the external feed she could see the eddies in the clouds from the downward passage of the harpoons. If just one of them hit the badly stressed hull the yacht would pop like a water balloon stabbed with a knife. AG smart munitions from the *Templar* were moving through the clouds like sharks seeking them, but the Monk knew that they had to stay at this depth until the AI had analysed the *Templar*'s actions enough to make a decent fist of predicting where the ship would be when they came out of Red Space.

Light and force lit up the clouds above them as rival smart munitions found each other and blossomed into explosively colliding submunitions. Waves of pressure buffeted the *Basilisk II*, further distending the hull. She knew they were dead. The Monk closed her eyes, which was foolish. She was still receiving the sensor feed, she just couldn't see the hull pressing in towards her.

Benedict/Scab could not work out the play. They could hide but then what? If they skipped to Red Space, the *Templar* could do the same. They could probably evade and run, but then what had they gained?

'Benedict?' Harold hissed. His first mate wanted to run silent, lace the clouds with AG munitions as intelligent mines, try and find them with passive sensors, but he knew there was a small chance they would miss a bridge opening if they did that.

'Continue the active scans. I want a laser spread tight enough to catch them. Can we seed the clouds?' He 'faced the question to the 'sect sensor operator; he wanted to drop a nano-screen over a wide area but he suspected he knew the answer.

'No, too much weather ... bridge!' the 'sect sensor operator 'faced just a moment behind the ship informing him of the energy signature. With a thought he ordered the ship to follow them into Red Space.

Blue light, a bloody red gash in the striated cloud. They were practically sucked through, helium and hydrogen venting and then dissipating into the crimson clouds. The hull flexed back to normal and then the ship lurched and went dead.

'Basil?' the Monk asked.

'I don't know what's wrong,' the AI said. She could hear the worry in its voice. 'It's not the ship, it's Talia. Her biometrics would suggest that she is upset.'

The Monk couldn't believe what she was hearing. Actually, she could. She was finding herself having some very uncharitable thoughts about her sister. She could hear 'faced questions from Vic and Scab. If this was to work she knew they would have to move quickly. Navigating away from the beacons, even for Church-built systems, was not an exact science, and even then they only had the best guess from the AI as to where the *Templar* would be. The ship moved. Subjectively it felt like they were going up. Now it was just a case of who would find whom first.

AG smart munitions had still been coming up out of the clouds at the *Templar* as they had opened the bridge. A number of the autonomous weapons had followed them through into Red Space. The light cruiser's lasers targeted the hail of submunitions as they passed through the glowing blue portal.

They saturated the surrounding area with active broad-spectrum scans. The personality-spayed AI was trying to predict where the other ship was when they felt the impacts. Little more than a slight tremor in the decks but the external feed showed a different story. Fusion warheads detonating as AG smart munitions breached their defences at short range. Kinetic harpoons impacted against their armoured hull and lasers lit up their energy dissipation grid.

The *Basilisk II* had come out of the red clouds subjectively below them. The yacht's weapon systems were concentrating fire on the *Templar*'s weapons, sensor arrays, and then the forward part of the ship. Benedict/Scab knew it was suicide. Surprise or not, they couldn't hope to go toe-to-toe with a ship like the *Templar*.

The airlock had grown out of the floor of the cargo bay, the smart matter arching around the three of them and pushing the feral Cystians aside. The cargo bay ramp had lowered with them on it. The Monk found herself looking out at the disquieting crimson clouds of Red Space. Not for the first time she wondered if the Destruction was some leech-like mechanism of this artificial universe sucking the life out of Known Space.

Light, force, kinetic and fusion energy were being exchanged between the two ships, further illuminating the red clouds. It was, for the moment, a one-sided exchange – somehow the *Basilisk II* had got the upper hand and targeted the *Templar*'s weapons. They were looking up at what was effectively the bottom of the light cruiser, but the larger craft's manoeuvring engines were burning as it started to turn to bring its larger weapons to bear.

The grapples were basically fat, cross-shaped pads with molecular hooks, similar to those on the feet of their combat armour. The same kind of pads that were currently adhering them to the cargo ramp as they were buffeted by the distant explosions. A guided AG motor towed the lines to the other ship. As soon as they made contact, Vic, Scab and the Monk leapt from the ramp. The winches clipped to their cloaked armour started dragging them towards the *Templar*. The AG motors on their P-sats, now in their more heavily armed and armoured combat chassis and clipped to the back of their armour, steadied their flight. Vic and Scab had had to assemble new P-sats after theirs had been destroyed in the Cathedral. The yacht's assembler had done its best, but they were not up to the specs the two bounty killers were used to.

The Monk couldn't help herself. This was exhilarating. Almost as soon as they had left the *Basilisk II*, the yacht opened a bridge back into the gas giant's atmosphere in Real Space.

Mr Hat had sunk the *Amuser* into the upper cloud layers. He had liberally laced the calmer upper clouds with nanites. He was also receiving tight-beam updates from the network of mini-satellites he had left in the lower layers of the orbital debris field that used to be the blockading Consortium fleet. He felt a little like the trap-door canine predators that had once lived on his home planet before it had been commercially exploited, though he was very much aware of the vast distance over which he'd had to spread his net.

The *Basilisk II* hit the web first, soaring upwards, dragging clouds of helium vapour behind it. The *Templar* followed, firing as many of its weapons as it could bring to bear, though the light cruiser's belly looked as though it was rippling as its carbon reservoirs tried to repair what looked like extensive damage. There was a near-constant wall of exploding fusion between the two craft, the result of colliding submunitions. Mr Hat knew this fight would go to whoever had the most AG smart munitions, which had to be the *Templar*.

This was bad; it wouldn't get Patron what he wanted, but this wasn't a firefight into which Mr Hat wished to interpose. After all, the *Basilisk II* was probably the *Amuser*'s match on its own.

Riding the putty-like substance through the liquid carbon the matter-hack had made of the *Templar*'s armour had been the worst. The Monk had felt the carbon harden into solid, explosive-fused reactive armour plate behind her. It was total sensory depriva-tion, combined with the knowledge that she would be trapped if it went wrong. She had required drugs to keep her calm, though they had only managed to downgrade sheer panic to deep unease at being consumed by the armoured skin of a warship.

Hitting the solid part of the hull and then seeing the glow of the powerful thermal seeds the putty was now tamping and, mostly, protecting them from almost came as a relief.

They spilled out of the hull in a shower of molten metal into a four-bunk sleeping quarters and a burst of ACR fire. The two possessed pirates in the bunkroom had seen the glow. They'd triggered the alarm, the security screen had triggered the alarm, and the sensors had triggered the alarm. It was just bad luck.

With a thought the Monk triggered her coherent energy field and took the brunt of the fire as she fell to the ground. Scab pounced on one of the pirates and did something horrible to him. The Monk extruded a blade from the field and cut the other pirate's legs off, before a power-assisted, taloned, insectile foot crushed his skull.

With another thought the Monk switched off the field. She wasn't going to be able to use it again until they had control of the ship because she couldn't 'face with the *Templar*'s systems from inside the field. She partitioned her mind and started the hack, dumping viruses and scatter-gunning attack programs to distract the ship's defences while she went looking for backdoors in any remaining Church programming that she had been cleared for. Scab was doing something similar, but cruder and more invasive.

The other part of her mind was all about combat. Had they not been discovered so quickly, had they been able to hide and try and subvert the ship's systems, use them to deal with the pirates, then they could have been less pro-active, less violent, but it hadn't played out that way. Now they went looking for Brother Benedict's body, and Scab's poisoned twin psyche. The Monk unclipped her dual weapon, a hybrid side-by-side automatic EM shotgun/laser carbine combination, with an underslung grenade launcher. Tiny AG motors compensated for the weapon's lack of balance. The shock-absorbing stock extended until it touched her shoulder, targeting graphics and weapon telemetry appearing in her vision.

Scab lifted his right arm up and the energy javelin shot out of it, cutting through the door like it was made of butter. A scream was choked off. Vic kicked the internal door off its hinges and stepped out into the corridor. His thorax rotated one way, his upper limbs firing the ACR and its grenade launcher. His abdomen rotated the other, his lower limbs firing the six-barrelled Gatling strobe gun. He was taking a lot of fire the moment he stepped out. The Monk was getting feed from Vic's P-sat. The corridor was wall-to-wall pychos. Vic's P-sat separated from his armour and rose over his head, its lasers shooting incoming grenades out of the air, EM-driven flechettes searching out unarmoured faces.

Scab reeled the E-javelin back, his automatic EM shotgun in one hand while with the other he grabbed the top of the doorway and swung up, his armoured feet adhering him to the ceiling. He was firing and being fired on the moment he left the sleeping quarters, his P-sat also separating from his armour.

The Monk was out behind Vic, covering their backs as they advanced down the corridor heading for the C&C. Vic threw the strobe gun up, its ambulatory spipod unfolding and sticking the weapon to the ceiling, the weapon still firing, covering their backs. Vic drew his lizard-made power disc and threw it with his lower left hand. His lower right was drawing his triple-barrelled shotgun pistol and firing three solid shot concussion rounds. They detonated in the corridor in front of Vic and Scab, giving them a moment's respite.

The Monk was firing underneath the strobe gun. Their enmeshed tactical software meant that she and the semi-autonomous rotating heavy laser were choosing complementary but not identical targets. Her S-sat separated from her armour, shooting grenades out of the air as it did so. She tried not to stagger as EM-driven 10mm armour piercing rounds, fired by the pirates from hacked Church ACRs, impacted her armour and exploded. She fired the four grenades from the launcher very rapidly, programming the solid-state tubular magazine for fragmentation and high explosive. The grenades battered those in armour with airbursts of concussive force and killed those without armour. She was triggering rapid bursts with the laser carbine and the EM shotgun simultaneously. The beams were hitting and superheating Church-issue armour, and then the EM-driven, fin-stabilised, penetrator flechettes pierced the weakened armour and exploded when they detected surrounding flesh. The strobe gun was like a scythe, a red mist forming at the end of the corridor from superheated blood.

The sensor feed from her P-sat was telling her where to put her feet so she didn't slip over on corpses. Her neunonics were receiving warning signs from her armour as she backed down the corridor. Her armour was being slowly eaten. Benedict/Scab had weaponised the nano-screens, turning them into nano-swarms.

The Monk was aware of the battery in her carbine running down, and the solid-state magazine in the EM auto-shotgun being eaten. Suddenly the strobe gun stopped firing. There was nobody moving behind them. Vic had stopped firing as well and Scab was just delivering *coups de grace*. They had killed everyone in the corridor but there were a lot more corridors between here and C&C, and the nano-swarm was eating their weapons and P-sats as well as their armour.

25
Ancient Britain

'Well, that's not for the faint hearted,' Anharad said, and sat back on her fur-lined chair. She looked as though even listening to Tangwen's plan had exhausted her. 'And you're sure about the giants and the lake?' she asked.

Tangwen, standing in front of her, nodded. She had asked for an audience with the Trinovantes noblewoman who was now the *frenhines*, or queen, of the Brigante. Britha knew that the young hunter had tried to keep the meeting to a minimum of people, those she knew and trusted. Britha wasn't sure if she was one of those or not; certainly Anharad wasn't happy to see her standing in the corner of the skin shelter. Germelqart was also trying to remain unnoticed next to her. Britha noticed that the Carthaginian's hand kept on creeping into the leather bag that contained the Red Chalice. Calgacus was there as well. Britha was translating in whispers for the Pecht *mormaer*. Garim, nominally in charge of the Brigante *cateran*, and Clust, the Trinovantes warleader, were both present too. Mabon stood at his grandmother's shoulder, hand on his sword.

Britha was worried because she had not yet seen Caithna and she needed to, to make sure the girl was well and would be looked after when Bladud came back and did whatever he was going to do. Tangwen had urged her to run and Calgacus had said that the Cait there present would stand by her, but she could feel how fragile Bladud's whole warband was. The cold had taken its toll with its bite, illness had done the same. Their supplies were holding up but the gathered warband were not happy. Divided along tribal lines with quick tempered and proud warriors, conflict was inevitable. Barely a day went by without another challenge fought and more often than not a body was left in the snow to feed the winter ravens. She did not wish to add to that strife but she could not run. To run took her further from Bress, which took her further from the rod, the Ubh Blaosc, and her daughter. She touched her belly. *You risk one child who is in you now for the vague hope of another.*

'The animals will not do what you ask of them,' Anharad said.

'We have a way, and we have those moonstruck enough to drive them,' Tangwen said, and grinned at Calgacus. Britha translated.

'She wants me,' the Pecht *mormaer* said wistfully.

'She'd break you, little man,' Britha told him, smiling herself.

'You have already started preparation, haven't you? It's why the Pecht left with Twrch,' Anharad asked, looking less than pleased. Tangwen pointed in the rough direction of the cave entrance to the Underworld.

'He doesn't care about us,' Tangwen said. 'He will leave us here to freeze, to rot, to let our supplies run out, to tear each other apart, because he doesn't care.'

'And what of his supplies?' Garim asked, a frown on his face.

'He is a lord of the land you call Annwn and was born in Cythrawl,' Britha said, using the gravelly voice of fear she had been taught in the groves. She looked over at the Brigante warrior. 'He does not eat what the likes of you and I eat. Would you know more of this?'

Garim spat and made the sign against evil. Anharad rolled her eyes at the spitting.

'What is he doing, then?' Anharad asked.

'Great works of magics,' Britha told the older woman, only half believing what she was saying. 'I think he means to make war on the Otherworld.'

'What business is that of ours?' Anharad asked. Britha could tell that the Trinovantes woman found what she was saying distasteful. Mabon's knuckles were white around the hilt of his sword. 'If he has no interest in us—' Anharad started.

'They sent a warrior and a great sorcerer to help us,' Britha said, through gritted teeth. 'You owe your life and freedom to them, because Crom Dhubh has come close to wiping us out twice now, and for the dead, for vengeance ...' She left it unsaid that the dead numbered Anharad's family.

Anharad looked suitably chagrined, though as *frenhines* she was right to look at all possibilities.

'Aye, you're right enough,' the Trinovantes noblewoman said. 'All we ask is to be in a position to act when Bladud returns, before we all freeze into one solid block of ice,' Tangwen said.

Anharad looked over at Britha and then back to Tangwen. 'And you're sure they don't know of your presence down there?'

'Yes, because neither Selbach nor myself were killed. The magics of the chalice hid us.'

'Very well. What will you do now?'

'We go to speak with Gofannon, the god in the Red Chalice.'

Britha frowned. It was similar to the name she had been told, Goibhniu, and very different to the name Germelqart knew the small god by. She remembered the twisted, red-haired dwarf she had seen the Carthaginian speaking to on the stairs the first time they had entered the chalice. She remembered the echoes of her movements.

'Why was not I informed of this meeting?' Ysgawyn demanded as he pushed his way into the shelter. Mabon and Clust both looked ready to draw their swords.

'Because you are a low person who nobody trusts,' Tangwen told him.

Britha was aware of Anharad sagging in her chair at the young hunter's words. Tangwen pushed past Ysgawyn. Calgacus very purposefully put his hand on Ysgawyn's chest and pushed him out of the way of the shelter's entrance. Ysgawyn was shaking with anger.

'You're not going to piss yourself again, are you?' Britha asked. She knew she shouldn't. She knew the more they humiliated him the more he would want revenge against them, though she suspected that was a foregone conclusion. Germelqart followed her out into the snow, one hand still in the bag with the chalice.

The Cait warriors hadn't liked the idea of such magics being done among them, but they had agreed to guard Germelqart, Tangwen and Britha while they visited Goibhniu. Britha remembered dripping her blood into the chalice and then falling back. She couldn't even remember her head reaching the snow.

It was not like the last time. In the realm inside the chalice the sun shone in a clear blue sky, warming her skin. She was on a ship, not the skin *curraghs* of her people, more like one of the handsomely carved wooden galleys of Germelqart's people. Unusually there was a forge underneath a raised platform at the rear of the galley. The forge would not have looked out of place back in Ardestie, though it was more elaborate, and had finer tools than those that had belonged to Brude, the Cirig's metal worker. Britha didn't recognise all of the tools, though she had little knowledge of the male creation magics.

The galley's oars rowed themselves. They were attached to some strange mechanism of red metal, but it was the sea that gave her pause. It was a sea of red liquid metal and there was no land in sight.

She could see Tangwen. She was up the stairs on the platform over the forge talking to something that looked like her serpent Father but who wore robes of burnished red copper. Its eyes were the vertical slits of an adder but held the colour of red gold.

Germelqart and the dwarf were nowhere to be seen. That made sense, for the Carthaginian's business with the god in the chalice was not of the type to be conducted under the bright sun.

'You are welcome on the Will of Ninegal,' Goibhniu told her. She closed her eyes, steeled herself and turned to face him. He was as Bress, except for the metallic red eyes and the hair of red gold. It felt like physical pain, a tightening in her chest, even though she was pretty sure that she was only here in spirit. She touched her stomach unconsciously. There was only one moon-struck moment when she thought of lying with the god.

'Ninegal?' Britha managed, completely forgetting the correct manners for addressing those of the Otherworld. Goibhniu smiled. Britha lifted her hand to her face and waved it around.

'My movements do not stay in the air any more, nor do yours,' she said. When she had first entered the chalice both she and Goibhniu had left echoes of themselves every time they had moved.

'It was pointed out to me that it was distracting for humans.'

Has Germelqart been coming here often? she wondered. She glanced over at Tangwen. She wasn't sure but she suspected that the younger woman had tears running down her cheeks.

'There are three of you here. You wish three boons?' he asked. Britha needed to focus but she could not stop staring at what seemed to be Bress's form.

'You wish to lie with me?' Goibhniu sounded half puzzled and half amused.

'What? No!' she snapped, flustered. 'And god or no god, I do not brook insolence.' Goibhniu's expression became neutral again. 'Look ... I'm sorry.'

'Your child is well.' It was not a question. Britha was struggling with the conversation, particularly as someone who was used to being in control. She wasn't sure if the god was wishing her well or simply stating a fact. She would have found it comforting, if he didn't keep wrong-footing her so.

'May we bargain?' she asked almost angrily.

'Why?' Goibhniu asked, confused.

'Because everything should have a cost or it will not be valued.'

The god thought on this. 'Tell me what you want,' he finally said.

'Weapons, or rather your power in our weapons, and changes made to them.'

'I have done this before, but it was a long time ago.'

Britha frowned. 'It was barely one moon ago,' she told him.

He turned to look down on her, concern on his face. 'What of the weapons you had of me?'

'We still have them but they are fierce, they drive warriors to madness.'

'To frenzy, blood madness, yes. They are weapons, should they not do this? The weapon and the wielder are the same, both are needed to kill.'

'But they are uncontrollable. They have the potential to cause more harm than good. They need to be less fierce, more controllable.'

'You cannot have the sword without the thirst, the need to see blood and bone. They are my fierce war-children.'

'They overwhelm us.' It was frustrating, as though he could not conceive of an inert, cold, and quiet weapon.

'You must be stronger. I can make swords and spears and arrows but they will be about their business. They cannot search out the hearts of your enemies, and inflict poisons on them that will war with their bodies, if there is no thirsting war-child holding the weapon itself. What you ask makes no sense, but my children respect strength. Show them strength.'

It seemed that Goibhniu did not wish to refuse her. He simply could not do what she asked.

'We need arrowheads, many of them,' she told him. He nodded. 'Sword blades, the less fierce the better.' He frowned and nodded. 'And spears. With long blades.' She wasn't quite sure how to explain this because she wasn't sure she had understood Tangwen properly herself. 'We fight giants ...' she began.

*

'We ask a lot,' she finally said some time later, after explaining all the things they wanted of the god in the chalice.

'Not too much,' Goibhniu said. 'Though I will need to remain on the ground throughout.'

'Will you drink of the earth like before?' she asked out of curiosity, but he shook his head.

'That was a great undertaking. No, I will grow roots into the earth like a tree and take what I need.'

Britha wasn't sure she liked the sound of this, but she nodded. 'Your price?' she asked.

Goibhniu regarded her carefully. The silence became uncomfortable.

'I am as you see me,' he said quietly. She closed her eyes as he reached out and ran the back of his hand down the side of her face. He felt warm. He smelled, not unpleasantly, of copper. He was nothing at all like Bress. She opened her eyes, looked up at him. The warm, metallic wind had caught her hair. He looked down. 'Is that enough of a cost?' He turned to walk away from her leaving her confused as to what, if anything, the cost had been.

'Wait,' she called after him. 'There is one more thing about the weapons ...'

Somehow the cold felt comfortable. She could lie here for a while with her eyes closed.

'Hello, Britha.'

She opened her eyes. They all seemed to be standing around her. A grim-faced Calgacus, an uncomfortable-looking Garim, Clust equally as uncomfortable, Anharad furious, Guidgen worried, Madawg and Ysgawyn grinning. She couldn't read Bladud's expression. It had been the Witch King who had spoken. He was still wearing his black robe, though he had his armour underneath it. He and Garim reached down for her and yanked her to her feet.

'Careful! She is with child!' Anharad snapped, despite herself Britha suspected. Mabon was a little way behind his grandmother. Garim and Bladud had a hold of her by her wrists and shoulders. She was not used to being manhandled like this. She wanted to order them to leave her be. She could have shaken them off. After all, they hadn't drunk from the chalice. She could kill them. Calgacus and his warriors would back her.

And you would be about Crom Dhubh's business once again.

'Did you order Madawg to kill Nils?' Britha asked Bladud. Staring at him. Trying to discern the truth in his eyes.

Madawg was playing the insulted victim. Ysgawyn was already turning her words, warning those listening that she was spinning magics with her tongue, trying to trick them. Guidgen was arguing. It was all noise. She shut it out. She wanted to know if Bladud had done this. He held her eyes. Then he looked down.

'You know I didn't do this, don't you?' she said.

'C'mon,' he said brusquely, and started dragging her towards the skin shelter that Anharad had received them in earlier in the day. The Brigante and Trinovantes warriors were trying to push through members of the Cait's *cateran* to get to Germelqart and Tangwen. Germelqart had been picked up by two of Calgacus's warriors. The Carthaginian still looked asleep. Tangwen was groggily climbing to her feet. She had the Red Chalice in her left hand. One of the bear skull- and fur-wearing Brigante made a grab for it. Tangwen snatched it away from him and then hit him across the bridge of the nose with the vessel. The man stumbled back and then sat down hard.

'What treachery is this?' Tangwen demanded, her hatchet in her right hand now. There was the unmistakable sound of a blade being drawn from a scabbard.

'Stop!' Calgacus shouted, in a rough approximation of the southern tongue. There was sufficient command in his voice that even Bladud gave pause. The Cait *cateran* stepped back as one and drew weapons.

'Translate for me,' Calgacus all but snapped at Britha.

'Cal ...' she started.

'Now!' This time he *had* snapped. Britha was more than a little taken aback. He turned to look at Bladud. 'You have come into my encampment, you have sought to take my guests, you have laid hands on a *drywl*' This last he almost screamed. 'Are you declaring war?' he demanded. Britha translated. Calgacus pointed at the amassed Brigante and Trinovantes. 'Have you grown tired of these? Do you wish to see what they look like on the inside? Do you wish to see them as food for the wolves and the ravens?'

One of the Brigante, a large but fat warrior, looked contemptuously at Calgacus and spat. One of the Cait broke his nose with the pommel of his sword. Then Britha knew that it was over. Now they would fight each other.

'Stop!' Calgacus shouted. He pointed at the warrior who had struck the blow. 'You kill them when I tell you to. You will be punished by me and you will pay compensation to that man.' Britha was still translating for him. Bladud's face was a mask of stone as Calgacus turned back to face him. 'Are we at war?' the Pecht asked.

It was only then that Britha realised that Calgacus, who had always seemed belligerent and warlike to her, was a lot cannier than he seemed. The last thing the Cait *mormaer* wanted was war with Bladud, now anyway, but this violation of his hospitality could not be allowed to stand. He had no choice but to retaliate. Laying hands on a *dryw* while she was under his hospitality was a grave insult. It was effectively an attack on the Cait.

'You are in my camp ...' Bladud started. Britha translated.

'No!' Calgacus cried. 'No more words. I asked you a question. If this is war then do not come slithering in here on your belly like one of them.' He gestured at the Corpse People present.

'Watch your tongue, northerner,' Madawg spat. Calgacus didn't even look at him and Britha didn't bother to translate.

'Draw a sword and go to work, if that is your wish!' Calgacus told the Witch King. Britha could feel Bladud gripping her arm tighter and tighter, he was shaking with anger. Calgacus was playing a dangerous game here. It had all gone very quiet. Not even Guidgen seemed prepared to say anything in case he pushed Bladud too far.

'I ...' Bladud swallowed hard. '... Apologise.' he managed, speaking in the Pecht tongue, Britha now translating for the southrons present. He still hadn't let go of her arm, neither had Garim.

Calgacus nodded. 'Would you like to discuss whatever troubles you?' he asked. Britha was aware of members of some of the other tribes present drifting in to hear what was happening. She saw Guidgen nod at one of the *gwyllion* who then turned and disappeared back into the crowd.

'This woman ...' Bladud started.

'You will have to unhand the *dryw*. We can't have that,' Calgacus said evenly.

'You go too far, northerner,' Bladud said. His voice was almost a whisper but it carried in the cold air.

'I am not manhandling a *ban draoi*,' Calgacus said. Britha translated. There were mutters of agreement.

'She is no longer a ...' Bladud started. Calgacus held up his hand.

'We can discuss this matter once things have been made right. If you do not agree then draw your sword.' There were more than a few sharp intakes of breath from the assembled crowd. 'In fact, let's not waste your warriors' lives. You have a grievance, you have wronged me, let's you and I sort this. Draw your blade.'

'Do you think I fear you?' Bladud asked quietly.

'No. You may even be a challenge, perhaps you will kill me.' Then Calgacus smiled. 'Why else would I be prepared to fight you?' Britha finished translating and it went quiet. 'Because we could do all the talking and posturing that seems to be so common. We could drip honeyed words, laced with venom, in each other's ears, but when it comes down to it, you say a thing is one way, I say it is another, and when all else has failed there is one final way to decide which of us is right. Or are the laws different down here?' Britha finished translating.

'The laws are the same,' Bladud acknowledged. There were nods from the crowd. Britha was aware of more of the *gwyllion* joining the crowd.

'Then we fight,' Calgacus said. 'Or you take your hands from the *ban draoi* and you can drink my *uisge beatha*, as my guest at my fire.'

Bladud let go of her arm.

'I am sorry that you feel wronged,' Bladud said. Calgacus nodded to his people, who stepped away from the Brigante and Trinovantes warriors and sheathed their weapons, but kept their hands on the hilts of their swords. Calgacus gestured Bladud towards his fire. 'I have my duties as *rhi*, as well.' Bladud sat on one of the logs around the fire and Calgacus handed him an earthen jug with the fiery clear liquid in it. Britha shook Garim's hand off her and went to stand on Calgacus's left shoulder, on the other side of the *mormaer* from where Bladud sat.

'But there is a right way to do things,' Calgacus said. 'There's always the sword and brand when the time comes.'

'I was tasked by Moren, arch *dryw* of Ynys Dywyll, to take Britha prisoner, to be delivered to him to be burned for her crimes.'

Calgacus nodded, playing the thoughtful *mormaer*. 'And what has she been accused of?' he asked.

'She is guilty of murdering Nils, the previous arch *dryw*,'

Bladud told Calgacus, raising his voice slightly. There were more gasps and mutterings. Britha was aware of eyes on her. Anharad was staring at her with undisguised hatred. She saw Guidgen whispering urgently to those around him.

'Guilty?' Calgacus asked.

'Aye, she was tried by Moren, who was forced to step into Nils' position,' Bladud continued. Britha could not help herself, she let out a snort of derision. 'She was tried by the arch *dryw*.'

'I see. This is grievous indeed.' Calgacus glanced up at Britha. 'Did you kill this man?'

'Of course not,' Britha said.

'She was seen by the arch *dryw* himself,' Bladud said. Calgacus was studying the Witch King as he spoke. This time he hadn't raised his voice to make the accusation, though he was speaking in the language of the Pecht.

'It was my warning cry that awoke Moren,' said Britha. 'I saw someone kneeling over Nils. I went to help the arch *dryw*, and whoever the figure was fled. I called for help. Moren made the accusation pretty much on the spot. A little while later Madawg came in the other door.'

'What's she saying?' Madawg demanded, having heard his name among the words spoken in Pecht. 'I have a right to know.'

'She seeks to cast blame on good warriors—' Ysgawyn started.

'Piss breeks, you may not speak in this camp,' Calgacus said. Britha translated, she saw Tangwen grin.

'How convenient,' Ysgawyn spat.

'He will kill you,' Britha warned him.

'Can you prove that Madawg did it?' Calgacus asked.

'No more than they can that I did,' Britha said.

'Then do not cast aspersions. You're better than that,' Calgacus said evenly. Britha stared at the Cait *mormaer*. He might as well have slapped her. 'I do not think that she did this,' Calgacus told Bladud.

'And I do not think that she is the person you once knew,' Bladud said. 'She ran because she feared the consequences.'

'I ran because Nils' death served Moren and yourself, and neither I or Guidgen could work out why you brought Madawg along with you.'

'What is she saying?' Madawg demanded.

'She's talking about how you murdered the arch *dryw* to profit his successor and Bladud,' Tangwen said in her southern Pretani tongue. A language that enough of them could understand. Now all eyes were on Bladud. The Witch King glared at the huntress, who held his look. He turned away first.

'Did you not learn your lesson?' Madawg asked, leering at Tangwen, expecting the young woman, his defeated foe, to look away from him. She didn't.

'Tangwen, can you prove what you say?' Calgacus demanded. The hunter stared at the Cait *mormaer*. 'Then you should not be making such insinuations either.' Tangwen looked unhappy but Britha noted that Calgacus had not interrupted her when she had raised suspicions about Madawg and the Witch King. She assumed that Bladud was under no illusions as to what was happening.

'I was there as well,' Guidgen started. Britha translated his words into the Pecht tongue for the Cait. 'It is as Britha says.'

'Prove it!' Ysgawyn demanded. Calgacus stood up and punched him very hard. Madawg and Gwynn, the other surviving member of the Corpse People, went for their swords.

'Enough!' Bladud roared before turning on Calgacus. 'The time for her to prove her innocence was on Ynys Dywyll!' Britha translated. Calgacus sat back down again.

'She would not have received a fair trial!' Guidgen cried. 'And when do we try you? And Madawg?'

'Try it, old man!' Madawg spat.

'So you would harm a *dryw*?' Tangwen asked loudly.

'I have the right to a trial by combat,' Britha said.

'I will stand for the arch *dryw*, I will avenge Nils!' Madawg cried.

'You cannot fight a *dryw*,' Guidgen said. There were a lot of muttered agreements.

'She is no longer a *dryw*,' Bladud said.

'That is not a decision that Moren can make,' Britha said, exasperated now. At best she saw this descending into shouting, at worst violence.

'See!' Madawg howled. 'She would defy the arch *dryw*!'

'I cast aside the protection of *ban draoi*! Let's you and I fight!' Britha screamed at Madawg. Almost immediately she knew she had let anger get the better of her. Calgacus was sitting quietly on his log looking at the fire, occasionally poking at it with a stick.

'Britha, you are with child!' Guidgen pointed out.

'I will stand as her champion!' Tangwen said quietly. It took a moment for her words to sink in, for the crowd to quieten down. Then mocking laughter filled the air.

'A fight I have already won,' Madawg finally said.

'Then it will not prove a challenge to you,' Tangwen said.

'I do not think that this is a good idea—' Calgacus started in Pecht.

'No,' Britha told the younger woman. Tangwen turned to look at the Pecht *dryw*.

'I always welcome your counsel, *ban draoi*,' Tangwen said, somewhat formally. 'But I do not think that this is your decision to make.'

'The time for trial by combat was at Ynys Dywyll—' Bladud started.

'She has the right to trial by combat and to a champion,' Guidgen said, sounding resigned. 'You know that is the case. If she is guilty then you have nothing to fear, Madawg will be triumphant.' Britha translated for Calgacus, who was looking between Tangwen and Madawg.

'This is foolish,' Madawg said. 'There is no need for a fight, the outcome is inevitable. I spared her once. She may as well kill herself and we can be about the arch *dryw*'s business.'

'Then you have nothing to fear,' Guidgen said again, though he sounded uneasy. Britha looked at Tangwen. The younger woman's face was expressionless. If she feared Madawg it was well hidden.

'Let me make this simple for you,' Tangwen told Madawg. 'I know, as the gods know, that you killed this Nils, and this will be proven when the gods judge you with my axe and knife.'

Madawg leant in towards Tangwen. Britha was aware of Tangwen recoiling slightly.

'This ... nonsense ... this insult to honour, is what comes of warriors not being allowed to take their rightful spoils, of not properly breaking their defeated—'

Tangwen spat in his face. Madawg went quiet, his face turning red, eyes bulging. Tangwen had a wry smile on her face.

'I will rape you as you lie dying!' he screamed. 'The last thing you will see is my f—'

'You really are frightened of me, aren't you?' Tangwen said. Madawg stared at her. He seemed to have lost the ability to speak. He went for his sword.

'No!' Ysgawyn screamed. Madawg's scream joined his master's

318

only to be cut off a moment later by a wet choking noise. Tangwen's axe had bit into his knee. The slash that opened his throat had looked almost casual, though Britha knew how difficult it was to cut a throat. Usually you had to saw at it. It took a lot of force to do what Tangwen had just done. She had half-severed the Corpse People warrior's head, with a dirk. Madawg staggered back, dripping red onto the snow beneath him. He let go of his sword, the blade sliding back into its sheath. He hadn't even half drawn it. Tangwen watched him impassively as he reached up for his own throat, the blood-drunk magics in Madawg's flesh warring with, and losing to, the chalice-forged venoms of Tangwen's dirk. He sank to his knees. Tangwen stepped to one side and he fell face-down to further stain the snow.

Calgacus also watched him fall.

'Well, I think that concludes that,' the Cait *mormaer* said.

Tangwen turned to make her way through the crowd. The warriors parted for her, eager to get out of the hunter's way. The Witch King was staring down at Madawg, horrified. He opened his mouth to protest.

'You clearly have the guilty party there,' Guidgen said loudly. Britha noticed that Calgacus was watching Tangwen leave, grinning. 'The gods must have acted through Tangwen because of Madawg's guilt, or how else would you explain her defeating someone we know was her better so easily? The only question remains is, did Madawg have any help?'

The murmurs of agreement among the assembled warriors and spear-carriers were increasing in volume. Bladud stood up and walked away with as much grace as he could muster.

'I think the little southron girl fooled us all,' Calgacus mused.

'And used Madawg's fear against him. He made a stupid mistake,' Britha said, but she too had been taken in by Tangwen's performance. The hunter had taken her life in her hands during the first challenge because she had taken Madawg seriously enough to see him as a threat, to go looking for a weakness.

Britha watched Bladud stalk into flurries of snow with Anharad and the rest of his retinue, Ysgawyn hurrying to catch up with the Witch King.

Calgacus followed her look.

'And I think it is a dangerous thing to humiliate a *rhi*,' he mused. Britha nodded. 'Do you think Tangwen will want the head?' Calgacus asked, looking at Madawg's body.

'No, it is an ugly thing,' Britha said, distracted. She had just realised that Germelqart was nowhere to be seen, nor was the chalice. She hadn't even seen Tangwen hand it off to the Carthaginian.

Germelqart understood enough about himself to know that it was not the snow that made him cold. He no longer felt the cold in that way. It was the sight of the snow and the trick his mind played on him. It was what the Greeks called the psyche that made him shiver under his furs.

He knew he shouldn't be out here on his own. It risked his discovery by the Lochlannach, but he had had enough of the noisy, violent, foul-smelling barbarians and their moonstruck ways for one day. He could make out the wards, drawn by the tiny glowing demons from the chalice, in the air. They would warn him if anyone approached.

He was sitting on a small rock outcrop looking down at the campfires. The night was mostly free of cloud. The stars and moonlight made the snow-covered valley glow. They were a fractious people. It occurred to him that what they really needed was a strong leader like Bladud, who they kept undermining, to truly bring them victory, tyrant or no. He thought of the Achaemenids. Sometimes what you needed was a bit of tyranny.

Germelqart closed his eyes. He felt along the threads the demons from the chalice had drawn subtly in the cold night air. He felt Selbach's fear ... no, his terror. The scout's trews were full of his own soil. He saw through the scout's eyes. Then the Carthaginian felt his heart start to hammer in his chest. He pushed down his own fear. Selbach was on Oeth, the island itself, standing on the highest level of the tower of bone. He felt strong, powerful fingers gripping his shoulder. Bress.

'I found him in the tunnels as I returned,' the tall, pale warrior from the Otherworld said.

'There's someone else looking through his eyes,' the tall man with skin the colour of obsidian said. 'Is that you, my old friend?'

Germelqart almost soiled himself. He was struggling to catch his breath. Selbach knew their plans! He had helped find the path. With a thought, tendrils grew from Selbach's demon eyes, gifted to him by the chalice. The tendrils sought the Cait scout's memories. The last thing Germelqart saw through Selbach's eyes was the Dark Man reaching for him. The Carthaginian withdrew and burned every demon between there and where he sat.

He felt a different kind of cold now. Now the Pretani barbarians needed to act. He stood and started running down the hill towards the camp.

Crom Dhubh was looking thoughtfully at the blank-faced, now-blind, drooling man. Bress assumed that he was some kind of scout. His face was painted grey like the rocks. His furs and other clothing were stained the same.

'They have found another way here?' Bress asked, looking around. The ice was so thick that the island was no longer the good defensive position it had been. His eyes lingered over the boned bodies frozen in the ice.

'It does not matter. They are no threat to us,' Crom Dhubh said.

'They stopped you at the wicker man and they destroyed the Muileartach's spawn,' Bress pointed out.

'Because we let them,' Crom Dhubh said. He didn't seem to be entirely paying attention. 'The Dragon's Voice?'

Bress opened the pouch on his belt and pulled out the smooth, faintly flesh-like, eight-sided stone that he had taken from the dead dragon he had found on the seabed between the three islands.

'This one is as good a vessel as any. He will sing the song to the Naga, he will call them.'

Crom Dhubh's touch made Bress feel nauseous as he took the stone and pressed it against the man's forehead. The stone started to grow through the captured scout's head. His body shook as he spat and drooled. Then the stone was gone. Skin grew over the man's eyes, as a reptilian eye grew in the centre of his head and his skin started to scale.

'Start the preparations. You will go with him,' Crom Dhubh said, and then turned to his silver-haired warrior-slave. 'You need only live long enough for him to sing his song.'

26
Now

Beth had thought it would be like driving through the movies, but it wasn't. It was clear this had been just another poor city with factories and slums, though at least the weather was nicer and there were palm trees.

She was wondering how much atrocity she would have to see before she became inured to it. She was sure that Bradford was the same, Portsmouth arguably worse, but there was just something about America: everything had to be bigger and better. Everything she saw made her want to close her eyes or to intervene, but they couldn't fight the whole city. Du Bois had made it clear that they were no longer the same species. For the majority of humanity only the flesh remained. *So that makes it okay, then?* she thought bitterly. *And what about the sane ones?*

She wondered why they weren't attacked. Sure, they were in an armoured military vehicle, but she had seen groups of marines, presumably from Camp Pendleton, the base between southern Los Angeles and San Diego, subjugating entire neighbourhoods as if they were in Iraq. But they had just watched them drive by in their stolen USAF vehicle. They were ridiculously well-armed, but they weren't that ridiculously well-armed. Did the insane know? Were they somehow aware of the alien tech circulating through Alexia's, du Bois's and her own veins? Were they top of the food chain in this city of atrocities? The idea seemed absurd. She could feel the biological nanites in the air, sporing from the ocean. It wasn't as overt as what had happened in Portsmouth, but she was starting to see the physiological changes to the people of LA. They were slowly being mutated. There was some kind of strange design ethos to the mutation. Du Bois had called it terraforming. Beth had thought he had said terror at first, until her neuralware had made her aware of the mistake. She suspected that even the city's architecture was starting to warp.

She should have gone to the moors. She had always liked the moors and now she knew how to survive there. Or she could have stayed in du Bois's castle. Or stayed in the desert, but it had been too late then. She had found out about her father. The worst thing was, she understood that it had just been another job for du Bois. It hadn't been personal to him. Somehow, despite how angry she was, despite her disgust at how easy it was for him to kill without a thought of the consequences, somehow she couldn't quite bring herself to hate him, which just made her feel all the guiltier. Now she was trapped in this city with little choice but to play this out as far as it went, to grudgingly cooperate with du Bois and his sister. At least Alexia showed some reaction to the horror around them.

They had come down out of the Hollywood Hills and back into the smog- and smoke-filled basin of the city proper. They had avoided the freeways because every time they got near them stray shots bounced off the ECV's armour. They had also avoided the strangely intact downtown. The city still had power. From the hills it had been like a map traced out in light. The skyscrapers still looked open for business despite the chaos. It was eerie.

They tried to keep reasonably close to the coast, avoiding areas that they had known to be dangerous before the Seeders had awoken, like South Central, but the LAX corridor was little more than a trench from multiple plane crashes, and parts of Inglewood, Culver City and Gardena were infernos. Where they could they had taken smoke-shrouded routes. Their augments meant they could still breathe where others couldn't. Amid the smoke they'd had to hide from military personnel with gas masks that had merged with their flesh.

They had crossed a channel and Beth had got a glimpse of Terminal Island, the artificial island split between the Port of Long Beach and the Port of Los Angeles. She knew there was a prison on the island. She wondered what it was like in there now. She supposed not that many of the prisoners would have had phones. Was the prison the last bastion of the sane? Had the prisoners escaped? Or had they just torn themselves apart anyway, without the direct influence of the Seeders?

They had turned off East Anaheim Street and onto an avenue that quickly became a dirt track, sandwiched between a used car lot and junkyards. The dirt road ended at train tracks, and beyond that she could see yellow mountains of sulphur. The whole area stank of rotten eggs. She scanned either side as they travelled down the dirt track. There was very little movement, though the ECV's passage scattered a pack of dogs, mostly pit bulls.

Alexia drove the vehicle down to the tracks and turned it around so it was facing out of the alleyway.

'You bring me to the nicest places,' she said quietly. There was little humour in her voice. Beth sort of liked the woman but she was sure that Alexia had been quite a frivolous person before this. She was worried that du Bois's sister was even less prepared for all this than she was. She felt a spike of anger when she considered for a moment that du Bois might actually be enjoying himself on some level. Then she remembered his response to La Calavera.

There was a line of old freight cars that had clearly been there for some time. At first she thought there were still homeless people living there. Sat round an unlit fire pit, or around trashcan braziers, but then she realised that they had been posed. Then she saw the head poles. Then she realised that the bodies had been decapitated … and the heads of goats sewn onto their necks.

'Hobo camp,' she heard du Bois say. 'Most of them wouldn't have had phones.' That didn't make it better.

Beth climbed down from the turret, grabbed her LMG and got out of the ECV. Her movement sent clouds of black flies into the air.

'Let's get on with this,' she snapped and started heading towards the freight cars. Du Bois grabbed her by the shoulder and almost got hit for his trouble. She turned on him.

'Look, I understand you hate me—' he started.

That's the problem, Beth thought. She knew she should, she just couldn't quite bring herself to do so. Her father's life, as far as she could tell, had been just one long streak of misery. He had given up a long time ago. He would not have survived any of this. He would have suffered. She knew that du Bois had done him a favour. Knowing this just made her feel worse.

'But if you're in this we still have to work together.'

'What do you want to do, sir?' she demanded, knowing that she was being petty. Du Bois just shook his head and turned towards the freight cars.

'So I think it's that one,' Alexia said grimly, pointing at one of the freight cars further down the line away from the hobo camp. It was full of bullet holes.

The three of them walked towards it, looking all around them, weapons at the ready, checking the freight cars they passed. As they got closer to the bullet-ridden freight car, Beth could see a lot of bullet cases glinting in the morning sun. Du Bois picked one up, briefly examining it.

'Five-point-fifty-six millimetre. Judging by the amount of them I'm guessing they were fired from fully automatic weapons. They just turned up and sprayed the place.'

Beth and Alexia covered him as he yanked the sliding door open and then climbed up into the dark interior.

'Anything nice?' Alexia asked.

'A flaying,' du Bois said.

'Nobody just kills anyone any more, do they?' Alexia said. 'I'll stay out here and mind the car.'

Beth glanced at her slightly irritably before climbing into the freight car. There were five bodies inside. The air was thick with flies. It looked like the victims, whoever they were, had been living there for a while. There were bedrolls on the ground, books, pornography, a camp stove, and a selection of unappetising looking ration packs. The bucket in the corner stank. All five of them had been carefully flayed. There wasn't a scrap of skin on them. In some ways that they'd only been flayed was a relief. That was when Beth really started to worry about herself.

Du Bois was gripping the blade of his tanto, releasing his blood-screen, presumably programmed for forensic analysis. There were some shell casings on the ground. Beth picked one up.

'Russian seven six two,' she said. 'Probably from an AK pattern weapon.'

Du Bois was looking inside one of the corpse's mouths. 'Eastern European dental work. I'm guessing these guys were ex-military.' He pointed at wounds in the flesh of one of the bodies. 'They were shot first. Someone turned up, maybe as many as ten shooters, emptied rounds into the car, then came in and did this.' He pointed at some scrape marks on the planks of the freight car's floor. 'They took something.' He concentrated. Beth was sure he was getting information back from his blood-screen. He pointed at one of the bodies. 'He was flayed alive ...'

'Nice.'

'The rest were done post mortem. Here's the thing, though – this happened a week ago.'

'This was done by sane people?'

'Obviously not, but they weren't subject to the Seeders' influence when it happened. Probably a gangland ritual killing, to warn them off retaliation.'

'The DAYP?'

Du Bois shook his head. 'They could have had someone do it for them, I suppose, but I suspect this happened before they knew they needed whatever it was that was here. Whoever did this has gone to some effort as well. The guards had discipline. Though why they don't just park these things in some garage in faceless suburbia I don't know.'

'Everyone is ... was ... looking for terrorists. Nobody cares about the people down here, and nobody would listen to them. Your blood-screen tell you what they were guarding? Nuclear? Biological?'

'Well, if the DAYP are interested then I'd guess the Russian mob had stumbled over S- or L-tech, possibly a weapon, which could be really bad news for us.'

'Could La Calavera have done this and then sent us on a wild goose chase?' Beth asked.

'Possibly, but why bother? Why not just tell us that he couldn't help us?'

'He didn't strike me as incredibly sane, and he'd definitely be capable of something like this.'

'Maybe he wanted to appear to be co-operative,' du Bois mused. 'Xipe Totec.' Beth had heard La Calavera mention Tezcatlipoca, one of the Aztec gods, but du Bois had seemed to think that the gangster had been referring to Mr Brown. Xipe Totec was the Aztec god who had been known as the 'Flayed One'. His sacrifices had involved ritual flaying.

'You want to go back to see La Calavera?' Beth asked.

'Not if I can help it. We go back there, I suspect one of us will kill the other.'

Beth wasn't in a hurry to go back there either.

'So?'

'I need a car battery.'

The current from the battery was just enough to kickstart the heart. The nanites from du Bois's blood were enough to do the rest. The nanites clustered together to provide artificial stimulus for an atrophied heart and neural pathways. Du Bois had programmed the nanites to kill signals from the man's nerve endings. He had picked the one who been flayed alive because he would have seen the most.

The flayed man opened his eyes. Beth had expected panic. His blue eyes were oddly calm, perhaps because of the lack of pain. He looked up at them both and then down at himself.

'How long?' he asked in Russian, which of course she understood now.

'A week,' du Bois told him, 'maybe a little more.' The man nodded. 'Can you tell us what you were guarding?'

'Could I have a drink?' he asked. A hip flask hit the boards of the freight car, thrown by Alexia. The flayed man picked it up and took a sip from it. 'I taste nothing.'

'You'll have to take my word for it, it's good stuff,' Alexia shouted from outside. In the distance Beth could hear dogs growling, fighting over something.

'What were you guarding?' du Bois asked again. The flayed man was staring at the bloody boards of the freight car's floor. Finally he looked up at Beth and du Bois.

'How long do I have?' he asked.

'Not long,' du Bois told him.

'I need a phone.'

'Things have—' du Bois started to explain.

'Once you have told us what we need to know,' Beth said. Du Bois frowned, looking over at her. 'What were you guarding?'

The flayed man was studying her. 'Even if I wanted to I couldn't tell you. It was a sealed crate. Not drugs. Not refrigerated. About four feet long by two across and two deep. No markings on the crate. Whatever it was it was important enough for them to get us to guard it all the way from Ukraine. I'm guessing a weapon of some kind.'

'Hermetically sealed?' du Bois asked. The flayed man shrugged. 'What happened here?'

'People turned up and shot us.' He gave his answer a little more consideration. 'A lot.'

'Who?' Beth asked.

He shrugged. 'We heard the sound of cars, performance engines by the sound of them. We grabbed our weapons and then there were a lot of bullets coming into the carriage.'

'Did you see any of them?' Beth asked.

'I got tagged pretty bad, in the shoulder, side, leg. I was in and

out but I saw the man with the black glass blade who did this.'
He gestured at his body, then he looked down. 'But he wore a
mask, like for ice hockey.'

'And you have no idea who they were?' du Bois asked.

'In my country yes, but here, I'm not so sure.'

Beth frowned. 'What do you mean?'

'We were under surveillance. We were sure it was FBI counter terrorism. In Russia the SVR ... if we had something they
wanted ...' He gestured at the sunlight shining through all the
bullet holes. 'Here I don't know ...'

Beth looked at du Bois. 'The FBI did not do this.'

'The CIA would do this,' the flayed man said. 'I worked with
them in Afghanistan, but they would not do it in America I think.
A phone?'

'You're sure it was government surveilling you? Some of the
Mexican cartels ...'

'It was government. A phone.'

Du Bois opened his mouth.

'What's your name?' Beth asked. The flayed man turned his
head to look up at her. She could see the sadness in his eyes. She
was pretty sure he knew what was coming next.

'Arkady.'

'I'm sorry, Arkady.' He was nodding when she shot him in the
head with the Colt OHWS.

Du Bois was moving away from her, bringing the carbine up.
Alexia had the ARX-170 pointed into the freight car.

'What did you do?' du Bois asked as she holstered the pistol.

'I'd rather he thought we were complete bastards than realised
what had happened to the world and anyone he cared about in
it,' she told him as she jumped down from the freight car and
started walking back towards the ECV. She felt the eyes of both
the du Bois siblings on her back.

It was the most ridiculous of long shots. Beth could see it in
du Bois's eyes, hear it in Alexia's voice. They were just going
through the motions now. Bothering the dead. They were in a
city of insane millions looking for sociopaths who were going to
fit right in.

As they left the Long Beach area they had heard what sounded
like a small war going on behind them. Artillery, tanks, helicopters, jets pounding the city to the south of them. Du Bois had

guessed that the Marines at Camp Pendleton had decided to take the city in force.

It had taken them the better part of the day to make their way back north towards the west Los Angeles district of Sawtelle. This time they had to fight. They had to run roadblocks. Small arms fire had bounced off the vehicle's armour. Du Bois had taken a round in the leg. Beth had also caught a ricochet in the arm. It had gone through her combats but not her hardened skin. It had still hurt.

She had known what the minigun's capabilities were but there was a difference between knowledge, using it for suppressing fire – as they had when they had been looking for La Calavera – and witnessing what it could do to a human body first-hand. She'd fired controlled bursts. Trying to limit it to between fifty to a hundred rounds each time she had depressed the trigger. The rotating six-barrelled weapon's rate of fire was horrific. It had filled the air with arcs of light from the tracers, chewing away at cars and SUVs in a shower of sparks. The people hit by the rounds looked like they had been disintegrated, they became smears on the concrete. Alexia and du Bois had popped smokes around the ECV to obscure the vehicle, though they could see through it themselves. Alexia used the weight of the armoured patrol vehicle to punch through the roadblocks. Du Bois and Beth fired at anyone, or anything, that looked like it posed a significant threat. It had happened more than once. It was as if the city had woken up to them. They were a disease and all the armed psychos were LA's antibodies. Their grace period was over.

'This is a fucking waste of time now,' Alexia muttered, sucking hard on the cigarette she was smoking. They were parked on a footpath among some trees on a lawn surrounding the Wilshire Federal Building, an ugly, white concrete, nineteen-storey tribute to bad sixties government architecture, close to the corner of Wilshire and Veteran. South of them, on the other side of the Federal Building's car park, was a real park. North of them, across the skyscraper-lined Wilshire Boulevard, were the neat rows of thousands of veterans' graves in the Los Angeles National Cemetery. To their west, though obscured by the Federal Building, was the VA West Los Angeles Medical Center. 'You're just playing soldier boy because you don't know what else to do.'

Du Bois and Beth were standing on either side of the ECV,

weapons ready, keeping watch. Beth was starting to realise that despite her new physiology, despite the ability to stay awake for prolonged periods of time, the constant need to remain alert, the constant tension, was starting to take its toll. She was only half listening to Alexia, who was leaning against the ECV's bullet-scored bonnet. The Federal Building looked strange, somehow. She was wondering if she was starting to hallucinate.

'We're just going to be fighting now, all the time. Eventually they'll get us, and if they can't kill us, then we're looking at suffering for a very long time.' She shivered, despite the temperature. The sun was going down but the evening was staying warm, low cloud and smog holding the heat in. Beth wasn't sure the other woman was wrong, though she was planning to put a nanite-tipped bullet in her own head before it came to that. 'We'll run out of ammunition eventually.' This was true. Beth had three cases of rounds left for the minigun, but she'd already burned through one case today alone.

'So will everyone else,' du Bois said. They could hear nearly constant gunfire now. If they watched then they could make out the distant flickering of muzzle flashes. They could still hear police sirens as well. Further east on Wilshire they had seen a mass battle going on between two forces in skyscrapers on opposite sides of the road, a spontaneous waste of ammunition, a battle thrown like it was a barbecue. 'This isn't going to end like this, Alexia,' he continued, gently. 'It's going to get worse.'

'How?' Beth was surprised to find that she'd asked the question. She couldn't imagine anything worse than this. There was something very wrong with the Federal Building.

'Imagine the thing you saw in the Solent. The Seeder. Many more of them, but more malign and insane.'

'So let's go somewhere better, somewhere isolated, and live out the time left as best we can,' Alexia said. There were tears in her eyes. 'I can't do this any more. There are exclusive resorts in the mountains, the desert, we could ...'

'Go there, clear them out?' Beth asked. Everything was stained with blood now.

'Oh God,' Alexia said and looked down.

'Maybe you should take the ECV, take Beth with you if she wants to go,' du Bois suggested. 'Let me know where you'll be and I'll come for ...'

'You bastard!' Alexia thumped him on the shoulder, staggering him a little. 'You know I won't leave you! Not now! We should both go! All go!' She turned to Beth. 'Will you tell him?'

Beth looked at Alexia and then used the excuse of being on watch to turn away from her. She wasn't sure what she wanted to do. Alexia's plan sounded attractive, no doubt, but she remembered the dead tourists in Portsmouth, the freaks who had taken her sister, the other Elizabeth in the warehouse in Cambridge. It might all be meaningless against the backdrop of all this insanity, but dealing with the DAYP was *her* part of the insanity, the small thing that she could put right.

'We're going to run out of places to look soon,' she said, still not looking at Alexia. 'We might as well check this out.'

'Christ, you're no better than he is!' Alexia spat. Now Beth turned to look at the other woman.

'Fuck off!' Beth snapped.

'Alexia,' du Bois cautioned.

'No! Because this isn't the last place you'll look, because if you don't get what you want here, you'll go back and fight that Calavera arsehole! And you might not know it yet, but you want to do it! You've got a taste for it. You don't know how many soldiers' eyes I've seen that look in.'

'You can go if you want,' Beth said as she passed Alexia, angry that the other woman had compared her to her father's murderer.

Beth wasn't sure who they were – employees, passers-by, maybe protestors. There were a few placards scattered around the plaza in front of the Federal Building. Whoever they were, they had fused with the concrete and glass of the building.

Du Bois was standing with his back to her as she stared at the building. The people trapped in the walls reminded her of the gargoyles that she had seen on old churches, except they were still moving, still somehow alive.

'Fuck this!' Beth said. Anger. Anger was better. The Model 0 LMG was up against her shoulder. She moved into the shadows, heading towards the door.

The glass was broken. The reception area had the coat of arms of the American government painted on the marble floor. The area didn't look too badly damaged, but the screaming and nausea-inducing flickering coming from the computer monitors reflecting off the marble was making it hard for her to concentrate. Du Bois moved forwards quickly and leapt over the reception desk, Beth covering him as he smashed the computers. Blood was running from his nose by the time he had finished.

They had taken the stairs, trying to ignore the begging, sobbing and muttered glossolalia of the unfortunates fused with the building. She wasn't sure, but she suspected some of them were whispering classified information. There was a moment of near hysteria where she thought about asking them what they knew. Du Bois had turned around to see what she was laughing at. The disapproving look on his face made it even more difficult not to laugh.

They had found the FBI's office. Beth and du Bois just stared. They were still at their desks in their suits, still working, though their monitors showed little but interference. Beth didn't like the things she was seeing in the corner of her eye in the interference, however. Skin had grown over the workers' eyes, ears and noses. Their skin moved as if breathing for them and they were wasting away.

Beth started laughing again. She turned to look at du Bois, grinning. 'Well, this was worth it.'

'It's an information network,' du Bois said. Beth's smile disappeared.

'You can't be fucking serious?' she said, but he had already put his .45, the carbine, the Purdey, his tanto and the belt buckle knife on a table and then stepped away from it. Beth actually jumped as all the phones in the room started ringing.

'Put the magazine of nanite rounds into your sidearm. If I come back wrong ...' he told her. She was shaking her head. He picked up the phone and held the screaming receiver to his head. His eyes filled with blood and then her vision was filled with light.

27

A Long Time After the Loss

Benedict/Scab was now in his hacked Church-issue body armour, wishing he had access to something a bit bigger than an ACR and two tumbler pistols. He was watching the fight. He supposed he should have known it would come down to this. He had a good idea of Vic and Scab's capability, but he had underestimated both the Monk and the resources they had brought to bear on the *Templar*. They had been tactically clever, using bottlenecked corridors to their advantage, but even so, three people shouldn't be able to hold off his crew like that. The pirates' main advantage, however, was the nano-swarm slowly eating the intruders' equipment. All of the boarding party were wounded now, their armour next to useless, their weapons about to fall apart, their own protective nano-screens overwhelmed by the weaponised Church swarm.

The electronic war in the ship's systems wasn't really going Benedict/Scab's way either. The crew of the *Templar* were mostly trying to deal with the overwhelming initial onslaught, which meant that Scab and the Monk got to sneak around causing trouble.

And then he'd been locked out of the *Templar*'s systems. That was when Benedict/Scab knew it was over. He was standing still on the walkway over the fouled dolphin pool in C&C as the S-sats turned on the rest of his crew. He was aware of the C&C nano-screen being weaponised and starting to eat the pirates as well, whether the hunting S-sats had caught them yet or not. The holography died, the various visual and telemetry feeds on the smart matter walls died. Benedict/Scab was aware of his own personal nano-screen, his armour and his weapons being eaten, but somehow he knew that neither the S-sats nor the nano-swarm would be what killed him. Beams, flechettes, EM-driven shotgun rounds fired by the S-sats impacted all around him but he stayed stock-still.

The door to C&C opened. He raised the ACR and fired. The first few rounds hit the Monk's coherent energy field before the weapon came apart in his hands. He was backing away. Harold threw himself at her, taking an EM shotgun blast in the back as he did so. She extruded blades from the field and trisected his lizard first mate in mid-air.

Scab leapt over the Monk. He was all but naked now, the nano-swarm having eaten his armour, though he still had his rotting tumbler pistol in one hand. Where the swarm had reached his skin it looked like he had contracted a flesh-eating virus. There was a hole in his cheek. His jaw and teeth were exposed. Another of the possessed pirates in C&C charged him. Scab rammed his metalforma knife into the visor of the pirate's rotting armour. The blade pierced the visor, stabbed into flesh and started to grow. Scab left it there.

Benedict/Scab drew both the tumbler pistols and fired them at his father/older self. They fired a bullet each before rotting away. Scab was cutting someone in two with his energy javelin just because they hadn't got out of his way quickly enough. The bullets impacted him, spinning through armoured skin and blowing out chunks of flesh. Scab barely seemed to notice. He was obviously being kept going by medical systems, narcotics, hatred and anger.

Benedict/Scab was aware of Vic running and leaping from one of the suspended catwalks to another over the fouled dolphin pool. The 'sect landed and started tearing apart any of the remaining crew with his power-assisted limbs. The Monk was moving around C&C with purpose, slicing up anyone she found with the L-tech energy blades she had extruded from her field.

The elder Scab stalked towards Benedict/Scab. The rotting flesh of his right arm glowed as the E-javelin was sucked back into its housing. His father/older self still held the, presumably useless, tumbler pistol in his right hand. Benedict/Scab had a metalforma knife in each hand now. The robust weapons would be the last to fall prey to the swarm that had been turned against them. He darted forwards to ram one into Scab. Scab blocked the arm and then broke his son/younger self's elbow through the rotting armour. Benedict/Scab howled as his internal medical systems attempted to deal with the damage and pain. He stabbed at his father/older self with the other blade. Scab did the same thing to the other elbow. It was obviously no effort for the elder Scab at all. He was staring at his son/younger self.

'Isn't this what you wanted?' Benedict/Scab managed through gritted teeth when his internal narcotics had taken the edge off the worst of the pain.

'Who do you think you are?' Scab asked, shaking his head. Benedict/Scab realised that the *Templar* had stopped moving. Through the open blast door he could hear screaming, and the sound of renewed fighting. The smart matter wall lit up again. His father/older self and the Monk were in charge of the ship now. He could see the *Basilisk II* had docked with the light cruiser. The Cystians, living weapons, once his – no, his father's – followers, had entered the ship. The nano-swarm had removed the possessed pirates' technological advantage. In close quarters mêlée the Cystians had the upper hand. It was just a slaughter now.

Benedict/Scab had allowed himself to be distracted by what the smart matter was showing him. His father/older self made him aware of this mistake by breaking his kneecap, and then hacking his neunonics to lock out his medical systems and internal drug supply. He lay on the catwalk over the fouled, empty dolphin pool, in a lot of pain. His cheek against the floor, he got to see the first of the Cystians reach C&C. They were red from head to foot.

Now he felt like one of the air-swimming avian cloud hunters from one of the low-G lizard worlds, pre-exploitation. Mr Hat had the *Amuser* just under the clouds, moving slowly and quietly, trying to minimise his signature, using the web of nanites he'd spread out across the clouds to backscatter and/or confuse any active scans coming from the stationary *Templar* and the docked *Basilisk II*. He was feeding passive scan information to the *Amuser*'s targeting systems, hoping it would be enough.

The automatons had already moved to the airlocks, which had been expanded to capacity. He was going to drop about a quarter of them through each of the airlocks. He doubted he would have time to do a second drop. The only way the initial drop would work was if the crews of both ships were too busy dealing with each other to notice him.

He was impressed, despite himself. He was not sure what they had done, or how they had done it, but Scab and his cohorts had disabled and successfully boarded the *Templar*.

The *Amuser* was within a mile of the other two ships now. Mr Hat accelerated. The ship rose out of the cloud cover, dragging vapour with it, forming eddies in the hydrogen and helium.

He launched two AG smart munitions, one of them travelling a lot faster than the other. He triggered the lasers and kinetic harpoons. They were travelling so quickly now it was practically point-blank range.

Submunitions blossomed but kept in tight together, multiple fusion warheads impacting against the rear of the *Basilisk II*, and for a moment there was only light. Then the yacht was gone. There was a very brief moment when Mr Hat thought he'd overdone it, destroyed his quarry, but the nano-web he'd sewn told him the yacht was heading down into the clouds again. He bombarded it with active scans, keen to remain aware of the other ship. He decelerated, manoeuvring engines burning brightly. He came around the *Templar*. The second AG-driven smart munition impacted exactly where the *Basilisk II* had been docked. The airlock. Waves of force battered into the *Amuser*, rocking it back, actually causing some damage, but he had to be this close for the plan to work. Mr Hat was firing almost blind into the light of multiple fusion explosions. The *Amuser* launched kinetic harpoon after kinetic harpoon, impacting the molten side of the light cruiser.

The first explosion rocked the *Templar* and the second impact sent the Monk flying. She switched off the coherent energy field with a thought, it didn't have much juice left in it anyway, and grabbed the edge of a catwalk as she fell towards the foul smelling, empty dolphin pool. The external feed playing on the smart matter walls was showing an odd ship. It looked like an up-ended squashed spider made of wrought iron and stained glass. It was firing on the *Templar* at very close range.

There was only a moment of panic when she noticed the *Basilisk II* was gone; then she was aware of it, damaged but fleeing down into the clouds. They had managed to lock Benedict/ Scab and the others out of the *Templar*'s systems but they didn't have total control of the ship, and after airlocks, weapons systems were often the hardest to hack, for obvious reasons.

They felt warm air blowing through the entrance to C&C as the blast doors started to close. The Monk swung back up onto the catwalk. Vic had dug his taloned feet into the composite materials underfoot. Scab had just dropped down onto all fours like an animal.

The Monk's audio systems filtered down the deafening

percussion of multiple kinetic harpoon hits. The internal feed showed the harpoons breaching the ship. One moment there was a corridor full of Cystians, the next moment they had ceased to exist.

The door to C&C stopped closing. The Monk heard horrible rasping laughter. She looked over to where Benedict/Scab was lying. His father/older self kicked the pirate leader hard in the head, cracking the rotting helmet of his son/younger self's combat armour, rendering him senseless.

'Just kill him!' the Monk snapped. She was trying to gain access to the weapon systems.

Mr Hat partitioned his mind. He could receive tactical audio-visual feeds from all his automatons if he chose to, and his neunonics could cope with the traffic, but he tended to choose one or two 'hero' automatons from each operations area. The *Amuser* was over the light cruiser now, both airlocks were open and his worshippers were dropping onto the *Templar*, scrambling for the breach the fusion warheads and the kinetic harpoons had made. The hull of the stolen light cruiser ran with liquid carbon from its reservoirs as the *Templar* attempted to seal the breach. His automatons looked like four-legged insects crawling over the grotesquely decorated ship.

None of the main weapons had fired but a few autonomous anti-personnel/boarder weapons had, mainly rail cannons and smaller lasers. Mr Hat was targeting the weapons systems, taking them out as quickly as he could, while continually firing at the breach to try and keep it open. The anti-personnel weapons destroyed more than a few of the automatons. Mr Hat stopped firing at the breach as the first of his worshippers, almost swimming vertically down through liquid carbon, made it into the *Templar*.

Without the coherent energy field the closest thing the Monk had to armour was the tattered remnants of her *gi*. She still had her two thermal blades, both a pitted mess, but her neunonics had run a diagnostic and they were functioning, though not optimally.

Someone had to get control of the *Templar*'s weapons systems, at the very least, to try and deal with the ship outside. She knew Scab would be trying as well. She would have to help him if they were to have a chance. She was also trying to find a way to undo Benedict/Scab's final 'fuck you', and get the blast doors closed. All of which meant she couldn't use the nearly exhausted co-herent energy field. So she was finding a place to hide. She was too soft and squishy for this fight. Arguably Scab was too squishy as well, but he at least had the E-javelin. Vic was their best bet against automatons. The 'sect had 'faced her the information on who was attacking them: a fellow bounty killer, top of the league tables, a rather weird diminutive lizard who wore a ridiculous stovepipe and went by the name Mr Hat.

'These will be full spec,' Vic 'faced to them both. 'Not as fragile as the ones on Cascade.'

They hadn't yet risked a direct feed from the *Templar* to their neunonics, but the smart matter walls were showing the auto-matons wading through the blood in the corridors, crawling along walls, the ceilings, creepy things dressed like male and female Victorian dolls, with featureless faces.

The Cystians had swarmed the automatons, but weapons of sharp, sculpted bone were of no use against armoured machines. The best they could do was slow them briefly before their broken bodies were cast aside. Their best hope was the *Templar*'s inter-nal security systems. The remaining S-sats were using hit and run tactics on the blank-faced automatons. They couldn't risk losing too many more of the S-sats by committing them fully. The weaponised nano-swarm was now targeted specifically on the automatons. They were starting to rot, robotic lepers, but it wasn't even slowing them down.

She was suddenly aware of operating without a safety net for the first time in a long time. If something mechanical came in here and pulled her head off, that was it for her. She would not be cloned this time. She grinned savagely.

Still, it's been a good innings, she thought.

In her head the Monk was aware of the defences the possess-ing psychos had added to the *Templar*'s weapon systems. They looked like a seething, wriggling mass of maggots. Her sword, the attack program she was using, burned with righteous fire.

Scab stabbed the first automaton in one of its rotting wounds with his metalforma knife. The smart matter blade branched out, fed matter from the carbon reservoir in its hilt. It pulled itself into the wound, looking for ways to disable the blank-faced machine.

Scab's right arm glowed and the next automaton through the door was cut in two by his energy javelin. Vic leapt up and grabbed another that was crawling along the wall, hammering it into the ground, holding it there as three clawed power-assisted hands thrust into its machine body and its mechanical innards were torn out. The automatons were already in the C&C, though, crawling up the walls and onto the ceiling to drop down behind Scab and Vic.

The S-sats in C&C were working hard in the target-rich environment, concentrating their fire until one of the automatons went down, then moving to the next and pouring fire onto that one. The S-sats were boxing clever, using their AG drives to stay out of reach of the automatons. One of the blank-faced machines, a female Victorian doll in widow's weeds, launched herself from the ceiling and dragged one of the S-sats out of the air. The automaton's energy dissipation grid glowed brightly as it was shot at point-blank range by the S-sat before the automaton managed to tear it to pieces.

In her partitioned mind, immersed in the *Templar*'s systems, the maggots were burrowing into the Monk's plate armour, breaching her defensive systems, trying to hack her neunonics, lobotomise, or kill her. She was feeling pain from biofeedback. A rat ran out of her lower leg. It was also wearing plate armour like her. A semi-autonomous, familiar program based on a pet she'd had in her late teens. The maggots didn't seem to notice it. The Monk sent the rat looking for a heavily encrypted backdoor that she hoped was still there.

Scab used the E-javelin to cut off the arm of another automaton, plunged it into the thing's chest and tore it up through its head. One of the blank-faced machines managed to grab him. He put the javelin through its head. Then another grabbed him, and another. He was screaming in rage as they bore him to the deck.

Vic was in a similar position; eight of them had hold of him and were trying to force the 'sect down onto the catwalk. Most of his armoured body was dented from the extensive beating he had received at the machines' hands.

The Monk had found a place between two of the couches used by the *Templar*'s sensor crew. There was a dead 'sect on one of the couches, the other was empty. Trembling slightly from the biofeedback, she looked up as one of the female automatons reached down for her.

Mr Hat targeted the incoming ship with lasers then, as it closed, kinetic harpoons. It was returning fire, burning hard to close the distance. Mr Hat moved the *Amuser* behind the *Templar* for cover, popping over and around it to fire and then ducking down behind the heavier ship.

The AG smart munitions bursting out of the cloud cover beneath the *Amuser* nearly caught him. They must have come in slow and stealthy, only accelerating at the last moment. He fired the rail cannons and lasers defensively as the AG-driven weapons burst into submunitions. The *Amuser* was caught in multiple explosions, and one or two of the submunitions made it through. His ship juddered and was thrown back from the force of the detonating fusion warheads as light engulfed his ship.

For a moment the *Basilisk II* disappeared, then he was taking fire again. The yacht had braked hard and was doing exactly the same thing as the *Amuser* had been doing, using the *Templar* for cover. They played hide-and-seek, circling the light cruiser, risking shots when they could, occasionally sending AG smart munitions arcing around the *Templar*.

The female automaton reached down just as the Monk started to spasm from the feedback. Counterattack programs and venomous viruses were poisoning the liquidware that ran through her brain. She managed to slash at one of the automaton's arms with a thermal blade. The blade bit into the machine's arm and got lodged there.

The blast door slid shut.

The Monk smiled at the blank-faced machine. With a thought she triggered the coherent energy field. The automaton let go of her, its fingers forced away from skin by the field. Extruded blades cut through the machine's legs. It toppled over. The Monk's neunonics showed her where to put the blade next to permanently destroy the automaton. Then she down-powered the energy field to save what little remaining power there was left in the L-tech device.

The familiar program had found the backdoor. It had shown Scab. Scab now controlled the *Templar*, and for once he didn't mess around, he immediately shared control with the Monk. She became aware of what was happening outside.

*

Mr Hat was aware of the *Templar*'s weapons activating. AG-driven smart munitions sprung from the light cruiser. He turned and ran, firing behind him, heading for the clouds. The *Basilisk II* kept firing as he fled but didn't pursue. The AG-driven smart munitions did, however.

The Monk flicked the energy field on and off. On when she was attacked, off the rest of the time to conserve power and monitor the ship. It was clear that the automatons were here to capture Vic and Scab and presumably her as well, as they could have been a lot more lethal than they had been.

She put the field up and extruded blades cut into those trying to hold down the still-screaming, writhing Scab.

He must love this, the Monk thought, smirking behind the field. As soon as his right arm was free he laid into the automatons with the E-javelin in a frenzy.

The field failed as she tried to free Vic. An automaton's fist caught her hard enough to powder the bone in her nose and much of her face. The force of the blow picked her up off her feet and sent her flying from the catwalk and into the befouled dolphin pool. Her systems tried to clamp down on the pain as much as possible, but she'd been beaten, shot, and partially eaten by nanites. Physically she just wanted to drop, give up. Instead she was treading water in the disgusting pool, looking for the maintenance ladder.

Vic burst out from under the pile of automatons that had been trying to hold him down. Scab was there with him, cutting up the still-rotting automatons with the E-javelin. Then everything was quiet and still. She could hear Scab breathing heavily and the water rippling. Vic looked down at her, kneeling on the catwalk.

'Do you want a hand?' he asked.

They had worked quickly. The Monk had ejected as many AG-driven smart munitions from the *Templar* as the *Basilisk II* could carry. Then Scab had set the controls of the stolen Church light cruiser for the heart of the sun. They had considered taking the larger, better-armed ship but they were too few to operate it anything close to optimally, though access to their military grade assemblers would have been useful, as the nano-swarm had eaten most of their gear. Instead it would be the funeral barge for dead Church members, the information forms from the Psycho

Bank that had possessed them, and the Cystians who had died aboard the vessel. But not for Benedict/Scab.

The Monk was sitting on one of the lower steps of the ziggurat, healing slowly as Scab dragged his howling son/younger self past her. The fused personality had been an abomination but so was Scab-senior's response. The mass killing never seemed to stop, and as much as she would have liked to lay this at Scab's door, it hadn't been him who had had Benedict possessed by a Psycho Bank copy of a younger Scab. This, the cover-ups when the Destruction had hit the systems, the fall of the Cathedral. How much was enough, she wondered? She should be appalled. No, she should have snapped a long time ago. How much had the tech really changed her? She felt like her, but surely a normal person couldn't cope with this. How many times had she been cloned? Was she just a simulacrum now? She felt numb as Scab cut his own son's heart out on top of the ziggurat and then held it up to show the silent masses of surviving Cystians who watched.

The Monk held her head in her hands. She felt a metallic claw on her shoulder. She looked up.

'Look,' Vic said. Flowers were growing out of the smart matter. They were sprouting out of the ziggurat and the walkway. She didn't want to look up at Scab. See his angry face confused at this moment of beauty.

'C'mon,' she said to Vic and stood up. She pushed her way through the Cystians, who ignored them. Towards where the *Basilisk II* was hovering, the cargo bay's ramp touching the flowering smart matter catwalk. Talia had flown them here but she had remained inside the *Basilisk II*'s smart matter, and had ignored Beth's attempts to communicate.

'A bridge has opened at the bridge point,' Basil, the ship's AI told them. 'No ship has come through.'

It could only mean one thing. An Elite. They hurried onto the ship, glancing behind her to see the Cystians had parted to let Scab pass as he ran towards them.

The ship was already peeling away from the catwalk as Scab reached the ramp. They had seconds at most. The *Basilisk II*'s sensor feed made them aware of the coherent energy field umbrella that the Mother was generating to try and hide the bridge opening, and then they were in planetary Red Space.

The Monk took control of the ship. Her Church experience made her the best Red Space navigator. Sensors and skill-sets only got you so far off the beacon paths. There was still a lot of intuition and experience involved.

'Talia, you need to come out now,' she said aloud, assuming that the ship would pass the message on.

The smart matter wall birthed her sister near to where the Monk was standing. Talia looked furious.

'What's wrong?' Vic asked.

What now? the Monk thought, uncharitably.

'You fucking bitch,' Talia said venomously, breathing hard. Then she looked at Scab. Even he seemed a little taken aback. 'In love with the ghost of the ship,' she said. The Monk frowned. Talia turned back to look at her. 'You knew, didn't you?' Talia demanded.

'What's she talking about?' Vic asked, looking between the two sisters.

This didn't make sense. There was no way she could know. There was no interface. Then she turned to look at Scab. He was smiling. That was when Talia went for her sister with her nails.

Alexia wept as the smart matter grew around her inside the ziggurat, engulfing her as she diffused her consciousness throughout the Cage around the dying world.

The Innocent walked among the flowers above the clouds and looked at the animals. They seemed to regard him as one of their own.

28
Ancient Britain

'That's not for the faint hearted.' Bladud had echoed his wife when Tangwen told him of the plan. He had always been careful in battle. He did not lack courage but he wished to triumph, and to take as many of his people back to their families as possible. He believed it was how you remained strong, though others felt that strength came from glory. It was surprising how often the glorious were defeated by the cautious. Tangwen's plan did not allow for much in the way of caution. Still, they would be able to look their gods in the eyes when they met them in the Underworld.

As they trudged through the snow towards the mouth of the cave, steam already rising from the warband's sweaty masses, Bladud was aware of the activity in the fort above and behind them. They could not use the horses to fight uphill so they advanced on the cave mouth, the entrance to the Underworld, on foot, and in a strange formation. It was strange because they had a shield wall at the front of the formation and another at the back. They were purposefully arranging for themselves to be trapped between two armies. It was beyond moonstruck.

The shield walls were made up of all the tribes, but the front wall mainly consisted of the Trinovantes, led by Clust. Anharad was among them, armoured and armed, and against her better judgement Mabon, her twelve-year-old grandson, was with them as well. The shield walls consisted of trained and, for the most part, experienced warriors. They carried their casting spears and their swords, but not their longspears. Behind them were the spear-carriers, the most experienced in the second rank just behind the shield wall. Their job was to fight over the warriors' shields, though many of the spear-carriers also had slings. In the middle of the two opposite facing forces were more warriors from a mixture of the tribes. They carried longspears but no shields. The warriors with the longspears were surrounded by bow-carrying *gwyllion*.

Guidgen was among the *gwyllion*, which Bladud was grateful for. He actually liked the old *dryw*. He just wished *gwyllion* didn't have to stand in the way all the time. He would have preferred to have Britha close by him because he didn't trust her further than he could spit a stone. He was pretty sure that Britha wouldn't know honour if she tripped over it. He had not liked what had happened on Ynys Dywyll. He had not liked how quickly Moren had capitalised on Nils' death. He did not like that Madawg had not been in his pallet asleep when it had happened. But as far as he was concerned Britha had shown her guilt when she had run. After all, she had worked for the enemy, slept with the enemy, she carried Bress's child in her belly, and by all accounts had changed sides more than once. There was just one small nagging doubt about Nils' death. Bladud could not quite shake the feeling that he believed Moren's version of events because he wanted to, because it was convenient.

Germelqart was with Guidgen. Bladud could not make out the Carthaginian. It was understandable that he was always quiet. He was so far from home, and surrounded by warriors and the inevitable chaos that accompanied them, but the foreigner had, if anything, become even more withdrawn of late. Bladud would have liked to have the Red Chalice out of the Carthaginian's hands and ideally back up in the north, in his home. They could not risk Germelqart and the chalice falling into the hands of the Lochlannach, so they were both in the centre of the warband. If they were taken it was too late anyway. Still, at least Germelqart had allowed those who had wished to drink of the chalice to do so, though only after Guidgen had delivered dire warnings about the consequences of such powerful magic. Surprisingly few warriors had volunteered. The Witch King could understand why. He had felt the panic when the molten metal had forced itself down his throat, the agonising burning, and then healing. He had felt fire course through his body. He could not remember ever feeling like this, even in his prime: he was stronger, faster, more aware. Part of him knew this was cheating, you should work for this, but he felt exhilarated, eager for the battle. His skin was feverish like the *riasterthae* frenzy he had heard stories of, though those stories always told of a golden age of warriors that none living seemed to be able to remember.

Most of the Brigante had followed his example, though Garim hadn't. He liked the man well enough, but he was no Nerthach.

He missed the big warrior, and cursed him for the stupidity of attacking Crom Dhubh by himself. The fact that the majority of the Brigante had drunk from the chalice would see them well after the battle, if any of them survived Tangwen's plan. He suspected she had come up with it while chewing on certain mushrooms.

Guidgen's warnings had scared most of the other warriors off drinking from the chalice. That and the stories of what the weapons had done. None of the Pecht had drunk of it, nor the *gwyllion*. This would also work in the Brigante's favour after the battle. He was suspicious of all the warnings, but he was a learned man, a strong man, favoured by the gods, or else he would not have accomplished so much, regardless of what Nils may have said.

Nils. He may not have liked the man. The arch *dryw* had been unable to see beyond his ancient laws. He did not know enough of the lands beyond his own cold, wet, beautiful island but he hadn't deserved his end.

Bladud glanced over at Ysgawyn and Gwynn of the Corpse People. The trial by combat came down to who was the best fighter. It had little to do with innocence or guilt, or the gods. Madawg had been a cagey fighter, unpleasant, but a warrior nonetheless. Bladud could not believe that he would have killed the arch *dryw*, though if he had, he had paid the price. Like most of the Brigante, Gwynn and Ysgawyn had drunk of the chalice as well. They may have been among Bladud's apparently staunchest allies, but sharing the power of the chalice with them made the Witch King uneasy. Tangwen had not looked pleased either, but she had said nothing.

Bladud still had the sword infused with the power of the chalice from the battle with the spawn of Andraste at the gwyllion's forest fort. Up until the morn of the battle it had lived in a skin that he had sewn up and inscribed with symbols of binding written in wolf's blood. A circle of salt had surrounded the skin. Now the sword was back in his hand whispering tales of gore to him again. As he saw the neat rows of Lochlannach moving towards them behind their shields, their own *carnyx* sounding their disquieting, ululating rasp, the sword started to shake with eagerness in his hand.

Like the Witch King, many of his warriors still had their weapons from fighting the spawn of Andraste. Those who did not had dipped their own in the Red Chalice. They were forged anew. The strands of molten metal climbed sword blades, spear and arrow-heads, even sling stones, giving them a red tinge, infusing them with the venom they would need to kill the warriors possessed by demons from Cythrawl.

Bladud was in the centre of the rear facing shield wall. It was where he expected the worst of the fighting to be. Cautious he might be, but you could not expect warriors to fight for you if you were not prepared to do what they did. With his body burning, and the sword thirsting for flesh, he did not feel cautious now. The Lochlannach moved towards them, still somehow managing to maintain their neat rows despite descending a steep snow-covered hill. Their discipline reminded the Witch King of the warbands of the city states that surrounded the sea on the other side of what the Greeks called the Pillars of Heracles.

The Brigante were still moving backwards as the Trinovantes warriors at the front of the warband made their way uphill towards the cave mouth. Bladud could hear threats and insults shouted from the front shield wall. Bladud suspected there was little point in engaging in the ritual insulting. The Lochlannach marching towards him certainly didn't look receptive to name-calling and slights on their sexual proclivities and parentage. If he weren't so eager for battle their blank expressions would have worried him.

'All of you remember this,' the Witch King cried. 'We defeated the children of gods! A god made the weapons we carry in our hands! These are just slaves, they are nothing to those of us who are mighty!' He was answered with cheering.

Behind them they heard shouted orders, the sound of taut bowstrings loosed in the cold air, stones and casting spears impacting into the leather-lined oak and magic of the shields borne by the Lochlannach in the cave mouth. Then came the first cries of pain as the Lochlannach in the cave mouth threw their own casting spears.

'Guidgen!' Bladud shouted. Moments later arrows shot overhead as half of the *gwyllion* present loosed. Most of the arrows ended up studding the approaching Lochlannach's shields but a few hit home. Bladud knew that the red-tipped arrows, imbued with the magics of the chalice, would grow inside the wounds. He saw a Lochlannach get hit in the leg, slow, falter and collapse into the snow, but the rest kept coming. He heard a roar behind him, then the sound of iron on wood, the sound of shields grinding together, the sound of cold metal finding warm flesh, and the sound of pain.

'Slings!' Bladud shouted. He hated the impractical weapons. The stones hummed just overhead, more than one hitting the helmets of warriors in front. One of the spear-carriers went down. He was passed back towards the centre of the warband, where Guidgen was with the warriors who carried the red spears that the chalice had forged whole.

Their line had stopped moving. Behind them they could hear the Trinovantes and the Lochlannach in the cave mouth battering each other's shields with spear and sword. The warriors of the various tribes were screaming at the silent Lochlannach. Bladud knew that some would be caught up in the moment, others overcome by the blood-thirst of their chalice-reforged weapons, others would just be very frightened, and among the war cries would be the howls of the wounded, trapped in the crush.

Arrows still flew overhead from the *gwyllion* archers. 'Spears!' Bladud shouted.

The Brigante moved, almost as one, the Iceni warriors with them likewise very disciplined. The other warriors were not so quick off the mark. The casting spears were shadows in the low winter sun as they flew over the snow, for the most part to thud into shields already studded with hungry arrows. The Brigante and Iceni warriors brought their shields up. The returning casting spears drove too deep into the wood of their shields for Bladud's taste. He heard oak split. There was a scream further down the line as one of his bear-skull-wearing warriors was flung back into the spear-carriers behind him by the force of the impact.

'One more!' Bladud shouted. He threw his second casting spear and saw it bite into a shield. 'Draw swords!' he cried. The Lochlannach shifted slightly as they marched through the snow, preparing to deal with warriors wielding swords. The Lochlannach had been listening to Bladud's orders and were taken by surprise by the third volley of hastily thrown casting spears. More than one went down with a spearhead spreading its hungry iron roots through their head. The *gwyllion* had loosed simultaneously, their arrows raining down on helmets. The false order was an old Brigante trick. He wished he hadn't had to teach it to the other tribes. Lochlannach dropped, but they closed lines and continued marching towards the shield wall. The Witch King's warriors hurriedly drew swords, and the occasional axe or iron-shod club.

The Lochlannach were so close now. It was the moment before shield walls met. Normally he would be frightened, but now he wanted this. Truly, he was a son of Codicius, the Red God, on this day. He decided on the one he was going to kill first. The Lochlannach were less than a few strides away now.

'Hold!' Bladud cried. Almost as one the shield wall stepped forwards. Another false order, an old tactic designed to break an enemy's advance. Swords fell. Most bit into wood. Some bit into flesh. Some of the Lochlannach fell. Bladud's shield hit the shield of the demon-slave he had decided to kill. The man was strong, and Bladud was pushed back in the snow. There was an excited scream in his head as chainmail exploded and his longsword found warm flesh to bury itself into. He would have to name the blade so he could have power over it.

'For Nerthach! Redden the snow!' he screamed, thoughts of his dead friend enraging him further. The front line was being pushed back. The spear-carriers in the rows behind them had not stepped forwards when the front line had. Now they did. Spears were shoved past Bladud's head, between him and the warriors pressing in on either side of him. One of the Lochlannach in front of him was hit in the temple, his head shoved back. The spearhead warped, growing into the Lochlannach's skull and the enemy warrior slumped, his body held up by the press of men. Bladud was aware of excited cries coming from behind him. He could smell the piss and shit as men and women lost control of bowel and bladder.

He saw the point of a spear getting larger in his vision. His sword was held above him so he could fight in the press. He brought the blade down, forcing the spearhead to hit his shield, scraping across it.

'And step!' Bladud cried. The shield wall tried to push, to throw the Lochlannach back to give them room. The Lochlannach didn't budge. That wasn't good. The Lochlannach stepped. The Witch King's own line went back. The problem was that they could only retreat as far as those in the shield wall at the mouth of the cave could advance. The Lochlannach stepped and pushed them back again.

Crom Dhubh sighed.

'And the thing is, I probably would have let them live had they been content to leave me in peace. They bring this upon themselves and then complain about the cruelties of dark gods.'

Bress was of the opinion that perhaps his master was getting a little carried away.

'Do you want me there?' Bress asked. *Perhaps see her one more time?* He hated how pathetic the thought sounded. Crom Dhubh frowned.

'You? No, you die soon. I need you here. Send the giants.'

'All of them?' Bress asked.

Getting the horses not to panic, to stay quiet, had been the difficult part. They had led them into darkness, through the twisting path deep under the hills that she and Selbach had finally managed to find. It had been Azmodeus who had suggested the answer. Alchemy. Which as far as Tangwen could tell was something like a cross between metalworking and herb working. Germelqart had used the chalice to make what he called an elixir that they had fed to the horses. The Pecht had been worried that the horses would be too docile, but the Carthaginian had ensured them that it would just make them obedient. Still, it was too much sorcery around the Cait warriors' valuable horseflesh for their tastes. Eurneid had certainly worked hard to instil a fear of magic in them.

Lowering the chariots down the crevice, by comparison, had been time consuming but much simpler. Selbach and Tangwen had observed Oeth for a long time to determine if the cave with the crevice in the roof was ever patrolled. It seemed that it wasn't. Crom Dhubh had too much confidence in his magical wards.

They had lowered the chariots by laying a smoothed-down tree trunk across the crevice. Then some of the burlier warriors had lowered the chariots using ropes curled round the trunk. They'd had warriors at the bottom of the crevice with another rope pulled taut to stop the chariots from bouncing off the rock. The chariots had also been wrapped in wool, furs, and hides to minimise the noise when they inevitably did bounce off walls of the crevice. It had been a bad mix of boring, tricky, and tense work, all carried out in near-pitch darkness, but in the end they had lowered the ten chariots into the cavern and hidden them far from the mouth. They'd had one or two worrying moments, but the biggest problem had been remembering that they still had to remain as quiet and careful lowering the tenth chariot as they had the first.

It was fortunate that the Pecht bred small, sturdy mountain garrons that were capable of handling the terrain of Annwn. Selbach and Tangwen had led the forty garrons through the Underworld, as they were the only ones who could see in the dark. It was left to Tangwen, however, to properly yoke the now-silent four-garron teams to the chariots. Selbach had disappeared. She was worried he might have been been captured. She knew the timid scout was braver than he thought he was, but Crom Dhubh made slaves of men with his magics. Tangwen was sure that they were discovered. Germelqart had assured her otherwise, and urged her to go on with the plan. He would not explain why he thought this was the case, however, and she'd had no time to press him.

The warriors and chariot drivers had gone down the morning of the planned attack on the cave mouth. The only illumination in the cavern had been the faint glow coming from Oeth reflecting off the white ice of the frozen lake, and the even fainter light from the pale sunlight that made it down the crevice above them. The Pecht, the lynx-headdress-wearing Iceni scouts, and some of the *gwyllion* had to be guided to the chariots. Most of the chariot crews were smeared with the ashes of the campfires to blacken their faces and the shinier parts of their armour. None of them wore any decoration. Tangwen could not believe their courage. She could see in the ghost world, as could Britha, who had helped where she could, but the rest of them were effectively blind. All of them looked empty-eyed in the grey and green ghost light, as though they were already dead, already spirits.

Tangwen had not been entirely happy about Britha's insistence on accompanying them. Not just because she was pregnant, but because it meant one less warrior with their meagre warband. Tangwen had offered to find what Britha needed, this rod, and bring it to the *ban draoi*, bring her Crom Dhubh's head, Bress's head, but it had not been enough for Britha. She had to be there. Tangwen was starting to think her hastily worded oath to help the Pecht *dryw* retrieve her daughter from the Otherworld had been a mistake.

Once they had finally managed to get in place they had waited and waited, and still none of them had made a sound. Tangwen had almost cried out, however, when the first huge arm had reached into the cave. The bottom of the crevice was a hole in the roof of the larger cavern; the giant's hand grabbed the rock lip and pulled itself in on its back, across ice and rock, blocking out the faint glow from Oeth. Gnarled, clawed hands reached for purchase as it dragged itself up the crevice and out of the cavern towards the surface. Tangwen was ready, longspear in hand. She heard movement from the other warriors. A whimper. The sound of piss splashing on stone. The smell of shit filling trews. The first giant showed no sign of being aware of their presence. Nor did the second. Nor the third. Tangwen had only seen the three on the ice. She waited. Then she moved forwards carefully and looked up the crevice. She could see the huge shapes clambering upwards to destroy Bladud's warband, dust and rock falling to the cavern floor in their wake. Tangwen watched until the last one had disappeared, then she crept back and organised everyone into place. The glow reflecting off the frozen lake provided them all with just enough light to see their way out of the cavern.

Tangwen passed the longspear to Calgacus and took her place in the lead chariot, notching an arrow on her bowstring. Each of the wicker and wood carts had a charioteer – Tangwen's was the silent, tall, scarred blonde woman – and an archer. The idea had been Germelqart's. He had told them of lands in the south where archers fought from chariots. This, however, left no room for the warriors themselves, so they rode on the yoke pole between the horses, crouched down so the charioteers could see. It was considered a warrior feat but it was mostly for champions to show off. In order for the horses to pull/carry three people, it had meant halving the number of chariots but doubling the horse teams for each chariot. Tangwen knelt down and wrapped one end of a braided leather thong around one of her thighs and the other around part of the chariot to help keep her in place.

The blonde charioteer turned to look at Tangwen in the faint light. Tangwen nodded. The charioteer snapped the reins. It was as if the four garron had suddenly awoken. Chariot wheels sparked off stone, and then they were onto the ice, and out of the cavern. Tangwen half expected them to be the only chariot, but she glanced behind her and saw the cavern filled with sparks flying from spike rimmed wheels and the garrons' studded shoes, all of which had been forged and fitted by Twrch. By the time they reached the ice they were almost up to full gallop. She heard Calgacus laughing. Others, behind, were howling battle cries. For a moment as the bright white ice shot by underneath her she had a savage grin on her face. Then she turned to face forwards and saw the bone obscenity of the tower reaching up towards the jagged, tooth-like rocks that lined the roof of the huge cavern containing the frozen lake.

Bladud's face was a grim rictus of exertion as he inched his sword arm forwards against the blank face of the Lochlannach in front of him. Then there was red on the demon-slave's face. Bladud started to saw his blade up and down; something hot and wet splashed across his face. The scream of exultation seemed to come from somewhere distant, from someone else. The bloody-faced Lochlannach in front of him stopped pushing against his arm, Bladud moved it back, and used the somehow still-sharp blade of his sword to bash the man's helmet in. The weapon, alive in his hand, bit through metal, into bone, and Bladud's face was splashed again.

The Witch King managed to lift his foot up and stand on the spear that was trying to stab him in the leg. In front of him a Lochlannach went down and was dragged through the Brigante shield wall to be killed by spear-carriers. Everything stank of blood, sweat and the ordure of ruptured bowels. The Lochlannach and Bladud's warband were jammed together, barely able to move. He'd seen opposing warriors pushed so close together that one had been able to chew the other's nose off. Daggers were sneaking in under shields to do the most damage. Intestines splattered to the ground, but their dead owners remained upright in the press. There was no snow beneath them now, just a red, churned up, stinking slurry.

Normally he hated a shield wall. There was no skill involved, it was just which warband was stronger, or hated the most, or just had enough people to wrap around the edges of the other's shield wall, but this? This he had been born to do. He put his shoulder into his shield, heaving, bringing the pommel of his sword down onto another one of the Lochlannach's noses. They weren't winning, but they weren't losing either. The bloody haft of a spear was slid across his face from behind. The spear's head found the face of a demon-slave warrior, deformed it with penetrating red iron, turned it crimson. The man to the right of him was dead, half his skull missing. Bladud was pretty sure that the corpse was still speaking to him, encouraging him to more acts of violence. Garim, on his left, was screaming and trying to push himself free enough to strike someone.

They felt the earth shake first. Then the warband was cast into shadow as the giants hove into view between the hills and strode towards them. The Witch King heard the cries of fear but didn't understand them. Some of the warband tried to break from the press of men and women, but most of them were cut down by the Lochlannach.

This is no time for fear, Bladud thought. He relished the stink of the slaughter, the steam rising from all of them. He just needed the warband to hold together that little bit longer.

The giants reached down to scoop up warriors and spear-carriers alike and crush them in huge gnarled hands. Casting spears and arrows rose up from the masses between the shield walls. One of the giants raised his foot and stamped down, turning more men and women into a mangled red mess.

'Break!' Bladud screamed.

29
Now

Du Bois was somewhere else. The building had breathing walls with veins. It looked like something out of a nightmarish version of the 1950s. A vast, open area of row after row of desks organised into concentric pentagons.

The 'people' sitting at the desks looked identical, regardless of gender, and they wore identical suits and hats. Skin had grown over their eyes and they had fused with the faintly insectile furniture as they typed on their similarly insectile, retro, typewriter-like keyboards. The glass panes of their monitors showed strange, unknown letters and other symbols. The symbols he did understand made him feel uncomfortable. The ones he did not understand hurt his head and made him feel nauseous. The computers were connected to each other and the fused bodies in the walls, floor and ceiling by a network of vein-like, black, shiny cables. The computer operators seemed to be the mutated, human biological components in some kind of vast machine. There was clearly some malign aesthetic to it. Du Bois couldn't shake the feeling that there was something huge pressing against the walls of this warehouse-like structure.

There was a figure sitting in the centre of the pentagonal arrangement of desks. Du Bois walked towards him. As he did he realised that he was unarmed. Every time he caught a glimpse of a screen his head hurt all the more and the urge to vomit became stronger. He could feel his neuralware shutting down parts of his mind to protect it. Blood was running out of his ear. There was more to this than was obvious on the surface. His internal systems were only letting him experience the data construct as three-dimensional to protect his mind, but at the very edge of his vision he was aware of the structure, the machine, curving away to impossible places he could not properly perceive. All that it left to experience was the unpleasant symbolism of his fragile mind trying to cope, it seemed.

There was definitely something huge pushing against the walls of the complex. Du Bois's breath quickened. He wasn't used to fear like this. The thing behind the wall, it wasn't just the size of it ... He looked away from the suggestion of strange limbs and appendages being pushed against semi-elastic walls.

'I don't know who you are,' the figure in the centre of the pentagon said. Du Bois had almost reached him. He was struggling to focus on the man. He looked nominally human but it was as if there was something that he couldn't see properly standing behind him. 'I should know who you are.'

Du Bois recognised the man, had known him, or at least he recognised the physical form. The figure looked out of time. He had the fleshy but serious look of a 1950s patrician, a politician, a policeman, or someone who played the like on black and white TV. Pain and nausea were preventing du Bois from remembering the man's name. He wore the skirt, blazer and bonnet of a respectable, upper middle class housewife. His make-up and nails were flawless.

'I have files on everyone, why not you?'

The chair he was sitting on looked alive. It had nut-brown skin. One of the arms of the chair had a tattoo, as did its legs, they were of horizontal lines forming complex patterns. The chair's face looked agonised, twisting as if it was trying to communicate.

'What's this? Some Kafkaesque comment on the fascism of government?' du Bois managed. The man in drag was holding something, leaning on it. A staff or pole, but it kept flickering in and out of view, in and out of existence. The top of the staff was a man's screaming, severed head.

'This is what you want, so this is what you get,' the man in drag said quickly.

Du Bois pointed at him. 'Do you know, I never liked you?' He remembered that much. The man in drag's face fell.

'Fear was enough,' he said. It clearly wasn't. Du Bois felt absurdly sorry for him, even though he knew he should be repelled. He couldn't shake the feeling that he had met the living chair before.

'There are still seeds. It hates life,' the chair said in a language that du Bois knew but couldn't place. South Pacific, he thought, through the pain.

'What do you want?' the man in drag asked. 'I should know. I had files but I don't now.'

Du Bois told him. The man was standing up, leaning on the pole that was sometimes there and sometimes not. He caught a glimpse of the thing behind the living chair. He did not like the angles of its physiognomy.

The man in drag walked among the rows of the suited, feature-less figures fused with the furniture and their odd computers. He ran his hand, with its painted nails, across their smooth faces.

'So beautiful,' he said wistfully. The screaming head on the staff had turned painfully around to scream at du Bois. The man in drag stopped by one of the fused figures, and pointed at him or her. 'They know,' he said. Then he searched in his handbag and pulled out a blade-edged silver dessert spoon. 'Do you want to use my spoon?'

Queasily, borderline hysterically, du Bois was reminded of the sugar skulls eaten on *Día de Muertos*, as he took the spoon and started to eat the information he needed.

Thunder, wind, light and pain. Something tore at his back, rip-ping at armour, forging a burning rent through flesh and making him roll across the floor. The air was full of dust and raining gore. Nearby he could see one of the faceless federal employees still sitting at his desk despite the destruction all around him. Tracers drew lines of light through the dusty red air, and the federal employee's head and chest ceased to exist. They were under fire. Du Bois knew that much.

Pain still lanced through his head, he still wanted to throw up, he still felt the fear, but this he understood, though it sounded bad. His vision was red. He tried to clear the blood from his eyes but it was behind the cornea. He would have to wait until it was healed.

His neuralware was separating the noises. He heard a GAU-19 firing. A triple-barrelled, rotary .50 calibre, electrically driven Gatling gun. The sound of rotors. Short bursts from an assault rifle. Single shots from at least two other rifles, and returning fire from Beth's Model 0 light machine gun, and he was unarmed. He felt the rotor wash from an aircraft hovering outside the Federal Building blowing the warm air from the desert Santa Ana winds into the office.

He could see through the red film now. He risked a look. The movement sent renewed pain lancing through his head and intensified his need to throw up. The telephone receiver he had picked up was still lying on the institutional carpet, screaming at him. He looked up over the desk he had fallen behind. He got shot twice. In the back and in the chest. He fell back to the floor. The bullets had been armour-piercing. They had gone through his nanite-reinforced clothing, and lodged in hardening skin, but his augmentations were such that he had seen enough. It had been as though everything had slowed down. A snapshot.

A CV-22B Osprey was slowly circling the building. The rotors on the aircraft were tilted upwards, allowing it to act as a helicopter. Rounds from the Osprey's belly-mounted GAU-19 were tearing through the open plan office. The powerful .50 calibre bullets had chewed through the windows and concrete of the building's exterior, and were turning the interior furniture into so much flying kindling, the still-working federal employees into so much flying meat.

Mueller, the German sniper, was standing at an open hatch in the side of the tiltrotor aircraft's fuselage. He had shot du Bois in the front. Beth was just behind du Bois's position, keeping low through the firestorm. She was firing at another two shooters behind and to her left. One of whom had just shot him in the back. He assumed that was Ezard, the American. The other shooter, he suspected, was Grace. The Pennangalan would stay close to Mr Brown.

If he was here then it was all over.

'Beth!' du Bois shouted. More pain. There was no chance of communicating via blood-screen in the rotor wash from the Osprey. The walls were moving like they had in the virtual space. The people fused with them were opening and closing their mouths like hungry koi. 'The Purdey!'

The LMG stopped firing for a moment, and his incredibly expensive rifle came sailing through the air towards him. He caught it and immediately started working the bolt, ejecting the five rounds the rifle was loaded with and reloading it as quickly as he could.

A .50 calibre round hit him in the calf. He screamed. Augmented physiology tried to cope with hydrostatic shock that wanted to tear the limb off. His system was flooded with endorphins, the information from the nerve endings in his leg were blocked. His leg was hanging on by a few strands of sinew and armoured skin;

du Bois kicked it around so it could heal back in place easier. He felt himself becoming radically thinner as matter was shifted through his body.

Du Bois finished reloading the Purdey as flesh, muscle, armoured skin, and bone knitted together. His augmented hearing picked up cries of pain and a thud as Beth was shot multiple times and fell over. He had to drag himself across the floor as the GAU-19 targeted his hiding place. Desks, part of the floor, and the remains of federal employees were torn apart where he had been a moment before. The noise from Beth's LMG had stopped. He heard his own SA58 carbine being fired instead. He pulled one of the 40mm HEAP grenades from a pouch on his webbing.

'Beth!' he shouted as he threw the grenade towards her position. He hoped she could work out the plan. He heard the pop of his carbine's underslung grenade launcher. Then the explosion of a 40mm fragmentation grenade at close range, presumably aimed at Grace and Ezard's position. Debris rained down on him. He was aware that the GAU-19 was no longer firing into the office, but it was still firing. The carbine had stopped. Du Bois hoped it was because Beth was loading the HEAP into the grenade launcher. He could hear more distant firing. The minigun on top of the ECV. Alexia. He estimated the range and dialled it into the Leupold telescopic sight attached to the Purdey.

Du Bois popped up from behind the desk, on one knee, not that he could stand if he wanted to. Mueller shot him in the face. The force of the bullet whipped his hair round, glancing off bone and armoured skin. Du Bois brought the rifle up to his shoulder. Behind him Beth was firing his carbine. Long bursts, suppressing fire. Rapidly burning through the rest of the thirty round magazine. Fireworks outside. Tracers from far below hitting the Osprey. The GAU-19 on the tiltrotor aircraft's belly firing downward. Mueller appeared in the scope, fire coming from the muzzle of his Heckler & Koch G3 rifle. Du Bois exhaled. Squeezed. The gun kicked back into his shoulder. Mueller's round hit him in the chest. He staggered back but didn't fall over.

'Now!' du Bois shouted. The 40mm HEAP grenade fired by Beth from the grenade launcher flew past him and impacted into Mueller. The German sniper flew backwards into the Osprey and the grenade exploded, blowing a hole in the side of the aircraft. He hoped that the nanite-tipped bullet he had shot Mueller with first would do the rest.

Du Bois managed to twist round. He got shot. He worked the bolt on the Purdey. He got shot again. He couldn't breathe. He was aware of fast-moving metal travelling through his body. Beth threw his carbine back towards him. He'd given her the weapon but he still had all the ammunition for it. It was effectively useless to her now. He saw the figure he was looking for. Ezard. Then he saw muzzle flash from the American's M14. He risked a snap shot from the Purdey. Another round caught him in the chest and he hit the ground. His own carbine landed on him.

Blood was bubbling out of his mouth. He was wasting away as any remaining fat was drained to try and heal a multitude of wounds. His neuralware made it known that he could just about put weight on his leg now. He reloaded the carbine. Muscle memory. It was practically autonomous as nanites struggled to rebuild enough of his body to make it a going concern. He could just about function, just about move.

Du Bois left the Purdey on the floor and rolled to his feet, leaking blood, carbine at his shoulder, firing at Ezard, advancing towards the American. Grace shifted aim, firing her N6 at him. Beth popped up from between bullet-riddled desks, her LMG hanging down her front on its sling, firing the compact Benelli shotgun rapidly at Grace as she advanced through the wreckage with du Bois. Ezard shook and stumbled back as he was hit by short burst after short burst from du Bois's carbine. The sniper staggered into a bullet-ridden partitioning wall and fell through it. Grace was knocked back by multiple impacts but didn't fall. Instead the punk girl ran for the door to the stairwell. She was staggered as more buckshot hit her, but she made it to the exit and all but fell through it.

Du Bois saw his Accurised .45 stuffed in the back of Beth's webbing. He swept his carbine to one side, letting it hang on its sling as he took his pistol back. Beth moved towards the exit to the stairwell. Du Bois ejected the magazine on the .45 and replaced it with the magazine of nanite-tipped rounds as he moved towards Ezard. The American was lying in the hole he had made in the partitioning wall, bleeding from multiple wounds, his bloody mouth opening and closing as he tried to reach for his own sidearm. It was clear that the snap shot, nanite-tipped round du Bois had fired from the Purdey had hit him. The nanites were already eating away at the sniper. Du Bois put two more nanite-tipped rounds into Ezard's face and the sniper was still.

Du Bois risked a glance behind him. The Osprey's GAU-19 had stopped firing. Mueller was nowhere to be seen. The hole in the side of the tiltrotor aircraft was smoking, but the aircraft was still hovering in the air.

He looked over at Beth. She had the shotgun at the ready and she was standing off and to one side of the door. Du Bois holstered the .45 and reloaded the carbine, bringing it up to cover Beth as she holstered the shotgun, changed belts on the LMG, and then reached for the door to the stairwell. Grace burst through the top part of the bullet-ridden door, legs curled up underneath her, her knees hitting Beth in the chest, sending her flying back. Du Bois heard something hit the carpet at his feet. He looked down at the grenade without its pin and spoon. He turned to run. The grenade exploded and sent him spinning through the air. The rest of the partitioning wall was demolished. He landed a reddened screaming mess. He was little more than pain now. Bullets were impacting into him. Grace was a shadow in the dust and smoke, fire in her hands from the two fully automatic Berettas. Low calibre rounds trying to beat the hardened bone and skin of his skull. Everything went black. Death felt like a blessed relief.

'How fucking servile are you? He killed your father!'

The relief hadn't lasted long. Now most of his nerve endings needed shutting down. He was living in pain despite the stimulated endorphin production. His neuralware was letting him know that he was broken. His body was eating itself as it tried to heal but he had taken a lot of damage. He needed matter and energy. He couldn't move, let alone fight, he couldn't even talk. He was a spectator now.

'I don't want to kill you, but I will. Why don't you put the knife away and let's go and cap dad together?' Grace's voice sounded strange. The punk girl had a fighting knife at the ready in each hand. The hilts of the weapons had knuckle-dusters built in to them. Part of the office was burning, but even through the smoke and dust he could see much of the flesh on the side of Grace's face was gone, he could see bone.

Beth was standing opposite her. She had lost the LMG. Her face was red with blood, deep slash marks in the skin and flesh. Her left arm was limp against her body. In her right hand she held a bloody World War I bayonet.

Du Bois tried to shout something. Instead he made a rattling

361

noise and bone clicked together. He shifted precious physiological resources to rebuild his mouth. His neuralware made him aware of how poor an idea this was.

'I don't think he did it,' Beth said quietly. 'I think he's done all kinds of bad things, but I don't think he did that. I think you know who put those memories in your mind, who raped you.'

Du Bois tried to speak again. He dribbled bloody drool down himself but he had made a noise. They ignored him.

'It's him I see!' Grace screamed, tears rolling down her face. 'Him I see pulling me out of the pile of corpses, protecting me, training me, making sure I got an education, and then, and then ... he was just fucking grooming me!'

'For how long?' Beth asked quietly. 'How long did you work with him before he suddenly changed?'

Du Bois didn't understand. Beth owed him nothing. Not after what he had done.

'But it's him I see! Every fucking time!' Grace was shaking her head. 'You've got to get out of my way.' She was practically begging Beth.

'I can't do that,' Beth said. 'It's not right.'

Grace stared at her. Du Bois could see the punk girl getting angry again, through the tears.

'Not right? Not right! He killed your fucking father!'

'And when it's time I'll deal with that, but I don't think he hurt you.'

'What? You've known him for maybe a week?' Grace demanded. Beth shrugged with one shoulder. 'I knew him over a century and he fooled ...' The sobs wracking her diaphragm looked positively painful. 'Move!' she shouted, snot running freely down her face. Du Bois read the punk girl's body language. She was about to attack. If Beth only had the use of one arm she wouldn't stand a chance.

'No!' It felt like the word had been torn from a raw throat. He managed to move and throw his .45 at Grace's feet. Both of the women looked down at it. Outside, the Osprey still hung in the sky, level with their floor, its rotors beating the warm night air. 'Nanite-tipped rounds,' he managed, pointing at the pistol. 'If it will give you peace.'

Du Bois was grateful that Beth said nothing. She was just looking between the two of them. Grace was staring at the pistol. Then it looked like she had to force herself to look at du Bois. He had no idea what it was that she saw there but she didn't attack Beth with knives. She didn't pick up the .45 and kill him. Instead she just sat down hard on the debris-strewn floor, knives falling from her fingers, and cradled her head in her hands.

Alexia crashed through the broken door to the stairwell, assault rifle at the ready. She looked around.

'Oh,' she said.

It had felt weird, Alexia carrying him down the stairs and out of the building once they had retrieved their various weapons. He was used to being the one looking after her, but Beth was too badly injured to help, and Grace obviously wouldn't touch him. *When did I stop thinking of Alexia as a he?* he wondered briefly.

'You really messed him up,' Alexia said. She had laid him against one of the ECV's wheels and hooked him up to a matter IV. He could feel his body starting to heal faster, filling out where it had cannibalised itself to remain functioning. The boot of the armoured patrol vehicle was open. Beth was sitting on the lip of it eating concentrated energy bar after concentrated energy bar.

The vehicle looked like it had taken a real beating. The armour was pitted and scored. Alexia had moved it from cover to get it into position and then fired the minigun up at the Osprey just enough to draw its fire. She had probably saved Beth and him.

'Were we friends?' Alexia asked Grace. Grace was also eating the energy bars. Regrown skin and flesh were slowly creeping across her face.

'Yeah, yeah we were,' Grace said a smiling ruefully. 'Once or twice more than that.'

Alexia stopped fussing with the IV and turned to look Grace up and down.

'You look like my type, y'know, when you're a bit less banged up.'

Normally when his sister spoke like this it made him feel uncomfortable but this time, there was something about the familiarity of it. He wished he could remember this strange, angry girl. Woman, he corrected himself. This, more than anything else, this piece of needless spite, this damage done, had made him realise just how much he hated Mr Brown.

'Sorry about your friends,' Beth said from the back of the ECV. Du Bois wished the three of them were paying more attention to what was going on around them.

'You get involved with violence ...' Grace said. 'I liked Josh but he was ...' She turned to look at du Bois, unable to keep the look of disgust off her face. Du Bois had known Ezard, the American, he had found the man pleasant enough, easy to work with, competent, but had always harboured a feeling of resentment towards him, he'd never been sure why. He hoped it wasn't anything as petty as the War of Independence. Naturalised British or not, he was still Norman French after all. 'Mueller, on the other hand—' Grace began.

'—Was an arsehole.' Du Bois had said it at the same time as her. She turned to regard him coolly.

'It would have been better if we could have spoken to Ezard,' du Bois said.

'Are you with us?' Alexia asked. Beth looked over at Grace.

'I want that fucker punished,' the punk said. 'I'd been having doubts since the Boneyard.' She shook her head. 'It was so real ...' She was still looking at him. The intensity of her stare was making him want to look away, making him feel ashamed, regardless of the truth. 'I'll help you get him,' Grace said, 'but I can't be near him.' She nodded at du Bois, and then finally looked away, much to his relief. 'Then I'm for the desert. Maybe I'll look for the City of Brass.' She tapped the side of her head. 'See if they can sort out what's real and what's bullshit up here.'

'Is that what we're doing?' Beth asked. 'Getting the bastard?'

'What else?' Alexia asked.

'An escape plan,' Grace said.

'I think there's a chance. When I answered the phone ...' du Bois started.

'When you spoke to the Seeders?' Grace said, sceptically.

'There was something there trying to communicate with me ...' du Bois said. 'I think there may still be uncorrupted seed pods.'

Alexia and Beth both had blank expressions on their faces. Grace looked dubious. Du Bois could see her point. Hearing it out loud it sounded like wishful thinking, the insidiousness of false hope. He looked down.

'Whatever we do, Mr Brown cannot be allowed to prosper,' he said quietly. Grace was nodding in agreement.

'Killing him might be doing him a favour,' Grace said. 'I'd only ever met Mr Brown a couple of times before, but recently I've spent more time with him. He's in a lot of pain. I mean, he gets through industrial amounts of synthetic morphine and he barely feels it.'

'What's wrong with him?' Alexia asked, straightening up and reaching for her assault rifle.

Grace shrugged. 'He's not a normal ...' Grace seemed to be searching for the right phrase as she reached for another one of the energy bars. ' ... thing.'

'Do we even know how to kill him?' Alexia asked, looking at du Bois.

'Well, the DAYP may have come up with an idea,' du Bois said. 'According to what I found out.' *What you ate*, he thought, but kept it to himself. 'The Russians were guarding a nuclear warhead. A suitcase bomb made from a Soviet nuclear-tipped artillery round. The FBI believed that La Calavera was acting as a middle man for the Mexican cartels, who were in turn looking to sell it to terrorists.'

'La Calavera double-crossed them?' Beth asked. Du Bois nodded.

'Why pay for it when you can get it for free, and he's insane. He doesn't care about the consequences.'

'So he's working for the DAYP?' Alexia asked. 'But then why send you to the scene of the crime?'

'Because he wanted time,' du Bois said.

'But he does want a confrontation,' Grace said. 'A challenge.'

Du Bois noticed Beth looking between the two of them.

'That doesn't make sense either,' Alexia said. 'Why would the DAYP want to blow up Mr Brown? What would they gain?'

'I don't think they do,' Grace said. 'But everybody has nothing to lose at the moment.'

Du Bois was nodding in agreement. 'They'll use it as a bargaining chip to make Mr Brown deal with them, rather than turning them inside-out and taking what he wants anyway,' he added.

'Do you know where he's going?' Beth asked Grace.

'No, only that he's here to meet with someone.'

'Where is he now?' Alexia asked.

'I don't know. Karma took out our spaceplane. We took the Osprey and came after you. We dropped Mr Brown and the Pennangalan some place in Bel Air. Looked like there was a car waiting for them.'

'How'd you find us?' Beth asked, narrowing her eyes. 'And why does Mr Brown care? We've got to be nothing more than an irritation to him now.'

'He didn't,' du Bois said.

'I did,' Grace said. 'We tracked you with our own satellites.'

'Keep all the really dangerous people fighting each other,' du Bois said.

'Which I'm guessing was the whole point,' Grace said quietly.

'What did he do to Karma?' Beth asked. 'It's like he rearranged his body with a thought. I liked him.'

'I don't know,' Grace said. 'I've never seen anything like that before. It's got to be some application of the tech.' She looked at du Bois but he just shook his head.

'Something's been bothering me,' Alexia said.

'Just the one thing?' Beth asked.

Alexia pointed up at the Osprey. 'Who's flying that?'

30

A Long Time After the Loss

Scab had wanted to see this confrontation between the two sisters. Vic had a big power-assisted claw on the Monk's shoulder. Talia was holding her bleeding, obviously broken nose.

'You didn't have to hit me!' the girl wailed. Scab was aware of how much shriller his life had become ever since they had found Talia. It was why he preferred the ghost. Why couldn't she be more like the ghost?

'I'm sorry. It was a reaction. You attacked me,' the Monk told her sister as she shrugged Vic's hand away. Scab knew this was a lie. The Monk had wanted to hurt Talia. He suspected she had felt this way since long before the Loss. He could understand why. Talia was very annoying, but it was more than that. Sometimes beauty was difficult to be around, and sometimes beauty hid spite.

'Let me see it,' Vic said, trying to pull Talia's hands away from her bleeding nose. Talia angrily tried to slap him away but hurt herself on his hard-tech body. Scab sat down on one of the armchairs in the *Basilisk II*'s lounge/C&C, and lit a cigarette. The chair moulded itself into what should be the most comfortable configuration for him. It was comfortable but he didn't like anything else making decisions for him.

'What did you do?' Talia demanded. Her voice had a nasal quality because of the broken nose.

'I don't know what you're talking about,' the Monk said.

'I saw the ghost!' Talia shouted. Then she pointed at Scab. 'The one he's in love with!'

Everyone turned to look at him for a moment. He didn't like it, but he just took another drag on the cigarette.

'I don't know what Elodie told you,' Vic said. 'But she was trying to manipulate all of us. That's not how Scab's built.'

I can love, Scab thought, but of course he could never say that.

'The bridge drive is alive, isn't it?' Talia demanded.

Now Vic turned to stare at the Monk. Scab cocked his head to one side and exhaled smoke through his nostrils. He thought about getting undressed. As he listened he was creating an unusually subtle, for him, search routine utilising some of the Pythian software they had bought previously.

'You can't ...' The Monk looked like her sister had actually managed to slap her, hard.

'Can't what?' Talia spat. 'I saw her. In the Drive. Looking back at me. Do you know who she looks like, Beth?'

Vic was looking between the two sisters, utterly mystified. 'Who?' he asked.

'The ghost looks like Talia,' Scab said quietly. 'I saw her for the first time after the Monks transferred the bridge drive from the *St Brendan's Fire* to the *Basilisk II*.'

'Fucking heretics,' the Monk said, shaking her head.

'Tell me, how many of the heresies were to do with self-determination for the bridge ghosts?' Scab asked. The Church's malice in this matter was as incidental as it was appalling, to someone else, that was, Scab thought. It did, however, prove that their sense of moral superiority was nothing more than rank hypocrisy.

'Well, the heresy that was sheltering you fucking wasn't!' the Monk said angrily, but it was guilty anger. Talia was staring at her older sister, furious. The Monk sighed. 'It's not the bridge. The bridge drives were derived from S-Tech, biotech. The ability to navigate was hidden in Talia's bloodline.'

'But surely it's your bloodline as well,' Vic said.

'They're not real sisters,' Scab said. The Monk turned to stare at him, but said nothing.

'Beth's parents kidnapped me when I was a baby,' Talia said.

'They didn't kidnap you. You were given to them by your real mum,' the Monk told her sister. 'We don't fully understand how the ships navigate in Red Space, it's instinctive as far as we can tell, but the navigation system is a biological computer.'

'Which apparently requires a consciousness,' Scab added.

'So they cloned slave Talia as hardware,' Talia said, and then turned to Scab. 'And you wanted me to see it.'

'I felt you should,' Scab said. People were always misunderstanding his intentions.

'Well, thank you for sharing your wank-fodder with me. A silent, submissive Talia.'

368

'She certainly whines less than you,' Scab admitted. He had never wanted to kill Talia more. In fact he wasn't sure why she was still here. Yes, she had piloted the ship, but both he and the Monk could do that. He couldn't see a use for her. 'We don't have a use for her any more,' he said out loud, pointing at Talia with the two fingers holding the smouldering cigarette.

Vic actually stepped in front of the girl.

The Monk sagged. 'This again?'

'Fuck you! I flew the ship!' Talia spat, looking around the side of Vic's massive, armoured, insectile form. 'Despite your little head fuck!'

Scab knew he was going to have to go or he would kill someone. He started to sink into the armchair and through the floor.

'You flew like a pro. How did you manage that?' Scab heard the Monk ask.

'I pretended I was playing a computer game, and don't change the fucking subject!'

It hadn't been as interesting as he had thought, Scab decided when he had sunk into the ship's smart matter. He assumed the Church, and presumably by extension the Monk, had just rationalised it. It would be why the ghosts were silent, unseen most of the time. They would have told themselves it wasn't happening. Made the consciousness into something else in their minds. It was how people who thought of themselves as 'good' worked. They weren't really good. Just less self-aware. As far as he could tell, the idea of being a good person was just about looking down on others and making them feel like shit. His revelation meant there would just be more arguing. There was always more arguing. He missed it being just him and a submissive Vic. If his search didn't come back with anything useful then he was going to have to come up with something else to do. If that happened he was going to kill everyone else on board.

He thought about going to see her. Just to watch her. He knew that she was aware of him, but Talia seeing her had spoiled it somehow, soiled the experience. Instead he decided to see what was in the immersion construct that Churchman had uploaded to the *Basilisk II* for the Monk.

The construct had been strange, almost frightening. It hadn't made any sense to him, but then he had always found reality easier to cope with than fantasy.

Now he was watching the Monk in her room, from inside the smart matter. She was getting undressed. He liked her body. It was spare and hard. There was no waste. She finished and stood in front of the bed, hands on her hips.

'Scab? Come out. I know you're watching.'

Scab tried to decide what to do. He had few weapons left. Most of them had been eaten by the *Templar*'s nano-swarm. His robust tumbler pistol was being reconditioned by the *Basilisk II*'s assembler. He still had his metalforma knife and straight edge razor somewhere in the smart matter. He could still kill her if need be, but she was naked, as though showing herself to him. He pushed his face through the ceiling's smart matter. She looked up at him.

'Come down, please,' she said. He wasn't sure why, but he extruded himself through the roof and dropped on to the convincing-looking smart matter replica of wooden boards that made up the floor in the Monk's room. They were warm. He wasn't sure why he was naked either, and he was surprised to find he was holding the inert form of the scorpion in his hand.

Where had that come from? He had given the remains to the *Basilisk II*'s assembler after the Innocent had destroyed it. He had known that the assembler could never fix it, make the weapon operational again, but it had put the shell back together. The Monk was looking down at it. Scab held it up for her to see.

'It's broken. Dead,' he explained. 'Given long enough, that's what happens.' She nodded. 'You like ... things?' he asked. He offered it to her.

'Scab, I can't take that. It's ... I don't know, it's precious to you, isn't it?'

'It's just a thing. It's no use any more. You like useless things. Your sister ...'

She laughed. 'Why do I get the feeling this is you trying to be nice?' She took the scorpion from him. 'Thank you. I do like useless things.' He grabbed her by the throat. She just looked at him. 'No,' she finally said, and pulled his hand away from her throat. He wasn't sure why he let her. She dropped the scorpion on her bed. Then she reached up and touched the side of his face. He couldn't quite read her expression. 'This is the last time anything like this ever happens.' She moved in closer to him, their skin touching. Her nipples brushed over his chest. She kissed him, gently. He only had a moment to suppress the worst of the toxins in his saliva. Even then he was sure the kiss must have burned.

Later, when they were lying together in bed, the Monk was looking at the scorpion. She had grown a table from the floor to put it on.

'If it's no longer of use, why did you reassemble it?' she asked.

'Don't do that,' he replied. 'Don't look for meaning.' She rolled over to look at him. Despite the question he felt calm.

'It's a connection, isn't it? Not something you care about exactly ...'

He started to climb out of bed. 'This will only weaken me.'

The Monk sat up. 'This will never happen again,' she told him, again. He wasn't even angry that someone was making decisions for him. He wasn't sure what he felt. For some reason he didn't leave. He just sat on the edge of the bed. 'We have to stop tearing at each other. All of us.'

He looked back at her and then pulled the covers off her and looked at her body, then shook his head. *What am I doing?*

'This is not what I'm here for,' he said quietly.

'Why the ghost?' Beth asked.

'Purity,' he whispered the word. 'I think I have to kill your sister.'

'That's just the romantic in you talking,' Beth told him. Scab turned to look at the Monk but there was no mockery in her words. 'People can't live up to that. Nobody's pure. Everybody compromises. Even you.' A tiny wisp of smoke arose from the mock-wooden floorboards. He unclenched his hands and saw where filed nails had penetrated the skin of his palms and drawn toxic blood. 'See, I think it's the other way around. The ghost has made you want the flesh, but you can't have the feelings, the connection to her. So you have to destroy.'

He looked back at her. 'So I settle for second best?' he asked, and gestured towards her.

The Monk laughed and put her hands behind her head. 'So Scab's back, then?' He stood up.

'Want to turn your insight on yourself?' Scab asked.

'I've no doubt I've done this for all sorts of shitty, fucked-up reasons. Or maybe it's just because I wanted to have sex, and you're the only non-insect on board. Or maybe I just wanted to ask you not to hurt my sister. Thinking about it, I've gone to great lengths to protect her in the past.'

Scab looked down. 'Asking is better,' he said quietly.

'Then can I ask you to stop tearing at us? Stop setting us against each other?'

He shrugged. 'I don't know,' he admitted. 'You can ask.'

'Your ... Benedict, we can't ...'

Scab held up a hand. 'Stop,' he said. She had been doing well but he knew she was about to tell him to do something. 'I ... feel things, intensely. People don't think I do but I do, but only in connection to myself.'

'That's because you're a psychopath,' the Monk said. He suspected that she had worked hard to keep the tone neutral, to remove the sympathy in her voice that would have led to murder.

'I am a virus. I have to stop the spread.'

'We can't just keep killing everyone. Even if Patron is practicing a scorched earth policy.'

'Then I'm the useless one.'

'You transmitted again,' Beth said.

'I'm being careful.'

'What are you doing?'

'I'm looking for the Ubh Blaosc.'

'Thank you.'

'It's not for you, or your sister, or that insipid fucking insect.' The anger had come from nowhere. A red wave the colour of space sweeping over him.

'The rage is starting to look a little impotent,' the Monk said.

Scab whipped round to stare at her. Shaking now. She held the look calmly.

'Until one of you leaves me with no choice. I am here, now, because I am curious. In terms of motivation, it's not much of one.'

'Do you know why we like you? Talia and I, and I suspect many of the women you've been with in your life?'

'Self loathing.'

'Woman are attracted to you because you are a vulnerable little boy, and some of us, and maybe it is self esteem problems, never seem to quite grow out of wanting to look after boys like you. To mother them.' His hands claws, he moved towards the bed. He wanted to taste the blood in her neck. 'Don't pretend. If you wanted to kill me you would have moved a lot faster. I'm not in any danger because you pride yourself on honesty. Even with yourself.' He stopped. He found himself not wanting to think about what she had said. 'You can't be pure if they changed you with brain surgery. It doesn't stop you from living a life.' He just turned and walked to the door. 'You could go through the wall, the ceiling, the floor, but you want her to know you've been with me, don't you? You want her to hurt.'

Scab turned back to the Monk. 'So do you,' he said quietly. The door opened and he walked out.

The door closed behind Scab. 'Only sometimes,' she said quietly. 'Fuck!' Beth got out of bed and grabbed her robe hanging from the side of the small, narrow wardrobe. 'Basil?' The ship's AI, looking like Churchman, appeared. Absurdly she found herself feeling guilty. She suppressed her blush response and had the bed make itself with a thought.

'Miss Luckwicke?' the image of the ship's AI, projecting itself into her neunonics, and through them to the visual centres of her brain, asked.

'Could you say something judgemental but paternal to me about my behaviour?' she asked. Basil smiled somewhat ruefully.

'I'm afraid not, Miss Luckwicke, not without extensive re-programming.'

'Please don't call me that, call me Beth,' the Monk said irritably.

'Are you sure that would help?' the AI asked.

'No, you're right,' she admitted. She wanted someone to judge her. She couldn't work out what she had been thinking? What she had hoped to achieve? *Orgasm?* a voice inside her enquired, and she smiled. 'Well, it certainly wasn't a newfound sense of self control.'

'Miss Luckwicke?'

'Christ, you're like a butler.'

'I could change my response parameters if you wish.'

'No, look, I'm sorry.'

'Miss Luckwicke, if you'll excuse me for saying I think you're still grieving. There are a number of options available to you, pharmacological, neural editing, immersion counselling ...'

'No!' Beth snapped. 'I'm fine,' she continued more softly.

'Will you be co-habiting with Mr Scab?' Basil enquired.

'No! No, god no. That will never happen again. I'm sorry to have bothered you, please can you leave me alone?'

The AI bowed. 'Of course, though the other Miss Luckwicke is coming this way.'

The Monk sagged. 'Let her in.' Basil disappeared and the door opened just as Talia reached it. The Monk went and sat on the bed and hugged her legs to her chest.

'If you've come to have another screaming match then I'm afraid you won't find much in the way of opposition.'

'I don't care about you and Scab,' Talia said. It was obviously a lie. What the Monk suspected she meant was that she couldn't understand why Scab had chosen Beth over her sister, which would, of course, make Talia feel jealous and shitty. Of course the Monk knew the truth, that Scab in fact preferred some perfect, idolised, unobtainable version of her sister, which made Beth feel shitty and jealous.

'I think the cool boy in school is making us both feel miserable,' Beth mused. It just made Talia look irritated. If not Scab, then Beth assumed her sister had come to shout at her some more about the Church's slavery of her cloned consciousness. She had honestly never thought about it that way, but even if Talia was right there was nothing she could do about it now except feel guiltier, and frankly she wasn't sure she could face the scale of it. To accept Talia's perspective meant that they were monsters, and had always been. Everything that they had done with the queasy rationale of the ends justifying the means had just been to perpetuate a monstrous crime. She could either try and process it, or get on with what they were trying to do.

Talia pointed towards the back of the ship. Beth guessed that was where she thought the bridge drive was. 'You know that's me, don't you? That's what I did for her.'

'Her?' the Monk asked.

'The other ship. The Seeder. She didn't have a name. It wasn't how we communicated. We just felt things.'

Beth took a deep breath. 'An apology doesn't quite seem to cut it,' the Monk said. She wished she knew more about bridge tech but it had been restricted knowledge. Perhaps that explained why Churchman had mostly used dolphins. They could be deeply unpleasant creatures when they wanted to. 'What do you want me to do about it?'

Eyes surrounded by dark make-up just stared at her.

'What's in the immersion you brought on board?' Talia asked.

'That bastard!' the Monk spat. *No, you can't have that. It's mine. Something for me. You take everything! Destroy everything you touch!* It was millennia-old resentment. She had known it was still there,

374

but had underestimated just how strong the feeling was. 'Scab told you?'

'He described, y'know, home before it all went tits up. It sounded like Maude and Uday.'

The Monk could feel it in her chest. She didn't want to share. *What? Your pets?* The question sounded harsh in her own head.

'We downloaded their personalities after you ... after the Seeder in the Solent woke up and spored. They were damaged. We tried to save what we could.' She found herself wondering if the City of Brass still existed. She hoped they were there, whole, cured, happy, cared for by people less selfish than the Luckwicke family.

'They might not want to see you,' the Monk said. She gathered her quilt around her miserably. *Because you turned Maude out, made her a porn star, a prostitute,* she thought viciously, and she really, really wanted to say it out loud. 'Wait a second, what do you mean he described?' Scab had been in the immersion. Cold panic spread through her chest.

'They were friends of mine,' Talia said. 'Well less Uday, but Maude.'

You lying bitch. The Monk was just about to tell her this, but then it occurred to her there was an easier way, because she was sure that the person Talia was telling the biggest lie to was herself. 'Fine,' she said. 'If Scab's left anything.' And if he had done anything to them this was all over. She would kill him, even with the memory of his touch all over her skin.

'Look, let me speak to them first, you're going to come as a bit of a shock to them, all right?' Beth said as they walked down the tree-lined Campbell Road. She was pleased that it didn't look like a post-apocalyptic hellscape after Scab's visit. It was a cold, bleak, late autumn day. The leaves were a damp mulch on the pavement, the sky was devoid of colour, but somehow it didn't bother her. She adjusted her ponytail and pulled her leather jacket tighter around her. Talia was looking at her. 'What?'

'I'd forgotten that you looked like that,' Talia said. 'I always really liked your jacket.'

Beth didn't say anything, she just kept walking. At the gateway to the small, overgrown, front garden Beth told her sister to wait. She bounded up the steps to the old townhouse that had been turned into flats, and put her key in the door. She wasn't sure why but she turned to look back at Talia. Her sister looked cold, wan, and pale standing by the gate. She looked like a ghost.

'Okay, come with me, but you need to stay in the hall until I've had a chance to have a chat with them. Assuming Scab hasn't done something awful,' she muttered. Talia smiled and ran up the steps.

Beth didn't like it. Normally walking into the flat was the best feeling in the world. Now she was scared and angry. Talia would talk them round, no matter what she'd done. Then Beth would have to share. Then the games would begin. Maybe this hadn't been such a good idea, she decided.

She heard the omnipresent TV, the ambient soundtrack of a student household. The smell of whatever had been cooked last. She motioned Talia to stay in the hall, and went in. So far there was no trace of Scab having done anything horrific. She could hear Uday and Maude talking to each other. She just hoped they weren't centipedes with human faces, or larvae of some kind. She steeled herself and walked into the lounge. Everything looked fine. Maude was sitting on the floor surrounded by folders full of coursework. Uday was stretched out on the sofa with a wet towel on his head, looking very dramatic.

'Hi Beth,' Maude said. 'Uday's had a funny turn.' She was grinning. Alarm bells were going off in Beth's head.

'I did not have a funny turn,' Uday said waspishly. 'I saw a ghost!' Maude was just smiling and shaking her head.

'Ghost?' Beth asked. Uday pushed himself up on the sofa.

'Oh my god, Beth, it was terrifying! I got back in from Uni and he was standing right there.' He pointed at the middle of the room. 'It was awful! The most malevolent looking man I have ever seen! He looked like ... looked like ... He looked like Olivier in *The Entertainer*, if Olivier had hated the world and wanted it to die in a fire.' Maude stifled a giggle. It was an interesting description of Scab, she conceded. 'And this little minx won't believe me!'

'I believe you,' Beth said, trying to suppress her own smile. 'What happened?'

'What? You mean after I shat my pants?'

'No, describe that process,' Beth said. 'Yes, after that.'

'Excuse me, I think you'll find I do the sarcasm around here, both you ladies are too gentle in temperament.'

'Uday!' Maude scolded.

'Well, he turned to look at me, and right then I knew I was dead. I mean, my heart stopped, and then he was gone.'

'Just like that?' Beth asked. She was struggling to imagine Uday and Scab meeting, but mostly she was pleased that he hadn't done anything too horrific.

'Attention seeking,' Maude said in a sing-song voice.

'Quiet, harridan,' Uday said imperiously. 'Seriously though, it gave me quite a fright.'

'Guys, look, I have something to tell you and I don't think ...'

Talia came through the front door and all but pushed past Beth. She cursed herself for not locking it behind her.

'Guys, I'm back!' Talia announced.

Maude curled up, shaking, into a foetal ball and burst into tears. Uday raised a trembling finger and pointed at her. 'The destroyer,' he managed. Talia looked between them and then fled. With a thought Beth froze the immersion.

Beth found Talia curled up in a corner on Fawcett Road, in an alleyway between a secondhand furniture shop and a takeaway. She crouched down next to her. Talia flinched when she touched her arm. She looked up, her face streaked with eyeliner from the tears.

'You turned them against me!' she spat. Beth didn't even feel angry now. She was going to have to go back and edit the encounter out of Uday and Maude's minds. It was for their own good, but it made her feel uncomfortable.

'The things you've done,' Beth said. 'Can you maybe think of a reason they would be angry with you?'

'They weren't angry. They were terrified,' Talia said, and started crying again. Beth just looked at her.

'You cause damage, Talia,' Beth finally said. 'You always have. You're like the social equivalent of Scab. Please stop.' Talia glared at Beth.

'You knew this was going to happen, didn't you?' Talia spat. Beth gave the question some thought.

'I had a pretty good idea but I knew that if I didn't bring you here I was looking at a future of screaming, arguments, wheedling, emotional blackmail and tears, wasn't I?'

Talia didn't say anything for a moment. 'You know it's sick, keeping them here like pets,' she said coldly. Beth looked away from her sister and down Fawcett Road at the frozen traffic and pedestrians.

'Maybe,' she admitted. Then she turned back to her sister. 'But I suspect that had that gone better you would have found a way to cope. Besides, do you think I should have erased them?'

Talia's face crumpled as she started to cry again. 'You didn't even know them!' she wailed.

'Probably not. Talia, stop crying. I'm sick of it.' There was no anger in Beth's voice. Talia looked up at her as if she had been slapped. 'I mean it.'

'Have you any idea what I've—'

'Maybe you should try using the words "I" and "me" less often as well. I know this is frightening. I know that all sorts of horrible things have happened to you, and nobody deserves that, regardless of how they behave. But that,' she pointed back towards Campbell Road, 'is all on you. As for the rest of it: I am here for you, whatever you do, as always, but you have to stop making it worse for yourself and everyone else.'

Talia stared up at her. Beth turned away and looked up at the blank sky. For the first time probably ever, she didn't want to be here.

'We should get back, see what fresh new hell Scab has prepared for us,' Beth muttered.

'Beth,' Talia said. Beth turned around. Her sister was standing up now.

'Thank you. For everything. I mean it.'

Beth pursed her lips but then nodded. Talia removed herself from the program with a thought.

The Monk opened her eyes and looked at Talia lying next to her on the bed. The branches of the superconducting material she had used for the brain/immersion interface was receding away from her ears and back into the walls. Talia sat up and wiped away the tears and snot with the back of her lace glove. Then she looked at Beth and smiled.

'Scab's found something,' Vic 'faced.

'About the Ubh Blaosc?' Beth asked.

'Maybe,' Vic replied.

31
Ancient Britain

Bress didn't think he had ever heard Crom Dhubh laugh before. It was oddly high-pitched. It didn't sound right. They watched the chariots emerge from the cave and speed towards them.

'They have nothing to offer us now but sport,' Crom Dhubh said. Bress felt his heart lurch. He knew she would be there before he saw her black-robed form, her half a head of red hair trailing her, like fire trails a comet. She had come for the rod.

'She is with them—' Bress started. The Dark Man turned to look at him. Any humour was now gone from his obsidian features.

'No,' he said, forestalling Bress's inevitable question. 'That was an amusement. Nothing more. She no longer wishes life for her, or the unborn child.' The child was a sickness, Bress knew that, but despite feeling Crom Dhubh's will crushing his own, he was not sure that he could kill her.

'I could show you a mercy. Kill her myself. There would be nothing left of her.' Something strange happened to the air in front of the Dark Man, and he was holding his black sword with the complex hilt, the blade edged with light. Bress lowered his head. Crom Dhubh's laugh was full of contempt.

'Should you risk yourself?' Bress asked, still not looking at his master.

'There is no risk. I cannot be killed. If anything I should be protecting you. You will be needed when the bridge is opened.'

'Should we bring the Lochlannach down from . . .'

'No, they remain in place.' Crom Dhubh turned and walked down onto the ice. Other than the children he had transformed as servitors, and the Lochlannach he would take to the Ubh Blaosc, they had no other forces on Oeth itself.

The chariots had formed a long column. It looked like they intended to circle the island. Spiked wheels on the chariots and

379

studded shoes on the sturdy garrons gave them purchase on the thick ice.

Bress followed his master. The strange sound of the hoof beats on ice echoed through the cavern. The first chariot passed. Bress thought he recognised the archer in the cart. She had been one of the warriors that had come here with Britha the last time. Arrows started to fly as the chariots passed. Many of them skittered across the ice but Bress had to dodge out of the way of a few of them. Several hit Crom Dhubh. The Dark Man plucked them from his body, their red metal heads still wriggling, trying to grow iron roots. Black dust fell from the wounds onto the ice as he cast the arrows aside.

Crom Dhubh pointed at one of the chariots. Something awful and nauseating happened to space. Bress looked away, pain lancing through his head.

Britha heard the sound of tortured horseflesh, human, and animals screaming, wood and metal splintering. One of the chariots ahead of her, the fifth in line, was tumbling across the ice. It looked like it had been picked up, crumpled together, fusing man, woman, horseflesh, and chariot, and then skimmed across the frozen lake. It reminded her of what Teardrop had done to the Corpse People at the gates of the Crown of Andraste. The other chariots were veering round it. Her charioteer had to steer the team so sharply the chariot came up on one wheel. Britha crouched and held onto the cart.

The warrior riding her chariot's yoke risked his life by holding on with one hand and throwing a casting spear with the other. It was an incredible throw, one worthy of stories and songs. It arced over the ice and hit the Dark Man dead centre in the chest. He didn't even try and dodge out of the way. He just reached up and tore it from crumbling flesh. That was when she knew they had lost.

The line broke. Bladud's order was easy to follow in the face of the giants' attack. It was messy. The front line, the Brigante and the Iceni, took the worst of it. Warriors and spear-carriers from all tribes ran. The Lochlannach surged forwards, pushing deep into the warband, hewing down any who got in the way. Some, in apparent panic, even ran towards the giants, mostly the *gwyllion* archers, and the warriors from various tribes carrying longspears but no shields.

Bladud opened his mouth to shout but suddenly his shield was sundered, his arm went numb. He screamed, more angry than in pain. The pommel of his sword slammed down into the corner of one of the Lochlannach's eyes, hard enough to break the bridge of the demon-possessed warrior's nose, and fill the eye socket with a red mess. With the same movement he scraped the red iron blade of his sword down across the man's face, opening it up. He stepped past the man, cutting at the back of his leg. The Lochlannach hit the ground. Bladud ran his sword through the possessed warrior's chest. The next one was nearly upon him.

'Murder these bastards!' Bladud screamed.

They were circling around the island now. Bress and Crom Dhubh were waiting for the chariots out on the ice. The lead chariot, Tangwen and Calgacus's, steered clear of them. That had been the whole point of using the chariots. Keep the warriors and archers away from the Dark Man and his destroying sword. Kill him with arrows and casting spears.

Tangwen, and the Iceni scouts, and *gwyllion* archers, were putting arrow after arrow into Crom Dhubh, but he just plucked them out.

Suddenly the Dark Man, his colour such a contrast to the pure white of the ice, darted forwards with incredible speed, the strangeness of his movement reminding her of Goibhniu somehow, and swung the black sword at the lead horse of the chariot two chariots in front of Britha's.

Everything went white. Something hit her, hard. *The baby!* she thought. Then she was in the air, followed by another hard impact. The cavern's ceiling was rushing past high above her as she was dragged across the ice. She had lost her spear. Somehow her charioteer was still in the cart. Britha was attached to the chariot by the leather she had used to secure herself to the frame. There was a hole in the ice where the chariot Crom Dhubh had hit had been. The chariot that had been behind the destroyed one, its horses burned and screaming, galloped straight into the rent in the ice. Water coursed over the lake's frozen surface, and Britha was dragged through it. The charioteer was wrestling with a panicked team, despite the 'elixir' the animals had imbibed. Britha managed to reach forward, grab the leather, and inch her way back towards the chariot. Even with the blessings of the chalice she struggled to pull herself back up into the cart once she had reached its frame.

The charioteer managed to control the team as they thundered past Crom Dhubh. He watched them pass. He was staring at her but she looked past him to Bress. He was crouched low, trying to avoid getting hit with arrows. Their eyes met. Britha saw pain. She knew he would see resolve.

'Take me close to him,' she told the charioteer, who nodded. The warrior who had ridden on the chariot's yoke had gone. Britha was looking around for her spear. They circled the other end of the island. Glancing behind she could see Tangwen's chariot catching up with them, Calgacus on the yoke, holding on for grim life.

Light shone through the ice from beneath them. It was emanating from where Britha had seen what looked like a circle of standing stones and some kind of structure on her previous visits.

She saw her spear. She pointed it out to the charioteer. He manipulated the reins, changing the team's direction. Britha crouched down, her hands all but skimming the ice; her finger caught the haft and she was armed again.

The timid Pict, the *gwyllion*, damn them, and the Iceni scouts had done their job well. They had counted the enemy. Bladud commanded more spears than they did. Tangwen's plan had called for the Lochlannach to be let among the warband on purpose.

'Form shield wall!' Bladud screamed. Behind him the spear-carriers dropped their spears, daggers were the order of the day. They fell upon the Lochlannach, cutting tendons, carrying them to the ground, stabbing and slashing. It had been a complex plan, too complex in Bladud's opinion, but it was working, somehow. He could not ever remember being as happy as he was when he saw the shield wall form again.

There was a cheer, followed by a crash that shook the gory, slush-covered ground. The spearmen had done their job. One of the giants had fallen. Tangwen had spoken with the god in the Red Chalice. This Gofannon had forged them spears designed for killing the huge creatures. Tangwen had told him that the giants had people in them. It hadn't made any sense, even to a trained *dryw*, but when rammed into the giants the spearheads would grow into roots that sought out the people inside the huge creatures. Bladud had suspected they would just slay the creature's last meal, but it looked like Tangwen had been right. The *gwyllion* archers had gone to cover the spearmen, shooting down any Lochlannach that attempted to aid their giant allies.

Bladud could hear the sound of killing being done behind him. In front of him the remaining Lochlannach were forming up. Someone else in the shield wall pitched forwards face-down into the churned-up red slurry.

'Let's charge these cunts!' Bladud screamed. The ragged, painted, blood-soaked Pretani warriors and spear-carriers screamed and charged the Lochlannach. Bladud slipped and almost went down. He felt feverish, he was growing hotter and hotter, but it felt good.

'Bastard!' Britha screamed and swung her spear, blade-first, at Bress. He leapt the blade. An arrow hit him in the shoulder in mid-air but glanced off his armour and they were past him. Another arrow shot past Britha as Tangwen, now behind her, loosed on Crom. Britha had to let go of her spear with one hand and grab the frame of the cart as it slewed violently to one side to avoid Crom Dhubh.

The near deafening sound of the ice breaking echoed through the cavern. At the tip of the island closest to where the light beneath the frozen lake was, a giant had just burst through the frozen surface of the lake underneath one of the chariots. The creature flung the team and cart up into the cavern's ceiling, bouncing it off tooth-like rocks. Britha stared in horror. It grabbed another chariot and dragged it, screaming horse team and all, into the hole it had made in the ice. The archer and the charioteer jumped clear but the yoke-riding warrior was caught in the huge creature's fingers. The archer fired arrow after arrow into the massive creature as it pulled itself out of the lake and onto the ice.

At first Britha had thought they were some kind of hunting creatures running from the island across the ice, but then she recognised the transformed children. The charioteer drew her sword, and the Iceni archer in her lynx headdress turned to loose arrows on them, but they were swarmed and pulled, screaming, down onto the ice, teeth and nails finding flesh.

Britha saw Tangwen's chariot veer towards Bress. Calgacus, standing unsteadily, put one foot on the back of a galloping horse and threw himself shield-first at Bress. This surprised even Bress. Calgacus's shield, with the Cait *mormaer*'s weight behind it, caught Bress in the face and chest. He went down hard, both of them sliding across the ice.

'You fool,' Britha said under her breath. 'Turn around! Get me to Bress, now!' she screamed at the charioteer. It was a question of whether or not the chariot could get there before Calgacus was killed.

They had ground the Lochlannach's numbers down at great cost to themselves. Soulless and unfeeling the demon-possessed warriors may have been, but they hadn't been expecting the charge. They probably hadn't been expecting them to fight the giants toe-to-toe either. Now it was a simple expedient of break their enemy up, and fight them two to one. Bladud knew they had to kill every single one of them.

Garim at his side, the Witch King stalked through the mêlée looking for a victim. Frankly he was glad of a moment to catch his breath, the magics of the chalice coursing through his body notwithstanding. It was eerie the way the Lochlannach didn't scream as they were borne to the ground and stabbed, slashed, or bludgeoned to death.

The spearmen were working together, attacking the giants from all sides. The *gwyllion* who had been supporting them had cast aside their bows. They ran between the giants' legs, even in the cold they fought nearly naked, throwing themselves high at the Lochlannach without regard for their safety, or they rolled under sword slashes to attack the demon-possessed warriors from behind. The *gwyllion* fought together, reminding Bladud of a wolf pack. They harried their foe, brought them down and killed them. He watched as a giant crushed one of the *gwyllion*, and then flung the broken body at their lines.

Bladud saw Germelqart sit down, the snow still white underneath him, surrounded by a group of painted *gwyllion* warriors. He was holding the Red Chalice in his hands, his eyes closed, concentrating.

Bladud saw Ysgawyn fighting two of the Lochlannach, his blade flicking out. The blade of a sickle penetrated the helmet of one of the demon-possessed warriors; the man shook and then collapsed to his knees. Guidgen was standing behind the Lochlannach. Ysgawyn darted forwards and finished the other enemy warrior, before bowing to the *gwyll dryw*. Even from as far away as he was Bladud could make out the mockery of the gesture. Ysgawyn turned and moved away from Guidgen, obscuring Bladud's view of the old *dryw*. Suddenly the *rhi* of the Corpse People stopped and went rigid. The Witch King stared as a sickle blade circled Ysgawyn's neck and then harvested his throat. The *rhi* fell into the red slurry. Guidgen was standing over him. The bloody red sickle in his left hand.

No! Bladud thought. *That cannot stand!* He had his suspicions as regards the Corpse People's part in Nils' murder – if Madawg had killed Nils it was unlikely he would have acted alone – but Guidgen couldn't just do as he pleased. Bladud was furious. Steam was rising as the slush melted around him. He felt the heat of the *riasterthae* frenzy that gripped him.

'Form here!' Tangwen screamed, and her charioteer slewed the chariot to a halt some hundred paces in front of Crom Dhubh as he advanced towards them. Britha rode between them and the Dark Man, arrows flying past her as Tangwen loosed again and again at the obsidian-skinned figure. The other remaining chariots were pulling up next to Tangwen, the archers also loosing at Crom Dhubh. The chariots were ready just behind the archers to carry them away when the Dark Man got too close. The warriors were grabbing their longspears, running to face the giant stalking across the ice towards them. There were only four warriors, four archers.

Britha turned to look ahead. Calgacus had stumbled to his feet first. Britha knew he needed to move, but the Cait *mormaer* looked dazed. She was aware of the light beneath the ice brightening. Calgacus had managed to draw his sword. He was looking around for Bress. The chariot was bearing down on the warrior from the Otherworld, spiked wheels and studded hooves kicking up chips of ice.

'Redden the ice!' Britha screamed. 'Run him down!' She noticed that Bress was carrying the case that contained Fachtna's terrible spear. At the last moment Bress rolled to one side and swung his sword up through the first horse on one side of the team, then the next. He cut through the frame of the cart, cut through the charioteer at his midriff. Britha had thrown herself back the moment she had seen him move. The blade of her spearhead cut through the leather she had tied herself to the frame of the chariot with. His blade flashed over her, narrowly missing. Then she hit the bloody ice and slid along after the mangled remains of the chariot and horse team.

Bress didn't know if he was trying to kill her or not any more. Tears stung his eyes as he straightened up. The warrior who had thrown himself at him looked like he had recovered enough to attack. He swung at Bress. It was a good swing, if Bress had been a normal human of this realm. Bress just leant back out of the way of the blade. His own sword cut the man's shield in two, and took his arm off at the elbow. Bress stepped back and let his opponent think about the situation for a moment. The man stared at the bleeding stump of his shield arm as though he didn't really believe what was happening. Then he swung again. Bress parried as he glanced back at Britha. He had learned not to let his lover get behind him when she was angry. She was still lying on the bloody ice. Beyond her was the wreckage of the chariot and team. Bress turned back to the man he was fighting. He swung low, cutting through both the man's legs at the knee. The man's body fell to the ice. Beyond his opponent he could see Crom Dhubh. His master had arrows sticking out all over him. Even from where Bress was standing he could see the living, iron roots moving in the Dark Man's flesh like a second, living skin of red metal. Bress turned back to his opponent, who was flopping around on the bloody ice waving his sword at him. Bress studied the man, trying to work out why he was still attempting to fight. Did the man feel hate as he did, or was he motivated by something else? He stepped to one side, sword at the ready as his erstwhile love walked past the wounded warrior on the ice. She rammed the head of her spear through his opponent's chest and twisted. The man lay still on the ice in a widening pool of red. Britha turned to face him.

'Assassins?' she demanded, her face a storm.

'I told you to get rid of the child.' He would not look her in the eyes. 'I could not do it myself.'

'Coward!' she spat.

'It would seem so,' he said, nodding. Then he looked up at her. 'But you cannot beat me. It's over.' Beyond her, Crom Dhubh was stumbling as arrow after arrow thudded into him. The archers stepped back onto the chariots, and the chariots moved further away from Crom Dhubh. The archers were still loosing. Bress frowned. Had his master badly misjudged these people again?

Bress watched as the giant swept a warrior aside, then picked up another and squeezed; a third it stamped on. The fourth tried to run but didn't get very far. Bress turned back to Britha. She was looking at the bright light shining through the ice.

'What's happening?' she demanded.

Bress risked another quick look towards Crom Dhubh. The giant was making its way towards the archers and the chariots. The Dark Man suddenly faltered, and knelt down on the ice. Bress frowned.

'Give me the rod!' Britha screamed at him. He looked back to her.

'I do not have it,' he said, and glanced at the light underneath the ice. Britha followed his gaze. Then she saw Crom Dhubh on his knees. She dropped her spear on the ice, and walked quickly to Bress.

'You promised. You can be free. Please.' She was begging now. He shook his head. Crom Dhubh's will was too great. The giant would reach the archers and kill them before they could ever do lasting harm to the Dark Man.

'I cannot,' he said. Then he looked down at her, at her stomach. He put his hand on her belly and swallowed, only faintly aware of the tears running down his face. 'What this starts ... you have to kill it ... promise me and I ...' Bress looked over at Crom Dhubh on his knees again. He liked that. He turned back to Britha. 'Swear to me you'll kill it?' She stared back at him. 'Swear it.'

'Yes,' she said. He wasn't sure of the truth of it.

'Make me believe it, or I'll kill you both now!' Bress shouted, shaking her. The archers were on the chariots again, loosing arrows up at the giant as it bore down on them, the chariots trying to get up to speed.

'Yes! Yes! I'll kill it! I'll kill your seed for my daughter! A child by a better man than you!' she screamed. Bress read the hate in her face. He could feel it as pain. He felt his own face hardening. He nodded, blinking away tears.

'You need to get very far away from me,' he said. Britha was backing away from him. 'Very far. The light will take you where you want to go.' He reached behind him for the case containing Fachtna's spear: the Spear of the Sun. The spear that Crom had wanted him to carry back to its home, the Ubh Blaosc, and use

387

against them. He was a slave. He had always been a slave. He could not break Crom Dhubh's control over him. The Dark Man had provided him with the magics that helped control the spear, which protected him from the insane mind inside the weapon. He couldn't fight Crom Dhubh, but if the spear possessed him, if he voluntarily dropped his defences ...

'Run!' he screamed at her. He opened the case and took out the hungry burning spear, and surrendered to it.

The last giant fell. The remaining Lochlannach were being hunted down and killed. There could be no mercy. Steam rose from the snow and slurry with every footfall as Bladud made his way towards Guidgen. He could see others now. Gwynn, the remaining Corpse People warrior, looked as though he was glowing from within as well.

The heat was agony now. He was burning from the inside as he managed to put one step in front of the other. The old *dryw* saw him coming. Bladud pointed at him with his sword.

'You!' he cried. He tried to swing his sword at the *dryw*. Guidgen stepped back. Bladud's sword, re-forged in the chalice, turned to dust, red dust. The Witch King stumbled and fell to his knees. Guidgen looked down at him sympathetically. Nearby Gwynn screamed as he burst into flames. Bladud was shaking his head. 'This is neither right nor fair.'

Guidgen swallowed hard. 'You wanted too much.'

Bladud looked down. The pain made him want to scream but he didn't.

'After all I have done,' he said. 'I did not deserve this.'

'No,' Guidgen admitted. 'No, you did not.' He knelt down in front of the Witch King. 'They are already singing of you in Annwn.' As the last of the Lochlannach died Bladud's warband's weapons turned to red dust. The Witch King could see beyond Guidgen to where Germelqart sat on still pristine, white snow, protected by the *gwyllion* warriors. More warriors burst into flames, those who had drunk from the chalice. They deserved better than this, as did their terrified friends and allies. Some tried to help, some ran in terror, others just watched, numb after everything they had seen and done today. Bladud looked up at Guidgen.

'So you and your little circle control the Red Chalice and all its magics?' he managed. Guidgen nodded. 'What makes you think you'll be any better than me?' He saw the doubt on Guidgen's face. Bladud burst into flames, but the Witch King did not scream.

Britha watched as Bress lit up from within, skin smoking, veins and eyes burning, the ice already starting to melt under him. The spear wreathed in flame. She was running now.

'Tangwen!' she screamed. The giant leant down and with one hand swept another of the chariots away, sending it spinning through the air to slam into the cavern wall. 'Tangwen!' She was trying to wave at the younger woman as she ran.

Bress threw the spear. It screamed in flight, seeming to suck all the air towards it. Britha couldn't have been heard over the spear, but for some reason Tangwen turned to look at her. The chariot changed direction. The spear flew through the giant leaving a burning hole, growing larger as its gnarled flesh melted in the weapon's wake. The giant was still, then it tottered, then it fell. The ice around the massive creature cracked, but it did not fall through.

Tangwen reached for Britha as the chariot thundered by. Britha grabbed the hunter's arm, the speed of the chariot trying to wrench her own arm off, and swung up into the cart. She knelt down on the boards of the chariot, clinging onto the frame for dear life.

The spear hit the roof of the cavern. Jagged, tooth-like rocks dropped through the ice and into the lake below. Cracks ran from the burning stone the spear had left behind it.

She watched as what had been Bress – for he was little more than a vessel for the demon, or the god, that lived in the burning spear now – turned to look at Crom Dhubh. The Dark Man had staggered to his feet and was slowly, painfully, pulling arrows with wriggling heads from his desiccated flesh. Bress started walking towards the obsidian figure. Tangwen's chariot rounded the island and they were lost from view.

The light at the other end of the island, under the ice, changed from warm amber to a cold, burning, bright blue. It refracted off the ice and now the whole cavern was that colour.

'Head towards that!' Britha shouted at the blonde, scarred charioteer. The woman glanced behind her at the *ban draoi*, but changed course. On the other side of the island there was another, really bright light. Ice and water were thrown up into the air. Some powerful, unseen force hit the chariot, causing it to skid in a spray of ice chips, but the spiked wheels found purchase again. They were nearly at the light. Britha had no idea what to do when they got there. Then the ice disappeared in a perfect circle above the stones. The circle was edged in bright blue fire. There was no water in the circle. The blonde charioteer was dragging on the reins trying to stop the team, but they were going too fast.

On the other side of the island something burst through the ice. Britha only caught a glimpse of it; she assumed she couldn't actually be seeing what she thought she was seeing. It looked like some kind of structure, like the one she had seen the edge of in the water, next to the standing stones, when she had first gone to Oeth.

The spear exploded back through the roof of the cavern, heading straight for the flying structure. Cracks shot out across the ice. Cracks appeared climbing up the rock wall of the cavern. The ice under their chariot collapsed. Cold lake water surged over the circle of blue fire, and they found themselves sliding down the ice as panicked horses desperately tried to backtrack. In the centre of the circle of blue fire they could see Lochlannach surrounding one figure. Everything seemed to slow down. The figure turned to look at her as the chariot and team slid down the ice. Skin covered its eyes, nostrils, mouth and ears, yet it looked familiar somehow. A vertical reptilian eye opened in its forehead. The chariot slid into the circle of blue fire from above.

The spear had left. It was no longer present in this place. At the last moment it had veered away from Crom Dhubh's vessel. The blue glow died. As water shifted violently beneath it, more cracks appeared in the frozen surface of the lake. Cracks ran up the cavern wall. More stalactites fell through the ice. Bress's head was white agony. His body felt like it was on fire. White light shot out from Crom Dhubh's vessel, its proximity setting Bress's skin on fire. The light turned stone to slag, burning and cutting through rock.

He had expected his master to kill him. He had outbid the Dark Man's control with the ancient power of long-forgotten gods, but Crom Dhubh had something else in mind. His erstwhile master's vessel moved into the hole it had carved, causing yet more damage to the structural integrity of the cavern.

Bress managed to roll onto his back just in time to see the roof collapse.

32
Now

Everything smelled of fuel or burning, everything sounded like gunfire. There were flames under all the letters on the Hollywood sign. This time when they came back into Laurel Canyon they came quietly. The streets of the canyon were empty except for dogs. Not the wild packs of street dogs in the city below, these looked more like spoilt pets who had no idea what to do now. They kept trying to make friends with Grace and du Bois as they walked ahead of the ECV. They were travelling slowly, the lights off. Beth was in the turret watching the two ex-Circle operatives. She was pretty sure that Grace wasn't a dog person. Du Bois, on the other hand, was struggling to shoo them away. She smiled. The smile disappeared when she remembered that while he might like dogs, he had no compunction about killing people.

Suddenly the dogs scattered. Du Bois held up his hand. Alexia brought the ECV to a halt. Du Bois and Grace crouched down, carbines at the ready. The dogs had been spooked by the presence of a bigger predator. The tiger stalked out of the undergrowth at the bottom of the built-up canyon wall. Its eyes glowed with reflected moonlight. It must have escaped, or been released, from a zoo or private menagerie. Du Bois and Grace brought their carbines up to bear on the beautiful animal.

'No,' Beth said simply from the turret. The big cat turned to look in their direction.

'You're not out here with it,' Grace said quietly through gritted teeth. The tiger let out a low throaty growl. Beth found herself wishing she had a camera. This beautiful predator out of place in the suburbs of a city she knew only from film. The tiger looked away from du Bois, Grace, the vehicle, and stalked into the undergrowth on the other side of the road. Grace kept the area covered as they moved slowly by.

Behind them were the lights of the LA basin and the distant

flames burning in and around what had been LAX. It looked like the sea was on fire. Up here it should have been peaceful, but she could still hear the heavy beat of the rap and heavy metal played aggressively loudly from La Calavera's castle further up the canyon.

They had picked the house because the driveway was big enough to park the ECV around the back, out of view of the road. It was on one of the streets that branched off from Laurel Canyon Boulevard, high on the canyon wall, and it provided them a distant view of La Calavera's castle. Beth had come to welcome the sound of the music now. It was preferable to the occasional screams they heard. The castle was lit up. SUVs and pickups, sporting armour and weapons, done up as technicals, or improvised fighting vehicles, were patrolling the neighbourhood, accompanied by motorcycle outriders.

Beth was watching this from the steep driveway while Grace broke in, quietly, through a side door, du Bois covering her. Alexia was leaning against the wall. Grace pushed open the door, drew one of her knives, and clutched the blade. The cut across her palm didn't bleed. She sheathed the fighting knife and concentrated.

'There's people in there,' she finally said.

'Find another house?' Alexia whispered.

'They already know we're here,' du Bois said, nodding at the dark shape of the ECV. He had wanted to recce the area on foot first but the ECV had been too exposed. Beth heard the sound of metal on metal. She glanced back and saw Grace and du Bois changing magazines on their carbines, and then screwing suppressors onto the barrels. It seemed they had chosen expedience.

'Perhaps another way?' Alexia suggested. She pushed past them both without a weapon drawn. Beth was already walking back up the hill. Du Bois went to follow his sister, but Beth's hand on his shoulder stopped him.

'Keep watch,' she told him. He looked like he was about to argue but thought the better of it.

'At least five people in the left-hand side back bedroom upstairs,' Grace told her. Beth nodded and followed Alexia. She slung the LMG down her front but drew her Colt OHWS, screwed the suppressor into the barrel, and changed the magazine for her only clip of subsonic ammo. She moved quickly, catching up with Alexia.

'I am so sick of this soldier girl bullshit,' the statuesque woman muttered. Beth suppressed a smile, but gestured towards the room that Grace had indicated. She tried to cover Alexia without making it too obvious she was covering her. If everything hadn't been so incredibly horrible she had to admit that she would have been enjoying all the soldier stuff. Alexia at least had the sense to stand to one side of the door when she tapped on it.

'Hello? If you're psychos there will probably be a horrible fight, but if not can we come in?'

On a whim Beth pushed open the door to the nearest room to her. There was a body in it. A teenaged boy. Blunt force trauma. It looked like someone had caved his head in with his own computer. The bloodstained tower was lying next to him.

'Alexia,' she whispered. Alexia turned to look at her, and Beth just pushed the door open further. Suddenly Beth wished she had cleared the house, instead of just relying on Grace's bloodscreen, but Alexia had been moving too quickly. Strange new military instincts were screaming at her that she was doing this wrong. She could hear movement in the room that Alexia had just knocked on. Beth signalled that she was going to check the other rooms. Alexia nodded and drew both her katana-like long knives. Her sidearm didn't have a suppressor. Beth went from bedroom to bedroom, quickly checking. She saw signs of habitation. In what she assumed was the master bedroom, she found bloodstains and signs of a struggle, but nobody else. She went back out into the hall and covered Alexia.

'Okay, I'm going to open the door now,' Alexia said. 'Broadly speaking I'm a nice lady, so please don't shoot me.' She turned the handle on the door and pushed. It opened a little way and then stuck. Beth heard a sob from inside. If they were infected with the insanity then they were really milking the tension. Alexia finally managed to push the door open. There were six of them: an old woman, two younger women, a man, a boy and a girl. They looked terrified. They obviously hadn't answered phones, watched TV, or been online. The old woman was pointing an archaic-looking shotgun at them.

'We're not mad,' Alexia told them. 'We're not here to hurt you, and while we're here nobody else will hurt you either.'

The woman who owned the house was called Eileen; the old lady with a shotgun, Dora, was her mother-in-law. Eileen had no idea where her husband or her other son were. All things considered she was holding it together pretty well. She had killed her youngest son when he had attacked her daughter, the little girl.

The man was called Ralph, and he was frantic about his partner who was a big-time Century City lawyer. The other woman was named Celia, and she was a neighbour. The boy hadn't spoken. They had no idea who he was, or where he was from, but he clearly wasn't insane so they had taken him in. They had pretty much been living in the back bedroom, staying away from the road to avoid the patrols from the castle. They were, of course, terrified of the heavily armed intruders in their home/hiding place.

Du Bois had joined them. Grace had remained on watch outside. It was clear from her body language that she didn't want to be anywhere near du Bois, which was understandable. It was also clear that her presence made du Bois very uncomfortable. False memory or not, Beth had less sympathy for him.

'After ...' Eileen stopped and looked towards the bedroom with the dead boy in it.

'It wasn't him,' Alexia told her.

The woman looked away. She had the look of a modern hippy. Someone who made her living doing something creative, Beth guessed. It made sense. Her understanding was that Laurel Canyon had been that kind of place.

'Well, everything just went mad, people we'd known ...'

'You'll find another body downstairs,' Dora, the old lady, said grimly.

'I hadn't wanted the gun in the house, Pete and I had a blazing row about it, but thank god,' Eileen continued, fighting tears. 'Mr Macintyre, we've known him since we moved here.'

'Lived on a farm,' Dora said matter-of-factly.

'We hid in the loft,' Eileen told the three of them.

'When did the people at the castle arrive?' du Bois asked softly.

Eileen shook her head, and looked down at her hands folded in her lap. 'I don't know. It felt like days after. It could have been hours. We stayed in the loft.' The tears came now. 'The things we heard.'

'I saw them,' Celia said. She was a middle-aged woman with laughter lines around her eyes. She looked like she smiled a lot. Beth suspected there was little cause for that now. 'They shot everyone who gave them trouble, took the rest with them. I'm not sure what for but we hear cheering and ...' She finished with a sob.

'They patrol the neighbourhood, looking for other people,' Ralph said. 'Are you people British military? Special forces or something? Is this only happening here?'

'We're a private concern,' du Bois told them.

'Mercenaries?' Dora asked. The tone of disapproval somehow made Beth like the old woman more. Du Bois opened his mouth to answer the question.

'This is happening everywhere,' Beth told them. 'I think you need to prepare yourself for the worst.'

'Your best bet is the desert, or the mountains, get as far away from everyone else as you can,' du Bois told them.

'Can you help us?' Ralph asked. The desperation in his voice was difficult to hear. She wondered if she would have been this helpless without all the augmentation. Not quite, she reckoned, but it wouldn't have been far off.

'I'm sorry.' Du Bois stood up and left the back bedroom.

Beth found him later in the garden. He had taken Eileen's son from his bedroom, and the body of the neighbour from the kitchen, and was digging graves for them.

'What we're doing now ...' Beth wasn't quite sure how to say what she was trying to say. 'We only have revenge or running away left, right?' Du Bois didn't answer her. 'Would it be so bad to help them, others like them, maybe find a place we could all stay? Rather than just killing all the people we're pissed off with?'

Du Bois threw down the spade and turned on her. 'What's the point?' he demanded.

'Keep your voice down,' Beth hissed.

'It only gets worse from here on, until there's nothing left. We're not even insects to these things. We're bits of dust.'

'So we keep killing, following your vision, sent by those insane things?' Beth asked. She wasn't sure who she was angry with.

'You want to stay and help these people, stay and help these people,' du Bois said. 'Be a good person.' He stormed past her and stopped suddenly. Beth turned to see Grace standing by the corner of the house; du Bois was staring at her, and then he continued on his way down the steep drive. Grace lit a cigarette.

'Revenge seems like a pretty good motivation to me,' the punk girl said. Beth leaned her LMG against the ECV, and picked up the spade.

'Do you want to help?' Beth asked.

'Can't, I'm on guard.' Beth got the feeling that she probably wouldn't have helped even if she hadn't been on guard. 'I don't think I've ever seen him that on edge.'

'It's a pretty extreme situation,' Beth said. The blade of the shovel bit into the earth as she started to dig. Above her she could hear faint piano music. Her neuralware told her it was Debussy. Her newfound military instincts wanted to go and tell whoever was playing to shut up, but she couldn't bring herself to do it.

Beth had finally managed to divest herself of all her weaponry, webbing and ammunition, though she was still carrying her pistol. She felt so much lighter. She'd even had a shower. Self-cleaning skin or not, she felt much better afterwards.

Alexia was sitting in the dark in the master bedroom playing an electric keyboard. The volume was turned down quite low. There were towels over the bloodstains. Beth leant on the doorframe and listened.

'Did we even ask them if we could stay?' Beth asked when Alexia had finished. She was aware of the other people in the house moving around quietly. Doors had been left open so they could hear Alexia play.

'Yes,' Alexia said. 'Of all the things I'm going to miss, dirty martinis, having my hair and nails done, breakfast at the Waldorf, music is the only thing I can't live without. I said that and Andrea, the little girl, went and got me the keyboard. This brave new world will be the poorer without music.'

In the distance they could hear the thump of the bass-heavy music from the castle.

'That first piece you played?' Beth asked.

'"Clair de lune", but then you'll know that. I think it's my brother's favourite.'

'You think?'

'Well, he's not exactly forthcoming, is he? You know, although I am a much better poly-musician, singer, lyricist and composer, and despite having devoted my life to music ... well, a little bit to hedonism and decadence ... well, okay, perhaps equal measures ... he's actually a better pianist than I am. I know! Heartbreaking, isn't it? Where is he anyway?'

'I think I upset him.'

Alexia brought her knees up to her chest, hugging her legs. 'You wouldn't have upset him, darling. This has upset him. He doesn't know what to do.'

Beth stared at her. 'He doesn't know ...?'

'He likes taking orders. We all do. It's hard thinking for yourself. I think he would just shut down except ...'

'Except?' Beth prompted.

'I think you might struggle to believe this from your perspective, but he is driven to do the right thing.'

Beth felt her face harden. 'Yes, you're right, that is difficult for me to believe.'

Alexia looked up her. 'He killed your father for what he thought was the right reason. Now he knows it's wrong. If he's off sulking then he's probably gone looking for a church to ask forgiveness of a god he, probably more than most on this planet, knows doesn't exist. Perhaps he's even self-flagellating again.'

'Doesn't help my father, does it?'

Alexia let go of her legs and leant against the headboard.

'Blame him, if you want, he has broad shoulders, but if you're not with us then you'll need to think of something else to do.' Alexia just watched her for a while. 'Everybody believes they think for themselves, don't they?'

Beth looked down, not saying anything. Alexia got off the bed.

'Get some rest, actual rest. I'm going to see if the other Patty Hearst wannabe will give me a fag.'

Beth stepped out of the doorway as Alexia passed. 'Do you mind me asking something?'

Alexia stopped.

'This is going to be one of those awkward conversations about the nature of my genitalia, isn't it?' Alexia turned and looked up at Beth. 'Darling, I can be whatever you want.'

Beth felt herself start to colour.

'No wait, I'm not ...'

'Not what, darling?'

'I wasn't ...' Beth tried again. Alexia was just smiling at her. 'Sorry.'

'It's my fault you know, that he's the way he is, that he does what he does. God, I was so innocent, suicidally naive like you wouldn't believe. I couldn't see the harm in it. Dressing like a girl, I looked so pretty, wanting to catch the eye of all the young men.'

'Du Bois told me that he had been alive for centuries,' Beth said. Alexia nodded.

'Oh yes, horrible men capable of much worse than anything I could dream of would have burned me; somehow I couldn't understand that. As for Malcolm, I was an abomination, against everything he stood for, but he never stopped protecting me. He was a proper knight, you see. We were both so naive. Do you know what he was doing when he first found the tech?' she asked. Beth shook her head. 'He was looking for the Holy Grail, I shit you not.'

Beth burst out laughing. Alexia smiled.

'Like in Monty Python?' Beth asked. Alexia nodded again.

'He wanted to cure me,' Alexia told her. Beth stopped laughing. 'But here's the thing. He didn't want me to turn into the younger brother he had always wanted, so I could become a soldier, or maybe a priest. Though I rather fancied the life of a wandering troubadour – as I said, I was hopelessly romantic. I didn't have a practical bone in my body, unless a nice young man put it there. He was going to turn me into a woman. He said it was because he wanted me to be happy, and I believe that, but on some level I think he knew that I was born in the wrong body.' Beth wasn't quite sure what to say. Suddenly the conversation seemed very serious. 'I think my brother has been horribly led astray, and I'm sorry about your father, but cut Malcolm some slack or just fuck off.' Alexia turned and walked down the stairs. 'Now I need to tell that to the other one, though I suspect she'll be less receptive.'

Beth was lying on the double bed in the master bedroom. Eileen hadn't wanted to sleep there because of the bloodstains. It was for the best, leave the unaugmented civilians in the back of the house, away from the road.

When did I start thinking of them as civilians? she wondered. She was drifting off to sleep when she heard movement. She opened her eyes to see Grace standing in the doorway, watching her. Beth sat up. It was the first time she had seen the punk girl look unsure of herself.

'Yeah?' Beth asked. It sounded harsher than she'd meant it to, but it wasn't that many hours ago that Grace had been cutting her up with her twin fighting knives.

Grace opened her mouth to speak, and then seemed to think

the better of it. 'Forget it,' she muttered, and turned and walked away. Beth got up and followed her. The doors to the back rooms were open. She could see the 'civilians' asleep in the beds, or on the floor on inflatable mattresses and camp beds. Eileen and Dora, whether they had intended to or not, had provided a safe oasis for the sane amid all the madness – even for them, at least for now. They hadn't needed to do that.

Alexia was now, presumably, on guard. If du Bois had come back she hadn't heard him and he wasn't upstairs.

'Hey,' Beth whispered. 'What's up?' Grace was making her way down the stairs. She stopped and looked up at Beth. She seemed to be struggling with whether or not she should say anything.

'Trust issues,' she finally said.

'Okay,' Beth said cautiously. It made sense, Grace had been made to think that she had been betrayed in the worst way possible by the person she was closest to, only to find out that she had in fact been betrayed and lied to by her employer. 'You don't know me.'

'I don't get a bad vibe from you.'

Beth knew it had to run a lot deeper than that but she was gratified. 'What do you need?' she asked.

'I don't like sleep,' Grace said. Beth nodded. 'I'm not trying to hit on you or anything ...'

'I'm not a lesbian,' Beth muttered. The only thing she minded about being mistaken for a lesbian was having to constantly explain she wasn't.

'Yeah, I know ...'

'You want to stay in my room?' Beth asked, though it wasn't really her room.

Grace looked less than pleased. Beth didn't think the punk liked having to ask anyone for anything. 'Yeah,' she said finally. 'I figured ...'

'That because he killed my dad I won't have any problem blowing his fucking head off if he tries anything?'

Grace considered her words. 'It didn't sound that calculating in my head, but pretty much.'

'You still think he did it?'

'I think there's a difference between what the head knows and the heart feels,' she said. The way her cockney accent mashed the word heart, it could have been hate.

'Course you can; in future, assuming there is one, you don't need to ask.' She would have no problem shooting du Bois.

Beth was awoken by the sound of the engines. The bedroom was softly half-lit by the still-working streetlights shining through the cracks in the thick curtains. Grace was already up, standing at the edge of the window, peering out onto the narrow residential road. She had the Noveske Rifleworks N6 carbine held in one hand, the suppressor still attached to the barrel. Beth didn't get out of bed. She did, however, grab her Colt from the bedside table. It still had the suppressor attached as well. She heard a child whimper from the back bedroom, an adult gently shush them.

'What have we got?' Beth asked. It was barely even a whisper.

'Low-riding muscle car with an MG, which has to be the world's least practical technical. Two motorcycle outriders. Four, no, five guns including the driver and MG gunner.'

'They coming in here?' Beth asked. She knew that Alexia was outside. She imagined du Bois's sibling would be covering the patrol from the castle as well.

'Just looking around at the moment. If they come in here we try and do them nice and quiet,' the punk girl said. It was kind of chilling. She looked younger than Beth. The problem was that Alexia didn't have any suppressed weapons. 'You take any inside. I deal with those outside.'

'Understood,' Beth said. After all, Grace had the experience, and as Alexia had said, it was nice when people made the decisions for you. They waited.

'Alexia give you her "be nice to my big brother" speech?' Grace asked quietly after a while.

'Yeah, she called you the other Patty Hearst,' Beth said, smiling.

'Me? I was never heir to a bucket of piss.'

'You mind me asking how old you are?' she asked.

'Maybe if I was a lady,' Grace said, though there was little humour in her smile. 'Not exactly sure, maybe a hundred-and-forty-five years old.'

'You look good—'

'Don't say it,' Grace told her. Beth went quiet. She couldn't think of a way to ask what she wanted to ask. Grace was still looking out of the window. Beth could hear rough voices shouting to each other in a mixture of Spanish and English. 'What?'

'Du Bois ... I mean other than the implanted memory ...'

'Let me make something very clear,' Grace said, her voice hard, though she didn't look away from the crack between the window and the edge of the curtain. 'I'm only ninety-five per cent sure it wasn't him. It's difficult to discount what feels like an experience. I find out it was him and your *compadre* is fucking dead.'

'He's not my friend. If he did it, I won't get in your way, I'll even help. I just don't know him.'

'You don't know what you're doing, do you?' Grace asked after a moment.

'I don't think you can understand just how far away all this crazy stuff is from my life.'

Grace thought for a moment. 'He's way too uptight. I mean, take the most uptight Catholic you've ever met and multiply them to the *n*th degree. The problem is, because of this, he seems to think there's some reward for hard work, loyalty, and trying to be a good person, but he was a good friend. He'd do anything for you.' Grace sniffed. 'Fucking bastards! What they did to my head ...' She went quiet again.

'So he was a good guy?'

Now Grace turned to look at her. Shaking her head.

'How fucking naive are you? Who do you think we are? We're mass murderers. Assassins. No, he was not a "good guy". He was a boot boy for the ultimate fascist conspiracy, but hey, Hitler liked animals.'

'You worked for them as well,' Beth said. It was almost a defensive reflex.

'Well, we all make mistakes, though his mistake happened over a period of eight hundred years.'

Engines were gunned. There was more shouting. Then Beth heard them drive away. A few moments later someone came in through the side door.

'It's Malc ... du Bois,' Grace told her. Beth headed downstairs. Grace followed.

Du Bois was in the kitchen. Through the open door Beth could see him putting two large sports bags on the kitchen counter. When he heard them on the stairs he grabbed his Purdey and joined them in the hall. Du Bois opened the side door and hissed his sister's name. Moments later she joined them.

'Well?' Grace asked.

'It looks like La Calavera's people are getting ready to leave. If they were military, I'd say they were planning a convoy.'

'So?' Grace demanded. 'Do we know that's anything to do with us?'

'I saw one of the DAYP. The demon-headed one with the stupid name.'

'Inflictor Doorstep?' Beth asked. He nodded.

'King Jeremy? La Calavera?' Grace asked.

'I didn't see them.'

'Plan?' Alexia asked.

'Hit them on the road,' Grace said. Du Bois nodded.

'They're armed to the teeth, but it's mostly small arms. There's not a lot of it that's going to trouble the ECV's armour. Their armour is mostly scratch built,' du Bois told them.

'Be nice if Karma had put a GMG or fifty cal on top. Still, boys and their toys,' Grace muttered.

'You said it was mostly scratch built armour,' Beth said.

'They've got a Cougar,' du Bois said.

'So she likes younger guys, who doesn't?' Alexia asked. Du Bois just looked exasperated. 'Pardon me for trying to lighten the mood.'

'That's where anything of import will be. The nuke, the DAYP, probably La Calavera,' du Bois continued.

'Or it's a decoy, or just a tank, and they're in something fast-moving,' Grace pointed out.

'Can we not just follow them to whatever meet they have with Mr Brown?' Beth said.

'We could do, but they've got a lot of screening vehicles, and we're going through significant bandit country, too big a risk of losing them. We need to control this. Control the nuke and get our hands on King Jeremy, and I can make him talk. That way at least we know what we're walking into when we go after Brown.'

'A chase through a well-armed LA playing Hell in the movie of the same name, against a convoy of heavily armed psychos? This doesn't sound very controlled,' Grace said.

'Give me another option,' du Bois said, clearly irritated.

Grace thought about that for a moment. 'Okay, I'm in, but I'm not riding with you,' she told him. Du Bois opened his mouth to object. 'You don't need another shooter in the ECV.' She turned and went upstairs. Beth thought that she was probably right.

33

A Long Time After the Loss

Vic was pretty sure that Scab was losing it. This scared him. They had travelled Red Space to an out of the way habitat that they knew was hip-deep in the black weapons trade. They had paid through the teeth to replace most of what they had lost. The reconfigured *Basilisk II* had passed the incoming bounty ships just inside Red Space. They were lucky it was only bounty hunters rather than one of the Elite that had traced them.

Scab had wanted to make examples on the habitat, though Vic was of the opinion that it had been inevitable that one of the black market arms dealers would sell them out. He had also wanted to make an example of one of the bounty killers' ships. The first one through had been a converted freighter, modified to be closer to a light cruiser in combat capabilities. It belonged to a bounty killer called Crabber. It was a bit too much ship for the *Basilisk II* to handle. The Monk had 'reasoned' with him and that was how Vic knew that Scab was losing it. This many lost opportunities for violence had to come out somewhere.

The Monarchist systems hadn't seemed that safe when everyone was after Talia. Now, however, they were falling into a shooting war with the Consortium. A war there was a good chance the Monarchists would lose, as they were currently one Elite down. To counter the imbalance the Monarchist systems had been offering succour to Church refugees fleeing Consortium persecution. The aristos had more to worry about than Talia and the secret of bridge technology now.

Scab's Pythian search programs had found only one reference to the Ubh Blaosc. It was in a suppressed report that the search program had to buy using one of their secure slush funds at not inconsiderable expense. They still had access to the funds from Talia's fake auction, but those funds had taken a battering recently.

The report was from a successful xeno-archaeologist, a job title that really meant S-tech prospector, who worked out of the Monarchist systems. All that the report said was that the archaeologist, a Dr Josef Ertl, was looking for an S-tech artefact called the Ubh Blaosc. Reading between the lines it sounded like he had been hired by one of the Blue Bloods – the Lords of the Monarchist systems. Dr Josef had gone missing. His ship had eventually floated into one of the beacon-guided routes through Red Space some three thousand years later, which made him one of the luckiest carbon-based life forms ever to have existed. The chances of a lost ship drifting into one of the routes were astronomically low. He was, of course, dead, but they had been able to retrieve his last backup and clone him, after the Blue Bloods had destroyed the current Dr Josef Ertl, who had been cloned after the original had gone missing. It was thought that the returned Dr Ertl would be much more interesting.

'So this Bedlam, it's a Psycho Bank?' Vic asked.

'Pretty much,' the Monk said. She was getting tired of answering the same question, but even with the information in his neunonics Vic wasn't getting it.

'But with real people?' the 'sect asked again.

'Yes,' Beth had snapped. Scab had wanted to go in guns blazing, but the Monk had suggested another way. She had reached out to her covert Church contacts in the Monarchist systems to see if a meeting could be arranged. More to the point, could it be arranged to their satisfaction that there wouldn't be any double cross. There had been some back and forth; Scab was less than pleased, but it looked like the Monarchists cared a lot more about fucking over the Consortium than they did about anything that Scab and any Church survivors were up to.

Even so, Talia was not happy that she had to go back into hiding. They could not know of her existence. Vic was of the opinion that if they were to stand a chance against the Monarchists' inevitable betrayal, she would be needed to pilot the *Basilisk II*. Telling her this had gone some way towards mollifying her.

'I was in a place like it back on Earth,' Talia said, looking down. Her sister turned to her.

'You were in a museum?' Vic asked, though he was struggling to deal with the concept.

'More like the secure wing of a hospital,' Talia said. The explanation didn't really help much.

'When?' the Monk asked.

Talia looked profoundly uncomfortable. Vic hoped that she wasn't going to start crying again. Though she had done a lot less of that recently, and she seemed to be getting on a lot better with her sister. Vic had even managed to spend some sexy time with her in one of the immersions she liked. With her non-invasive superconducting connection to the *Basilisk II*'s systems she was able to get a lot more out of the programs now.

'Y'know, after ...'

'I went to prison?'

'Well, I was going to say after you killed Davey, but yeah,' Talia said. The Monk opened her mouth to ask something. 'I don't want to talk about it,' Talia said quickly. Vic was wondering why she had brought it up in the first place. Vic opened his mandibles to ask for another explanation.

'The entire planet is a museum,' Beth said in exasperation. 'It's basically a place where they keep the material remains of the past on display, in the belief that it will be of interest, both in terms of education and entertainment, to the people of the present and the future.'

And this was the bit that Vic didn't get. Surely most of what they needed to know was in their neunonics? And if it wasn't then they could 'face for it. He started to ask the question but Beth cut him off again. 'There's a number of arcologies spread out across the planet; each arcology has a theme and it stores, displays, and explains the artefacts of each theme. There's an arcology called Earth, that's supposed to be all pre-Loss artefacts. I know for a fact most of them are fake. Though I've always hoped that it's the real *Voyager II* they've got. We even talked about stealing it.'

'Then there's the Mausoleum, where you can apparently talk with the reanimated corpses of interesting, but ultimately dead, people,' Talia said with mock enthusiasm. 'Which nobody seems to think is odd but me.'

'Do they have Vic Matto?' Vic asked.

'No, I checked,' Talia said. He felt funny inside at the thought of her doing that for him. 'They claim to have Elvis though,' she said. 'Which sort of cheapens it all, makes it like Vegas.'

'You never went to Vegas,' Beth said.

'Blackpool, then,' Talia said, in exasperation.

'It's not the real Elvis,' the Monk said, then she frowned. 'At least I hope it isn't. That would have been a waste of space and made him a lot more evil than I thought he was.'

'Ooh, they have Walt Disney!' Talia said.

'Now that makes sense,' the Monk said. 'They have a number of arcologies for the diaspora, the colonial era, the exploitation, post-colonial era and recent history, though personally I think the last five thousand years have just sort of blurred together. There's another arcology for the Seeders, the Church, the history of space travel, Red Space, the Art Wars and so on. Then there's the Bedlam – that's a museum of mental illness and interesting mad people, in which they are keeping Dr Ertl.'

'See, that's what I don't get,' Vic said. 'If it's a Psycho Bank, why have live ones? Isn't that dangerous?'

'The virtual ones can be as well,' the Monk muttered.

'So why bother?'

'So people can go there and study and learn from them,' Talia said. Vic just shook his head. Talia patted him on the arm. 'Bless.'

He knew she was patronising him but somehow he found it very endearing.

'It's for entertainment, Vic,' the Monk told him. 'Entertainment.'

He brightened. 'Look at the funny mad people? Yes, that makes sense.'

The Monk was just shaking her head.

'Is he still looking at the bridge ghost and wanking?' Talia asked.

'No, I'm looking forward to our inevitable betrayal,' Scab said, emerging from the carpeted and wood-panelled corridor that ran between their private rooms. Talia actually squealed, but Vic was gratified that she moved behind him and not her sister.

'Your plan wouldn't have worked,' the Monk said. 'The security's too high.'

'We've hit Blue Bloods before, even hunted them,' Scab said. Vic was nodding. He had to admit he was with Scab on this one. They were basically walking into a trap.

'So we just go and kill everyone?' the Monk asked. 'Look, this place is set up more like a Citadel, or even the Cathedral, in terms of security. I don't think we could even get the ship inside.'

'Worked well for the Cathedral.' It was out of Vic's mouth before he realised what he was saying. Talia was looking up at him ruefully.

'We don't have entire battle fleets and three Elite with us,' the Monk pointed out.

'I've broken into a Citadel,' Scab said. The Monk narrowed her eyes.

'He has,' Vic said. 'Got me killed, though, by a fucking Elite no less.'

'Ludwig?' the Monk asked. Vic nodded.

'But you had the godsware,' Vic said to Scab.

'The Marduk implant?' the Monk asked. Scab nodded. 'Still got it?' Scab didn't say anything. 'Look, I know this is a shitty situation. I know we can't trust Pallas, and believe me I know that better than anyone, but as far as we can tell he's on the level.' Pallas was the Blue Blood who owned the system. 'They're desperate. They know as soon as the Consortium are finished mopping up the Church, they are going to properly turn their sights on the Monarchist systems. The Blue Bloods are outnumbered, outgunned and one Elite down. We've sold this to them on fucking the Consortium over.'

'Have you met him before?' Scab asked.

'That's a complicated question,' the Monk said.

'Give me a simple answer.'

'Maybe.'

'Are we meeting him?' Vic asked.

'He's getting cloned especially,' the Monk told them.

'Well, aren't we special,' Scab said. The blatant sarcasm worried Vic as well. It wasn't really Scab's style. Most of the time his sense of irony was either deficient, or too well developed for Vic to understand.

'Hey!' Talia snapped. 'If you're going to stick your dick in my sister then at least you can be nice to her!' The Monk blinked.

Scab narrowed his eyes, Vic suspected more as the result of confusion than anything else.

'Thank you, Talia,' the Monk managed.

'They say Pallas might be the Prime,' Vic said, meaning the progenitor of the Blue Bloods.

'They said that about the Elder of the Living City, and the Absolute. I think if the Prime still exists he's well hidden, and we'll never see him. More likely he was eaten by his children a long time ago. I'm pretty sure that Pallas is first generation, though,' the Monk told them.

'What a waste,' Scab muttered. Vic wondered what he was referring to.

*

Ridiculously ornamental, retro-looking warships tracked them the moment they emerged from the bridge point. Similarly overly-decorated orbital weapons platforms tracked them as soon as they entered Black Athena's planetary space. The arcologies' security systems locked on as well, once the *Basilisk II* entered the atmosphere.

Black Athena was a designer garden world. All the land was carefully laid out, manicured parkland interspersed with shallow waterscaped seas. The baroque pyramid arcologies dotted the planet, dwarfing even the landscaped, snow-capped mountain ranges. Though the arcologies did not break the atmosphere.

The planet had a tiny permanent population, despite its vast security forces. It also had a vast transient population of wealthy tourists from the Monarchist systems and, until recently, the Consortium. Some of the more influential Consortium tourists were now hostages being used as an uplift shield.

As they made for Bedlam, the near, yellow sun was sinking below the equator, casting the designer world into a strangely bright twilight. Vic was enjoying the scenery, just before he died, from his new biomechanical-style seat. The Mother had 'faced the design specs to the *Basilisk II*, but somehow the chair wasn't as comfortable as it had been on Cyst. Much of the ship's hull was transparent and he was receiving visual feed from the ship's sensors, which he had overlaid with a suitably inspiring sound-scape.

Talia was safely cocooned again, deep in the ship's smart matter. They were going to keep 'face silence unless things went really badly. She brought the ship circling around the Bedlam arcology, he suspected so she could check out the view, and brought it in to land on the designated landing pad close to the top of the arcology. Apparently Pallas kept penthouse suites on the top several floors of all the arcologies.

They stepped out onto the landing pad into freezing temperatures and howling winds. Both Scab and Monk had stipulated no umbilical connection to the ship. Molecular hooks on Vic's feet kept him adhered to the pad as he made his way with the Monk and Scab to the airlock.

The outward sloping, transparent, smart matter walls of the lowest floor of the penthouse suite looked down on a massive, empty space thousands of storeys above the ground. Vic hadn't expected the arcology to be hollow, somehow. His neunonics had long rid him of the agoraphobia that hive-born worker 'sects were conditioned with, but the massive drop was making him a little uncomfortable. A structure this size, Vic knew, would have to have internal weather control.

The 'exhibits' were in 'displays' on successive floors that ran up the inside walls of the megastructure. Ornate lifts made of smart matter designed to look like something called 'decorative wrought iron' ran at regular intervals up each wall. Similarly archaic-looking maglevs ran around each level, presumably to take tourists to their favourite psychopath or recreational killer. Vic didn't think he would like the idea of being one of the exhibits. He could see some of the closer levels on maximum magnification. The inmates didn't look happy. However, there were no tourists today. It seemed like the museum had been closed to the public for their visit.

Vic turned away from the transparent smart matter wall. He still didn't quite get the entertainment value of the place. The lowest floor of the penthouse suite didn't make sense to him either. Everything was red and gold. The furniture looked flimsy, impractical, and all of it was dumb. It was the sort of place that only the deranged mind of a hairless monkey could come up with and think of as clever. Apparently it was supposed to be the recreation of something called a reception room, belonging to someone called a Russian Tsar. Scab was playing with what looked like a jewelled egg.

'Please be careful, Mr Scab, that is the only remaining Fabergé egg.' The man who spoke was surprisingly nondescript. He reminded Vic of the Elder of the Living Cities in some ways. He appeared to be baseline male human: tousled, dark blond/light brown hair, pale green eyes. He was wearing a pair of red cords, a padded yellow smoking jacket with a red lining, and a cravat. Vic's neunonics had to supply him with the names of these items of clothing. He was also wearing a pair of red-gold-rimmed half-moon glasses, and he had a cigarette burning in a holder that looked like it was made from the bone or horn of some kind of rare animal. The Monk had rolled her eyes at the mention of Fabergé, and Vic's human body language database suggested that she was struggling to keep the revulsion from her face. She sighed when Scab twisted the egg until it broke and dropped it onto the floor.

'What an excellent way to start,' Pallas said. 'I had expected more than petty spite.'

'That surprises me, considering you claim to have the original me down there,' Scab said quietly. Vic and the Monk turned to look at the human killer. Menace had infested every last uttered syllable.

'I checked,' the Monk said.

'Obviously I removed any mention of it from anything you were going to see,' Scab said.

'He's just a clone,' Vic said.

'The hyperbole of an over-excited marketing department, nothing more,' Pallas said.

'I'm not happy about you having a cheap copy here either,' Scab said.

'Hardly cheap, Mr Scab, I assure you. Though he has come in useful to your compatriot here,' Pallas said smoothly, and nodded at the Monk.

'The copy that we downloaded into Benedict came from a Psycho Bank the museum sold us,' the Monk told Scab. 'Seriously, we don't need any help to be at each other's throats.'

'Destroy it,' Scab told Pallas.

'Of course,' he concentrated. 'It is done. I've 'faced evidence of the clone's destruction to you. Let me know if you require anything else in terms of proof. Would you like a seat? Can I offer you some refreshment, perhaps even food? I would certainly love to hear about your adventures, they sound terribly exciting.' The three of them just stared at him. 'Dr Ertl, then?'

Given the distances involved, the elevator and the maglev ride had been surprisingly fast. They were walking along beside the transparent-fronted cells, accompanied by their new P-sats, looking at the various inmates. Some looked comfortable. Others were restrained. Few looked happy. Vic guessed a number of them were displaying aberrant behaviour, but it was difficult to be completely sure because he had spent so much time with Scab. The inmates' silence made the massive structure seem somewhat sepulchral to Vic, though Pallas was keeping up a running commentary on each exhibit they passed. It was kind of annoying.

They walked past a fat lizard mumbling to himself, obviously an adult uplift, though there was something childlike about his behaviour. The next cell contained a restrained worker 'sect, which was odd as the worker caste were so heavily conditioned as part of their genetic engineering that it was quite difficult for them to be mentally ill, except by design. One cell had the disassembled, but somehow still moving, components of what had once been a rather baroque automaton. The human half-and-half in the next cell reached out to them, displaying the stigmata he/she had chewed in his/her palms.

Each of the cells was decorated with an aesthetic presumably meant to showcase the inmate's particular symptoms. Holograms showed teaser trailers of the inmates' immersion mindscapes. Some were abstract and alien, others disturbing but less so than one of Scab's custom torture immersions. A few were surprisingly beautiful. The latter often seemed to belong to those inmates showing the most external signs of being disturbed.

Vic didn't think he was the best judge of what was right or wrong. He was mostly of the opinion it was all right to do things that got you what you wanted, but there was no need to be as big a prick as Scab was about it. Bedlam, however, he was pretty sure, was wrong. This was mental illness as pornography.

'Dr Ertl,' Pallas said, and gestured into an exhibit. The chamber was very sparse, just a bed and a chair. The human sitting in the chair looked like he had once been a man-plus, but everything had sagged. His flesh was pale and unhealthy looking. He wore a robe. His eyes were dead and he was staring at nothing. His lips were moving, but according to Vic's neunonics he was just mouthing nonsense syllables. The plain cell was painted blood-red. The teaser trailer for his mindscape was a burning, bleeding, crimson star.

'You could have cloned him, run time-dilated counselling, hell, a surgical redesign, he doesn't have to be like this,' the Monk said, clearly angry.

'Well, we're doing a kind of an exploitation-era retrospective. He's well medicated. Besides, he is more interesting this way.'

'Oh yes, he should be able to tell us a great deal,' the Monk muttered.

'There's an immersion version of his mindscape,' Pallas pointed out. 'Just 'face with the exhibit. It's our latest attraction.'

Vic was ignoring Dr Ertl's red cell. He was looking in the next cell. It contained another worker 'sect done up in very human-looking drag. The 'sect appeared to be doing some kind of mundane domestic task in a pre-Loss, dumb matter, human environment.

411

'Is that supposed to be me?' Vic blurted out, more surprised than anything else.

'On Suburbia,' Pallas supplied. 'Artistic licence, of course.' The Monk walked past the fake Vic to the next cell/exhibit: a human girl, dark hair, too much eye make-up. The base female human inmate was wearing striped tights, platform boots and a strait jacket. One needle-tracked arm, with a badly scarred wrist, had managed to slip free of her restraints. She was drawing on the white floor of her cell with charcoal held in her free hand. The picture was of a falling tower hit by lightning. There were thousands of overlapping words scrawled on the walls. Vic's neunonics were able to translate a few of them. Slut, whore, junkie, victim. In what looked like blood, someone had written over the other words with the phrase: the Empire never ended.

'Is that supposed to be Talia?' Vic demanded. Both the Monk and Scab looked at him sharply. Pallas was smiling.

'You could have fucking 'faced the mindscape,' Scab snapped at Pallas.

'Would have rendered the trap sort of pointless, wouldn't it?' Pallas explained. The sad thing was, the confirmation it was a trap did not come as a surprise to Vic.

'Scab,' the Monk said, looking at the cell beyond fake Talia's. Scab backed up so he could see what she was talking about. It was obviously one of his clones. Suspended by chains, no arms, no legs, a scar where his genitals should be, eyes and mouth sewn shut. Helpless.

Vic was aware of an elevator moving up the closest shaft towards their level. Then Vic started to realise how much his erstwhile partner had lost it when Scab started to laugh. Vic saw the smug expression on Pallas's face falter.

'I think you might be trying too hard,' Scab said.

'Yeah, I mean talk about labouring the point,' the Monk agreed.

'Few can stand your mindscape for long, Mr Scab,' Pallas told them. 'Most need psychosurgery, or at least counselling afterwards.'

'That's tourists for you,' Scab muttered.

'Perhaps Miss Luckwicke would care to see the next cell?' Pallas asked.

'Let me guess, is it another petty headfuck?' the Monk asked. She walked past the neutered and chained Scab clone that evidently hadn't been destroyed after all.

'You arsehole,' the Monk snapped. She genuinely sounded upset. Vic moved to join her. It took a moment for him to realise that the bearded human figure in a loincloth and a crown of thorns, nailed to a cross, looked like the *Basilisk II*'s AI. It was weird. Vic wasn't sure why it bothered the Church operative so much.

'Congratulations, you've managed to irritate us,' Scab said. Pallas's smile was back.

'Why go to all this trouble? The Consortium aren't friends of yours,' the Monk demanded.

Vic sent his P-sat out over the huge drop. None of his sensors had been able to pierce the smart matter of the exhibits. Some of them had opened, however, and figures had spilled out and started climbing towards them. Vic recognised them.

'The price of peace,' Pallas said.

'Really? The girl died at the Cathedral,' the Monk said.

'Your sister is in the ship,' Pallas said contemptuously. 'And they don't want her. She should have been mine to start with. They want him.' He pointed at Scab. 'Oh really, Mr Scab. I'm a clone ...' Scab shot the Pallas clone with his tumbler pistol.

'Does nobody understand the benefit of catharsis?' Scab wondered out loud. All three of them had weapons in their hands now.

'Still a prick!' the Monk said, looking down at the body of Pallas's clone. The door to the elevator slid open. 'For what it's worth, you were right. I'm sorry.' Scab ignored her.

'Not. This. Way,' Scab managed through gritted teeth. He sounded angry with himself.

'Should we kill ourselves?' Vic asked hopefully. The Monk and Scab turned to look at him. 'It was worth a try.'

Butterflies, thousands of them, were fluttering out of the cavernous mouth of the open elevator. Vic saw both the humans frown. Their neunonics were being 'faced with target locks from the arcology's internal security systems. The first of the blank-faced automatons, in their laced finery and long-tailed suits and hats, were pulling themselves over the mock-wrought-iron railings. Mr Hat walked out of the elevator. The top of the diminutive lizard bounty hunter's huge stovepipe hat was open. More butterflies were emerging from it. Vic focused on the butterflies and magnified. Beyond razor-sharp monomolecular wings, he assumed they were dripping with powerful toxins and/or virals.

The 'sect was less than pleased to see the small bounty killer was carrying a squat, bulky S-tech de-coherence gun. Maybe the Monk's coherent energy field would stop the weapon as it pulled them apart at a molecular level, but maybe not.

'Mr Scab, Mr Matto, and I'm afraid I do not know your name,' the short lizard said to the Monk. She didn't answer. 'Miss Negrinotti sends her greetings. She was well rewarded, and is back on Ubaste. This has been a merry chase. One of the most challenging of my career. It is over.'

'I think you're right,' Scab said. Vic and the Monk were looking around for any way out. Vic was aware of the Monk desperately 'facing the Basilisk II, but there was no reply from Talia. 'I think all that remains is to make sure that you are never, ever, successfully cloned again.'

This level of threat wasn't really Scab at his finest, Vic thought. The human killer was biding time, but the 'sect couldn't understand why. Then he realised. Scab was hacking the exhibit. Scab was either downloading Dr Ertl's mindscape, or possibly even neurally auditing the inmate/exhibit. Optimism wasn't a trait Vic normally associated with Scab. Mr Hat frowned. Vic didn't think the lizard had quite bought the threat either.

'Mr Scab, I don't think you quite understand the gravity of your situation,' Mr Hat said.

'Seriously,' the Monk said. 'Let's skip the supervillain bullshit and get to the, presumably brief, gunfight.'

'This isn't a colonial immersion,' Mr Hat said, 'and I brought a friend.'

Vic tried to shut himself down there and then. Scab overrode and scrambled the suicide solution order the 'sect had sent to his own neunonics. Ludwig rose up through the floor. Vic's neunonics flooded his system with drugs in an attempt to maintain some form of functionality in the face of abject terror.

'You can be reasonable or unreasonable,' Mr Hat said. 'The only people it will make any difference to are yourselves. This is over now. You were good sport. Console yourselves that you've made me a very wealthy lizard.'

'You get that you're still just as miserable as the rest of us? Right?' More than anything, Vic was surprised that he could speak in the presence of the Elite. He was talking to Mr Hat, but he couldn't take his compound eyes off Ludwig. It was the visual feed from his P-sat, and the sensor feed from his antennae, that made Vic aware of Mr Hat's moment of hesitation at his words. Vic forced himself to look away from the terrible, black machine, and to the diminutive lizard. 'What if, just for once, we could have had something better?' Vic asked. The lizard frowned.

Scab started to move. There was black light. Ash fell to the ground like snow. Mr Hat, the automatons, the butterflies, were all gone. There were no more target lock warnings on his neunonics. Even Scab was staring at Ludwig. Vic did not think that he had ever seen his partner look surprised before.

– I wish to come with you. Even though the words had been 'faced, they were deafening. Vic and the Monk cried out, clutching their heads. Scab grimaced. Their perception had shaken with each syllable.

'What if we say no?' Scab asked.

'Don't engage him in conversation!' Vic cried.

– I wish to come with you.

'Don't do that again!' the Monk shouted at Scab. 'Yes, fine, whatever!' she told Ludwig. Vic could hear an edge of hysteria in the Monk's voice that he'd never heard before. Vic was desperately running diagnostics on his neunonics to find out why the incoming 'faces were hurting as they turned and walked quickly back towards the elevator, accompanied by Ludwig. Vic noted that Scab couldn't even be bothered to kill his own clone.

The orbital defences, the fleet, all of them had left the *Basilisk II* alone, presumably because they thought that Ludwig was escorting them somewhere, but Talia remained in charge of the craft.

'Em ...' Talia said when she saw the machine Elite hovering in the *Basilisk II*'s lounge. They were stationary, close to one of the less visited beacons in Red Space. 'Did we get the information?'

'Yes,' Vic answered.

'Okay. Can we keep him?' Talia asked.

'No!' the Monk and Vic said at the same time.

Vic was pretty sure that Talia didn't fully appreciate just how dangerous the augmented alien killing machine was.

'But, I mean, it's going to be easy now. If we have the information we need, I mean. The flying bin can destroy anything that gets in our way.'

Vic stared at her, appalled. '"Easy?" Why would you say something like that?' The 'sect wondered when he had become so superstitious. It was pleasingly human.

Scab was stretched out in an armchair, a cigarette with a long ash tail hanging precariously off it held between two fingers. He had stripped to the waist but still wore his hat and braces. He was immersed, looking at Ertl's mindscape.

Finally Scab emerged from the immersion. The Monk, giving Ludwig a wide berth, moved closer to Scab.

'Well?' she asked. 'Do you know the way to the Ubh Blaosc?'

'No,' Scab said. Now Vic knew his ex-partner had lost it. Scab was smiling.

34
Ubh Blaosc

The inevitability of the fall. More like riding over a cliff than into a lake through ice. The water was gone. Everything seemed to slow down, thanks to the gifts of the blood she had drunk from Britha. The instinct was to hold onto the chariot but, thinking quicker than she ever had before, Tangwen knew that would just mean she would join the collision of horseflesh, wood and metal. She leapt off the chariot.

Everything was moving too quickly for her to process. What she saw in the air, over the Lochlannach warriors, made no sense. Below the ice was another world wreathed in blue fire. A stone circle, but not the one she had seen in the crystal clear water during her previous visit to Oeth. There were dark armoured shapes just beyond the light. She had seen the blank-faced figure with the single serpent eye, and somehow she had known it was Selbach. He had been cursed by the magics of her Father's people. All the Lochlannach were trying to protect him.

She practically landed on several of the demon-possessed warriors, carrying two of them to the ground. Once the impact would have broken her body. Now she rolled. She felt the impact of the chariot and its horse team, an explosion of dirt, screaming horseflesh, the mangled bodies of the Lochlannach. *Britha?*

She had less than a moment to think. Her body was already healing the damage she had taken in the fall. She kicked out, her foot contacting with one of the Lochlannach, and rolled away from him and onto her feet. She still had her bow in hand. She grabbed at an arrow from her quiver. It was broken. She grabbed at another as one of the Lochlannach tackled her around the waist, picking her up off the ground and slamming her into one of the stones. She screamed out as her hair and exposed skin burned. The stone was hot. Her furs were smouldering. She heard shouting in the language of the Goidel, and another language she understood but didn't recognise. There was screaming from above. She saw the monstrous burning spear that had slain the giant speeding towards them, and above the spear the toothed roof of the cavern Oeth was in. Cracks appeared in the rock far above them and raining stone crushed several of the Lochlannach. The screaming spear was caught in a net of lightning. This only seemed to make it angry. Tangwen dropped her bow and arrow. She grabbed the hilt of her dagger and dragged it from its sheath. She rammed the chalice-re-forged blade into the Lochlannach's head. Her furs and hair caught fire. The Lochlannach dropped her and she shoved him back so she could move away from the stone. She dodged a spear-thrust from another Lochlannach. She closed with the man, drawing her hatchet as she did. He dropped the spear and reached for his sword, but the hatchet impacted into the side of his face. Tangwen kicked him into two more of the Lochlannach who were trying to get to her. She dropped the hatchet and the dagger, reached back for her bow, at the same time finding an unbroken arrow in her quiver by touch. Then she charged the Lochlannach.

'Not the women!' a familiar voice shouted in the unfamiliar tongue. Tangwen was moving too fast to register the pain of the flames yet. The Lochlannach had formed a circle around Selbach, protected by their large shields, bristling with spears. She spun, dancing past the spearheads, getting inside their reach. Something had been done to Selbach, something bad, but more obviously something important to Crom's plans. She leapt up. Her foot touched the rim of one of the Lochlannach's shields. She bent her knee and then threw herself into the air. The cavern, the falling rock, the ice and the water above her disappeared, and with it the blue fire, and suddenly she was falling up into a twilight sky. Panic came close to overwhelming her. The bowstring was already drawn back. She loosed. Then she was flying back towards the ground and Lochlannach blades. She saw Britha close to the stones, curled in a ball, trying to protect her stomach. The arrow took Selbach in the head. He disappeared under his guards. Lightning arced out, joining the stones to the Lochlannach warriors, their flesh blackening, their eyes cooking, their armour fusing in an instant. They collapsed in rows beneath her as she hit the ground. She tried to burrow her way through the smoking dead, to grab at the earth so she would not fall into the sky beneath her. Above her the living spear screamed, and tried to force its way down through the lightning to kill her and all else.

A figure walked between the stones, a woman in the robes of a *dryw*. Tangwen wanted to spit and make the sign against evil, but she didn't dare let go of the earth lest she fall into the sky. The *dryw* wore the skull of a horse on her head. It covered her face. She was the *Láir Bhán*, the White Mare, the horse that was death and winter. A flickering light glowed within the skull. She carried a staff in one hand, her other was raised up towards the spear. Tangwen could feel the magics in the air on her skin. It was like the moment before a storm. She was still burning. Tangwen rolled onto her back. Panic nearly overwhelmed her again as she found herself looking down into the sky below her, and at the god whose wings blocked out the sun.

With difficulty she managed to put the flames out. The lightning had gone, though she still saw remnants of its light in her vision. The spear was no longer in the sky above them. She crawled through the smoking bodies, feeling little of the pain of her burned back, clutching at the earth, making her way towards Britha. Tangwen grabbed one of the Lochlannach's swords as she went. She tried not to look at the wreckage of the chariot. The horses had, mercifully, been hit by the lightning as well. The blonde charioteer's body lay broken, her limbs arranged at horrible angles. Tangwen made it to Britha, and all but lay across her, sword at the ready to defend her pregnant friend. Trying not to look down into the sky.

The figure that walked slowly towards them looked too bulky for a man, even a man wearing armour. He was clad in thick plates of ornately decorated metal, the likes of which Tangwen had never seen before. His helm was that of a metal raven, and it covered his entire head. She screamed as the helm folded away from his face, over his head and disappeared into his armour, seemingly of its own accord. His face was in shadow, but it looked like he had long, dark, braided hair, with feathers, bones, and other items woven into it. Behind him the *Láir Bhán* held the writhing spear in one hand. The spear was shrinking, as other armoured figures helped wrestle the weapon into a case.

'Are you well?' The familiar voice again. She pointed the sword towards him. 'I mean you no harm, and you are not going to fall into the sky.' He knelt down, his features in light now.

The entire bottom part of his face was painted with black dye, and there were red and white markings painted around his eyes.

Tangwen's eyes flicked to the *Láir Bhán*. She had walked to the centre of the circle, and was kneeling over Selbach's corpse, knife in hand. There was a wet crunch as the horse-skulled figure cut into Selbach's head.

'Teardrop?' Tangwen asked, her eyes welling with tears.

He shook his head sadly. 'That is my name, but I am not the man you knew. When we die we come back in the spring.' He smiled at her. 'I think that both of you have wounds that need seeing to.' Tangwen could feel Britha uncurling beneath her. She moved so the *ban draoi* could sit up.

'My child,' was all Britha said.

'We will see to it,' Teardrop said.

'Like you did the last one?' Britha demanded. Suddenly the *ban draoi* had a dagger in her hand.

'That was ... regrettable,' Teardrop said. He glanced behind him at the horse-skulled *dryw*.

'Anyone who tries to harm or steal her child, I'll kill them,' Tangwen spat, sounding more fierce and less afraid than she felt.

Teardrop just nodded, though Tangwen suspected that he wasn't particularly worried. She felt a thrill of fear run through her as the *Láir Bhán* approached.

'Just kill her,' the horse-skulled *dryw* said. Her voice was not that of a woman. It was strange and full of authority and hate. She held something dripping in the hand not holding her staff.

'She is with child,' Teardrop said, exasperation in his voice. The *Láir Bhán* said nothing. The moments stretched out uncomfortably. Light flickered within the skull around the impenetrable black eye sockets. Then the *dryw* removed the skull from her head. She was one of the oldest people that Tangwen had ever seen. Her skin was like leather, but she still looked vital and full of life despite the sheen of sweat covering her face.

'Whose child?' she demanded. Her voice sounded normal now, though still angry.

'Fachtna's,' Britha lied. Tangwen tried not to react. It wasn't often she heard fear in the northern woman's voice. Falsehood was a little more common. The *dryw* studied her. 'We'll harvest this child and then she burns.' Tangwen was aware of Britha tensing, but she said nothing.

'I do not know how things are among the sons and the

daughters of Mael Duin, Grainne, but among the Croatan there are laws,' Teardrop told the old woman.

'We have laws against murdering a *drui*, for example,' the *dryw*, apparently called Grainne, spat.

'Fachtna killed Sainrith,' Britha told the other woman evenly. 'And I killed him for it, and you will give me my daughter back because there is no law that says you had the right to take her.' Teardrop had sagged as he heard of Fachtna's death.

'She had her part in it!' Grainne said.

'I was asleep when it happened. He killed Sainrith trying to stop you both from stealing my child!' Britha shouted at the other *dryw*. Teardrop held up his hands.

'Peace, please.' He turned to Grainne. 'They are under my hospitality. Don't we have more important things to do this night?' He nodded at the bleeding thing in Grainne's hand. It looked like a stone of some kind.

'I will lodge a complaint with the Medicine Societies.'

'That is your right,' Teardrop said.

'And by coming here they have killed us,' Grainne said. 'The changed one sang his mindsong. The Naga now know where we are.'

It had taken some convincing but Tangwen finally knew that she was not going to fall into the sky when she stood up. There was a remarkable difference between what she knew, and what all her senses were screaming at her. She was walking very carefully on the ground. She had retrieved her weapons, though re-forged in the chalice or not, they looked small and frail in comparison to the oversized spears, swords, clubs, hammers, and axes the bulky armoured figures bore. Some of the armour was decorated in ways similar to the metalwork of the Gauls, the Goidels, and her own people. Other armour, like Teardrop's, she didn't recognise the patterns of at all, though parts of the decoration seemed to represent beasts; some she recognised, others she didn't. Those who wore the more strangely decorated armour were darker skinned, and had dark hair. She assumed that they were from the Croatan, the same tribe as Teardrop.

Tangwen had cried out again when Teardrop's armour had folded away, like his helmet had, into a small metal pack attached to the back of his belt. Underneath his armour he wore deerskin leggings, soft-soled boots, and a loincloth. His shoulders, upper arms, and parts of his back and chest were decorated with tattoos that just formed shapes. If they represented anything, then Tangwen couldn't work it out.

The circle of stones was nestled in the mouth of a canyon surrounded by sandy coloured rock. An outcrop gave views over a vast plain that reminded her a little of the reeds in her marshes at home, though without the hidden, and sometime treacherous, water channels.

They had been given food, which Tangwen hadn't wanted to eat until she had assurance that it came with no obligation. It was known that you shouldn't take food from the fair folk. After watching Britha get stuck in, however, she had followed suit. It had been delicious, filling, and had helped her body heal itself.

Teardrop had touched Britha's belly and closed his eyes, concentrating. 'I think if you were a normal mortal you would have lost the child by now,' he had told Britha ruefully. 'But all is well, as far as I can tell. Though you would do well to let a *drui*, or a medicine woman, examine you.' Britha had just shaken her head.

Later, Britha had recovered her spear. She had asked Teardrop if Calgacus's blonde charioteer, whose name neither of them knew, could be put in the cauldron. Tangwen had heard of such things, magical cauldrons that could bring the dead back to life. Grainne had refused. She had claimed that they would need all their magics for the war. To Tangwen's ears the refusal had sounded partly motivated by spite, but it seemed that her Father's people were coming to this land, and her Father had always feared his own kind. He had said that they had been turned mad and evil.

Tangwen hadn't wanted to get on the 'chariot'. Magics were one thing, but the vehicle was a crime against sense, and all that was natural. Made of smooth dark wood on the top, and lighter wood underneath, it was roughly shaped like a long-necked, short-bodied amphora, of the sort they traded for when the ships came from the lands to the east of the sea. It was sleek, however, reminding her of an arrow as well. The back opened for them, but she knew that people weren't meant to fly like that. Britha wasn't happy about it either, but it was the *ban draoi* who eventually talked Tangwen into climbing on board. She had almost soiled herself when it dropped away from the earth and into the sky.

The Otherworld was a strange inside-out place so vast it was difficult to understand. The sun was in the middle of the Otherworld, closer, larger, and warmer on her skin than Belenus, the sun god who shone in the sky high above Ynys Prydain. The land sloped up and away from her on all sides. She saw seas high above her, and she could not work out why the water was not running down the side of the huge curving land. It looked empty. If it hadn't been so strange it would have been beautiful. She saw distant mountains. She had never seen mountains before. They must have been huge but they looked tiny. White lands, presumably covered in snow.

Tangwen could see through part of the chariot's cart, though it covered them completely. They were rising up, the vehicle turning in the air. It shot forwards, but she didn't feel a lurch. She knew that the charioteer controlled the vehicle from a small area at the other end of the neck. She was sitting on a comfortable seat, in fact one of the most comfortable that she had ever sat on. They were soaring through clouds now. Her eyes widened as they passed floating rocks, and spherical trees. Strange creatures, some like birds, others not, flapped or glided through the air, many of them much larger than any creature in the air had a right to be. Entire lands shot by beneath them.

'I know it's difficult, but you must understand that you are completely safe up here,' Teardrop said. He had referred to the comfortable compartment in the rear of the chariot as the cupola. On some level she knew this was wondrous, thrilling even, but she couldn't quite shake the fear. Britha looked uncomfortable, but not as frightened as Tangwen was.

Now more than ever she found herself missing the reassurance of her Father's mindsong. With everyone looking to her, with all of the killing that had been necessary, the guardianship of the cursed chalice, she had never felt more lost. She had hoped to go home and see if her Father still lived. That did not seem likely. They were travelling so fast now.

'I was saddened to hear that Fachtna is dead,' Teardrop said. 'I understand what he did, though I do not condone it. I had hoped that you had found a place away from here to live your lives in peace.'

'There is no peace in a land with Crom Dhubh in it,' Britha said.

'He is the cause of much suffering, I think. Did he send the changed one?' he asked.

'We tried to stop him,' Britha said.

'We tried to kill him,' Tangwen managed.

'Tried?' Teardrop asked. The two women looked at each other.

'I don't know,' Britha finally said.

'The cavern collapsed. If he cannot be killed then he must have been trapped,' Tangwen said, but even to her own ears it sounded like something that she wanted to believe, rather than something that she knew to be.

'Tell me how Fachtna died,' Teardrop asked.

'I told you ...' Britha snapped, but Tangwen could tell the anger was to cover something she did not wish to talk of.

'It would take very powerful magics indeed to kill my friend. How did you do it?'

'If you want vengeance—' Britha started. Tangwen could see her trying to hold something back.

Teardrop help up his hand. 'My wife might, but I just want to know.'

Much of the land passing by so quickly below them looked empty. It was vast, but devoid of people, at least as far as she could tell.

'When we returned to Ynys Prydain I did try to kill him for what he had done. The *dryw* exist for a reason. Without them the tribes would murder each other. There must be laws, judgement, sense in the face of the warriors' greed and lust for blood. They look to glory. We enforce honour. Without us then all are as the Corpse People,' Britha told him. He nodded, though Tangwen did not think that he completely agreed with her words. 'I ran him through with his own sword. I ... I have had cause to regret this.'

'Was the sword singing at the time?' he asked. She shook her head. It was obvious that she was wrestling with her emotions.

'No,' Britha said eventually, squirming slightly in her low seat.

'Then you did not kill him.' Tangwen could hear the hope in his voice.

'He is dead. He was diseased by the Muileartach. I think he had become the goddess's champion.' Teardrop considered her words and then finally simply nodded. His face was impassive. The sadness was all in his dark eyes. 'I killed him for the control rod.'

Teardrop regarded her carefully. 'How?' he finally said.

'The spear.'

'You could not wield the Spear of Lug. Who helped you?' It was clear that he had already worked out the answer. Britha looked down, unable to look him in the eyes.

'I wanted my daughter back,' she said quietly. Tangwen knew that Teardrop was clever enough to work out that the death of Fachtna was the reason the rod had come to be in Crom Dhubh's possession. Why his people were now about to go to war with her Father's people. They were circling down over vast riverlands. In the distance was a sprawling structure, easily the size of the largest longhall she had ever seen, made of handsomely carved wood, standing on an island among the rivers. The island was in the centre of a network of causeways. Once again the reminder of home was unwelcome.

As they circled closer to the structure Tangwen could see a man – even from this distance he did not look Croatan, though he was dressed like Teardrop had first been when she had met him – and a woman, who obviously was Croatan, and four children waiting for them.

'I apologise in advance if my wife tries to kill you,' he said.

'Can a god survive a hill falling on him?' Guidgen asked, and looked to Germelqart, but the Carthaginian said nothing. The ravine in the southern hills was larger now. He knew that their friends were buried underneath all that rock, along with the Pecht, the Iceni scouts, and some of his own people. Britha was lost, but she was too strange and distant to ever have been a friend; too untrustworthy as well, though he had come to value her. She was just a little too selfish to be a *dryw*, in his opinion. She made decisions with her heart.

Their plan had worked. At least he hoped that it had. He had prayed to Cuda, the mother, and Arawn, king of the underworld, that they should keep Crom Dhubh, that the Dark Man was at least trapped, if not dead, though hopefully the latter. He admonished himself as he found himself thinking that if Crom Dhubh wasn't gone permanently, then he hoped the Dark Man wouldn't return while Guidgen yet lived. Let him be a curse on future generations. It was an uncharitable thought. Besides, the old *gwyll dryw* had a sneaking feeling that he was immortal now.

They had served Bladud ill, and many of the other warriors who had drunk from the chalice, too, though he would not mourn the death of the Corpse People. They had walked a very narrow path, but Gofannon had honoured their agreement. People had to fear such magics. There had to be a price to such power, or it would destroy the land. It was just a shame that they could not have burned the Lochlannach who had drunk from the chalice as well. This would have spared them all the trouble, but Crom Dhubh had made a different pact with the god in the chalice, and Gofannon honoured all his agreements. Those who still had their weapons from the fight with the spawn of Andraste had, for the most part, been eager to give them to Guidgen for safekeeping after they had seen those who had drunk from the chalice burn and the way the newer weapons had crumbled to red dust.

From his vantage point high on the slopes of one of the southern hills Guidgen could see the survivors splitting up. Each of the tribes would be making their own way back towards their lands. The idea of a united Ynys Prydain had died with Bladud. *Which is good*, Guidgen thought, as it was a strange and unnatural idea.

As the surviving guardians of the Red Chalice, Guidgen and Germelqart had been looked on with fear and distrust, but only Anharad yet had the power to move against them, and Guidgen was still a *dryw*. The Trinovantes noblewoman had seen her future snatched away from her again, this time by their actions, not by those of Otherworldly raiders. He could count the shame and the guilt he felt over his actions, and yet he knew that the five of them, Germelqart, Tangwen, Calgacus, Britha and himself, had done the right thing.

Garim was now the king of the Brigante. He would make a weak king. Such things happened. When he died maybe the next king would be stronger.

Germelqart was going to return with him to the *gwyllion*'s land. Hide in what the spawn of Andraste had left of it. He suspected that Moren would hunt for the power they had. With the *gwyllion*'s abilities as warriors, their knowledge of the land, the Red Chalice, and the original chalice-re-forged weapons, they would be fine. Where possible they would hide rather than fight. They would keep guardianship of the Otherworldly power. They would use it against threats like Crom Dhubh, and the other gods that wished the Pretani ill. They would form a new circle.

It was Tangwen that he would miss the most.

35
Now

Grace had spoken to Eileen and the other survivors, and then she had gone looking around the Laurel Canyon neighbourhood for alternative transport, much to du Bois's annoyance. He could hear the engines being revved in the castle now. La Calavera's vehicles sounded all muscle, clouds of exhaust rising up from the courtyard in the mock castle.

The ECV was sitting on the steep sloping driveway. La Calavera's people were too occupied to send patrols up into the residential streets overlooking Laurel Canyon Boulevard now. It was a beautiful day.

The Cougar, the six-wheeled armoured truck, was the first to leave the mock castle and roll onto the boulevard. Motorcycle outriders shot out from the castle, and overtook the military vehicle. Next up was a Cadillac Escalade pickup truck with thick, ugly metal plates wielded to its bodywork, a heavy machine gun in the truck bed. Then an armoured Mustang, and then a succession of muscle cars, SUVs, pickups, and dune buggies, all armoured, all being used as platforms for weapons. They had turned the civilian vehicles into technicals, improvised fighting vehicles. The motorcycles buzzed around the main convoy.

'If she's not back, then we go without her,' du Bois said from the passenger seat.

'Or we call it off. There's too many of them,' Alexia said, shaking her head. Du Bois suppressed his feeling of irritation. He glanced behind him but all he could see was Beth's legs, as she was manning the turret. The minigun had just less than one box of ammunition left, fewer than a thousand rounds. He wished that the ECV had been armed with a more practical weapon. The convoy was now snaking its way down the winding road.

'Okay, we roll,' du Bois said, not acknowledging his sister's suggestion. Alexia hesitated but then started the engine, its deep bass rumble lost under the noise of all the engines in Laurel Canyon this morning. The ECV rolled down the steep drive and out onto the side street. Du Bois didn't look back at the house. He tried not to think about Eileen and the other survivors. *No, he thought, not survivors, just not victims yet.* He hoped the food and other supplies he had scavenged would do them some good, though he was starting to wish that he'd had more sleep. His augmented physiology could keep going for much longer than a normal human, but it had its limits.

The side street had houses on one side, the other side looked down onto another residential street, and then below that, Laurel Canyon Boulevard. They were running parallel with the boulevard. Du Bois had his SA58 OSW carbine in hand. A 40mm HEAP grenade was loaded into the grenade launcher. The M240 machine gun on the swing mount could not comfortably achieve the angle to fire down onto the convoy. Still, he hoped that nobody in the vehicles below would look up. He heard the sound of a bike and glanced in the rear-view mirror. Grace was behind them on a stolen Harley Davidson Night Rod. He could see where she had taped pistol magazines and grenades to the bike for easy access.

Someone in the convoy looked up, and he heard the staccato rattle of small arms fire, and the deeper, slower sound of heavier machine guns. Tracer rounds flew across the road in front of them. He heard the change in the pitch of the engines below. They didn't return fire. Beth didn't have the angle in the turret either. Du Bois shrank back into his seat as rounds bounced off the ECV's armour. They were firing at his side of the vehicle, and he didn't have a door. Alexia accelerated, and moved as far to the right on the narrow road as she could. Grace accelerated, moving behind the ECV on the left-hand side, using the armoured vehicle to protect herself from the gunfire.

Alexia wrestled the heavy vehicle around the twists and turns of the residential street. Ahead of them they could see the junction with Laurel Canyon Boulevard. They started taking much heavier fire now as each of La Calavera's vehicles passed the junction. Grace braked hard and moved the bike in behind the ECV. Du Bois heard the tearing sound of the minigun firing. Tracers shot out overhead. Some of them glanced off the vehicles, but the armour-piercing rounds ate through jury-rigged armour. Cars filled with red mist and spun out of control. Du Bois leaned out of the ECV, bullets whipping past him, and fired the HEAP grenade from his carbine's underslung launcher. The grenade caught a custom low rider in the side, penetrated the metal plates wielded to it, and detonated. The car careened across the road and into the canyon wall.

Alexia depressed the accelerator. The ECV lurched forwards. Du Bois rapidly reloaded the M320 grenade launcher with his last HEAP round, and then braced. The ECV hit an SUV in the side. The technical buckled from the force of the heavier vehicle's impact; it was lifted off its wheels and tumbled onto its roof as Alexia slewed the armoured patrol vehicle hard left onto Laurel Canyon Boulevard. Grace shot by them on the inside. They were close to the tail-end of the convoy, only three more vehicles and some motorcyclists behind them. More ripping noises. Beth was firing short, controlled bursts from the minigun. It didn't matter. Its ferocious rate of fire would quickly chew through ammunition. The vehicles behind them careened off the road. Some of the drivers and crew would have been hit, others just frightened off by the volume of incoming fire. It didn't matter how insane you were, it was difficult to be on the wrong end of a minigun.

As they shot past the turn-off for Hollywood Boulevard, du Bois grabbed the M240, nestled the butt against his shoulder and started firing. He kept his field of fire to the right. Grace kept to the left of the ECV. She had one hand on the handlebars, the other was firing one of her Beretta M92Fs, converted to full automatic, with remarkable accuracy. Motorcycle outriders spilled off their bikes and tumbled across the asphalt. Du Bois barely felt the bump as the ECV ran across them. The rear vehicle in the convoy now was a muscle car. Gunmen leaned out of the vehicle, firing at Grace. Du Bois fired the M240, tracers tracked the shots into the vehicle. Holes started appearing in its ad hoc armour; he saw a limb spin out of the passenger window. The vehicle shot across the road and slammed into the canyon wall. Grace, no longer holding a pistol, slewed hard right across the road. Du Bois cursed and stopped firing. The gunners in the pickup truck technical that had been in front of the muscle car started firing at the Night Rod and the ECV. Sparks filled du Bois's vision. He didn't have a clear shot. A bullet grazed his skull as he leant out. He caught a glimpse of something flying from Grace's hand. A moment later the truck bed of the pickup exploded, gunmen's bodies flying through the air. Grace was right next to the truck's cab, one of her Berettas practically stuck through a firing slit in the armour. The pickup truck started to wobble. The pistol disappeared inside her leather jacket and she braked hard. The ECV shot past her and crashed through the pickup. Grace swerved in behind them. The Cougar and a number of other vehicles swerved right across Laurel Canyon Boulevard, and took Selma Avenue. The rest remained on Laurel.

'Follow them!' du Bois shouted, pointing at the vehicles that had gone down Selma. 'Beth, conserve ammunition. They're trying to get behind us.'

They sped down curving Selma Avenue. Du Bois risked a few bursts with the MG. They received a lot of inaccurate fire in return. Alexia brutally dropped a gear, and floored the accelerator du Bois almost cried out. The ECV lurched forwards and hit the left-hand rear side of the armoured van in front of them at the corner of Sunset Boulevard. The van spun out. Du Bois pulled himself back into the cab as the van bounced off the ECV again and came close to tearing the door gun off. Alexia braked hard as she tried to wrestle with the armoured patrol vehicle as it shot across Sunset, smashing through a car coming the other way. Du Bois caught a glimpse of some kind of fire ceremony at the Chateau Marmont, naked, painted guests turning to look at the chase.

'Fuck's sake!' du Bois shouted. Angry because his sister's driving had frightened him.

'I used to like the Marmont,' Alexia said, moving through the gears rapidly, keeping her foot depressed between shifts. The bit of Sunset that they were on was broad and straight, so she could build up speed. 'Less traffic than there used to be.'

'Really?' du Bois shouted. There were other vehicles on the road, but driven by the insane or not, they were doing everything they possibly could to stay out of the way of the heavily armed chase. Alexia was using the whole broad road, weaving in and out of the sparse traffic. Beth was firing the Mod 0 LMG now, conserving the ammunition in the minigun, tracers arcing overhead. Grace nearly lost control of the bike as she braked one-handed, still firing one of her full automatic Berettas. The ECV shot by her. She swapped the pistol over to the other hand, accelerating, ejecting the spent high capacity magazine from the Beretta, and replacing it with another one that was taped to the handlebars.

They were speeding past Sunset Plaza now, the street lined with billboards for a world that no longer existed. Part of the

Hollywood Hills were burning up on their right. They exchanged fire with the convoy as the road curved onto the Sunset Strip. Everything seemed to be for sale on either side of the Strip: drugs, sex, slaves, alcohol, hair care products for anachronistic street tribes, all of it being documented by film crews. The rock bars and clubs were orgies spilling out onto the street. They were taking fire from pedestrians. Du Bois grunted as his leather coat stopped more than one round.

Some of the vehicles they were chasing were faster, but the slower vehicles in the convoy limited their speed. Alexia was more than able to keep up with them, though they were taking so much fire she had to look through a veil of sparks to see the road. The bullet-resistant glass of the windscreen was being chipped away in parts. Behind them the muscle cars, SUVs and pickup truck technicals that had split off when part of the convoy had turned off onto Selma were catching up.

Sunset curved round to the left again as the road entered Beverly Hills. Ahead of them they could see a wall of wrecked cars stretched across Sunset. There was a withering hail of fire from the defenders behind the blockade as they lit up the convoy. Some of the convoy vehicles careened off the road, colliding into each other. Du Bois watched as the armoured Cougar rammed through the blockade at speed, sending the wrecked, vehicular building blocks, and the Beverly Hills defenders, flying. Another of the convoy's vehicles slammed into the blockade and went spinning through the air into someone's landscaped, manicured lawn. A bike hit one of the wrecks and the rider flew over the burned out car. They were receiving fire from the vehicles behind them. The ripping sound of the minigun answered. Alexia nudged a wreck with the front of the ECV and sent it sliding into another, and then they were through the barricade.

Both their armoured patrol vehicle and La Calavera's convoy were taking a lot of incoming small arms fire from smartly dressed private security people, whose uniform had something of the SS about it, and from people wearing the merchandise of an exclusive local gun club. Ahead of them the M2 .50 calibre heavy machine gun in the CROWS remotely operated turret atop the Cougar was returning fire, making large craters in manicured lawns. If a round hit someone they exploded. The hydrostatic shock popped limbs and heads off.

Du Bois cried out as round after round hit him. Armoured

clothing and hardening skin stopped most of them. It didn't mean they didn't hurt. His head snapped round as a bullet tore open his face. There were sparks inside the ECV's cab. He heard Alexia cry out and the vehicle wobbled, but she held it. The convoy's outriding bikes were just being mown down. A badly injured dismounted rider staggered out in front of the ECV. There was a thump and he disappeared under the patrol vehicle, leaving a red stain on the bonnet.

For a moment everything seemed to slow down for du Bois. It was clear what kind of micro society they had been trying to build behind their barricades. Slaves dropped down onto lawns to avoid the gunfire, their mounted overseers sliding off panicked horses and seeking cover, humans on leads being used as human shields, bodies hanging from trees. Yet all the lawns were immaculate, the cars gleamed. Du Bois's finger curved around the trigger of the door gun and squeezed.

Beth dropped down into the main cab of the ECV, and grunted as a ricocheting round caught her. She was putting a fresh belt of rounds into the Model 0. 'The minigun's empty!' Another round hit her, and she slumped, but then struggled back up and climbed into the turret. He had no idea where Grace was. Beverly Hills was a bad place to be exposed on a bike. Ahead of them an SUV technical exploded. They bumped through the wreckage, fire and debris raining down on them. The ECV suddenly jumped as something exploded against it. Flame rolled over du Bois's side of the vehicle, and the overpressure tried to suck him out of the cab. Behind him Beth ducked back down into the cab as the explosion rolled over the top of the vehicle as well. The ECV was surrounded by fire. Alexia drove through it. The convoy was turning right onto North Hillcrest Road. As Alexia slewed the armoured patrol vehicle round the corner, du Bois leaned out of the vehicle and looked back. There was a still-smoking crater in the armour towards the rear of the vehicle. He guessed it was from a 40mm high explosive grenade fired from a launcher. Had it been a HEAP he suspected the chase would have been over.

They roared past more large houses with swimming pools and well-manicured lawns. There was less of an armed response on Hillcrest. A gate to one of the big houses exploded, parts of it bouncing off the ECV, and Grace's Night Rod swerved onto the road behind them. The door MG ran dry. Du Bois started replacing the belt as quickly as he could, and got shot several more times in the process.

Two of the remaining motorcycle outriders, in fact, possibly the only two remaining outriders, were falling back towards them. There weren't that many vehicles left ahead of them: a couple of the dune buggies, a four-wheel-drive flatbed light lorry, armoured, with spikes, chains, skulls, and flayed skin hanging off it. It was enough to make du Bois think that they were trying too hard. Then there was still the Escalade with the HMG in the back and the Cougar.

Alexia swerved towards one of the motorcycle outriders. The ECV clipped the bike, but the rider was already reaching for the bonnet of the armoured patrol vehicle. He grabbed the bull bar as his bike disappeared under the ECV. The outrider was holding on for dear life, his boots bouncing off the ground. He was stripped to the waist, his body and shaved head covered in gothic script. Alexia was looking for wreckage to scrape him off on. Du Bois reached for his carbine, but the other outrider was suddenly next to him, grabbing for the doorframe. Du Bois cried out as a large, very sharp knife was rammed into his right arm. A fist covered in rings hit him in the face. He could smell the man, see his flesh desecrated with rusted nails, human skin covering his mouth and nose, his hair shaved into a triple mohican. The second out-rider leaned back for a kick. Du Bois drew his tanto, somewhat awkwardly, with his left hand. The folded steel of the Japanese blade sliced up through the outrider's side and then through the tendons of his arm in a C-shaped cut. Alexia swerved the ECV up onto the pavement as the outrider was falling back. He hit a lamppost at speed.

Alexia slewed the vehicle round onto Santa Monica Boulevard, following what remained of La Calavera's convoy. The gothic script outrider swung one-handed through the passenger door-way and kicked du Bois in the face. The two-footed kick hit him with enough force to knock him towards Alexia, but his seatbelt caught him. The man was almost sat in his lap now, reaching for the Glock in his waistband. Du Bois's hearing cut out for a moment. The sound of the Colt OHWS held right by his head was deafening. Blood splattered the windscreen and gothic script was a dead weight on his lap. Du Bois could barely move.

'Malcolm!' Alexia shouted. He had no idea what she was warning him about. Beth stood up again, opening the hatch to the turret. Du Bois heaved, and screamed as blood squirted out of the knife wound in his arm. Gothic script flopped out of the ECV. Du Bois had to lean out of the vehicle for a clear view, then he saw what Alexia was shouting about. The flatbed lorry and the two dune buggies were dropping back towards their armoured patrol vehicle, gunmen and women hanging off them or waiting in the lorry's flatbed. It sort of made sense – the majority of their small arms could do little to the ECV's armour, but du Bois still couldn't shake the feeling that they were going through the motions of some post-apocalyptic fantasy. They were insane but they seemed to be obeying some obscene set of rules.

Du Bois screamed again as he removed the blade from his arm, and dropped it onto the asphalt. The wound was already starting to close, his body feeding on itself, yet again. He had not had a chance to finish reloading the door MG. He heard submachine gunfire and Beth cursing. The dune buggy on his side of the ECV was almost on him, the hangers-on reaching with one hand for their vehicle. Du Bois drew his .45 with his weak right hand, and started firing at them. With his left he opened the grenade launcher on his carbine and removed the HEAP grenade. One of the hangers-on fell between the two speeding vehicles, shot multiple times. Du Bois found a 40mm flechette grenade on his webbing. Another of the gunmen leapt from the dune buggy, firing a MAC-10 submachine gun one-handed as he did. It was inaccurate, the weapon's recoil making it climb too quickly. Bullets sparked off armour, but a ricochet went through the back of his seat. His armour stopped the bullet, but it still felt like getting hit with a hammer. He emptied the rest of the .45's magazine at the gunman, who bounced off the ECV and fell under its wheels. Du Bois slid the flechette grenade into the launcher, and clicked it shut. He dropped the .45 into the footwell, and brought the carbine up, firing the grenade launcher. Needle-like flechettes filled the air between the ECV and the dune buggy. One of the gunmen fell off the other vehicle. The driver slumped forwards and the dune buggy swerved towards the ECV. The patrol vehicle clipped it and it went spinning.

The flatbed lorry was bumper-to-bumper with them now. People were climbing onto the ECV's bonnet. Others were jumping onto Alexia's side of the vehicle from the other dune buggy. Du Bois heard the LMG firing from the turret. Boarders tumbled down the windscreen and rolled off the bonnet. Alexia was driving blind now, her face splattered in blood. A bearded boarder swung in and kicked du Bois in the face. He continued across, catching Alexia. The ECV swerved violently. A sawn-off double-barrelled shotgun was pointed at Alexia. Du Bois grabbed the hand with the shotgun and pushed it up. Both barrels fired. Alexia cried out but the blast missed her. Buckshot bounced off the cracked armoured windscreen and the interior superstructure, some of it catching Alexia in the face. The ECV cut violently to the right, but she managed to wrestle back control. Du Bois punched the man in the groin. If it hurt the bearded boarder he showed no sign of it. Another boarder leaned in and shot du Bois twice. He cried out as he was slammed back into his seat. His still-healing right arm went numb. The boarder lying across Alexia and du Bois was screaming and thrashing, repeatedly kicking Alexia in the head as she struggled to control the vehicle. Du Bois managed to get the punch blade from his belt buckle. He rammed it repeatedly into the man's crotch, changing the pitch of the boarder's screams. His vision filled with fire as he was shot in the face at point-blank range, his head pushed violently around. The bullet beat his hardening skin, and all but tore off his reinforced jawbone. He was screaming now, pain, anger, and probably fear. The boarder lying across them got stabbed in the face and then the throat. He grabbed Alexia's pistol from her hip holster. She was sobbing through the blood of her torn-open face. Alexia jumped when du Bois shot the gunman inside the cab with them through the bottom of his jaw, twice. He swapped Alexia's pistol into his right hand and leant out of the ECV, getting shot in the shoulder again in the process. He put another two rounds into the boarder kneeling on the boot with the pistol. He pushed at the one inside the vehicle with his left hand, shooting at anybody who tried to get in the cab with Alexia's pistol. The bearded boarder's head hit the asphalt, and he was dragged out of the cab. Du Bois dropped Alexia's now empty pistol into the footwell. Behind him Beth was thrashing around in the turret. The LMG had gone silent. Du Bois was finally able to grab his carbine again. Someone tried to swing in and took a three-round burst in the stomach before du Bois helped him off the armoured patrol vehicle with his boot. He leant out of the ECV. There was an explosion on the other side of the vehicle. He caught a glimpse of the other dune buggy, a tumbling, smoking wreckage in the rear view mirror. He desperately needed breathing room.

He could hear his sister sobbing next to him. No time to deal with that now.

'This is fucking crazy!' she screamed at him. Du Bois leaned out and started firing burst after burst from the carbine, shooting the boarders on the bonnet who were trying to clamber up the windscreen, firing on the other gunmen in the back of the flatbed lorry, cutting them down.

Breathing room! The carbine ran dry. He flipped open the grenade launcher, the spent flechette round ejected. More gunmen were jumping from the back of the lorry and onto the ECV.

'Fuck off! Fuck off!' Beth screamed from the turret. He was vaguely aware of blood spattering the back of his neck from above. The boarders clinging on to the right-hand side, the driver's side of the ECV, fell away as one of Grace's fully automatic Berettas sounded. Du Bois leant down to grab his last HEAP grenade from the footwell. Someone hit him in the shoulder with a machete hard enough to get through armour and hardening skin. He howled out in pain and sat back, hard, in his seat. He had a moment to take in the grinning face of an obviously drug-fuelled muscle-bound psycho, as he swung the machete at him again. Du Bois parried the blow by hitting the boarder in the arm with the collapsible stock of his carbine hard enough to push the man backwards. He then rammed the stock into the boarder's fingers, breaking them. He barely felt the bump as they ran over him. Du Bois grabbed the HEAP and slid it home. He leaned out of the ECV. One of the boarders was running across the bonnet towards him. Du Bois fired the grenade launcher. The velocity of the HEAP grenade flew through the boarder's leg, taking it off at the knee. It flew across the flatbed, through the cab and into the engine block of the lorry. Then it blew. The ECV crashed into it. Du Bois threw himself back into the cab, narrowly avoiding being torn out of it by twisted wreckage. The ECV lurched horribly. Alexia screamed. It felt like the armoured patrol vehicle was in the air for a moment. A bloodied Beth was suddenly sat in the back of the cab, sidearm in hand, pointing it up at the hatch. The ECV landed, bounced. There was the sound of screaming metal, and then they were clear. There was wreckage and a body on the bonnet of their vehicle.

'I'm stopping! I'm stopping!' Alexia screamed. The roof hatch for the turret opened and Beth fired her pistol up through it.

Du Bois tried to tell his sister to keep going, but it came out a slurred mush as he spat blood down himself. He reached up and pushed his jaw back into place, the flesh growing around it, holding it in place as his body auto-cannibalised for the matter to heal itself. The ECV was slowing down. It would be a few moments before he could speak. It was just the Escalade and the Cougar in front of them now. Tracer fire drew lines of phosphorescent light between the Escalade, the Cougar and their own vehicle. Sparks filled their vision again as rounds from the heavy machine gun in the Cougar's remotely operated turret, and what sounded like a Russian made DShK from the Escalade technical, scored holes in the ECV's armour, and cracked the windscreen. The body had been spread all over the bonnet by the impact of the large calibre rounds. As the ricochets spun off the armour, du Bois knew that there was only so much the ECV could take. Grace had swerved in behind them, riding close to use them as cover.

Du Bois put his hand on Alexia's shoulder. 'If you stop now, this was for nothing,' he managed through his not-fully-healed jaw, slurring some of the words. Then he turned away from her and reloaded the door gun. The heavy rounds slowly chewing through the armour sounded like a thousand jackhammers pounding on the ECV. He purposely didn't look at Alexia.

On his left was what had once been a golf course. It looked like a battle had been fought on it. The course was pockmarked with craters and even burned-out vehicles. On the other side of the boulevard were skyscrapers, a commercial district of some kind. It looked strangely open for business. One of the buildings had bodies hanging out of most of the windows. They were taking fire from another of the buildings. They had the road to themselves, however. It seemed this was too intense even for the crazies.

He finished reloading. He looked back at Beth. She was holding her LMG now, her face healing under the blood. She was losing weight as he watched. It looked like she had been slashed, shot and extensively beaten with blunt instruments. Her right arm was bloody to the elbow. She nodded to him. Grace roared right up next to him.

'Draw their fire!' He only heard her because of his augmented hearing filtering out the gunfire and roaring engines. The gunners on the Escalade tried to target her, tracers chasing the fast-moving Harley Night Rod. Du Bois started firing long burst after long burst at the Escalade, tracers and armour piercing rounds sparking off the road and the pickup truck technical as he tried to suppress the gunners. He was aware of Beth climbing back into the turret. He saw tracers fired from above arcing over the Escalade to bounce off the Cougar's thick armour.

The Night Rod's engine screamed as Grace dropped a gear and twisted the throttle. She cut a hard left across the front of the ECV, leaning in so low her shoulder all but touched the asphalt. The gunners in the Escalade followed her with tracers. The large rounds dug up the road before spinning into the air. Du Bois poured on the fire. The DShK gunner turned his attention back to the ECV. The other gunwoman in the Escalade's truck bed was firing an M16 at Grace. The Night Rod wobbled as it took hits. Grace jerked and nearly lost the bike as she was shot as well. She straightened up. A pistol in her hand now, she emptied a magazine into the two gunners in the back of the Escalade. Both of them staggered back. The DShK gunner fell out of the truck bed and bounced along the road. The woman sat down hard. Grace's pistol disappeared inside her leather jacket and she stood up on the bike's seat, holding onto the handlebars. Then she leapt. She seemed to hang in the air for a long time. The bike fell away, tumbling along the road. Then she landed on the truck bed, grabbing onto the bolted down DShK. Going down on one knee she drew the Beretta from inside her leather, reloaded it, and put a three round burst into the gunwoman's head. Du Bois was concentrating his fire on the Cougar now. Both the rear and the front passenger doors on the Escalade opened, gunmen leaning out of them, aiming weapons back at Grace. She calmly transferred the Beretta to her left hand, and stood up holding onto the heavy machine gun's tripod. She put a burst into the two gunmen on the right-hand side of the vehicle. More bodies hit the road. A shotgun blast almost blew her out of the back of the Escalade but she managed to hold on. She crouched down and put three bursts into the final gunman, leaving him hanging out of the door, trailing along the road, leaving a red smear behind him on the asphalt.

They shot underneath the San Diego Freeway. The houses were smaller, cheaper-looking on either side of the road now. Many of them had been burned out, badly damaged by small arms fire or explosives. There were few people on the street and even fewer on the road, and those were giving them a wide berth, though a few were taking opportunistic shots at the three remaining vehicles.

The Escalade started weaving across the road, trying to shake Grace out of it. Du Bois was wondering what she was trying to achieve here. If she killed the driver then she was out of the fight, even if she took his place. The best thing the driver could do was stop, but that put the Escalade out of play as well. Grace knelt down and pulled her N6 carbine around her body on its sling, gripping onto the pickup with one hand, reloading the weapon's grenade launcher with the other. The .50 calibre HMG in the Cougar's turret was still firing at the ECV. Alexia had taken to weaving their vehicle back and forth across the lanes of Santa Monica Boulevard, trying to avoid being caught in a constant hail of large calibre weapons fire. Du Bois and Beth had stopped bouncing rounds off the Cougar's superior armour. Grace, kneeling down, brought the carbine to her shoulder and fired the grenade launcher. The grenade hit the remotely operated CROWS turret on the armoured truck, and the 40mm HEAP grenade exploded. Flame blossomed on top of the Cougar, whipped back by the speed of the vehicle. The HMG was just so much mangled metal now. The heat of the explosion cooked off the rounds, sending .50 calibre bullets flying off in every direction. The Escalade almost turned over trying to shake Grace off as she clung on for dear life.

There was movement in the smoke, on the roof of the Cougar. Du Bois sighted the M240 door gun. The squat, huge, two-headed, off-kilter shape of La Calavera appeared through the smoke and quickly knelt down. Du Bois started firing the door gun. Tracers rushed to meet the gangland warlord. His new second head was female and screaming. La Calavera was stripped to the waist, his impossibly muscled torso on display, all visible skin covered by the skeleton tattoo. He beckoned the Escalade technical closer. The door gun rounds were driving furrows through his flesh. They were joined by rounds from Beth's LMG fired from up in the turret, but the wounds were closing almost immediately. Du Bois had never seen such efficient healing on anybody, regardless of how much S-tech they had running through their bodies. Grace quickly reloaded one of her Berettas, holstered it and grabbed the DShK, and started firing at the Cougar as the Escalade closed with it. The heavy machine gun put craters in the truck's armour. La Calavera brought a squat, heavy-looking weapon to his shoulder. An Objective Individual Combat Weapon, a hybrid assault rifle and semi-automatic 25mm grenade launcher. He pointed the weapon down, and fired the overbarrel grenade launcher twice at the Escalade's truck bed. He raised the weapon and fired the grenade launcher twice more at the ECV's turret, and then he shifted it again and fired at du Bois. An explosion blossomed above the Escalade's truck bed, and then another, engulfing Grace. La Calavera leapt off the back of the Cougar, powerful leg muscles carrying him high into the air.

Beth appeared in the back of the ECV's cab, slamming the turret's hatch closed as the air-bursting smart grenade exploded above the vehicle, the wave of force pushing it down on its suspension, flames rolling over the vehicle. The final two grenades exploded all but next to du Bois. Force battered him back into the ECV, only the seatbelt stopping him from flying into Alexia. The overpressure hit his augmented – but still mostly liquid – body. Waves coursed through his frame, hydrostatic shock breaking bones, rupturing organs. His body shielded Alexia from the worst of it, but the cab's armoured frame guided the shockwave, bouncing her and Beth around. Flame filled the cab for a moment. Everything went black.

Du Bois came to screaming and in pain. His overtaxed internal medical systems were desperately trying to return him to something resembling functional, using his body's fat reserves so quickly he was practically deflating. Alexia was unconscious. Beth had leant in between brother and sister to steer the ECV. She was blackened, and had a compound fracture of the cheekbone, but seemed the best off of the three of them. As he lolled about in the passenger seat, feeling like a sack of water filled with broken twigs, he could see Beth's cheekbone sucked back through her skin, and the wound close.

They were speeding towards the Cougar and the smoking Escalade. The DShK was now just so much mangled wreckage. Grace was hanging off the Escalade's tailgate, being dragged behind the pickup. She was firing one of her Berettas, short burst after short burst, at La Calavera as he clambered over the pickup's cab towards her. These wounds weren't closing as quickly. She had reloaded her pistol with a magazine of nanite-tipped rounds. How she had the presence of mind to keep firing as she was dragged along, du Bois had no idea. He supposed her armoured bike leathers helped, and she hadn't been caught in an enclosed area by the explosions, but he wasn't sure he could have done the same.

Du Bois found himself able to speak again. 'Alexia!' *Brilliant,* du Bois thought, *nothing brings round the unconscious like shouting,* but his sister was stirring. Suddenly she sat bolt upright and screamed, flailing around in her seat. Beth nearly lost control of the ECV. It shot across the road, and was heading towards a surf shop. Du Bois managed to move and drag the wheel towards him so sharply he thought for a minute the vehicle might turn over.

'We need to get Grace!' Beth shouted, trying to restrain Alexia as du Bois steered badly. La Calavera reached through the gunfire and grabbed Grace, one hugely muscled arm lifting her, easily, up off the road. She fired the last of her pistol's rounds into him at point-blank range. Du Bois could see the nanites doing their work. It looked like parts of his flesh were being eaten from within.

'I've got it!' Alexia shouted. She had calmed down and had the steering wheel again. The ECV was accelerating towards the back of the Escalade.

With her free hand Grace drew one of her knuckleduster-hilted fighting knives. Du Bois was able to move enough to reload the SA58 carbine with the magazine of nanite-tipped bullets. La Calavera punched Grace in the face hard enough to make her whole body shake. She looked dazed but she managed to hold on to her weapons. She rammed the fighting knife into his mouth, yanked it out, and then stabbed him in the throat. The ECV was catching up. Grace pulled the blade out of his throat, and then rammed it up into his arm and started sawing. He let go of her. She landed on the truck bed, tore her blade free, bent her legs and threw herself backwards into a somersault. Alexia dropped a gear, and the ECV's engine screamed as she accelerated, the patrol vehicle surging forwards. La Calavera swung his OICW up to his shoulder. Du Bois leaned out of the ECV, sighting past the mangled remains of the door gun. The ECV was under Grace now. La Calavera fired the OICW's underslung assault rifle. Rounds impacted into Grace. Du Bois fired a three-round burst. The bullets hit La Calavera's central mass. The huge two-headed figure stumbled back. Grace landed on her back, hard, on the ECV's bonnet. Du Bois fired another three-round burst. La Calavera sat down in the truck bed. Grace started to slip off the bonnet. Du Bois dropped his carbine into the footwell onto the other discarded weapons, and grabbed for her. Outstretched fingers got the neck of her leather jacket. Then he screamed as the road caught her, and she was yanked back. Du Bois's arm was all but pulled out of its socket. He found himself looking down at her. She was looking up. Hate gone. Replaced by fear, and something else. He was aware of movement inside the ECV, then the sound of Beth firing her Model 0 LMG from the turret. The armoured patrol vehicle was dragging Grace along now. Du Bois knew she could survive if he let go, but somehow that felt like a betrayal. She was kicking out with leather-armoured legs, trying to stop herself from going under the rear wheel. Du Bois screamed out again as, at an awkward angle, he pulled her close to him. She grabbed the edge of the doorway, and he helped her into the cab until she was practically sat in his lap.

'Get your fuckin' hands off me!' she screamed, and clambered off him, seething, into the back of the ECV. Du Bois turned back to focus on the vehicles ahead. La Calavera, his flesh being eaten from within, was clambering over the Escalade's cab and onto its bonnet. His back was blossoming in little plumes of blood which closed a moment later, as Beth put round after useless round into his rotting body from the turret above. He leapt from the Escalade as Alexia drew level with the vehicle. Beth started firing at the pickup truck's engine block. La Calavera caught the rungs on the ladder on the back of the Cougar. Du Bois had his carbine in his hands again. He leaned out of the ECV, the asphalt shooting past underneath him. In the distance he could see the ocean. It looked wrong, much darker than it should be for the clear blue skies above it. Alexia sideswiped the Escalade, pushing it across four lanes and into the edge of a building. La Calavera had reached the top of the ladder. Du Bois put another nanite-tipped round into his back, aimed, and did the same again. La Calavera sprawled face-first on the roof of the truck, but then managed to pull himself out of view.

It was just a chase now. They had nothing that could go through the Cougar's armour, and the Cougar's HMG was out of action. All the weight was on the side of the 6×6 armoured truck, so they couldn't try forcing it off the road either. Du Bois picked the various weapons out of the footwell, cleaned and sheathed the knives, checked and reloaded the pistols, returning his sister's Beretta to the holster riding her hip.

There were hotels on either side of them. One hotel had all its windows open, curtains billowing in the wind coming off the Pacific. Another had bloody smears down its whitewashed walls, multiple bungee cords hanging from the roof. The road snaked through a park, people wandering through it in a daze, a number of them looking like they had been the victims of something horrific. The road dipped under Ocean Avenue, where hanged bodies scraped across the roof of their vehicles, swastikas painted in blood on the tunnel walls along with the words 'surfing is for whites'. Out of the tunnel and into the bright sunlight, then they were on the beachfront running parallel with the ocean.

It seemed quiet, all they could hear were the odd gunshots and a few screams over their engines. Behind them was Santa Monica Pier. The big wheel was burning, but still going round; bodies hung off it in a way that reminded du Bois of a child's mobile.

The Cougar cut across the car park, its armoured bulk knocking vehicles out of the way. Du Bois had reloaded his carbine with normal rounds, but put a magazine of nanite-tipped .45 calibre rounds into his pistol. Beth had done something similar. Grace was ready with her weapon. Alexia just looked pale and sick.

Surfboards stood up in the sand like gravestones as far as they could see, all along the beach, bodies strapped to them, swastikas carved into their flesh. There was a moderate swell in the water. A lot of surfers were sitting out on their boards looking to the east. Du Bois thought he could hear chanting. The water still didn't look right, too dark.

The Cougar had stopped dead down by the water. Du Bois could see the strange demon-headed member of the DAYP, the one called Inflictor Doorstep for some odd reason. He had on a wetsuit and he was jumping down from the back of the armoured truck. A number of aggressively blond and tanned surfer types with swastika, SS, and death's head tattoos were running towards him. One of them had on a spiked World War One German helmet. Du Bois guessed that they were surf Nazis, surfing-regionalism taken to a ridiculous degree. The apocalypse seemed a little literal in Los Angeles. The surf Nazis skidded to a halt when they got a good look at Inflictor as he pulled a surfboard out of the back of the Cougar. He walked to the water, and started paddling out as Alexia brought the ECV to a halt next to the Cougar, just in the water line.

'Get the fuck off our beach!' the surf Nazi with the helmet snapped. Du Bois glanced at them as he climbed out of the vehicle.

They were both armed but weren't bringing their weapons up.

'Alexia!' du Bois called. His sister climbed out of the ECV and levelled her ARX-170 rifle at them. Du Bois, Grace and Beth – with the Benelli shotgun, rather than her LMG, he noticed – made straight for the Cougar. Inflictor was paddling out to sea.

Inflictor had left the side door to the armoured truck open. The back was filled with all sorts of detritus. La Calavera, still clutching the OICW, lay among the detritus, rotting away. Grace covered as Beth climbed into the rear of the vehicle. A shotgun blast put La Calavera's most recent victim, his second head, out of her misery. Then Grace drew her pistol, and put two nanite-tipped rounds into La Calavera's actual head. Du Bois, carbine at the ready, moved to the truck's cab. The door was unlocked. He yanked it open. It was empty. No Dracimus, no King Jeremy.

'Is the nuke in the back?' du Bois demanded, but he knew the answer before Beth told him.

'Where was the Mustang that left with them?' Grace asked.

'Fuck!' du Bois screamed. He stalked back to the ECV.

'This was for fucking nothing?' Alexia sounded broken.

'Get out of here!' du Bois ordered the two surf Nazis.

'This is our beach, motherf—'

Du Bois shot them both. He glared out at Inflictor lying on his board, paddling out into the swell. He needed to eat soon. Replace some mass. He was emaciated, and it felt like his body was about to cave in on itself. Beth had followed him round to his side of the ECV.

'Are you having fun?' she asked, looking at the two dead surfers. 'Is that what we just did all that for?' Du Bois ignored her. He reached into the ECV and pulled out the Purdey. He worked the bolt mechanism on the custom rifle to eject all the rounds in it, and then took the magazine for the SA58 with the nanite-tipped rounds in it. He pushed five of them out of the magazine and loaded them quickly into the Purdey, as Inflictor got further away. He heard Alexia retch. There was a dune buggy and two quad bikes speeding towards the ECV, leaving a cloud of sand behind them. The vehicles were all decorated with severed heads hanging from chains.

'Were we just playing war for the sake of it?' Beth demanded. Du Bois removed the scope from the top of the rifle. Multiple explosions had rendered it so much broken glass. Grace was kneeling down, using the ECV as cover, bringing her carbine up to aim at the incoming vehicles. Du Bois took aim at Inflictor. The rifle was yanked from his grip.

'What the fuck?' he demanded, rounding on Beth.

'He is the last person who might know where King Jeremy and Mr Brown are.'

'He's not a person!' du Bois screamed.

'Oh right, are we the cleansing fire here to punish the infidel, or are we trying to accomplish something with this ... mass murder?'

'It's a battle,' du Bois managed, the anger slowly leaking out of him, his words sounding hollow in his own ears. 'He won't speak to you.'

'What did we do?' he heard his sister howl.

'Shut the fuck up please, Alexia,' Grace said through gritted teeth.

'We've got to try,' Beth said.

Inflictor Doorstep had gone surfing.

36
A Long Time After the Loss

It was the colour that had driven the xeno-archaeologist mad. Doubtless Dr Josef Ertl had felt trapped in the blood-coloured space, but it was red that had pushed him over the edge and nothing else. There had been just too much of it. It had been inescapable. The ship that the doctor and his crew had used had been quite primitive. They hadn't been able to tint the fixed transparent parts of the hull. Scab smiled as he thought about this. Red would have been all they could see. They would have bathed in it. They would have felt it outside the ship, pressing against the hull. He could understand that. Red Space had a palpable presence. Many people felt it. He felt it. Ertl's cannibalism of his fellow crewmembers made sense. The cannibalism of the ship, programming small parts of the smart matter hull to turn into beetles he could hunt and eat, less so. The doctor's mind had turned in on itself, cycled through fantasy to cope. Scab felt Ertl had taken the coward's way out. He'd tried to hide from Red Space rather than embrace it. Known Space was the skin, Red Space was the blood underneath.

Dr Ertl had found the artefact many years after he had become lost. He had made marionettes of his fellow crewmembers' bones; both the ship and the doctor were little more than husks by this point. That was why, other than a few cursory expeditions, nobody had ever truly believed his story. Except the entity that Ertl had allegedly spoken to claimed to have been from the 'Ubh Blaosc'. That was what had caught Scab's intelligent search program's attention. It was slim. Nobody else had ever been able to substantiate Dr Ertl's claims, though another ship, some five hundred years later, had claimed to have seen four black suns arranged in some kind of regular pattern within Red Space. It was the only corroborating information.

It was thin. Really thin. Ertl's reverse-calculated coordinates had been vague, even by Red Space standards, and had borne no fruit for the few speculative expeditions that had taken Ertl semi-seriously in the past. This had caused yet another argument among the crew of the *Basilisk II*, but their choices were to become lost in Red Space, or be hunted down and killed, at best, by the Consortium.

Being lost in Red Space wouldn't be that bad, though he would probably have to kill some of the others. He wasn't sure that he would kill the Monk. He feared what she had said about him being a vulnerable child. He was self-aware. He had few delusions about who and what he was, but if he feared what she said then there was probably more truth in her words than he was prepared to admit. He couldn't kill her until he had investigated what had been said, and either discounted it or come to terms with it. Anything else would be petty.

He wasn't sure what to make of Ludwig. The Elite had remained silent and still since he had come on board the *Basilisk II*. The others feared the Monarchist Elite, which made sense. Scab was mostly angry that it was yet another thing that he couldn't control. That said, it wasn't doing anything, other than slightly affecting very local gravity.

Vic had to go.

He wasn't sure what to do with Talia. There was no denying that she was very annoying, but she looked so much like his ghost. He wondered what would happen if he reduced Talia to a more primal state, perhaps if he peeled her? Though he suspected it would lead to shrillness. People seemed to lack self-awareness in the face of a straight-edge razor. It was depressing. If only he could take her physical form and have her possessed by the entity that haunted the bridge drive. It was probably this fantasy that had kept Talia alive for so long.

He was watching her now, his senses neunonically 'faced with the ship, spread through the molecularly-bonded dense smart matter surrounding the glowing blue drive. She lived as a flickering image, so much less real than a hologram, little more than a discharge of energy, but with definite shape and form. She had a simpler, more childlike nature than Talia, Scab could tell. There was something pure about her, not the façade of purity like the Innocent. This was real. *Or a story you have told to comfort yourself because all the compromise has weakened you.*

The ghost's image started to distort, as if something had snagged her and pulled, a silent scream. He felt it like a cold knife made of panic slipped between his ribs. *Ludwig,* was his first thought, but 'faced information from the ship's sensors reached him faster than the thought blaming their Elite stowaway. Significant gravitic forces acting on the *Basilisk II.* Far more gravity than was usual anywhere in Red Space. He had the ship's smart matter squeeze him through it like live food travelling down a gullet. With a thought he disconnected his life support connections to the ship as it extruded him into the yacht's lounge/command and control. The other three were already there, staring through the magnified, transparent smart matter hull at visual information that was probably minutes old now. Ludwig was still where he had last seen him. Something about the alien automaton made Scab think of a miniature singularity, and not just because the machine's Elite-tech was powered by a network of entangled micro black holes.

'I think we've found your black suns,' Vic said. The 'sect still sounded scared, presumably despite drugs and neunonic control of his physiology. Scab realised that he must have been slipping in recent decades. He should have known, perhaps after New Coventry, that his 'sect partner had become too human to be of use to him. He should have started looking for a new partner then. Something tugged just at the back of his mind, some doubt, watered and fed by the Monk. Perhaps it was sentimentality. Perhaps he did need Vic in some unknown way. It was another thought he didn't want to have right now.

Instead he focused on what was in front of him. Ten black suns arranged in a circle. They were Red Space echoes. They were static, according to the ship's sensors, and obviously arranged by some kind of intelligence. He wondered if this was played out in Real Space somewhere unknown, or hidden from them by the Church. The suns burned with their own fire. His eyes were drawn to the centre of them as he watched. Like Red Space itself, he had convinced himself that he could feel them as some kind of palpable presence.

Sometimes clouds of gas obscured the suns, but for the most part the area encircled by the black suns was clear and open, untouched by the billowing clouds.

'It's a trap,' the Monk said.

'Just once I'd like to go somewhere and not hear that,' Talia said.

Scab marveled at the power involved in keeping the ten suns in place, at their seemingly qliphothic nature; they were the opposite of life-giving stars, they were anti-life. There was a beauty to it.

'Not for us,' the Monk said.

'Makes a change,' Talia muttered.

The smart matter hull magnified the object in the centre of the suns. It was about the size of a capital ship, but did not conform to the design of any of the uplift ships he was aware of. It didn't belong to any of the three factions, and from what little he could remember of the serpents – most of his memory from his Elite days had been classified, and virally removed – it didn't resemble what he had seen of their S-tech either. It was tube-like in shape, one end rounded, the other blunt, and its hull was formed of interwoven strands of some kind of metal. It looked like rope of the kind he had seen in some of Vic's colonial immersions.

'I think it's L-tech,' the Monk said.

'You think?' Vic asked. 'Weren't you supposed to have been experts on this kind of thing?'

'Yes, but we've never found a ship before. We didn't think they had any. We thought they travelled in different ways,' the Monk explained.

'Like what?' Talia asked, frowning.

The Monk shrugged. 'We didn't know, perhaps point-to-point wormholes.'

'So if it's not transport?' Vic said. 'A weapon?'

'Maybe, maybe defence like this guy,' the Monk said, and pointed at Ludwig with her thumb. Vic almost flinched.

Scab didn't see what the fuss was about. He had killed Vic more often than Ludwig had.

'Or exploration, like a probe,' the Monk suggested.

'Big probe,' Vic mused.

'Or a lifeboat,' Talia suggested. 'Why isn't it being torn apart by the forces involved?' Even Scab turned to stare at the girl. 'Yes, I am from before the Loss, but no, I am not a complete moron, and yes, I can understand telemetry.'

'The material it's made from is really dense,' the Monk said. 'It has its own gravity well.' Her sister nodded.

'It wanted us to find it,' Scab found himself saying. 'Or something did. This was too easy.'

'What or who?' Talia asked. She looked less than pleased when

449

Scab glanced towards the part of the ship where the bridge drive was encased by smart and dumb matter. The Monk, however, kept looking at Ludwig.

'We have to go there,' Scab said. 'Talia flies.'

'Go to what? It's a solid mass.'

'Ertl spoke with something,' Scab said.

'Via the ship's comms, and that's assuming it wasn't a hallucination.'

'You're the one looking for this Ubh Blaosc,' Scab said, starting to get exasperated.

'Agreed, but let's try communicating with it first, because at the moment there's nothing there, and assuming that we could survive the trip, and going over the *Basilisk*'s specs I'm not sure of that, it's a one-way trip. We don't have anything like the energy to break free of the Black Suns once we get there.'

'We need to go there.' Scab realised he was suddenly very sure of this. He just wasn't sure why.

'Well, I'm glad we've discussed this in a reasonable manner,' the Monk said.

'Beth, this is Scab, Scab, this is Beth,' Vic said. Scab felt a vein on his neck flutter as he tried to control his anger.

'Presumably now we need some threats, call some bluffs, and all the other tiresome bullshit that passes for decision-making on this ship?' the Monk asked. 'You want what we want. Just let us explore some other avenues first before we reach for weapons, yes?'

The smart matter on the walls suddenly extruded raised symbols, the same ones repeated over and over. Scab's neunonics told him that this was writing, an archaic and very slow form of communication. It was a pre-Loss human dialect. His neunonics translated the 'words' for him: 'Please take me there. It is safe.' All four of them turned to look at Ludwig.

'See,' Scab said, though he was less than pleased about the liberties the machine Elite had taken with the *Basilisk II*.

'It's hardly fucking validation, is it?' the Monk shouted at him.

They all knew that Elite-tech provided a near instinctual understanding of its environment. The ghost of Scab's memory of this feeling was maddening. Talia was doing the flying. All of them, including Ludwig, who had submitted to it silently, were encased in smart matter. The *Basilisk II* had reconfigured itself

450

into a compact arrowhead and got rid of all its cavities. With the exception of their extensively cushioned bodies, the yacht was now one solid mass. Even so, receiving the stress telemetry from the ship was beginning to make him wonder if he had made a mistake. He was so heavily 'faced with the yacht that he actually felt the forces working on the craft, distending its hull. He assumed that the feedback that Talia was receiving would be quite painful.

In the normal human visual spectrum it looked like they were plummeting towards the Lloigor craft as if they had fallen from a great height. It was only when his neunonics superimposed the interplay of the waves of force against the hull that he came close to understanding what was happening. The ship felt like it was being squeezed. It was taking the path of least resistance against the gravity. Talia was only hardening the hull and using the engines when they were necessary to stop the ship being torn apart.

Then the woven metal of the truly alien ship was suddenly much bigger in his vision. He felt a thrill of the unknown, not unlike the way he had felt when he seen the Seeder Ship that Talia had been linked to, and killed it. The metal of the ship started to uncoil. It grew, changing shape, blossoming like a vast metal flower. According to their sensors and Basil's AI-modelled predictions, the ship was becoming less dense as it grew open spaces inside it. Outside of the sheer power of an Elite, Scab was struggling to think of a more awesome display of technology. Basil was feeding information on the stresses the hull of the other ship would be subject to from the ten black suns. The ship was easily the size of some planets now. It was a vast, metallic craft that had clearly been designed as much for aesthetics as anything else. It looked like something from an older, grander time. A craft fit for the titanic servants of heretical gods, or godlike aliens anyway.

And suddenly it filled their view completely and the gravity had gone. They were moving at great speed towards its hull. Even Scab's sphincter clenched for a moment. He was aware of the panicked 'face exchange of communications. The *Basilisk II* was burning hard to try and bleed off its speed before it hit the edge of the ship. It took Scab a moment to work out what had just happened. Then it took him a moment or two to come to terms with the information. It seemed that the Lloigor ship in its current configuration had just grown big enough that it would have been torn apart by gravitic forces, so it had protected itself with a coherent energy field. The amount of energy that would have been involved was incredible. He wondered where it got its power.

Part of the hull opened in front of them like an eye blinking, and then they were inside. Everything was smooth and curved. Inside was a vast open and lonely space that felt like it should be filled with smaller craft. It was like the blank-faced ghost of a thousand cities. Every internal structure looked as if a vast crew had just left, and the ship itself had slowly erased the material signs of their presence, but left hints.

The *Basilisk II* was reconfiguring itself. Rooms and the lounge/command and control were reassembled. All of them were extruded out of the smart matter. A badly bruised Talia disconnected herself from the ship, and her sister took over, flying the yacht neunonically. Ludwig was still where he had been since he came aboard. All were silent, all were staring through the transparent hull. Talia wasn't even complaining.

Scab might not have completely understood the emotion, but he felt the atmosphere. There was an overwhelming feeling of sadness about the place.

'Find a place to land,' he said.

'Why?' Vic demanded. Scab was tiring of the 'sect only ever being able to see things in terms of his own fear. He turned to look at his erstwhile partner.

'Because we're in an alien spaceship,' he suggested. He could tell that the 'sect didn't think that was a good enough reason. The Monk seemed to, however.

'Well, we're going to have some time to get used to it,' the Monk muttered.

Scab had the *Basilisk II* check for any kind of communications coming to or from their ship. If anything was happening then the ship's excellent sensor suite couldn't detect it. Suddenly Scab couldn't shake the feeling that Ludwig was watching him. It took him a moment or two to recognise the sensation as discomfort.

He felt the *Basilisk II* touch down on a relatively flat piece of the Lloigor ship's interior, between two massive curving bits of the metallic substance that made up the ship's superstructure. The curving metal structures managed to simultaneously look a bit like pipes, and a bit like hills. They were nestled among windowless towers. The atmosphere outside seemed to be breathable, and gravity was pointing the right way. Scab made his way towards the cargo bay and the fore airlock.

'Wait,' the Monk said. Scab turned to look at her.

'For what?' he asked. 'All the First Contact bureaucracy in the world isn't going to make any difference. We are stranded here.' He continued towards the cargo bay. He could hear the Monk complaining as Talia followed him. Then he was aware of the presence of Ludwig just behind them as well.

Vic was the last to leave the ship. He had his weapons drawn.

'Just for once, maybe?' Talia asked, pointing at the guns. Scab could see the 'sect was conflicted; he wanted to please Talia, but he wanted to live in fear as well.

'That's the sort of nice idea that gets you into trouble,' Vic muttered, but holstered his pistols.

'I don't think it would make much difference,' the Monk said, looking around. The whole ship was illuminated by a not unpleasant blueish-white twilight, though it further added to the somewhat melancholy nature of the place. It stretched out as far as Scab's augmented eyes could see in all directions. It was like some vast subterranean world. The only thing that bothered him was that it reminded him a little of the Cathedral.

'Well, if we can find a source of food and water, or even just matter, living here won't be so bad,' Vic said. 'At least we'll get some peace and quiet.' Both the human women were staring at him. 'What?'

'Why would you tempt fate like that?' Talia demanded.

Scab was wondering why there had to be talking. It was odd but he didn't want a cigarette.

'So it's very nice and all, but now what?' Despite Talia's words Scab could hear awe in her voice as she looked around.

There was nothing one moment, and then suddenly it was in the air above them. It was a floating, three-faced head; then a scruffy, long-haired human in a trench coat with awful teeth; a multi-armed, part-insect part-human-female black-skinned death goddess; a wedge-headed Seeder servitor on a cross; a hooded old man with a beard and only one eye; a young man with a crown of thorns crucified on a tesseract; an androgynous-looking human with ginger hair and different coloured eyes; a horrific caricature of Scab. The flickering images were vast and ever changing.

Talia had backed away so quickly she had fallen over. Vic had weapons in his hands again. Scab was just watching.

'It's a display of power,' the Monk said, but Scab didn't think so. It was trying to communicate, trying to find a frame of reference. It may have wanted to negotiate from a position of strength, but who didn't?

'Who are you?' Scab asked quietly.

The words hurt and seemed to make everything shake, much like communication with Ludwig. The answer was a mash of many different words. He managed to make some of them out, but most of them were nonsense to him: Durga, the Leveller, hive Kali, Seeders, Odin, Bowie, God and other names.

'I think I'll call you Oz!' Talia shouted into the thunder of words. The words stopped.

– Please focus.

The words hurt again. He, Talia and the Monk were staggered, capillaries in eyes burst, ears bled. This time it was Ludwig who had spoken. Talia closed her eyes and looked like she was concentrating. The images had gone, and an old man with a great beard and a ragged grey robe was standing in front of them. His palms were bleeding from holes in them. His eyes were different colours.

'You are unfocused, chaotic, difficult to understand and always have been,' the old man said.

'So what's your name?' Vic asked.

'Oz,' the figure and Talia said at the same time, the human girl sounding a little exasperated.

'What are you?' Talia asked. 'Are you the ship?'

'I am as you are, a three-dimensional machine designed to serve the creators. Mine are hypothetical five-dimensional beings that probably ascended a long time before the death of their universe, and the birth of yours. My essence, my beginning, is only seven thousand, four hundred, and thirty two iterations from the microscopic vessel that breached the walls with the last of the old universe's energy.'

Scab was pretty sure that the words meant he was from somewhere else, but beyond that he didn't really care.

'We're not machines,' Talia said. 'We're biological, natural.'

'There's nothing natural about biological life,' Oz said. He seemed to be studying them with a kind of detached curiosity. 'You had a creator. You were programmed to evolve, just like machines. Biological life is not indigenous to this universe. It spread. Like a fungal infection.'

'But the Seeders must have evolved,' the Monk said. 'Or did they come from somewhere else?' Oz turned to look at her, a blank expression on his face. 'You don't know, do you?'

'I had nothing to add,' Oz said, nodding towards Ludwig. 'I am trying to fix your raven's mind, but he has been badly hurt, and changed, and much is missing.' They all turned to look at the machine Elite.

'He's not really ours,' Talia said.

'Yes,' Oz said.

Scab was reasonably sure that Oz wasn't purposely trying to be difficult. It was just a communications problem. It didn't stop it from being annoying.

'No, he's really not,' Talia persevered.

'The ravens are like myself. They are grown in times of need to protect the adopted great-grandchildren. You remind us of our masters a long time before they ascended. Well, at least until you lost your way.'

'Protect us from what?'

'Níðhöggr, your insane progenitors.'

'There is a Destruction, something that consumes everything it touches,' the Monk said. 'Do you know of it?'

Oz concentrated. 'The Screaming?'

'Would you protect us from that?' the Monk asked. Scab let out a dry chuckle.

'Nothing can protect you from that.'

'Do you know what it is?' the Monk asked.

'I know it belongs in your universe.'

'So you'll help us?' Talia asked.

'I am trapped.'

'You can't get free of this place?' Talia asked.

'I will wait until one or more of the black suns die,' Oz said. 'I have changed the strange programming in the raven. Those that changed him no longer control it. It will protect you, though it wants to go home. As do we all. Once I carried many tens of thousands of ravens.' It was the first time Oz had shown anything approaching human emotion, just a slight wistfulness in his voice.

'What happened?' the Monk asked.

He shook its head. 'I was damaged and I did not know this red place.'

'Is that how the black suns trapped you?' Talia asked.

'They hold me here, or perhaps they dance around me like demons to the sound of some mad piper?'

Scab narrowed his eyes. He was aware of the Monk tensing. That hadn't sounded right. It had been a departure from its previous very literal speech patterns. Oz turned around and there was another younger, slyer face growing out of the back of his head. Vic took a step back. There was something serpentine about its features.

'We should get back on the ship.' Scab heard the words over a 'face link that he hadn't given permission for and he didn't recognise the voice. He assumed it was the new Ludwig. The Elite, or raven, or whatever he was, had just gone through his 'face security like it hadn't existed. It was just one more reminder for Scab that he needed power, and then he needed to make examples.

'How will that help?' Vic asked over the 'face link. 'He is the ship and we are all trapped.'

'He will make a path for us while he can still fight the Yig virus,' Ludwig said.

The metallic material of the ship had started to take on a faint, but noticeable, scaled appearance.

Talia was backing towards the ship. The Monk was doing the same, though she moved between this new serpentine Oz and her sister in a way that suggested to Scab she had no idea of the gravity of the situation. That made him smile. There was, however, something that Oz had said earlier in the conversation that had been nagging him.

'What life is natural?' Scab asked. Oz turned to look at him. His eyes were reptilian slits now, but they were still different colours.

'You think us monsters.'

'Scab, what are you doing?' Vic 'faced.

Questioning, Scab thought but didn't say.

'Don't presume to know my mind,' Scab said, and then pointed at serpentine Oz. 'I've seen your kind before, serpents I mean, though I've seen a ship's AI before as well. You're just another eating, shitting, murdering race of uplifts who presumably think you're clever because you managed to reverse engineer obviously user-friendly, advanced technology.'

'We know the truth,' serpentine Oz said.

Scab's sigh was audible. 'There is no truth,' Scab said. 'Just the lies people tell themselves to get through the day.'

'Scab!' Talia hissed.

Parts of the massive Lloigor ship had started to move, he could feel it under his feet. The movement reminded him of a serpent's constricting coils.

'And where are we going to run?' Scab demanded.

'There is no need to run,' serpentine Oz said. 'I am a generous god. I have shown your ship the way, I will release you from my prison.'

Scab didn't like this. He didn't like it at all. It was too easy, and easy things never worked out. He almost registered the in-trusion warnings from his neunonics before his defences were overwhelmed.

Scab was surrounded by cold, hard, black vacuum. He was among the stars. Moving at speed through a nebula, he was aware of faint signals, communications between distant particles, a network, a hive mind. The movement of what was unknown space sped up, and he found himself somewhere else. He screamed despite himself as he was plunged into the heart of a star where sentient fire played. Then he was far beneath the ice of a moon, bacteria-like silicon colonies leaching sustenance from faint heat sources. A crystalline virus that could sing, infecting rock, thought forms that created bodies of liquid hydrocarbons, clustered gas colony minds, unnoticed because unlooked for. If they ever had been able to, then the uplifted races could no longer see beyond their own frame of reference.

It was beautiful. It was the universe that Scab had always wanted to see. It was pure.

'You are the lie,' Oz said. 'The tyranny of biology.'

Scab was sitting in his favourite chair in the lounge/command and control on the *Basilisk II*. The others were there as well, including Ludwig. His neunonics held no trace of his time in the very real-feeling immersion that the serpentine Oz had presum-ably uploaded into him. The memory was all in his meat.

The yacht was flying through the narrowing but still-cavernous structure of the Lloigor ship. Olfactory and visual analysis of the other crewmembers, excepting Ludwig, suggested tension rather than panic. Scab lit up a cigarette, his vision polarising to cope with what looked like a dull red sunset round the next bend in the craft's vast superstructure. Then, as they rounded the bend, at the end of the huge – but constricting – cavern, he could see what looked like a partial view of a dull red star. The star had black rings of some kind of tech running around it, displays of energy crackling from it. He assumed this was the craft's power plant, a fading artificial sun.

Scab 'faced with the *Basilisk II*. He was less than pleased that Ludwig was flying. The machine was looking for a way out of the huge Lloigor craft, and it was being guided through the shrinking tunnels by some invasive force in the yacht's systems. The virus looked like a carpet of snakes. It was all but ignoring the yacht's defences, suborning system after system. There was a sinuous beauty to it, Scab thought. He took a sample, imprisoned one of the constituent snake-like pieces of code in the most secure Pythian software he had, and stored it in his own neuronic memory. He wasn't quite sure why he did it. It was a huge risk and if/when it got free it could turn him into that which he most feared, a slave, but the virus was subtle, all-pervasive, sinuous, beautiful and powerful.

On a whim he looked for the Monk's immersion program, the one she seemed to think was so precious. It had not fallen to the writhing carpet of snakes, yet. He transferred that as well. The virtual environment took up a lot of his neuronic memory. Then Ludwig broke his 'face link with the ship. Scab sat in his chair, exhaling smoke. He could hear warning shouts from the Monk, cries of borderline panic from Talia and Vic. Scab ran a diagnostic to see if he had been infected by it. He hadn't, as far as he could tell. Then he turned to look at where he knew the bridge drive was. Where his ghost was.

The Lloigor ship shrank down to a more manageable size and extruded a tunnel of coherent energy wide enough for Ludwig, still battling the Yig virus in the ship's – and now presumably his own – systems, to fly down, taking them far past the gravity of the black suns. It had been the virus that provided them with the coordinates. It was the virus that would show them the way to the Ubh Blaosc. A tear ran down the side of Scab's face. The serpents had taken his love's purity.

37
Ubh Blaosc

Serpentine minds encased in armoured forms, flesh and vessel one and the same, hung dormant in the red clouds of their adopted home, far from the black screaming and the cold. Lightning crackled across thick, pitted, built-up, protective dead skin as muscles unused for millennia flexed. Awareness stretched out across huge distances in the red realm. Níðhöggr, the nagaraja-class behemoth, the idiot god, awakened along with billions of his children. Fires burned in their tails as the largest of the dragons moved. They had heard the mindsong. It was time to enter the pain realm and feed again.

Britha frowned as she looked between Teardrop, his family, and their pale servant. Both she and Tangwen had been introduced to Raven's Laughter, Teardrop's wife, a short woman with laughter lines around dark eyes, her long, grey-streaked hair in a braid running down her back. She did not seem pleased to see either of the 'mortal' women. The children – Rain, the eldest, a tall, rangy girl who took after her father; River, the second oldest, who had all the poise and beauty of a noblewoman; and the boy and girl twins, Bear and Sky – had been banished, despite protests, from the main chamber of Teardrop and Raven's Laughter's home. Their home bothered Britha. It was the size of a longhall, which made sense if Teardrop was a *mormaer* among his people, but then his people should share the space. For just the one family it was too much in terms of resources. The chamber looked comfortable enough, smooth, curved, shining wood, furs and skins to rest on; it let in a great deal of light from the Forge shining high above the riverlands. It reminded her a little of a cave, but a very pleasant one.

'He is not a Goidel,' Britha said of the servant. He had an odd name: Oliver. He was dressed a little like Teardrop had been the first time she had met him, when his head had been swollen with the crystal things that had finally consumed him. Except all of Oliver's clothes were black and he wore a tall hat with a seemingly superfluous buckle on it. 'And he is not one of your people.' Teardrop and his wife exchanged a look. Britha thought they looked a little like children caught doing something naughty.

'I am from a place called Roanoke,' Oliver said. His accent was unlike anything she had ever heard before, yet he spoke the Goidel tongue. 'We were colonists from another land.'

Tangwen opened her mouth to ask a question.

'The Croatan, my people, took Oliver's people as slaves,' Teardrop said. 'It took us a long time to learn that this was not the right thing to do.'

Britha frowned. There was nothing wrong with taking slaves if their own tribes were not strong enough to protect them. They were well treated and protected by the laws, and most were released after an allotted time, but she had learned a long time ago it was not a good thing to judge another people, regardless of how strange their ways were.

'And yet you still serve?' Tangwen asked.

'I choose to. We are as free as anyone else, though few of us are warriors and we choose not to engage in the blasphemy of the *drui*, and the medicine societies,' said Oliver.

'They have their own gods,' Teardrop said.

'God,' Oliver corrected.

'Despite the evidence,' Raven's Laughter said, rolling her eyes. 'So. You killed my friend?' she asked Britha.

'Yes. Is there strife between us?' Britha asked bluntly. Tangwen tensed slightly, hands close to her weapons. They were standing just in front of the entrance to Teardrop's home, silhouetted in the Forge's red twilight. They had not been invited in or offered food and drink. So far, Britha was less than impressed with Raven's Laughter's hospitality.

'Picking fights when you're with child?' Raven's Laughter asked.

'She's not picking the fight,' Tangwen said.

'I'll not stay where I'm not welcome,' Britha said.

'Laughs,' Teardrop said quietly, not looking at his wife. 'They were trying to stop the Naga's mindsong.' Raven's Laughter seemed to sag.

'With your permission,' Oliver said. Raven's Laughter nodded.

'I will stop the children listening, and then prepare food. The cured venison, and flat bread with sweet potatoes I think?' Raven's Laughter just nodded again. Oliver turned, and Britha took a step back as part of the wall swung open, and he made to move through it.

'Oliver,' Teardrop said quietly. The servant stopped and turned his head slightly.

'Arm the children?' Oliver asked. Teardrop nodded. The servant looked to Raven's Laughter. She hesitated, and then nodded as well. The wall swung shut behind the servant and they heard raised voices and children complaining.

'I am sorry,' Raven's Laughter said. Suddenly Britha could see how close to breaking down the woman was. 'Each time the Naga come they are stronger. We wipe out every last one of the brood, but the next one we meet has learned from the previous one through the mindsong. Lug moves us after each attack so they cannot find us so easily, but it weakens the Forge.' She turned to her husband. 'We did this.' Her hand flew to her mouth and a tear ran from her eye. 'Excuse me.' She turned and fled the chamber through one of the curving passages that led deeper into their home. Teardrop looked stricken. There was something about the way she had said it that had made it sound like an accusation.

'You must forgive her,' Teardrop said. 'It is unlikely we can fight them off this time.'

'We will stand with you,' Tangwen said, though Britha could hear just how tired the younger woman was.

Teardrop smiled. 'Thank you.' He sighed. 'Welcome to my home. Please sit down. We will bring you food and drink. You should rest and then we can talk.'

Britha sat down on a pile of furs. It was only then, as the tension bled out of her, that she started to realise how tired she was. Her muscles did not ache as they had when she used to fight in battles before Cliodna's gift, however, before eating the flesh of the Lochlannach, before drinking from the chalice. She reached up to touch her throat.

Tangwen had collapsed onto the furs of a creature that Britha did not recognise when a more composed Raven's Laughter bustled back into the chamber, and handed Britha a leather cup full of milk.

'I do not wish to sound ungrateful, but you don't have anything stronger? Heather ale, perhaps, or *uisge beatha*?' Britha asked. Raven's Laughter frowned as she handed a cup to Tangwen.

'That's not good for your child,' Raven's Laughter admonished. Britha frowned. This was clearly nonsense. Pecht children had been born regardless of how much their mothers had drunk for years, but she decided to respect their odd beliefs. Raven's Laughter sat down. Teardrop did the same, putting his arm around his wife.

'You have come for your child?' she asked. Britha nodded. 'Grainne has her?'

'Yes; she and Sainrith stole my daughter from my womb.'

'They would have stored her in the earth,' Raven's Laughter mused.

Britha struggled to retain her composure. Her stomach had lurched as she had heard the words.

'We cannot steal from the *drui*,' Teardrop told his wife. Britha knew that Teardrop was not a timid man, but she was sure that she heard a little fear in his voice.

'We wouldn't be stealing anything,' Raven's Laughter said, irritably. 'Will Grainne listen to reason?'

'She blames me for the death of Sainrith,' Britha said. Raven's Laughter looked at her.

'Fachtna must have loved you a great deal. You paid him well for it.'

Again Britha had to fight to maintain her composure. She opened her mouth to say something, and then closed it again. She deserved Raven's Laughter's barbs, and probably worse.

'We will speak to Grainne,' Teardrop said. 'Perhaps she will see it differently now ...'

'Now that it doesn't matter any more?' Raven's Laughter demanded. 'Tell me, when you have what you want, what then? Would you go home?' Britha nodded. 'You understand that every time we open one of the trods we weaken the Forge that sustains us all?'

'How would she know that?' Teardrop asked.

Britha felt a flash of anger at being patronised. She knew that everything had a cost. She had been taught that in the groves. The question was whether or not the benefits outweighed the price.

'You are under no obligation to help us,' Tangwen said. Britha knew that it was fatigue making the warrior more than a little brittle.

462

Raven's Laughter turned to look at Tangwen. 'We will help because what they have done is wrong, but even if we are successful then I think all that will happen is you will carry both your children until the Naga turn up and consume us all.' She turned to look at her husband. 'But it will keep us busy instead of just sitting here waiting for the inevitable. Which is what I think my husband intended, but if this means I am not with my children at the last then the Talking God himself will not be able to protect him from my wrath.'

At first they were tiny metal buds against the vast outer skin of the Ubh Blaosc. Huge vessels like straight coils of rope as they started to grow. The children of Lug awoke to life deep within the metal shells of the enormous craft. In each of the mighty vessels tens of thousands of ravens, weapons with minds of their own, the grandchildren of Lug, were born. Their minds connected to their brothers, sisters and their parent craft. They were eager for their short lives and destructive ends. They were conceived in metal wombs hating their serpent enemy.

Bloody gashes appeared in the night that surrounded the Ubh Blaosc, obscuring the pinpricks of light from distant stars. The maws of the first and mightiest of the dragons appeared, fire between their teeth.

Teardrop concentrated for a moment. 'It's started,' he said. His face was expressionless, but Britha could see the helplessness in his eyes. She had no idea how it had come to this. It had not been long ago that she had been looking after her tribe's needs. Now she was to be present at the end of the Otherworld. Raven's Laughter looked away. The top part of the back of the chariot they were travelling in was clear like water, but solid, though not cold like ice. She could see out into the blue sky they were soaring through. Tangwen had her eyes closed tight. Britha was somehow more able to cope with the flying chariot, perhaps because during the last trip she had taken in one of these craft she had been bleeding to death after the trees had come to life and tried to kill her. This trip was far more pleasant in comparison. She was less than pleased that there didn't seem to be a charioteer at the other end of the craft's long neck, however.

They were circling down towards a familiar-looking wooded, mountainous land. She was tensing, and even though they were travelling towards a grove to see a *dryw*, she wished she had a spear and not just the chalice-re-forged dirk at her waist. Somehow, here, she felt foolish wearing her black robes.

They were sinking down past the tops of oak trees. Britha couldn't shake the feeling that they had shifted aside slightly for the chariot. The back of the vehicle split open. It hadn't landed, but it remained steady just above the earth.

Grainne was waiting for them as the *Láir Bhán* in her horse skull. She was standing on a rock outcrop between the trees, the light of the Forge directly behind her. Everything was set up to awe them. Britha had used similar ploys herself.

'Oh, take the skull off, you silly woman!' Raven's Laughter snapped, shielding her eyes with her hand. The attempt to awe them didn't seem to have worked on the Croatan woman. Britha saw Teardrop suppress a smile even as his face became stern.

'Laughs!' he admonished before turning to Grainne. 'I apologise for my wife's behaviour.'

'I am more than capable of apologising for myself when it's warranted,' Raven's Laughter snapped. Britha did not think that the Croatan women liked her very much. She, on the other hand, was growing very fond of Teardrop's wife.

'I shall overlook this rudeness,' Grainne said. 'I can only assume that you have come to deliver the mortal for punishment.'

'She has broken no law,' Teardrop said. 'You know this.'

Grainne turned to walk away.

'You have, though,' Raven's Laughter said. Grainne stopped.

'Careful, Croatan. You may not come under my responsibility but we work closely with your medicine societies.'

'You have stolen her child, and have not even seen fit to replace it with a changeling,' Tangwen said uneasily. The horse's skull moved as though it was sniffing the air.

'What's this? Her kin comes calling, and yet a serpent child walks free?' the *drui* asked. Raven's Laughter and Teardrop turned to look at the young warrior.

'My father hid from the evil of his people, he was not as they are.'

'But you were there when the Naga were called ...' Grainne left the accusation unsaid.

'And now you speak with a forked tongue,' Raven's Laughter pointed out.

'There's nothing wrong with a forked tongue,' Tangwen muttered.

'You had no right to take my child,' Britha said. 'No law gives you the right. I made no agreement, no bargain.' She pointed at the other *drui*. 'I say that I have the right to stand in judgement of you.'

'You have no authority in our circle. You are little more than a slatternly landswoman, complicit in the murder of your betters, as far as I am concerned. Your presence insults me and I tire of it. For all of your mortal bleating you seem to forget the trouble that you have brought us. There are more important things.'

Suddenly Britha felt very tired. 'Then what difference does it make?' she demanded. 'It is easily within your power to grant me what I ask, isn't it?'

'Have you forgotten that we were as they are?' Teardrop demanded.

'No more! Now leave this place!'

'Stop hiding!' Raven's Laughter screamed at the woman. 'We slatternly landsfolk have our ways as well. I know that Sainrith was your lover for many years.'

'We were *drui*, at festivals and rituals ...' Grainne started, the authority in her voice faltering slightly. This was starting to make more sense to Britha. Sex was fine between *dryw*, or with warriors, *mormaers*, and even landsfolk and foreigners, for ritual reasons, or even just pleasure, but bonds could not be allowed to form, as how then could they deal fairly and impartially with all? Grainne had been guilty of a crime herself, it would seem.

'Take off the skull,' Raven's Laughter shouted, 'or I will come up there and slap it off you!'

'How dare you ... !'

'It doesn't matter any more!' Raven's Laughter was almost bent double screaming at Grainne, drool dripping from her mouth. 'Complain all you want to the medicine societies, we will all be in the bellies of the serpents before they can punish me. You, her, my husband, me, my children! All of us!'

Britha looked nervously around as the trees seemed to shift slightly. Tangwen screamed. Britha's head shot round. It took a lot to make Tangwen scream. Bristly spines were growing through Raven's Laughter's skin, piercing the simple dress of deerskin she wore.

'You'll be dead before the first branch touches us,' Raven's

Laughter said. Britha actually took a few steps back. The horse's skull fell to the ground. Grainne lifted an arm and pointed a finger at Raven's Laughter. It was a simple movement, the curse behind it obvious.

'Please, both of you,' Teardrop said, glancing at his wife, clearly worried. 'We should not be fighting among each other, not now.'

'Where is the child?' Tangwen asked, continually glancing at Raven's Laughter's now animalistic features. Then she cried out as the branches of the oaks moved sinuously closer to her. It was more than enough for Tangwen. She had her hatchet and dirk in hand now.

'It's not that simple,' Britha muttered. 'She is held by magics and was unborn when she was taken.'

'Oh,' Tangwen said, trying to move away from Raven's Laughter and the moving branches without showing too much fear.

'We protect our people. The child was taken because she has the key to the red realms, where the Naga hide from us, inside her. It was a decision made by the Circle for the good of all in the Ubh Blaosc,' Grainne said. 'You do not defy only me in this, you defy all.'

'It can't make any difference now,' Teardrop said. 'It's too late.'

Grainne's smile was full of malice. 'Then speak to the Circle. They may be busy with the attack. It might have to wait until afterwards.'

Britha found herself looking around. There was certainly no evidence of an attack. She turned back to find Grainne shaking her head with a look of contempt.

'Why?' Teardrop asked. Britha knew why. She could see it written all over the other *dryw*'s face. She knew that she would never see her child while this woman had anything to do with it.

'As I burn it will give me great pleasure to know that she too burns, as does her child, forever apart!'

Raven's Laughter turned and stalked back to the chariot. Britha knew that she should be as angry as the small Croatan woman was, but she couldn't muster it. She knew she should scream and rant at the other *dryw*, threaten her, strike or even kill her. A mother's child had to outweigh corrupt authority like this, surely? Instead she just felt tired and sad. Sometimes it felt, even when the land burned, that men and women were only capable of making decisions through spite.

'I'm sorry,' Teardrop said. He sounded as sad as she felt. He turned and followed his seething, spiny wife. Britha felt a hand on her shoulder. She turned around to see Tangwen. The younger woman was obviously terrified of everything she saw in this strange place, but she was here for Britha. The Pecht *dryw* didn't think she had ever felt more grateful. Britha turned back to look up at Grainne. The horse's skull may have been gone but now the old *dryw* wore a mask of malice.

'I'm sorry for your pain,' Britha said. Then she turned with Tangwen and walked away.

The night surrounding the Ubh Blaosc burned, as did parts of the shell itself, as the largest of the serpent dragons breathed on it. Thorn-like spores rained down on the shell, bursting into seeds of fire, seeds that warped the shell, ate into it, or transformed it, infecting it with hideous new life that then started to feed.

The huge vessels, piloted by the minds of Lug's children, sped towards the giant dragon. They lit up the night with bright lances fuelled by the suns that beat at the vessels' hearts. The lances blackened the armoured flesh of the dragons, and ruptured impossibly ancient flesh.

The behemoths turned on Lug's children, wreathing them in fire like gods of the sun, night becoming day. They made the black bleed, tricking Lug's children into their red realm. Into traps laid when all was yet still young and easier to manipulate. They sent the ghosts of serpents to crawl through their enemies' minds.

The barrel-like ravens sought out the smaller dragons, their own swords of light reaching for the swarming flesh of the Naga creatures like grasping fingers. Or they worked together against the larger dragons, dying in their fiery breath, or like exploding stars if they reached the flesh of their ancient enemies.

'I am not sure I was needed here,' Tangwen said as they walked towards the back of the chariot. Britha stopped and turned to the hunter. Tangwen's features looked gaunt, hollow. Britha reached up to touch the other woman's face. Tangwen's face softened a little.

'I cannot repay this debt,' Britha said, letting her hand drop. Tangwen shrugged.

'It's better than having a cave land on you,' she said. Britha wasn't entirely sure that the serpent child believed this. They could hear Raven's Laughter as they continued towards the back of the chariot.

'She is a mother!' the Croatan woman shouted as Britha and Tangwen climbed into the comfortable cupola at the rear of the chariot. The back of the vehicle had opened in a way that reminded Britha of a beetle's carapace. 'We have done this! It is our people who have wronged her ...'

'But what were you thinking, threatening a *drui*?' Teardrop asked, more exasperated than angry.

'She would not have given me back my child,' Britha said, climbing up into the back of the chariot. 'But I thank you for trying.'

The rear of the chariot folded shut.

'How can we steal this unborn child?' Tangwen asked. Teardrop was shaking his head. Raven's Laughter's spines were retracting as she climbed into the neck of the chariot and started crawling along it.

'What are you ...?' Teardrop started.

'There is one more that we can ask,' she shouted behind herself.

'Over this? He would not see us now.' But the chariot was already rising into the sky. Teardrop turned to Britha and Tangwen. 'I think you should get some sleep.'

Ibic ÓLug was a progeny grown from the body of the ship that the mind Ebliu MacLug inhabited. Focused gravity propelled the raven through vacuum as he wove through beams of plasma aimed at the larger ships and the burning breach point on the vast shell of the Ubh Blaosc.

The barrel-shaped construct knew his life would be short, but oh so bright, if he could just break through the defences and reach one of the vast biomechanical ships. The rage, the programmed fury, at the serpents' transgression, their attack on his creator's home, their wish to consume everything, drove him on.

He was on the edge of a vast swathe of plasma projected from the hive godship, Níðhöggr itself. Ibic ÓLug felt his own armour start to melt and run. The raven left near-invisible molten drops of himself as a trail behind him, like burning tears, but the frenzied need to hurt the enemies of his people drove him on.

Beams of fusion lanced out at the smaller, faster, biomechanical craft that closed with him, and the thorns that chased him. He banked hard, shooting beneath a large, ponderous dragon, his fusion beams doing little more than scoring a line in the millennia of dead skin built up as armour protecting the behemoth's flesh. He saw Níðhöggr ahead of him in all its multi-spectrum glory, but the godship, now subjectively above him, fired a hail of thorn-like spores that rained down on the barrel-like construct. He burned with an inner light, so many fusion beams shooting out from him he must have looked like a tiny sun for a moment, but one of the thorns made it through and exploded.

Ibic ÓLug screamed, more from his failure than the pain of the burning plasma, as he tumbled away from the battle, away from his home, and into cold space.

Teardrop had given them something to drink. He had told them it would enable them to sleep through the journey. When Britha awoke she could not see through the material of the chariot's cupola. She suspected that was for the best. Tangwen had jerked awake suddenly. She had fallen asleep next to Britha on one of the benches in the back. Britha was aware of the chariot moving. She didn't think it was moving quickly.

'You do not think this is a good idea?' Britha asked Teardrop, who was sitting opposite her. She did not think this was a good idea. It was not the sort of thing that the Pecht did. In fact they avoided it.

'It bothers me that with everything going on he agreed,' Teardrop told her.

The chariot had stopped. Raven's Laughter pulled herself out of the neck and into the cupola as the rear of the vehicle split open. Tangwen was sitting up. She had the look of a wild animal that could bolt at any moment. Laughter and Teardrop stepped down from the chariot. Britha followed, cautiously, Tangwen more so. The air smelled of copper and fire. The floor was a flat plain of copper stretching out into the distance. They were in a massive, odd-shaped chamber that reached up farther than they could see. There were clouds high above them. Behind them they could see a huge opening that looked out on blue sky but was surrounded by a nimbus of fire. In the distance they could make out chariots, and other, larger, craft, surrounded by tiny-looking figures.

'We are inside a god, aren't we?' Tangwen asked, her voice

sounding small. She bent her legs slightly, like someone who wasn't sure of how steady the floor was beneath her.

Everything stopped. Tangwen, Raven's Laughter and Teardrop were perfectly still. Everything was melting, even the air itself. Britha took a step back as the figure appeared. It was difficult to look at, painful, not least because of the bright glare coming from it. Its head shone like the sun, but he appeared to be a beautiful Goidel warrior, equipped for war. He was more attractive than Fachtna, even more so than Bress, but there was something unreal and therefore false about the beauty. The figure seemed to be constantly folding in on itself, and then rebuilding its form.

'You will never see your children.' The voice was like music in her head. The figure's mouth had not moved. The other three were still frozen. They had not reacted to Lug's appearance. Britha felt the lurch inside her at his words, but tried not to show any response. She was also resisting the urge to avert her eyes from the light. 'But they may live if you will it.'

'Why will I not see my children?'

'Because your enemy still lives, and your people, all people, need your service still.'

'You mean serve you? We do not do the bidding of gods. We do not want their attention.'

'There is nothing here to serve. I am no god. I am mostly imagination, an echo of a ghost. I cannot even remember what I once was. I merely have perspective.'

'What would you have of me?' Britha asked, swallowing hard. Her eyes felt wet.

'I would have you kill that which you call the Llwglyd Diddymder, the Hungry Nothingness, the black screaming that eats the sky.'

Britha spat and made the sign against evil. It was not something that she had done much recently, but she remembered the squirming blackness in the sky over the burning wicker man.

'I cannot fight such a thing ...' she started. 'There are others, stronger than I ... the power that you have here in the Otherworld.'

'You will not fight it. You will poison it. You will die. You will be consumed. All will be destroyed. That does not matter. If you could see things as I do you would understand.' In front of him a glittering structure that looked like a very complex spider web made of fragile crystal appeared. Its strands did not seem to exist fully in the world and, like Lug himself, it hurt to look at. Parts of it were obviously missing. 'My Croatan Children call this Grandmother Spider's Web. The Hungry Nothingness lives where the arrow of fire is weak, where all is cold chaos, and its pain is the least. It lashes out from the end of all things, collapsing and consuming the strands of the web. It is not the way of things. It stops those who would, those who can, from becoming the sublime, from becoming as gods. It threatens not just this realm, but all realms. Its insane servants travel through the holes in the web, spinning new strands, each intrinsically more corrupt, more resistant to resistance, worse than the one it branched off from, and more conducive to its inevitable destruction.'

Britha did not understand what Lug was saying. This was clearly the work of the gods. She had no business being involved. She wanted to scream, bolt, finally break down. Instead she tried to hide the trembling from him as she shook her head.

'No,' she finally managed.

'Then your children and mine have no chance anywhere,' Lug said.

'How will my children live if this place falls?' she demanded. 'If I am gone?'

'They can be carried from this place. I will make a sacrifice for them.'

Britha found herself looking at Tangwen, frozen in place.

'Then send someone else,' she said desperately. She knew it was cowardice, but now the tears of red metal ran down the side of her face only to be sucked back into her skin. After all of it, the battles, the betrayals, and the sacrifices, suddenly she knew what it had been for. Why she was still fighting after her people had been killed. Two unborn children. Two people she did not know and might never meet. For whatever reason, to her, they were all that mattered.

'You are a weapon now. One of the Llwglyd Diddymder's children sewed part of their essence into you. You can become one with the city.'

She had heard the word city before, from Germelqart, but it was unfamiliar. Cities sounded like hateful places.

She shook her head. It made no sense. It was too big. Her head felt as though it was about to split.

'No,' she said, shaking her head again. Lug held up a closed fist, and then opened it. The crystalline tendrils reached for her.

The other end of them was in unseen space, difficult, painful to look at. She knew that they did not come from here, not from the Otherworld, or her realm. They were parasites from some other place, Cythrawl perhaps, like Bress. They had granted Teardrop his power when she had first met him in her world. They had consumed him.

'You will do this. We understand you. You want your children to live. This is the only way.'

She did not move away but she tried to keep her mouth shut. Her nostrils flared in panic, her eyes widened, but at last she succumbed to her fear and opened her mouth to scream and the crystal tendrils forced their way into her eyes, up her nose.

'You are a poison. You must consume the Llwglyd Diddymder from within. You must truly learn to hate.' Lug's words were lost among the agony. The crystal tendrils silenced the scream as they surged into her mouth. Then they started to eat.

Tangwen's eyes rolled up into her skull and she collapsed to the warm copper ground. Britha was convulsing nearby, her eyes turning silver. Teardrop looked down at the Pecht *drui*, pity and guilt warring on his face.

'Did you know?' Raven's Laughter asked, his wife's voice filled with disgust. The veins on Britha's head bulged as something pushed its way through her veins, her head already starting to swell.

'We have to take them both to the Cauldron,' Teardrop said.

'Did you know?' Raven's Laughter demanded. Teardrop turned to his wife.

'Do you think I would do this? That I could?' he shouted.

'We could defy him,' Raven's Laughter said, but Teardrop could tell his wife knew that it was already too late. He crouched down and gathered Britha into his arms, carrying her back towards the chariot. He was disgusted with the gods, his people, and himself. Moments later he heard his Raven's Laughter pick up Tangwen and follow.

The seas surrounding the continent boiled first, then they turned to steam. Internal pressure, and water rushing in from further afield, sent plumes of water vapour shooting thousands of miles into the sky. Then the land, the entire land burst into flames. Fountains of blackened slag, ash and lava flew into the atmosphere as though from a continent-sized volcano.

Níðhöggr, the behemoth, the living ship, the Nagas' bio-mechanical hive god's serpentine, maw-like prow emerged first through the breach, surrounded by vast jets of molten matter. Other smaller craft, looking like shoals of fish in the fire, shot past the huge ship, spreading out quickly, sporing.

The eggshell had been cracked.

38
Now

Lodup was shaking, though he didn't feel the cold any more. Germelqart's severed head, on the end of the pole, was linked to the breathing stone by tendrils of flesh: a hardwired connection. The Mwoakilloan salvage diver had watched the tendrils grow through Germelqart's head, pushing themselves beneath the skin, cracking through skull. The severed head was still screaming in glossolalia. It was little more than an interface for them. A mutated larynx had grown from the now organic-looking pole that the head was impaled on. It did not look like a human organ. It was clearly designed to accommodate the twisted vocabulary of an alien language. It worried Lodup that he was starting to understand the words.

It had been through the head that they had risked looking for sane minds in Earth's now insane and extensively redesigned communications network. He wasn't sure if he had made contact with someone or not. He was sure that he couldn't take another attempt.

Command and Control stank. Lodup had no idea how long they had been living there for. They had intermittent power, and the lower deck of the habitat had been partially flooded when the structure had shifted. He knew there had been significant changes outside. He had felt them, just like he felt the still-slowly-wakening minds. Something was protecting him. Some vestige of how they had once been before they had made contact with the thing that lived through the tear in the sky, before Germelqart had unwittingly sacrificed the boy to it. Lidakika, the octopus god who in myth had created Lodup's island home of Mwoakilloa, was the name the protecting entity had taken. Whether it was literal or not he did not know. Lidakika's protection felt like a thin membrane with the immensity of the sleeping minds pressing against it. The city was a palpable presence, glowing with energy, crawling with life, an unseen surrounding pressure.

They hadn't gone back into the water since they had seen the congregation of clones around the waking, living city. Since they had seen the black thing from the cold sump, growing like a tree, the thing that they all somehow knew, from ancient racial memory, hated life.

They had mostly been left alone in C&C. Sometimes Siraja, the dragon-faced AI, would appear and watch them through many eyes. Each time, his appearance was more warped than the last. Yaroslav screamed, drooled, and reacted the only way he could remember, with violence, even though the AI was just an image in the cracked smart matter of the wall, and then ricochets would fill C&C for a while. They had seen some of the wedge-headed creatures, reborn out of the city's stone, but those had left them alone as well. Other times the black-eyed clones, who had once worked on the city, came to stand and watch them from the moon pool, or even out in the corridor. Yaroslav fired on them when they were close enough. They stood there taking round after round until their physiology gave up and they collapsed to the floor.

The worst times were when Sal came on her own to stand in the Moon Pool and look up at C&C's oval window. Even when he hid from the window she knew he was there.

Yaroslav, the once taciturn Russian security chief, was pushing for a suicide pact. It seemed like he had been talking for days now, mostly in Russian. He was very enthusiastic about it, ranting, waving his gun around. Sometimes he curled up in a corner and rocked back and forwards, switching between nonsense words in English, Russian and German. He seemed to be reliving something from his past. Lodup kept hearing the word Leningrad.

It was Siska, however, who he was most frightened of. She was mostly silent now. She stayed in the darkest corner of C&C, moving little, but when she did she moved sinuously. He had only caught a glimpse of her eyes recently. They were reptilian slits. Her skin was starting to scale, and the few words that she had muttered had put emphasis on the sibilants. She made him feel like prey.

This was survival as a habit. Lodup was half convinced that Yaroslav was right, though the solidly built Russian hadn't taken his own life yet. The only thing that stopped Lodup putting a gun in his mouth was the knowledge that the modified seedpods were still there. There was a chance they could leave this place. Lidakika had told him this. He was learning to despise hope.

The sky was the colour of a bruise, and a strange storm was coming in from the Pacific. The sea was unnaturally dark. Beth didn't like having to dip her arms into the water to paddle the surfboard. She had stripped off her jacket and boots and much of her webbing, transferring the pistol holster and the pouches for clips to the belt of her combat trousers. The OHWS was loaded with the magazine of nanite-tipped rounds.

She was wondering how much of what was going on she was able to deal with, because it all felt so unreal, like she was in a film. She might understand that the people she had killed were already dead, little more than vessels for alien madness, but they still felt human when flesh impacted on flesh, when warm blood splashed across her face. The sound of shouted warnings and crying was becoming fainter now. She felt weak, emaciated, her body feeding on itself to heal her various wounds. She knew she should have eaten some of the energy bars before she paddled out.

She was coming to the conclusion that the sea calmed her. This wasn't like Southsea, however. There was the constant feeling of a presence under the water, though she supposed it had been the same in the Solent. Even though she was being glared at by surfers with crude swastikas carved into their flesh, many of them wearing skin masks cut from the faces of their victims, paddling out on the water was still the calmest she had felt since she had arrived in LA.

The surfboard tipped into a shallow trough between waves – it felt like she was sliding downhill – and then she was next to Inflictor Doorstep. He was sitting on his board, bobbing up and down in the swell. He paid her little attention. He looked the same as he had the last time she had seen him up close. Monstrous physiology on the edge of what the human frame could support: tough looking leathery skin, and the inhuman features of a comic book-demon. The only differences were the wetsuit, the dreadlock-like tendrils of flesh hanging off his head, and this time he wasn't pointing a massive pistol at her. She thought about drawing the OHWS to cover him, but he didn't seem very interested in her, and he was unarmed. He was just looking out to the east. The sun was a red ball just above the horizon, its reflection a path of fire across the surface of the dark water.

'What are you waiting for?' It hadn't been the question she had meant to ask.

'A break from the tedium, same as ever.' He still didn't look at her. 'It's the apocalypse, and everyone has been assigned their roles by central casting. It's like we all still think that we're living in a reality TV show.' His chuckle was a dry rasp. 'The real reason for a surveillance society.' This was little more than a whisper. 'Maybe in Norway it's like Ragnarok, or in Africa ... they're doing ... African ... things, but here it's the apocalypse and we all know how to act because we've played the games, seen it on TV, watched it at the movies.'

'You're bored?' Beth asked incredulously. Now his monstrous head turned to look at her.

'Yeah,' he nodded. 'They've made madness boring, how the fuck'd they manage that?'

'You don't feel special any more?' Beth asked. Demonic eyes regarded her. She suspected he was trying to work out if he was being mocked or not. He was. Gunshots rang out over the water from the beach, but neither of them turned around.

'We used to be monsters,' he said quietly.

You used to be bullied kids with ridiculous levels of entitlement, Beth thought. 'Now you're just the same as everyone else. Where's King Jeremy? Where's the nuke?'

Inflictor turned back to look out to sea. 'You know they're burning A-list actors in wicker men up by the Hollywood sign? It's being done by every waitress, office clerk and bathroom attendant who never got a break. In Beverly Hills the plastic surgeons are operating on people's larynxes so they can speak the new language. It's this year's big thing, like breast enlargements, or the latest smartphone. In the valley, porn stars lived next door to soccer moms. Sometimes they were the same person – or was that just a fantasy? Now the whole valley is one big orgy, one big orgasm, one big organism. This is what we want. A Pavlovian response to pornography: violent, sexual, both. Everyone wants to rape someone, just to prove they can. It's the dominant social discourse of the twenty-first century. It's an alien invasion, right? Bullshit. They've been here longer than us. They're that thing, foetus-curled around my brain stem, the old reptilian part. This is all just supply and demand.'

'How much more of this shit am I going to have to listen to?' Beth demanded. What was getting to her was that that Inflictor had made himself this way without any alien involvement. 'Where's King Jeremy?'

'Tell du Bois I let Silas go.'

'He knows,' Beth told him. Inflictor's frown lasted for a moment.

'They're supposed to have driven us mad? All they've done is put everything that was on the inside, and not that well fucking hidden, on the outside. Nothing's changed. We're the alien invasion, have been for a while. Maybe since we first felt that satisfying thud running up our arm, the warm salt spray of blood when we took a rock and used it to cave in some Neanderthal's head.'

'You've given this a lot of thought,' Beth said. *Pseudo-intellectual, philosophical bullshit!* 'Do you understand that I don't care? To me you're just another sociopathic little shit. Now, what do you want to do? Talk or get shot?'

'It's a small price to pay,' he said. She wasn't quite sure what he was talking about.

'This isn't a confessional,' she told him. She again considered drawing the OHWS but she was beginning to suspect that he was well beyond threatening.

'No, but it is a church. I understand why you hate me, fear me ...'

'It's more disgust,' Beth said, but she foresaw a monologue and made herself comfortable. She was trying to decide how much of it she was going to put up with before shooting him in the head.

'... but nothing we did matters now. They would have ended up the same way.'

Beth thought back to Elizabeth in the warehouse in Massachusetts. She just about managed not to draw the pistol and kill him then and there.

'You've been superseded?' Beth said. 'Poor baby.' *This wanker thinks he's in some kind of atrocity competition.*

He turned to look at her again. 'Tiger shark embryos fight in the womb. The winner gets to be born. We're not going to be the winners.'

'Do you owe King Jeremy anything?' Beth asked, her voice brittle.

'Everything, in some ways, but he's a motherfucker. He's at

Terminal Island. Look for a submarine. That's all I know.'

Beth drew the pistol and pointed it at Inflictor's head. He showed no reaction whatsoever.

'You know, don't you?' she asked. He didn't answer. 'Doesn't matter what you've become, what you've done, the power you think you have, you're still the same frightened little boy, aren't you?' He said nothing. Beth holstered the pistol. He couldn't cause any more damage, he was right about that at least. The worst he could do was just join in. She turned the surfboard around and started paddling back towards the shore.

'Don't you want to surf?' he called after her.

They cleared most of the rubbish out of the back of the Cougar and took that. It was less damaged than the ECV. They made their way south-east along the Appian Way. Beth's last glimpse of the ocean was of the surfers rising on a large swell, the water obscuring something dark and huge just underneath the surface.

Things that looked like a cross between tendrils and vines shot from the water, taking root in the ground, climbing up buildings, explosively making trenches in the beach sand. They burst open, the spores just about visible, like a heavy pollen fall in the haze of the morning sunshine and smog. The buildings started to warp and change, splitting open as if to reveal a new world inside, independent life growing from the matter and tearing itself free.

Alexia steered away from the sea front. Du Bois ran his tanto over her skin. The cut didn't bleed. He cleaned the blade and did the same to himself. Grace was doing likewise. Beth could feel the blood-screens filling the armoured vehicle. The Seeder spores from the sea were like a bad itch. She drew her grandfather's bayonet and used it to release her own blood-screen to help fight the spores and wished things were different.

They drove towards the smoke and fire still surrounding the ruins of LAX.

They were in a gun shop. She knew where she was geographically, but the place names were pretty meaningless now, just raw information that had only been relevant before the Seeders woke up. The place had been pretty extensively looted, unsurprisingly. Beth was trying to ignore the dead bodies, but one of them had been run through with a hunting rifle. She couldn't stop smiling at the absurdity of this. She was starting to worry about herself.

'Fuck!' Grace screamed and kicked at one of the display cases. She had managed to retrieve the fighting knife she had been holding when she'd hit the bonnet of the ECV during the chase. It had got lodged in the grill at the front of the vehicle. She had, however, lost one of her Berettas. 'It's like balance, y'know?' Beth didn't know. The punk girl continued searching through the detritus. Alexia was by the door, crouched down, leaning against the wall, chain smoking.

'I don't think you're going to find what you're looking for,' du Bois said. They hadn't come here looking for another Beretta; they were pretty sure that most of the guns would have already been stolen. Instead they had come for another scope for the Purdey. At some level it annoyed Beth that she knew the replacement scope for the custom weapon wasn't as good as the first one, which had been destroyed during the chase. She didn't want to know this much about guns and military stuff, let alone have to utilise the knowledge. Though she was managing it better than Alexia, it would seem.

It's because you've always liked fighting. She tried to ignore the thought.

'We need to get moving,' du Bois said. He was affixing the new sight to the Purdey. Grace glared at him, and then went back to kicking boxes around with the toe of her motorcycle boot.

'Why? What are we going to do?' Alexia asked. 'Everyone's already killing everyone else. What more have we got to offer?'

Grace straightened up and looked over at Alexia.

'We're killing Mr Brown,' she said simply. Beth was aware of du Bois taking a deep breath. She looked over at him. Grace saw the look.

'Why pick a fight with him?' Alexia demanded.

'What's going on?' Grace asked du Bois.

'There's a way out,' he said. Grace choked off incredulous laughter.

'There *might* be a way out,' Beth corrected.

'There's a way out if we can get to Kanamwayso,' Grace said, pointing towards where she knew the ocean was, 'where all the bad shit out there is coming from; and your evidence that there's a way out is the hallucination you had during a psychotic episode, brought on by contact with the same fucking Seeders at the Federal Building. You know if we fucking hesitate here Mr Brown gets away!'

'How are we going to kill him?' Alexia demanded.

'The nuke,' Grace said irritably, barely glancing at Alexia before turning back towards du Bois.

'You're out of your mind,' Alexia said. Grace rounded on her.

'What did you fucking think we were doing?' she shouted, making Alexia flinch. 'Did you think we were all going to become fucking astronauts? Grow up!'

'That's enough,' du Bois said.

'Is it? This was why I was fucking helping you! Were you lying to me?'

'It's a bit more complicated than th—' du Bois started.

'Were you lying to me?' she screamed at him.

'We misled you,' Beth said. Grace turned round to look at her. The punk had shifted her carbine so she could more easily bring it to bear. Beth was pretty sure it was an unconscious gesture but it made her uneasy. She tried not to do the same with the LMG hanging down her front on its sling. 'Not entirely on purpose. We're making this up as we go along.'

'So what's your plan?' Grace asked. She looked between the three of them.

'Palm Springs,' Alexia finally suggested, but nobody laughed.

'We use King Jeremy's leverage—' du Bois started. Grace nodded.

'Negotiate?' Grace asked quietly. Du Bois didn't answer. 'The leverage is a threat. In order for it to work he needs to know there's a possibility he can survive. You're going to let him live, aren't you?' Du Bois still didn't answer her. 'Want to hold me down so he can rape me again wearing your face?' she asked very quietly. Du Bois looked away from her. 'Look me in the eyes, you cowardly piece of shit!' Du Bois didn't.

'Tell her,' Beth said.

'Tell me what?' Grace asked.

'Remember when we thought we were doing good work?' du Bois asked, though Beth was pretty sure he was still struggling with the punk girl's actual existence and couldn't remember what they had actually done together. 'When we thought we were saving the souls of the best of humanity, the scientists, artists, engineers, poets, musicians?' Grace barely nodded. Du Bois tapped his head. 'I have them. Up here. The Brass City stole them. Hamad gave them to me when I killed him, and then I hid the knowledge, even from myself.'

'And?' Beth prompted.

'And the City of Brass found them,' du Bois said.

'They're like the Library of Alexandria,' Grace surprised Beth a little by saying. 'They would have taken a copy.' Du Bois nodded, still struggling to look at her. 'So they're safe.'

'They're not human in there,' du Bois said.

'They only exist until they are compromised,' Beth added.

'So?'

'This is hope,' du Bois said, finally managing to look at her.

'No,' Grace said. 'This is an out-of-control messianic complex and one too many Charlton Heston films. "Let my people go," Malcolm? Really?'

She was right. Beth knew she was right.

'So our last act is just to try and kill everyone? Stop anyone from getting off this yeast infection of a planet?' Alexia asked. She was scratching at her skin.

Beth could see the pollen-like Seeder spores in the air. She was pretty sure that she was only able to do this because of her augments.

'Even in the highly unlikely chance it works ...'

'Evacuation was what the Circle was geared up to do,' du Bois pointed out.

'Before the Seeders woke up, but if by some miracle this does work, all you do is give that fucker a much larger playground.'

'What is "hope" for you, then?' Beth asked.

'The slight chance I can survive being reasonably close to a tactical nuclear explosion, and then I go looking for the Brass City.'

Du Bois opened his mouth to retort.

Beth held up her hand. 'Okay, we're going in to talk to them. You cover us. When you've had enough then you pull the trigger,' Beth told her. Grace stared at her. Du Bois opened his mouth again. 'No. She's got a point.' She cut him off and then turned to Grace. 'You get to decide.'

Of course it might not matter. The deal could have already been struck. Mr Brown and the DAYP could already be on their way, though if the nuke had gone off they would have seen it. It had started to rain. The rain was gritty, unpleasant, and tasted of salt. They had risked the motorway, *freeway*, Beth corrected herself. It was the fastest route. Du Bois was driving now. With the CROWS turret out of action there was no requirement for gunners. He was using the weight of the vehicle, and its superior armour, to barrel through other vehicles and roadblocks. She convinced herself that the bullets hitting the armour sounded like the rain.

As they came over the Vincent Thomas Bridge, being pursued by an armoured tow truck with a snowplough attached to the front, Beth could almost convince herself things were normal. The Port of Los Angeles, and the Port of Long Beach, looked reasonably untouched. Except for the root-like tendrils that had grown up the bridge's suspension towers. Their dark mottled flesh had burst where they had released their spores. Except for the two container ships and the oil tanker that had been partially dragged by the tendrils down into the water, a black puddle spreading outwards from the tanker. Except for the smoke rising from the Federal Correctional Institution out on one of the artificial islands, bodies hanging from its walls. Even if the inmates had weathered the initial electronic attack through the communications network they would have succumbed to the spores by now. Except the helicopters in the air over Long Beach, and further south, Huntington and Laguna Beach, much of it burning as the Marines from Camp Pendleton slowly 'took back' the city. The shape of the helicopters looked wrong somehow.

They had caught a glimpse of the submarine from the bridge. It was docked on the north side of the farthest, boot-shaped, artificial island in the Port of Los Angeles. A modified Virginia-class nuclear-powered fast-attack boat.

They had come off the freeway and headed down Navy Way next to the train lines and onto the artificial island. It was a bumpy ride where the tendrils had grown through the road and taken root in the concrete of the actual island itself. They could see the overgrown cranes, places where the stacked containers had fallen over.

They drove past the entrance to the container yard and pulled up. Grace climbed out of the back. She had swapped weapons with Beth. She was carrying the Model 0 LMG and the last of the belted ammunition. Beth, in turn, was carrying the punk girl's N6 carbine, magazines for the weapon, and the remaining grenades for the grenade launcher. Grace also had du Bois's Purdey. It had looked like it had been a wrench for him to hand the weapon over until his sister had snapped at him, pointing out that it was only a gun. The punk girl had four of the 7.62mm nanite-tipped bullets for the sniper rifle.

'How long?' du Bois asked. Beth was pretty sure that Mr Brown knew they were there. There was only one road onto this part of the port. His erstwhile employer would be a fool not to have Navy Way under observation.

'Half an hour,' Grace said. Du Bois was already shaking his head. Half an hour wasn't a long time to effect a stealth infiltration. 'Fifteen minutes.' Then she turned and ran into the rain towards the stacks of containers.

'This is fucking stupid,' Alexia muttered. Beth wasn't sure that she disagreed.

'If we can get out, if we can do something here, then I want you with me,' du Bois said. 'But you're right. This will probably end badly. If you want to go, go.' Alexia didn't say anything. Instead she reached over and hugged her brother.

It had seemed like a very long fifteen minutes, then they had started towards the submarine's berth. They had not got very far before they had started taking fire. Most of the incoming fire was from small arms and machine guns. Alexia jumped and swore when first a fifty calibre round, and then a 40mm grenade, exploded against the armour, rocking the heavy vehicle. A rocket exploded nearby, another in the air, but the larger weapons never seemed to hit them. Beth assumed that this was because Grace was doing her job of providing sniper cover, taking out the heavier weapons that could actually damage the Cougar. Through the rain and gunfire she caught glimpses of their attackers. They were clearly military trained, but their uniforms looked wrong. They were dressed like somebody's idea of post-apocalyptic pirates. She guessed that the surviving members of the DAYP had customised some of the Marines from Camp Pendleton to fit in with their new environment when they had slaved them. It smacked of the DAYP's video game reality. The white sheet they were hanging off the armoured 6×6 truck as a white flag had to be in tatters now.

In the headlights of the Cougar, Beth could make out figures standing by the submarine's boarding ramp, her eyes cutting through the rain and general gloom of the day. She saw a gunman take cover behind an armoured Mustang muscle car. The woman with the silver mask – du Bois and Grace had referred to her as the Pennangalan – and Mr Brown, leaning on a staff with drips hanging from it, were both there. Mr Brown's hand shaded his eyes as he peered into the truck's headlights. Du Bois drove steadily and slowly towards the obsidian figure of his old boss. Beth was now sure there were two figures hiding behind the Mustang, both dressed in ridiculous post-apocalyptic outfits she suspected that they had seen in a film, or in a computer game.

Du Bois stopped as close as he dared get to Mr Brown, parking the Cougar next to a stack of cargo containers, and waited. Bullets rained down on their armour. If they hadn't been able to filter out most of the noise it would have been deafening. Suddenly Beth started laughing. Du Bois and Alexia turned around to look at her as if she was mad.

'I think you've both been doing this too long,' she told them. Mr Brown looked like he was having a shouted conversation with one of the figures behind the muscle car. The figure stood up and waved his hands around, apparently to illustrate his point. He had a large and heavy-looking rucksack on his back.

'That's the nuke, isn't it?' Alexia said as the gunfire stopped. Du Bois just nodded. Without the gunfire they could make out the four figures in front of them better. King Jeremy, aka Weldon Rush, and Dracimus, aka Torsten Elling. Both of them looked like Aryan high school jocks at a *Mad Max* fancy dress party. Dracimus was aiming an AR-10, modified to fire enormous .50 calibre Beowulf rounds, at their truck. King Jeremy had a .50 calibre Desert Eagle in his right hand. She had to magnify her vision to work out what he was holding in his left hand. A dead man's switch, presumably attached to the nuke in his backpack. Du Bois had called it correctly. Anything happened to King Jeremy and his thumb came off the button, then everyone died. It seemed that the Do As You Please clan had found something that actually threatened Mr Brown. Beth looked down at King Jeremy's face. The insanity was written all over it, it was in his cold green eyes, and she suspected that at this moment it stemmed from fear as much as anything else. She knew that Grace would be looking through a scope at King Jeremy right now. At any moment she expected a bullet to hit the DAYP clan leader, and then there would be a very bright light, and she would cease to exist, but nothing happened. Strangely, she didn't feel frightened. More resigned. She almost wished it was over because this, all of this, she could almost understand. If their plan worked then she knew that she would have no frame of reference for whatever happened next.

Du Bois looked over at her, then his sister. She nodded, as did Alexia. Beth drew and checked her OHWS, du Bois did the same with his .45. They opened the doors and jumped out into light, raised weapons, and shouting. Lots of shouting. The air was thick with nanites. The Seeder spores were in conflict with what Beth could only imagine was some kind of industrial-strength blood-screen. She suspected that Mr Brown must have some kind of S- or L-tech nanite factory nearby, protecting the area from the Seeder spores.

Beth had her pistol levelled at King Jeremy, and nothing would have given her more pleasure than to squeeze the trigger. Du Bois's weapon was aimed at Dracimus. Alexia's ARX-170 was aimed at the Pennangalan, for all the good it would do. Dracimus, despite, presumably, being extensively augmented himself, looked terrified. The Beowulf rifle was steady, however, as it was aimed back at du Bois. The silver-masked woman had her weapon up and was aiming it at Beth. King Jeremy had raised his pistol. He looked more tense than frightened right now. Marines in post-apocalyptic pirate chic also surrounded them. Everyone was shouting at them to put their guns down, except for Mr Brown and the Pennangalan. The three of them waited, expecting to be cut down in a hail of gunfire. Expecting to see King Jeremy die and his thumb slip off the dead man's switch. Nothing happened. Nobody shot. Eventually Mr Brown motioned for everyone to be quiet.

'Malcolm, a surprise, but a pleasure,' he said when there was finally quiet. Beth had to will herself not to get turned on by his deep voice.

'The Marines are your people?' Malcolm asked King Jeremy, ignoring Mr Brown.

'Go and fuck yourself,' King Jeremy snapped. 'Kill this mother-fucker!' he ordered a slightly pained-looking Mr Brown.

'Weldon,' Mr Brown said. 'You need to order your people not to shoot.'

'What? Why?' King Jeremy demanded. It was the voice of a spoilt child. He was already grating on Beth. Her finger curled round the trigger of her pistol, she remembered the manticore, and she almost fired.

'Because I understand what is happening, but you will require a demonstration.'

'Or,' King Jeremy started as if he was talking to a particularly

486

stupid child, 'we kill him and get on with our day.'

'Do you want to live?' du Bois asked the sociopathic man-child. King Jeremy held up the dead man's switch and smiled.

'You're too fucking stupid to know what this is, aren't you?'

'Oh for goodness' sake,' Alexia muttered. 'I thought he was supposed to be some kind of prodigy.'

'Apparently not when it comes to reading people,' Mr Brown muttered, rubbing the bridge of his nose with thumb and forefinger. 'Calculate what they have to lose,' he told King Jeremy, sounding pained. 'Then perhaps we can "get on with our day".'

'You'll be fine, nobody's going to hurt you,' du Bois told King Jeremy.

'Okay, nobody shoot,' King Jeremy said.

'No matter what happens,' du Bois added. King Jeremy repeated him. Du Bois shot Dracimus twice in the face. Dracimus staggered back, the nanite-tipped rounds already eating away at the inside of his head. Du Bois shifted his aim to King Jeremy as Dracimus collapsed to the ground, his head now looking like a half-eaten bowl. There was more shouting and threats. The three of them waited patiently, as did Mr Brown, until it all died down.

'Now you're thinking that maybe you can get us in a rush, before we fire?' du Bois said, and then raised his left hand. Another shot rang out from a distance and the Pennangalan staggered back and then sat down. She was up on one knee, the Sig 716 carbine at the ready, in a moment. 'The next round is nanite-tipped and goes in Weldon's head, understand?' Du Bois shouted.

'I'm going to fucking kill you!' King Jeremy spat.

'So you have suborned Grace,' Mr Brown mused. 'If she believes you then she must be very angry with me. I'm surprised she hasn't already killed Mr Rush.'

'Don't call me that!' the already on-edge King Jeremy snapped. Beth was half starting to think that in his anger he would forget to keep the dead man's switch's button depressed. Mr Brown had a point, though. It seemed that Grace was playing along with their plan.

'Would the nuke kill you?' du Bois asked.

'I honestly don't know,' Mr Brown said after a moment's consideration. 'It's enough of a doubt that I am willing to consider partners, although there was always a place for you, Malcolm.'

'This is how it works,' du Bois said through gritted teeth. 'King Jeremy drops his gun and stays with us at all times. We go into the sub. I'm in front. Beth is behind. He is always covered. I even suspect something is happening, conventional or your magic bullshit, we kill him and everyone dies.'

Mr Brown had looked even more pained at the mention of magic. 'You must want to live a great deal. Tell me, will Miss Soggins be joining us?' Nobody answered.

'You're not serious?' King Jeremy demanded.

'Shut up, Weldon,' Mr Brown told the sociopath, and then turned to du Bois, Beth and Alexia: 'Well then, you'd better come on board, I suppose.'

39
A Long Time After the Loss

It had been the longest journey that the Monk had ever experienced in Red Space, and it had happened far from the Church beacons. To the Monk's mind they might as well have been lost among the blood-coloured clouds of the supposedly coterminous universe. More than thirty standard days, with the ship acting more and more strangely each day. They had neunonically cut their connections to the *Basilisk II*. They couldn't take the risk of the Yig virus suborning their neunonics, and meat-hacking them. The *Basilisk II* was seemingly flying itself. They had resorted to voice commands to communicate with the ship. It responded to them sluggishly, if at all. The Monk had half expected the craft to take on more serpentine qualities, perhaps influenced by Scab's tale of the bridge drive ghost being infected by the Yig virus, but that hadn't happened. Instead there had been a subtle change in the interior design, and in the texture of furnishings, as if the ship had reconfigured itself to cause a constant feeling of unease. She was pleased that as far as she could tell it hadn't corrupted the food supplies, yet.

They hadn't summoned Basil since the Yig virus had infected the bridge drive's navigation biocomputer. The biocomputer was S-tech, it was an isolated system, it shouldn't have been possible to hack but then Naga-tech was also derived from S-tech, and had been given more of an opportunity to evolve. As good as the security was on the heavily modified yacht, the ship's AI wouldn't have stood a chance. Nobody had seen Basil since, although Talia swore blind that she had seen a hunched figure creeping around the corridor by the bedrooms.

They couldn't even immerse. That was the worst thing. Maude and Uday were either gone, or horribly corrupted by Yig. The Monk had been able to lock away the loss of the Cathedral while they were careening from one disaster to the next. Now she had all the time she needed to think about it. She had books, movies, music contained in her internal liquidware, accessible through her neunonics, much of it from before the Loss. She had spent a lot of time lying on her now tactilely unpleasant bed, clutching her legs to her chest, listening to sad music, or watching old films in her mind's eye without time compression, despite having perfect recall of them, wishing she could cry. She was trying to process her emotions, but using drugs to moderate her moods so she could function. All the while expecting the ship to turn on them, or to learn that they were forever lost in Red Space at any moment.

Their hope mostly lay with Ludwig. The L-tech automaton Elite was monitoring the ship as best it could. It had been quite open in admitting that in doing so it had caught the Yig virus. Like Oz, Ludwig was trying to fight the virus off, and seemed in control of himself, which was fortunate, as after the bridge ghost had been infected with Yig, Scab had suffered a psychotic break. The human killer was in a permanent fury. Ludwig had to restrain him. This loss of control only made Scab worse. The Monk felt like she was back in prison and banged up with a real psycho.

The Monk hoped the infected *Basilisk II* was going to the Ubh Blaosc, and she hoped there were answers there. If not, it had been a long hard road for nothing. After thirty days she wondered what was happening in Real Space. Had the rest of the Church been hunted down? With the Monarchist systems down to one Elite now, had the war begun? Or was it already over? What was Patron doing?

She felt the changes in the ship. She had become attuned to it during the long voyage. The main systems were powering down, so it could bleed off heat and limit its EM signature. It was reconfiguring to make it more difficult to detect. Then she was aware of the slight change in the atmosphere, the background noise, as the bridge drive was activated. The Monk stopped the music in her head, rolled off her bed and onto her feet.

'Door.' Nothing happened. 'Door! Please.' The door opened. Talia was walking by, Vic trailing after her. The hard-tech augmented 'sect had spent all of the voyage either with Talia, or in a semi-hibernated state. It seemed that he was not able to cope with boredom very well without access to immersions. He turned to look at her as they passed. She suppressed a shiver. She had never been able to cope well with the inhuman movements of 'sects. It was like their heads were mounted on swivels.

The lounge/C&C was bathed in red light, the smart matter hull completely transparent. Ahead of them she could see the blue rip of a bridge point and beyond that Real Space. She tried to feel relief but there was still too much unknown, though she was hoping for an advanced but benevolent race that would help them. She wasn't sure what was wrong, but the ship's flight felt off somehow.

'What's that?' she asked.

'Gravity,' Ludwig said. He had learned how to communicate verbally. She suspected he was using a dialled-down sonic weapon application of the Elite-tech to do so. Scab hung limp in front of him, held in a coherent energy field that must have been using a significant amount of the automaton's entangled energy feed. At least Scab wasn't trying to thrash about. 'There is something with a huge mass just the other side of the bridge point.'

The *Basilisk II* slid through the rip into space. There was a glow from beneath the ship, manoeuvring engines compensating for the pull of gravity. At first the Monk thought they were above a vast plane. It stretched as far as they could see in all directions. The bridge closed behind them, and the ship started to rise. It wasn't visible to the naked eye, but neunonic analysis suggested that there was a slight curvature. The *Basilisk II* continued to rise. The 'serpent witch' mind of the bridge drive's navigation systems had brought them out very close to the object, whatever it was. It was clear that it had been constructed, despite its vast size. It had to be L-tech.

'Any scans, comms?' the Monk asked Ludwig.

'Nothing,' the automaton answered after a moment. She hadn't liked how long it had taken the Elite to get an answer from the Yig-infected ship. Then came the realisation of what it was.

'It's a Dyson Sphere,' she said. Talia frowned. Vic concentrated for a moment and then opened his mandibles in his 'sect replication of human surprise.

'That's like a star encased in a structure, right?' Talia said. The Monk was a little less surprised at her sister's knowledge this time. Her neunonics were trying to do the maths on the amount of matter involved, although it was just estimates because she couldn't risk accessing the *Basilisk II*'s systems. The builders would have had to cannibalise multiple star systems for this much matter. She looked up through the transparent hull and yes, Known Space seemed lacking in nearby stars. Her neunonics had no frame of reference to plot location. They were in deep space. She suspected between galaxies. This suggested that the megastructure had been moved, somehow.

'A stellar engine?' she asked Ludwig. The machine didn't answer. 'Is this your home?'

'I think so,' Ludwig said. It sounded like the sort of thing an uplift would say; she didn't like that it sounded unsure. 'Mr Scab wishes to speak with you,' the automaton said. The Monk glanced at the others. Vic sagged. She couldn't read Talia's expression, despite neunonic analysis. The Monk nodded. There was a shift in the air around Scab's face, though he was still hanging limp in front of the cylindrical floating automaton, suspended in mid-air.

'You have to let me go,' Scab said. His tone was flat, but it still sounded the closest to desperation she had ever heard from him. It chilled her, and reminded her of just how vulnerable she suspected he truly was. 'I need to kill.'

Vic let out an affected laugh.

'You're not really convincing us,' the Monk said.

'I don't think it will be you. I'm ready. I want to kill it. Shoot me like a bullet into god.'

'Let him go,' Talia surprised the Monk by saying.

There was nothing, it was dead, inert, as far as they could tell, though even active scans wouldn't have got through the dense shell of the Dyson Sphere. There was no activity on the surface that they could see, and the *Basilisk II*'s AG system was strained to its maximum tolerances with them being as close as they were. Ludwig managed to coax the truculent possessed yacht out further. They did a fast fly-by, stealthy as they could, passive scans only. Four and a half standard hours later all they had seen was a lot of smooth grey matter.

'We have something,' Ludwig said. As a precaution they did not 'face with Ludwig either, though if he was overcome by the Yig virus then his Elite-tech would easily overwhelm their neunonic security. When he fell they all fell. Part of the transparent hull magnified. They were far enough away from the sphere now that she could make out the curvature more clearly. The ship was a gnat staring at a mountain.

'I don't see it,' the Monk said. Talia came to stand by her side, peering at the magnified part of the hull. Vic wasn't far behind. Scab was sitting in his chair, smoking. The ship upped the magnification on the hull. The Monk's augmented eyes could now make out a very faint red glow. The magnified square of the hull switched to the infrared spectrum. There was a faint emanation of heat from the area.

'Can we send in one of the AG submunitions?' the Monk asked. 'Use it for passive scans and then return to the ship and report?' They couldn't risk transmissions.

'In theory,' Ludwig said. 'But like all the ship's systems they are infected, and it will be beyond my influence unless we transmit and give away our position.'

'Do you know the way back?' Scab asked, and then took a drag on his cigarette. The Monk just looked at him. 'Then let's get this over and done with.'

The Monk turned to Talia. 'You still want neunonics? Soft-machine augments?' Suddenly her sister didn't look so sure of herself. Scab opened his mouth, but then didn't say anything.

'Now wait a minute ...' Vic started.

'It's not up to you,' the Monk snapped. For just a moment Talia looked frightened.

'I'm not so special out here, am I?' she said. The Monk laughed. 'I've no idea where here is.' Even with all her experience she couldn't quite get her head around how far the two of them were from Bradford. Talia just hugged her sister. For that moment she found herself feeling profoundly grateful. Her sister knew that she needed help. 'How much do we trust the assembler?' she asked Ludwig. The automaton reeled off some impressively large number as the probability against Yig infecting any neunonics they assembled.

'Yay! Now I can be a superhero too,' Talia said weakly. Some part of the Monk felt bad. It felt like she was polluting her sister, but she was also increasing her chances of survival. Talia's systems would be high-end civilian/mid-range military/bounty killer – the *Basilisk II*'s assembler was good, but not much use for the custom illegal hard- and software that the likes of herself, Vic and Scab had within them. They would do their best to fabricate armour and weapons. She would have artificial skills provided by the software, but they wouldn't have time to properly integrate them with her body, even after it had been augmented, and artificial skills were no match for experience and training.

They had put Talia under and laid her on her bed. The neunonics and liquid hardware had been fed into the brain membrane through the eyes and ears, and most of the assembled soft-machine augments had been injected intramuscularly. They had left to let them grow and integrate. Talia had been ravenous when she had woken. They had run her through some simple integration exercises. Scab had started to pace impatiently. Ludwig had remained a still presence in the lounge/C&C, though Beth knew he was fighting an unseen electronic war within his own systems and the *Basilisk II*'s.

Then they had put on the new armour bought from the black market habitat on the way to Black Athena. They had run diagnostics and simulations with the as-yet unused weapons systems. There was something more than a little off-putting about seeing Talia armed and armoured. The Monk suspected it was the assumption that her younger sister had no sense of responsibility whatsoever, and that giving her weapons was just an act of lunacy. Still, the softwired neunonic skills made her look at least competent. Beth was also pleased that Talia had Vic looking after her, though she tried not to think too hard about their 'relationship'. She saw Scab casting her sister the odd strange look. She had even felt a momentary pang of jealousy, but then found herself shaking her head and smiling at the ridiculousness of it.

Ludwig had brought the *Basilisk II* down as close to the Dyson Sphere as the AG and manoeuvring systems could manage. Subjectively the sphere looked like a huge, flat mountain stretching away from them in all directions. They were too close to make out the curvature. They made their way towards the escaping heat as stealthily as they could.

It reminded Beth of someone having taken a spoon to crack a boiled egg, but that was perhaps because she knew the translation of the name the Ubh Blaosc. It was a huge, ragged tear in the shell of the Dyson Sphere. From inside they could make out the faint red glow.

'Plasma damage,' Vic said, looking at the melted and fused smart matter surrounding the hole in the shell. 'It must have had the force of a sun.'

494

'An Elite?' the Monk asked.

'Too much even for them,' Vic said.

'The dragons breathe fire,' Ludwig told them. Even Scab turned to stare at the automaton.

'Are you all right?' the Monk asked Talia. Her younger sister was looking uncomfortable in her skin.

'It's strange,' she said. 'It's like I'm trying to get used to things that are already instinct.'

They were over the hole now, the ship struggling with a strange interplay of gravitic forces, tiny against the backdrop of the massive rift. It began to sink into the hole, into the Dyson Sphere, into what she assumed was the Ubh Blaosc.

Inside was vast, dark and empty, illuminated by the faint red light. She guessed there would be no atmosphere. Even with a hole this size it would take a very long time to evacuate all the air from a structure like the Dyson Sphere, but this had happened a very long time ago. The entire surface of the sphere seemed to be made up of mountainous ridges and valleys. Magnification showed the landscape consisted of segmented, organic, resinous-looking material. From their perspective the ridges climbed up the huge vertical-looking walls of the sphere's interior, disappearing into the darkness above and below. In the red light it looked like Hell.

'Is that a fucking statue?' Talia asked. The light was coming from a fading, final sequence G-type star that looked small and distant in the centre of the Dyson Sphere. The light from the dim star was obscured by what did appear to be a massive statue, though the word didn't really do it justice, of an ancient warrior with wings. The Monk had no idea what to make of that.

'The Naga would have consumed all the matter, transforming it at a molecular level for their own purposes,' Ludwig told them. The Monk noticed that the ship was starting to move towards the statue and the fading sun.

'Then why not the statue?' Talia asked.

'He is a god,' Ludwig said. Even Scab turned to stare at the automaton. It was not something that the Monk had ever wanted to hear a machine say.

'Where are we going?' Vic asked.

'Lug,' Ludwig told him. The 'sect opened his mandibles to ask another question. 'Extremophile Naga spores are attaching themselves to the ship.'

'Are they doing anything?' the Monk asked.

'Is there movement down there?' Vic asked. The Monk had been thinking the same thing. Parts of the transparent hull were magnified. The mountains seemed to be shifting, parts of them uncoiling, flashes of light from engine fire as hibernating, bio-mechanical Naga ships started to awake.

'If they know we're here let's speed up,' the Monk said.

'Speed up?' Vic demanded incredulously. 'Let's just fucking leave!' Movement was spreading like a forest fire beneath them.

'There's nowhere to run now,' Scab said. The Monk glanced at him, his face in shadow, the rest of him illuminated by the faint red light.

'They know something is happening but I don't think they know exactly where we are yet,' Ludwig said. The Monk wondered just how much the automaton had been compromised.

'Can we go any faster?' the Monk asked.

'The faster we move the greater the likelihood of disco—' Ludwig went quiet. The Monk stared at the floating cylindrical automaton. It was one of the Elite. They were capable of fighting entire fleets on their own, of destroying habitats, rendering worlds uninhabitable, and something had just made it go quiet. The air in the yacht's lounge/C&C was suddenly filled with the funk of Vic's pheromonic terror. She knew how he felt.

'Is there safety with Lug?' the Monk demanded. Ludwig didn't answer.

'Beth?' Talia said, clearly frightened. The biomechanical ships, the Naga's 'dragons', were separating themselves from their resin-like environment. The *Basilisk II* surged forwards, dramatically increasing its speed. Beth found herself using her neunonics to estimate how long it would take them to get to Lug, assuming that Lug was the statue, and how fast the biomechanical dragons would have to go to catch up with them. She abandoned it for the useless speculation it was. She had only come into contact with the Naga twice before. The first time had resulted in tens of thousands of deaths, and the sterilisation and subsequent destruction of an entire habitat. The second time it had nearly killed her. The serpent uplifts were voracious, and utterly inimical to all other forms of biological life. Suddenly this vast sphere had become claustrophobic. 'Beth!' Talia cried. The Monk almost snapped in response until she saw what her younger sister was pointing at. The Lounge/C&C's carpet had developed scales. The faint red light was getting brighter. Suddenly Scab had stood up as if his armchair had just bitten him, his EM auto-shotgun in hand and his combat armour helmet growing over his head, the black visor sliding down over his face.

'Seal up,' Beth told her sister as her own helmet grew around her head. Talia's eyes went wide.

'Shit!' the girl swore and ran towards her bedroom. The ship was reconfiguring, changing shape. The flexing of the smart matter hull was more sinuous than normal.

'Talia!' the Monk screamed just as her visor slid down. Her new P-sat clicked into the clip on her new armour's shoulder. She could see the dragons burning towards the yacht now. At least they had some distance to travel from the shell to the huge warrior-shaped structure partially obscuring the faint red sun. Talia emerged from the corridor that led to the bedrooms. She was tucking what looked like a stainless steel rose into one of the compartments on her recently assembled armour.

'Close your fucking helmet!' Beth 'faced. Talia actually flinched. It was perhaps a little harsh for her sister's first 'face communication, but at least Talia was closing her helmet.

The yacht was heading straight for Lug's huge open mouth. It had to be hundreds of miles high, thousands across and then it filled their vision. The floor of the yacht shifted beneath them.

'The ship has fallen,' Ludwig announced in a matter-of-fact tone. The ship was slowing. There was a flash of black light, and then Beth was tumbling through the sky heading straight towards Lug. The AG motor in her P-sat could do nothing to slow her. She was aware of several parts of the mutating *Basilisk II* falling away from her far below. Something took hold of her and she started to slow down. Then she became aware of the heat. Despite the late sequence of the star, despite the huge structure of the warrior in its way, they were still in the corona of a star. Her armour was right on the edge of its material tolerances. Then the heat went away. The four of them were being carried in some kind of coherent energy field projected by Ludwig, who was just above and behind them. Once again Beth found herself wondering just how compromised by the Yig virus the ancient automaton was. She was still getting AV feed from her P-sat. The fire of the dragon's engines seemed to fill the sphere all around them.

Hanging underneath Ludwig, approaching the huge statue,

all she could really see of it was the cavernous darkness inside the mouth. Beth suddenly felt calm. Then her augmented vision illuminated the interior of the enormous head. It was filled with the same resinous material that coated the Dyson Sphere's inner shell. There was movement everywhere on the resin. The serpent uplifts, themselves slaves to one of the hive-minds in the huge Nagaraja-class capital ships, were uncoiling from their resinous nests.

'You've killed us, Ludwig,' Beth said to herself. A 'face transmission wouldn't have reached him through the E-field. She wished she could comfort her sister. Talia would be very afraid right now.

Ludwig dropped them on the very edge of the open mouth. The Monk had a ninety million mile drop to her back. The E-field came down.

'I'll be outside,' Ludwig told them.

They went through the motions. Flashes of laser light lost in the huge cavernous darkness of the mouth. The serpents, and other, scuttling, biomechanical weapons, rushed towards them. The most target-rich of environments. Not even Talia hesitated. Targeting systems told them where to aim: the closest first and then work their way out. Beth fired her hybrid EM shotgun/ laser carbine combination, cycling quickly between the side-by-side weapons. Superheated flesh exploded where the laser hit. The auto-shotgun's solid-state magazine was assembled into fin-stabilised, armoured-piercing rounds, designed to go through the serpents' thick, armoured hide, and explode when they detected warm flesh. Her P-sat was firing its laser over her shoulder at incoming projectiles. She would save the grenades in the under-slung launcher until they needed breathing space.

Vic's strobe gun was a scythe of red light. The rotary weapon was in his lower limbs as he swivelled his abdomen one way and then back again. His thorax swivelled independently, his upper limbs firing his advanced combat rifle. The ACR ran dry. He quickly reloaded and started firing again, the diminishing magazine looking like it was being eaten by the rifle. It was clear that he was compensating for Talia, trying to keep her safe. The Monk's younger sister, however, was holding her ground. She didn't have anything like the firepower of the rest of them, and was presumably only able to function through the fear due to the chemicals her soft-machine augments would have dumped into her blood, but she was firing burst after burst from her double-barrelled laser carbine.

Scab was a picture of efficiency. One shot with his EM auto-shotgun and a serpent fell. Then the next and the next; he was moving with startling speed, his targeting systems prioritising threats. His P-sat, clipped to his armour, was stabbing out at the Naga as well.

Of course it was a waste of time. They were just postponing the inevitable. Behind her the Monk was aware of fire. It illuminated the interior of Lug's head. It looked like a vast living plane of serpents writhing across the resinous landscape towards them. Her armour and the P-sat sent the images of what was happening outside to her neunonics. Ludwig was fighting the vast fleet of dragons coming up behind them. They bathed the automaton in their plasma fire. In return, black light projected out of him like a prism, slicing open ancient biomechanical machines, spilling their contents like guts. Out-of-phase ghost bullets went looking for minds, dragons de-cohered into vast showers of dust, DNA was hacked and Naga-craft fed on their own energy to regress to protoplasmic states. Viruses infected flesh, dragons turned on one another, projected high-energy particles, disrupted atomic structures. Ludwig was a ghost, wreathed in a corona of fire, moving between them, through them.

The Monk's combat armour 'faced structural integrity warnings as she was bathed in plasma fire. There was only so much the energy dissipation grids could do as molecularly-bonded hardened composites took on a semi-liquid state and started to melt and run. As one, the four of them fired their grenade launchers. They surrounded themselves with explosions to give themselves room, to buy another moment of time.

The Monk was aware of Naga spores trying to infect her armour. It would make no difference. Their initial onslaught had caught the Naga before they could fire, but eventually the serpent plasma weapons would turn them to so much slag. It would be over quickly. She was just pleased that the Naga didn't seem to be using electronic warfare of any kind.

The serpents were charging her now, firing. At the last she would move to Talia and give her sister the coherent energy field generator. She should have done that beforehand. She 'faced over the operation codes and instructions. She could see them up close now. Tall, thin, bipedal forms in biomechanical armour fused to scaled flesh. They carried organic-looking plasma weapons, and barbed spears that she knew were for injecting eggs – effectively voracious biological nanite factories – into host flesh. There were too many of them. The shotgun ran dry. She fired the carbine one-handed, the weapon partially melted, as she reached for another solid-state magazine. The closest serpent was almost upon her, appearing through the fire, its spear reaching for her. The magazine slid home, she dropped her hybrid weapon, and reached for both her thermal blades. It was the wrong decision. She should have triggered her P-sat. The spear touched her armour. Everything stopped. Her vision was filled with frozen fire.

And Beth was in darkness. There was a moment of panic. This shouldn't happen. Her eyes should always be able to see, no matter what her condition. Torches burst into life. They were in a low, dome-shaped, stone and earth structure. Jewellery and ancient weapons were laid out around the chamber. There was even a chariot. She guessed it was supposed to be the representation of a burial mound, similar to those found in Ireland before the Loss.

She was dressed the way she used to dress so many millennia ago, her hair in a ponytail, boots, the leather jacket. Her sister was standing next to her. Scab was in his suit and hat, but it took her a moment to realise that the nominally human-looking figure, dressed as anachronistically as Scab, with four arms and compound insect eyes, was probably Vic.

'An improvement?' Talia said hopefully. She was pale and shaking.

'Fuck!' odd human Vic shouted. 'It's an immersion.' Now the Monk was starting to get worried. Whoever or whatever had done this had gone straight through their neunonic security like it hadn't existed.

'So?' Talia said. 'Still better.'

'Even sped up as fast as our brains can interpret the data, time still passes, events still happen, no matter how quick this is. It's just postponing the inevitable,' Vic explained.

'We will arm you, armour you.' The voice sounded like old paper being rustled. The corpse sat up on a stone bench, ancient leathery skin spread across bone, the tattered remnants of fine clothes hanging off its frame. It was difficult to look at, as though it kept folding in on itself. Its movements left permanent fractal images behind it, somehow reminding the Monk of a pupa. Talia let out a little scream, and her hand clamped over her mouth. 'My grandchild knows what to do.'

Talia turned away from the corpse-like entity. 'Your hair's come back,' she said to her sister. Vic turned to stare at the pair of them. 'Oh calm down, we're dead anyway.'

'Are you Lug?' the Monk asked. She was struggling to look at the corpse-like entity.

'We need to get back,' Scab said, looking around the burial chamber as if he could find a way out.

'What is it?' Vic asked quietly. It took a moment for the Monk to realise that the 'sect was talking about the Destruction.

'We don't know. Different intelligences have different names for it. The Screaming, the Destruction, the Hungry Nothingness. Somewhere in the fire and pressure of the birth of your universe was some kind of sentience. It was born into pain and light, like all of us. As we cannot even begin to imagine the extent of its sentience, we cannot begin to understand the depths of its suffering. Its existence was agony.'

'Is it God?' Talia asked, awed.

'It was born with, it did not give birth to, the universe. Perhaps to your species it is, as it is responsible for your creation.'

'I thought that was the Seeders,' the Monk said.

'In fleeting moments of what passed for clarity, it created the Seeders. It wished company. It sought to soothe itself, to matter, to not be alone.'

'Well, that worked out well,' Vic muttered, his body language displaying his impatience in a very human manner that the Monk thought, in other circumstances, the 'sect would be very pleased with.

'They severed links with their creator to protect themselves, and I suspect that may have driven it over the edge. Then something went wrong and contact was re-established.'

'And it drove the Seeders and anything linked to them, like the Naga, insane,' the Monk said. Lug nodded.

'So it is God?' Talia asked.

'No, it is just another form of life. It did not create us, and there are many other forms of life it did not create. I do not think that there are gods. I think that there is only nature.'

Beth found herself thinking briefly of Churchman.

'So now it will consume the universe?' Talia asked.

'Seriously, we need to—' Scab started. Beth rounded on him.

'Look, we've lost that fight. I want to know what happens next before I trigger every last piece of ammunition on me to cook off so I don't get turned into a Naga egg sac!'

'It has already consumed the universe, many times.' Suddenly Lug had even Scab's attention. 'Eventually, as the expanding universe cooled, the Destruction was able, over billions of years, to marshal its thoughts, to understand the nature of its pain. Using the meagre remaining energy resources it could marshal it was able to open a wormhole, a bridge into the red universe that the minds of the Seeders had expanded from the quantum foam. Utilising the energy of the younger universe, the chaotic space, and the now-weak thermodynamic arrow of time, it went back and started to consume. It collapsed each branch, each possible universe, in on itself at progressively earlier times, each going further and further back, until eventually ...'

'The Universe never gets born?' Vic asked quietly.

'Yes,' Lug said. There were tears on Beth's face. She wasn't sure why. The whole thing still sounded too large, too abstract, even after all these years.

'That poor thing,' Talia said. Vic was staring at her as though she was mad. Beth glanced at Scab. He looked completely passive. This bothered her.

'So nothing can be done?' Vic asked. He sounded almost relieved.

'Each time we try,' Lug said. 'Each time we fail.'

'Because this Screaming has servants,' the Monk said.

'Broken things, mad with the pain that leaks into them, that try and stop any agencies who would prevent the consumption of dark energy that leads to the collapse. Their instinctive understanding of five-dimensional physics, however, provides them with a great deal of power.'

'Like Patron?' Beth asked.

'He is always there. Each time he sends people back to help him make things worse for the future, to make resistance all the harder.' Lug pointed at Scab. 'And each time it makes him worse.' Scab remained completely still. 'Your strand will be the last time that the universe gets this old.'

'Are you saying that this is our last chance?' the Monk asked.

'I do not know, but I suspect it to be the case.'

'Why do you care?' Scab asked. Beth was worried Lug's neck skin would tear open when the strange collapsing entity turned to look at the human killer.

'Nothing will have time to ascend, to move beyond. So what will be the point?' Lug asked. Beth frowned, she wasn't quite sure she followed, but the answer seemed to amuse, if not satisfy, Scab.

'If we're the last chance then it's over,' Vic said. 'We're fucked.'

'My grandchild will help, and I will lay myself out on an altar for you,' Lug told the 'sect. The look of confusion on Vic's immersed humanesque face was quite comical. Lug turned to look at Beth. 'I'm sorry,' he said. Then she died.

Talia saw it on her periphery first. Just a movement. A distraction from the targeting schematics overlaid on her vision, from her burst-firing, double-barrelled laser carbine, from the chemically suppressed fear, from the chemically suppressed pain as her skin bubbled due to the heat leaking through her partially melted armour. Despite everything seeming to move so slowly, and her thoughts moving so fast, it still took her a moment to translate the image into actual information. Her sister on the end of a barbed spear held up high, one-handed, by a serpent in biomechanical armour. Beth's armour was already fusing with her body, the biological nanites modifying matter at a molecular level, auto-cannibalising what they needed for the energy to give the new form growing out of her sister's dead flesh life.

It took Talia a further moment to realise that the screaming was her own.

40
Ubh Blaosc

Wherever Tangwen was, it was dark. It felt like she was in water but it was warm and safe somehow. She could rest. She hadn't felt that way in a very long time. She didn't want to leave.

Then everything was hard light and cold metal against bare skin. The metal underneath her felt rounded, like the bottom of a cauldron, but it was huge. Various figures and symbols protruded from the metal. It was odd, they obviously didn't mean to cook her, as the cauldron was otherwise empty, except for Britha. The *ban draoi* was naked, like Tangwen, her knees drawn up to her chest. Her head didn't look right somehow. The shaved half of it looked bulbous, the veins bulging. *Like ...*

Britha looked up.

Tangwen stared. She had quicksilver eyes, like Teardrop's had been towards the end, tears the same colour sinking into the *ban draoi*'s cheek, and Tangwen didn't think she had ever seen anyone look so guilty.

'What? What's happened?' The last thing she remembered they had been standing in the god's head. Had she fallen asleep? More tears. 'What have you done?' Tangwen asked. She felt different somehow.

Britha opened her mouth to speak, but only a strangled noise came out. 'I'm sorry,' the Pecht woman finally managed.

Then Tangwen knew. She wasn't sure she would have known, been this aware of her body, before she had drunk of Britha's blood. She stood up and jumped for the lip of the cauldron and pulled herself out of it. 'Tangwen!'

She collapsed onto the too-even wooden floor of the too-pristine longhall. She staggered away from the cauldron, fell onto all fours, and threw up. Teardrop-on-Fire and Raven's Laughter moved towards her, hands outstretched.

'Get away from me!' Teardrop was dressed for war: he wore

only skin trews and a loincloth, tattoos on his back, chest, and upper arms; the bottom part of his face painted, symbols picked out in the design; his hair tied back and braided. The pack for his magical armour was affixed just over his left shoulder this time. There was a knife sheathed at his hip, and he carried the case that she had seen Fachtna carry: the case for the giant-killing spear that Bress had wielded at Oeth. There was just a moment of confusion. The last person she had seen handling the horrific weapon was Grainne, but that thought was quickly swept away by her anger.

Raven's Laughter wore thicker hides, but Tangwen had seen the short, dark-haired woman transform. She knew her for a monster. Her weapons were spines that grew through the skin, though the Croatan woman had an axe, not unlike her own, through her belt, and a knife on her hip as well.

'What did you do to me?' The guilt was clear on both the Croatans' faces as well.

'It was not them, it was me.' Britha's voice from behind her. Tangwen turned around. The guilt was still there, but the Pecht *dryw* looked more inhuman than ever. Tangwen stared at her, shaking her head, trying to think of something to say. 'You'll make a better mother than me.'

Tangwen couldn't quite believe what she had just heard. She stormed across the longhall to the *dryw*. 'When?' she barked. 'When my head's split open by a Trinovantes club? Or when I take a spear in my guts during a raid on the Cantiaci? I'm a warrior! I eat tansy cake after I lie with any man!' She slapped Britha, hard. The *ban draoi* looked more shocked than hurt, so Tangwen punched her. Britha stumbled back and bumped into the cauldron before losing her footing and sitting down hard.

'I am a *dryw*!' Britha shouted. 'You cannot lay a hand on a—'

'No!' Tangwen said, looming over Britha. 'You make excuses, avoid your responsibilities, and then hide behind your black robes, hoping that being strange and threatening will get you what you want! You wreak destruction wherever you go! I wish I'd never met you!' There were tears in the young hunter's eyes. 'And now I'm pregnant with your changeling baby! You're a coward!' She was screaming now, face purple with rage.

'Both,' Britha said. Tangwen stared at her.

'What?' Tangwen asked, very quietly. She was aware of Teardrop and Raven's Laughter moving closer to her.

'Both my unborn children,' Britha said, her face crumpling. There were more quicksilver tears running down her cheek only to be sucked back into her skin. Something about them reminded Tangwen of engorged ticks. Tangwen straightened up, looking down at Britha, her swollen head, her silver eyes, the red metal of her once-woad tattoos.

'Look what you've done to yourself,' Tangwen said. 'Has it been worth it?' She knelt down next to Britha. 'I want you to know I'll cut his child out of me,' she whispered. Then she went looking for her hatchet to bury in the *dryw*'s head. Teardrop's armour unfolded, encasing him in metal, his helmet completely covering his head. Shaped like a raven, the helm reminded Tangwen of an *enchendach*. Even with all their strength, and the magics of the fair folk at their disposal, Teardrop and Raven's Laughter struggled to stop Tangwen from killing Britha.

Outside, the noise hit Tangwen like a wall of thunder. The Otherworld was falling. High above her a land, on what she thought of as the wall of this inside-out world, burned. A fountain of fire, wreathed in smoke and steam from the oceans surrounding it. She didn't understand how she could see so much that was so far away. Amid the fire and burning rock she could make out the enormous, monstrous shape of a dragon that surely must have been the size of Ynys Prydain itself. Her bowels turned to liquid, and it was only with the greatest difficulty that she did not soil herself. She wanted to go back into the longhall. They had heard nothing of this great storm outside, presumably because of more fair folk magic. She stood frozen, vaguely aware of Britha doing much the same. They should not be here. This was no place for mortals.

'Come on,' Raven's Laughter tried to coax her. 'We'll take you home.'

Fire rained down from the hole in the Otherworld, the glow reflecting in Teardrop's impossible metal armour. Tangwen tried to make sense of the small, fast-moving dots spreading out from the fire. Bright spears of light existed for less than moments in the distance, while closer to them lightning played across tree-tops. She ducked down, hand on her axe, as two vessels, much larger than their chariot, shot by overhead.

'They are ours,' Teardrop said gently. Tangwen had felt fear before. She had almost not made it onto the wicker man, but this was too much. There had been a chance against the Lochlannach, against the spawn of Andraste, even against Crom Dhubh. There was no chance here against such power.

'These are my Father's people?' Tangwen asked. She could not equate this madness with the gentle creature that lived in the crystal cave beneath her village. Raven's Laughter was affixing another metal plate to Britha's shoulder, which the hunter knew could grow to become the same sort of armour that protected Teardrop. Raven's Laughter exchanged a look with her armoured husband.

'Your Father's people are the Naga?' the Croatan woman asked.

'He is a serpent, but not like this.' She could hear the desperation in her own voice.

'I think Tangwen's Father was spared the madness,' Teardrop said, his voice sounding strange coming from the armour.

'You met him!' Tangwen shouted. 'You know! Fachtna did not like him!'

'I know this is hard to understand.' Teardrop had to shout to be heard. 'But that was a different Teardrop.'

'Another changeling!' Tangwen shouted. Raven's Laughter turned away from a concerned-looking Britha, and moved towards Tangwen. The hunter stepped back, a hatchet and blade in her hands now. 'Get away from me!'

'We just want to take you home,' Raven's Laughter said.

'No! You'll do something else!'

'Tangwen, please,' Britha said.

'I will kill you,' she warned. 'I don't care about the consequences!' Then the area was bathed in flickering blue and white light. Tangwen looked behind her at the vast wood. Lightning was surging up from blackening, glowing, smoking treetops. The closest trees to her were shrivelling. The lightning wreathed the form of a winged dragon, just above the roof of the forest, fire in its tail, its maw glowing. Where the lightning touched, flesh was charred. Moving things, armoured creatures, were growing and leaping out of the dragon's armoured skin and dropping into the trees, the lightning hitting many, but not all of them as they fell. Tangwen's head whipped around as she felt a hand on her shoulder.

'We have no time for your fear,' Raven's Laughter told her. She noticed the small Croatan woman's hand was on her own axe. Tangwen swallowed and nodded. Britha and Teardrop were already rushing towards the chariot, the rear of the vehicle peeling open for them. Raven's Laughter and Tangwen followed. Tangwen's stomach lurched as the chariot started to rise the moment they were on board, though there was no one controlling it as far as she could see. She felt something at her waist. She looked down. Raven's Laughter was attaching a strangely shaped box, made of an oddly coloured metal that Tangwen didn't recognise, to her belt.

'What are you doing?' Tangwen demanded.

'This is a shield, this is Teardrop's shield.' Raven's Laughter shifted to show a similar piece of metal on her hip. 'You must not get hit by any of the Naga's weapons. You will know when the shield is up because you will be surrounded by light. Nothing can harm you then, but you will not be able to harm them either. You can still move, however. Do you understand?' She didn't but she nodded anyway. She screamed as she was suddenly able to see through the rear of the chariot. Raven's Laughter was crawling along the neck of the vehicle. Teardrop was looking out of the back. In the distance the huge monster was through the spewing fire. It looked like things were falling off it as it made its way through the sky. Spears of light and lightning were answered with fire as the Otherworldly vessels fought with the dragons.

'Manitou Pass or the New Pool?' Raven's Laughter called from the chariot's neck.

'The Pass is closer,' Teardrop called. Tangwen let out another scream as the chariot veered sideways sharply, and she found herself looking straight down at the land below, yet she did not fall. It was if she was standing flat on the ground.

'New Pool is safer,' Raven's Laughter called back.

'Not if the dragons catch us in the air.'

Tangwen's stomach lurched as the chariot levelled out. She edged back towards the benches that ran around the cupola.

It was the circle of stones where they had first arrived in the Otherworld, nestled in the canyon mouth, the rock outcrop looking out over a vast plain in the shadow of the huge god whose wings obscured the sun. She could see dragons over the plain. These ones did not have wings like the one over the forest. They looked like armoured, ridged, flying slugs, with fire in their rears. A hard, thick, dark rain fell from them, and where it landed the plain died as though diseased, and new land grew. The new land looked like hardened tree sap. Occasionally lightning would arc up from the land, always answered by gouts of white flame.

Tangwen stumbled out of the back of the open chariot. Teardrop was out next. He was carrying the case that bore Fachtna's screaming spear of the sun. He made for the outcrop, and started climbing up it. Britha climbed out next, the metal armour unfolding all around her, her helm also shaped like a raven. She was carrying a strange-looking spear. Finally Raven's Laughter climbed out and thrust a large, strange, and very ornate bow into Tangwen's hands. It looked like a bow fit for a god.

'Now listen to me. If you can see them, you can hit them, but don't draw attention to us. Only use it if you're sure they are going to attack. Aim at what you want to hit, not above it, the arrows won't drop. Understand?' the Croatan woman asked. Tangwen most certainly didn't, again, but she could do what Raven's Laughter asked, so she nodded. The Croatan woman did not look convinced, but handed her a quiver of thick-shafted arrows. 'It can also call and guide the lightning ... but you probably don't want to worry about that. There is a spirit bound into the bow. If you let it, the bow will teach you how to use it best.'

'What happens now?' Tangwen asked. 'The stones. You open a trod?' Raven's Laughter looked up into the sky, through the spears of light and the fire, towards the sun that was too large, felt too close, and the god that obscured its light.

'We don't have a control rod. It is with him now.' She nodded towards the sun. 'Look!' The Croatan woman pointed over the plain. Four of the slug-like dragons were turning towards the canyon. Tangwen was aware of light shining through the earth from below the stones. The air felt like it did before storms swept in from the sea over the marshes at home. She jumped when the spear started screaming. Teardrop was knelt on the outcrop. He had opened the case, the spear's fire reflecting in his shining raven armour. Raven's Laughter was reaching into the back of the chariot and pulling out another bow. The moment she had it the rear of the vehicle sealed itself, and the chariot, of its own accord, flew out over the diseased plain. Lightning shot up from the earth into the chariot in a constant stream. The vehicle started to glow, and then a thick stream of lightning-wreathed light shot out from the front of it. The light pierced the flesh of one of the slugs, went straight through it like a spear shoved through flesh. Smoking, the slug-like dragon started to fall from the sky. Flame lit up the twilight, burning the chariot as it banked hard and fled the breath of the three remaining dragons.

'Tangwen!' Raven's Laughter shouted. She had one of the thickly-shafted arrows notched. Tangwen did the same thing. Teardrop threw the screaming spear, it left a path of flame over the plain. Tangwen pulled the bowstring back to her cheek. The bow had no pull, the heavy arrow would fly little distance if at all. Then she heard the whispering in her mind, the spirit of the bow, eager for the hunt. She flinched as symbols of light appeared in her vision with promise of where the arrow would hit her prey, the whispering describing how to slay a dragon. *Give in to fear and you will die here. You know how to hunt,* she told herself, and suddenly the unfamiliar bow didn't feel all that unfamiliar. This she knew. This she understood. She listened to the whispers. She listened to herself. She held her breath. The screaming, the flames, all of it went away. It was a perfect moment of calm. She loosed. Then she breathed.

The slug-like dragon was as far away as a trader's ship close to the horizon back home. Once she had loosed she knew that the arrow could not hit, but the arrow flew from the bow so quickly it seemed to disappear. Things were happening to the other two remaining dragons, but she remained focused on her own. There was a gout of what looked like liquid metal from a forge on the dragon's hide. Then it lurched in the air. Then it was as though a white sun had burst from inside it, and smoking lumps of flesh rained down on the plain. There was another white sun, and another of the dragons was gone. The fourth one was lit from inside by fire as it too fell smoking from the sky. The screaming spear burst out of it, making its way back towards Teardrop. Once the weapon had terrified her. Now, in the face of the dragons, it seemed reasonable.

The stones in the circle behind her were glowing from within, lighting up the strange symbols inscribed on the rock. Lightning jumped between them.

A pale amber light sprang up around her, and then she was surrounded in white, liquid flame. She had no idea what was happening. She went down on one knee as though the fire had weight. The flame receded, though the surrounding rocks had turned into still burning molten pools. Britha was kneeling down as well; the metal of her armour looked partially melted. The boots of the armour were eating into the rock, and it started to heal itself in the way that metal shouldn't be able to. A winged dragon curved over them and came to a stop in the sky in front of Teardrop. The Croatan warrior's hand was outstretched, waiting for the screaming spear to return, thunder echoing over the plain as the weapon sped back to him. Tangwen reached for another arrow.

'Tang ...!' Tangwen turned to see Raven's Laughter wreathed in the amber light as a much smaller gout of the white liquid flame hit her. The serpents were running down the canyon walls. They wore what looked like armour made of living flesh. Some carried long, barbed-looking spears, others strange weapons that she only recognised as such because of the way the walking snakes carried them, and then because they belched the liquid fire. Despite the armour she recognised their shape. There were differences but underneath the living armour she knew they would look like her Father.

She thought of the lightning. She listened to the whispers of the spirit in the bow. Lightning leapt from the ground, from the stones, to the bow. She pulled the bowstring, lightning became an arrow, and she loosed, and she loosed, and she loosed again, and her Father's people fell from the canyon wall. In her periphery the dragon breathed. Teardrop was engulfed in the constant stream of fire, molten rock shot up into the air. A hand reached out of the stream of liquid flame. He caught the returning spear. The amber light surrounded Tangwen again and the lightning died, as some of the remaining Naga warriors used their weapons on her. She turned, protected by the fair folk's magic. She could make out Teardrop, a silhouette in the flames as he threw the spear into the dragon's maw. As the amber light faded the lightning returned to her bow. Tangwen felt another change in the atmosphere. She turned to see a circle of blue light contained within the glowing stones, and in that circle a blood-red land. She was aware of the dragon drifting away from the outcrop, burning inside, slowly dropping towards the floor of the plain far below. She was aware of Teardrop's smoking, blackened body as it fell from the now molten outcrop to hit the ground.

Raven's Laughter glanced behind at the body and then continued firing lightning from her bow as she moved towards Britha. The raven-headed *dryw* was fighting like a demon. One arm was held high, the glowing spear in her metal fist bearing an impaled Naga warrior on the end of it. She was crushing another's head with her armoured fist, as a third charged her. She flung the impaled Naga off her spear. Light sprang from the weapon's tip and pierced the charging serpent straight through. Tangwen loosed, and another Naga warrior fell.

'Go!' Raven's Laughter shouted. Then the amber light was again protecting her from the fire weapons. Tangwen loosed again, and again, killing those attacking the Croatan woman.

'Tangwen first!' Britha shouted.

Fool! Tangwen thought. Raven's Laughter was growing spines through her flesh. There were too many of the Naga. Britha suddenly sank to her knees, gripping her head. Screaming, though it sounded wrong through the armour, like the ringing of metal. Britha held out an open hand, and suddenly her fingers were curling around the haft of the burning, screaming spear. Tangwen saw Raven's Laughter unclip the strange metal object which provided her shield from her belt, attach it to Britha's armour, and then push the Pecht *dryw* towards the circle.

'Go! Or this is for nothing!' Raven's Laughter screamed. There were Naga caught in the lightning around the stone circle. Britha stumbled between the stones and into the blue fire and fell into the red world, surely Cythrawl, Tangwen thought. *Good.* The blue fire disappeared and with it the red world, leaving an afterglow in her eyes.

Tangwen loosed lightning at a Naga charging Raven's Laughter, and it fell. The Croatan woman leapt over a spear thrust, and landed on the serpent wielding the weapon. Frenzied axe and blade blows bit through armour and into snake flesh.

Tangwen loosed lightning into a Naga warrior that had almost reached her, leaving its face a smoking hole. She dropped her bow, and grabbed her hatchet and dagger. Amber light surrounded her, the spear thrust sent her tumbling backwards, then everything was fire again. She rolled over but was struggling to get up. The protective magics didn't quite let her touch the ground. She managed to stand and ran through the flame. The stones were glowing, smoking, trembling. Above them the sun flickered like a burning brand in the wind. The amber light disappeared. There was a warrior in front of her. She rammed her chalice-re-forged dagger into its head, forcing it to the ground. She side-stepped a low spear thrust, stepped onto a non-barbed part of the weapon's haft, and launched herself into the air. She kneed the spear-wielding serpent in the bottom of its jutting, helmeted maw as she brought the axe down into its head with a satisfying, echoing crunch, spraying herself in its surprisingly red blood.

In the air she saw Raven's Laughter's barbs shoot from her flesh, impaling the surrounding Naga warriors. Almost immediately their living armour started to rot, they staggered and fell. Tangwen landed and rolled forwards under a spear-thrust. She pushed the barbed weapon away from her with the blade of her dagger, and swung the hatchet into the Naga's neck as she rolled to her feet. The blue flame illuminated the glowing stones again. She felt warm sunlight on her skin. She could see a green land through the trod, in the circle of stones. She ran. The chariot was in the air again, taking lightning from the earth and raining it down on the Naga. The rotted Naga killed by Raven's Laughter's spines were climbing to their feet, turning on the other snakes. Raven's Laughter tumbled sideways, fire burning the rock where she had been standing. Tangwen pulled the strange metal object from her belt, and leapt for the green promise in the circle of stones. Tangwen threw the magical shield towards Raven's Laughter as she flew over the circle of blue fire, and closed her eyes.

She hit the ground hard enough to have the wind knocked from her. Then she thought of the life she carried within her, her hand involuntarily moving towards her stomach. She felt the warmth of the sun on her skin, grass against her cheek. Tangwen opened her eyes. She was lying in a circle of stones that she did not recognise, under a clear blue sky. The air felt like it did just after a summer storm.

The chariot and the Naga *Tei-Pai-Wanka* that she had enslaved when her spines had infected them with disease finished off the rest of the snakes. Raven's Laughter went to stand over the blackened body of her husband, fused with his armour. The chariot came down to hover close to the crumbling stones in the now useless circle, the rear of the cupola splitting open. Raven's Laughter burst into tears.

The chariot had flown across the burning Riverlands, taking Teardrop-on-Fire home for the last time. Raven's Laughter had carried him from the chariot and into their home, the children and Oliver, all armed and armoured, watching her as she laid him down. Her eyes were red but no longer wet. The children, and even Oliver, were sobbing. They could only be allowed to do so for so long. It was clear the Ubh Blaosc was lost. She had flown over the diseased sourland that the Naga were creating, but this was their home, you had to protect your home, and she had seen the shadowy forms of the serpents close by.

41
Now

The clone had strayed too close to C&C. Yaroslav had been terrified, Lodup had seen it on his face, but the Russian security chief
had risked leaving C&C to snatch the clone and bring him back.
Lodup had recognised him, or rather who he was a clone of,
vaguely. A Danish diver he had worked with on oil platforms off
the coast of California. The clone stared blankly up as Yaroslav
slowly beat him to death, a grin on the Russian's blood-spattered
face. Lodup was curled up in a ball close to where the pole that
Germelqart's head was mounted on had grown into the floor.
He flinched with every blow, but he supposed it was the first
time that Yaroslav had felt in control for a very long time. Lodup
closed his eyes. Thought about killing Yaroslav, and not for the
first time. Some of it was fear, but some of it was pity. He wanted
to put the Russian security chief out of his misery. He was too
frightened to act, and after all the clone wasn't human any more,
if it ever had been. Just another hollowed out, flesh satellite of
the city. Also he couldn't be sure how Siska, now little more
than a brooding, predatory presence in her corner, would react.
Instead he closed his eyes, and tried to find a pattern in the muttered nonsense spouting from Germelqart's severed head.

'It's not a city,' the severed head managed in halting English, as
if it were a language freshly learned, as if he was talking through
a great deal of pain.

'What?' Lodup whispered back.

'It is an apparatus, a tool.'

'What for?' Lodup couldn't believe what he was hearing,
though he had no idea who he was talking to: a lingering fragment of Germelqart's psyche, Lidakika, or some other fragmented
mind, even Siraja, the habitat's corrupted AI. It could just be a
cruel trick.

'Transmission. A huge machine used to focus the minds of the

Seeders, one of many across the universe. It was used to help build the red realm when Earth was but cooling chunks of molten rock. It was meant for ascension. To leave the flesh behind ...'

'What are you doing?' Siska came stalking out of her corner, her long unbound hair obscuring her face, reminding Lodup of the *Yūrei*, the vengeful spirits of Japanese folklore.

'Nothing,' he said. Not quite willing to look up in case he saw more of the serpent in her than he wished to. He tried to push himself further into the wall.

'Don't speak to it. It talks for the city now. It will drive you mad.'

Lodup wanted to laugh. He just wasn't sure that he could stop if he started.

It looked like the conn of a normal submarine, but there was no crew, which gave it a somewhat haunted feel. An AI piloted the vessel. Du Bois was thankful for the L-tech-derived machine mind's discretion. Most of the AIs he had ever come into contact with had been quirky, to put it mildly, and he wasn't in the mood. Thankfully his arms didn't ache from covering King Jeremy; his augmented physiology had taken into account that he was going to be locked in this position for a significant amount of time and had made allowances for it.

'Well, this is nice,' Mr Brown said. 'Though a little tense. Could I offer anyone some refreshment, or are we all too macho for that?' He had replenished the drip bags full of synthetic morphine hanging from his T-shaped staff. The Pennangalan, her featureless silver mask covering her face, carbine in hand, remained by her master's side. King Jeremy was staring at du Bois with a look of utter hatred. 'I am interested to know what you are going to do when we get there. Assuming that we're not killed out of hand.'

'The same thing you are,' du Bois said.

'Which is?' Mr Brown asked.

'Leave. Nothing has changed,' du Bois said. 'If we can't get out, then you can't get out. Who knows, a nuclear explosion in Kanamwayso might be good for everyone.'

Mr Brown started laughing. 'You've always been an amusing fellow, Malcolm. Your naiveté is only outweighed by your childish sense of *noblesse oblige*. Strange qualities for an assassin and mass murderer, don't you think?'

'Why don't you shut up?' Alexia suggested. She was leaning against the bulkhead, smoking a cigarette. She seemed to have recovered a little from the chase, and all the violence. Du Bois was used to his sister looking glamorous, though he'd picked her up off the floor after her indulgences had really got her into trouble a few times, and she hadn't looked quite so good then. Now, however, she looked haggard, as if the last few days had aged her. 'It's been a long, shitty day in a very difficult week. Nobody's happy about the situation, so let's deal with it as best we can, but let's deal with it quietly.'

'See, you look rapeable, but I think you're some kind of freak, aren't you?' King Jeremy said.

'Oh, for goodness' sake,' Alexia muttered. Beth just shook her head a little. Du Bois would have quite liked to have pulled the trigger there and then. 'I suppose that pistol whipping is out of the question?' she asked her brother.

'He does have his thumb on the dead man's switch of a nuclear weapon,' du Bois pointed out.

'It's just one ridiculous cock substitution after another with you boys, isn't it?' Alexia asked. Once the comment would have angered du Bois. Now he had to smile.

'Seriously now,' du Bois told King Jeremy. 'Please just be quiet.'

'And she's too ugly,' King Jeremy said, nodding towards Beth.

'Thank God,' Beth muttered. 'Maybe you should have a look under the silver mask,' she suggested. King Jeremy glanced back at the Pennangalan, who didn't react in any way. There was just a moment of unease on the boy's face, and then his mask of spite was back.

'You're going to pay for what you did to Dracimus,' he spat.

'You mean young Mr Elling?' du Bois asked. 'You're incapable of empathy, so don't pretend you care about what happened to him.'

'By the way, Inflictor ... stupid name, what was he really called?' Beth asked.

'Kyle Nethercott,' du Bois supplied, 'and this here is young Mr Weldon Rush.'

'Don't call me that!' King Jeremy demanded.

'It's just your name, darling,' Alexia said.

'And I don't think you understand,' Beth said. 'You're not in control here.'

'I have a nuclear bomb!'

'And yet you're somehow still inadequate, but well done, very Dr Strangelove,' Alexia said.

'I should point out that Mr Rush may actually be unstable enough to take his thumb off the dead man's switch if you continue mocking him,' Mr Brown said, though he sounded more resigned than nervous.

'Why don't you control your ugly bitches?' King Jeremy asked du Bois, grinning maliciously.

'Well, this is terribly constructive. There's nothing like having priorities,' Mr Brown observed.

'Why don't you control us?' Beth suggested to King Jeremy. 'Pass the dead man's switch off to a responsible adult ...'

'I'll hold it for you,' Mr Brown offered.

'I'll make them both fucking suffer, you can watch, see a prodigious imagination at work—' began King Jeremy.

'Weldon,' du Bois said. He was more profoundly depressed at the state of today's youth than seriously angry. 'You're not a comic book villain, you're just an angry young man. I'm sorry that your comfortable middle class upbringing in one of the wealthiest nations on the planet was hard. I am sorry you felt like an outsider, or were bullied, alienated, had cruel or unfeeling parents, I really am, but you have to see, for your own sake, that there are more constructive ways of handling it than becoming an entitled little sociopath. I know you think that these threats sound horrific and frightening, but to us they just sound like you waving around all your insecurities.' The expression of malice on the boy's handsomely sculpted face faltered for a moment. It would have been funny if it hadn't been so heartbreakingly pathetic the way he looked to Mr Brown for reassurance. Mr Brown's expression was sympathetic, but he was nodding in agreement with du Bois. Then the mask of malice was back and du Bois knew that he had barely made a dent.

'Fuck you and your whores,' King Jeremy spat.

'I'm his sister, you little freak,' Alexia said in disgust.

Beth leant in closer to him, though still keeping him covered. Du Bois was pleased to see that her finger was back around the trigger guard and not the trigger itself, however. 'There's something I've always wanted to ask people like you,' she told him. 'What are you so afraid of?'

It was clear he didn't have an answer. Or if he did he didn't want to share it.

'So nobody wants tea then?' Mr Brown asked.

Du Bois wasn't sure what it was, some change in the background noise, but he knew they were within the borders of the city. He was aware of it at a primal level, a mounting fear. He was pleased he could not see beyond the sub, any external views having been mercifully switched off. He could see his own fear reflected more openly on King Jeremy's face. He suspected it was only due to extensive augmentation that the boy was able to cope with having weapons pointed at him, let alone deal with the city. It was a place that you needed brain surgery to work in. He half expected King Jeremy to panic, and then all this would end in a bright flash of light. He had only ever visited Kanamwayso once before. Just before the Boxer Rebellion. He hadn't liked it then. It would be infinitely worse now the Seeders had awoken.

The sub moved quickly, far faster than a conventional sub, which unfortunately made them noisy in the water, but they had still been locked in the same position for the better part of three days. All of them were more than capable of it physically, but it would still take a toll on their bodies. It was just fortunate that they had near perfect control of their bodily functions.

He had reviewed what he knew of the evacuation craft, the spayed seedpods of the once-slumbering alien intellects that inhabited the sunken city. Each of them could effectively act as a colonisation ship. There were millions of frozen embryos, vast stores of human, Seeder, and what they knew of Lloigor knowledge. They were equipped with a great deal of the tech, certainly enough to start assembling what they would need if they could find the raw materials. Du Bois was sure that he could work out a way of dumping all the slave minds that Mr Brown had uploaded, and all the evil greedy bastards that he had recruited, and replace them with the minds that Hamad had stolen and Azmodeus had rediscovered. All that was missing was Talia's genetic material to run the ship's biomechanical navigation systems. King Jeremy had the sample of genetic material. After nearly three days of thinking on this du Bois was still no closer to solving the problem.

'So this is your plan?' du Bois asked Mr Brown. 'Just have the sub take us there?'

'Did you think I would have a password? They are alien, in the true sense of the word. Alien as any god. I personally think that you're too small to worry about. They are possibly aware of humanity, on some level, like you are aware of a fungal infection, but your destruction was little more than a spasmodic reflex action. Your problem in this, as it is in your defiance of me, is hubris. You desperately want to matter. You don't.'

Alexia laughed.

'Calm down,' Beth said. 'We only wanted to know if you had a plan.' He was both impressed with and grateful to his sister and Beth. This was his world, a twisted and perverse version of it in some ways, or perhaps just a more honest version, but both of them were handling it. They might not have been as inured to the violence as he was, but he knew he could trust them. Though he suspected neither of them would struggle to kill King Jeremy, or mourn for Mr Brown if it came down to it.

'There's nothing certain here,' Mr Brown told them.

Something scraped against the hull. King Jeremy screamed, and du Bois didn't like the way the boy's thumb slipped a little on the switch. Alexia came off the bulkhead like she had been electrocuted. Beth flinched. Du Bois felt his sphincter tighten.

Mr Brown was just smiling. 'Would you like to see?' he asked. 'It must be extraordinary.' Du Bois nodded towards the boy. Under the best of circumstances it could drive someone like King Jeremy over the edge. This wasn't the best of circumstances. 'You're quite right of course.'

Somehow a nuclear explosion was starting to seem like the easy way out. Something else brushed against the sub. Something about the contact reminded du Bois of an unwelcome caress.

Du Bois climbed out of the hatch and onto the bridge of the modified Virginia-class sub's sail. He had clambered up the ladder one-handed, his Accursed .45, with the magazine of nanite-tipped bullets in it, pointing down at King Jeremy who was out next. He couldn't risk looking around, not yet, but his peripheral vision was telling him that something was very off in the huge moon pool. The moon pool was part of the underwater habitat that the Circle had used as a base of operations to plunder the S-tech from Kanamwayso, the city of gods, the name they had given to the petrified city. The name had been taken from Pohnpeian mythology.

'Come on, out of there,' he snapped. He felt vulnerable now and didn't like it.

'It's hard. I've only got one hand,' King Jeremy whined. Du Bois had to resist the quite strong urge to slap the boy. Beth was out next, covering King Jeremy, then Alexia, who initially seemed eager to get out of the sub, and then less so as she looked around, appalled.

'Jesus Christ,' his sister said.

'Keep him covered,' du Bois said. Beth nodded. He looked around.

'Normally the *Victoria* doesn't dock here, it's too busy, and we had to raise the habitat to do so, but that's less of an issue now,' Mr Brown said as he climbed after them with fresh morphine drips attached to his staff.

They had pushed up a number of the pontoon jetties in the huge open moon pool as they had surfaced. The *Victoria*, as the submarine seemed to be called, was now wearing the pontoons around her hull like a necklace. The light was flickering but his vision was compensating for it. Above him the rotary weapons systems looked rotted. The submersibles, the robot-like atmospheric diving suits, were all twisted and warped, as if things had grown out of their matter and pulled their way clear. On one of the larger submersibles something had grown from the condensed adamantine hull, a stillborn monster frozen in amber.

On one of the walls a tall, thin man had been crucified. Spikes had grown from the habitat's hull through his wrists, and his side. His left hand was missing. Crabs were eating his legs and lower torso, leaving the rest of his body alone. The crabs looked wrong somehow, they were albino, had never seen the sun, but they were too large for this depth and shouldn't have been able to walk up walls.

On the bulkhead above the crucified man, the words: *I died for your fucking sins* had been written in a thick smear of blood. *Your fucking sins* had been crossed out and replaced with the words: *nothing at all.*

'Is that Deane?' du Bois asked, more for something to say than anything else. He knew it was. Mr Brown nodded anyway. Deane had been the dive supervisor in the habitat.

They could feel the spore-like nanites of the city testing their own blood-screens which all of them, bar Mr Brown, had refreshed before leaving the sub. His skin was itching like mad. It felt badly inflamed.

'How far underwater are we?' Beth asked in a small voice.

'Some four thousand metres,' Mr Brown said cheerfully. 'A little under three miles of water over our heads, or four hundred atmospheres if you prefer. That is to say that the pressure down here is four hundred times what it is on the surface.'

'I don't feel that much different,' Beth said, glancing around at their surroundings, obviously less than happy.

'Your body is adapting to it,' du Bois said. 'The nanites are scrubbing the nitrogen build up, your lungs are modifying to breathe the gas and deal with oxygen toxicity, your joints are being reinforced ...'

'Not to mention modifying your larynx so you don't sound like a cartoon character,' Mr Brown added. 'Though you'll not be as suited for operations here as the crew were.'

'Where's the Pennangalan?' du Bois suddenly demanded.

'Ah,' said Mr Brown. 'You noticed.'

'Of course I fucking noticed,' du Bois snapped. 'Alexia, keep watch.' His sister nodded, her ARX-170 rifle at the ready.

'Malcolm, you need to remain calm—' Mr Brown started.

'You need to tell me where she is, right now,' du Bois said. Something loped out of the hatch. Alexia swung round, her rifle coming up to her shoulder. Beth's pistol wavered for a moment, as she almost took it off King Jeremy and pointed it at the thing. Du Bois was similarly tempted. At first he had thought it was a large, pale greyhound, except that greyhounds can't climb submarine ladders. Then he realised it was a broadly human form, but sexless, emaciated, with chalk-white skin, its physiology modified to better enable it to move on all four of its spindly limbs. Its face seemed vaguely familiar. It went to Mr Brown's side and nuzzled against him. Du Bois looked up at his ex-employer as the Pennangalan finally climbed out of the hatch.

'What's wrong with you?' du Bois asked.

'His name is Silas,' Mr Brown said, smiling, patting the creature that seemed eager for his attention. 'Yes it is, yes it is!'

'Silas Scab? The clockmaker?' du Bois asked. He had killed him. A Swiss child murderer who'd had access to the tech somehow, though he hadn't been affiliated with the Circle or the City of Brass.

'His son,' Mr Brown said impatiently.

'Azmodeus mentioned him, so did Inflictor ... Nethercott. He said he had freed him,' Beth said. Mr Brown turned to look at King Jeremy.

'I didn't know anything about that,' King Jeremy said, shaking his head.

'What's it doing here?' du Bois demanded, his voice tight. Even King Jeremy looked disgusted.

'He contains genetic material that I am interested in. I didn't reveal him, well more *it* really, earlier because I knew it would upset you.'

'What do you want with his DNA?' du Bois asked.

Mr Brown sighed. 'Does it really matter right now?'

'Malcolm!' Alexia said sharply. She had her rifle trained on a figure standing in one of the corners. A female, blonde hair tied back, wearing a ragged beige coverall. Her eyes were completely black.

'One of the clones,' Mr Brown told them. 'I think you can probably assume that she is controlled by whatever minds control the city.'

'Is she a threat?' Alexia asked. Mr Brown laughed.

'The window,' Beth said. She nodded towards the oval window that looked out from C&C over the moon pool. Du Bois recognised Siska. The Pennangalan's sister, though rumour had it that they could both lay claim to that title. Her hair covered most of her face. It had only been a quick glance, but du Bois was pretty sure that under the hair something was wrong. He had worked with her closely, very closely, in Sumatra and the South Seas during the late eighteenth century. He hoped he didn't have to kill her.

'I go down first,' du Bois told King Jeremy. 'Don't slip, you don't want to fall into that water.' The boy swallowed and then nodded.

'You fucking bastard!' Lodup Satakano shouted at him as soon as they moved into Command and Control. The room stank, it seemed that the habitat's recycling had ceased to work. The Mwoakilloan salvage diver looked ill-used, gaunt, wide eyed. Du Bois could understand his anger.

He recognised Piotr Yaroslav, he had been a *Rota Osobogo Naznacheniya* combat diver during the war. Du Bois had helped recruit him after they had worked together hunting SS Werewolf units that had gained access to stolen S-tech. He was not sure about the security chief's new steroid abuser physique, however.

Siska looked worse closer up. There was something wrong

with her skin, and he was pretty sure he didn't want to see her eyes right now.

'Malcolm,' she said as he entered.

'Can you get us out of here?' Lodup demanded. 'My family ...'

'Your family are gone,' Yaroslav snapped, and then raised his futuristic-looking Vector SMG to his shoulder when Silas bounded into the room. 'What the fuck is that?'

'No, you see my family didn't have much in the way of phones and computers, internet access ...' Lodup started.

Du Bois didn't have the heart to tell him that Mwoakilloa and Pohnpei were among some of the first places that the spores would have reached. If his family were lucky they were dead, if not then they weren't his family any more.

'He is mine, Piotr,' Mr Brown said as he walked into Command & Control. Yaroslav screamed and cowered, backing away from Mr Brown. Du Bois hadn't been expecting that. The man had seen some of the worst excesses that the Eastern Front had to offer. He was no coward. His fear of Mr Brown, however, looked almost religious in nature. What had happened to them? It was obvious they had been there for a while. He looked at the remains of their meals, empty water containers, the partially absorbed sewage they had seen running down the stairs. It made sense. The Seeders here would have started to awake from their slumber at the same time the one in the Solent had. There was a body lying on the floor, the carpet-like grass analogue growing into and around it. The body had the same black eyes as the woman they had seen in the moon pool. One of the clones. He had been beaten to death.

Lodup took a step back from Mr Brown as well, presumably somewhat cowed by Yaroslav's reaction. The big Russian was hiding under the elliptical hardwood table on the raised area, just in front of the oval window. Silas was trying to lick the Russian's face.

'Who are you?' Lodup demanded. 'Why are they pointing guns at that guy? And why's he dressed like that?' King Jeremy was still wearing his post-apocalyptic gear. He looked even more foolish down here. Mr Brown ignored him. Instead he was looking around, and what he saw didn't seem to please him.

Siska rushed over to the Pennangalan, and embraced her silver-masked sister. Du Bois's enhanced hearing picked out the hissing quality to Siska's whispered Khmer.

Mr Brown's gaze had come to rest on a spot on the wall, an expression of disgust on his face.

'What the fuck is that?' Alexia demanded, the butt of her rifle against her shoulder, half raised. Du Bois risked taking his eyes off King Jeremy for a moment. It was a severed head. A middle-aged man he didn't recognise, slightly chubby face, goatee beard, his swarthy skin suggesting a Mediterranean heritage perhaps. The head was impaled on an organic-looking staff, and there were strange organs where the staff met the head. Some of them were inflating and deflating like lungs, another he suspected was some kind of larynx, the rest of them he didn't recognise. They didn't look human. Dreadlock-like tendrils of flesh grew through his white-streaked black hair, connecting him to the wall, where the semi-intelligent, condensed adamantine matter had taken on a partly flesh-like appearance.

'No, no, no, no,' Mr Brown said, shaking his head. Both Silas and Yaroslav made a whimpering noise. 'This will not do.' Mr Brown walked across C&C to the severed head. Both Beth and du Bois shuffled round, looking between King Jeremy, who they were still covering, and his ex-boss. The severed head on the pole looked up at Mr Brown. Du Bois didn't see fear in the eyes. He saw pity.

'I'm sorry,' the head on the pole said. Mr Brown nodded as though he understood. Then he tore the head off the pole and crushed it with his bare hands.

'No!' Lodup shouted, reaching for one of the Vector sub-machine guns. Du Bois grimaced, Beth flinched but neither of them shifted their aim from King Jeremy. Yaroslav continued whimpering and Silas licked his face some more, Alexia turned away, Siska just watched. Before Lodup could bring the SMG to his shoulder the Pennangalan's Sig 716 carbine was levelled at the salvage diver's head.

'She'll kill you. Lower the weapon,' du Bois warned him.

'What the fuck is going on? Who are these people?' Lodup demanded.

'He's your boss,' Siska hissed. 'We work for him.' Mr Brown turned slowly to look at Lodup.

Du Bois found himself taking a step away. The expression on the obsidian-skinned 'man's' face had gone beyond malevolent. His skin seemed to twitch with a life of its own. It wasn't a human face, not any more, if it ever had been.

'May I remind you, Mr Satakano, that man betrayed all of us,' Mr Brown said, presumably meaning the owner of the severed head. His erstwhile employer gestured all around. 'He must bear responsibility for much of the misfortune that we are now beset by. We must, however, find a new interface. Communication is so important, don't you think?'

Lodup was staring at Mr Brown. Then his eyes went wide. He opened his mouth to scream. Something complicated happened in the air between Lodup and Mr Brown. Lodup's head fell off, and dropped to the grass-like carpet.

'No!' Siska cried. She had her Sig P220 pistols in each hand now, but she couldn't seem to bring herself to point them at Mr Brown. The Pennangalan moved away from her sister, her featureless mask of beaten silver looking between Siska and Mr Brown. Du Bois tightened his grip on the .45, but still didn't dare move it from King Jeremy. He could tell that the boy was only just starting to realise how out of his depth he was. Du Bois wasn't quite sure how Mr Brown could do what he could do, but one thing was clear to him: they were only alive because Mr Brown wasn't entirely sure he could stop du Bois and/or Beth from pulling the trigger, and then survive the resulting nuclear explosion. Du Bois nearly pulled the trigger. Despite everything else that was going on, it was clear that Mr Brown was an abomination. He couldn't be allowed to live, to spread his corruption beyond Earth, but du Bois wanted to live. Right there and then du Bois understood just how much of a coward he was.

'No more,' du Bois managed. He saw his terrified sister glance over at him. He didn't think she had liked the fear she had heard in his voice. Mr Brown ignored him and picked up Lodup's head. He walked back to the pole. There was a crunch as he impaled the head. The tendrils that had connected the previous severed head to the wall of the habitat were waving around like the tentacles of a sea anemone. Wet sounds came from the pole as it grew up through Lodup's neck stump. Eyes rolled down, and there was awareness. The strange organs started to work again. The mouth opened and closed but made no sound. Du Bois flinched at more crunching noises as tendrils pierced the back of Lodup's skull.

'You used to have the stomach to do what was required, Malcolm,' Mr Brown muttered, distracted. 'This is where your actions have led you. Take responsibility.'

'You have come for our murdered children? The ones whose

corpses you mutilated?' The severed head spoke with a multitude of voices.

Yaroslav was repeating one line of a Russian nursery rhyme over and over again. A tear rolled down King Jeremy's cheek.

'Yes,' Mr Brown said brusquely, the drip bags of synthetic morphine nearly empty. 'What is required? A sacrifice?'

'What if we ask for a first edition of Borges's *Manual de zoología fantástica*, a left-handed rubber glove with six fingers, the foreskin of Christ, the second season of *Studio 60 on the Sunset Strip*, Tantalus's tantalus?'

'I'm afraid I have limited resources at this moment,' Mr Brown said impatiently. 'I can offer you a beautiful hermaphrodite.'

'That's not going to happen,' du Bois told him. The severed head's eyes moved unnaturally in their sockets to look at du Bois.

'Come to terms with what you want to achieve here,' Mr Brown told du Bois without looking at him. He could feel his sister's eyes on him.

'One of us gets hurt, everyone dies,' du Bois told him.

Lodup's severed head spoke again, but this time it was in the Mwoakilloan's own voice. 'What if we asked for you?' he said to Mr Brown.

'You're too late. I have already been laid out on a stone altar in this town. What if I offered contact?' There was silence. Du Bois remembered what Azmodeus had told him. The contact that had broken Mr Brown's mind and driven the Seeders mad.

'You will go unnoticed,' the head finally said in a multitude of voices.

Mr Brown nodded. Then he turned to du Bois. 'And your sacrifice?' Du Bois had the sense of the steel teeth of a trap closing around him.

'What?' du Bois asked. Beth glanced at him and then quickly back to King Jeremy.

'The S-tech in your bodies can adapt the younger Miss Luckwicke's DNA, accept it, allow it to replicate, but the resulting mutations will almost certainly be lethal. Which one of you is to die in agony? Is this why you brought the elder Miss Luckwicke along? To turn her into her sister? Or perhaps the brother you always considered to be a perverse abomination against your non-existent god?' Mr Brown asked.

Now Beth and Alexia were both staring at him.

'What's he talking about?' Beth demanded. She was no longer looking at King Jeremy.

'We can use one of the clones in the seed ships,' du Bois said. He knew he was clutching at straws. Mr Brown was already shaking his head.

'It would be a convenient murder, I grant you, but you don't have the time to bring one to maturity,' he told them.

'You're not turning me into my sister,' Beth said. Du Bois was pretty sure she was close to turning her gun on him.

'You never said anything about this,' King Jeremy said.

'It's very simple, Mr Rush, you take one of the sisters and I take the other,' Mr Brown said. The Pennangalan looked up at him sharply.

'No ... !' Siska shouted.

'Quiet!' Mr Brown snapped. Du Bois heard the authority in his voice. He felt it. Even he wanted to obey.

'Me,' du Bois said. 'I'm the sacrifice.'

'Malcolm ...' Alexia started.

'Please, let's get this done,' du Bois said. He wanted the tension to end, one way or another.

'What about him?' Beth asked, nodding towards Yaroslav. Du Bois could tell that she hadn't wanted to make the suggestion.

'His mind is near gone,' Mr Brown said. 'By all means hook up a madman to one of the seed ships. I should be interested in the results. If you have the slightest trace of common decency in you, you'll put a bullet in his head.'

'Piotr?' du Bois asked. The Russian just shook his head. 'Piotr, please, we're leaving this place.' He spoke gently, in Russian. Yaroslav continued shaking his head.

'I don't want to become something else,' the Russian begged.

'We're not going to do anything to you. You'll be safe with us. Please, Piotr, we need you to get up.' Du Bois tried to ignore the sound of Silas licking the Russian's face. The Pennangalan turned and walked out of C&C.

'Where's she going?' Beth demanded. Mr Brown turned to look at the Yorkshirewoman.

'Show some sympathy. She has just learned that she is going to die. She has gone to compose herself, but she will return. She is a good servant.'

*

Du Bois wanted to squeeze his eyes shut, and not see what he was seeing. The vast, labyrinthine city was so much larger than the last time he had been here. Living sepulchres, city-sized ziggurats and pyramids. Every angle just wrong enough to induce nausea, every angle leading to somewhere unseen. The twisted multi-storey bridges, made for huge and non-human physiologies, ran between structures grown for un-guessable purposes. The city had roots. It grew like an infection: a saprophyte urban sprawl. It crawled with warped life, but the armoured, multi-limbed, wedge-headed servitors, and the increasingly piscine-looking clones, were little more than cells in a vast organism. And among this urban infection they caught glimpses of the Seeders, though they could feel their presence pushing on their own membranous minds. Vast shadows, all unmistakably life, but so different to anything they really understood. The Seeders' physiology existed in other places. Their armoured, biomechanical flesh the result of an evolutionary process violated by pain and madness. Each showing some warped elements of the templates of rudimentary biological life.

Du Bois's mind wanted to shatter like so much brittle glass. He kept his eyes on the near-hysterical King Jeremy, but he was aware of all of this in his periphery. He cursed the technology that augmented his senses, and found himself wishing for blindness and a rude, dumb intelligence.

Yaroslav was curled up in a ball in the only working submersible they could find, water slowly rising around him. He was clutching the Vector SMG like a child clutching a teddy bear. Du Bois knew he would have to do something about removing the weapon from the Russian, but right now he just wanted this over with. He wanted to be somewhere else.

Alexia was leaning against the leaking submersible's bulkhead, her eyes squeezed shut in a way that made du Bois envious. King Jeremy was making whimpering noises as he sobbed. The submersible piloted itself. It knew its way through the twisted geometry of the city's living architecture. It moved like a wounded fish. Its superstructure was badly warped from where something had tried to grow out of it.

The submersible had been accompanied by something that looked like a cybernetic whale for part of the journey. Its battleship-armoured body was covered in living eyes watching their vehicle.

Mr Brown had stayed in C&C. After all, the threat stayed the same. If du Bois took the DNA sample, then King Jeremy detonated the nuke. If King Jeremy double-crossed them, or Mr Brown interfered, then Beth and du Bois shot King Jeremy, and the nuke was detonated, and if Mr Brown lived then he was trapped, the DNA lost. Eventually they would have to let King Jeremy go. At least this way they would be some distance from Mr Brown.

The submersible had surfaced in a smooth black cavern. The ceiling and edges of the cavern were obscured in darkness. The edges were either too far away or somewhere else entirely as a result of the strange geometry. The moment they left the submersible their protective blood-screens were being eaten by the city's aggressive biomechanical nano-spores. Alexia had to coax Yaroslav out of the mutated vehicle. The illumination in the strange cavern flickered like a broken strip light as the five of them made their way across the rubbery texture of the floor. They could see the biomechanical ship, the mentally spayed offspring of the Seeders, a panspermic, extremophile organism turned into an escape pod for a species. It looked like a cross between the seedpod it was and a bottom-feeding marine creature of some sort. It was easily the size of one of the larger football stadiums. The airlocks, the lenses protruding through its skin, were violations of its alien flesh.

'Malcolm,' Alexia whispered. She was looking around frantically, her rifle at the ready. He could feel it too. Even their augmented eyes could not penetrate the darkness at the edge of their vision, which seemed to expand as the light flickered out. He had the impression, just afterimages in the light, of people, many of them, perhaps thousands, in the darkness, just out of sight, watching them.

'What's that?' King Jeremy screamed, making the rest of them jump. The young sociopath was pointing at a figure on the edge of the blackness. A man with a dragon's head, he was wearing a finely tailored suit. The suit was covered in hundreds of mouths opening and closing, as if engaged in conversation. Du Bois recognised the figure as Siraja Odap-odap, the habitat's AI. The darkness seeming to eddy around and behind the dragon-headed figure.

They increased the pace. The airlock door was already opening for them. Du Bois suspected it was a false promise of safety, but it was all they had. They stopped when they reached the air-lock. Despite the airlock's presence in alien flesh, the technology looked human, falsely comforting.

'Give it to me,' du Bois said. King Jeremy shook his head. Yaroslav flinched as he did so.

'I will fucking shoot you in the head,' Beth told him.

'I can't be here on my own,' he pleaded, looking around, terri-fied. 'I can't go back through ...'

'For Christ's sake,' Alexia muttered. Du Bois half expected a warped vision of Christ to appear.

'Come with us,' du Bois said. Alexia and Beth turned to stare at him. He could tell from the expression on King Jeremy's face that he wanted to.

'Are you out of your fucking mind?' Beth demanded. 'Do you know what he's done?'

'Strand Mr Brown here, in this place,' du Bois said, ignoring Beth. King Jeremy could be dealt with the moment his thumb was off the button. King Jeremy looked between the three of them. Yaroslav's whimpering was becoming more urgent.

'No,' King Jeremy said, shaking his head. 'You'll kill me the first chance you get.'

Damn!

King Jeremy took out the vial. Its contents looked like a clear liquid, presumably the subtle, ancient, powerful S-tech reverting to its base biological nanite form. The vial extruded a needle. Du Bois held out a hand. King Jeremy pressed the needle into his flesh. Then he held up the hand with the dead man's switch in it, and started backing away from them.

They stepped into the airlock and it hissed shut. Beth, Alexia and du Bois sagged. Du Bois holstered his pistol and leant against the metal wall. Yaroslav looked around with the mounting panic of a trapped animal. The inner airlock hissed open. The four of them staggered into the huge, stadium-sized chamber. It was coated in what looked like stainless steel, the metal covering what looked like a rib cage. Du Bois felt like Jonah. Then he hit the floor, hard.

'Malcolm!' Alexia screamed, kneeling down next to him. All-pervasive, ancient, powerful biotechnology started to break down and change a body that was not meant to host it. Turning bubbling flesh protean. Putting it in flux. He screamed, growing new organs, his physiology constantly resetting itself as it tried to find a form that could cope. As the pain became too much, du Bois went away.

Alexia stared at du Bois, his flesh running like liquid. He had stopped screaming now. The noise he was making was more like keening. It changed resonance as his mouth took on different forms.

'Wha—' Beth started. Alexia was looking around frantically. She pointed towards the front of the craft, a wall of stainless steel-like material that covered what looked a little like organs, presumably the biomechanical working of the creature/ship.

'He needs to be linked to the ship,' she said. It was the only thing she could think of. Her only hope was the craft would recognise her brother as a living component, and stabilise him. If it could keep him alive, keep his consciousness alive, then something else could be worked out later.

His body was difficult and disgusting to grasp. She felt turgid, sludge-like shifting flesh against her grip as Beth helped her manhandle him towards another airlock-style door in the steel. Yaroslav trotted after them, still clutching his Vector SMG.

The airlock opened for them, and they made their way into a tangled warren of corridors between organ-like biomechanical machinery coated with the steel-like material. Alexia had only the vaguest idea of where she was going, other than forwards. She was on the left of her brother, Beth the right. She only caught a glimpse of the silver-masked figure leaning out of an intersecting corridor and heard the pop of the underslung grenade launcher firing. Beth pushed all three of them into a narrow passage on the left-hand side of the corridor. Du Bois's sticky, protean form practically landed on Alexia. There was an explosion further down the corridor. Her augmented hearing protected her from the worst of the blast and allowed her to hear the thump of a body landing hard on the floor. She felt Beth's weight move off them.

Beth had the N6 carbine up. She was kneeling beside the corner of the cramped passage she had shoved them into. Alexia was struggling to her feet, trying to pull her brother's difficult, shifting form further down the passage. Beth risked glancing out into the main corridor. Almost immediately she was taking fire. The Pennangalan was marching towards them, firing short bursts from her carbine. Beth took one in the shoulder. The armour-piercing round, slowed by her armour, lodged in her hardening flesh. The force knocked her back. The wound started to heal almost immediately. In the momentary glance she had seen Yaroslav lying face-first on the floor of the corridor, his back a bloody, blackened, smoking mess. It had been a 40mm fragmentation grenade. It must have exploded behind Yaroslav and thrown him forwards. Beth leaned round the corner and fired the N6's grenade launcher directly at the Pennangalan. The silver-masked woman threw herself into another branching passage further ahead. Beth was up, holding the N6 one-handed as she marched towards the corridor intersection. The fragmentation grenade exploded in the distance; shockwaves buffeted her, shrapnel embedded itself in her hardening clothing and opened up the skin on her flesh, which, again, healed almost immediately. Another three-round burst caught her in the chest as the Pennangalan appeared around the corner, crouched down low. Beth fired the N6 rapidly and clumsily with one hand, bullets sparking off the metal as she opened the grenade launcher, ejecting the case of the previous grenade, loaded it with a high-explosive, armour-piercing grenade, and clicked the launcher shut. The Pennangalan was firing bursts so rapid they were almost full automatic. Beth felt round after round hit her. Some were stopped by her armour, her hardening flesh, some grazed off her armoured skull, tore into her jaw. Others beat her armour and tore hot channels through her body. Each one was like getting hit by a hammer. The worst beating you could ever receive in a high velocity instant. She staggered, almost went down, but forced herself forwards, still firing. More than a few of her rounds hit home, staggering the silver-masked killer. Both of them ran out of ammunition. The Pennangalan disappeared from the corner, back into the other passage. Beth threw herself into the air past the intersection. The Pennangalan was backing away, a Sig P220 pistol in each hand, firing the moment she saw Beth, hitting the Yorkshirewoman as she fell through the air. Beth fired the grenade launcher. The HEAP grenade caught the Pennangalan in the stomach, she flew backwards into the air, and the grenade exploded. The concussion wave hit Beth, bounced her off some of the metal-coated organic machinery, and she hit the ground, a wounded, bleeding mess. She let out a primal scream of pain before forcing herself to her feet. She let the N6 hang from its sling and drew the OHWS, still loaded with nanite-tipped rounds. She limped slowly down the corridor towards the Pennangalan. The silver-masked killer looked like she had been hollowed out. Beth could see her spine, but somehow the other woman was still moving. Still trying to reload one of her Sig pistols with her own magazine of nanite-tipped rounds. Beth raised her pistol and put two rounds into what remained of the Pennangalan's chest. The nanites started to eat away at flesh. It looked like she was being slowly dissolved. Beth continued to limp towards her, covering her with the pistol. She had a perverse need to see the face under the silver mask.

Alexia struggled to drag her brother along the corridor away from the sounds of gunfire. She looked up as she sensed movement. Yaroslav was standing there. There was smoke coming from his back, but he looked more together. He was holding his SMG as though it was an actual weapon now.

'Piotr, help me!' she pleaded. He looked down at du Bois's protean form, seemed to come to a decision, and walked towards her, sweeping his Vector to one side, letting it hang down on its sling. Too late Alexia realised there was something wrong, too late she recognised the look in his eyes. She let go of du Bois, and grabbed for her rifle, but Piotr had already reached for it and taken hold of it himself. She heard an explosion from further down the corridor, the shockwave buffeting them as a huge, calloused fist hit her hard in the face, slamming her back into the steel-covered organic machinery.

Under the mask the Pennangalan looked like her sister, but she was younger, her face softer, more innocent, except for the vertical slits of her reptilian eyes. Beth really wanted to just sit down and bleed. She was so badly damaged, had so many injuries, that she was amazed she could still move, let alone function. The alien nanotech in her body was killing the pain signals to her brain, auto-cannibalising her flesh to synthesise endorphins to help kill the pain. There was an odd vinegary smell coming from the body. Through the lessening pain she remembered that she was supposed to double tap. She raised the pistol to shoot the body twice in the head. Something wasn't right. The acrid vinegar smell was nearly overwhelming. The physiology of the corpse, even allowing for the grenade that had gone off inside it, didn't seem right. Something slithered inside the body. Beth's eyes widened, her finger tightening on the pistol's trigger. An intestine-like tendril whipped out through the dissolving chest cavity and around her wrist. Beth screamed as acid burned her skin. She lost her grip on the pistol and it tumbled to the floor. Another tendril wrapped around her neck, then another around her face, acid burning her screaming mouth. Hissing, a long serpent tongue flickered past rows of serpent teeth as the head separated itself from the body, dragging healing organs that emitted a phosphorescent glow, like fireflies, behind it. The head leapt on intestinal tendrils towards Beth's face.

Alexia had been hit before, but it had been a while since she had been hit that hard. She almost blacked out. A feeling of nausea was suppressed by her augmented biology. She shook off the effects of the blow as she felt rough fingers around her throat, choking her. Then she was hit again.

'Got to get it back, get it back,' Yaroslav was muttering in Russian over and over again.

'Piotr,' she managed. He hit her again. The third time he hit her she did black out.

She came to on the ground as Yaroslav was replacing the magazine in his pistol. A cry of pain echoed through the metal corridors.

'Beth,' she tried to call out weakly, climbing unsteadily onto all fours. Yaroslav kicked her in the stomach. The force of the kick sent her flying into the machinery. Hands around her neck again, picking her up onto her feet, and slamming her into the metal. 'What are you doing, Piotr?' she said, trying to recover her breath. He just hit her again.

'I am not the victim. I'm not the fucking victim!' He let go of her neck and she felt him undoing her jeans.

'No, Piotr! No!' He jammed the barrel of his pistol into her face.

'Shut up!' he screamed. Then he yanked her jeans and panties down.

It was like being strangled at the same time as someone tried to burn your head off. She had managed to get her left hand in between the Pennangalan's head and her own. Needle-like serpent teeth sank into her flesh, emptying their venom into her body. She could feel herself weakening, her neuralware making her aware of just how fucked she was. The thing was making a keening, hissing noise, despite having a mouthful of her flesh. The Pennangalan's jaw dislocated, her mouth distending, trying to swallow Beth's hand. In a blind panic, Beth managed to tear her smoking right hand free of the acidic, intestinal tendril that had wrapped itself around her arm. Her leather jacket was melting away where the acid was dripping onto it. She reached into a hole in the nanite-reinforced leather. The Balisong blade clicked open, and she rammed it again and again into the screaming thing's separated head. She dropped the blade and pushed against the burning tendril, bringing her foot up and levering it in between herself and the separated head and organs. She pushed with her foot with all her might. The tendrils left smoking welts on her flesh. She rammed the head against the organic machinery on the other side of the narrow corridor, leant forwards, and dragged the shotgun from its back scabbard. Beth jammed the weapon through the flailing tendrils, against the thing's head and pulled the trigger, and again, and again, and again. Shells ejected from the shotgun as the head came apart in a spray of buckshot. Beth screamed as she blew half of her own foot off. The tendrils stopped whipping around. Beth crawled away from it and grabbed for her dropped pistol. She rolled over and fired three rounds into the already healing head. It stopped healing. The nanite loads started to eat away at the Pennangalan. Beth lay down, pain overwhelming what her systems could cope with. She wanted to sob. Then she heard an inhuman scream.

Yaroslav was staring at her genitalia, shaking his head.

'I'm not gay,' he said.

'Okay, okay.' Alexia tried to reason with him. 'You're not gay, so why don't we just ...' Both of the long knives that her brother had brought back from Japan were in a horizontal double sheath on her webbing. She drew them quickly while he was distracted. The first blade opened up Yaroslav's arm, the one holding the gun, down to the bone. He dropped the weapon. The second she rammed into his groin with as much force as she could muster. She felt resistance from his armoured clothes, from his hardening skin, but they were no match for the five-hundred-year-old folded steel. She buried the blade in his crotch. His scream sounded inhuman. Somehow he still had the presence of mind to backhand her hard enough to knock her off her feet. She landed next to her brother's protean form. His clothes and webbing acting as an ineffectual bag for his bubbling flesh, she grabbed his pistol from its holster, and rolled back to face Yaroslav. The Russian was just looking down at the hilt of the blade protruding from his groin. The targeting symbols in her vision told her where to aim. She fired again, and again, and again until the slide locked back on the pistol, the magazine empty. Yaroslav stood there for a few more moments, staring at her, uncomprehending, then he collapsed to the ground. The nanite-tipped bullets were already starting to break his body down. Alexia dragged her jeans up and curled up against the metal-covered machinery.

'You fucking bastard!' she screamed at the corpse. She had made herself different. It had been a choice. It had been done on her terms. It wasn't his place to make her feel like a freak. She had liked him, he had looked muscle-bound, big and dumb, she went for that sort of thing sometimes, though she knew he couldn't have been unintelligent working for the Circle. She had wanted to look after him. He had seemed so frightened, and then this. She burst into tears.

Beth appeared at the end of the narrow corridor. She was bleeding, burned, leaning against the machinery to stay upright. Her pistol was held in both hands. Alexia looked up at the other woman through her tears. Beth just nodded, and then slid down the metal covering to sit on the floor. Alexia looked at her brother's constantly transforming body as it struggled to cope with powerful biotechnology from a previously female line.

'Transitions are always difficult,' Alexia said quietly.

They were watching the mutated submersible surface in the moon pool.

'You're not going to put the DNA into us, are you?' Siska asked.

'No,' Mr Brown said. She tried not to flinch at the sound of his beautiful voice. 'The Naga-tech would reject it and probably kill you. The seed ships can leave the atmosphere. We have time to grow a clone to sufficient maturity. It amused me not to tell Malcolm the truth. I wanted to see what he would do.'

'And the boy?' Siska asked.

'We will suggest the same thing to Mr Rush. The ship's systems themselves will guide him in the cloning process. Unless he kills himself I expect great things of him. He has the potential to make kingdoms of madness, sublime entertainment.'

'And you knew that Yaroslav was about to go thatch?'

537

'Long overdue.'

'But why did you send my sister?' Siska asked. A terrified-looking King Jeremy was climbing out of the submersible. She did flinch as Mr Brown reached out to stroke her head.

'Because you wouldn't have killed them. Malcolm is out of the picture. It's left to fate now, though I rather doubt that Alexia and Miss Luckwicke are a match for your sister. Besides she was so servile, so slavish in her obedience. It becomes boring.' Siska tried desperately not to show any reaction, though her breathing sounded ragged to her own ears.

'I can't go out there again,' King Jeremy said from the door. He was weeping. Siska suspected the only reason he had been able to tolerate as much exposure as he had was because of the S- and L-tech augments the ridiculously dressed boy had managed to get hold of somehow. Mr Brown was striding across the room towards King Jeremy, a hand outstretched. The boy's expression was one of abject terror. He held up the dead man's switch. Mr Brown reached for it. Siska turned away as the air between Mr Brown and King Jeremy's hand became nauseating and painful to look at. Silas yelped and ran whimpering for a corner. There were multiple wet cracking noises. King Jeremy howled in agony. Siska looked back. Bones stuck out of the flesh of his arm in multiple places. His hand and the dead man's switch had fused. Mr Brown stroked the boy's face with his two long-fingered, obsidian-skinned hands.

'Shhh!' Mr Brown said gently. 'Don't you scream, don't you ever scream. You know nothing about pain and never will.' King Jeremy managed to make do with just whimpering. 'I find you repellent, Mr Rush, in so many ways. You are an abject lesson in what happens when the weak and the frightened gain power. I should extinguish you, but I suspect you will serve a purpose. I think that you will make things worse.' Silas padded up to King Jeremy, and nuzzled against him.

'P ... p ... please ...' King Jeremy managed.

'Please what?'

'I don't want to be on my own ...'

'We all have to live with the consequences of our actions.'

Du Bois wasn't sure how he got there. Presumably his sister and Beth had carried him to one of the couches in what was supposed to be the seed ship's cockpit, but which was, in fact, little more than a place for humans to try and monitor the organism. The ship had known what to do. It had wrapped in him in a cocoon of metallic, intelligent matter. It had injected him with more S-tech in a bid to control the biological flux his body was held in. It had helped his mind dissociate from his body, and instead associate with the now rudimentary intelligence of the biomechanical craft.

They were rising through the Pacific. Something about the ocean made him think of amniotic fluid. He shared awareness with the ship. The bodies of the Pennangalan and Yaroslav were significantly less disturbing than what he saw through the lenses on the exterior of the seed ship. Huge, twisting empty spires, reaching for and breaching the surface of the ocean, screaming human faces as a skin disease on the living basalt. Vast charnel buttresses, each one a contradictory living necropolis, crawling across the ocean floor. Twisted simulacra of existing cities growing, fruiting, and bursting; feedback from the inflicted insanity as alien minds failed to understand, or even fully acknowledge, the fading human presence on their planet. From the matter of the city vast, screaming effigies grew and, like the cities, fruited and burst into infectious spores: a piscine Christ, a piscine Buddha, a piscine Krishna, more that were less familiar to du Bois's already overwhelmed mind.

The ship rose from the clinging ocean, between the towers of the sunken city, and into a dawn of strange light. The ring of bright, flickering blue fire was a terminator. Before it was blue sky, behind it all was red and gaseous. The Seeders were taking their world somewhere else. The sun was turning black, being eaten by what looked like vast, squirming bacteria. The seed lurched as du Bois's battered mind was overwhelmed by religious terror. After all, the God he claimed as his own was a solar deity.

He took the seed ship, with its cargo of human clones, and the minds he carried in his own head, away from the diseased and lost planet.

Lodup was in total darkness now, but it wasn't frightening. He felt safe for the first time in a long while. There was light, like a spotlight on an empty stage. Sal was standing next to him. She turned to look at him with her black eyes.

'Thank you,' she told him. 'We wished to spread.' Then she disappeared with the light.

42
The City

Ludwig was home. Except that wasn't his name. His name had been Ibic ÓLug, a raven, a weapon, one of many, created to hate and kill his enemy. They had failed and his home had fallen. The Ubh Blaosc was now the home of serpents. Oz had broken the false programming that the Monarchists had given him when he had become an Elite. He was free, but not for long. He felt the pain of the Yig virus he had contracted from Oz eating away at him, at what he was, at what he had tried so hard to remember. He no longer had a home, but he could still hear his grand-creator's mindsong.

One of the uplifts was dead. He did not think he liked any of them, but then he was a weapon, it was not his purpose to like. Hovering just outside the huge head of the sun god, Ibic knew that it was only a matter of time before even he would be overwhelmed. The Naga did not fight like the other uplifts. They swarmed until their enemy was overcome. There was no false concern for the lives of their warriors – only victory, consumption mattered. They bathed him in their plasma fire. Any Elite would struggle in the heart of a sun. Still their ships fell like rain, sundered, diseased, controlled so they turned on one another. Phased bullets sought crucial system organs.

Grandfather Lug told the raven his plan. The remaining uplifts staggered as the sun god had spikes, filled with the seeds of Lloigor technology, grow through the serpent's extruded crust of resin and inject their bounty into Scab, Vic and Talia's otherwise mundane armour. It would be the sun god's final gift. Through the mindsong Ibic saw the three remaining uplifts about to fall. The Forge, the dying red sun, started to flicker, creating arcs of weak coronal ejection. He saw and felt the particle spray flow around him, a vast fountain of sparks in inhuman vision.

Goodbye, his grandfather told him.

Ibic's coherent energy fields reached out for the uplifts and enveloped them. Ibic ÓLug exuded the black, liquid glass exotic material of his armour and then accelerated. He drew vast amounts of energy from the network of proto-black holes that powered him through the entangled link. He flickered in and out of phase, dragging the three uplifts with him. He avoided the Naga through speed, stealth, and just not existing in the same physical state as them. Lug's seeds grew like a virus through the uplifts' equipment, transforming it. Their new armour then injected further seeds into the uplifts themselves. He could not hear their screams through the coherent energy field that enveloped them, but he was aware of their agonized contortions, at least in as much as he was instinctively aware of everything.

Six standard minutes as the uplifts measured time, a gift from humanity. Six minutes from the head of the sun god to their destination. He had hoped speed and stealth would be enough, but he could see Naga craft moving towards the destination. Perhaps they could feel the energies building, or perhaps it was just a function of enormous biomechanical minds playing the odds. The surface around the pool had come to life, much of it taking to the air. Níðhöggr itself, this hive fleet's own behemoth god, was making its way towards their destination. The huge biomechanical ship's movements looked ponderous, but it had been closer, and was moving fast enough that it would get there first. Ibic ÓLug wished that he could kill the snake's god, a god that the machine weapon/warrior had been created to hate, but knew he did not have the power, even now. The Níðhöggr was no mere Consortium capital ship.

Alchemy in machine guts. He used his own precious matter, and diverted his own precious energy feed, to create the three items. He knew these would be his own final gifts, and his death, as he plummeted towards the Naga godship.

Ibic ÓLug plunged into the Níðhöggr in a different physical state. He could not see through the godship, but he had been aware of the lines of energy snaking under the behemoth, meeting in the pool on the surface of Ubh Blaosc. Instinctively Ibic could feel what was happening in the pool. The Níðhöggr's defensive fields tore at the raven, shredding him in the way that no Lloigor-derived Consortium or Church shield could. He was screaming as the serpent god flayed him. All of his power went to keeping him in the different physical state that was protecting his uplift cargo in the flickering, shifting coherent energy fields clutched to him like a mother holding newborns. He saw the guts of the serpent ship, armoured bone superstructure, vast biomechanical organs. He saw the sparks fly through its vast nervous system, its children squeezed rapidly through its veins. He wished he could reach out and harm this thing he had been created to fight.

And then suddenly he was beneath the Níðhöggr, in its vast shadow. He could see the glow of the stones in the black water, the lightning playing across them. This had to be timed just right. He came to a halt, and bled off the kinetic energy that tried to act on the three shielded uplifts, their flesh and armour still changing. He drank the kinetic energy; every little bit helped. In his vision the forces at play looked like a tiny star going nova, and then space bent away from him and his instinctive understanding failed him as the trod was opened. He switched off the coherent energy fields, and the three uplifts dropped.

He ejected his gift. Three coherent field generators made as best he could in the time he had. The field generators attached themselves to the falling uplifts' transforming armour.

Ibic ÓLug was now shieldless, but now he could cause hurt.

It looked like he had exploded. Ghost bullets with virulent S-tech biological virals, and potent L-tech nanotech virals, intelligently sought crucial organs. Black light, fusion lances, de-coherence beams undid molecular bonds, and dust rained down on the resinous plain. DNA hacks regressed complex biomechanical organisms into protoplasmic slime. It lasted less than a moment. The black water drained from the pool. For a moment the glowing stones were visible, a ring of blue fire within, a red world beyond. In the sky above, the Forge flickered. Then the Níðhöggr breathed, and introduced Ibic ÓLug to the conditions at the heart of a sun. Then a star collapsed.

Patron was sure that the concentric rings of stone where the Lloigor machines had set up this particular trod, one of the few in Red Space, were the petrified ribs of some unknown creature.

All three of the Elite were there. The Innocent, his newest, was wearing only a pair of loose, baggy, white cotton trousers as he sat on the edge of the rock, dangling his feet over crimson gases. Hedetet, the hive queen he'd had violate her own form by remaking her as an arachnid, an eight-limbed, stinger-tailed, humanoid scorpion, was coated in her black, liquid glass armour, hiding the shame of her form. She was leaning on her weapon, which was configured as a spear.

Patron ran his hand over his favourite's cobra-like head. She flinched at his touch less these days. All his hand felt was the exotic matter of her armour. Like Hedetet, the surviving Pennangalan sister was ashamed of her form. She was the most covert of the Consortium Elite. She had to be. She was not a full Naga, only a tech-infused hybrid. It still would have been more than enough to cause difficult questions in board meetings, and public outcry, such as it was, if her existence became common knowledge. Uplifts just weren't self-aware enough to embrace their own destruction.

'I am surprised they have got this far,' Patron mused. It wasn't their individual abilities he had doubted, more their ability to work as a group, or even in their own best interest. The stones glowed from within, picking out the symbols in the rock that even Patron struggled to understand. A ring of blue fire appeared within the circle.

Britha hit the ground hard. The blue fire, reflecting on the silver of the raven-headed armour, winked out. She felt the change in the power. She wanted to throw up from the pain. The raven-shaped helm folded away from her face but she was only dry heaving. The spear was screaming at her, her head felt like it wanted to burst. The parasite thing living within her seemed always just out of reach, teasing her as it hid.

'Quiet!' she screamed. She felt calmness flood through her in an unnatural way, but it allowed her the presence of mind to sing the mindsong that contained the magic, to calm the spear. She could feel the heat from the haft even through her armour. Its screaming rage subsided to a simmering fury, and it became almost manageable. She was aware of the crystal parasite creeping through her mind, eating what she was, what she had been. Her red hair drifted to the black ground as it fell out of her swollen skull.

She stood up and knew that she was in Cythrawl. She could still see the fiercely glowing magic burning within the stones, feel it. Beyond the stones a city, like the terrifying stories that Germelqart and Kush had once told her of their 'civilisation'. Vast, dark structures, spires and towers that looked like barbed, spear-shaped brochs, reached up for the red sky. The angles were impossible, their shadowed parts reached to elsewhere. Once it would have hurt to even see such a thing; now, instinctively, she understood that those were paths she could walk. That was when she realised that she was little more than an echo now. Britha was no more. Her body was just a vessel. She was just a memory in a demon's mind.

There were things there, vast creatures that had grown into the rock. She saw the power they drank as glowing lines coming from deep in the earth. She knew them as kin to the Muileartach. Somehow she could hear their minds echoing through the crystalline tendrils branching out from her head, and into other places. The minds might have been hopelessly moonstruck, but they were cold and languid. There was little for them to eat now. She was barely aware of the other smaller minds, the people who crawled across this city as lice crawled across skin.

There was something else here. Something that burned the tendrils of her crystalline awareness, made them shrink away from it. Something that she knew to fear more than a god, a sleeping mind whose desire to wake she could feel. On the horizon a huge, black, squirming and very close sun was rising.

Lightning started to play amid the circle of stones. Lug's spear caught fire. The stones glowed from within, picking out the symbols in the rock. Part of her wanted to stay in the circle, journey by trod away from this terrible place, but she could see the power at play here, and stepped out of the circle just as the ring of blue fire appeared.

The blue fire faded. There were four of them. Two were clothed in a material not unlike the black shining rocks that the traders had once brought to her people. Rocks that they swore came from the insides of burning mountains. One such stood more than two heads taller than her. She had six arms, carried a strange-looking spear, and had a long, segmented tail that ended in a stinger. The other had the head of a hooded snake. Britha did not recognise the weapon she held, but it was easy to see that it was one. The third figure was unmistakeably Crom Dhubh, though his clothes were strange. She felt hate flare in her for all that he had done to her people. The parasite in her head showed him what he really was, a man-shaped squirming hole in space.

She felt something in her chest when she saw the fourth figure. It was Bress as a young man, with very short hair. He was nowhere near as tall, but it was unmistakably him. Though the innocence of his features, the childlike expression of wonder as he looked around at this horrible place, seemed very out of place on what were, ostensibly, her lover's features. Britha's hand shot to her mouth, and a quicksilver tear ran down her cheek, only to be absorbed through her skin a moment later. Then young Bress seemed to fall asleep, though he remained standing. His sleep did not look restful; he jerked and swung his arms around as the black shining material leaked through his skin like oil and coated his flesh. A long, black-bladed sword grew from nowhere and he let it drag on the ground.

There was no point in hiding. Crom Dhubh surely knew she was there, just as she could feel him, and see him for what he was. She stepped out from between the stones. Her helmet was still folded away from her face. There was just a flicker of surprise on his face.

'I had not thought to see you here,' he said, glancing at the spear. He was speaking in the tongue of the Pecht. It felt like an insult hearing him use the tongue of her people. He concentrated, and then looked away from her. 'The same trick? Lug has been infecting his pets with parasites again.'

'Why aren't you dead?' she demanded.

'Am I not? Perhaps it's just not something that happens to me. I should thank you. I used to think so small. Without you it would have been over before it had even started.'

'You've destroyed so much!' she cried, tears of quicksilver running down her cheek again.

'You cannot possibly understand how little that matters.' Then he concentrated. Britha could see it again. The light burning in the smoking stones. She could see the power branching out into places it had not been before, the magics of the stones overtaxed. Crom Dhubh and the three black, shining, stone-clad warriors walked out of the circle, away from Britha.

She thought of her people, the Cirig, Cliodna, her lover, Fachtna, her lover, Kush, Teardrop-on-Fire, Raven's Laughter, their children, all the people of the Ubh Blaosc, that burning Otherworld. She thought of her children whom she would never see, now. Perhaps Crom Dhubh had a plan, but all the harm he had caused had only ever seemed to be done on a spiteful whim to her. He had found another Bress, an Otherworldly changeling perhaps, and enslaved him as well. She watched the changeling dragging the huge blade behind him. Crom Dhubh would turn him into a monster as well, like the Bress she knew, if he had not already done so.

What do you love, Crom Dhubh? The thought was a whisper in her mind. It sounded like her voice. She saw echoes of past movement stretching out and away from Crom Dhubh. The black-skinned man's hand touching the snake-headed woman. The energies in the circle coalesced, and blue fire filled the ring of stones once again. The raven head flipped down over her face. She felt her armoured feet branch into the earth, anchoring her, as the deluge of black water tried to wash her away. The Spear of Lug made a path of steam through the water as Britha threw it.

Fury as a state of being, fury at loss of control. Things were being done to him against his will. He had felt this before, or something like it. Some fragmented remainder of a surgically removed memory in the scar tissue that passed for his mind. He was being turned into an Elite, or something very similar. The awareness of everything returned as his senses spread out, only to become confounded by the architecture of the strange city he found himself in, on this world in Red Space.

He lacked the superior biotech of S-tech, though the invasive Lloigor nanites were doing the best they could to improve his own soft-machine augments. Lug's gift, which had turned his combat armour and weapons into liquid and reformed them, was not the cobbled together, jury-rigged scavenging of ancient technology that the Elite-tech was. They were fresh from their creators: armour, weapons and flesh now just components in the same fighting machine.

Energy was the problem. Wherever they were it seemed in short supply. He was aware of an entangled link feeding him energy from ancient machines. The feed was sluggish in a way that suggested a radical change in physics. He was aware that the energy on demand was severely limited.

He pushed himself up onto one knee in the deluge as it surged out and away from the centre of the circle. His internal systems turned the wave of nausea, brought on by the twisted architecture, into little more than a fleeting piece of information. He felt the three Consortium Elite. If he had known the scorpion and the snake then he had long ago forgotten them, but he recognised the Innocent, and he knew Patron for what he was: a screaming hole in space.

'No!' He wasn't sure how he heard the scream, but he saw the path of steam the burning spear made through the water. Even he was surprised when the spear exploded through one of the still-glowing stones, creating a fountain of energy, and hit the snake-headed Elite. The Elite flew backwards, pushed by the spear's screaming, burning head. It hit a thick pedestal of strange-looking stone. The horrible, tentacled statue atop the pedestal was moving slowly, lines of energy and the instinctive knowledge of the existence of a vast and languid mind telling Scab that it was actually alive. The spear drove the Elite deep into the stone, and then passed through her. Scab was appalled. There was just a moment of fear. No, not fear, awe. It had been Patron who had been screaming. Scab didn't care. He wanted to kill the Innocent.

His armour bulged as it sucked strange matter from the ground, an infection of nanites transforming it at a molecular level into payloads. From the time he had torn the egg from the flesh of his first kill on Cyst and it had grown into his tumbler pistol, he had preferred bullet to beam. His weapon was an ergonomically optimised carbine. The barrel was widened and flattened. The armour fed it the ghost discs, using much of the available entangled energy feed to enable the discs to flicker in and out of different physical states, some of them even forming micro-bridges, or attempting quantum tunnelling to pass through the Innocent's armour. Each of the ghost discs would fragment into voracious nanites if they returned to this hard reality inside the Innocent. It was a distraction, nothing more.

They were bathed in a cold, hard rain of white light and something past ultraviolet: focused particle beam weapons, X-ray lasers. This blackened planet under its red sky had an orbital defence network. Scab was aware of it being S-tech, biomechanical satellites and habitats with living weapons, and Patron was in control of them. A flickering nimbus of amber energy surrounded him as he kicked off through accelerated particles, warping gravity around his armoured form to provide flight. He was aware of Vic standing over Talia, both similarly protected by coherent energy fields as the earth around them ceased to exist, and another figure in raven-headed armour, the spear-thrower, kneeling, protected by her own field. Scab did not know her but she was familiar somehow.

The Innocent was moving, surrounded by his own flickering light, the exotic matter of the liquid glass that encased him rippling as the discs hit it and the armour transported them elsewhere. The rain of hard light and particles stopped. Both Scab and the Innocent dropped their coherent energy fields so they could harm each other. Scab still had his energy javelin: it was, after all, L-tech as well. The armour covering the palm of his hand parted to let the E-javelin out as Scab covered the distance to the Innocent. The Elite swung his oversized sword, making it look as if the weapon overbalanced him. It was a lie. The black blade, inimical to life, cut at Scab as he closed in. Scab's new armour cut him open, pushing itself into his flesh, wounding him so it was armour the blade cut through, and not fragile – despite augmentation – flesh. Scab lashed out with the E-javelin. The Innocent parried with his blade. All the technology in the world couldn't compensate for experience and sneakiness. Scab's 'weapon', which had been shaped like a carbine, was now a knife in his other hand. He stabbed it towards the Innocent, who was suddenly surrounded by the amber light again. Scab gritted his teeth as he slowly inched the exotic matter of the blade into the Elite's coherent energy field. The blade flickered between different physical states as it edged through the shield.

The spear disappeared like a screaming comet into the red sky. Scab understood its flight path. Behind him he was aware of black light and lances of fusion. He heard buildings crumble. He was also aware of, and then disappointed by, the attempts at electronic warfare. It demeaned them all, though he would seek any opportunity to prove himself hypocrite in this. The Innocent launched himself into the air. Scab raked his blade down through the amber light of the Elite's shield, and made ripples in the liquid glass armour. A foot caught him in the head with enough power to powder armour plate. Scab bounced off the top of one of the smoking stones in the circle. His spine snapped and then reknit almost immediately. He impacted with the edge of the warped, tomb-like structure, creating a Scab-shaped imprint in basalt. The Innocent chased the burning spear. Scab cloaked himself in gravity and followed.

*

The feeling of power was overwhelming, after his new systems made the pain go away. Now Vic knew what it was like to be one of the Elite. New-found senses made him aware of the city's scurrying, parasitical life already fleeing. A moment of shock as he saw an Elite killed with what looked like an archaic weapon. He was aware of the other two Elite, but did not fear them. Whether that was from a new sense of power, new conditioning, or both, he wasn't sure. He was aware of the woman in the raven-headed armour who had thrown the spear. She might not be on their side, but she didn't seem to be a friend of the Elite, and had already killed one. Only Patron gave him pause.

Then came the orbital bombardment. Talia was kneeling on the ground. He moved to stand over her. Both of them were encased in amber light as they fell into the newly made crater. In the Thunder Squads he had worked with teammates to destroy cities. Now he could do it himself. Now he *wanted* to do it himself. One of the Elite was a female 'sect: a shrunken hive queen with an arachnid augment. Despite all the changes he had made to himself, despite the fact that he'd been a worker playing at being a warrior, his own deeply held prejudices made him disgusted at this violation of the insect form. The storm of accelerated particles and hard light passed. His 'weapon' was still in a shape he was comfortable with, that of a strobe gun. His coherent energy field flickered off and on to let the rotating weapon fire beams of fusion energy, black light mixed with the more discreet, exotic bandwidth lasers phasing in and out of this space, trying to confuse the scorpion Elite's defences. Beams were refracted off the arachnid, more disappeared into the man-shaped screaming black hole that Patron had become. The beams scythed through twisted towers and spires started to fall. He was aware of vast, ancient, insane, somnambulant minds screaming out in pain through esoteric frequencies.

The scorpion Elite was in the air. Vic's weapon followed her, leaving paths of destruction through the city as it did so. His awareness told him of discrete carrier beams containing a DNA hack striking him, which further enraged him. A de-coherence beam tried to loosen the molecular bonds in his reformed armour, sneaking through his coherent energy field while it flickered to allow his weapon to fire, but the armour's matter was too clever for it. It pulled new matter from the ground, nanites transforming it into useful material. Vic was aware of Scab and the Innocent taking to the air after the burning, screaming spear that had killed one of the Consortium Elite.

The arachnid plunged though Vic's barrage of energy and hit him in the chest, driving him into the earth. His bones were powdered and re-healed almost instantly, the pain momentary but overwhelming. He came to a halt. She was striking at him with her spear through the surrounding rock. Each blow was doing something to the coherent energy field, somehow sucking the energy from it. He could see root-like lines of light in the rock around him, conduits of energy for the stone circle. He thrust his hand through rock and grabbed one of the branches, then he dropped the energy field and grabbed the Elite. He was screaming as the energy coursed through him, his armour fusing with his flesh. His upgraded neunonics, too slow to switch off all his nerve endings, took his mind away somewhere else for a moment. The scorpion had gone. Vic was healed, his armour still smoking. He became aware of the arachnid hive queen's location. He exploded out of the stone through a tower. Its geometry didn't make sense, he was somewhere other than he should have been and he hit another building hard. He changed state, but the cold, old, living city tore at him. Screaming, he emerged, fantasies of godlike power somewhat tarnished, but he continued after the scorpion Elite at hypersonic speeds, towards the rising carrion sun, and the squirming parasites feeding on it.

Britha was knocked off her feet by the impact of the eight-limbed, black-armoured creature slamming one of the newcomers, this one with six limbs, deep into the ground. One of the other newcomers had taken off, following the one like Bress. Both of them chasing her spear as it flew towards the castle in the sky that kept on trying to harm them with its storm of light.

The third newcomer, who had the right number of limbs, and who wore armour like the other two, which had obviously been made in Ubh Blaosc, was lying in the centre of the deep crater made by the storm of light. Britha spared her a glance, feeling a strange kinship towards her. Then she looked back to Crom Dhubh.

Britha knew she should be afraid, and even after everything she had seen she was still appalled. She perceived him as a hole in space, crackling with black lightning. She felt him take energy from somewhere else, dark places, and feed it to his remaining black-clad warriors. Britha reached out through the tendrils to stop this, to sour the milk of an already poisoned teat. A whip-like tendril lashed out from within the man-shaped hole in a blur, the crystal cracked, the entities feeding off her screamed, and she echoed their scream. He began pulling down the crystal-line branches growing out of her. The tendrils receded into her head, and back through holes to unseen places that it hurt to look towards.

The eight-limbed, black-clad, insectile warrior burst from the earth. Moments later the six-limbed newcomer followed, careen-ing through the odd geometry of the city. The six-limbed crea-ture was taken elsewhere for a moment, vanishing even from the awareness of the crystalline entities.

Crom Dhubh glided through the air towards the last armoured newcomer as she rolled to her feet. Britha reached down, pulling at the new strings of dark energy he was trying to set up to feed the magics to his warriors, and with a thought she rearranged the arm reaching for the girl in as painful and debilitating a way as she could manage. The crystalline parasites surged down through her head, consuming more of her, and she screamed. The girl was in the air, bouncing off useless buildings as she sought to get away. Britha heard Crom Dhubh's scream in her head, it made the crystal vibrate. Then the Dark Man showed the *ban draoi* what he really looked like. He unfolded into different places, displayed the impossibility of his form. He wanted her to see all of him in the knowledge that she could not understand his shape and all of its possibilities.

Quicksilver and blood burst from her eyes, ears, and nose. She almost shut down, the parasites pushing through her head as they tried to translate what he, it, was to a human mind. More of the crystal tendrils growing from her were torn away. The para-sites were frightened now. He reached for her with limbs and appendages unseen and impossible, and rearranged her through her armour. Her shield of light did not even activate, as it did not seem to be aware of the existence of parts of Crom Dhubh's form. No time to cry out. He left her alive so she could appreciate pain as he reached for her with his other arm. She hadn't even been aware of him moving in front of her, as he healed the dam-age she had done to him. Her armour carried her into one of the buildings, and ran for a shadowed corner that seemed to stretch away forever.

Britha came to on a balcony high above the crater. She had no idea how she had got there. She knew only that there were things in the dark places between the city's strange geometry. She knew now that she could not kill Crom Dhubh. The Dark Man was a god. His human form was just a disguise. She was not sure that even the Spear of Lug could kill him. The crystalline entities knew her mind and whimpered. Already wounded, some of them dead, they curled away from the direction of Crom Dhubh's presence. Crystalline branches grew through what was left of the meat of her brain. She was little more than a wilful, living memory held in crystal now, forcing the parasites to do her bidding.

It was sword and shield. The Innocent broadcast his most sophisticated hacks at the spear. They were L-tech-derived programs and viruses that had been further developed by Pythia. Scab then tried to block the electronic warfare, upgrading his own bag of tricks on the fly with newly uploaded L-tech software. So far Scab and the spear's own not-inconsiderable defences were winning out. Occasionally either the Innocent or Scab would risk an attack, but energy was at a premium for both of them.

The city was far below them now. It was a huge, black, fragmented scar in a vast rift valley. It spread out like a parasitical starfish, growing onto the two continent-sized plateaus to the east and west.

They left the atmosphere. The small, orbital habitat looked like a petrified biomechanical egg to Scab. He understood the lines of energy within. It was getting ready to rain down more hard light, though it was sluggish, and newly awakened. His senses made him aware of a diminishing reservoir of qubits within. Presumably it was communicating via quantum entanglement with other orbital weapon platforms that remained in orbit. Soon the network would concentrate fire on Patron's enemies.

The spear reached the habitat, burst into it, and began its destruction. The Innocent looked almost graceful as it reached the exterior of the orbital and started to fling pieces of it at Scab using a mixture of brute strength and manipulated gravity. They were easy to avoid. It felt like a childish tantrum in some ways.

'Why do you hate me?' the Innocent asked in a reasonably innocuous transmission. Scab didn't have an immediate answer. He wasn't sure it mattered here, now, but he wanted his clone dead anyway.

'Self loathing,' he transmitted back. It wasn't entirely a lie.

'I'm sorry,' the Innocent said. 'I can't wake up.'

Below them the bits of the habitat burned as they hit the fragile atmosphere. The spear passed him, veering a little as though it wanted to attack, but then continuing its flight back towards the city.

Scab's energy feed was diminishing rapidly. The Innocent was using the wreckage of the ancient S-tech satellite to try and hide from him. The planetary horizon was lit up as other awakening habitats started to fire down on the city. He had to stop them.

Why? he asked himself. Did he want to see Patron fail, destroyed? Did he want to kill the closest thing to God Known Space had ever seen, just to say he had? Did he care?

He audited his neunonic memory to see what the Lloigor's violation of his technological and biological privacy had left him. His memory capacity was still there. The Monk's, Beth's, construct was still there, a worrying symptom of sentimentality. The snippet he had taken of the Yig virus from the *Basilisk II*'s systems had to be gone. It had been a tiny piece. It had been imprisoned with the best Pythian software, but he had known it would slither through in the end. Why had he done it? He knew that eventually it would make him something else. It wasn't even suicide. In taking the sample he had given himself up to eventual sequestration, eventual slavery.

He thought back to his mother on Cyst, the Church's manipulations, Patron's manipulations. *Were you ever anything other than a slave, a puppet?* Perhaps the honesty of the Naga's wish to consume remained the only pure thing left.

Surely Lug would have destroyed the sample of the Yig virus? Suffer not a serpent to live. But it was still there in his upgraded neunonics. It was represented as a serpent beast, in a tower, on an island. The beast was swathed in chains of cold iron. It looked like a secure L-tech program had reinforced Scab's own Pythian prison. Scab knew that the virus couldn't be controlled or defeated by anything they had available, but he wondered if it could be lied to, spoofed.

Scab shifted physical state as he phased through the mostly intact top of the S-tech satellite. He felt its barely-awake living defences tear at him, try to strip away his own defences, diminish him. It was like the Marduk implant all over again, he saw with a god's eyes. He was an embodiment of godsware. *Who would give something like me this sort of power?* His voice was incredulous in his own head.

The smooth organic interior flashed past him, and he was out the other side of the habitat. The Innocent was standing on the skin of the habitat's hull, both of them at right angles to the dead planet far below. The Innocent held his sword. Scab saw his own face encased in the black liquid glass. For once he didn't see a monster. He shook his head. It didn't matter. He used his own software to create a virus that told as convincing a lie as he was capable of, and sent that and the Yig virus to half the satellites in the defence network. He told the Yig virus that the remaining satellites were Lloigor in design. Then he sent transmissions to the uninfected satellites, telling them that the rest of their net-work was infected.

'I don't want to fight,' the Innocent said, high above the dead planet. Scab just shook his head. He had access to precious little energy. He was going to have to do this the old-fashioned way, the nasty way. Once that thought would have given him pleasure. He ran at the Innocent and tackled him. He warped gravity, tilting the wreckage of the habitat, and they plummeted back towards the city. He was going to kill this clone imposter, and then Patron. There was just a nagging moment of doubt in the back of his mind. They were wreathed in fire as they hit the atmosphere. Above them the red clouds were lit up in various spectrums as the satellites started to fire at each other.

The city kept on wrong-footing him. Vic's godsware awareness wasn't all that it was cracked up to be. The strange geometry had him colliding with buildings, sending rubble tumbling through the levels below, sending the strange creatures that inhabited this place scurrying, or just crushing them. He disappeared into what he had thought was an optical illusion, which should have been impossible at his level of awareness. He travelled through a screaming total darkness, another thing that should have been impossible, full of shapes and noises. It had almost been a relief to come back out in the city.

The scorpion Elite was above and behind him. She was in the best possible position for a dogfight. The further they got away from the stones, the more crumbling and ruined the city was. At hypersonic speeds the constant thunder of their passing sounded off, oddly muted amid the strange architecture. Buildings tumbled in their wake as accelerated particles and de-coherence beams cut through once-living basalt, and broke molecular bonds. Vic rolled and retaliated with fusion beams and exotic lasers. The arachnid banked and the destructive beams scythed through the tops of towers. They passed over vast buttresses, their destructive forces creating huge rents in them, revealing layer after layer of skeletons fused with the sculpted rock.

Behind them, Vic was aware of the fury of another orbital bombardment, much more destructive than the first. He heard, felt, alien screaming on strange bandwidths. There could be little left of the centre of the city now.

The city left behind, they were over the eastern continent-sized plateau. Quadruped herd creatures with a passing resemblance to humans fled in their wake, though Vic saw little else in the way of life on the dead planet as they sped over a vast mountain range, the spine of the plateau.

There were craters and smaller valleys that Vic suspected might once have been lakes, or seas. Neither of them could risk using their own matter for ordnance while they were separated from the earth in flight, and Vic found himself using his weapon sparingly, conserving energy. The arachnid was doing likewise, though every barrage gouged blackened trenches in the dead world's surface, sending tonnes of dirt and debris flying into the sky. Energy was at a premium on this strange world. In order to deal with the scorpion Elite, Vic knew he was going to have to close with her.

Neither of them were firing now. The arachnid was transmitting various electronic warfare attacks, but Vic's L-tech defences were more than a match for them. They were over another huge rift valley between the two major continental plateaus. Vic was flying with his back to the ground, looking up at the scorpion Elite as he propelled himself with the powerful AG field. There was a moment of realisation. As deeply ingrained as his hatred of arachnid augments was, he had no idea what had led the Elite to transfigure herself in this way, just as the warrior-caste 'sects that hated him had no idea what had made Vic the way he was. Though, Vic reflected, that had mostly been the desire to embrace behaviour deemed deviant by his staid society. He knew that it was thoughts like this, and the hesitation they caused, that led to inevitable death, but for all his apparent power, nothing was happening in this titanic battle. It was kind of pointless. Then he remembered Talia. He had got carried away with his new-found power. He had to kill the abomination to protect her.

The red sky lit up in a coronal display, as accelerated particles played across the magnetosphere accompanied by flashes of X-rays and deep UV. The orbital weapons platforms were duelling with each other. The atmosphere flared as wreckage started to fall to earth in various parts of the sky. Vic's weapon turned to a double-ended spear – he'd seen his namesake use one in an immersion – and he closed with the scorpion Elite in the sky. She exuded blades from the black, liquid glass armour, and they collided violently.

Britha's body hadn't so much healed itself as rebuilt itself. As the sky lit up again she stepped back into an odd angle where the balcony met the tower and found herself in pitch, living darkness. There were things there, tearing at her. She cried silent screams as she tumbled out of another shadowed corner. The building, and much of the city surrounding the stones, simply ceased to exist in another rain of the hard light. She heard the vast minds in the city, malevolent siblings of the Muileartach, scream in their half-asleep state. She knew that Crom Dhubh was searching for her, reaching out for her. His senses and his strange, unfolding, fragmented form were one and the same now. The only place she could hide from him was in the screaming darkness, and she could not bring herself to go back there.

There was a black lake. Her new-found senses had made her aware of it. There was something in that lake, something that the crystal parasites curled away from, whimpering, something that even the minds of the city's sleeping gods seemed to fear as they whispered to her that it could kill Crom Dhubh if she would but call to it. She closed her eyes, and in the single moment before she sang the mindsong to the thing in the lake, she wondered how all had come to this madness. The thing's answering mindsong was like a disease among the crystal, turning it to blackened dust. She collapsed, her body spasming and cramping, her guts feeling like they were crammed full of rusty and broken blades. The pain somehow still less damaging than the fear that the thing in the lake was aware of her existence.

Something like thick, smooth, black mud surged from the black lake. Her new-found awareness wanted nothing to do with it. Britha threw up blood as she guided the oozing, viscous

556

black thing towards her enemy through the nonsensical, tangled warren of the labyrinthine streets. She was aware of the city's inhabitants trying to flee before it. It consumed those who were too slow. It annihilated them on some fundamental level. Perhaps it could kill Crom Dhubh, but it was too late now. He had found her. Britha managed to stand in the shadow of the Dark Man's monstrous form, look up at him defiantly, though he was little more than a fragmented man-shaped hole in the air. Then the spear returned to her hand. She tried to smile. It was more of an agonised grimace. A whip-like tentacle lashed out from inside Crom Dhubh's strange form. Agony lanced through Britha's head as more of the crystalline branches were torn away from her. Something like a hand reached for her. Britha threw the spear. It was a weak throw, but the sun god's spear knew its business. The spear disappeared inside the Dark Man's impossible form. She felt the mindsong connection with the weapon break. Little more than a lump of blackened spear-shaped carbon landed on the ground. Britha sank to her knees, weeping tears of blood and quicksilver. She had come here to do something. She tried to form the memory through the pain. She had been supposed to poison the Hungry Nothingness. She hadn't even had a chance.

Talia knew she had been changed. She was aware of what was happening, though the insane city played with her new-found awareness, disrupting it. She understood she had power, but she had always seemed several steps behind everything else they were facing. Inasmuch as she could process the bewildering sensory information, she couldn't understand it, or more precisely she couldn't cope with it. After the first orbital bombardment, where she had felt oddly subdued terror, she had relied on a tried and true tactic she had used many times in the past: she had run and hid.

She had tried to hide in a corner and found that the edges of the corner hadn't met. She had fallen through. The darkness had pulled at her. She had landed somewhere else in a confusing, multi-level labyrinth, in another part of the city. She didn't want to go back into the darkness. Once she would have screamed at the grotesques that were staring at her, but she realised that they were just very frightened. She heard the sound of buildings falling, the cries of the alien minds that in many ways were the city. Talia giggled. She was sure that it was only technology that was keeping her sane.

The bombardment of her senses, the need to keep moving, was good. It meant she didn't have to think about Beth.

Talia was aware of the thing from the lake before she saw it. The strange inhabitants of the city fled before it. A flickering, ghostly figure in a robe was standing on a needlessly complicated corner, watching its approach. The tech, in her body, in the armour, told Talia that the ghost was feeding sensory information to huge, barely functioning servers in various parts of this world. The servers contained the corrupted ruins of some kind of VR environment, an immersion as Vic called them. Then the thing surged around the corners of the city into view like a wave of turgid oil. A pseudopod of the viscous material flicked out, and the robed ghost ceased to exist. Chemicals and technology suppressed primal fear, but Talia knew this thing was beyond wrong even as those it touched dissolved, as it pulled them into its body. Talia looked around for a way out of the labyrinth, and then remembered she could fly. Pseudopods reached out for her as she rapidly accelerated, bouncing off the unexpected protrusions of the city's strange masonry. It was like trying to fly through a very solid optical illusion.

Her eyes widened as another, more extensive orbital bombardment lit up the city, destroying the centre around the stones, badly wounding one of the minds, judging by the filtered signals she was receiving. The thing from the lake surged through the streets beneath her. She saw another monster moving between broken, smoking, twisted spires. It took her a moment to come to terms with what her new senses were telling her, that this unfolded hole in reality was Patron. It was hard to look at him. She was aware of one of the oily, viscous, anti-life thing's pseudopods reaching up for her. She moved away from it. The orbital bombardment had stopped. Now the sky was lit up like the northern lights. She saw shooting stars. She looked between the two monsters.

'Oh, this is ridiculous,' she muttered in her narcotic- and technologically-aided calmness. She flew back towards the centre of the city, towards the destruction. She was aware of wrestling figures tumbling from the sky, through buildings, to impact with the ground. Scab was a blur, fighting with the Innocent. Vic was a blur, fighting with the scorpion-like Elite. They were wrestling, stabbing, slashing, punching, kicking, the Elite's armour extruding blades in all sorts of places. It might have been happening in a bewildering blur that she could only really understand because of her augmented perception, but it looked little different from a brawl on the dance floor of a Bradford nightclub. With a thought she ran through her own weapon options and found what she was looking for.

'Stop!' she screamed.

43
The City

'Stop!' It was a sonic weapon, it broadcast throughout the sound spectrum from infrasound to ultrasound wavelengths. Talia wanted them to take notice. Ancient masonry crumbled, towers fell, any of the city's inhabitants within range of her weaponised voice went deaf, blood exploding from ears, noses and eyes. It was enough to get their attention, just for a moment. She knew that Vic would listen because she was asking. Warily he paused in his attack. She gave thanks that the scorpion Elite was reasonable enough to do the same. Patron stopped, she assumed out of curiosity.

Scab continued fighting, of course. He was intent on driving a black blade through the Innocent's armour. 'Scab!'

He ignored her, too intent on the kill. 'Vic?' she asked. Vic held up all four of his limbs to show the scorpion Elite that he meant no harm, his weapon absorbed by the armour. The scorpion Elite nodded.

Talia glanced behind her. She could see the first of the pseudopods of the black, viscous thing. Vic flew across to where Scab was trying to kill the Innocent. Scab didn't even glance his way. He probably hadn't expected Vic to kick him into a massive block of basalt. Scab came out of the crater in the side of the wall. His armour appeared to be reacting to his mood. More than ever he looked ready to kill; he looked like a weapon.

'Scab, please!' Talia begged. 'We can kill each other later, but please, just for a few moments.' The screams caused by the oil-like creature's attacks on the city's strange inhabitants sounded less than human. 'Can we make that thing go away?' she asked.

'Leave it to do its work,' the woman in the raven-headed armour said as she climbed to her feet. All around them was a smoking ruin. The creature surged closer.

'Okay, okay, look, please, we can all go back to this massive fight in a moment, I just want some time to talk first. Seriously, I'll even join in on your side.'

The helmet unfolded away from the woman's head. Talia took a step back at the woman's appearance. She wasn't sure why, after all she had seen. The woman was bald, her head unnaturally swollen, eyes like mercury, tears of quicksilver and blood on her cheeks. Talia could see the pain etched into her features. She could also see the resemblance. It was faint but there was enough for Talia to recognise some of Britha in her own features.

'No,' the woman said. 'You do not know his crimes. He must die.'

Talia sighed. Patron was a distended shadow folding itself down into a mostly human shape that existed, at least partly, in their space.

'Everyone's such a fucking hard-arse,' Talia muttered, sagging. She wished her sister was here, though she wasn't sure if Beth would be part of the solution or the problem. She felt tears in her eyes as she tried to suppress the memory of her sister on the end of a spear, the serpent's 'eggs' already growing inside her.

'Look, this is ridiculous ...' She glanced behind her at the viscous thing's seeping progress, though she constantly felt its presence. 'This ... I don't know, your fighting's kind of become abstract. Do you honestly think it means anything in the face of *that*?' She used her thumb to point at the thing. Everyone was staring at her and she started to feel self-conscious.

'I think this is beyond your understanding, girl,' the woman with the swollen head said, though Talia thought there was something in the way the silver eyes regarded her, perhaps recognition. She glanced behind her again. The thing from the lake was much closer. She knew that she could create a weapon-like focus for the offensive powers of her armour. She intended to use it on the anti-life thing, but she was struggling with what it should look like. She could only think of amorphous blobs of shifting matter for some reason.

'We need to get back to it now. We have other things to do,' Scab told her over a private secure link.

Talia was aware that neither Patron nor the two Consortium Elite were making any move. Patron's strange shadow form seemed to be looking at her. He had to know that the thing from the black lake would be making straight for him.

'Oh yeah, more killing,' Talia said out loud. She pointed at the anti-life thing. 'That's better at it than you. Can't you feel it?'

'Maybe she's got a point,' Vic said. Talia felt a surge of gratitude, but it was mixed with the expectation that he probably wouldn't be of much help. 'Maybe if we could all just talk a bit, yeah?' She had been right. Even Patron looked a little embarrassed for the 'sect as he resumed a more human form, and turned back to the swollen-headed woman.

Something burst out of a shadowed angle high above them. For a moment it looked like a moving piece of inky darkness, drifting away like smoke at the edges of its form, as if it didn't completely belong. Then she was able to make out a vague, faceless, humanoid form, gliding on bat-like wings, trailing a smoky, whip-like tail behind it. There was someone on its back, clinging on, riding it: a tall, thin, pale man with long platinum hair trailing behind him. He was dressed in armour, and had a sword strapped to his back. The sensors in Talia's armour were letting her know that the man in question had significant biological augmentations, and that both his armour and sword were of a tech level equivalent to the sort of weapons that Vic, Scab and her sister had carried. It was all information that she just suddenly knew. She was also aware that the man's base form had been extensively sculpted, but he was, in fact, another Scab clone.

'We are blessed,' Talia muttered to herself. 'This should calm things right down.'

Patron started to laugh as the inky, bat-like, humanoid thing circled down through the red air to land.

'Bress?' the swollen-headed woman called.

'Why am I tall and attractive?' Scab demanded as the figure clambered down from the humanoid's back. The creature's face reminded Talia of a caul. She couldn't shake the feeling that there was a mouth underneath it trying to scream. It bolted for a corner the moment 'Bress's' boots touched the ground.

'Britha,' he said. 'What have you done?'

Talia turned around and looked at pseudopods creeping towards them, burning the smoking ground with their touch. She backed away. Vic and Scab both took to the air. The two remaining Elite did likewise. With a thought Talia made the helmet of her armour fold away. She seemed to remember that sometimes it was important to let people see your eyes.

'Okay, seriously—' she started.

'Britha, can you stop it?' Bress asked.

'If I do he's won,' the woman, apparently called Britha, said, very quietly.

'I will kill you and be gone before it catches me anyway,' Patron said. 'I may even have your lover do it.' There was something about the way he made the threat, as if it was a reflex, as if his heart wasn't in it. Bress glanced at Patron, but turned back to Britha.

'Please, the girl is right. We need to stop fighting. She is a descendant of Fachtna and yours. She can save us.' Britha glanced over at her. Talia tried to fly, to move away from the crawling thing, but bumped into protruding masonry.

'Ow!'

'Are you still his slave?' Britha asked him. Bress kissed her.

'Priorities!' Talia shouted. Scab was muttering to himself. Talia was quite surprised that Patron hadn't just killed them all.

'Please,' Bress whispered as he pulled away from Britha. She nodded, mercury tears in her eyes.

'I ... I ... if this is a trick ...' Britha started.

'It is not a trick,' Bress promised her. Patron was staring at the tall, thin man.

'I will speak with the city,' Britha said and closed her eyes.

'This changes nothing,' Patron said. 'She killed Siska.' Bress turned around to look at the tall, obsidian-skinned figure. Patron was becoming easier to look at, his lines more defined.

'And how long was she your slave?' Bress asked.

'She was not—' Patron started, but Bress was shaking his head. The unsure expression on Patron's face looked out of place. Talia found that she was hovering in the air now. She turned to look at the anti-life thing. It had become sluggish, slower, and finally had seemed to come to a bubbling stop, seething and roiling in place as though something had caged it. Britha opened her eyes.

'For now,' she told them. Talia touched gently down and walked towards Patron, Bress and Britha. Vic floated over to join them as well. Scab was looking between the remaining Elite.

'Look, we can resort to violence any time we want. Let's just try and have a bit of a conversation first, agreed?' Talia suggested.

Patron's laugh was without humour. 'As far as it goes.'

'Scab, do you want to join us?' Talia called. He did not answer and remained hanging in the air until, with a final glance between the two Elite, he floated over to join them, his helmet peeling back away from his face. Vic had also lowered his helmet.

'Do you want to bring the other two over?' Talia asked Patron, meaning the two Elite.

'There's no need,' Patron said, glancing at Bress as he spoke.

'How did you get here?' Britha asked Bress. She had hold of one of his arms, but it was tentative, as if she couldn't quite believe he was there. 'I thought you were dead. Nobody could withstand that, surely?'

'I was trapped under stone, mostly crushed, for ... for so long. Most of the time the magics in my body made me sleep, to try and heal with what little resources I had, to preserve what they could of my mind. It didn't help. I was mad for millennia. I've lived entirely delusional and hallucinatory lifetimes. Shifting tectonic plates, erosion and entropy freed me. Then it took me further millennia to reassemble my shattered mind, but somehow I could still remember you.' There were more quicksilver tears in Britha's eyes.

'Aw,' Talia said as her cynicism was overwhelmed by her sense of romance. Scab was staring at her in disgust, but Talia couldn't help but think that there was something else there. Jealousy?

'Well, that's very nice,' Patron said. 'But your presence here is irrelevant. We kill you and then get on with our day. If you want to spend some time together, then by all means leave the city ...'

'Why leave the city?' Bress asked.

'Because he knows that if we stay in the city we can use it to contact the Destruction,' Talia said. Scab glared at her. Patron turned to look at the young human woman.

'That will not go well for you. Look around. Do you know where you are?' he asked. Vic and Scab were looking at him blankly.

'Our land,' Britha said. Patron looked impressed despite himself. 'You took our world to Cythrawl,' Britha said.

'This isn't Hell,' Scab said. 'It's just Red Space.'

'And if we're no threat, why do you want us to leave?' Bress asked. Patron narrowed his eyes.

'You've broken your programming,' Patron said.

'I think you underestimate just how much time I've had,' Bress said.

'So can we start killing each other again?' Scab asked impatiently. Patron started to nod.

'Wait!' Talia shouted. 'What exactly do you want?'

Patron was starting to look exasperated now. It was clear that curiosity had been the reason he had stayed his hand, but he had not heard anything he considered interesting or persuasive. 'It is irrelevant,' Patron said.

'No it's not,' Bress said. 'If it was you wouldn't be here. Look at this place. You know there's not enough energy to send you back. It's not as bad as it is in our universe, but we're all stuck here now. You've sacrificed yourself. You wouldn't have come here if it wasn't decisive.'

Talia felt her stomach lurch. She had known she was stuck here but hadn't heard it spelled out like that.

'My actions might be decisive, but don't fool yourself into thinking this is a fight. This is an execution. You cannot stand against me. I only came here because I knew I would not fail. Though I have to admit I was surprised you got this far.'

'Tell that to the dead snake,' Scab said. Vic was nodding.

'And you did not expect to see me,' Britha said.

Patron sighed. 'There is no you. There is just a crystalline lattice comprised of individual five-dimensional parasites which vaguely remember you.'

Talia saw Bress try and hide his stricken expression. He almost managed it.

'Then what difference does it make if you tell her?' Bress demanded. 'Or is it just, even now, even after all the pain, you know how ridiculous "I want to destroy everything" will sound?'

'It's not that simple,' Patron started.

'It fucking is if you're one of the poor fuckers about to not exist,' Vic said. 'I mean seriously, man, grow up.' Patron turned to look at him. Talia wasn't sure she had ever seen a look that more supremely defined cold anger. Vic took a step back. Talia found herself doing the same.

'Vic,' Talia said, putting her hand on his arm. His armour was still warm. 'If it's more complicated ...' she started.

'I ... we ... just want the pain to end,' Patron snapped. Then Talia saw it. It was etched all over his face.

'We can end the suffering,' Scab said.

Patron was shaking his head. 'It's not enough. Memory.'

'We need to compromise now,' Talia said, and found Scab's dead eyes staring at her. 'That way everyone's equally unhappy,' she said weakly.

'I do its bidding—' Patron started.

'But neither you nor it are thinking straight,' Bress said. 'This is a pain response. You're aeons old, the only thing holding you together is ill-will, unintentional masochism, and an instinctive understanding of how to manipulate fundamental forces. You want the pain to end, then end it.'

'It would never allow me—' Patron started. There was desperation in his voice, but something else as well. Hope. Talia's eyes felt wet.

'It's a wounded animal, lashing out,' Bress pleaded. Talia couldn't help but glance at Scab. 'Even if it had control of you in the past, here? Now? It's so cold back in our universe that the simplest of its thought processes could take millions of years. You're trapped in a cycle of your own pain and madness, but everyone around you is either afraid of you, or under your control, and nobody dares tell you this. You can end it with a thought.'

Patron stared at Bress. Realisation broke over his face. Suddenly he looked younger. Then he turned to dust.

All of them stared at where he had been standing. Even Scab. Talia was aware of tension leaking from Bress's frame, tears running down his face. Britha watched the dust drifting to the ground, her face a mask of fury, as though she had been cheated, then she sagged as relief broke across her pained features like a wave.

'Oh,' Talia managed.

'That was a lot easier than I'd thought,' Vic said.

'We need to kill the other two ...' Scab said, turning to the two remaining Elite. Talia lost her temper.

'What the fuck is the matter with you?' she demanded at him. Scab turned back to look at her. 'Your fucking violence, and fighting, and all your hate, and anger, a complete waste of everyone's fucking time! Do you not see that now?'

Everyone looked a little awkward, except for Scab, who looked furious.

'Do you have anything to offer other than words ...' he started.

'Words just fucking stopped us from getting killed!' Talia screamed at him.

Scab pointed at the Innocent. 'He has to—'

'It doesn't fucking matter!' she shouted in his face. Straight away she knew she had gone too far, but she was past caring. Scab moved very quickly, but Vic was there between them.

'Maybe you'll win, maybe you won't,' the 'sect said evenly, 'but you risk not being able to kill god.'

Scab was seething, trying to control himself.

'I really was a fool,' Bress mused. Scab's head shot round to glare at him.

'I'll pierce your body with your own bones before you touch him,' Britha spat at Scab. She reminded Talia of a witch in a children's book. Scab looked like he was desperately trying to control his breathing. Britha turned back to Bress. 'Is he some hellish fetch made in your image?'

'There is only me,' Scab shouted. 'You're a fucking copy, nothing more.'

'Change a broom's handle and its brush enough times, is it the same broom?' Talia said, trying to calm down herself.

Bress sighed. 'No, he is me, as was, and is one of our descendants.' Now Scab was staring at Britha.

'Do you know how much suffering I've caused?' he demanded. 'You should have drowned your child at birth.' Talia found herself thinking of her teenaged temper tantrums.

'I was not there at their birth,' Britha said, though that did not make any sense.

'The pain you've caused ...'

'You make the decisions!' Bress snapped. 'Stop making excuses!'

'In fairness to him,' Talia said, 'he's clearly mentally ill.'

'He's an entitled little prick, you mean,' Vic muttered. Scab turned to stare at the 'sect. 'I know: rage, rage, rage, threat, threat, threat. She's right.' He nodded to Talia. 'None of this matters here ... Can we get on and ...'

'Excuse me.' All of them turned to look at the scorpion Elite. 'I'm going to take young Woodbine here—' She nodded at the sleeping Innocent. Scab bristled at the sound of his name '—and go. Okay?'

Nobody said anything. The silence stretched out. Talia's enhanced awareness allowed her to notice both Scab and Vic tensing.

'Sure,' Talia finally said. The scorpion Elite walked over to the Innocent. The way she picked him up, cradling him in four of her arms, reminded Talia of a mother with her child. She looked around at the city, at the broiling seething mass that was the thing from the black lake.

'He trapped us here,' the Elite said. 'But there has to be something for us as well.'

'What do you want?' Vic asked, unable to keep the disgust out of his voice. The arachnid hesitated.

'You know, I haven't thought in those terms for such a long time,' she said.

'I want to rest,' the sleeping Innocent said in her arms. The arachnid looked down at the human Elite, and then back towards Talia, Vic, Scab, Bress and Britha.

'I don't think we want to fight any more today,' she finally said, and then took off. They watched her fly through the city's strange crumbling spires until she was out of sight. According to Talia's new-found senses the two remaining Consortium Elite were making for low orbit.

'I know how to kill it,' Britha suddenly said. Talia assumed that she was talking about the Destruction. 'To poison it. This city can act as a trod, send me, somehow, to the Hungry Nothingness.'

'We have a way as well,' Vic said. 'We think we can make it kill itself.' The 'sect glanced at Scab. 'No harm in doubling up.'

'I have come a long way to find you,' Bress told Britha. 'Please don't just go now.' There were no tears. He spoke without his voice breaking, but Talia could hear the strain in his words.

Britha touched her swollen head. 'It's too late,' she said. 'I thought you were ...'

Something was nagging Talia at the back of her mind. This didn't seem right somehow.

'For fuck's sake,' Scab snapped. 'Can we just get on with it?'

'Shut up, you vicious little prick!' Talia screamed at him. 'After everything you've seen, done, is that all that you can offer? Self-pity and suicide?' Scab was staring at her, breathing heavily. It reminded her of a panic attack.

'You have to stop speaking to me like that,' he managed. She saw Vic open his mandibles to counter-threaten.

'Vic, don't,' she said. 'Look, there has to be a better way than this. Has anybody tried talking to it?' The moment the words were out of her mouth she remembered Portsmouth, the destruction it had wrought.

'It's not Crom Dhubh,' Britha said. It took Talia a moment to realise that she meant Patron. 'I have seen it, it ate the sky.'

'It's not something you can communicate with,' Bress said gently. Talia noticed that he was holding onto Britha now, very tightly.

'Patron must have,' Talia said.

'It didn't work out well for him,' Scab snapped.

'Maybe she's got a point,' Vic said, though even he sounded sceptical.

'Maybe you just agree with everything she says,' Scab spat.

'It's what Churchman was trying to tell us. I mean, all the violence and shittiness, it just played into Patron's hands, which played into the Destruction's hands, didn't it? Created the kind of society that deserved to be destroyed, that wouldn't resist. I mean, where has it got us?'

'Here,' Scab said. He sounded bored now.

'Okay, fine. Patron and the Destruction were driven mad by pain. They couldn't see beyond that. Can you?' Vic asked his partner. He was sounding less sceptical now.

'Your time is terrifying, Scab,' Talia said. 'But what about your ghost? What about what Oz showed you? I saw your face afterwards.'

'I'm all for a better world,' Scab said, eyes on the ground, then he looked up at her. 'I just don't think I have a place in it.' Bress laughed. Talia felt like slapping him. Just for a moment she felt profoundly sorry for Scab. He turned to Britha. 'We should both go, to be sure.'

'I'm going, on my own,' Talia said, simply.

'No,' Vic said immediately. Talia looked down.

'You're not in love with me, Vic. It's just the side effects of your brain surgery, and I don't love you. I just needed someone.' When she looked up he had a very human-looking expression of hurt on his insect face.

'And you're going to do ... what?' Scab demanded.

'Try and communicate.'

'This is stupid,' Scab spat.

'Oh yeah,' Talia said. 'It's stupid to talk about things. Much better to poison your problems, and try and get them to commit suicide.'

'It's trying to destroy everything!' Scab shouted at her.

'Do you care?' Vic asked. It shut Scab up for a moment.

'I want to do something,' he said.

'You have,' Talia told him. 'A great deal.' She turned to Britha. 'The city, it can ... I don't know ... send me or something?' Britha looked unsure but nodded. 'So what do we do?'

'I'm coming,' Vic said. Talia sighed. 'I don't care about what you said. I just want to go where you go.' Talia opened her mouth

569

to argue, then she nodded. She wondered what would have happened if her sister had been here. She probably wouldn't have let her try this. She was absurdly pleased that Vic was coming. It was selfish, she knew. It would probably end in instant oblivion, but she had never liked being on her own. Scab was shaking his head in disgusted disbelief.

Britha sat down in the ashes and debris and closed her eyes.

'Vic,' Scab said. Talia heard something in his voice and looked over at him. His armour was peeling open across his chest. He reached in and withdrew the large revolver he carried with him. Talia had an inkling that it was important to him somehow. The armour resealed as he walked over to Vic. 'I've had enough now. I think you should do it. Use this.' He held the revolver out to the 'sect. Vic looked down at it. Talia opened her mouth to say something, but thought better of it as Vic made his own weapon grow out of his armour. It looked like a three-barrelled sawn-off shotgun. Talia glanced at Bress. He was watching the exchange. She could not read the expression on his face. Vic put the gun to Scab's head. Talia squeezed her eyes shut.

'Fuck you, Scab,' she heard her insect lover say, and then tensed for the shot. Nothing happened. She opened an eye. Vic was lowering the three-barrelled weapon. Scab looked stricken.

'Don't get jealous,' Talia told the big 'sect as she walked over to Scab and kissed him. He tasted of cigarettes. It was somehow comforting. She broke away from him. 'I'm sorry I'm not her,' she whispered and moved back to Vic, taking one of his hands in her own.

A complex, shining, crystal flower blossomed from Britha's head. Talia and Vic both collapsed to the ground.

44
The City

Vic had the impression that he was standing on the floor in a broad room with a low ceiling, but the walls – if there were such – and the ceiling were lost in darkness. He was not sure where the light was coming from. Talia was standing next to him, and despite what she had said about not loving him, which he was sure she had meant, and she was probably right, she looked grateful for his company. There were two other figures in the room. One was a well-built human male with very short hair and light brown skin. He was wearing a grass skirt and his body and limbs were covered in tattoos composed of horizontal lines. At first Vic thought the hairless monkey was wearing a cloak made from some kind of tentacled creature. An octopus, according to his neunonics, but then he saw it move and realised that the octopus didn't quite look right. Some of its tentacles were digging into the man's flesh, and their two bodies looked at least partially fused.

The other figure was frail, his skin grey, loose and spotted. He was in a wheelchair, an oxygen tank attached to the back of it. He looked familiar to Vic. He had seen the man in one of Talia's attempts at programming an immersion.

'Dad!' she cried, and ran to him, hugging him. 'I'm sorry, I'm so sorry!' Weak, sickly hands stroked her hair. 'Vic, it's my dad.' She was smiling, despite the tears. Vic was loath to cause her pain, but he reached for her, trying to pull her away, though she resisted.

'Talia, I don't think that's your father,' he told her. She turned to look at the old man.

'He is correct,' the human in the grass skirt said. Talia pushed the hand of her father's doppelganger away, and stood up. The figure in the wheelchair just watched her.

'Who are you?' Vic asked the human in the grass skirt.

'I am, or I was, Lodup Satakano.' He nodded towards the octopus fused with his back. 'This is Lidakika.' Talia had backed towards Vic, and he had put his arms around her. It was funny but he didn't feel frightened here, just very protective.

'You're one of the Seeders, aren't you?' Talia said.

'No,' Lodup said. 'I was a human. I worked in the city a very long time ago. I was, I guess, sacrificed to it. Lidakika, however, is a fragment of one of the minds that you call Seeders. She protected me, made a place for me. We spoke with Britha, who like you is connected to one of Lidakika's sisters.'

Talia nodded. There were tears again, but Vic suspected that these weren't the tears of self-pity, anger and frustration he was used to seeing from her.

'I miss her,' Talia said. Lodup smiled and nodded. Vic wasn't sure if Talia meant the Seeder ship she had once been merged with, or her sister.

'Which means that you are the Destruction,' Vic said, turning to look at the figure shaped like Talia's father. Lodup nodded.

'As Britha asked, we have facilitated communication,' Lodup said.

'He's not quite the raging inferno of hate, pain and oblivion I expected,' Vic admitted.

'This is how the communication has been translated. It is so you can understand it. The minds in the city attempted communication once before, but now they mostly sleep. Everything is cold now. Pain can only burn so hot in a time like this.' Lodup's voice sounded different, more feminine. His posture had changed. Vic wondered if they were talking with Lidakika now.

'We need you to stop trying to destroy everything,' Talia said. 'Please.'

'Existence is pain, there is only pain, and therefore there is no reason for it,' the sick old man said.

'Look, we can't possibly imagine what it was like for you, but what about now? Surely it's over?'

'Only now can I think enough to understand what has happened to me,' he said.

'And the pain?' Talia asked.

'It is manageable. It is the memory. Physics is so cruel, and should not have been allowed to exist.'

Talia went quiet, thinking, clearly not sure what to say next.

'But you've done extraordinary things,' Vic said. 'Look, the

Seeders may not have worked out, but they did extraordinary things. They made her, me, all the other uplifts. You should see the things they can do. I mean they ... we can be real fuckers, but they're capable of other things as well. Living Cities, immersions, alcohol ...'

'Their accomplishments were taken from older races,' the old man said.

'Their culture wasn't,' Lodup said. His voice was back to its original masculine sound.

'Music, art, poetry, literature, even the tech and science in my time, it was, to all intents and purposes, innovation: imagination and hard work building on itself,' Talia said.

'There is still sanity among your children,' Lodup said, his voice turning feminine again. 'It is there in the beauty of their minds, their accomplishments. They built entire ecosystems, created sentient species, they made an entire universe for you to hide from the pain.'

'Look,' Talia said. 'Maybe we all seem fierce, and violent, and horrible, but the truth is, all the worst things just tend to be caused by a minority. Admittedly they are a minority with a disproportionate amount of power, but still. Maybe things changed after my time because they were socially engineered that way, but there were billions of unnoticed acts of kindness every day, billions of people caring for each other. Sure, we get distracted, we get caught up in our own selfish shit, and our insecurities make us want to find someone to look down on, and our fear has us looking for someone to blame, but that's not really us. Not all the time.' Her voice had become small and tapered away at the end. Vic wasn't sure that the humans she was talking about still existed by the time he had been hatched.

'I saw the look of wonder on a killer's face,' Vic said. He wasn't sure where this was coming from. 'Worst person I ever knew. He had probably killed millions, possibly billions in his lifetime. As an Elite he had been a one-man extinction event.'

Talia turned to look up at him. 'Way to sell the species,' she muttered.

'Truth be told I wasn't much better myself, just smaller scale, and less of an arsehole, but the Lloigor machine showed him something. Life in other places, in the hearts of stars, beneath the ice ...' Now he dried up.

'He fell in love with a spaceship ghost as well,' Talia added weakly.

'There's life in the dark matter, isn't there? Things that we can only ever guess at but never see,' feminine Lodup asked. 'In the spaces between.' The old man nodded, very slowly. 'I'm sorry, but we do not have much time ...' The voice was masculine now. Very suddenly the octopus looked old and sickly.

'What does that mean?' Talia demanded. Vic held her tighter.

'Lidakika suggests you contact the last of the Lloigor machines, see what they have seen, the life they have observed, which was nothing to do with you or your children ...' masculine Lodup said, ignoring Talia's question.

'Only the hated universe,' the old man said. Vic felt hope slipping away. Then wondered why he was so engaged. It could make little difference now, but he desperately wanted to convince the old man. Perhaps he just wanted to see Talia happy, possibly for the last time.

'She says to look through her eyes, for the last time, see the racial memories of your grandchildren. Perhaps it will help you take comfort.' Lodup reached over, touched the old man, and then died. Collapsed to the floor. Talia rushed over to him. Vic followed more slowly.

'What happened?' Talia asked.

The old man waited a beat before answering. 'The city died millions of years ago now. I carry your minds, I carry what you were.'

Talia stood up and staggered back from the old man. Vic was just staring. The words of Bress, Scab's much nicer clone, came back to him: *It's so cold back in our universe that the simplest of its thought processes could take millions of years.*

'How long?' Talia asked, appalled.

The old man shrugged. 'Billions of years, as you measure things.'

'What will you do?' Vic asked, suddenly extremely frightened of the answer.

'A long time ago I made a mistake. My children tried to talk to me and I lashed out and hurt them, and nobody would ever speak to me again because they were afraid. I cannot go back to change events now. There is not the energy left.'

'You'll stop collapsing possible universes?' Talia asked. There was hope in her voice despite the knowledge that she could never go back.

'I made the decision when I understood your sacrifice,' he said. He swallowed hard as he struggled to speak. 'Only here, now, can I see the great beauty of it all, and it is only a memory, but it is a memory greater than the pain.'

'If only we knew then ...' Vic said quietly. The old man looked up at them, both his eyes glistening with tears.

'I do not deserve it, but will you stay with me?' he asked. Talia nodded and moved to his chair. She reached down to touch the side of his face with her hand.

Epilogue
Ancient Britain

Tangwen went walking in the woods. The child was making noise, but that didn't bother her. Unless the forest spirits turned on her there was little that could threaten them. She had her bow, her hatchet, and her dagger for bears, lynxes and wolves, though the land was slowly returning to normal, and the animals mostly left people alone.

All had tried to give her advice on being a mother. In the end she had decided to do what she felt was right once she had worked out how to keep them both alive, though only the girl was with her now. She had given birth to the twins that were not twins in early winter, in Gaul, where she had found the rest of her tribe. Come summer she had deemed the girl strong enough to travel. Tangwen had named her Kush. It probably wasn't a girl's name in the hot southern lands, but she did not care. Kush deserved to be remembered. Love of her children, well Kush anyway, did not stop her from still being very angry with Britha. The boy she had named Fachtna. A revenge against his father.

Shortly after Fachtna's birth the brass scorpion had turned up. Tangwen had tried to get rid of it. Tried everything, including violence, but the thing would not leave the boy's side. It at least had the sense to hide when others were present.

The scorpion was one of a number of reasons that Fachtna frightened her. She knew it was not good to feel that way about a child, but she couldn't help it. The child never cried. He just stared. A *dryw* from one of the Gaulish tribes had advised her to drown Fachtna in the river, an offering to the gods. She had told him that she had seen the gods. The death of a child seemed of little interest to them.

When she had returned to Ynys Prydain she had gone to the lands of the Trinovantes, and visited with Anharad. The woman who had done so much to keep them together, to keep them alive when they had fled from the spawn of Andraste, was little more than a shell now. She had lost so much, and the still-silent Mabon was well on his way to becoming a warrior. He would soon be rushing off to risk himself for honour and glory in disputes and squabbles that seemed so petty after she had seen the Otherworld burn. More and more the memories came to seem little more than bad dreams. Anharad's one solace was Caithna. Tangwen had considered taking the girl back north to her people, the strange and fierce Pecht, but if what Britha had said was true then little of her tribe was left. The girl might have been the tribe's only survivor. Still, she was starting to come alive, and her presence in turn enlivened Anharad. Despite everything Tangwen had left Anharad as a friend.

One day I will go north, she thought. *If Caithna is of an age, and wishes it, she can accompany me. I will take Kush with me and we can meet these fierce, moonstruck northerners.* But for now, a walk in the woods.

She had looked for her Father, but the crystal cave had been empty.

She had smelled the bodies before she found them. They had been drained of blood and then flayed. A warning. She smiled.

'I know you're there!' she called. 'Take me to him.' The blood-painted, ash-covered *gwyllion* seemed to grow out of the trees like the forest ghosts they were feared to be.

She was marched through the woods blindfolded. They had even blindfolded Kush because they knew no better. They had taken her upriver in log dugout boats. Finally they had removed the blindfold, and mother and child had crawled through the tunnel and into the earthen cave supported by the root structure of a mighty oak. It was where she and Kush had first spoken with Guidgen. The weapons that had been blessed by the chalice were leant against the earthen walls, oiled and wrapped in skins. The Red Chalice was in the centre of the fire. She realised then how much she hated the thing. The old *dryw* was there, sat on the other side of the fire, Germelqart too. Both of them looked fatter and happier than when she had last seen them. They took turns embracing her. It was difficult in the cramped confines of the earthen cave.

'I had not thought to see you again, Tangwen Serpent-Child,' Germelqart said. He was watching Kush wriggle in her lap.

'It takes more than a hill falling on top of me to kill me,' she said, smiling.

'May I hold her?' Guidgen asked. Tangwen nodded and the old *dryw* lifted the child out of her lap and started fussing over her, making her laugh and smile. 'What did you name her?'

'Kush,' she said quietly. Germelqart nodded in gratitude and then had to turn away with tears in his eyes.

'She has the blood of the gods in her veins,' Guidgen said, tickling Kush's belly, making her laugh and kick her legs about. 'Yes you do! Yes you do!'

'The boy?' Germelqart asked. Tangwen considered asking him how he knew.

'Fostered by my people,' Tangwen said, trying to suppress the guilt she felt for baby Fachtna. 'He will be trained as a warrior, though if he shows aptitude he will be given the opportunity to become a *dryw*.' Germelqart nodded. Neither of them commented on the fact that it sounded like Tangwen was planning on having little to do with Fachtna.

'But it is Kush who has the blood of Andraste in her? Who is the child of the goddess as much as she was the child of Fachtna, Britha, and yourself?' Guidgen asked. Britha frowned. The old *dryw* had made Kush's parentage sound so complicated, and it was, she had been born of magic. It was much simpler for Tangwen, however. Kush was her daughter.

'We need to protect your daughter and her line,' Germelqart said. Tangwen gritted her teeth. She did not like the way that they were making plans for the child already when she was but seven moons old. 'And the chalice, and the weapons.'

'We need to look to the threats against Ynys Prydain. There are other items of great magic out there, others who carry the blood of the gods in their veins, the unquiet dead of the Underworld, the magics of the fair folk from the Otherworld ...'

'The Otherworld is fallen. I saw it burn,' Tangwen told them. Both of them stared at her, clearly not sure what to say to that.

'Will you help us?' Germelqart asked. Guidgen had drawn an iron-bladed knife and held it against the palm of his hand, away from the wriggling Kush. Tangwen thought on it. It could never be harder than the winter before last had been, surely. At least now they knew what they faced. She nodded. The cold iron scored a line of blood on the old man's palm.

'We will make a Circle,' Guidgen said.

Terminal Island, Los Angeles – Now –

Grace breathed in and held it. Her finger squeezed the trigger. The rifle kicked back into her shoulder, and the crack of the bullet echoed out across the water between the artificial islands. The Pennangalan fell over, but she would get back up. Grace had hidden herself as well as she could with the time she'd had, but the ridiculously dressed post-apocalyptic pirate marines had a good idea where she was now. They were holding off, presumably as a result of du Bois's negotiations. She could hear the shouting.

Grace looked through the Purdey's new scope, settling the crosshairs on Mr Brown. A bullet, even a nanite-tipped one, would do no good. She shifted the scope so it settled on du Bois. Even now it still felt like it had been him. Pretty much the ultimate betrayal, and behaviour at odds with everything she knew about du Bois since he had helped her out of the blood-soaked ruins in Spitalfields. She moved the rifle again until it settled on King Jeremy. A sociopathic little prick who used people as his playthings. It would be so easy to squeeze the trigger. Mr Brown had to die in a nuclear explosion. Had to. It would kill her, and the others, but frankly their plan was stupid and doomed to failure. They were going right into the heart of the madness. She didn't want to die, but she didn't think this was going to be much of a world to live in, and Brown deserved to be destroyed for what he'd done. She wasn't quite sure how old she was, because nobody had thought to remember the date she'd been born in the rookery she'd grown up in, but she was more than a hundred-and-forty years old. It was a good innings in anybody's book.

They were turning now, moving towards the submarine. Her throat was suddenly dry. The crosshairs were over the back of King Jeremy's head. Her finger curled round the trigger, started to squeeze. Then she relaxed, looked up from the scope and smiled. *No.* If she died, if she further harmed her life in any other way, then he won. He'd implanted the memories to split her and du Bois up. She still wasn't sure why he had done that, but she wanted to make sure he had failed.

Working quickly she packed the Purdey back into its case, and strapped it to her webbing, all the while looking around. Patron, du Bois, and the others had disappeared into the sub, and now she suspected that all bets were off as far as the pirate marines went. She picked up Beth's LMG that she'd swapped for her carbine, checked it, and clipped it to its sling. She could see some movement, but nobody had started shooting yet. Grace had picked her position on the cargo containers not just because it provided a clear view of the kill-zone, but because it provided a straight run to the Cougar.

'All right, boys,' she muttered to herself. 'You don't shoot me, I won't shoot you.' She started to run, leaping from container to container. Immediately she was taking sporadic, but annoyingly accurate, fire. She felt the hammer blows of the bullets impacting her nanite-reinforced bike armour, staggering her, but she kept running. She leapt off a stack of three containers, dropping onto a stack of two. Stopping to suppress some of the heavier and more accurate fire, she aimed up at a sniper position on one of the cranes. Tracers flew upwards, sparking off superstructure or arcing off over the water. She was running again, dropping down from a stack of two to a stack of one, bullets flying past her from gunmen between the stacks. A bullet creased her armoured skull, and she almost went down. She fired on the run, inaccurately trying to suppress the most concentrated areas of fire and the sniper. She reached the end of the container and leapt, getting shot in the legs from below before landing and collapsing, with a cry of pain, on the roof of the Cougar.

'Fuck!' she screamed. She pulled a fragmentation grenade from her webbing, pulled the pin, let the spoon flick off, cooked it for several seconds, and then dropped it between the Cougar and the container. The explosion rocked the armoured vehicle. She saw a body bounce off the lip of the armoured truck's roof. *This is going to hurt.* She rolled off the top of the vehicle and dropped to the ground. She screamed out and collapsed. She was getting shot again. She sent a long, undisciplined burst of fire past the front of the vehicle, and then another past the back, just trying to keep the pirate marines' heads down. She staggered to her feet and dragged the door of the Cougar open, swinging on it, which was the reason that the marine sitting in the driver's seat missed her with the two rounds from the Beretta M9A1. Grace dragged him down from the vehicle and stamped on his face, sending pain lancing up her legs. She grabbed the pistol. It would replace the one she'd lost in the chase, and she could convert it to full automatic if she ever found the tools. Grace climbed into the relative armoured safety of the Cougar, slamming the door and locking it behind her. The submarine was pulling away from the dock as she drove away in a hail of gunfire.

Grace had used the weight and armour of the Cougar to bully her way through LA. The streets were filled with the dead as the inhabitants killed more and more of each other in a constant no-holds-barred riot. Closer to the sea the city had already started to warp and mutate, the result of what Grace thought was the awakened Seeders' terraforming process. Kanamwayso had infected LA like a virus, replicating even as it killed.

She had healed as much as she could, relying on the energy bars and drinks rather than wasting any of the remaining drips. She had taken a little fire as she had driven into the castle in Laurel Canyon. Most of the gunmen had died in the chase. The fight to clear the structure was very one-sided. Then she had taken all the food, water, fuel, ammunition, and anything else useful she could find, and loaded it into the back of the Cougar.

'Eileen!' Grace shouted as she entered the house. 'It's Grace, it's safe to come down.' She looked up as Eileen, Dora, with her shotgun, and Ralph appeared at the top of the stairs.

'Grace?' Eileen said.

'We can't stay here,' Grace said. 'Get everyone, gather what you need, but only what you need. I have a vehicle and supplies, but we need to get going.'

'Where are we going?' Eileen asked. Andrea had come out to hug her mother. Grace looked at the frightened little girl for a moment before answering. 'We're going to find a safe place out in the desert.' Eileen turned and started organising everyone. Grace went out to stand watch by the Cougar. Soon they would drive out of the canyon. The sun was setting on LA.

The City

Scab stared down at Talia and Vic's bodies. He still felt the touch of Talia's lips on his own. Bress, his nauseating clone, reached down and checked the pulse in Talia's neck.

'Dead,' he said. Scab didn't like that. He wasn't sure why. Bress was pushing open Talia's eyes, examining them as though he was looking for something.

'Leave her alone,' somebody said. Scab was surprised to find that it had been him. Bress turned to look up at him, studying him. Scab's grip tightened on his tumbler pistol. The black roiling mass of hate was receding back the way it had come through the city, like a tide going out.

'The city took their spirits,' the human woman said. Her name was Britha. She was holding her swollen head, clearly pained. His clone moved to comfort her in a way he knew he never could. He just watched. 'It sent them somewhere else.'

'Did it work?' Scab asked. It suddenly seemed important. Not because of existence – that was meaningless, abstract nonsense – but because for him to lose Vic and Talia it had to be worth something.

'I don't know,' Bress said as he helped Britha to her feet. She was clearly in a lot of pain. It wasn't a very comforting answer.

'I don't think I have much longer,' she said.

'Even here there are people, well, things really, that might be able to help.' They started to walk away, Bress helping Britha.

'Hey,' Scab said. They stopped, and Bress looked back. 'Where are you going?'

'What it took me the longest time to learn was that I made myself unhappy. You try too hard,' Bress told him, then he turned away from Scab and both of them walked deeper into the city. It was easy for him to say, his mind had had aeons to be destroyed and rebuilt. Scab turned back to look at his two dead ... friends. With a thought his armour folded away and he looked around at the city. His new home. He took his cigarette case from the breast pocket of his suit, took out a cigarette, and lit it. He didn't like the taste. He needed a purpose.

Woodbine sat down between Talia and Vic's bodies in the ruins, and accessed the Monk's, *Beth's*, immersion construct.

He was standing on a pebble beach on a primitive pre-Loss Earth, next to a terminal for primitive ground effect vehicles. Beyond the terminal were the bright lights of some kind of entertainment area. Over the water he could see an island; behind him, the lights of a tiny city. The air smelled funny here.

The immersion had translated his image reasonably faithfully, though his tech was era-compliant. He reached into his suit and pulled out the revolver, the immersion replacement for his tumbler pistol. He looked at it for a long time and then he threw it into the water. Slowly he removed the rest of his weapons and threw them into the water. He kept the straight-edge razor because, well, you never know. Then he knelt by the water and washed the make-up off. He thought about stripping off naked, but it was a little cold, and he suspected it was against the local social norms. You could take symbolism too far.

The immersion's predictive routine had guided him once it had understood what Woodbine wanted. As far as he could tell it was a place where people came to 'learn', which was some kind of inefficient way of imparting skills and knowledge. He was walking through an area where the learners, or students as they were apparently called, met to eat and socialise.

She was sitting on her own. She was dressed similarly to how Talia had dressed, but that was where the similarity ended. She was poring over her work, and was alone. Scab was sure she was called Maude. She looked up as Scab sat opposite her.

'I would like a friend, but I am not sure how to go about it,' he said. Her face scrunched up in consternation. Then she smiled.

Acknowledgements

A Thanks to Dave Arnott for astrophysics advice, it is not his fault that I've ignored him and just made shit up.

Thank you again, for the time and effort put in by Chloe Isherwood of Chloe Isherwood Photography, and Gabriella Howson as Britha.

Thanks, as ever, to Matt Bryant for continuing support, tech and otherwise. (Finally got your prize dude!)

To Jason & Katy Wheatley and their amazing family for advice (I am listening, even if it doesn't always seem that way!) and a refuge of strangely peaceful anarchy.

To Film Night, Cat Hallsworth, Chris Edwards (A full service postie!), the noncontributing Dan Kendall, Becky Kendall and the occasional Dave Hurst, for providing a place of respite and an often much needed break.

Continuing thanks for advice, ranting, encouragement and drinks (strange how the latter is often a theme) to M.D. Lachlan, Peter F. Hamilton, Anthony Jones, my arch-nemesis and not-a-real man (it's a long story) Hannu Rajaneimi. To Chris Wooding and Bill Thomas for their feedback and suggestions. And to relative newcomers (though Worldcon veterans) Jon Wallace and ewok-loving Edward Cox.

Thank you to Abigail Nathan for her extensive copyediting skills.

And to the Gollancz crew: Charlie Panayiotou, Gillian Redfearn and the amazing Sophie Calder (even though she sent me to Manchester for some reason), and of course my long suffering editor Marcus Gipps. It might not seem it sometimes but I do appreciate all your hard work.

A big thanks to the hardest-working agent ever: Robert Dinsdale of AM Heath.

Thanks to all my friends, I realise I've mostly been a social media mate recently and not seen enough of everyone, hoping to change that and looking forward to seeing more of you all in the near future.

My family who have gone above and beyond recently providing everything from proof reading and marketing support, to concept artwork, mechanical skills and DIY: Mum, Dad, Nicola, Simon, Nell & Amelie -thank you!

(Oh and Yvonne, but the book is dedicated to her, so I'm hoping that she'll notice that.)

And finally thank you very much to everyone who bought or loaned-out a copy of any of my books, it is always greatly appreciated. I don't think I'm terribly good at social media (My much neglected blog!) but I particularly want to thanks to everyone who follows, contacts, comments etc. (bear with me, I'm getting better) and all those who have taken the time to review, good or bad, in print and online.

Gavin G. Smith, Woking (where the Martians landed), 2015
www.gavingsmith.com